MISSION R&AW

INDIA'S SECRET SERVICES UNRAVELED

MISSION R&AW

INDIA'S SECRET SERVICES UNRAVELED

R. K. YADAV

Former R&AW Officer

Published by
PRABHAT PRAKASHAN PVT. LTD.
4/19 Asaf Ali Road,
New Delhi-110 002 (INDIA)
e-mail: prabhatbooks@gmail.com

ISBN 978-93-5562-861-9

MISSION R&AW: INDIA'S SECRET SERVICES UNRAVELED
By R. K. Yadav, Former R&AW Officer

First Edition
2026

Price
₹ 800 (Rupees Eight Hundred Only)

Printed at
R-Tech Offset Printers, Delhi

Preface to Second Edition

Without any hesitation, I should affirm that R&AW is a panic-creating word for its adversaries. But it is more hysterical and frightening to R&AW itself implying its hierarchy when it comes in public domain. Lot of research is done at R&AW when it appears anywhere in India as to how it originated and who are the "anti-national" elements behind this conspiracy. Later, a post-mortem is also conducted before its final burial after wasting tons of energy, resources and manipulations. It is usual practice in R&AW for which a big branch is existential with worst composition of known notoriety. This rhetoric is obvious because my mobile was disturbed for years by them but now it is feeling comfortable after January, 2015.

In this polemical scenario, a book written on R&AW was bound to be a hot potato for their appetite. But to their utter dismay, I outwitted them. It was never known to Alok Joshi, the then R&AW Chief and his bumbling compatriots till it appeared in market in the first week of April, 2014.

Electioneering for 16th Lok Sabha was in full swing when this book became public. I decided to release it formally but no political stalwart was ready to perform this venturesome job fearing his own future after the outcome of Parliament results. Multiple options were attempted without any success. One alternative was to rope in some former R&AW Chief. There were two apprehensions in this context for these stalwarts. First, most of them lacked knowledge regarding facts of full text of the book. Second, they were scared of two words, R&AW and R K Yadav. I thought it better not to get disturbed the mental peace of these old species. No politician knowing anything about R&AW was found on national watch list. Out of film personalities, Amitabh Bachchan was also discussed but there were doubts he would burn his fingers in R&AW affairs. Madan Lokur, Hon'ble Supreme Court Judge, my old friend, was found fully engaged around that period of time. Obviously so. Thus, wait and watch policy was temporarily weighed.

In May, 2014, Narendra Modi got a massive majority. I was delighted because I knew many big personalities in BJP who could become Chief Guest in release ceremony of this book. Unfortunately, no one in BJP was ready to be part of this release function including Subramaniam Swamy. Perhaps new PM Modi was enigmatic in his assertion to his new South Block job and no one wanted to be pin-pointed to release a book on R&AW which is under the PM. Assured that no one was ready to swallow this bitter pill, I requested Sharad Yadav and Natwar Singh along with my two journalist friends Ram Bahadur Rai and Rajat Sharma to release this book on 17 July, 2014 at Constitution Club in New Delhi. They readily agreed to do it because of my personal relations with them. Despite some hiccups, the release was smooth and media gave huge publicity to it.

I was expecting legal repercussions of violation of Official Secret Act but R&AW authorities preferred not to intervene thereafter fearing more controversies which they faced when Major General V K Singh was put to such action. Rest is apart of history now. There was no controversy related to the issues evaluated by me from the archives of Indian Intelligence and from the experiences of our stalwarts which I tried to elaborate to the best of my ability. I was much pleased to hear when some seniors, who were denied their elevation to the top by manipulators, that even they were not aware of many revelations which they found in this book. This was really a great compliment for me to hear from these highly-acclaimed intelligence honchos.

This book received worldwide acclamation particularly in Pakistan. CIA reviewed it from every nook and corner. It was highly appreciable from their point of view as the MUST READ material on Indian Intelligence. Many articles on burning issues between Indian and Pakistan history were highlighted at length. Obviously, Pakistani readers reacted vociferously on being pushed to wall on disclosure of 1965 war debacles and atrocities committed in 1971 war by Pakistan army on Bengali population in East Pakistan. I was approached by Pakistani media to speak personally on news channels which I avoided in view of fragile India-Pakistan relations particularly when new Government was finalizing its agenda on Pakistan.

Prior to the elevation of Modi as Prime Minister, I stated in an interview that he would be new in the South Block and as such his exposure on internal and external security matter would have to be handled by some able intelligence officer. Fortunately, he appointed Ajit Doval as his National Security Advisor who has proved his mettle. In this book I have exposed as to how the previous NSAs were spoilers. It have added a new chapter on Ajit Doval so that Indian public should weigh the pros and cons of what I adduced on this issue. Profiles of three new R&AW Chiefs have also been included in view of what I opined about their predecessors. Some bizarre incidents too are part of this book.

Not out of any sheer enmity but of mere curiosity, I have no hesitation to question the decision of Modi Government on intelligence matters. National Technical Research Organization (NTRO) was created in 2004 under mysterious circumstances in the sense it was duplicity of what the all powerful Technical wing of R&AW is meant for. What it may but why it was made the post-retirement refuge of some spent forces. One P V Kumar overlooked for R&AW Chief post was installed here. He was a non-technical man. Alok Joshi who retired from R&AW after 62 years of age was imposed as NTRO head till 65 years of his age. How these manipulations are allowed to be maneuvered by bureaucrats of Narendra Modi is questionable. I have been given to understand that a Britisher close to PMO recommended appointment of Alok Joshi. Now Anil Dhasmana another R&AW Chief is head of NTRO. If Modi's otherwise performance is judged, this is something indigestible to me the least. This department should be meant for cyber and technical experts who could infuse new dimensions in view of many researches going on worldwide on this very sensitive subject.

But I should unhesitatingly admit that after Ajit Doval became National Security Advisor, there has been no major terrorist attack like 26/11 in any part of India. Jammu and Kashmir is always exception in view of Pakistan's continuous infiltration of terrorists to target Indian security forces. But now situation is changing dramatically in Valley. Three R&AW Chiefs who worked under Doval too proved their worth and many trans-border operations were conducted inside Pakistan which is the best hotpursuit after 1971 war and Balakot airstrike is the daring example of it. I hope Doval would continue to work in that ardent manner despite his advancing age but I am told he is ever refreshing and an institution in himself.

❑

Preface to First Edition

When I joined R&AW in 1973, I never thought I would write this book. With my simple nature and rural background I was never destined to pass judgment on people like Pakistani Field Marshal Ayub Khan, Indian General J.N. Chaudhri, politicians and bureaucrats which I have dared to do knowing fully well that I am trying to swim against the tide. Nor was I meant to critically analyse the working of intelligence wizard R N Kao, the founder of R&AW and take head on his 19 successors who helmed this organization. All this happened due to my deeper perception of this outfit, closer proximity with Kao, better accessibility withtop bosses of R&AW and my irresistible passion for the welfare of its employees. I know for certain that I would face rough weather after the launch of this book but I was made to do all these idiosyncratic depictions due to the umbrageous bureaucratic system of Indian administration in general and R&AW in particular. Further, I have used my innate outrage against this system to illustrate some of the uncanny incidents which would ablaze someone for which I should be excused and which should be taken in the right earnest. I should, however, like to take the credit which I never deserve for unfolding the unimaginable aspects of our intelligence system, leave alone certain sordid affairs which I encountered while serving in this prestigious organization.

Just after joining R&AW as a middle level officer, I was singled out from among my batch-mates for posting at Jodhpur in Rajasthan. Obviously, I was agonized for this step-motherly treatment because I did not have any Godfather which wasintegral to one's survival in R&AW. During my stay in Rajasthan, as a young man, I witnessed a number of weird and nasty incidents in the office. Since I was on probation, I had no option but to adapt to this new working culture of our intelligence which was in sharp contrast to what we generally see in other bureaucratic set ups. It was a very good experience which partly groomed me to serve this department better in future.

After spending three years in Rajasthan, I somehow got myself transferred to Delhi Headquarterss. Fortunately, a positive opinion was formed about my brilliance, sincerity, hard working nature added with straight-forwardness and stubborn attitude. In balance of these positive and negative aspects of my personality, I was fortunate to know that Kao's Secretariat had requisitioned my services which was a prestigious and honorable posting for every R&AW man. Arun Bhagat, who later became Director of Intelligence Bureau, was then Under Secretary in R&AW and was in charge of my posting, preferred to keep me with him since he was in need of a good replacement in his branch. I had a very smooth working with Arun Bhagat till he went on a foreign assignment. Arvind Dave, who later became R&AW Chief,

replaced Arun Bhagat. I had little uneasy time with Dave but somehow it ended smoothly.

After serving some years in that Branch, I was posted to China Branch thereafter. P V Kumar, who later became head of National Technical Research Organisation (NTRO), was incharge of China Branch. He was usually victim of his own deeds and I was able to manage with him in that perspective. Fortunately, I passed my time very smoothly in China Branch later when I was placed with a suave person K.C.Puri who deliberately assigned me heavy task in order to utilize my talent effectively in stead of resorting to confrontation on petty issues.

At that time R&AW was passing through a tumultuous period because in 1977 Morarji Desai, the Janta Party Prime Minister, ordered drastic reduction of R&AW's staff strength in view of a false notion that this agency was misused by Indira Gandhi during the Emergency period in India. Full details in this regard are available in chapter "Revolt in R&AW". A chaotic atmosphere of uncertainty was prevalent in R&AW. Worried about their future prospectus every employee was looking for new options in life. There was no mechanism in R&AW to take care of the administrative problems of the employees. I discussed the implications of this imbroglio with some of my friends who too were scared to outline any sort of solution to this alarming situation. When they asked my opinion in this regard, I suggested that we should form a union of employees in R&AW which should work on the pattern similar to other Government departments in India. Many of my friends vanished from the scene after listening to the idea of forming a union in R&AW — a most sensitive department of the Government of India. I did not relent and with the help of some of my hardcore colleagues secretly formed a union in R&AW which was duly registered with Delhi Government on June 30, 1980.

When the news of formation of this union broke out, there was an uproar in R&AW and the top hierarchy was hell-bent to crush the founders of this outfit of which I was the first one. But they became scared when they assessed the ground realities and tried to mend fences with me. However, an untoward incident, as explained in the book, took place in R&AW when Delhi Police and CRPF were called inside the Headquarterss where the employees were agitating on an administrative issue. 33 employees were arrested on November 27, 1980. I was also arrested by the police and taken to Lodhi Road police station. Special arrangements were made for me by R&AW top brasses for the police treatment which affected my body for several days. There was a pen down strike for 12 days all over India resulting in suspension and dismissal of around 80 employees. This was the beginning of an end.

A dynamite was thrown on the roads of the capital of the Indian Union. I was supposed to take care of all the suspended and dismissed employees. At the same time, I was responsible to interact with lawyers for various criminal and civil cases which were got registered against all these employees. There was a lot of hue and cry in the print media over this incident in R&AW. There were allegations and counter-allegations between the union and the R&AW authorities. A state of limbo xi was prevailing inside the agency.

I had no option but to narrate the true picture of this incident to media and politicians in Delhi. In this scenario, I developed good contact with a number of journalists and politicians which continued for a long time. R&AW was an unheard ghost for the journalists and the politicians till that time. Among the politicians with whom I was constantly in contact were Atal Bihari Vajpayee, Charan Singh, H N Bahuguna, L K Advani, Chandershekhar, Prof. Madhu Dandvate, P Upendra, S B Chavan, R K Dhawan, Prafulla Mahant and many others. Prof. Dandvate once told me that he was worried about the safety of my life. Among the journalists, veteran Kuldip Nayyar and Inder Malhotra took up our cause with the Government. I would never forget the efforts of Ram Bahadur Rai and Rajat Sharma who relentlessly raised our voice with the Government and in public. Both of them are my personal friends even today. But the most significant of these developments however was my personal equation with R N Kao. These details have also been elaborated in the book.

Two attempts were made on my life by some unscrupulous R&AW officers in the hit and run incidents when my scooter was hit on the roads of Delhi. In one accident, my collar bone was broken and I was hospitalized for a few days. But God provided me with extra strength to take on the mighty R&AW bosses, although some of them were anxious to resolve the crisis.

After restoring the services of all my suspended and dismissed colleagues, I thought it proper to bring the intelligence agencies of this country under Parliamentary scrutiny for which various politicians and journalists were provided materials pertaining to the basic discrepancies of R&AW. Although the Government did not take credence to these facts so far but my efforts are continuing and would last only when I achieved success in this regard.

It is shameful that despite availability of huge resources in IB, R&AW and other central and state level intelligence/security related agencies, we have to frequently witness acts of terror and other gruesome incidents across the country. R&AW, which over the years, have won laurels for its commendable work of national interest, is routinely charged with lack of transparency and accountability in its working. It is also publicly alleged that IB is reckoned as a Government Thana — police station — which is always used by incumbent regimes for witch-hunting and settling scores with their political rivals. Further, the work culture of R&AW has completely degenerated which has severely affected the morale of its employees. This is mainly attributed to filling key positions of this outfit with people having police background. Earlier, the focus of recruitment in R&AW was confined to professionals. While writing this preface, I get nostalgic about the of days of R N Kao, the architect of Indian intelligence service in India and founder of R&AW, when people of this organization used to work in great harmony as a composite unit. Being a part of this outfit, I feel extremely aggrieved about the present state of affairs in R&AW. It is against this background, I have written this book recalling the good work done by R&AW and

how some of its subsequent heads have brutalized this organization.

I should be sympathized to my children, Anjali and Amit who bore the brunt of my struggle from their school days and never raised any hue and cry even during my difficult days. Now, they are blessed with two sons each. Aditya and Adhyan to Anjali and Arjun and Angad to Amit. Lovingly, I call these four grand children as terrorists since they created lot of noise and disturbed me while I was busy writing this book. I can not ignore the strength and support of my wife Kamla who coped with the hostile situation created against me. I would never forget the help given by my friend N K Sood, a R&AW colleague, who provided several important tips for this book. Over and above, I am grateful to my elder brotherly figure Prof. D S Arora who not only edited a major part of this book but intensely propped me to work for this venture.

In the end, I am grateful to late R N Kao who inspired me greatly to work for the cause of R&AW and provided some insights which have been used in the book. I have only one regret that Kao, who by his exemplary uprightness did unprecedented and unparallel intelligence work for India and who helped several of his officers to win medals and awards for their achievements, has remained unnoticed nationally. Similarly, the Bangladesh Government has also erred to take note of Kao who was the brain behind their liberation war of 1971. It is high time that the concerned authorities both in India and Bangladesh shed their political reservations and bestow the much desired honour on this unsung hero of Indian intelligence I would also never forget the support and motivation provided by K Sankaran Nair number two of kao who helped me a lot in writing this book and gave lot of information based on my various questionnaires structured on the different aspects of R&AW. He gave me a video interview which I would share with some old foxes of R&AW. Besides these two wizards, I am also grateful to many former R&AW officers who do not want to be named in the book but gave me vital information which has been of immense value for this book.

❑

Contents

Employees of the Research and Analysis Wing at the Prime Minister's house on Wednesday when they presented a memorandum on their grievances and demands. — Express photograph.

PERSPECTIVE STATESMAN – 28 March, 2009 NEW DELHI S

'RAW deal'

THE SATURDAY INTERVIEW

RK Yadav

"I'm only concerned about the misuse of secret funds. Since no agency checks misuse of secret funds, I'm bringing it to public notice."

– R.K. YADAV, FORMER RAW OFFICER -INDIA TODAY

Author Giving an Interview to ABP News Channel, New South Block, Delhi

K.Sankaram Nair (Former Secretary R&AW) & Author

कारंट

गुप्तचर संस्था 'रा' में फेरबदल अवश्यंभावी, जहां ३५ अधिकारी २००० कर्मचारियों पर शासन करते हैं

५

२७ दिसम्बर, १९८०

'रा' का बहुमंजिला भवन : 'रा' कर्मचारियों को संबोधित करते हुये आर. के. यादव

R N Kao — Founder of R&AW

Rameshwar Nath Kao was born in a Kashmiri Pandit family on May 10, 1918 at Banaras i.e. Varanasi. One of his ancestors was a Dewan with one of the Nawabas of Lucknow. His father was Deputy Collector in the UP Civil Service. His father died when Kao was five years of age after which he was brought up by his grandfather and uncle under the strict discipline of his mother. According to Kao, due to the death of his father at the young age of 29, his entire family particularly his mother did not recover from the tragedy which ultimately coloured his own outlook during his childhood which was rather cheerless and lonely. But his uncle looked after Kao very well like his own son. He did his schooling at various places after the death of his father due to various family circumstances. He wanted to become an Engineer or driver of a steam locomotive during his childhood. Kao completed his graduation from Lucknow University in 1936. He then took admission for M.A. in English Literature at Allahabad University. He secured first position in M.A. for which a gold medal was awarded to him. He qualified in the Federal Public Commission in 1940 for the Indian Police and was allotted U.P. Cadre. He joined this service on April 7, 1940 at Moradabad for training. For a short stint in between, he served as a Lecturer of English at Allahabad University.

According to Kao, during the course of police training at Moradabad, the British officers used to encourage the Indian origin trainees to affect a contemptuous attitude towards the average Indian. In this pursuit, the Indians were asked to assiduously reflect the views and opinions of their British colleagues who were also receiving training with them. Their contempt towards the national movement of Indian National Congress was reflected from the fact when Kao was single out by the principal of the training school for reading

Hindustan Times newspaper which was not allowed inside the school for spearheading the news in this regard.

After independence, Intelligence Bureau (IB) was set up with some police officers taken on deputation from various states and he joined IB in 1948 as Assistant Director in charge of security and posted as the security officer of Pandit Jawaharlal Nehru.

In the early phase of his career, in April, 1955, he was assigned a very ticklish intelligence operation. Chinese government chartered an Air India Super Constellation plane, "The Kashmir Princess" from Hong Kong for Jakarta, the capital of Indonesia where the first ever conference of Non Aligned countries was to be held in a citycalled Bandung. It was believed that Chou En Lai, the Prime Minister of China was to travel to Indonesia in this plane but due to health problem he abandoned his visit temporarily.

On April 11, 1955, this plane "Kashmir Princess" took off from the Hong Kong airport with Chinese delegates and some press correspondents and crashed in the Indonesian sea as a result of a sabotage which was engineered by Taiwan Intelligence (Formosa at that time). China Government raised a big hue and cry over this crash and Chou En Lai insisted Pandit Jawaharlal Nehru at Bandung conference that Indian Intelligence should be a party to the investigation in Hong Kong as he neither had faith in Hong Kong nor in the British authorities. Nehru directed B N Mullik, the then Director of IB to depute a capable officer to participate in the investigation at Hong Kong. Mullik assigned this arduous and sensitive assignment to the young R N Kao. He performed this assignment to the full satisfaction of Chou En Lai and briefed him at Beijing personally. Chou En Lai presented Kao his personal seal as souvenir when Kao met him in his office.

Kwame Nkrumah, Prime Minister of Ghana, was very friendly with the Indian Prime Minister Jawahar Lal Nehru. Nkrumah sought help from Nehru to set up his security organization in Ghana since it became independent from the colonial rule and was confronting serious internal and external problems. R N Kao was selected for this job and in a span of one year he not only formed the security structure of Ghana but also groomed two officers of that country to head it in the coming future. Nkrumah wanted him to continue for this job for another year but Kao declined and returned to India and promised to send another suitable officer in his place. Subsequently, K. Sankaran Nair, a very capable officer, was sent to Ghana to complete the remaining work of Kao.

Formation of R&AW

After the death of Lal Bahadur Shastri, Mrs. Indira Gandhi became Prime Minister of India in early 1966. In 1968, she decided to form a separate external intelligence department based on CIA of USA and MI6 of Britain. She selected R N Kao who was Joint Director in the IB, for this job. She wanted a loyal man of known integrity. Kao had served as the personal security officer of Pandit Nehru and accompanied Queen Elizabeth and Chou En Lai as Security Officer when they visited India first time in the regime of Nehru. Many eyebrows were raised on the selection of Kao of his being Kashmiri Pandit origin like that of Gandhi but she was firm in her decision. Indira Gandhi gave Kao a free hand, except for two conditions that the new organization should be multi-disciplined one and should not draw its higher personnel exclusively from the IPS. Secondly the top two posts should be filled at the discretion of the Prime Minister from within the organization or outside. Kao prepared a blue print for the new intelligence set up based on detailed studies of CIA, MI6, French intelligence, Mossad and Japanese intelligence which was accepted by the Cabinet and the new external intelligence agency R&AW was created on September 21, 1968 with a skeleton staff of 250 taken from the IB. K. Sankaran Nair, another able officer from IB, was selected as his deputy. The then Director of IB M M Hooja fought tooth and nail to deny the new agency the chattels of office, like buildings, furniture, accounts staff and food personnel but with the help of another capable army officer, I S Hassanwalia, and R&AW started firing on all cylinders within one year.

In the new outfit, Kao, introduced many new divisions based on his studies of various international intelligence agencies. Economic intelligence was a distant idea of that era because there was no such concept in the erstwhile IB. This division was then created to monitor various economic developments in the neighboring countries which could affect the Indian interest particularly in the fields of defence, security and science and technology. Similarly, Information Division, Science and Technology Division, code-breaking branch, Satellite Monitoring Division etc. were also the new chapters opened in R&AW. Prior to this, Aviation Research Centre (ARC) was his brainchild in IB after the 1962 war with China. Later on, in the early eighties, terrorism in Punjab reached to its peak and the Government needed a guerrilla outfit which was created by Kao in the form of National Security Guard (NSG) in 1984.

When Pakistan army started its brutality in East Pakistan in March, 1971, millions of refugees thronged India and caused several major problems for India. When Indira Gandhi did not find a political solution to sort out this grievous situation, she asked the Army Chief, General Manekshaw to get the Indian army ready for liberation of Bangladesh who sought six months time for the preparation. Kao was asked by Indira Gandhi to prepare ground work for the army before the final assault and use R&AW to its optimum in this operation. Kao with the help of his able colleagues, built up a formidable guerilla force of more than one lakh Bangladesh refugees, Mukti Bahini which created havoc for the Pakistani army in East Pakistan. Besides that R&AW penetrated deep into all the establishments of East and West Pakistan and when the Indian army went for the final war on December 3, 1971, 93,000 soldiers of Pakistan army were hauled up in Dacca and made to surrender to the Indian army before Lt. General J S Aurora on December 16, 1971 i.e. within two weeks of the start of army action. This was the biggest and historical landmark for R&AW under R N Kao in the intelligence history of India.

In the North East of India, Sikkim was a strategic state in between India and China. There were some internal problems between the ruler of Sikkim and the local population which was beyond the control of the ruler. R N Kao advised Indira Gandhi to merge Sikkim for which she agreed. In this bloodless operation of R&AW, Sikkim was merged with India as the 22nd State without the intervention of defence forces. This was another feather in the cap of R N Kao.

Nuclear Explosion

In May, 1974, India exploded its first nuclear blast at Pokhran in Rajasthan to the utter surprise of many countries, particularly USA. CIA had received 26 reports in 1972 that India was on the verge of exploding a nuclear device or was capable of doing so. R N Kao was coordinating with the Scientists for this operation on security matters. It must be to his credit that he kept the entire programme under wrap and did not allow to get a wind of it to other nations for any penetratation. Only after the explosion, Pakistan radio made a broadcast at 1 PM on that day and the rest of the World started probing the truth about it. This was another major achievement of this elite Intelligence Officer of India.

Foreign Assisments

R N Kao had excellent rapport with his counterparts in other countries. He was a good friend of George Bush Senior, who was Director of CIA in the mid seventies. Likewise, during this period, Sir Maurice, Old-field head of MI6 was a personal friend of Kao and he shared views with him on various art and cultural matters besides the routine intelligence sharing. He was the model for 'Mr', James Bonds secret service chief in the 007 novels of Ian Fleming. He used to come on long vacations in India as personal guest of Kao in the mid seventies and visited important towns like Jaipur or Jaisalmer on the verge of the desert for relaxation. Mossad Chief and French Intelligence Head also had excellent rapport with Kao during this period. When Sewsagar Ramgoolam, the Prime Minister of Mauritius, visited India in the early seventies, he requested Indira Gandhi to help his ruling party to fight the Movement Militant Mauritian of Paul Beranger. Ramgoolam's party was largely ethnic Indian in composition while Beranger's was the party of the Ceroles, the Africans of the island who spoke "patoix", a mixture of French and African languages. K. Sankaran Nair, the number two in R&AW, was deputed by Kao to provide all sort of help to Ramgoolam and he won the next election.

Wali Khan, son of Khan Abdul Ghaffar Khan, the Frontier Gandhi and a stalwart in the Independence Movement, was living in exile at London in the early seventies. He was bitter opponent of Bhutto, the new Prime Minister of Pakistan because the North West Frontier Pathans were demanding autonomy which was oppressed by the central Government of Pakistan. Wali Khan wanted moral, political and other support from Mrs. Indira Gandhi. R N Kao sent his deputy Sankaran Nair to negotiate as the Indian representative. Since Pakistani Embassy at London was keeping watch on the movements of Wali Khan, the rendezvous was shifted to Copenhagen in Denmark where Nair and another R&AW man of Indian mission, I.S. Hassanwalia met Wali Khan. Subsequently all sort of support was given to Wali Khan by the Indian Government till 1977 when Indira Gandhi lost election.

Unsung Hero

Indira Gandhi imposed Emergency in India in June, 1975 and arrested most of the opposition leaders all over the country. There were charges of brutality and torture against these leaders. Ultimately, when in March, 1977, she lifted Emergency and held parliament election, she was routed in whole of North India and Morarji Desai of Janata Party became the new Prime Minister of India. Since, most of these leaders were recently released from jail, they apprehended that R&AW was misused by Mrs. Indira Gandhi during emergency against these leaders. R N Kao, who was on extension of his service, was unceremoniously asked by Morarji Desai to proceed on leave because he suspected him as the prime accused during Emergency. Charan Singh, the then Home Minister of India, appointed a one man committee headed by S P Singh to find out the involvement of R&AW in the internal affairs of the country during Emergency in 1975-77. This committee gave clean chit to R&AW in this regard and Kao was honourably exonerated for his involvement in Emergency.

After Indira Gandhi became Prime Minister in 1980, she called Kao from his retirement and appointed him as her senior advisor on internal and external developments. She used to consult him on political and intelligence matters. His professional guidance was of general nature. In one major development, when Indira Gandhi wanted to go USA she was not getting her choice of date of appointment with the US President through External Affairs Ministry channels. R N Kao through his friend George Bush Senior arranged her meeting with the US President.

When Indira Gandhi was assassinated, he was upset over her death and resigned on morale grounds. There were charges against Kao that he did not guide Indira Gandhi against a possible assassination attack from her security guards which were not substantiated in the Judicial Commission which was appointed subsequently to probe the assassination. Principal Secretary of Indira Gandhi, P C Alexander, was jealous of Kao's brilliance. His close proximity with Indira Gandhi was also a reason of his being envious to Kao. When Rajiv Gandhi became Prime Minister, Alexander used to mouth and misguide him against Kao. In this working culture, Kao found himself uncomfortable and sent his resignation to Rajiv Gandhi which was accepted by him.

R N Kao was very affectionately and emotionally linked to his younger brother who suffered a heart attack. He went to see him in the hospital and fainted there after visiting his ailing brother. Kao too had a massive heart failure and died on the spot along with his brother on January 20, 2002. This unsung hero was forgotten by the Indian government for his sterling contribution to India which has no parallel in this hidden society of intelligence community. He gave a lot to the country but got nothing. However, he got so many of his juniors decorated with numerous awards and rewards of the government.

❑

Formation of IB and R&AW

Formation of IB and RAW

In the aftermath of 1857 mutiny, the British rulers in India wanted a separate police force which should be totally loyal to them and serve their vested interest. This was done by passing a Police Act of 1861. The outfit thus created was anti-people and reactionary which fully served their purpose under all circumstances. This system functioned until 1885, when the Indian National Congress was formed for having a balanced equation between the British and the Indian public.

Freedom Struggle

By the end of 19th century, Delhi and its hinterland witnessed a number of cheating incidents which proliferated with the passage of time. The victims in most of these events included British and their loyalists. When the police were unable to control the situation, the British created the "Thuggi and Dacoity Department" which was manned by civilian police force. In 1904, this department was renamed as Central Criminal Intelligence Department which started assisting the local police in the whole of India on criminal matters. In 1918, it was changed into Intelligence Department with the principal objective of collecting political intelligence against those involved in freedom struggle. In 1920, when voice of freedom was raised in every corner of the country, it was again reorganized and made into the Directorate of Intelligence Bureau (DIB) for collecting intelligence on matters relating to internal as well as external security. By this time, the National Movement for independence had spread like a wild fire all over the country under the leadership of Mahatma Gandhi. Simultaneously, there erupted violent activities of Bhagat Singh and his associates, which made the British suspicious of every Indian in general and Hindus and Sikhs, in particular. Later on, Quit India movement compounded the problem further for DIB. The situation, however, became more vulnerable with the formation of Indian National Army (INA) under Subhash Chander Bose in league with the Japanese and Germans which was hell bent to overthrow the rule of British by force. The INA had set up its own intelligence cell to monitor the British intelligence which was on their feet to counter their violent activities. The DIB was keeping a tab on INA activists to checkmate their proliferation in the country. When the Second World War broke out, DIB's responsibilities increased further and its domain of activities got extended to all parts of India particularly towards the INA. Till 1947, most of the officers were either British nationals or Muslims from the regular police force of India. While there was no let-up in their regular law and order duties, they concentrated mainly on acquainting themselves with the political situation and trends and kept a track of any threat arising to the British Raj.

After the partition, the DIB was trifurcated. British went to their country and most of the Muslim officers opted for Pakistan leaving only a skeleton staff in India. However, before leaving for England and Pakistan, these British and Muslim officers burnt all records of Intelligence Bureau (IB) all over India which were prepared on the private lives of the Maharajas and the Congress leaders who were involved in the freedom movement. These Maharajas were blackmailed by the British rulers on the basis of these records. Dossiers of the sources of the British police were also destroyed in order to avoid any controversies for the Indian Government.

Shift of Power

The Indian officers who stepped into their shoes on the eve of Independence also came from the Indian Police of British and its successors, the Indian Police Service. They too had done their stints in the regular police. But in sharp contrast to their British predecessors; they were required to keep themselves completely away from politics. The sole political tendency expected, encouraged and rewarded was loyalty to the ruling party. Therefore, the men who came to be at the helm of the IB after independence were hardboiled policemen to whom crime and criminals were familiar and politics was a taboo. In fact, they were trained by their British masters to look upon every Indian politicians, who were opposed to the British Raj, a little better than criminals. Neither did the rules change significantly to usher in a transformation in the character of the new organization nor in its purpose of functioning. The transfer of power was meant to them a shift of loyalty from the British to the Congress party which had come to power after the British left India. A logical consequence followed thereafter. Political spying started on those who were opposed to the party in power. In the working of intelligence too, these men were totally at sea. Trained in and accustomed for long years to the use of police executive powers, they were at a complete loss in a set-up which first stripped them of their uniform and their powers and then asked them to show results. To operate unseen, went against their achievements.

Indian IB was first headed by an Indian T J Sanjievi Pillai after the partition. Hence, from the Thuggi and Dacoity of 1890 it became IB in 1947 which is still continuing to look after the internal security matters of the country. This Thuggi and Dacoity became so synonymous for intelligence gathering in North India during the pre-partition days that still the Shimla office of IB located at Dormers Building is known as Thuggi house to the local population.

IB Formed

Sanjievi Pillai, the first Director of IB after partition wanted to make a cadre for IB and started recruitment for the rank of Sub Inspectors of highly qualified personnel with the ultimate aim of creating an independent intelligence department of a purely civil nature. To make a beginning in this regard, he visited Washington in 1949 to study the organizational set up of CIA with the consent of then government. He conceived the idea of an independent intelligence cadre drawn mostly from universities. The scheme attracted students with good academic record. The idea was to train these youngsters and finally pass the reins of the organization to them. Sanjievi demanded executive powers which were resented by the government on the plea that executive powers to a secret service were incompatible with the principles of democracy. However, due to these differences with the then Home Minister Sardar Patel, he was replaced by B N Mullick who continued to rule IB till 1965. Political bosses, be of that period or of now, in the seats of power were perfectly content the Bureau's spying on its political opponents. Even today, the entire work and division of work of the IB is based on political necessity of the party in power. The candidates recruited in IB and RAW for any post are asked to fill a declaration if they or any of their near relatives are associated with the Communists or the Rashtriya Swayamsevak Sangh of the Bhartiya Janta Party. If the reply is in affirmative, they are not recruited in these departments due to their allegiance to these groups. Surprisingly, when Inderjit Gupta was Home Minister under the Deve Gowda and I.S.Gujral Government, he did not remove this column of the Communists. Even when NDA Government under Atal Bihari Vajpayee ruled for five years up to 2004 and a RSS cadre man L K Advani was Home Minister, the column of RSS was never removed from the recruitment form for the reasons best known to them. It implies that a RSS man and a Communist can become the Home Minister of India but he can not get a job in IB and RAW due to this linkage. This is the most intriguing aspect of ruling this country when these politicians are in power, they are denied any chance to the kiths and kin of their cadre to join IB and RAW at the behest of Indian bureaucracy.

Police Monopoly

Mullick too continued the scheme of direct recruitment of youngsters from the universities but his preoccupation with important political and military problems did not allow him time to reorganize the intelligence administration. No worthwhile attention was paid to cadre planning. The induction of police personnel continued much to the disliking of the better educated direct recruits from the universities. There were instances, which still continue, when the recruits from the police ranks tried to boss over their understudies posted along with, or under them, for training. A feeling developed in a section that IB had become a police organization with direct recruits from open market forming a neglected minority. Mullick had promised the newly direct recruits confirmation in the Indian Police Service within a span of 20 years which was never done. No separate cadre was earmarked for them.

This trend continued in RAW also at later stage. It would be worthwhile to mention here that in spite of these efforts by Sanjievi, Mullick in IB and later on by R N Kao in RAW, no direct recruit has been allowed to head these organizations due to the persistent monopoly of IPS officers. Slowly vested interests developed and IB became a close preserve of the faithful of its Chief, with their own, cliques and deeds, shrouded under the garb of secrecy. As police cadres were favoured by their state bosses, their proportion increased alarmingly. Deputation of these police officers as per rule for one year continued for 30 years or till their retirement. This trend further demoralized the capable and distinguished officers of IB who surrendered to their fate. A police culture grown over the years has virtually replaced government control over the agency. And at a time when the mash between security threat and democratic dissent was getting increasingly blurred, the IB had become all powerful with no public accountability till Mullick was Director and Pandit Nehru was the Prime Minister. The structure of the IB has been ambiguous. It is usually described as a civilian department, a central police organization and a wing of the Home Ministry. Unlike the CIA, FBI or the erstwhile KGB, the IB does not exist under any act of Parliament nor does it follow the rules applicable to other department of the government. Similar situation is prevalent in RAW. The absence of legal sanction has resulted in the misuse of power. There is still a confusion among the employees of these two departments as to whether they belong to a central police organization or a civilian department. This unaccountability had made them immune to public criticism or parliamentary scrutiny. It has thus made them an easy prey to political pressure.

According to K Sankaran Nair, the number two under R N Kao in RAW, he worked for many years under B N Mullick and found him a formidable and iconic leader of the IB but he committed a blunder. Prior to his retirement, there was a rumour in IB that M.M.L. Hooja would succeed him but one Sharda Prasad

Verma from Bihar IPS cadre was brought as his understudy and became IB Director after his retirement much to the resentment of Hooja. For the first time, a hidden rivalry started taking roots among the top hierarchy of IB as a result of this action of Mullick. Verma continued to consult Mullick on all important matters even after his re-employment as Director General, Security in charge of the Aviation Research Centre (ARC). Ultimately, Hooja became Director of IB when Verma completed his term.

After the unwarranted blame on IB that it failed to provide adequate intelligence in 1962 and 1965 war, the then Prime Minister, Mrs. Indira Gandhi wanted to create an external intelligence outfit under a loyal man of known integrity. Initially, she was considered a weak Prime Minister hounded by senior Congressmen who worked with her father Pandit Jawahar Lal Nehru. Y B Chavan, the then Home Minister of India was then considered a very powerful man in the Cabinet. He wanted to resist this move by Indira Gandhi. However, when Chavan was Defence Minister of India, after the 1965 war, a paper was prepared at his behest that army wanted their own intelligence comprising of academies and army officers in various field. Indira Gandhi used this paper against Chavan and decided to form an external intelligence agency. R N Kao a known Kashmiri Pandit who was the Security Officer of Pandit Jawahar Lal Nehru was selected for this job. Indira Gandhi knew Kao personally for a long time. Kao was known to be near to the Nehru family because his mother was childhood friend of Kamla Nahru, wife of Pandit Jawahar Lal Nehru. His father in law Justice A N Mulla was also a close friend of Moti Lal Nehru. He was from I.P. cadre of 1940. Being Kashmiri was an added advantage to the elevation of this post for Kao beside the full confidence Indira Gandhi reposed in him due to his long association with Nehru family.

There was yet another feather in the cap of R N Kao in his operational capability. During his younger days as an intelligence officer, in 1955, he was instrumental to avert a major political mishap when he participated in the investigation of the sabotage of an Air India plane "Kashmir Princess" by the agents of Taiwan. This plane chartered by the Chinese government was supposed to carry their Prime Minister Chou-en-Lai from Hong Kong for Bandung Conference of Non-aligned countries in Indonesia in April, 1955. This plane crashed in the Indonesian sea. Fortunately, Chou-en-Lai did not travel in this plane on that day. Obviously, Chinese government raised a hue and cry on this sabotage and demanded a tripartite inquiry by including an Indian intelligence officer along with the Hong Kong and British police into this sabotage. R N Kao was selected by Indian government to participate in this inquiry. He ably convinced the Chinese Prime Minister Chou-en-Lai on the proceedings of the investigation and lauded by him for the work he did in Hong Kong and presented a personal souvenir to him for his ability. Pandit Nehru, the then Indian Prime Minister showered all praises on

Kao for this successful assignment. Indira Gandhi was aware of this achievement of young Kao and as such he was found as the only suitable intelligence officer to head the new external intelligence outfit of the country.

IB Bifurcated

Kao was on official tour in England in November 1967 when the then Cabinet Secretary Joshi called him and conveyed the decision of the Cabinet that IB would be bifurcated and a new organization for external intelligence would be created. He wanted a scheme on this proposal based on his past experiment because he created the intelligence department of Ghana a coastal country in Africa during 1959-60 on the request of the then President of that country Kwame Nkrumah to Pandit Jawahar Lal Nehru. R N Kao, a Post Graduate in English, studied the intelligence system of various democratic countries because Indira Gandhi did not want to replicate IB functioning which in her opinion was an old wine in new bottle. Because of her past experience, she specifically told Kao not to create a police organization but a modernized intelligence based on latest developments all over the World. Kao deeply studied the working system of the USA, British, KGB of USSR, German, Japanese, French and Israel intelligence outfits and based on the available resources prepared a pilot scheme which was flexible enough to include any intelligence requirement and was not in any way rigid in its functioning.

Bureaucratic Rivalry

There was an extreme bureaucratic rivalry in IB at that time when it was decided to bifurcate for its external intelligence. When Kao discussed this scheme with the then senior officers of IB, S P Verma, the Director and M M L Hooja, both of them tried to thwart this scheme on one plea or the other and never cooperated with Kao. Ultimately, Kao submitted the blue print for creating a new external intelligence department as Research and Analysis Wing, RAW to the then Cabinet Secretary who appointed Kao as Officer on Special Duty in Cabinet Secretariat severing all his link with the IB. S P Verma retired in February, 1968 and M M L Hooja succeeded him who fought tooth and nail to scuttle any move of R N Kao to take help from the IB on any matter in the formation of new intelligence outfit RAW. Not a single officer working on foreign desk was transferred to RAW by him. Kao wanted to appoint K.S. Sankran Nair, a competent officer of IB, as his deputy which was delayed by Hooja by denying him the promotion so that Kao could not have a smooth sailing in his new venture. However, with the help of the Principal Secretary P N Haksar and the then Foreign Secretary T N Kaul who both were also Kashmiri Pandits, every thing was sorted out and Sankaran Nair was asked to join as number two in RAW though on a lower rank to which he agreed during a lunch meeting with Kao. He was subsequently promoted as Additional Director.

RAW Established

With this background, RAW was formally established on 21 Sept., 1968. This name was selected on the basis of a wing of CIA. Kao demanded some staff from IB working on foreign desks which was vehemently resisted by Hooja. About 250 staff of IB whom Hooja considered as sub-standard, was transferred to RAW. Sensitive branches like foreign language experts, forensic experts, crypto and cipher officials and even accounts knowing personnel were not transferred to RAW. Initially, there were lots of difficulties even in the disbursement of monthly salary of the staff due to paucity of trained staff at the disposal of Kao. However, calm and sagacious Kao with the help of flamboyant Sankaran Nair and Sardar I S Hassanwalia, won over all these problems in a short spell of time. A number of private buildings were hired in South Delhi for official purposes of RAW. Indira Gandhi arranged an office for Kao in South Block for his functioning. Indira Gandhi gave him free hand to organize the new department.

In order to organize the functions of RAW in important countries where Indian interests were of urgent importance, Kao took help of the then Foreign Secretary T N Kaul who fully cooperated with him. New posts for RAW officials were created in the neighboring countries and in USA, UK, and other strategic countries of Europe and in South East Asia. Many police officers and Army officers were taken on deputation to man these postings. Many new divisions like Information, Economic, Science and Technology etc. were created by Kao on the pattern of other foreign intelligence agencies. Structure of RAW was exclusively a new one and amalgam of

whatever Kao thought was good from all the advanced foreign intelligence agencies, although there are apprehensions that it is having some resemblance to CIA of USA. Hence, from this skeleton staff of 250 members in 1968, Kao started RAW which ultimately did some excellence job for the country in the coming future. Although no policeman in western democracies is heading intelligence outfit, but in RAW and IB, initially there was no option for the then Government to appoint Police officers for these posts which is currently proving detrimental to the effective working of these organizations.

❑

3

Rebellion of Sheikh Abdullah

Brief history of the major events of Jammu and Kashmir is summarized as under:-

1846: Gulab Singh bought Jammu and Kashmir from the East India Company for Rs.75,00,000 (Seventy Five Lakhs) under the treaty of Amritsar on 16th March, 1846 and the state of Jammu and Kashmir came into being.

1932: Sheikh Mohammed Abdullah and Mirwaiz Yusuf Shah formed the All Jammu and Kashmir Muslim Conference.

1939: Muslim Conference dissolved by Sheikh Abdullah and Jammu and Kashmir National Conference came into being.

1946: National Conference launched Quit Kashmir movement against the Maharaja and demanded the abrogation of the Treaty of Amritsar. Sheikh Abdullah arrested.

1947: Sheikh Abdullah released on 29th September.

1947: Pakistan sponsored tribesmen entered Kashmir on 22nd October.

1947: Maharaja Hari Singh signed the Instrument of Accession acceding Kashmir to the Indian Union on 27th October. Indian Army entered the state to repel the Pakistan raiders; Sheikh Abdullah appointed head of the Emergency Administration.

1948: India took the Kashmir problem in the United Nations Security Council on 1st January and offered to hold a plebiscite under UN supervision after the raiders were moved back, the plebiscite administrator took his officer under the Jammu and Kashmir Govt. and the Pakistanis were not given the chance to consolidate their hold on the areas which they had illegally occupied.

1948: On 13th August, a UN commission proposed the future of the state would be decided in accordance with the will of the people after the territory occupied by the Pakistani tribesmen is vacated. This was accepted by Pakistan on 20th December.

1949: A ceasefire between India and Pakistan left 84000 sq. km. of Kashmir under Pakistani control out of which 5180 sq. km. was ceded to China by Pakistan later.

1949: On 17th October, the Indian Constituent Assembly adopts Article 370 of the Constitution ensuring a special status for Jammu and Kashmir.

1951: An interim constitution for the state came into force in November.

1952: An agreement is arrived at on 24th July between Sheikh Abdullah and the Government of India which provided the state's autonomy within India.

1953: On 9th August, Sheikh Abdullah Govt. dismissed and he was arrested for treason. Bakshi Ghulam Mohammed became the Prime Minister of state.

1956: State Constituent Assembly adopted a constitution for the state which had a provision making it an integral part of the Indian Union.

1963: After the disappearance of holy relic from the Hazratbal shrine, large scale violence and demonstrations took place across the Valley.

1964: Holy relic recovered on 4 January.

1964: Sheikh Abdullah released on 8th April after the conspiracy case was withdrawn.

1964: On 29th April, Prime Minister Jawahar Lal Nehru and Sheikh Abdullah held talks.

1964: Sheikh Abdullah was sent to Pakistan on 25th May by Nehru for talks with Field Marshal Ayub Khan.

1964: Jawahar Lal Nehru died on 27th May.

1965: India and Pakistan war began after armed Pakistani infiltrators crossed the ceasefire line on 5th August and the international border in Chhamb in September. The war ended in a ceasefire on 23rd September.

1971: Bangladesh war started on 3rd December. Pakistani forces surrendeedr in two weeks and East Pakistan became Bangladesh.

1972: India and Pakistan signed the Shimla Agreement on 2nd July by Mrs. Indira Gandhi and Zulfiqar Ali Bhutto with provision for establishment of durable peace and normalization of relations including final settlement of

Jammu and Kashmir and resumption of diplomatic relations between India and Pakistan.

1974: Kashmir accord signed on 3rd November by G. Parthasarthy for Indira Gandhi and Mirza Mohammad Afzal Beg for Sheikh Abdullah. Certain constitutional commitments were accepted.

1975: Sheikh Abdullah sworn in as Chief Minister on 25th February with the support of the Congress.

1977: Sheikh Abdullah resigned after Congress withdrew support on 27th March and the Assembly was dissolved. Elections were held on 30th June and National Conference got 47 out of 76 seats.

1982: Sheikh Abdullah died on 8th September and his son Farooq became the Chief Minister.

Plebiscite

There had been much criticism within India against Prime Minister Jawaharlal Nehru's decision of taking the Kashmir issue in the Security Council of the United Nations in 1948 and acceptance of the principle of plebiscite which is still hounding the Kashmir problem. This was done under some compelling circumstances of that period which led Nehru to refer this case in the Security Council and to accept to hold plebiscite although the Indian army was capable of driving the raiders out of Jammu and Kashmir. Certain questions were also raised about the acquiescence to a plebiscite by India when the Maharaja of Kashmir had legally acceded to India by signing the instrument of accession. These issues could not be objectively criticized subsequently and those events had to be recapitulated which forced Nehru to take such drastic and questionable decisions at that time.

After the declaration of independence and feeling encouraged with the events of Hyderabad and Junagarh, the Pakistanis invaded Jammu and Kashmir in October, 1947. Indian troops were sent in the valley immediately after the instrument of accession was signed by Maharaja Hari Singh with the Indian Govt. Since, Indian army was not familiar with the terrain of the valley, it became difficult for it to get vacated immediately certain areas in the deep which were occupied by the Pakistani raiders. The winter season was round the corner due to which there was apprehension that combat operations would be extremely difficult and unmanageable for the Indian army which was ill-equipped and not well organized a result of the partition of the country. Further, it was apprehended that additional contingents of such raiders would be pushed into the valley in the winter by Pakistan that would make this regional fight into a long drawn war which India could ill afford in view of the problem faced in the northern region as a result of the influx of large refugees from West Pakistan. Also, there was a belief that Security Council might give its final verdict in a short period which was subsequently stalled at the behest of the Americans and the British.

Further, the Indian Govt. had taken a general stand that accession of every State would be decided on the wishes of the people of that State and not on the will of the ruler. This is the reason that the Indian Govt. had taken military action in Hyderabad whose Nawab had declared his state independent and Junagarh whose ruler had decided to accede his state with Pakistan. Hence, merger of all these three states had to be considered together and not in isolation because if India could have claimed that instrument of accession signed with the Maharaja of Kashmir was final merger then they had to accept the Pakistani claim over Junagarh and also tolerate Hyderabad as an independent state within India. The Hyderabad and Junagarh issues were also taken in the Security Council but due to the majority population of Hindus in these states, the Security Council had little doubt of their annexation with India and did not pursue the matter. Whereas in Kashmir the case was just reverse where the majority population was Muslim but ruler was Hindu whose desire to merge with India could not be taken for granted and initially Maharaja Hari Singh also showed his reservations to merge with India for a long time. Hence, if India did not accept to hold plebiscite in Jammu and Kashmir, the Junagarh case could be re-opened and India's stand on Hyderabad would have been weakened. So, tactically the decision to accept the plebiscite formula was correct due to the prevalent political scenario of accession of that period. However, India had been able to accept the condition of plebiscite only after the whole of the territory of Jammu and Kashmir is vacated from the raiders of Pakistan, which ultimately has not been done till today. At that time Pakistanis knew that people's movement in Jammu and Kashmir was pro-Indian than pro-Pakistani and the leaders of that movement led by Sheikh Abdulla acknowledged their allegiance to Gandhi and Nehru so they purposely did not get the territory vacated from the raiders to prolong the political solution on the basis of plebiscite. There was no criticism of the ceasefire as a result of the intervention of the Security Council at that time but the criticism came up subsequently when the Security Council failed to force Pakistan to withdraw intruders from the illegally occupied territory of Kashmir due to the imperialist intrigues.

If India had accepted to hold plebiscite some time in 1949, there was a good chance of its merger with India because the atrocities committed by the Pakistani intruders on the peaceful people of Kashmir were still fresh in their minds and India was held in much high esteem as their savior. Military intervention by India at that juncture was considered as timely help[for which India was hailed as savior of Kashmiri population. The National Conference was also a united body and had complete control over Kashmiri psyche in the valley. He declared in a convention of his party in October 1948 that political, social and cultural background of Kashmir required its immediateaccession with India alone. On the other hand, Nehru's prestige amongst the Kashmiris was very high because they still remembered that he had gone to Kashmir in support of the people's liberation struggle and had courted arrest for their cause. Even the British assessment at that time was that there was an even chance for India to succeed in the plebiscite if held at that time.

Sheikh Abdullah, at the same time, was deadly opposed to the plebiscite in Kashmir. His autocratic attitude imbibed a feeling in him that he was the sole representative of the people of Kashmir and whatever he would decide should be acceptable to them. So, he had formed a firm opinion that it was futile to opt for plebiscite when he had taken the final decision to merge Kashmir with India. He considered it would hurt his prestige if some outsider should come as the Plebiscite Administrator in his State to find out their views because he had opted for accession with India and that had to be the final decision of every Kashmiri. The Indian Govt. was in a dilemmatic situation as it had accepted the United Nations Commission for India & Pakistan (UNCIP) resolution for a plebiscite which was vehemently opposed by Sheikh Abdullah who was pampered by Nehru as the sole leader of Kashmir.

Overall political situation in Kashmir was murky because conflicting reports were received by Indian Government about other leaders of Kashmir on the matter of plebiscite. Sheikh Abdullah had a long-drawn enmity with the Maharaja Hari Singh which ultimately infused animosity against the Dogra community. Kashmiri Pandits who wielded much influence in the kingdom were scared for their own existence in the rule of Sheikh Abdullah. Minority Hindu population thus was apprehensive about the basic communalism of Sheikh Abdullah because he always raised the issue of Muslims who fled to Pakistan after violence in Jammu but was hardly concerned about the non-Muslim refugees who were living in pathetic conditions in Jammu and adjoining areas. There was absolute suspicion in the mind of Maharaja and other Hindu leaders that Sheikh Abdullah's much hyped friendship was delusive to strengthen his own political ascendancy in the state so that he could call his own shots in future. In Delhi, there was a strong apprehension among politicians that Sardar Patel and Pandit Nehru had divergent opinion about the integrity of Sheikh Abdullah and his future motives as Sardar Patel never gave credence to the intentions of Sheikh Abdullah. At later stage stage of the history, Sardar Patel was proved right whereas Jawaharlal Nehru was considered incorrect in their assessment.

Turbulence Brewed

In January, 1949, IB sent a report to the government that Sheikh Abdullah had given an interview to two foreign correspondents, Davidson and Ward Price in which he visualized the possibility of an independent Kashmir which was subsequently indicated by Karanjia in his weekly Blitz from Bombay on these lines. When details of the interview were enquired from Sheikh Abdullah, he came to know of this report of the IB. He demanded withdrawal of the IB officer from the valley who had sent that report or else he would be put under detention by him. Since, political situation in Kashmir was volatile at that time which Sheikh Abdullah was exploiting on his whims and fancies, the Government had no option but to withdraw that IB officer from the State on the threat of Sheikh. IB Director vehemently opposed this action of the Government. Subsequently, a capable Sikh army officer Ijwant Singh Hassanwalia was posted as Assistant Director in-charge of IB in Jammu and Kashmir with the approval of Sheikh Abdullah. This was blessing in disguise for the Government because Hassanwalia proved his worth as the most capable and fearless officer who was later instrumental in exposting the treason and treachery of Sheikh Abdullah against India.

While all these suspicious intrigues were making rounds, Sheikh Abdullah started fired a salvo and demanded that either the Maharaja should either abdicate or else face an enquiry in connection with charge of connivance on the massacre of Muslims in Jammu and adjoining areas. Government of India was aware of this mendacious accusation of Sheikh but helplessly bowed to the autocratic demand knowing well that instrument of accession was signed by the Maharaja which could have adverse implication in the Security Council. However, no Indian politicians had the guts to counter the illegitimate demands of Sheikh at that critical juncture. So, in view of his unflinching high stature in Kashmir valley where his own party was toeing his dictated lines, a compromise formula was devised. In May, 1949, Maharaja was forced to leave Kashmir and his son Yuvraj Karan Singh took over his place and assigned the status to work as an agent of the Maharaja. This was an intolerable humiliation for both of them. This action further emboldened the Sheikh who perceived that Government of India was at his mercy and he fully exploited this situation in his nefarious designs.

In the meantime, the Security Council nominated Admiral Nimtiz as the Plebiscite Administrator for Kashmir which was vehemently opposed by Sheikh Abdullah on the ground that he was the undisputed leader of Kashmiri population and no plebiscite of any sort was required in Kashmir. Indian Government devised a formula with Sheikh Abdullah to counter the proposal of plebiscite and suggested to form a Constituent Assembly for the Kashmir wherein its people would be responsible to define their own destiny on all subjects related to them. This was an intelligent move by Indian Govt. because Pakistan had not withdrawal the troops from the Indian territory which was a pre-condition to plebiscite as decided by the Security Council. Thus, legally India was absolutely correct in not pursuing the proposal of plebiscite on this ground only.

In order to give their distorted version, Indian Prime Minister Jawaharlal Nehru was getting conflicting reports from sycophants and detractors of Sheikh Abdullah on the ground realities prevailing in Kashmir about both the Hindu and Muslim population in general and Sheikh Abdullah in particular. IB was asked to submit the assessment in this regard. IB Director Mullik gave a report wherein he pointed out he general opinion that there was no suspicion about the faith and intention of Sheikh Abdullah in this accession of Kashmir in the Indian territory. General public was reported to be totally in favour of the accession. Other leaders like Bakshi Ghulam Mohd. and D P Dhar were not doubting the genuine intentions of Sheikh and they strongly advocated the unity of Kashmir with India for its betterment rather than with Pakistan apprehending thrust of tribal across the border which would change the identity of Kashmir. Nehru circulated this report to all missions abroad and also sent a copy to the Permannent Representative at the UNO so that he could project wishes of Kashmiri people at the world for a. When this report was sent to Sardar Patel, the Indian Home Minister, he countered it by cautioning that Sheikh Abdullah would let down India and Jawaharlal Nehru and his antipathy towards Dogra community was inborn which ultimately would be hostile towards the majority community in India.

I S Hassanwalia, head of the Jammu and Kashmir unit of IB, under the cover of the army, opened many posts in whole of Jammu and Kashmir which improved the intelligence gathering on political and security of the State as Pakistan was bent upon increasing acts of subversion in Kashmir. These IB posts were opened clandestinely in army area without knowledge of Sheikh Abdullah because he was suspicious of the activities of IB and put all sort of obstructions in its expansion. Due to disintegration in the National Conference which was autocratically ruled by Sheikh Abdullah, Ghulam Mohiuddin Karra, who was of equal status as that of Sheikh was deliberately denied the Cabinet birth by him left National Conference. Karra was a stooge of Pakistan and with their financial support formed a political outfit the Kashmir Political Conference which demanded the accession of Kashmir with Pakistan. Pakistan resorted to subversive activities inside the valley by financing some anti-Indian elements and Karra was one of them. Pakistan devised this new subversive policy because there was remote possibility of any additional aggression from their army due to the presence of Indian army at all vantage points on the frontiers. UN observers were posted all over Kashmir and in this scenario, Pakistan army had no chance for direct infiltration to face these two factors.

IB reported to the government. the internal subversion and sabotage activities which Pakistan had initiated through anti-Indian groups and individuals and also financed several mushrooming subversive organizations. Karra's party and one Pir Maqbool Gilani were the chief architects of these activities. Moreover, many Muslims who had fled to Pakistan from Jammu and Kashmir were sent back by

Pakistan by imparting training of sabotage. IB had to operate with extreme caution because Sheikh was wary of IB's activities in Kashmir and was a stumbling block in its smooth functioning. Hassanwalia penetrated all anti-Indian groups through their communication channels and their contacts and Delhi Headquarterss of IB was able to suggest counter-measures to Government on the basis of the reports of its Kashmir office. Hassanwalia was thus able to be one step ahead of these covert organizations and exposed the arrival of first consignment of arms and explosives from Pakistan amongst the pro-Pakistani agents.

When IB reported the infiltration of Pakistani trained Muslim Kashmiris, the state government ignored this fact. State Govt. rather affirmed that the refugees had the right to come back and should be allowed to do so because as per the Land Reform Act, which was passed in the Constituent Assembly without the consent of Centre, empowered the Muslims who had migrated to Pakistan could return to Jammu and Kashmir and occupy the land according to terms of the UN resolution. Most of the holders of these lands were Hindu. Surprisingly, no permanent provision was made for the settlement of Hindus and Sikh refugees from Pakistan occupied territory though they were living in utter misery in many parts of the State. They were given only temporary leases of evacuee property and as such their future remained uncertain compared to other refugees who migrated from Punjab, Sindh and NWF Provinces of Pakistan to India. These Hindu and Sikh refugees were discriminated on the ground that the land belonging to the Muslims migrated to Pakistan could not be transferred as per UN resolution which authorised them to come back and resettle in these lands. This open invitation to these migrated Muslims to resettle in India gave clandestine opportunity to Pakistan to infiltrate trained saboteurs and propagandists whose number swelled in the years to come. This legislation passed by the State Government gave ample opportunity to Pakistan to increase infiltration of saboeterus under the garb of refugees which was a new headache for the IB to acertain their real identity.

Constituent Assembly Constituted

The idea to constitute the Constituent Assembly with the consent of Sheikh Abdullah was mooted by the Indian Government to thwart any incursion in Kashmir. The architect of this strategy was Gopalswamy Iyengar, the then State Home Minister. Indian Government logically took the advantage in this planning because Security Council could not force Pakistan to withdraw its intruders from the illegally occupied territory in Kashmir and creat conducive atmosphere for plebiscite. Sheikh Abdullah was hoodwinked this opportunity to suit his hidden agenda. He affirmed his supremacy logically under this umbrella and in a meeting of General Council of his party in October, 1950 wanted to end any drift and uncertainty to create a democratic set-up for the people of Kashmir. In the resolution passed in this meeting on the initiative of Sheikh Abdullah, it was affirmed that Kashmir's accession to India was perfectly valid legally, morally and politically and the people of Kashmir had the right of social progress being part and parcel of the Indian Union. A mandate was thus given to the party under the leadership of Sheikh Abdullah to convene the Constituent Assembly which would be the constitutional authority to decide the fate of Kashmiri population with regard to future course of actions.

On April 4, 1951, Yuvraj issued a proclamation directing that a Constituent Assembly should be constituted forthwith for the purpose of framing a constitution for the State which was resisted by an Anglo-US draft resolution. In the elections held in September, 1951, seventy five members were elected which gave massive majority to the National Conference. Some members who were opposed to Sheikh got elected from the Hindu majority area of Jammu. Subsequently, the rule of the Maharaja was abolished and replaced by the Sadar-e-Riyasat (Governor). Yuvraj Karan Singh was elected the first Sadar-e-Riyasat on November 17, 1952. The Assembly also approved a separate flag for the State and restricted the use of Indian National Flag on formal functions. A Basic Principles Committee was also appointed which finalized its final draft of accession to India in March, 1953 which created rift in the National Conference. While a group headed by Bakshi Ghulam Mohammand, G M Sadiq, D P Dhar and Harbans Singh Azad tried hard to bring about Kashmir's integration with India, Sheikh Abdullah although agreed to accession as logical wanted to keep Kashmir as autonomous as possible with only defence, communications and foreign affairs to be handled by the Indian Government.

Confrontation

Australian Judge, Sir Owen Dixon was appointed as UN representative after the departure of UNCIP in 1948. His final recommendation to the UN was that it was not possible to hold overall plebiscite for whole of Jammu and Kashmir including the area occupied by Pakistan. He suggested that the Jammu and the adjoining Hindu majority area could merge with India and the Pakistan occupied Kashmir along with the contiguous Muslim majority areas like Pooch, Rajouri, Mendhar etc. could merge with Pakistan. He further recommended that a plebiscite could be held in the Kashmir valley alone under the auspices of the UN to determine its future. Sir Owen Dixon was greatly influenced by Dr. Edmonds, the Principal of C.M.S. Mission School of Kashmir and a close confidant of Sheikh Abdullah. It was suspected that these proposal were mooted at the behest of Sheikh Abdullah. This fact was reported by the IB office in Kashmir to Indian Government. So, Sheikh had dubious intention in his mind about the accession in spite of the fact that he approved the logical inclusion with India in the newly formed Constituent Assembly.

Although, Sheikh Abdullah maintained cordial relations with Nehru but became autocratic in heeding to the advice of Indian Government. When the Indian Government suggested that the jurisdiction of the Comptroller and Auditor General be extended to Jammu and Kashmir, he resented this move and accused the Government of wanting him to sign a promissory note in their favour. He was poignant on this move of the Indian Government and gave a highly provocative anti-Indian speech at Ranbirsinghpura wherein his outburst was coloured with his own ill designs.. He described the accession as of restricted nature and full application of Indian Constitution was unrealistic, childish and savouring of lunacy. In another speech, he retorted that it would be better to die than to submit to the taunt that India was their bread-giver and Kashmir was not begging for India's aid. These outrageous postures of Sheikh were duly reported by the IB to the Prime Minister who mildly rebuked him for this provocation. A draft proposal about certain constitutional ties with India was to be signed by Sheikh Abdullah which he delayed to assess the consent of other Assembly members. When he was convinced that majority of members were against him, he reluctantly signed this agreement on the initiation of Bakshi and Sadiq. IB kept Prime Minister informed almost all these political developments, favourable or otherwise, that were taking place in Kashmir. Developments within the Constituent Assembly and in the Basic Principles Committee were duly communicated by the IB to the Prime Minister which he mildly pointed out to Sheikh Abdullah either directly or through Bakshi and other only on matters pertaining to the development against India in Kashmir.

In another important incident of political repercussions, IB reported a deliberate attempt on the part of Sheikh to ignore the people of Ladakh and deny their leader Kushak Bakula his rightful place in the political set-up. There was a strong resentment among the Buddhists as a result of this deliberate neglect of their reion by the Sheikh Government. IB report was endorsed by Sadar-e-Riyasat in his own report to the Indian Government. Several steps were then taken by the Indian Government to improve economic situation of Ladakh. Thereafter, IB organized patrol parties which were sent to the borders with Tibet and Sinkiang through uninhabited region of North and North-East Ladakh to which Kashmir Government never gave any strategic importance. To the discomfiture of many Hindu leaders, Sheikh carved out Muslim majority areas of Doda and Kishwar as separate district detaching from the Hindu majority district of Udhampur which was an instinct of communal bias of Hindus in Sheikh Abdullah. He was testing the patience of Indian Government by indulging in every matter and deliberately created a hostile situation which Nehru ignored with the hope that Sheikh would play a bigger role in Indian politics which was his weirdly dream. Sheikh suspected that IB was responsible for his exposure to Nehru. So, he demanded the withdrawal of two officers from Kashmir which was vehemently restented by IB Director since such unfounded allegation could demoralize the IB cadre which was working in worst conditions on the borders where neither Kashmir police nor army had ever operated. This confrontation was diffused on the invervention of senior leaders, Bakshi and Dhar, who convinced Sheikh on this matter.

In the winter of 1952-53, the Praja Parishad started agitation in Jammu demanding full integration of Jammu and Kashmir with India on the basis of one constitution, one flag and one President because abolition of Maharaja had deeply hurt the Hindu community of that area. The pathetic conditions of Hindu and Sikh refugees at various places in Jammu and Kashmir added fuel to the fire. This agitation was brutally handled by the police at the behest of Sheikh Abdullah. Similar agitation was started in Delhi by the newly formed Jana Sangh party of Shyama Prasad Mukherji which was also countered by Delhi administration. Sheikh became very hostile on these agitations and categorized this as Hindu revivalism which was trying to harm the Muslims of Kashmir. Although, Nehru justified the views of Jana Sangh and Praja Mandal but he could not ignore the prevalent international opinions on it engineered by Pakistan in Security Council. IB under Hassanwalia and with the active role of its Director Mullik helped the State Govt. to contain this agitation and diffused the ignited situation successfully.

Sheikh Abdullah was trying to use this agitation as an excuse to stall his previous commitment of accession to India in all fairness. He openly challenged India's secularism on this incident and put forward an argument that integration of Jammu and Kashmir and particularly of the Kashmir valley and certain adjoining parts which had Muslim majority with Hindu India would not be in the interest of the Muslims of Kashmir. Thereafter, he openly professed for a special status for Kashmir. He misconceived a weirdly illusion after meeting two prominent foreign visitors during this period that Kashmir should be developed like Switzerland whose security could be guaranteed by big powers, where tourist from various parts of the World would improve its economy and he would be the ultimate beneficiary as the undisputed ruler of this territory. His hostile diatribe against India increased day by day and he used every occasion particularly Friday gatherings at the Hazratbal Mosque to spread the his venom through vicious propaganda against Indian Government. IB was keeping a close vigil on his activities and duly informed the Indian Government on his day to day hostility. Nehru cross-checked these reports of IB with D P Dhar and Karan Singh who corroborated IB's assessment.

In this volte-face, Sheikh Abdullah got arrested Dr. Shyama Prasad Mukherji, founder of Jana Sangh, on 8 May, 1953 for defying ban on the entry into Jammu and Kashmir and was taken to Srinagar and put under house arrest. There was lot of criticism in India on this arrest. But Sheikh became more defiant in spite of the fact that his other Muslim colleague Bakshi, Sadiq, Mir Qasim and Masoodi refused to accept his anti-Indian propaganda. Nehru was against any confrontation against him and invited him to Delhi to remove all sort of misunderstanding but Sheikh spurned the invitation. His recalcitrant behaviour continued to haunt Delhi.

Visualizing the broader implication of this complex imbroglio engineered by Sheikh, Nehru went to Srinagar in May 1953 and met Sheikh and all other assembly members at the residence of Sheikh. He briefed them in detail on the prevalent internal and international implications on Kashmir and stressed the importance of its merger with India for security and prosperity. Nehru warned them of serious consequences towards its destruction — culturally, economically and politically — to adopt any other alternative. But Sheikh did not relent and remained defiant as before, Nehru returned to Delhi, fully dejected due to failure in his mission. IB was wary of this situation in their assessment about Sheikh Abdullah after monitoring all his activities since the beginning of Jan Sangh agitation. Nehru later disclosed that Sheikh who was outwardly very friendly with him but indulged in making false charges against India and had finally said that in spite of his personal friendship and regard for him, the time had come when this personal interest had to be sacrificed in the interest of the country.

In another attempt to break the deadlock, Nehru sent Maulana Abul Kalam Azad to Srinagar to convince him not to betray the aspiration of Kashmiri people but he too was ignored by Sheikh and even insulted him at the Id meeting. On his return to Delhi, Maulana advised Nehru to dismiss Sheikh before he committed any offence against Indian Union. After that Nehru had made up his mind to take drastic action against him with little hope that Sheikh would change his attitude as he has done on several occasions in the past. He asked IB to gear up their intelligence network in full swing in Kashmir in order to take appropriate action in the present unfavourable political situation.

Dr. Shyama Prasad Mukherji died in detention in Srinagar on 23rd June, 1953 due to prolonged illness. There was countrywide criticism of Sheikh Abdullah for denying the proper medical treatment to him. Instead of expressing any repentance on the death, Sheikh justified detention of Shyama Prasad Mukherji to support Praja Parishad's agitation for complete integration in the Indian Union which was against his wishes. He brushed aside all the criticism against him in this case and gave little importance to any political outcry. Nehru was in London at that time attending the Commonwealth Prime Minister's conference. He was briefed appropriately about the developments in India by Mullik, Director IB who was keeping constant watch on the situation in Kashmir. IB briefed Nehru that Sheikh was not planning to merge Jammu and Kashmir with Pakistan but was aspiring for a special status just short of independence. He was aware that he would be a dwarf in Pakistan politics in case he would opt for it. That is why he arrested his former colleague G M Kaara in June

1953 when he came out openly in favour of Pakistan and shouted Pakistan Zindabad at a public meeting. But his mental framework was Hindu biased. Nehru stressed the need to further strengthen IB in Kashmir in view of the hostile attitude of Sheikh. Hassanwalia through his sources deeply penetrated into all vital links of Sheikh Abdullah and spread his network in whole of the valley to give first hand information to Central Government about political development and infiltration from Pakistan.

Sheikh Abdullah Arrested

During the first week of June, 1953, the Basic Principles Committee's report about determining the status of Kashmir in India was referred to a Council comprising important Kashmiri leaders which was vehemently opposed by Sheikh Abdullah. He had some other designs in this matter. Due to the stubborn attitude of Sheikh Abdullah on Kashmir's relations with India who wanted a special status, the final decision was postponed till the return of Pandit Nehru from London. IB informed Nehru that Sheikh was in minority in the inner coterie of the National Conference and even in the Constituent Assembly he had few supporters who would support him for an anti-India stance. Thus, there was a possibility of his becoming a fierce dictator due to his isolation in his own party. IB also reported that Sheikh might arrest leaders of all prominent parties who were opposed to his lineage on the future of Kashmir. In the last attempt for reconciliation, Rafi Ahmed Kidwai, a reputed Muslim leader in Nehru Cabinet, wen to meet Sheikh but he also failed to make any impact on his hostility. Thereafter, Kidwai and D P Dhar met Nehru and acquainted him with the grave situation and advocated strong measures. When Nehru asked for it, Kidwai recommended dismissal of Sheikh.

Although, Nehru had made up his mind to dismiss Sheikh Abdullah and install Bakshi Ghulam Mohammand as his successor but he started taking all possibilities into considerationas a fall out of this decision. Before taking final action, Nehru summoned IB chief to give his assessment of the situation in Jammu and Kashmir after the dismissal of Sheikh. A senior officer D W Mehra was sent to work with I S Hassanwalia who had complete control of the developments in the Kashmir valley through his intelligence network. Hassanwalia had also informed that after the dismissal of Sheikh, his followers and pro-Pakistani elements could spread wide scale violence. He suggested the and the Army should be put on high alert to cope with the impending situation of maintaining law and order. Nehru ordered the army to be put on high alert to meet all sorts of consequences in general and take control of the Kashmir Militia, the pro-Pakistan outfits. Rafi Ahmed Kidwai was looking after the affairs of Kashmir in Delhi during this period.

Government made full preparations to handle the post-dismissal situation of Sheikh Abdullah. But Sheikh himself committed the hara-kiri and ordered Sham Lal Saraf a senior leader to resign from the Cabinet. When he refused to resign, Sheikh dismissed him but Sadar-e-Riyasat refused to oblige him. All other senior leaders like Bakshi, Sadiq, Dogra, D P Dhar and Masoodi were against Sheikh for this action and supported Saraf. Due to his anti-India tirate he had lost majority in all the three bodies i.e. the National Conference, the Constituent Assembly and the Cabinet. Constitutionally he was in minority and there was a bleak chance for him to rule Kashmir on any other alternative even with the help of Pakistan. He could never dare to depose the Sadar-e-Riyasat because of the strong presence of Indian Army.

In this hostile political scenario, Sheikh Abdullah, tried to get help from the pro- Pakistani elements. Hassanwalia got information that Pir Maqbool Gilani, a confidant of Sheikh, had established contacts with Pakistan to help Sheikh and that an emissary from Pakistan was coming to meet Sheikh at Tanmarg near Gulmarg. In the morning of August 8, 1953. Sheikh suddenly left for Tanmarg, the rendezvous fixed for the Pakistani emissary ostensibly to hatch a plan for a coup. So, in the evening, Sadar-e-Riyasat issued orders dismissing Sheikh Abdullah and invited Bakshi Ghulam Mohd. to form the ministry. Bakshi refused to take oath until Sheikh Abdullah was arrested. On getting nod from Delhi, Sadar-e-Riyasat issued orders for the arrest of Sheikh as his meeting with the Pakistani emissary would constitute a grave danger to the security of the State. At 4 O'clock in the morning of August 9, Baksh took the oath to become Prime Minister of Kashmir in place of Sheikh Abdullah. Sheikh was arrested along . Mohd. Akbar and a few others including couple of Hindus and taken to Udhampur. There were sporadic incidents of violence in the valley after his arrest. Bakshi along with D P Dhar controlled with Afzal Beg, Ch the situation remarkably with the help of Indian Army and IB. The violence could not continue for long because there was a general feeling in the valley that Sheikh was not much liked by the people except for his type of politics. The disturbances lasted for three weeks and sixty people were killed in the firing by the police and militia mostly in the Srinagar city.

Kashmir ultimately got reconciled to the arrest of Sheikh and a decade of comparative peace lasted in the valley during which the State made a phenomenal progress in all spheres of its economy and education. New road-link were developed which increased the influx of tourists in the valley. A tunnel was made through Banihal which smoothened the traffic during winter season. All these developments contributed a lot to the economic prosperity of Kashmir which Sheikh had negled due to his false ego and a sense of distrust towards his own political colleagues. Constitutionally, Government took measures to integrate the higher administrative and police services with the all India services. Jurisdiction of Supreme Court was extended to Jammu and Kashmir and integration in many other fields progressed at the behest of Bakshi and D P Dhar.

New Political Options

After the exist of Dixon as UN representative, Frank Graham the new incumbent realized the ground realities that now plebiscite was not feasible after a lapse of more than six years. He suggested that both India and Pakistan should suggest means by which this could be done. Surprisingly, Security Council, perhaps at the behest of some super powers, tried to put the blame of impasse on India rather than holding Pakistan responsible for not withdrawing the troops from POK, which was the precondition in this issue. India vociferously opposed this manoeuvring and got the resolution restricted to the fact that the two countries should establish direct contact to settle the issue.

After several meetings between the Prime Ministers of two countries, an understanding was reached when they met at the time of the Queen's coronation in June, 1953 in London. In September, 1953, Mohd. Ali Bogra visited India. Nehru and Bogra decided to hold an impartial and regional plebiscite under the Plebiscite Administrator of a small country rather than from USA or UK which had political interest in this region. Mohd. Ali Bogra, unfortunately, could not get this proposal approved by his Cabinet. USA too put pressure on him to retain Admiral Nimitz as the Plebiscite Ambassador. Bogra, thus, backed out of this agreement which was an unfortunate development and the permanent solution of this dispute was left in limbo and still persists. This suggestion of Nehru was overlooked in the subsequent deliberation of the Security Council obviously at the behest of of super powers.

This political situation took a total U-turn when Pakistan-USA Aid Pact in 1954 was signed by both the countries. Pakistan was further pampered by the super powers when it was made member of the UK-USA sponsored Middle East and SEATO pacts with the result many countries came to the side of Pakistan which further emboldened to defy it any move on the solution of this problem. In March, 1957, another UN representative Jarring visited both sides of the cease-fire line and after long talks with leaders of both countries realized that the plebiscite suggested in

1948 was now unrealistic and not feasible because both the countries had stabilized their position in the area under their control and it would be dangerous to upset the status quo.

In 1955, Russian leaders Khurushchev and Bulganin visited India and appreciated the progress India as a democratic country achieved in all fields of Industry, agriculture, education etc. Khrushchev also visited Srinagar and declared there that Kashmir was an integral part of India as per the wishes of their people. Thereafter, Russia vetoed all resolution mooted by the Anglo-American block which were detrimental to India's interest.

Bakshi released G M Karra who was arrested by Sheikh earlier, in December, 1954. Bakshi tried to convince him to change his pro-Pakistani stand but he did not relent and continued his clandestine activities against India with financial and other help from across the border. Mirza Afzal Beg who was arrested along with Sheikh was also released in November, 1954 and he too continued his subversive activities against India for accession of Kashmir with Pakistan. At the instigation of Pakistan, he formed a political outfit, the Plebiscite Front to raise the issue of ascertaining the wishes of the people which in favour of accession with Pakistan although National Conference to which he belonged had refused such action. Hassanwalia was keeping proper track surveillance of Beg and after it was established that he had plans to overthrow the present Government in Kashmir, he was re-arrested in 1955. At the time of his arrest some incriminating letters were found in his possession which proved that he was part of aconspiracy to bring about a state of armed rebellion in Jammu and Kashmir with the help of Pakistan.

IB Strengthened

In August, 1952, when Nehru visited the valley, Hassanwalia the IB in charge at Srinagar met him at Sonamarg and briefed on the ongoing problem of infiltration and sabotage activities in far-flung areas of the valley which were financed by Pakistan. Nehru immediately ordered the strengthening of intelligence set up and new check-posts of IB were opened in the army area from Kargil to Ranbir Singh Pura to keep a tab on the activities of saboteurs and apprised the army about across border activities of Pakistani army because after the ceasefire both sides had agreed not to enter 500 yards within area of the line of control. Opening of these posts proved very useful for the ultimate aim of the army to check the infiltrators and provide intelligence of vital importance for the security of the border areas. After strenuous efforts of I S Hassanwalia with full support from Director IB, Mullik, IB was able to make significant progress on three aspects i.e. forward intelligence, counter-intelligence and setting up of armed police check posts to identify the infiltrators. Thus, IB was in total command to tackle all the anti-national activities sponsored by Pakistan through her agents for subversion, sabotage and political conspiracy inside Kashmir. Many infiltrators were arrested and from their interrogation further information was obtained about Pakistan's massive effort at perpetrating a series of explosions and sabotage activities in the valley. It was a conspiracy to raise the matter in the Security Council that the Kashimiris were still rebellious because of India's refusal to hold the plebiscite.

In the Security Council, a discussion on the Jarring Report was held to decide the issue of holding plebiscite in Kashmir. Jarring prepared this report as UN observer on the recommendation of the Security Council, IB gave exhaustive and exclusive details with documentary evidences of the continued attempts of Pakistan-sponsored activities of sabotage and subversions in the valley. As a result of this intelligence back up, Krishna Menon, the flamboyant Indian Foreign Minister, took a frontal aggressive posture in the Security Council and refuted all false allegations of Pakistan about the wishes of the people of Kashmir for a plebiscite. He listed full details of violation of ceasefire agreement by Pakistan and asked pointedly to the Security Council as to what steps were being taken by them to stop the continued aggression and violation of the ceasefire agreement. The Security Council had no answer to the vehement opposition of Krishna Menon against holding plebiscite in such a hostile condition. After the valiant efforts of Krishnan Menon on this issue, any further discussion was not allowed by the Soviet Union which vetoed these attempts as unwarranted and unjustified. This process was made possible in the UNO only due to the proper intelligence gathering in the valley by IB Assistant Director, Hassanwalia with the help of his dedicated team and further analytical corroborations of all these intelligence reports at IB Headquarters under the able leadership of Director Mullik that India was able to block the Security Council to pass any resolution which was not in the interest of India. Thereafter, the Security Council did no intervene effectively in the Kashmir issue except to maintain the observers on the ceasefire line. This was the first major achievement of IB on the international arena particularly so when it was in the emboryonic stages of its inception.

Traitors Neutralized

Hassanwalia, the bold and articulate Sikh handling IB in Srinagar through his sources was able to penetrate in three important Pakistani channels who were involved in assisting the Plebiscite Front of Miraz Afzal Beg and the War Council which was formed shortly after the arrest of Sheikh Abdullah. One of these channels was in Hillan in Pakistan Occupied Kashmir via Nilakanth Gali into Srinagar and the second from Lipa via Tangdhar to Srinagar. These two channels provided crucial information about the clandestine assistance these two organization were receiving from Pakistan. In Delhi, the IB sleuths recruited an officer of Pakistan Embassy as its important source who gave vital details of High Commission officials activities in Kashmir. Through these penetrations, IB was able to unearth many other links of Pakistan which were in operation inside Kashmir. IB was thus able to neutralize them with the help of these sources. In another bold operation, IB officials were above to take possession of several documents from a Pakistani intelligence post in Occupied Kashmir wherein valuable information about the plants of sabotage and subversion by infiltrators inside the valley were detected. Numerous Sheikh supporters were arrested on the basis of incriminating documents seized from the couriers infiltrated from Pakistan. These supporters were found involved in league with Pakistan intelligence eliciting support for their conspiratorial activities. Leaders of Plebiscite Front and War Council were discreetly maintaining contacts with Sheikh who was giving instructions to them to launch anti-Indian activities not only in Kashmir but at international for a through Pakistan. Documents seized from the possession of Afzal Beg indicated that Sheikh Abdullah had sent instructions to raise the banner of autonomous status for Kashmir equating Pakistan with India in future deliberations. Another document gave evidence to IB that Sheikh was approaching the Security Council for a plebiscite in Kashmir. This document was given wide publicity by Pakistani press. Seizure of other documents disclosed that large number of weapons were already brought inside the valley but due to non-availability of saboteurs, these weapons could not be used for subversive activities. Sheikh Abdullah and other leaders were mentioned in pseudo names and codes were devised to deceive the Indian intelligence. One Pakistani Intelligence Officer escaped the arrest by IB in August, 1955 while he was in Srinagar on a clandestine mission to channelise Pakistani assistance to the Plebiscite Front operatives. Pakistan was extending all possible support to various factions involved in subverstive activities. In addition to providing all sorts of support to Plebiscite Front of Afzal Beg, financial support was also provided to other factions including Kashmir Political Conference of Karra.

IB deliberately did not bust some of these Pakistani channels and allowed to work with these to remain functional with their agents in Kashmir so that a full proof case could be prepared against the conspirators including Sheikh Abdullah. Certain communications intercepted by the IB showed that there was a regular link between the leaders outside and those inside the jail who were working with the assistance of Pakistan. These contacts used to pass messages of Pakistan intelligence officials to Sheikh Abdullah who was in prison at Kud. Jail staff was aware of these activities but deliberately did not follow the rules strictly inside for Sheikh whose diktat ruled the roost. Even his wife was allowed to stay with him at times during night hours. Sheikh Abdullah's instructions were regularly conveyed to the conspirators outside prison by his supporters and even by jail staff. In one of the intercepted letters written by Afzal Beg to Pir Abdul Ghani it was clearly mentioned that Sheikh Abdullah was in league with one Pakistani intelligence officer in Rawalpindi. It was written in this letter that it would be important if Pakistan could get Sheikh Abdullah summoned before the Security Council to put his defence in favrour of Pakistan. Other communications intercepted by the IB revealed that by 1956, large amount of money in Indian currency started coming from Pakistan to the supporters of Sheikh Abdullah and other hostile groups in the valley. In another significant development, Masoodi was able to launch a pro-Sheikh lobby in Delhi with the help of Mridula Sarabahi, one time Secretary of Mahatma Gandhi, who was staunch loyal to Sheikh Abdullah for reasons best known to both of them. This lady belonged to a patriotic family of Gujarat which was involved in the freedom movement. IB had gathered information that Sheikh was having very intimate relations with this lady. Her house was used as hub to make contacts with the Pakistan High Commission in Delhi for anti-Indian activities. Even huge amount of money was enrooted from her house to finance activities of Plebiscite Front. IB informed all these details to the Prime Minister and the Home Minister.

In order to prepare a foolproof case against those anti-Indian leaders including Sheikh, substantial amount of money was allowed to reach the hands of supporters of Sheikh Abdullah and even to Begum Abdullah with the full knowledge of the Home Minister and the Prime Minister. IB was gathering vital proof and evidences of these hostile activities against India. Both the Prime Minister and the Home Minister did not want to linger on this matter and wanted to investigate the possibility of launching a case of conspiracy against these conspirators as early as possible on the basis of the material already collected and assessed properly by IB to decide how far these leaders had individually and collectively indulged in the conspiracy. IB further got valuable from several culprits who were arrested in those years for subversive activities to which they were engaged at the behest of Sheikh. These confessions further gave considerable weight in this conspiracy against India.

IB was burning mid-night oil in this case in Srinagar where its Director Mullik with the impeccable insight of Hassanwalia and other legal experts were draewing together all available material to prepare a foolproof case against the conspirators. By October, 1957, all these evidences were collated together to prepare the First Information Report on charge of conspiracy against eleven leaders of the Plebiscite Front including Mirza Afzal Beg, Pir Maqbool Gilali, Begum Abdullah etc. They all were charged for revolt against the State through violent revolution and a conspiracy was hatched in Jammu and Kashmir to overthrow the Government. Sheikh Abdullah was not included in this FIR as the evidence against him were inconclusive because some of the documents recovered from the couriers were still to be decoded. Prime Minister, Home Minister and G M Bakshi approved the action of IB to finalise the FIR. Hassanwalia played a pivotal role in preparing this case because of his intimate knowledge of all the events that had taken place in Kashmir since 1953. He was the only one involved in the arrest of conspirators, searches and the consequent recoveries of documents. He worked hard to fix the dates as well as extract the hidden meanings and purpose from the decoded communications. There was problem to place the meaning of Pushto and Persian words which frequently appeared in the seized documents. By the month of January, 1958, the IB built up a strong case against all the accused mentioned in the FIR and also against Sheikh Abdullah and several others whose names had not been included in it. After completion of the legal scrutiny of these evidences by March 1958, the charge-sheet was completed by IB and filed a case in the court.

The Magistrate in his judgment committed the accused to the Court of Sessions for trial on conspiracy to wage a war against the country. The Magistrate in his order mentioned that soon after the arrest of Sheikh Abdullah on August 9, 1953, his friends, relatives and sympathizers resorted to violence which could be controlled in three to four weeks by the security forces. He further said that these people incited communal feelings and provoked disharmony in the State to disturb its peace and tranquility to bring a public disorder to foster hostile feelings against the people of India. He found the main campaigners in this case as Begum Abdullah, Khawaja Ali Shah, Saeeda Begum, Ghulam Hassan Kanth, all relatives of Sheikh Abdullah and several other workers of National Conference. They were involved in establishing an outfit called War Council to carry out these activities against the State. This War Council started nefarious activities all over the State and issued posters, pamphlets, slogans and wall writings and even incited the people to kill Bakshi Ghulam Mohd. Court observed that Begum Abdullah supplied the cyclostyling machine for preparing the required material. She was in league with the Pakistani agents whose emissary was captured by the IB. While this conspiracy was in progress, Begum Abdullah visited Sheikh Abdullah in Udhampur Jail in October, 1963 and illegally stayed there for several days which was purported to be a move to brief him on the progress of her contacts with Pakistan. War Council with the aid of Pakistan started arousing communal disharmony in the valley by distributing incriminating pamphlets. Pir Mazbool Gilani worked as a conduit between Pakistan and Sheikh Abdullah in jail. When Mirza Afzal Beg was released on medical grounds, he at the behest of Sheikh Abdullah changed the name of the War Council to Plebiscite Front on August 9, 1955. Beg was also found in contact with a Pakistani intelligence officer. Thereafter, financial aid started pouring from Pakistan to Plebiscite Front and Begum Abdullah. Many letters written at the instance of Sheikh Abdullah from jail intercepted by the IB smacked of a clear conspiracy against India. A letter written by Sheikh Abdullah was smuggled out to Security Council through Pakistan. When Miraz Afzal Beg was re-arrested in September, 1956, a letter was recovered from his posession which proved that the conspirators had planned to import arms and explosives as well as Razakars, the terrorists, from Pakistan. One of the conspirators went to Lahore on the pretext of seeing a cricket test match but brought back a lakh of rupees from the Pakistani Intelligence. Two other conspirators received a consignment of arms at Yus Maidan from a Pakistani emissary. False and fabricated stories were built up and sent regularly about genocide and suppression of Muslims of the Kashmir to Pakistan which was broadcast from Pakistan and Azad Kashmir radios to defame India particularly in Muslim Countries. When all this propaganda did not yield any results, Sheikh Abdullah tried to incite the people of Kahsmir in the name of Hazrat Mohammad. Pakistan continued the financing of this conspiracy by pumping in large sums of money and also sent large quantities of arms and ammunition. Court further mentioned that on the basis of information received from the conspirators, Pakistan sent large groups of infiltrators who carried out a series of explosions and sabotages in which several lives were lost. Some of these attempts were foiled by the IB on the information provided by its sources which frustrated these Kashmiri leaders and Pakistan who had conspired to bring a state of anarchy and disorder in Kashmir by large scale violence and killings with a view to overthrow the lawfully constituted Government of Jammu and Kashmir. Police vigilance and intelligence maneuvering by the IB, thwarted all these plans of the conspirators. The uncooperative attitude of the majority of Kashmiri people to this propaganda helped the administration to bring these people to criminal justice.

Sheikh Released/Re-arrested

In this hostile situation, for some unknown reasons Pandit Jawaharlal Nehru ordered release of Sheikh Abdullah on January 9, 1958. His release at this juncture hampered the investigation against him because he was the main conspirator and if he was not made accused, it would facilitate in weakening the case against other accused persons. He returned to Srinagar and delivered public speeches against Bakshi rule and the Government of India. He even challenged the right of the Government of India to be the arbiters of Kashmir's fate and demanded that Kashmiris should be given the right to decide their fate. He gave a call for a mammoth meeting on January 17, at Pathar Masjid in front of Mujahid Manzil, the Headquarters of National Conference. He ostensibly wanted to capture this building by force to jolt the smooth functioning of Bakshi Government. Administration made elaborate police arrangement on that day to counter any such move on the part of Sheikh and his supporters. More than 20,000 people gathered on that day and kept on waiting for Sheikh Abdullah's arrival at Pathar Masjid but his courage failed and he did not turn up sensing large scale bloodshed and his ultimate arrest. Rather, he went to Hazratbal and poured his venom in a bitter speech against Bakshi and against the Government of India and also asked the people to boycott the Republic Day celebrations on January 26. Bakshi wanted to celebrate this day with full State honour to show his strength to Sheikh. IB was keeping strict vigil on all his activities and informing the Government of India on daily basis. With local police, IB made elaborate arrangements for peaceful celebrations of Republic Day. Supporters of Sheikh did not dare to create any disturbance and his call to boycott the function remained unheeded. On that day more than 40,000 people gathered in the Civil Lines where Bakshi Ghulam Mohammad gave a speech and complimented them for the celebrations in spite of the adverse propaganda unleashed at the behest of Sheikh and his supporters. This celebration boosted the morale of Bakshi who was feeling politically uncomfortable after the release of Sheikh Abdullah. Nehru and Home Minister Pant were informed by IB on the successful celebration of Republic Day.

Hereinafter, desperate Sheikh Abdullah continued to hold propaganda meeting and inciting the people through inflammatory speeches to rise against the Government of Jammu and Kashmir and religiously cited passages from Quran comparing Bakshi Ghulam Mohammad and his supporters as infidels. During regular Friday meetings at Hazratbal Masjid he unleashed pernicious propaganda against Indian Government provoking the Kashmiri people to starve rather then accept economic aid from Delhi. Secretly, he sent instructions in other part of the State to recruit Razakars for rebellion. This was all recorded by the IB meticulously for the consumption of Delhi Hqrs. On February 21, 1958, he incited his supporters for violence as a result of which some of them tried to ransack the National Conference office at Raj Bagh where one worker was killed and about thirty were injured. One jeep of National Conference was burnt, one police wireless vehicle was damaged and many shops were destroyed. Police arrested his supporters and cases filed against them which created fear among them and most of them refrained from indulging in any such incidents in the coming future.

During this period, Sheikh Abdullah was secretly planning to demand a plebiscite for merger of Kashmir with Pakistan with the help of large scale recruitment of Razakars. These ultras were trained in subversive activities to plant bombs and resort to violent activities with arms and ammunitions received from Pakistan. The IB through its sources was keeping tab on all his activities. Large amount of money was being received by Sheikh supporters from the Deputy High Commission of Pakistan at Chandigarh and directly from Pakistan. A major portion of this money was received directly by Begum Abdullah. When the Government felt that the situation was becoming from bad to worst and it was apparent that the Sheikh was bent upon joining hands with Pakistan by creating chaos and disorder in the State to give an excuse to Pakistan to intervene directly, he was re-arrested on April 30, 1958. The IB recovered a draft of the Plebiscite Front resolution dated April 7, 1958 from his house, which revealed that Sheikh Abdullah had made corrections in his own hand writing wherein it was mentioned to give a clear call for breaking the ties with India and more or less accepted accession to Pakistan as the aim of the Fron. This was an ample proof to justify his arrest because he again indulged in the activities which was detrimental to security and integrity of India.

Conspiracy Case

The IB had already prepared the charge-sheet against Sheikh Abdullah, Begum Abdullah, Afzal Beg and others in the March of 1958. After the release of Sheikh, it was withheld and was not filed in the court knowing well that he would indulge in such activities which could enable them to add further direct evidences in the chargesheet. Later on, these evidences were gathered in the form of his inflammatory speeches, his attempts to raise Razakars, the Hazratbal rioting at his instigation and murder of a National Conference worker, the Plebiscite Front manifesto to revolt against India and receipt of large sums of money from Pakistan by his wife during his presence in the house, which further strengthened the court case. He could even be indicted on the basis of his activities during the period of his brief freedom from January to April 1958 which made the IB fully satisfied that it had built-up an unassailable case against him. Hassanwalia and Balbir Singh, Joint Director, in charge of Kashmir at Delhi Headquarters of IB along with other legal experts relentlessly worked for many months to prepare a charge-sheet of more than 1,600 pages which was sent to the Government of India and other legal experts for scrutiny and suggestion in view of various ramifications of this big conspiracy. This was ostensibly necessary because many of the original documents were in Urdu, Pushto, Persian written mostly in cryptic language using code names since IB was working on this case since 1953 connecting oblique and even vague references received from time to time. When the final charge-sheet was placed before Nehru, Pant, Bakshi and the Law Minister by Mullik, Bakshi took a firm stand that Begum Abdullah who was regarded as Madr-e-Meharban in the valley, should not be included in the charge-sheet as the Muslim population of Kashmir would turned against him if she was made one of the accused in this case. Although Director IB insisted of her inclusion as she was the main conduit between Pakistan and the conspirators for transferring money, but due to pressure from Bakshi, her name was omitted from the charge-sheet. Surprisingly, after a couple of days, Nehru decided that Sheikh Abdullah should also not be prosecuted even though his offences were very grave. Many arguments were put before Nehru that his exclusion would create doubt on the ultimate success of the case but Nehru's stature prevailed upon others to agree to him to drop Sheikh also. Ultimately on May 21, 1958, a complaint was filed in the court of the Special Magistrate, Jammu, under section 121-A and 120-B of the Ranbir Penal Code and Section 32 of the Security Rules against 25 conspirators, including Mirza Afzal Beg, Pir Mazbool Gilani, Pir Maqbool Wigland and others. Five Pakistanis were also included in the case. There were 40 others co-conspirators who were not included in the charge-sheet but their names were mentioned in the complaint. However, on October 23, 1958, on the recommendation of the Prosecution Counsel, Sheikh Abdullah was also included in the supplementary charge-sheet, after Nehru and Pant were convinced on the legal ramification of the case. Since Sheikh was not an absconder and was under detention and as such not to produce him as an accused for open trial, when he was the main conspirator in this conspiracy, could constitute a serious and irremediable flaw in the ultimate success of this case. This legal apprehension by the legal experts made Nehru and Pant to agree for the inclusion of Sheikh in the supplementary charge-sheet.

Pakistan Government helped the conspirators and provided legal help of a famous British lawyer, Dingle Foot, of international fame along-with his junior J O Kellock who stayed at Jammu to defend them in this case. Huge amount of money to Begum Abdullah directly from Pakistan and through the Pakistan High Commission in Delhi for conducting the defence. Mirudla Sarabahi, a staunch follower of Sheikh Abdullah in Delhi, carried on an unrelenting propaganda against the Bakshi Government, the Government of India, the IB and the Security Forces in Kashmir, calling them the conspirators responsible for filing a false and fabricated case against Sheikh and others. She even succeeded in convincing some Members of Parliament who demanded withdrawal of this case against Sheikh. Nehru tolerated all her activities knowing well that this move was supported by false arguments. When her activities reached the boiling point after the escape of Pir Maqbook Gilarni to Pakistan with her connivance, she was arrested under the Preventive Detention Act on the order of the Home Minister much to the reluctance of Nehru.

When the Court proceedings started, the accused resorted to delaying tactics by taking the matter to the High Court and Supreme Court on flimsy grounds which ultimately did not succeed. Hassanwalia too deposed and made his statement indicting Sheikh Abdullah for waging a war against the nation. However, after examining 229 witnesses and exhibiting nearly 300 documents, the case was completed for final verdict in October, 1961. Only one man who was convicted in a bomb case turned hostile and all the others remained true to their statements they made during the investigation. They did not turn hostile while deposing against Sheikh Abdullah, the Shere-e-Kashmir, who was supposed to be the undisputed leader of the valley and on whose behalf persistent threats and intimidations were hurled on these witnesses by the members of the Plebiscite Front. Even all possible delaying tactics adopted by the accused person, by creating scenes, shouting anti-India slogans and insulting prosecution counsels, adopted by the conspirators did not deter the Magistrate in the finalization of this case. The Judge also being a Kashmiri tolerated their unruly behavior in the court premises. Finally, on January 25, 1962, the magistrate passed orders committing all the accused persons to the Court of Sessions. The following extracts from the committal order would show that the Prosecution had been able to establish a prima facie case against the accused persons:

"The evidence-oral and documentary-discussed heretofore, and the circumstances of the case, would appear to make a prima facie case and sufficient grounds for holding the conspiracy proved as alleged by the prosecution, to hold that the accused present in the court, and the absconding accused, as also the Pakistani officials who are accused in this case were, among others, members of this conspiracy. In short, the prosecution would appear to have prima facie proved this conspiracy against these accused persons to warrant these accused persons being committed to the Court of Sessions to stand their trial for a charge under section 121-A Ranbir Penal Code and under section 12-B Ranbir Penal Code read with Rule 32 of the J and K Security Rules, Samvat 1996 and under that rule 32."

An offence under section 121-A of the Ranbir Penal Code was punishable with sentence for life and that under section 120-B of the Ranbir Penal Code would be punishable with death or life imprisonment as in this case several murders had been committed in furtherance of the conspiracy against India.

In April, 1962, Pandit Nehru was ill and he wanted to withdraw this case which was opposed by Bakshi, Sadar-e-Riyassat, Dr. Karan Singh and Mullik. Karan Singh stressed that if Government of India felt the necessity, they could pardon the accused but only after the conclusion of trial as withdrawal of the case at that stage would invite charges of accusations against the Indian Government from many quarters. Pandit Nehru realized the gravity of the situation and relented to withdraw the case. However, the trial in the Session Court took considerable time due to the delaying tactics of the conspirators particularly after the Chinese aggression of October 1962, they hoped that Governmentt would politically settle the Kashmir issue and in this imbroglio this case would also be withdrawn. Sheikh Abdullah also wrote a letter to Nehru from jail wherein he showed no sympathy towards this tragic incident and rather impressed upon the need to improve an understanding between India, Pakistan and Kashmir. IB had advance information that while in jail Sheikh was not only disparaging India but denigrating Nehru also for the catastrophe.

Around this time, the British and the American offered aid against China but exerted pressure on Nehru to concede the unreasonable demands of Pakistan to which Nehru made up his mind to make up with Sheikh Abdullah to counter this pressure. However, Morarji Desai bluntly refused the overtures of these countries and asserted that aid or no aid, India would not concede to the unreasonable demands of Pakistan. Again in September, 1963, Nehru wanted to withdraw the case after 49 Members of Parliament including Jayaprakash Narayan wrote to him in this regard. This move was engineered at the behest of Mirdula Sarabhai who launched a virulent propaganda not only against the Bakshi Govt. but against the IB officers for delaying tactics. Due to stiff opposition from Bakshi Ghulam Mohammad and other Kashmiri leaders — G M Sadiq, D P Dhar, Mir Qasim,

Bakshi Abdul Rasid — and even the Sadar-e-Riyasat, Dr. Karan Singh who said that if Sheikh Abdullah would be released without trial at that time, he and his friends would revert to their old activities against India. It would be then extremely illogical to put them on trial again and many unwarranted problems would be created for IB and the Government of Kashmir. Nehru realized the ground situation and allowed the case to continue for its logical conclusion.

Holy Relic

A person named Hazrat Syed Abdullah, a Shia Muslim, who claimed that till lately he had been the Mutwali of the main shrine at Medina and came to Bijapur in South India in 1635. He said that he left Madina because he fell apart with the Sultan who banished him from the country after he defied his orders to appear in his Court on the complaint of his cousin. Hazrat Syed Abdullah claimed that he was a direct descendant of the Prophet and he had with him a strand of the holy hair of Prophet (Moo-e-Muquaddash or the Holy Relic). This Holy Relic came in inheritance to Hazrat Imam Hassan, grandson of the Prophet and in this lineage it came in to his possession in 1633 A.D. King of Bijapur was also a Shia like Syed Abdullah and believed his story. In generosity to the high status which Syed Abdullah claimed, the king donated a "Jagir" to him in his State where he died twenty-three years later. This "Jagir" later passed on to his son, Syed Hamid and he inherited this Holy Relic. In 1686, Aurangzeb attacked Bijapur and Syed Hamid lost his estate and fled to Jahanabad where he came into contact with a Kashmir trader Noor-ud-din Ashwari who became friendly with him. When Ashwari was told by Hamid that he was in possession of the holy relic of the Prophet, he requested Hamid to give him the holy relic to which Hamid did not agree. Tthe same night he had a dream in which the Prophet asked him to hand over the holy relic to Ashwari, which he did. After a few days, Ashwari had a dream in which he was asked by the Prophet to take the Holy Relic to Kashmir and establish it there on the bank of a lake. So, Ashwari closed his business at Jahanabad and with this precious possession, he started for Kashmir giving Deedar (exposition) of the holy relic at various places before he reached Lahore. This news reached to Aurangzeb who ordered that the Holy Relic should be produced before him and imprisoned Noor-ud-Din Ashwari. Medanish, servant of Noor-ud-Din brought the Holy Relic to Aurangzeb who after testing it in the traditional manner, was convinced that Relic was a strand of the Prophet's hair. He ordered it to be taken away from Medanish and placed at Dargah Sahen at Ajmer for preservation. After the Holy Relic was installed at the Dargah, Aurangzeb also had a dream in which the Prophet commanded him to restore the Holy Relic to Ashwari and sent it to Kashmir immediately. Soon thereafter, Aurangzeb restored it to Medanish and sent his force to escort him to Kashmir. In the meantime, Ashwari died in prison due to shock of being dispossessed of the Holy Relic. Medanish along with the exhumed body of Ashwari and the Holy Relic arrived in Kashmir in 1700 A.D. where he was received by the Governor Mir Fazir Khan with full honour. On the order of the Governor, the Holy Relic was placed outside the town at Bagh-e-Sadiq Khan built by Shah Jahan on the bank of the Dal Lake which subsequently acquired the name Hazratbal Mosque due to the presence of the Holy Relic i.e. Moe-e-Muqaddas.

Theft of Holy Relic

Even when placed in the mosque, the descendants of Noor-ud-Din Ashwari kept control over the Holy Relic, the Moe-e-Muqaddas and they were the only people who were entitled to exhibit the Holy Relic to the public and they, therefore, gradually came to be known as the Nishan Dez or the persons who could exhibit it. There are only ten days in the year which are connected to some events in the life of the Prophet. When the Relic is shown to the people, the method of exhibition of the relic was that on any of these days, the Nishan Dez would bring the quartz tube containing the Moe-e-Muqaddas on the balcony of the Hazratbal mosque and from there show it to thousands of pilgrims congregated in the huge yard in the front. Only those in the balcony could see the tube but except the Nishan Dez none could see the strand of the hair as it could be seen from only one side and by holding the quartz tube quite near the eyes. Nishan Dez used to give private exhibitions in return for a substantial amount on these fixed days which was their personal income and did not go to the mosque fund.

On Friday following the Miraj-e-Alam, on December 20, 1963, a Deedar of the Moe-e-Muqaddas had been given to the public after which it was placed at its original place by the Senior Nishan Dez, Rahim Bandey. On December 26, a private exposition was given to a person by the same Nishan Dez and latter claimed to have placed the Moe-e-Muqaddas at the proper place. In the early morning of 27th December, Rahim Bandey found that the side dour of the passage leading to the room housing the Moe-e-Muqadass had been broken open and both locks of the inner door leading to the sanctuary had also been forced open. The lock of the front door of the passage had also been forced open from inside. The wooden box containing the Moe-e-Muqadass had been taken out from the small wooden shelf in which it had been kept and after forcibly opening the shelf and the small bag containing the tube with the Moe-e-Muqaddas inside had been removed leaving the velvet covering, the trappings and the wooden box behind in the shelf.

The news about the theft of Moe-e-Muqaddas spread like a wild fire throughout the valley. Large crowd gathered at the Hazratbal mosque in the morning and thousands of people started marching in Srinagar streets indulging in violence. There was a spontaneous strike against this sacrilege committed in respect of the relic which they held to be highly sacred and dearer than their lives. Local authorities failed to control the situation and the crowd attacked Bakshi Abdul Rashid, General Secretary of the National Conference who tried to convince the gathering that Relic would be recovered soon and they should disperse. One Hotel and a cinema hall owned by brother of Bakshi were set on fire by the public. When the police tried to intervene, the crowd attacked the police and burnt the Kothibagh Police Station whereupon the police opened fire killing three persons. The incident turned the anger of the entire Kashmiri population against the Bakshi family in particular and the Kashmir Government in general. A rumour was floated by some vested interest that Bakshi family was responsible for this outrage. There was complete strike throughout the valley thereafter. A senior officer of IB was rushed from Delhi to assess the ongoing hostile situation and to investigate the case. In the meantime, the entire Kashmir valley was up in arms. there was a plan even to attack the All India Radio Station at Srinagar at the news broadcast of Pakistan Radio which blamed the Government of India for having engineered the theft of the Moe-e-Muqaddas in order to humiliate and completely suppress the Muslims of the Kashmir valley. When situation became grave and starting deteriorating every day, Punjab Armed force from Jullundur and a CRP battalion from Neemuch was rushed to Kashmir immediately. On December 30

1963, Nehru through a radio broadcast appealed to the people of Kashmir to restore the normalcy as he was sending a senior IB officer to take charge of this case and to recover the Holy Relic and punish the culprits. IB Director Mullik arrived in Srinagar on that day to take control of the investigation.

Entire valley looked like a deserted region due to strike. Schools, offices, shops, cinemas, and restaurants did not open fearing disturbances. An Action Committee was formed with Maulavi Mohd. Farooq as its head to monitor and regulate the day-to-day proceedings since normal life was paralysed. All roads were blocked and the traffic came to standstill because there could not be any movement without the permission of the Action Committee. All the Ministers werevirtual prisoners confined to their houses with police protecting them from the danger of being lynchedby the public. All public institutions and offices were guarded by armed police since the mob was on rampage. Government functioning came to a grinding halt and most of the staff was in support of the crowd participating in the ongoing strike.

IB Investigation

IB worked tirelessly after this incident of theft. Its staff was confronted with extremely dangerous situation in Srinagar and elsewhere in the valley when went to take assessment of the situation. Mullik along with other IB officers visited the Hazratbal mosque and inspected the spot from where the relic was stolen. Surprisingly, the crowd gathered at that place did not create any hindrance and rather offered all sorts of help and promised full cooperation in the future too. IB team headed by Mullik againt visited Hazratbal Mosque on January 1, 1964. They concluded investigation for three hours and during the course of searches some clues about conspiracy behind this theft and identification of the possible culprits were received. Their investigation revealed the modus operandi of the theft at the place where the Holy Relic was originally placed. They reached the conclusion that unless the culprit knew how and where exactly the Holy Relic was kept, it would have been difficult for an outside burglar to take it away easily. Only the bag containing the glass tube with Holy Relic in it was removed leaving even the velvet covering and the silver trapping behind it. The thief must have been one whose movement in any part of the mosque including the passage in front of the sanctuary at any time of the night was freely allowed without any suspicion. He must have ensured himself prior to indulging in this theft that no one took notice of his presence in this big mosque since many people were sleeping elsewhere. .

The Action Committee which was regulating the strike also met the investigation team headed by Mullik and exerted pressure to arrest Bakshi Ghulam Mohammad on suspicion in this theft. Since there was no truth in this accusation and IB did not have any proof in this regard, they rejected their demand. At the instigation of followers of Sheikh, a sinister propaganda was unleashed by them in public meetings to release him who could restore peace and stability in the valley. They all spearheaded a campaign that the people of Kashmir would not accept the words or the leadership of any other leader in this tense situation except the Sheikh. This was an oblique inference that even the leadership of Nehru was not acceptable to them. There was a hidden agenda of Action Committee in all such outbursts because Chairman Maulvi Farooq's uncle Maulavi Yusuf was an accused in the Kashmir Conspiracy Case. This Committee was in league with the real Mirwaiz of Kashmir, who had run away to Pakistan and was carrying on anti-Indian activities and propaganda through Pakistan and Azad Kashmir radios with the help of Pakistan. Supporters of Sheikh included one of his bitter rivals Mohiuddin Karra, some Plebiscite Front leaders and armed Razakars whom Sheikh Abdullah recruited in 1958 before his arrest. They all came to the forefront and made arrangements for all processions, meetings, hartals and langars for the striking people. At the same time, they issued threats and intimidated those who were loyal to the Government. These elements tried to internationalize the Kashmir issue by releasing posters and leaflets that it was not part of Indian territory. They also raised the banner of revolt against the accession and demanded the intervention of Muslim countries including Pakistan to take up the matter at the United Nations.

Pakistan and Azad Kashmir radios were indulging in the most virlent propaganda accusing India solely responsible for disappearance of the Moe-e-Muquaddas. In order to arouse anti-Indian feelings among the Muslim population, theft of the relic was cited as an attempt by the Indian Government to demoralize the Muslims of the whole country. These broadcasts were airmed at raising Jehad and whipping up religious feeling against the Hindu rulers of India who had outraged Islam. They also tried to instigate the Indian Muslims in the name of Islam that all the Muslim countries were in their favour and it was the right time to break shackles and get independence forever from the Hindu community. All pro-Pakistan elements sitting in Pakistan and in Kashmir united in this mission to tarnish the image of Indian democracy in the world. IB was keeping full watch on the happenings and regularly informed the Prime Minister and the Home Minister on the developments as a result of this hostile propaganda unleashed by Pakistan from other side of the border. Action Committee was obviously trying to achieve their evil designs in the garb of this sinister propaganda and take advantage of the prevalent volatile situation in the valley. It was absolutely impossible to take any preventive mesures against the crowd which immobilized life in the valley. Majority of the population did not bother about politics but had been deeply hurt by this sacrilege and use of force at this juncture would have construed as interference in the religion, and a propaganda throughout the Muslim world could be spread that the Hindu police had used force against peaceful Muslim crowds which had collected only to express their concern at the loss of the Holy Relic, the Moe-e-Muqaddas. Pakistan and her agents in Kashmir were systematically exploiting the Muslim mind in the valley to use as a lever if any action of the security forces against the crowd, in the Security Council and in the Muslim world elsewhere. The Indian Government kept full patience and held the nerves on this grim situation created by Pakistan through their agents. The pattern of the conspiracy was clear. Pakistan had tried many steps since accession of Kashmir including the invasion by tribal, outright attack by the Pakistani army, innumerable sabotages, explosions and conspiracies but had not been able to bring about any large scale disturbances in the placid atmosphere of the valley but by this single relic episode put the entire valley into a state of turmoil and people's anger was fully aroused. Release of Sheikh who was identified with the pro-Pakistani groups and detained under the Kashmir Conspiracy case and arrest of a loyal Indian Bakshi was demanded which was part of the deep routed Pakistani conspiracy.

A couple of months earlier, the IB thwarted the move of an agent of Pir Mazbool Gilani, an absconder in the Kashmir Conspiracy Case, to create the similar mischief in another mosque at the behest of Pakistan. IB fully apprised of all the developments and processed the demands for further assistance in men and materials from the Indian Government. Additional enforcement to control any worsening of the law and order situation, was sent to Kashmir. There was a move to impose the rule of Sadar-e-Riyasat which was dissuaded by Mullick, the IB Director because such action would have brought a heavy blood bath in the valley in view of the hostile atmosphere created by the Action Committee members in league with Pakistani agents. However, IB had by then collected enough material evidence against Pakistan sponsored conspiracy in the disappearance of the Relic.

IB with the help of the Kashmir Police started an interrogation centre to examine all suspects and intelligence was further strengthened to track down the culprits. A large number of persons were interrogated. IB thoroughly checked and analysed the facts and circumstances to reach at logical conclusion that that investigation was on the right track After acute brain-storming it became evident that Pakistan through Pir Maqbool Gilarni with the assistance of some of his important contacts in Kashmir, who had received money for this purpose from Pakistan, were involved in the removal of the Moe-e-Muqaddas. There was every possibility that this could not have been done without the knowledge and connivance of one or more of the custodians of the Relic. Even though the Moe-e-Muqaddas had been removed, there was absolutely no chance of it being taken out of Kashmir and even out of Srinagar town. IB concluded that it was still close to the Hazratbal Mosque. Even the damnable conspirators in Kashmir would not allow the Moe-e-Muqaddas to let it reach to Pakistani because in that case the importance and sanctity of Hazratbal would be lost altogether along with depriving the means of living of a large number of people who depended on the income they derived from the pilgrims. IB was able to tighten the noose around them and the culprits were finding it difficult to keep the Moe-e-Muqaddas any more in their possession. When the pro-Pakistani elements became abundantly sure that the recovery of the Relic was imminent, a demand was raised by that the very recovery of the Moe-e-Muqaddas should take place under the supervision of Sheikh Abdullah who should be immediately released. The culprits concerned with this theft realized that they have been identified and they would soon be trapped and arrested. However there was a strong apprehension among the IB top brass that if driven to the wall, there was a danger that the culprits might even throw the Moe-e-Muqaddas into the Dal Lake or bury it somewhere in the ground. Though they would not deliberately destroy it but either these steps would lead to its destruction and it would be impossible to recover it then forever. Hence an option for the culprit to retrieve the Holy Relic was kept open to return the Moe-e-Muqaddas honorably to its original place of rest. This practice was followed earlier also when it disappeared on two previous occasions and retrieved by the perpetrators. In a planned strategt, on January 3, 1964, all guards were withdrawn from the mosque and people were given free access to the place. IB realized that arrest of culprit without the Moe-e-Muqaddas was of no consequences to them and if the Moe-e-Muqaddas was recovered, whether the culprit was punished or not would be a matter of little importance.

Relic Recovered

In a most secretly guarded operation which could not be disclosed in the interest of the security of the State, the IB was able to get the of Moe-e-Muqaddash replaced at 5 p.m on January 4, 1964 and it was found placed at the same place from where it was removed on December 27. This operation was never disclosed for obvious reasons because such a disclosure could bring many unwarranted controversies inviting many repercussions not only for the state but also for the Indian Government. When the IB team entered the Hazratbal Mosque, they found the Holy Relic resting in its old wooden box although found broken. Holy Relic was taken by the IB Director to their Headquarterss in Srinagar after displaying it to the gathering which jumped in excitement to celebrate the occasion. Prime Minister and Sadar-e-Riyasat were informed that the Holy Relic had been recovered by the IB. All India Radio was given this news to broadcast to the whole world. In order to ascertain its originlity, Nishan Dez were called one by one to identify the Moe-e-Muqaddas. They confirmed that it was original and no suspicion in this regard should be raised. Members of the Action Committee were given information by the IB about this recovery. Next day, the law and order problem was over. Strike was called off in the valley and offices and other establishments were re-opened. Public transport started moving and life in the valley returned to normal. Black flags disappeared and the Razakars and other Pakistani agents went into hiding. A serious calamity was averted by IB in a totally hostile and anti-Hindu climax created by Pakistan which too some extent succeeded in East Pakistan where Hindu community was targeted on the Relic theft. It would be pertinent to mention here that one of the two Kashmiri officers involved in this operation of IB was a Muslim, Ghulam Qadir, the CID chief.

On January 5, 1964, on the direction of the District Magistrate, the Moe-e-Muqaddas was placed in a big hall in the first floor of Shergarhi police station for regular prayers amid tight security arrangements. Members of the Aukaf Committee who had seen it from close quarters by paying special fees and Nishan Dez along- with twelve other persons including some Pirs identified the Moe-e-Muqaddas as the original one. This identification continued for five days. Members of the Action Committee were informed of this fact by the IB who did not raise any eyebrow on its recovery in spite of the fact that Pakistan Radio started a propaganda that the Relic recovered was not original and a fraud was committed on the people of Kashmir and instigated them to continue the agitation. Action Committee could not dare to do so in view of the peace returned to the valley after the recovery of the Relic. Its dictatorial approach which continued for eight days was a damp squid and none of its sinister design succeeded thereafter because the District Magistrate issued prohibitory orders in Srinagar to maintain the law and order.

District Magistrate duly recorded full proceedings in full public view and there was not a single voice against the originality of the relic. Political leaders of Kashmir advised the IB Director Mullick that since the investigation and trial in this case would consume considerable time, it will be ill advised if the the Moe-e-Muqaddas was kept away from the Hazratbal shrine. On 10th January, the Moe-e-Muqaddas was placed at its original place in the Hazratbal Mosque in the presence of large crowd and the District Magistrate put his seal on the premises which was reinforced by iron doors and steel bars. It was decided that on the 6th February on the occasion of Urs-Char-Yar, the customary Deedar day, exposition of the holy relic would be given to the general public by the Nishan Dez.

So, the IB foiled the conspiracy of Pakistan with the recovery of Moe-e-Muqaddas because it was stolen by the pro-Pakistani agents to destabilize the Kashmir Government to incite violence and chaos in the valley. They succeeded to some extent in their mission for seven days of its disappearance when whole of the valley became standstill and violence erupted in many areas due to this theft. However, after its recovery, none of the anti-Indian objectives dictated by Pakistan to Action Committee could be achieved. Whole dram to get released Sheikh Abdullah in the garb of this theft did not attain any success. The Kashmir Government did not change and Bakshi was not arrested which was hidden motive behind this conspiracy. There was no bloodshed and situation in Kashmir became normal under the firm control of India. So, in order to revive the violent agitation in valley, Pakistan and Azad Kashmir radios started persistent propaganda that the Moe-e-Muqaddas recovered by the IB was not genuine and a fake Relic had been placed in the mosque which was an act of the greatest sacrilege by the Kafir officers of India. They even rejected the claim of the most respected Fazir of Kashmir, Syed Mirak Shah of Shalemar who said that in his dream, Hazrat Mohammad told him that he had returned to the shrine and the people of Kashmir should celebrate it.

Special Deedar

As a result of the instigation by Pakistan, members of the Action Committee and agents of Pakistan raised a demand for the special Deedar by them to establish the true identity of the Holy Relic. It was not acceptable to the Government because there was every apprehension that the members of the Action Committee would negate the originality of Moe-e-Muqaddas. However, the continued propaganda of Pakistani and Azad Kashmir radio and the agitation of the Action Committee with the help of Pakistani agents and Razakars provoked violent trouble in Srinagar. The general public was instigated to make insulting remarks on the Indian Armed Police and false charges were propagated against them. Sikh soldiers were special targets of taunting and a strong demand was raised to withdraw the Punjab Armed police from Srinagar. The Action Committee planned virulent confrontation on January 26,

1964, the Republic Day of India. On January 25, while the mob was coming out from the mosque after prayer, hooligans of Action Committee aided by pro-Pakistan agents attacked Punjab Armed Police personnel on duty in the vicinity of mosque and in other area of Srinagar. Obviously, the armed personnel reacted in self defence and in the ensuing retaliation of police firing, seven civilians were killed. Soon thereafter, curfew was imposed in the troubled area to control the situation.

Prime Minister Nehru deputed IB Director Mullik and Home Secretary to make on the spot assessment of the law and order situation in Srinagar after this violence. On reaching Srinagar, they met the members of the Action Committee who demanded an enquiry commission to determine the justification for police firing which was rejected out-rightly.They also demanded special Deedar to satisfy them of the originality of the Relic. It was also not agreed as the next Deedar would be held on February 6 on the customary day which was nearing after few days. Understandably there was every apprehension that the demand for the special Deedar of the Action Committee to determine the sanctity of the Moe-e-Muqaddas was coloured politically and not on the merits. These Pakistani agents were determined to declare that the Relic was spurious as a result of which the people of valley would rise in revolt on the so called sacrilege committed by the Indian authorities. Their demand was not accepted by IB and Home Ministry of India officers on the plea that the District Magistrate had already completed all these formalities in public view. Sadar-e-Riyasat also agreed on the suggestion of these officers. On that night, the administration arrested most of the members of the Action Committee and many other agents including Razakars and suspected elements were taken into custody and security was put on high alert to avoid any untoward incident all over the valley till February 6, 1964, the day of deposition of Holy Relic before the general public.

Weather condition in the valley was deteriorating due to winter season. In spite of these adverse chilling conditions when temperature had dipped to below zero degree, the brave Punjab Police Armed soldiers not only maintained law and order in Srinagar but in other cities of Kashmir also. They maintained law and order situation flawlessly and all the evil designs of Pakistan and their stooges in Kashmir were outwitted by this brave force of Punjab soldiers and their commanders. IB clandestinely brought thousands of genuine pilgrims from the villages of the valley to counter the presence of the Pakistan sponsored elements who were bound to create trouble on February 6, 1964, the day Moe-e-Muqaddas was to be exhibited to the general public. This was planned by IB to remove whatsoever doubts were raised by anti-Indian elements regarding the original Relic. Security forces were posted at all vantage pointsto maintain lawand order in the city. Additional police in plain clothes with IB staff were deployed all over Srinagar to get inside view of any untoward incident. IB also made elaborate arrangements to counter the efforts of divisive elements who were in town with the help of Pakistan. All Kashmir politicians were in support of the strategy of IB and other government officials to meet the alarming situation. General public of Kashmir, be it Hindu or Muslim, completely supported action of the Government to hold the customary Deedar on February 6, 1964 in a peaceful manner to teach a lesson to the Pakistan and their agents. However, this could not happen in view of some unexpected political developments which was in the offing.

Prime Minister Nehru was restless and fingers-crossed while watching the whole situation in the valley. In order to diffuse this controversy forever, he intervened and deputed Lal Bahadur Shastri who was Minister without Portfolio, to make the Kashmiri public aware about the veracity of the matter. Shastri was assigned the responsibility to conduct the proceedings in his presence to hold Special Deedar of Moe-e-Muqaddas for the public. Home Minister Gulzari Lal Nanda protested against the Special Deedar but writ of Nehru again prevailed. IB Director too was opposed to such a display of the relic but he extended full support to Shastri in this political mission. He however stressed a condition that if special Deedar was to be held, it must be confined to only religious leaders and no member of the Action Committee should be included in the identification process. According to him in this process a message would go that this identification was conducted on religious basis and not on political compulsions. Shastri accepted these suggestions. However, the Action Committee was authorized to select the team for identification and any interference of Kashmir Government was ruled out in this process. The Action Committee after much dilly-dallying sent a list of 14 identifiers for this job.

IB had made elaborate arrangements to maintain law and order in the state on the day of identification which was scheduled on February 3, 1964 to meet all consequences as a result of the impending aftermath of identification. Armed police was deployed to control the situation near Hazratbal mosque and Dal lake. Administration and police all over the all over the valley were put on the high alert to maintain law and order. IB was fully prepared to face the possible show-down created by the Action Committee because till the last moment they did not disclose their names of identifiers to Shastri.

However, in spite of all these odd conditions, the special Deedar was held as scheduled at the Hazratbal mosque. Before giving their verdict, each of the 14 members of the committee of identifiers were given a copy of the holy Quran to swear by it that they would speak the truth. All those members took the oath accordingly. The acting Chief Nishan Dez, Noor Din Bandey narrated the background knowledge of the holiness of the Relic and its history and gave its description from the books for the purpose of identification. Thereafter, amidst total silence, the District Magistrate broke open the seal of the safe and the Nishan Dez brought the holy Relic with its trapping in full view of the public. He took the tube where Relic was kept to each of the fourteen members by turn and held it near his eyes so that each of these could have a clear view of it. Although there were some reservations put forward by the IB about the identifiers but in the presence of Shastri and Shamsuddin, the Chief Minister of Jammu and Kashmir all these fourteen holy persons from Kashmir including the highest Pir Mirak Shah and the Chief Nishan Dez, Noor Din Bandey gave unanimous verdict that the Moe-e-Muqaddas recovered by the IB was genuine. Faquir Mirak Shah, the holiest of the holy men in Kashmir was the first of the identifiers who uttered the single word “Haq” meaning right. After the identification, the large crowd watching the proceedings silently jumped into the excitement and celebrated with joy. Shamsuddin, the Chief Minister of Kashmir was in tears. With this declaration, the 37 days uncertainty prevailing in the valley, ended in a happy note much to the relief of the Kashmir and India Government both. The Action Committee members were crestfallen and left the venue in a huff without even the courtesy to thank Shashri. The news was telecast by the Srinagar Radio so that AIR, Delhi could further telecast and inform the whole of the World about the reality of the false propaganda raised by the Pakistani leaders and their agents in the valley. IB thus temporarily thwarted the sinister design of Pakistan to destabilize the Kashmir Government in a totally hostile situation. Later, on the February 6, normal Deedar of Moe-e-Muqaddas was held where more than 60,000 people congregated. The Deedar was successfully conducted four times to the jubilant pilgrims. Prime Minister Nehru duly complimented Mullik and his staff in Kashmir for displaying utmost devotion and capability in this difficult task which they fulfilled in absolute adverse conditions.

Subsequently, on February 9, 1964 Nehru sought full details of this whole affair from Mullik. He told him that all these developments which were taking up in valley was a clear indication that Kashmir was still not a part of India in all realities. Mullik briefed Nehru there was genuine cause behind this large stage agitation by the Kashmiri people but there was absolutely no reason to either blame the state Government or the Central Government for this incident. Even after the recovery of the Holy Relic, Pakistan knowing fully well that Relic was genuine, could arouse the people of Kashmir against India by false propaganda spearheaded through their agents as a result of which the Special Deedar had to be held to assuage the feelings of Kashmiris. This provocation was a clear indication that pro-Indian leaders were either fence sitters or incapable to check all such evil designs of Pakistan. Hence, a new rethinking had to be taken on the policy of Kashmir in such adverse circumstances to which Prime Minister was totally convinced and thought of its reorientation henceforth.

Sheikh Released

However, with the passage of time there was political squabbling among the Kashmiri leaders after the Kamraj Plan when Bakshi resigned from the Chief Ministerial post to work for the strengthening of the party in Jammu and Kashmir at the behest of Nehru. There were all speculations that release of Sheikh Abdullah was imminent. All those Kashmiri leaders who opposed Prime Minister Nehru in Sept., 1963 on the release of Sheikh, took a volte-face and made strong appeal of his release. They were apprehensive that he was to be released soon and as such wanted to take personal credit in this regard. They were aware that ultimately Sheikh Abdullah would become Chief Minister after his release and in that scenario they should champion the cause of his release for their own benefit in Kashmir politics.

Session trial of Sheikh Abdullah was in progress. But in this political uncertainty many of the witnesses in Kashmir Conspiracy case were victimized by the so-called Action Committee formed by the Plebiscite Front leaders. There were numerous cases of intimidation and assault on them. IB Director wrote to the Government to issue clear direction because with the rumour of impending release of Sheikh Abdullah, witnesses of the case were not steady fearing saftely for their life. On April 4, 1964, the Prosecution Counsel sent an urgent message to the Government and also raised a similar apprehension but no one was prepared to take any initiative in this regard. IB head of Jammu on April 5, informed Delhi Headquarters that G M Sadiq Chief Minister had issued a press statement to the effect that the case against Sheikh Abdullah would be withdrawn immediately. IB duly informed the Prime Minister, Home Minister and Shastri in this regard.

Soon thereafter, an emergency Cabinet Committee under the Chairmanship of Nehru met in Delhi. Quoting the episode of Moe-e-Muquaddas, Nehru stressed that even after fifteen years of accession, the situation in Kashmir was unstable and as such some radical changes were required in the valley. He added that in spite of what he did for Kashmir, the people were still dissatisfied which could be due to the lack of governance of state leadership. He stressed that Sheikh Abdullah had a strong base in the valley and in the changed circumstances it was imperative to bring him into the main streamline of the state politics and as such should be released forthwith. In this regard, Prime Minister sought the opinion of all those present in the meeting. Home Minister G L Nanda mildly protested but did not persist firmly. Other politicians and bureaucrats were silent spectators except the IB Director, Mullik who analyzed the events subsequent to the Moe-e-Muquaddas episode. He opined that the Kashmir policy required a caution approach because in his opinion Sheikh had not changed his attitude towards India. He affirmed there was a cast-iron case against Sheikh and his acquittal was beyond imagination of all legal experts. He stressed that if the case was withdrawn, he could never be prosecuted again on these charges if he would hatch any such conspiracy against India. He further warned that while unveiling this conspiracy, many of sensitive agents of IB would be exposed and their life in valley would be totally unsafe. IB Director or the Government should issue a firm statement that the case would not be withdrawn and if this could not be done then it was difficult for them to keep the witnesses firm and steady any longer. Even some of the IB officers working in Kashmir had to be withdrawn prematurely because their continuance would jeopardize their life since they were exposed to the public and media.

After all these deliberations, Prime Minister Nehru consulted G M Sadiq and other legal experts. In spite of the apprehensions raised by IB Director, Nehru decided to withdraw the case and release Sheikh Abdullah. Thus diktat of Nehru again prevailed and the water-tight case of Kashmir Conspiracy was withdrawn and Sheikh Abdullah was released on April 8, 1964 along with other accused. His supporters welcomed him as the Lion of Kashmir. Even the Praja Parishad, the staunch opponent of Sheikh, also hailed his release. He reached Srinagar after release from Jammu and revived the anti-Indian forum Plebiscite Front and started making speeches against the Indian Government.

Sheikh in Pakistan

Pandit Nehru called Sheikh Abdullah on April 29, 1964 to Delhi and suggested him to forget the past and look to the future and sought his suggestion for an everlasting solution of the problem of Kashmir. In order to reform his attitude towards India, Nehru asked Sheikh to visit Pakistan and assess the conditions of Muslims there. He wanted him to have exact view of the prevalent political situation in that country before coming to any definite conclusion. Nehru wanted Sheikh to get him back to a proper frame of mind so that he could take a decision whether his association with India was more beneficial in comparison to Pakistan and his dream of independent Kashmir was realistic. Sheikh Abdullah went to Pakistan on May 25, 1964. He was disturbed to see pitiable conditions in which the Kashmir refugees were living there. Azad Kashmir leaders in Pakistan Occupied Kashmir informed him that Pakistan had a lukewarm attitude to form any elected Government for them. Sheikh Abdullah was further disillusioned when he did not get any encouragement for his dream of independent Kashmir from Pakistan leadership. Although, he got the crystal frame of picture that association of Kashmir with India would be more beneficial but he had the inherent desire to rule Kashmir independently. Due to the sudden death of Pandit Nehru on May 27, 1964, he abruptly cut short his visit to Pakistan and participated in his funeral in Delhi. His emotional link with India broke away with the untimely death of Nehru. He considered himself as the undisputed ruler of Kashmir and did not tolerate any sub-ordination to any other leader of India after the death of Nehru. He considered these leaders inferior to him.

Hence, the purpose for which Nehru sent him to Pakistan was defeated after his death. Sheikh did not change his past stance and soon thereafter treacherously resumed his anti-Indian propaganda in Kashmir. Rest is history and the Kashmir issue is still raked day in and day out even by petty Kashmiri leaders for their own political aims and cheap publicity. The Kashmir Conspiracy case wherein Sheikh Abdullah was certain to be convicted for lodging war against India, died an unnatural death due to the pliable political attitude of the Central Government after the departure of Bakshi Ghulam Mohammad as Chief Minister of Kashmir. This case could also not be completed in time due to the tactical handling of the case by the conspirators who deliberately prolonged it for several years by intimidating and threatening the witnesses in one way or the other who could not sustain these threats for their own and for their family's safety. IB deserved all kudos to prepare a water tight case in view of the hostile local population and cross border help from Pakistan. Nehru too was liberal to Sheikh and due to political pressure on him from all quarters on him from all quarters, IB could not prolong this case further and was forced to withdraw prematurely. However, this was a landmark achievement for the newly created IB which in spite of all adverse material and political situation, could prevail upon the odds and put up a brave face by prosecuting a leader of the stature of Sheikh Abdullah in Kashmir. B N Mullik, Director, Balbir Singh, Joint Director and above all the young Sikh army officer I S Hassanwalia, who built up the IB in Jammu and Kashmir from a scratch to a formidable unit, deserved a remarkable place in the IB history whose achievements date were above all other such operations in the country till date.

❑

Sabotage of "Kashmir Princess"

April 11, 1955 has gone down in history as a day of worldwide agony, consternation and puzzlement, for it witnessed the crash of the Kashmir Princess — an Air India International Super Constellation plane, registration No. VT-DEP, in the sea, 100 miles short of Indonesia-China sea near Natuna Islands which are territory of Indonesian Republic. Kashmir Princess had been chartered by the Chinese Government for some of its delegates to the Afro-Asian Conference scheduled to be held in Bandung, Indonesia from April 18 to 24. Jawaharlal Nehru, Indian Prime Minister, was the main architect in organizing this conference of 25 newly independent countries of Asia and Africa. Indonesia, Burma, Ceylon and Pakistan were the other countries which helped Nehru to host this summit. The Bandung conference was the first ever summit meet of Afro-Asian Heads of State/Government after Second World War to promote Non-aligned Movement, So, all eyes in the world were focused on the approaching events that were to culminate in its materialization of world politics hereinafter.

This plane arrived from Bangkok at 12.15 hrs. on April 11, 1955 at Kai Tak airport in Hong Kong, where its new Captain Datar was in command of the flight. At Hong Kong, in the normal transit drill, it was cleaned and refueled in the presence of Flight Engineer A N Karnik. During the course of discussion among crew members, one of its co-pilot, Godbole revealed that he would be lucky to see the Prime Minister of China Chou En-lai travelling in this plane. He got this information from the staff of airport who were cleaning and refueling this plane. From Hong Kong this plane was on a non-scheduled international chartered flight for Chinese delegates. Hence, this was an open secret in Hong Kong that the Chinese Prime Minister was to travel in this plane for which only the Chinese Govt. was responsible to this leakage in media since this news should have been kept secret keeping in view the large presence of anti-Chinese KMT agents of Formosa (now Taiwan) in Hong Kong at that time.

According to the secret documents of Chinese Government released in 2004, the Chinese Prime Minister, to his good fortune, could not board this plane as he had to undergo an operation of Appendices in Peking due to which he delayed his visit to Bandung. After three days of this crash, Chou En-lai went to Rangoon where he met Indian Prime Minister Jawaharlal Nehru and Burmese Premier U Nu. Thereafter, he went to Bandung for the first Afro-Asian Conference in the aircraft of Jawaharlal Nehru. The crash of Kashmir Princess in this context became not only a historic event but a contentious matter in the internal relation of China with India and Britain. The wreckage was almost total. The flight of Kashmir Princess was to last seven hours and thirty minutes. About five hours after its departure from Hong Kong, when it was flying about 18,000 feet over sea, it exploded and fell into the sea. The aircraft was burnt and destroyed with all its passengers and crew. The passengers numbering 11 were — a Polish correspondent Jeremi Starec, an Austrian correspondent of Der Oesterreiche Volkstimme newspaper, Fredrick Jensen, a Vietminh official delegation Vuong Minh Phuong and eight Chinese delegates, Shen Chien-Tu of Hsinhua News Agency, Hwang Tso-Nei also of Hsinhua News agency, Tuhung, a corrospendent of the Central People's Republic Broadcasting Station of Peking and Vice-Secretary General of the All India China Joirnalists Association, Li Ping another correspondent of Hsinhua news agency, Ho Zeng-ke, photographer of the Central News Reel and Documentary Films Studio of Peking, Shih Chih-Ang, Li Chao Chi and Chung Pu-Yun, all staff members of the Chinese delegation. They met an instantaneous death and of the eight crew members, five perished. Three crew members, Flight navigator Pathak, Aircraft Mechanical Engineer Karnik and co-pilot Dixit survived. The captain of the aircraft, Captain Datar, one of the most experienced pilots of Air India International, died and found in his seat when salvage operations took place later. The 960 miles journey of Kashmir Princess was thus cut short tragically after about two thirds of it had been traversed. Of the three crew members, Aircraft Mechanical Engineer Karnik, who survived after swimming for nine hours and reached an island that was inhabited. His ordeal ended when he was per chance rescued by the fishermen and lifted by British warship to Singapore. Later, he was decorated with the highest civilian award of Ashok Chakra and promised an allowance of Rupees Forty per month in 1972 by Indian Government which was never paid to him due to official wrangling and red-tapism of Indian executive system. Though, Chinese Government gave a citation of Rupees Fifty Thousand to Karnik but Indian Government never cared to honour this unsung hero financially. The survived crew members later recalled that they heard of rumours of sabotage at Hong Kong but no authorities took due credence to these rumours. Neither the plane was re-checked by any security personnel thereafter nor any security drill took place. According to them the plane ditched near Natuna group of island after a struggle of ten minutes from an approximate height of 18,000 feet. Soon after the explosion, smoke started entering the cabin and fire was detected in the star board ring behind number three engine nasal. Captain of the air-craft decided to ditch the aeroplane and the prescribed drill was methodically carried. The descent was rapid and its final stage was carried out under difficult circumstances. The aeroplane fell into the sea, the star hitting first and the nose sank almost immediately. It burnt and destroyed as a result of the impact. One of the air hostesses, Miss Glori Asphonson acted heroically and prior to the accident, she issued life belts to every passenger and crew members as per the underlying safety procedure.

The world consternation was all the greater because all sorts of rumours had been afloating in Hong Kong before Kashmir Princess's departure, that the Chinese Prime Minister, Chou En-Lai, would be flying by it. The crash of Kashmir Princess was seen in this context as pre-mediated conspiracy to kill the Chinese Prime Minister. Chou En-lai flew to Bandung later by and was thus spared of a ghastly end. This did not mitigate the gravity of situation. The crucial questions were : who perpetrated the crime? With what motives? And how?

Four nations were involved in a big way — three mainly the UK, China and India. The fourth one, Indoesia, was also involved because Kashmir Princess had crashed in the Indonesia waters. The Chinese were concerned most of all because the sabotage of Kashmir Princess seemed to aimed solely at their Prime Minister and most of the passengers were Chinese. Government of India was not directly concerned with this case because the aircraft was Indian but diplomatically Indian role was of paramount importance since at that time in 1955, the Chinese did not have any regular diplomatic relations with the British. They sent their officers to Hong Kong to gather first-hand information. They also insisted vociferously that some experienced intelligence officers from India must also be associated with the investigation authorities in Hong Kong. The Chinese Premier Chou En-Lai was so incensed that he took personal interest in the investigation proceedings from the very beginning and getting uncontrollably impatient on occasions at its tardy progress subsequently.

Sensing the Chinese impatience and the thick air of suspicion in the minds of the Afro-Asian statesmen attending Bandung meet, the UK Prime Minister, Sir Anthony Eden, solemnly assured the Prime Ministers of China and India that UK Government would spare no effort to trace the culprits and bring them to book. As for India, the newspaper editorial-writers vied with one another in demanding identification of marauders and demanded exemplary punishment to them. Prime Minister Jawahar Lal Nehru declared even before his departure for Bandung that senior Intelligence officer would be sent to Hong Kong for thorough enquiry. In pursuance of his directive, R N Kao, Assistant Director incharge of Security, was selected by B N Mullik, Director of Indian Intelligence

Bureau with the concurrence of higher authorities for this challenging assignment. Another team of three officers of Civil Aviation Department was constituted to assist Kao in this mission. Kao took his loyal Chandra Pal Singh, Deputy Central Intelligence Officer to assist him in the investigation. He also selected Vishwanathan, an engineer from the Hindustan Aircraft Factory to apprise him on technical aspects of the investigation. Indian Prime Minister Nehru informed his British counterpart, Sir Anthony Eden about the nomination of R N Kao for this investigation in Hong Kong.

Soon after his deputation to this challenging task, Kao left Bombay on April 20, 1955 to meet the surviving crew members of Kashmir Princess Dixit, co-pilot and Karnik, the engineer. They had swum a considerable distance from the place of mishap. Kao asked them searching questions about the explosion in the aircraft and the subsequent crash in the sea. After getting their version of how tragedy struck Kashmir Princess, He also got the details of the persons who got access to the aircraft prior to its taking off at Kai Tak airport in Hong Kong. Kao went to Singapore, where the salvage operation of the debris of the unfortunate Air India Super constellation plane was in progress. He met Dr. Raha, Director General, Civil Aviation, Government of India, who was supervising the salvage operation. Dr. Raha briefed him fully about the sabotage and the type of the time-device used in the blast.

From Singapore, he flew to Indonesia and traveled then to Bandung by car. On April 23, 1955 he called on Jawaharlal Nehru and briefed him about the information he had collected from the surviving crew members and Dr. Raha, incharge of the salvage operation. Jawaharlal Nehru introduced him to Chou En Lai and said that he was one of the best investigating officers in India and had been specially selected by him to be associated with the enquiries regarding the Kashmir Princess. Chou En-lai asked Kao to meet him at the place he was staying in Bandung in the evening. Kao met Chou En-lai who spoke to him through an interpreter. He asked Kao to give him up-to-date information which he learnt from the survivors. Kao briefed him the details of explosion and wanted to make a sketch of actual place where fire broke out in the plane. While doing so, ink of his fountain pen spread on his fingers which he tried to wipe with a paper. To his utter surprise, Chou En-lai left the room and returned in a while accompanied by an attendant who was carrying neatly folded wet towel in the tray to get wiped the ink spread on the fingers of Kao. He was too impressed by the courtesy and generous gesture bestowed by such a big stature political figure like Chou En-lai to a lower level officer. He asked Kao to get more information from his government and insisted he should not inform the British authorities about this meeting. Chou En-lai invited Kao to Beijing for sharing with him the information in the possession of the Chinese Government about the sabotage. Later in the evening, Kao briefed Jawahar Lal Nehru about what transpired in the meeting with Chou En-lai. Nehru asked Kao to proceed straight to Hong Kong to participate in the investigation.

The wreckage of Kashmir Princess was salvaged by the Indonesian maritime authorities with the assistance of Royal Naval Survey Frigates and the Far East Air Force Command based in Singapore. A scientific examination and analysis of it led to one and only one conclusion that a time-bomb was inserted in the under-carriage wheel bay. This having established, the next crucial question was: who did this? Chinese Government claimed that they had definite information that this sabotage was engineered by the KMT, the Formosa intelligence, through their agents. Initially, Hong Kong authorities did not accept this Chinese version. On April 13, the Hong Kong Government issued a press statement that they had received information from the British Charge d' in Beijing a few days earlier that some Chinese nationalist sympathizers would create trouble for a group of delegates leaving Hong Kong for the Bandung Conference by Air India International plane, Kashmir Princess. The Government was requested to take appropriate precaution. It was admitted in the press release that a representative of the New China News Agency in Hong Kong had telephoned a senior police officer to inform him that 11 delegate would be travelling by an Air India aircraft on April 11. This aircraft was chartered on behalf of the party by the China Travel Service office in Hong Kong. Further, according to them, the plane arrived on schedule flight few minutes in the afternoon. Additional security steps were taken to ensure that there should not be any sort of physical assault to the delegates due to board this flight at Kai Tak airport. According to press statement, plane took off at 1.26 p.m. without any untoward incident and nothing suspicious was detected. Hong Kong authorities considered the likelihood of anything having been planted inside plane as extremely remote. However, New China Agency responsible for handling of passengers and checking up with the crew the route to be taken, did not do this exercise. It would be pertinent to mention here that on April 10, i.e. one day before the accident, the Chinese foreign office sent for the Counselor of the British Embassy in Beijing and informed him of Chinese fear regarding the departure of the party next day through Kashmir Princess. Both Chinese and British agreed to this meeting during investigation of the case. Beyond this, while the Chinese asserted that they forewarned the British of apprehended sabotage, the British only admitted that they were warned of some trouble at the time of the departure of the party which they took to being demonstrations against the passengers and the Hong Kong authorities averred that they had taken suitable steps to ward off any such trouble. Rather a story also floated in Hong Kong by representative of western media honchos that there was possibility that the Chinese deliberately leaked out information about their chartering the Kashmir Princess in Hong Kong for 11 passengers as a kind of a blind to mislead their enemies and in fact Chou En-lai and his party left Beijing via Kunming and proceeded by an Indian Airlines Skymaster from Rangoon to

Jakarta. Some American newspapers even went on describing that the Kashmir Princess was not air-worthy and crew members had doubts about it before they commenced the journey from Bombay. As a corollary, the insinuation was also being made that the Government of India and the Indian Air Lines Corporation had intentionally been neglectful in this matter so that Chinese interest might be harmed. In India, this was construed as a crude attempt to create disruption between India and China diplomatically. Chinese ignored such false propaganda and People's Daily reported that the Chinese people were expressing profound sympathy for the loss of life of five Indians in this accident.

Another logical claim highlighted at that time was that if the Chinese, as they claimed after the accident, knew that there was a possibility of a sabotage of the plane, they should have informed the Indian Government, Indian Embassy and the Air India International instead of merely conveying this information in some vague terms to the British Charge d' in Beijing. If this information had been conveyed in a more precise form, may be the Government of India would also have taken some more positive steps to ensure the security and safety of the plane. The British on the other hand seemed to have underestimated the danger and must in any case accepted the constitutional responsibility for faulty security arrangements which enabled the saboteur to place a time bomb inside the plane which caused this ghastly accident.

On April 17, Air India issued a press statement that the crash had occurred as a result of an explosion caused by an extraneous source. Initially there was some doubt as to where the explosion had occurred and the fire which followed it started. But subsequently, on the statement of the survived crew members, Dixit and Karnik and on the eventual discovery of the infernal machine and the time mechanism from the wheel bay of the wrecked aircraft after the salvage operation, there was little doubt that a time bomb was placed in the star board wheel bay of the aircraft and the explosion had occurred there followed by a fire which engulfed the engine and the trailing edge of the star-board's wing.

Immediately after receiving the news of crash of Kashmir Princess, Hong Kong police started enquiry by recording the statement of all the persons who had access to the aircraft while it was at Kai Tak (Hong Kong) airport. Kao gave them the statement of the survived crew members. After two weeks when it was confirmed that the explosion had occurred in the star-board under carriage wheel bay, Hong Kong police concentrated on five employees of the Hong Kong Aircraft Engineering Company who had access to this part of the aircraft. According to the Chinese Government, the main culprit who had placed the bomb was a KMT agent, called Chou Chu alias Chou Tacming. Initially the Hong Kong police were unable to confirm the presence of this man in the group which had access to the wheel bay of the aircraft.

Intensive investigations for an objective answer to this sabotage were made by Kao. A firm believer in team work and a dutiful, humble man with no ego, he won the confidence of Sir Alexender Grantham, British Governor and his team of seasoned sleuths, on the one hand, and Hsiung Hsiang-hu, Deputy Director of Information, Ministry of Foreign Affairs, China, later on posted in Hong Kong by Chau En-lai to unravel the truth and to liaise with Kao, on the other.

Since Hsiung stubbornly and consistently declined any direct contact with the British intelligence authorities, much less a face-to-face meeting with them, Kao worked as an honest communication link between the two. Supplementing his own first-hand information, which was by no means inconsiderable, with that collected by him from the British and Chinese intelligence sources, which worked independently of each other, Kao gathered encyclopedic information about the crash of Kashmir Princess. Armed with knowledge and encouraged by his superiors in New Delhi, whose confidence he enjoyed is a full measure and whom he always kept fully in picture, he went about his intelligence investigation with a thoroughness and finesse that was both envy and despair of even World known acknowledged authorities on intelligence.

To cut it short, according to Kao, his findings, supplemented by other independent sources and supported by circumstantial evidence, revealed that Wu, a senior KMT intelligence officer in Hong Kong, surreptitiously purchased the services of Chou Chu, alias Chou Tse Ming, alias Chau Kui, an employee of the Hong Kong Aircraft Engineering company, whose responsibility was to service the aircraft at Kai Tak Airport of Hong Kong. on April 11, 1955. This operation of KMT of Formosa started in second week of March,1955 when heavy media reporting highlighted the possibility of a strong delegation of China for the Bandung Non-Aligned Conference in Bandung, Indonesia. Around this period, Wu got in touch the Fifth Liaison group of the KMT Intelligence network at Temple Street, Hong Kong. Wu contacted Kwan Tsau Kee and Tsang Yat Nin and enquired whether they had a relative or friend working at the Hong Kong Airport who could undertake a job of national importance for him. They discussed this matter with another person Chou Tsang Yu who said he knew one Chou Chu working there. This was confirmed by these three persons on 18 March to Wu. In a subsequent meeting on March 25, Wu asked Chou Tsang Yu to enquire whether Chou Chu would be willing to do a job for him. In the following three days, Chou Tsang Yu and Chou Chu met regularly and then Chou Chu was introduced to Wu. On conclusion of the informal discussions, Wu after securing the confidence of Chou Chu, finally asked him whether he would undertake to sabotage a communist plane. He was promised substantial rewards and safety in Taiwan. Initially Chou Chu did not agree to plant the bomb in the plane but when he was offered huge money of $600,000 for this job, he agreed. Several meetings took place thereafter in various Hotels between Wu and Chou

Chu and two others whom Chou Chu named at one occasion as Vhy Ng and on another Kam and Wong. At these meetings Chou Chu was given various sums of money. Later on, he was given a training to plant the bomb by one of the juniors of Wu. He was then given a time bomb and Chou Chu with the help of another man Wong, quietly placed it in a cavity of one of the wings near the petrol tank while ostensibly servicing it. Two days after the sabotage, Chou Chu met Wu in Hong Kong who gave him only $200 and asked him to wait for the next instalment of the reward. After some time, Chou Chu, under influence of alcohol confessed to his father that he was involved in this sabotage.

On May 18, 1955, Chou Chu made good his escape from Hong Kong by a US Civil Transport plane as a stowaway. After Chou Chu had escaped, Yu Pui another employee of the Hong Kong Aircraft Engineering Company, who was in charge of Chou Chu's group, punched Chou Chu's card in the company office, showing him as gone off duty. No sooner did he landed in Formosa than the KMT intelligence whisked him away. Nothing was heard of him later.

According to Kao there were some interesting details about the identity of Wu, mastermind of this operation of sabotage. He was described by different witnesses with whom he came in touch in connection with the plot as the man from Shanghai with characteristic physical peculiarities, like a heavy jowl and protruding teeth. In the beginning, he could not be positively identified but it was believed that he was identical with the man, named Kam, mentioned by Chou Chu in his confessions to his father, Chow Tsu Vy and his room mate Chou Tse Hok. Through various witnesses examined by Hong Kong Police, there was no doubt about the identity of Wu who carried through this operation through Chou Chu in the sense that all referred to him as the key accused. On the basis of the information given by Tsang Yat Nin, Wu was believed to be identical with a man called Wu Yichin. On the basis of the information given by him, Wu's movements were traced by the Hong Kong Police and they were able to establish his last known address in September, 1954 as 8, Tsing Wah Street, First Floor, Hong Kong. Further investigations by Hong Kong police revealed that the elusive Wu stayed in Hong Kong from July, 1954 to May, 1955. Although there was no confirmation of the whereabouts of Wu but Hong Kong Police vaguely concluded that he too fled away to Formosa, never to be seen or heard later. Hong Kong could not compel the Government of Formosa to extradite Chou Chu and Wu for their alleged crimes, because it had no extradition treaty with Formosa. India too was equally helpless, for it had no diplomatic relations with Formosa. There were thus no means now to get at the neck of the culprits. Hong Kong police however arrested large number of persons on the suspicion of owing allegiance to the KMT Intelligence but the real culprits were never caught and put to criminal trial.

In Beijing, on May 7, 1955 Kao called on Chou En-Lai, who warned him of the grave danger to his life and safety in Hong Kong. With a view to pre-empting any attack on his life, Chou asked him to arrange some security for himself. Kao respectfully regretted his inability to go in for armed guards. Convinced of an impending attempt on Kao's life, Chou En-lai sent nevertheless telegram on the matter to the Governor of Hong Kong. Brave Kao, willing to walk cheerfully with the shadow of death as his constant companion in Hong Kong, could not, of course, prevent the Chinese Premier from taking pre-emptive measures for his safety, for even a word of suggestion on his part to deflect Chou En-lai from this course would have been impolite, impolitic and imprudent. Kao was received by Director of Special Branch on China-Hong Kong border who informed him that he had been instructed by the Governor to make adequate security arrangements for his security and a British inspector would be deployed during his stay in Hong Kong for his security along with an unmarked police vehicle. Later Chou En-lai on two occasions sent word through Psiung, the Chinese assisting in investigation, to Kao that according to the information available with the Chinese Government, his assassination was imminent. Keeping in mind the veracity of the report of Chinese Government about the sabotage of Kashmir Princess, Kao some time became uncomfortable on the warnings of Chou En-lai. He took some precautions for his safety. Although, Kao tried to keep his cover job secret but due to his long stay in Hong Kong, he was exposed to many persons including some KMT agents.

Having built a bridge of understanding with Chou En-Lai in this initial meeting, according to Kao when called on him three times during his stay in Beijing, every time he met Chou En-Lai, he was received with all esteem and understanding. One such meeting took place in the presence of Indian Foreign Minister Krishna Menon when Kao attended a dinner which Chou en-Lai hosted in the Peking Hotel. It was clear from these initial parleys with the highest Chinese authority, the Chinese Prime Minister, that the letter was convinced of the sincerity of purpose, personal integrity and professional caliber of Kao. On May 11, Chou En-lai gave a written note to Kao wherein whatever information the Chinese had gathered about the sabotage of the Kashmir Princess was elaborated. This report named Chou Chu alias Chou Tacming as the main culprit. Chou En-lai advised Kao to hand over personally the copy of this note to Sir Alexander Grantham, Governor of Hong Kong which was duly done by him. Most intriguing part of the meeting which Kao had with the Chinese at Beijing was that so far as they were concerned, the matter seemed to have been dealt with only at higher level. This was evident due to the fact that they attached the greatest importance to this case. Kao was personally briefed by Chou En-lai in this case and no other person interacted during his stay in Peking. Hsuing, who was to liaise with Kao in Hong Kong, was introduced to him only on the last day and that too lasted for a while.

In the light of this information given to the Hong Kong police, two persons could be correctly identified i.e. Chou Chu and his uncle who was known as Percy Chou, who were connected to the ground maintenance crew of the Hong

Kong Aircraft Engineering Company. Thereafter, Hong Kong police carried out various searches and arrests but Chou Chu could not be traced in Hong Kong. On May 19, during dinner at his residence, Maxwell, Commissioner of Police informed Kao that one American national, Jones who was working as a Security Officer of the Civil Air Transport Company, registered in Taiwan, gave a report in which he claimed that Chou Chu had escaped to Formosa as a stowaway on the aircraft of the Company on May 18, at 10 a.m. from Kai Tak airport. It is a strange irony that Chou Chu whom the Chinese claimed the main suspect, escaped from Hong Kong just six hours before the arrival of Kao in Hong Kong from Beijing and the time when he handed over the report to the Governor. Maxwell told Kao that if the information about Chou Chu had been given earlier, he would have been arrested by the Hong Kong police. Hong Kong police further confirmed to Kao that the Chinese had well established information through their sources but they give it in small dots and too late.

In Beijing, Chou En Lai also informed Kao that he would depute some officers of his Government in Hong Kong who would liaise with him closely in the investigation. He desired that these officers should maintain contact with the Hong Kong police through Kao and not directly due to some political considerations. This team of three persons was headed by one Hsiung Hsiang Hui who was introduced as Deputy Director of Information, Ministry of External Affairs, to Kao. The Delhi Headquarterss of IB was fully kept informed by Kao of the going-on in Beijing. Needless to mention, that his superiors were highly pleased with the success of his debut in this sensitive enquiry and looked upon it as indeed it was, a success for Indian diplomacy with the help of an Intelligence officer.

On May 18, 1955 Kao proceeded to Hong Kong by car. A British Inspector was posted by the Hong Kong authorities in Hotel Miramar, where he stayed during the course of his investigation. Initially, there was some misunderstanding with the Chinese Intelligence Officer, because both the sides were working with the help of interpreters. The talks were unavoidably time-consuming and lot of confusion prevailed due to the travails inherent in interpretation. This was, however, a transitory phase. Convinced of Kao's sincerity and capability, the Chinese side soon settled down to a better understanding and working relationship with him. Around this period, Chou En-lai also visited Hong Kong. He held discussion with the Governor of Hong Kong and also obtained a brief from Kao. Later, Chou En-lai wrote to Jawaharlal Nehru in this regard and praised Kao for the manner in which he had set about the task and its implementation in a shrouded atmosphere of two different political mindsets. According to Kao, Chinese were stubborn and hard negotiators with least faith in the British counterparts in this investigation.

Meanwhile, an interesting development took place. Chou En-lai complained to Jawaharlal Nehru about the tardiness of the investigations. Chinese were skeptical about the British intentions and the plea of rules of law by the Hong Kong Police did not convince them. Therefore, Krishna Menon suggested to Jawaharlal Nehru to send B N Mullick, Director of Intelligence Bureau to Hong Kong which would have good effect on the Hong Kong authorities and certainly go down well with the Chinese. Jawaharlal Nehru himself too was not quite sure, if the British were pursuing the enquiry with the vigor and verve so characteristic of them. So, with a view to putting "more life into the investigations" he asked B N Mullik, Kao's immediate superior, to proceed to Hong Kong. Mullik reached Hong Kong on Ist June. No sooner did he reach Hong Kong than he plunged himself into intensive discussions with Kao, the chief British Intelligence Officer from South East Asia, the commissioner of Police and the Hong Kong special Branch, and the Governor, Sir Alexander Grantham, who had been under orders of British Prime Minister to work without stint for the arrest of the culprits. He meticulously went through the police records as well. Above all, Mullick and Kao had daily sessions of bilateral discussions with Hsiung at the latter's place. No amount of persuasion on their part could make Hsiung budge an inch from his known stand on two issues., namely, his refusal to see the British Intelligence Officers and his obduracy for arrest of several hundred people branded as KMT agents, who had anything, however remote, to do with Chou Chu and Wu, their subsequent trial and handing over to the Beijing Government. However, Mullick was satisfied that the British and the Hong Kong police were making genuine efforts to investigate the case. Chinese were unhappy citing that the British were too secretive to give details of the sabotage and KMT network operations. Mullick was appreciative of the efforts of Kao in Hong Kong.

Finding himself at the dead end of a blind alley, Mullik rushed homewards on June 4 to apprise Prime Minister Nehru next day at the Bombay Airport on the course the enquiry ran under his stewardship. His meeting with the Prime Minister on the eve of his long tour of the USSR, some other socialist countries of East Europe and the UK was considered crucial, for it updated the PM's knowledge on the Kashmir Princess tragedy—an issue that was likely to come up during his discussions with the European leaders.

On hearing Mullik's report, Nehru was happy with him. But then something very unexpected happened almost like bolt from the blue. The Indian ambassador in China sent a long cable to Indian foreign secretary, conveying Chou En-Lai's umbrage at Mullik's performance. Chou En-Lai accused Mullik of being partial to the British in the matter of the investigation of this case. He even charged Mullick being on the pay role of the British/US imperialists. Under instructions from Jawaharlal Nehru, who was then in Prague, capital of Czechoslovakia, Indian Ambassador in China was asked to defend Mullik. Despite that, a second telegram was received by the Foreign Secretary from the Indian Embassy in Beijing, conveying the Chinese reiteration of their accusations against Mullik and their demand for action against him. Under instructions from Nehru, who had reached Moscow, the Indian Ambassador in Beijing was again asked to defend Mullik. Then Nehru sent a message to Chou En- lai wherein he emphatically denied that there was any collusion between Mullick and the British and stated that there was no question of any Indian official let alone Mullik acting either as an apologist of the Hong Kong Government or condoning any wrong action taken by them. Nehru reiterated that the object of his Government in sending Mullik to Hong Kong was not only to emphasize the Hong Kong authorities the importance of the case but also to help them with suggestion as to how further investigations could be conducted. He further added that it was very unfortunate that some misunderstanding should have arisen about the attitude of Mullik. The Chinese then relented.

Why did Mullick's higher-level effort, which was ordered to soothe Chou En-Lai, boomerang with such fury, turning out thus to be counter-productive? Probably, it was the very short duration of his enquiry which gave the Chinese an impression of casualness or cover-up attempt on his part, or probably it was his sudden departure from Hong Kong and head long homeward rush to call on Nehru ostensibly on the urgency to brief him about the success of his mission. Though Nehru defended Mullik in the cables of the Indian Foreign Secretary to India's Ambassador against Chou En- lai tirades yet he too did not understand the cause of China's ire with Mullick. This is clear from the fact that when in July 1955, Mullick met Nehru in London; the latter asked him why Chou En-Lai was so enraged with him? Leaving Hong Kong on June

4, 1955 Mullick felt that extension of his stay in Hong Kong would be futile, yet he did not disturb Kao and asked him to stay on in Hong Kong to finalize the enquiry. This had also Nehru's approval. Kao worked like a busy bee, burning midnight oil and shuttling tirelessly between Hsiung of China and the British Intelligence Officers, there being no direct contact between them. His self-effacement, comeliness total commitment to the job in hand vi-a-vis. the enquiry, won him the esteem of all his counterparts—even the Chinese led by implacable Hsiung. Jawaharlal Nehru was no less impressed. When Mullick reported him the progress of enquiry into the crash of Kashmir Princess at the Bombay Airport on June 5, he took care to congratulate not only Mullick but also Kao on the good work done. Although Mullik was prime to self-praise, yet he was obliged to records: ".... Prime Minister Nehru had complete trust in both me and Kao and he knew that we must have done everything that was possible in the circumstances. He also knew us too well even to harbor the remotest suspicion of our collision with foreign country." Again, when Mullik called on Nehru during the latter's official visit to the UK on July 7, Nehru enquired to him about Kao and his future programme, indicating that Kao did have at least a small niche in his heart.

In the meantime on June 12, Hong Kong Police publically announced a reward of 100,000/- dollars to any person giving information leading to the arrest of the persons responsible for the sabotage of Kashmir Princess. On the suggestion of Willcox, Director of Special Bureau, Hong Kong, Kao gave this information in advance to Hsiung. On June 20, Willcox informed Kao that one Chou Si Hok who used to share the room with the main culprit Chou Chu and who had been arrested on May 19 and released after interrogation, reappeared before the Police on June 15 and said that he wanted to make a statement regarding the Kashmir Princess, in order to qualify for the reward of Hong Kong $100,000. He informed the Hong Kong police that on April 30, 1955 Chou Chu returned to his room late in the night in a state of great agitation. After taking a few puffs of heroine lost control over his tongue and began to boast that his days of difficulty and poverty were over and went on to reveal that he had sabotaged the Kashmir Princess in return for which he was expecting a handsome reward of money of $600,000/-. He also revealed that he had been put in touch with two KMT agents called Wong and Kam who had given him money and met him on several occasions. Night before the sabotage occurred, Chou Chu was called in Movieland Hotel where a time bomb wrapped in a brown paper was given to him. Next day on April 11, he was taken by the KMT agents in a car which dropped him at the gate of the airport. Then while cleaning the fuselage of the Kashmir Princess from outside, he had pushed the parcel containing the time bomb because he heard the ticking noise, in a cavity above the right wheel. Chou Chu further said that when he went to the KMT agents to collect the reward for the sabotage, he was told that since Chou En-lai was not in the plane, the amount he would get would not be what had been promised to him originally. However, he was assured that it would be safer for him to get the money in Formosa. Chou Si Hok further revealed that a few days later after the April 30, Chou Chu told him that he wanted to go to Formosa on the 16th of May which he changed to 18 subsequently. Chow Si Hok was further reported to have disclosed to the Hong Kong Police that Chou Chu had told him that the KMT agents had informed him that they had been planning against Chou En-lai's life for some time. Their original plan apparently was to assassinate him the previous year on way back from Geneva via Hong Kong which did not succeed. Later they decided to concentrate their efforts on assassinating Kuo Mo Ju who went to India as the Head of the Chinese delegation for the Asian Conference. However, about the same time they heard of the rumoured possibility of Chou en-Lai going to Bandung via Hong Kong. Therefore, they changed their plans in an attempt to sabotage the plane concerned at Hong Kong. In the light of these statement, Hong Kong police reoriented their enquiries and arrested some more suspects connected with an electrical shop at 113, Temple Street which was said to be one of the hubs of KMT intelligence activities in Hong Kong. Owner of this shop one Kwan Tsau Kee was connected to the KMT intelligence organization called as the 5th Liaison Group. From the statements of these suspects and the documents recovered from their possession, it was clear that the large KMT secret organization had been functioning in Hong Kong. Another information given by Hong Kong Police to Kao that KMT station was working there under the cover of the Christian Catholic Mission, the Headquarters of which was in Taiwan. Hong Kong Police further revealed that this station had been receiving $4000/- per month from Taiwan for its operations.

On June 27, one reliable source of Kao in the British MI5 at Hong Kong told him that there was little for him to do in Hong Kong and suggested him to write to Delhi for his return. About this time, the British authorities also informed Kao that their efforts to persuade the Formosans to return Chou Chu to Hong Kong had not been fruitful. Kao could not assess the seriousness of the British in this regard. However, from the beginning it was clear to him that the Formosans would never agree to return Chou Chu to Hong Kong to stand a trial for the sabotage case against him. Later, Willcox, Director of Special Branch, Hong Kong, admitted before Kao that extradition of Chou Chu to Hong Kong at that stage would be a source of embarrassment to the Hong Kong Government rather than any thing else. Later source of Kao in MI5 confirmed that Hong Kong authorities had decided not to pursue the matter for the repatriation of Chou Chu and the matter be allowed to rest. Chou en-Lai, on the basis of a note handed over by Hong Kong Police, took strong exception to their conclusion that on the basis of available evidences, there were dim chances of Chou Chu being convicted in the Court of Law. He attributed this change of attitude on the part of British based on political considerations. He charged some officers of Hong Kong Police as agents of Formosa Government. When Indian Government sought Chinese reaction to the withdrawal of Kao from investigation at that stage, Chou en- Lai personally intervened that Kao should remain in Hong Kong till the investigation was over and desired that prior to his return to Delhi, he should visit Beijing to personally brief him in this case.

It would be interesting and pertinent to mention here that the British MI5 officers were aware of the fact that Kao had established credible liaison with the Chinese in Hong Kong. They wanted to exploit these credentials politically. They wanted through Kao to get better idea of the Chinese policy towards Indo-China, Burma (now Myanmar), Siam (now Thailand), Formosa (now Taiwan) and South Korea. They wanted to know through Kao, his opinion or the Chinese view about their relations with the Russians, the extent of Russian aid to China and behaviour of Russians in their dealing with Chinese. They were curious to know whether the Chinese would be keen to attend the forthcoming Summit talks which were to be held in Geneva in the coming future. Above all, they were keen to kersuade him to have some whisky peg proved futile in order to elicit any information in this regard although he maintained very cordial relations with them during his rest of life. Also, when it became crystal clear that Kao would be meeting Chou En-Lai in Beijing prior to his return to India, attitude of the British officers and Hong Kong Police suddenly changed dramatically. Henceforth, they had almost stopped discussion on the progress of the case. They wanted Kao to give a favourable report and wanted to bail them out before Chou En-lai by explaining the inability of the Hong Kong authorities to prosecute the KMT intelligence suspects. Indian Government informed Kao not to make any personal comment on this subject while holding discussion with the Chinese.

Kao reached Beijing on August 26. He met Chou En-lai on August 27 where Chinese Vice Foreign Minister Chang Han Phu and Hsuing were also present. He gave him report of the Hong Kong Government .This meeting lasted for more than two and half hours. After a prolonged polemical statement Chou En-lai asked Kao his final appraisement of the situation and his view whether anything would result ultimately. Chou En-lai himself gave the impression that there was little hope of the British being able to carry the case to a successful conclusion. Keeping in view the instructions given by Government of India, Kao confined his reply to merely a technical appraisal of the state of the investigation and informed him that he felt that considerable progress had been made and he was convinced of a positive result. Kao informed Chou En-lai that the Hong Kong Police had informed him after the departure of Hsuing on August 20 that they had every hope of making out a prima facie case against Chou Chu. Kao also informed him that he had been unofficially told that Hong Kong Government was finalizing a report, a copy of which would be submitted to him. This of course, did not satisfy Chou En-lai and he was doubtful about the real intention of the Hong Kong Government whether they would give a detailed account of the investigation to the Chinese Government. He was of the opinion that they would close the case by the year end because they were assessing the political situation and if it suited them they would relapse into inactivity. Kao preferred not to comment on political situation. However he assured Chou En-lai that in spite of being disheartened many times due to apparent lack of communication on the part of the Hong Kong Police regarding day-to-day happening, his overall impression was that they had not relaxed in their efforts to unravel the case.

However after prolonged deliberations on the arrest, investigation, legal difficulty and KMT agents in Hong Kong Police, Chou en-Lai finally observed "I cannot conceive with the Hong Kong Government is so inefficient. Unless there are political reasons of some pressure from outside, it is difficult to find adequate reasons for delay on the part of the Hong Kong Government". His conclusion was based on the observation made by the British Charge d' O'Neill who informed him that according to British Law, no person could be convicted in his absence. Chou En-lai had every apprehension that the main accused Chou Chu, in this background, was deliberately smuggled away in a CAT plane from

Hong Kong to Taiwan with the connivance of both the British and Hong Kong authorities to diminish the legal conclusion of the case. He was of the opinion that Chou Chu did not perceive any personal hatred against those people who were in Kashmir Princess and the sabotage must have been carried out for political reasons. Kao gave his personal opinion on the investigation of the case on factual circumstances which did not further convince Chou En-lai who retorted "Can we put it this way? The Hong Kong authorities knew that you were going to leave Hong Kong and would return to India via Peking. Is it possible that they wanted to "bluff " you regarding the present state of investigation". Kao replied that anything was possible but his personal assessment was that substantial progress had been made in the investigation of the case. This reply slightly angered Chou En-lai as he felt that Kao was questioning his assessment and averred with some heat that if in the event he proved right that it would mean that Kao had been deceived by the Hong Kong Government. He further averred and repeated that his Government had definite information that the Hong Kong administration was riddled with KMT agents, two of whom were in the Special Branch itself and British Intelligence had direct association with the Taiwan Intelligence. He finally concluded on a positive note by saying that if the British Government had the honest intention, this case could be solved and assured that they would continue to help as before and give more time to them. In case there intention is different, we must be on guard and not be deceived and that was the central idea of his approach.

Before closing the meeting, Chou En-lai requested Kao as Hsuing had worked with him for three months, he would like that they both write a joint report to the Indian and the Chinese Government. Chou En-lai said that this report could constitute a basis for Prime Minister Nehru and him to consult one another on their attitude regarding the future depending on the developments pertaining to what the British did. Kao did not agree on the plea that he would need the permission of his Government to do so for which he sent a formal request through Indian Embassy.

In the evening, Premier Chou En-lai hosted a dinner for Kao at a place know as summer palace some distance away from Peking. This was a special signal honour he did to Kao who was too junior an officer of Indian Intelligence capable to be bestowed by such a big dignitary. Chinese Vice Foreign Minister, Chang Han Phu, Madame Kung, Director of Information, Foreign Ministry, Hsuing and Indian Ambassador were present in the dinner. Nothing regarding the sabotage case of Kashmir Princess was discussed during the dinner. Hsuing informed Kao that Madam Kung was his immediate boss in the Ministry. According to the sources of Kao, this charming lady was girl friend of Chou en-Lai, although he did not believe those sources because for some reason Kao informed the author that he had an opinion about Chou En-lai that he seemed to him quite an asexual.

Indian Government did not accord permission to Kao to sign a joint report with the Chinese. Later on, as a compromise relating to the joint report, the Chinese suggested that Kao might discuss with Hsuing his report and suggest changes, if there any in the investigation. On September 3 and 4, Kao had detailed consultations with Hsuing and his report seemed to him as factually correct. He gave Kao a copy of his report. However, the Chinese expressed surprise and regret at the time taken by the Hong Kong police in bringing the investigation to the conclusion. According to them, a case like this over which the Hong Kong police spent more than five months, under Chinese system, would have been worked out in few weeks of time.

Kao left Beijing on September 6 and reached Hong Kong on 7. He stayed there for a week. He had excellent liaison with the officers of British Intelligence MI5. These officers confirmed to Kao that in their opinion it was clear that Chou Chu, the main culprit, had been helped by one or more persons belonging to the Hong Kong Aircraft Engineering Company to hide in the CAT plane to be able to run away to Formosa. In this important field of enquiry, the Hong Kong Police did not appear to have made much progress. He met the officers of the Special Branch who assured him that unremitting efforts to investigate the case continued. He collected copies of various statements and documents prepared by the Hong Kong police and called for the last time on the Governor of Hong Kong on September 12 and others, he left for Delhi on the September 14 reaching there next day.

In December, 1955, Kao got the report from Hong Kong police that this case had finally been wound up and the necessary legal action also completed in the Court. Although, the main culprit was never caught and his guilt was not conclusively proved but his accomplices were kept under detention for various period of time and were ultimately 31 were let off and put up on a ship from Hong Kong on January

15, 1956 for Formosa. In the middle of 1956, the remaining 13 suspects were also let off by Hong Kong Police since they had decided to close the matter for the time being but it was for ever. On January 11, 1956, the British Government in London announced that the KMT authorities in Formosa had finally refused to hand over to the Hong Kong authorities Chao Tse Ming alias Chou Chu against whom the Hong Kong authorities had issued a warrant of arrest for conspiracy for murder. That seemed to put an end to all hope of bringing the main criminal for trial.

Some-time after the middle of the year 1956, Sir Alexander Grantham was in Delhi and R N Kao met him at the house of the British High Commissioner. When Kao discussed with him the Kashmir Princess case, his reaction was elusive and it appeared that he did not show any anxiety in it. Kao further gathered from the MI5 representative in Delhi that although there was no question of their having lost interest in the case but a dead end appeared to have been reached. Since all the co-accused had been deported, the British authorities in Hong Kong appeared to have closed this case. Having reached to this conclusion, Kao recalled the assessment of Chou En-lai in Peking about the British authorities as correct, which somehow Kao confronted, that the British would not prosecute the main culprit Chou Chu nor the chief conspirator Wu and the case would be put under the carpet.

Soon after his return from Hong Kong, one afternoon Nehru invited .Kao over tea at Teen Murti House to get full details of the case personally. He wanted his impression on the attitudes of the British and the Chinese authorities about the progress of the case. Kao gave the detailed account of the investigation to Jawaharlal Nehru since he met him at Bandung in April, 1955. At the end of this meeting Kao told Nehru that he was much impressed with the courtesy and personal considerations which Chou en-Lai and other Chinese officials had shown to him. Reply of Nehru was significant and its importance was clearer later on in the mind of Kao in the subsequent events which unfolded later culminating in the armed conflict between China and India in 1962. Kao distinctly remembered that in reply to the observation of Kao about Chou en-Lai and the Chinese officials, Jawaharlal Nehru said "Yes, when they want to, the Chinese can be very polite and charming".

Thus ended the journey of this tiring investigation of Kao from April to September that gave him enormous experience which later on proved of monumental help to become the head of R&AW, the external intelligence of India on September 21, 1968 i.e. after 13 years of this incident. His interaction with the Chinese and the British at high level and his first hand experience of the convoluted game of intelligence which these power played, proved asset for him subsequently. This is long and short of the investigation conducted by Kao along with the Hong Kong and Chinese authorities. It would be worthwhile to mention here that Kao had made up his mind to revert to his parent cadre of UP police from IB prior to this incident because he was disillusioned with his desk in IB but prefer to stay for some time due to some personal reasons.

On two scores, Kao came a cropper. First, he could not make Hsuing, his Chinese counterpart; agree to direct talks with their British counterparts in Hong Kong — not even informally at a meal to be hosted by him when B N Mullik, reached Hong Kong to oversee the progress of this investigation. Second, the star culprits, Chou Chu and Wu, having made good their escape to Farmosa when the British authorities in Hong Kong had reached the dead end of the enquiry. Hsiung clamored for the arrest of hundreds of persons, who might have ever come into contact with them, however nebulous and fragile that contact might be, and their subsequent trial or handing over to the Chinese Government. This was, however, contrary to the Hong Kong laws and could not, therefore, be agreed to by the British authorities in Hong Kong. Hsiung expected Kao to make them to toe the drastic line of action proposed by him—an expectation that Kao could not fulfill because it meant a flagrant contravention of Hong Kong laws. These aberrations, uncontrollable and external to Kao, notwithstanding, he persevered in the sluggish investigations, cooperating to the hilt with his Chinese and British counterparts and bringing into the bargains credit to India.

At no stage was there any rumour or any unpleasant reference in Chou En Lai's conversations with Kao in Beiing. During Kao's last meeting in the dinner with him, Chou En-lai presented Kao a seal as personal souvenir — a tribute to Kao and country he represented during a sensitive period of growing suspicious political atmosphere between India and China. Kao proudly showed this seal to the author of this book at his residence where still it is placed near his head which he sculpted after his retirement. Kao also showed the writer the picture of his visit to the Great Wall of China, which was arranged by Premier Chou en-Lai, where Kao was standing wearing, as usual meticulous as he used to, white cotton trousers and a white shirt and a light weight jacket with boat high, like the Chinese do. Kao also informed this writer that surprisingly cutting across all the protocol barriers which Chinese strictly follows, he was, on his request, allowed to visit the forbidden city and a divorce case proceedings in a Chinese Court in Peking. Kao's request to show a prison in Peking was, however, not agreed by them. Rather, they allowed him to visit a hospital where children were treated.

Subsequently, at the behest of the author, R N Kao carried out a brief review of the whole investigation from the time the crash took place in April, 1955 to the conclusion of his last meeting with Chou En-lai and other Chinese official in September beginning. There was no official announcement that Premier Chou en Lai would travel by Kashmir Princess for the Bandung Conference but there was a general belief in Hong Kong that he might do so. Originally this plane was booked by the China Travel Services for forty delegates which was subsequently reduced to 25 with 3,500 pounds of baggage. Later this was again brought down to 11 passengers and 500 Kg. of baggage. On the 10th April in the afternoon the Air India were informed that there was a further change and in fact only 13 passengers with a small amount of luggage were to travel by the plane. According to him the Hong Kong police soon after the crash, their enquiry concentrated on five employees of the Hong Kong Aircraft Engineering Company who had access to the aircraft prior to take off for Bandung. When he visited Beijing in the first half of May he was given definite information by Chou En-lai about the responsibility of KMT agents for the sabotage of the Kashmir Princess upon which swift action was taken by Hong Kong police but surprisingly the main suspect Chou Chu escaped six hours before his arrival there. Chinese official Hsiung through Kao passed on detailed information about the KMT agents in Hong Kong on which proper action was taken by the Hong Kong police. In

Beijing, Chou En-lai personally informed Kao the presence of two Chinese origin inspectors, who according to Chinese, were KMT agents. On Hsiung's demand one of this inspectors of Special Branch of Hong police was transferred out which was suspected to be a KMT agent. Kao was acting on selective basis to pass information from Hong Kong authorities to Hsiung and vice versa keeping the sensitiveness of the matter in mind. After the Indonesian Government issued a report on the sabotage of the aircraft, Hsiung further wanted the Hong Kong authorities to confirm their reporting on this matter that Kashmir Princess was sabotaged by KMT agents. Hsuing further claimed that according to their informants, the Taiwanese were trying to persuade the Hong Kong authorities through the US channels to secure quick deportation of the suspects whom the Hong Kong police had suspected, in order to hide their culpability. Around middle of June, flow of information from Hong Kong authorities to Kao almost stopped which annoyed the Chinese representative Hsuing and an atmosphere of uncertainty prevailed. Chinese Government through Hsiung continued to pass on bits and pieces of information to Kao which would seek to confirm their original report that the sabotage had been organized by the KMT agents and the Hong Kong police without revealing the full details, kept protesting self-righteously that they were doing everything possible according to their own law and procedures. Hong Kong police duly informed Kao about the confession of Chou Si Hok, involvement of Chou Chu in sabotage and arrest of many suspects of KMT. In the third week of July Kao received instruction from Delhi that he should visit Beijing once again before returning home. Kao discussed about this with his counterpart of Maxwell of the Special Branch who advised him to delay this visit because the available evidence against Chou Chu were being assessed by the Attorney General and a report was still under preparation. In the meantime, reports and photographs of the wreckage from the Indonesian Government were received by the Hong Kong authorities which were given to Kao by them on the promise of not being given to the Chinese. On August 10, Kao was informed by the Director of Special Branch, Maxwell that the Attorney General, Hong Kong had confirmed that there was a prime facie case against Chou Chu and they were preparing a summay account of the whole inquiry covering all the aspects including the enquiry regarding the KMT intelligence network and copies of the report would, in due course, be given to the Government of India and China. Maxwell further informed Kao that no decision had been taken regarding disposal of the suspects connected with the KMT intelligence network. He wanted Kao to postpone his Beijing visit pending completion of the report so that he should be able to convince the Chinese Government on behalf of the Hong Kong authorities the legal limits under which they had to function. Eventually Hong Kong authorities gave the report to Kao in the last week of August with a copy in seal cover for the British Charge d' in Beijing.

Unanswered Questions

During the 1950s, the Kuomintang (KMT), several network of Taiwan Intelligence secret agents in Hong Kong were directly under the control of the trusted aide of Chiang Kai-shek, his son Chiang Ching-kuo. Chou En-lai's much hyped visit to Bandung through Hong Kong gave them a golden opportunity in selecting their target to fulfill their political dreams that too where they could execute their plan with number of available resources at their disposal. Available evidence in the sabotage of Kashmir Princess revealed that Chou En-lai was aware of the plot of the KMT beforehand and secretly changed his travel plans but surprisingly he did not stop a decoy delegation of lesser cadres from taking his place. This fact raised few intriguing and important questions. What were the motives of KMT? How much did the Chinese Government and Chou En-lai knew before the crash? Why did they not cancel the flight or divert it to a more safer airport inside China? Was U.S. intelligence CIA involved as Chinese propaganda alleged?

Objective Assessment of the Sabotage of Kashmir Princess

According to discussion with R N Kao by the author, Chiang Kai-shek, the ousted Chinese ruler then head of Taiwan, certainly wanted to kill Chou En-lai when it was publically known that he would be attending the Bandung Conference and take a chartered flight from the Kai Tak airport of Hong Kong. This sabotage was the result of the ongoing political rivalry between the People' Republic of China i.e. Communists region and Republic of China i.e. previously Formosa and now Taiwan where Chiang Kai-shek established his Government after he was ousted from the mainland by the People's Liberation Army of Communist China. Bandung Conference of Non-Aligned Countries was going to be an acid test for Chou En-lai to make his presence felt on the international arena as the strong leader of his region. Chiang Kai-shek never wanted that to be projected at any cost. In September, 1954, Chou- En-Lai's army attacked some islands held by the Formosa Govt. off the cost of Fujian and Zhejiang. This attracted world wide denunciation for the Communist China particularly so when a Mutual Defence Treaty was signed between the United State of America and Taiwan prior to these attacks. Under a political operation "Oracle", on the initiative of British Commonwealth, Britain and New Zealand, this Taiwan Straits Crisis was taken to the Security Council in order to defuse the conflict. New Zealand was member of the Security Council at that time and being a Pacific country had the legitimate right not to allow any danger to the peace of that region. In this background of political uncertainty, Chiang Kai-shek of Taiwan assessed that Chou En-lai had deliberately changed his tack in 1955 by portraying the peaceful initiatives vis-à-vis Taiwan. In Chiang Kai-shek's eyes Chou En-lai had two objectives i.e. to persuade the USA to negotiate with the China, isolate his regime and neutralize the effect of the recently signed Mutual Defence Treaty by his Government with USA and ultimately gain entry to the United Nations. He wanted to thwart this hidden agenda of Chou En-lai. In his calculation, Chou En-lai's peace offensive and the British Commonwealth's Operation Oracle were at least as dangerous as, if not more grievous than, the military confrontation in the Taiwan Straits. He suspected the prospect of a successful Afro-Asian Conference in Bandung with Chou En-lai, the architect of the China's peace initiative, again capturing the imagination of World, could only weaken the precarious position of Taiwan further. In the circumstances, Chiang Kai-shek had every incentive to assassinate Chou En-lai, who could cause greater havoc for him in comparison to the Chinese army. A successful operation by assassinating Chou En-lai would not only avenge the recent loss of Da Ahen, Yijangashan, Nan Zhi islands to China but also would boost the morale of the KMT in Hong Kong and China. This would also undermine the peace offensives of China. An attempt on the life of Chou En-lai in British Hong Kong, whether successful or not, could have the added advantage of driving a wedge between the British and the Chinese and put an end on their diplomatic flirtation. It would also provoke China to accuse the USA of complicity, thus stiffening American resolve against admitting the China to United Nations. So in this political game plan, there were indications that the order to sabotage Kashmir Princess was given in early March, 1955 to the Kuomintang i.e. KMT operative Wu Yi-chin by Chiang Ching-kuo son of Chiang Kai- shek. Although, the available evidence linking the attempt on the life of Chou En-lai to Chiang Kai shek were circumstantial and insufficient to prove that Chiang ordered it himself. But the huge payment offered to the saboteur indicates that these orders had high level authorization. Moreover, Chinag's past record had legitimate linkage that he liquidated his political opponents by one way or other. Thus, it was always inconceivable that a matter as important as killing Chou En-lai, which would invite World wide political provocations, could have been authorized by none other than Chiang Kai-shek.

Authenticity and motive of his unsuccessful attempt to assassinate Chou En-lai by the Taiwan head Chiang Kai-shek was further corroborated by a 1979 classified U.S. Senate International report which disclosed that in 1971 KMT planned another assassination operation to eliminate Chou En-lai. The report quoted this plot as bizarre as it was elaborate because a trained dog wearing a remote-controlled bomb was to be blown to kill Chou En-lai. According to this report, the KMT sent an agent to Switzerland to make payment to an Italian neo-fascist group to carry out this plan while Chou-En- Lai would be visiting Paris. KMT agents had acquired linens that Chou En-lai had used in a hotel outside China. They used them to train a police dog named Kelly to learn Chou En-lai's scent. The dog was to be outfitted with a remote-control bomb which would be detonated when Kelly made contact with Chou En-lai. This attempt of

KMT did not succeed because China cancelled the trip of Chou En-lai to Paris. This plot further corroborate that sabotage of Kashmir Princess was the motive and mastermind of KMT to assassinate Chou En-lai who till last moment was supposed to travel by it.

Why and What for China Took the Risk at Hong Kong?

Chinese Government in general and Chou En-lai in particular were aware of the murder plot before it happened yet they chose not to take all the necessary measures to prevent it. They had prior intelligence knowledge at least by April 9 that KMT agents might sabotage the aircraft. This fact clearly asserted that their intelligence network in Hong Kong was of top quality and in full swing. Subsequent incidents revealed that John Tsang, at that time the most senior ethnic Chinese officer in the Hong Kong police, who had served as a police aide-de-camp to Governor Sir Alexander Grantham was, for example, a Chinese Communist spy. The ability of the Chinese secret service to name the KMT agents and identify the means by which the time bomb was delivered also pointed not to incompetence but to efficiency and effectiveness. After all, had there been a failure of intelligence or in transmission to the top leaders until April 9, Foreign Ministry of China should have been rehearsing with checking the reliability of the intelligence and working out an emergency exit.

If the Chinese really wanted to forestall the sabotage, it could have given the British authorities more notice or more specific warnings or at least conveyed the importance while in communication with them and then on April 10 or the Hong Kong police the next day. Alternatively, the Chinese either could have cancelled the journey on this date or should have diverted the flight from Hong Kong airport from a secure airport i.e. Bai Yun airport in the nearby Guangdong province of China which was a safer zone for this flight where runway was even 1,000 feet longer than the Hong Kong airport. Instead, Chou En-lai allowed the KMT agents to execute their sinister plot of sabotage at Hong Kong airport and did not take risk to travel on this aircraft for his life and for the other high power delegation including Vice-Premier Chen Yi, Minister of Foreign Trade Ye Zhichuang and Vice-Foreign Minister Zhang Hanfu. Some journalists and low cadre delegates were purposely selected to take journey from this aircraft. The aircraft was originally chartered for April 18. On April 2, when the Chinese definitely knew of the plot, the date of the flight was changed to April 11 and the passenger list was revised on April 7, a day before Chou En-lai claimed knowledge of the plot. It was highly unlikely that a special flight for Chou En-lai could have been allocated to some junior delegates and his travel plans were changed without his permission. The Chinese never gave any explanation as to why the identity of these delegates and journalists was not revealed until after the crash of aircraft. Had these details were made public in advance, the KMT agents might have cancelled this sabotage in view of the fact that Chou En-lai and other senior delegations members were not travelling through this aircraft and this mishap could have been averted. Nor the Chinese explained why they asked the British to treat the journalists as if they were senior members of the Bandung delegation headed by Chou En Lai when they were passing through Hong Kong. The most plausible reason was that they were dispensable and were used as bait. There was no evidence available to suggest that the Chinese knew the precise plan of the plot minutely even than they suspected that the saboteurs would try to blow the aircraft. They deliberately exaggerated the prior knowledge of the plot. Chou En-lai did not change his travel plans on the basis of this plot but on diplomatic considerations. He decided on April 7 to go to Djakarta by way of Rangoon where he was to meet the Indian Prime Minister Jawaharlal Nehru and Burmese Prime Minister U No on April 14. Once the travel route were changed on April 7, the flight from Hong Kong could have been cancelled in view of the knowledge of the plot. Had this rescheduling of the travel plan known publically, KMT agents were unlikely interested in killing junior delegates and journalists.

Chou En-lai and his government had two motives behind risking, and indeed sacrificing, the victims. The first and foremost was to use this opportunity to expose the KMT secret service network in Hong Kong and to dismantle it. If the Kashmir Princess had been diverted to Guangdong province or simply cancelled, the agents would have had to abort the operation. So there was no reason left for the Chinese to smash the intelligence network of the KMT at that time. The secondary motive was to exploit the propaganda value of such an incident. Immediately after a day the crash occurred, the Chinese Foreign Ministry started this campaign by issuing a statement that the USA and Chiang Kai-shek had jointly planned this sabotage to assassinate their delegation for the Bandung Conference. Surprisingly, British were not shown as in collusion in this plot and the Hong Kong government was charged only for negligence. Subsequent events during the course of investigations in this case revealed that Chinese were able to strengthen their relations with the British and Hong Kong Governments in the guise of this case.

Suspected Involvement of CIA in the Sabotage

Initially just after the sabotage on April 11, the Chinese government and media virulently accused the CIA of collaborating and master-minding the sabotage of Kashmir Princess. These accusations were not supported with any facts or documents. Further investigations by the Hong Kong police in this case did not find any evidence of involvement of CIA in this sabotage. This fact was too confirmed by R N Kao to the author during the course of discussion on this subject. The Chinese government, in spite of the presence of moles in Hong Kong police, could not furnish any details about the possible collusion of CIA with KMT in this sabotage except that the time bomb used was American made and was one of a batch smuggled to Hong Kong from Taiwan. The timer for the bomb, a "mark 3" firing device, was probably made in the USA but that too was widely available. Further, the American were initially keen but on the British request they tried to persuade the Taiwan to deport Chou Chu, the main suspect of sabotage of Kashmir Princess to Hong Kong police to face trial but Taiwan refused to acknowledge him as KMT agent. These facts absolve CIA of any complicity in collusion with KMT in this sabotage. Most importantly, American national interest did not coincide with that of Taiwan on that occasion. USA like Chiang Kai-shek never shared the worry of peace offensives of Chou En-lai at that time. Their primary interest in East Asia were peace and security. Moderate attitude of Chou En Lai in comparison to other Chinese leaders actually made him valuable rather than dangerous to the United States. However, one former CIA operative John Discoe Smith, who defected to Soviet Union in 1967, wrote in his memoirs "I was an agent of CIA" gave some details of his adventures in CIA. He claimed in his memoirs that in 1955, Jack Curran, a CIA officer attached to the US Embassy in New Delhi, asked him to deliver a bag to one Wang Feng at the Maidens Hotel in the Indian capital. Smith claimed it was a bomb, the one used to sabotage Kashmir Princess. It is a fact that this hotel existed in New Delhi and now part of Oberoi Group of Hotels but there were no further evidence to prove that how this bomb was transported from New Delhi to Hong Kong when it was planted in the aircraft. Hence there were no corroborative evidence to prove the indulgence of CIA in this sabotage as claimed by Smith.

There were reports which indicated that the CIA believed that Chou En-lai planned to use the Bandung Conference to project him leader of a world power. In order to cover it, CIA sent agents pausing as journalists. Eleven years later i.e. in 1966, a U.S. Senate committee investigating CIA operations heard testimony that gave murky details of a CIA plot to assassinate an "East Asian leader" attending a Asian conference. The identity of the leader was shrouded for another 11 years. In 1977, William Corson, a retired U.S. Marine Corps intelligence officer who served in Asia, published "Armies of Ignorance" in which he identified this leader as Chou En-lai. Corson informed the review committee that Gen. Lucien Truscott had brought the operation to a halt. Soon after his appointment as the Deputy Director of CIA in 1954, Troscott discovered that CIA was planning to assassinate Chou En-lai. During the final banquet in Bandung, a CIA agent would slip a poison into the rice bowl of Chou En-lai which would not take effect for 48 hours, allowing for his return to China. According to Corson, Truscott confronted the then CIA Director, Allen Dulles, forcing him to terminate the operation to assassinate Chou-En- Lai.

❑

Establishment of Ghana Intelligence

Ghana, a coastal African country formerly known as Gold Coast, got independence from the colonial rule of Great Britain on March 6, 1957. Dr. Kwameh Nkrumah, leader of the Convention People Party (CPP) which had a leftist ideology, first became President and later Prime Minister of Ghana. Nkrumah met Jwaharlal Nehru in Commonwealth Prime Minister's Conference at London in July 1957. Both of them became very friendly because Nehru was propagating for a third force parallel to NATO and Communist Eastern Block of newly independent countries of Asia, Africa and Europe in the form of Non Aligned Movement (NAM). Since Nkrumah was a powerful leader of Africa, he supported Nehru in this cause as a result of which he and Nehru decided to work jointly for this movement.

In Ghana, elections were held in early 1956 to decide as to which party would rule the country. Dr, Nkrumah's CPP got absolute majority. Main rival party of CPP was National Liberation Movement (NLM) of Dr. Kofi Abrefa Busia who was defeated with huge margin in that election. Ghana was sharply divided between the CPP and other opposition parties in all the five regions. Dr. Busai of NLM did not want Nkrumah to rule the country since the former was very ambitious to become Prime Minister of Ghana. He even went to London to persuade the British government to defer their plan to transfer power to Nkrumah to which the British did not agree. Under these circumstances, in the face of a hostile opposition of some of his own countrymen, Nkrumah became the President of Ghana. He was conferred the Ghanaian title "Osagyafo" i.e. the Redeemer by his countrymen, out of great respect for him.

Nkrumah wanted a socialist reconstruction of his country which was opposed by his own party men. He wanted the Marxist analysis of the political and economic development of his party and tried to check the reactionary trends which had surfaced in the party against his vision. Further, he inherited the civil service including police of colonial British period which was not trustworthy in the mind of Nkrumah. During one of his speeches, he called them "neo-colonialist forces", unpatriotic and anti-government. But due to lack of qualified or experienced senior officers among the Ghanaians, he had no option but to keep the British officers in a number of high posts due to their past experience. What was most compelling for Nkrumah to bother was the presence of British Intelligence officers from MI5 at the British High Commission in Accra. Nkrumah was actively encouraging and inspiring freedom struggle in other African countries like South Africa, Namibia and Swaziland. He was funding liberation movements of these countries out of huge foreign exchange reserves which Ghana was earning out of Cocoa exports. Nkrumah felt that British Intelligence, on the pretext of helping Ghana, was actually covering internal affairs of the country and closely monitoring the help it was giving to the freedom movements in Africa.

In this atmosphere of uncertainty, Nkrumah was unable to keep tab on his political opponents, his own party men who were opposed to his own ideas, the bureaucratic set up, presence of British Intelligence officers and the police. Additionally, he was championing the cause of independence of other African countries on the platform of NAM where he found Pandit Nehru as the main supporter. Since, he was unsure of his political survival in his own country, he discussed this matter with Nehru in a meeting with him at the Commonwealth Conference in London in 1957. Nkrumah informed him that the British officers who ruled Ghana had continued to remain in the country even after its independence and by virtue of close connections with the Ghanaian security set up they could manipulate matters against the country and also they could get to know all the information of what he was doing after taking over in Ghana. Nehru advised him to have an effective intelligence apparatus in his country which would prove vital to him for ruling his country and would also help him in the freedom movements of other countries in Africa. Nkrumah sought help from Nehru on this issue because there was no intelligence department in his country after the colonial independence. Nehru agreed to help him in this regard. Nkrumah sent a formal letter to Nehru in October, 1957 wherein he proposed to send two of his officers for training in India. He also requested Nehru to send an expert of IB to create an intelligence outfit of Ghana.

Nehru discussed this matter with the Director of IB, B N Mullick and directed him to take necessary steps in this regard. This matter was earlier discussed by Daniel A. Chapman, Secretary to Nkrumah with B N Mullick when they met in London while attending the Commonwealth Security Conference prior to the meeting of the two Prime Ministers. Nkrumah's suggestion was examined in the Ministries of Home and External Affairs as also by Mullick, who was at a service to service level also in contact with his counterparts in London, particularly because this matter related to the establishment of a service in a Commonwealth country.

Nehru suggested three phased proposal to Nkrumah for setting up the Ghanaian intelligence agency. First, Director of IB, Mullick would visit Ghana to prepare the detailed plan after examining the ground realities. Thereafter, two Ghanaians would be imparted training in India by the IB and later an Indian expert would be sent for a year to set up the intelligence apparatus of Ghana. These two trained officers of Ghana would help the Indian expert to set up the service, select the staff and arrange for their local training. It was decided that the job of Indian expert would be of advisory nature and not as head of the Ghana Intelligence Services.

Nkrumah promptly accepted the scheme forwarded by Nehru and in April 1958, sent two of his trusted officers from the Special Branch, Paul Yanki and Ben Forjoe to India for training with IB, the prime intelligence agency of India. They belonged to the Nzima tribe of which Nkrumah himself was a part. They enjoyed the personal confidence of Nkrumah and were intensely loyal to him. Both these officers worked in the Colonial police in the ranks and had risen to officers cadre due to sheer intelligence and guts. Officers of the IB from various disciplines trained these Ghanaians in the art of security and intelligence, internal as well as external. Paul Yankee was destined to become Chief of Intelligence of Ghana.

Mullik selected R N Kao in February, 1958 to go to Ghana as the Indian expert to set up the intelligence agency. Kao, who was Deputy Director in IB at that time, was immediately relieved of his routine work and put on special duty in connection with this assignment. British counterparts were envious of this arrangement because Nkrumah sought Nehru's assistance in this endeavour instead of taking their help. Mullik's departure to Ghana did not materialize due to his pre-occupations and phase two of the scheme i.e. training of the two Ghanaians was set in motion. There was much wrangling with regard to the status and emoluments of Kao between Mullik and Ministry of External Affairs but ultimately diktat of Mullick prevailed and Kao was given clearance for his new appointment.

After Yanki and Forjoe completed their training and returned Ghana, Kao went for this new assignment in October 1958. Although Kao was on deputation to the Government of Ghana, he was getting salary from Indian Mission. This was a sort of financial aid given to Nkrumah by Nehru as a friendly gesture. It was an open assignment and not a cover job. He had the services of two junior officers in the initial stages. They were Krishnan Nair and H J Kriplani who were also sent to Accra to assist Kao. He started from a scratch since no other staff was available in that country of this expertise. Kao formed the Foreign Service Research Bureau(FSRB) of Ghana which was an external and internal intelligence wing of Ghana. He also got his other supporting staff of junior cadre from IB of India to assist him in Ghana. He was provided a beautiful colonial officer's bungalow on the Fifth Circular Road and a new Opel car for his official and personal use. Although out of sheer jealousy, officers of the Indian Mission in Accra denied all the privileges that other countrymen were getting in Ghana but Nkrumah directed his Foreign Office to extend all those privileges and perks to Kao. With his pleasant manners and good personality, Kao was an instant hit with Nkrumah and other officers with whom he had to work.

Both Yankee and Forjoe informed Kao that they had done absolutely nothing since their arrival from India not even reported to their government bout the training they received in India. They obviously kept every future plans pending till the arrival of an expert from India. So, Kao made a beginning starting from naught. There was nothing on the ground whatsoever not even an office table or stationery or a typist. However, everybody present in the services of Kao at Accra was cheerful, unfailingly courteous and devoted.

Kao met Dr. Nkrumah the day after his arrival in Accra. Kao explained the reason for cancellation of Mullick's visit to Accra and assured him that having been instructed in detail by him, he would try to do his best until his arrival. Nkrumah was most gracious to Kao and told him that they had no experience of foreign intelligence work and his government would be guided by his advice. He informed Kao that what was happening in Ghana was of great significance to the rest of Africa. He briefed the targets for foreign intelligence work to Kao and in that priority the first one was to take care of the French occupied territory which surrounded Ghana on three sides. The next in importance was to be United Arab Republic whose Embassy in Accra had been doing a lot of offensive intelligence work. He further added that, studying of the intelligence activities of the British and the Americans should come in order of priority. Regarding communism, Nkrumah informed Kao that that did not constitute an immediate problem but he was under pressure from the Soviets who wanted to establish an Embassy in Accra. He reaffirmed that until then, he had resisted the Russian overture but he would be interested in getting Kao's assessment or reviews of Russian design and international communist activities in that order. He informed that on communism, the British had offered help to him. Kao promptly briefed Nkrumah of his methods of work and the difference in the scope of positive intelligence and counter-intelligence. Nkrumah desired to advise him on both and asked Kao to take charge of the Special Branch which was working under him. Kao impressed upon Nkrumah the importance of training and hinted that he had to get some staff for this assignment from India and also some office hands to organize the main registry. He asked Kao to prepare the scheme and promised all assistance.

Kao first met Nkrumah in his castle where he maintained his office also. This was the official residence of the British Governor during colonial days and located on picturesque Atlantic Ocean. Kao painted a perfect pen picture of Dr. Nkrumah. According to him, he was a well-dressed person of medium height and built. He had a prominent forehead and bright large eyes. He had friendly manners though of course he could be brushed and loo when he wanted to be so. Kao found him of great self-assurance which was obvious because he considered himself a man of destiny who was to lead Africa in the struggle to realize its own distinctive personality. Nkrumah spoke and wrote English with great facility and a public speaker particularly in his own language he was very eloquent and managed to sway the masses. However, like other Africans, Nkrumah was too intriguing because he was acutely conscious of his mission in life and the fact that he was man of destiny.

Nkrumah selected 21 persons who were to be taken into the organization which was placed under Kao for training. Their ages ranged from 21 to 49 years. None of them was graduate. All of them were employed in different capacities in various departments. Curiously, there was not a single police officer in the list. One amongst them was working in the trade union congress and another was an employee of the CPP which was then ruling party in Accra.

For one year Kao, exceptionally the brilliant officer of IB, worked in Accra on this venture and built up the basic framework of intelligence set up of Ghana. Nkrumah directed his Principal Secretary A L. Adu to give all sort of help to Kao which he readily provided. Kao spent day and night on this assignment and worked out the fool proof blue print for the Ghanaian intelligence. He recruited local personnel in FSRB and put them through training courses on the pattern of IB. Yanki and Forjoe were his No. 1 and 2 Ghanaian deputies.

After one year, he was called back to IB in India. Nkrumah did not want to relieve him and he even offered him citizenship of Ghana with much more than the salary and perks which Kao was getting in India but Kao refused it and came to India. Nkrumah was very friendly with Kao and used to walk in his office which was located near to Christian Coastal Sea shore to enquire about any sort of help he required for his work. Kao established the entire intelligence set up of Ghana on the basis of its geographical need.

R N Kao returned to India in December, 1959. K Sankaran Nair, another able officer of IB was selected to succeed him for completing the work which Kao had left prior to his returning India. Initially, Nair was reluctant to go to Ghana but on persuasion by Kao, he agreed. He met Nkrumah who expressed the confidence that he would continue the excellent work of his predecessor Kao. Nair encouraged Yanki and Forjoe to run the intelligence operations on their own. Other officers were trained to learn how to assess reports from the field, how to filter the truths from the reports of agents and how to prepare the finished material for the consumers, primarily the Foreign Ministry and importantly, but not always, the President. Nair stayed in Ghana for another one- and- half years and with the help of Paul Yankee and Ben Forjoe completed the work which Kao had started. Paul Yankee who was to take over as Chief of FSRB, died in a road accident. When Nair was confidant that next in seniority, Bne Forjoe was capable to work independently as Chief of intelligence of Ghana, he sought permission from Nkrumah to return to India. Although Nkrumah was reluctant to relieve Nair but he returned to India in June 1961 after spending one-and-half year in Ghana on this assignment. Towards the end of his tenure in Ghana, Nair persuaded Nkrumah to visit the FSRB office to which he agreed and spent half a day there patiently listening to an explanation of its structure, objectives and methods of working. He also met and shook hands with all the staff from the highest ranking to the office boys and the receptionist girl, charming all of them with his warm and wide smile. Thereafter, he attended an evening party at the Nair's bungalow where some Indian, European and Ghanaians from various ranks and files were invited. According to Nair, Nkrumah was more involved in African affairs. Initially, he depended on Russia and China for arms training of police and army which was not successful. Israel too tried to come near him. Net result was internally people of Ghana were disgruntled particularly with the army.

R N Kao and K S Nair met Nkrumah at Palam Airport in New Delhi in February 1966, when he was going on an official visit to China via Delhi. Three spent some time together at the Airport which was not on the protocol of the Ministry of External Affairs. He greeted both Kao and Nair with warm hug. Nkrumah again appreciated the job done by these two officers in Ghana. While he was in Peking, there was a military coup in Ghana and Nkrumah was overthrown from power. He took asylum with Sekon Toure, President of Guinea and died there due to cancer – a forgotten hero. Nkrumah was a great pioneer of the African freedom struggle against European colonial rule in the continent. If Africa is free today, a lot of credit for this must go to him. Unfortunately, today he is hardly remembered even in his own country.

This was the first major venture of IB of India which these two most capable officers carried out on a foreign soil in Africa on the face of the fact that other agencies like CIA, MI6 or Mossad of Israel did not get this privilege leave aside other agencies of Asia.

❑

War of China

Historical background of territorial dispute with China

Tibet as a nation was united from various tribes in 127 B.C. by king Nya-Tri-Tempo who was succeeded by forty generations of kings. Original religion of Tibet was Bon which was subsequently taken over by Buddhism by thirty-third king, Song- Tsen, Gampo who took his boundary from the present area known either as Inner or Outer Tibet. He married a Chinese and a Nepalese princess. He died in 650 A.D. and his successors carried their conquests deep into Chinese territory and extended Budhism further. They conquered Chinese Turkistan, whole of Ladakh, Nepal, Sikkim and some portions of North Bengal. They also captured several provinces of China. A stone pillar standing in front of the Potala gave ample proof of these victories in China.

Budhism Promoted

Thi-Song-Deu-Tsen, the thirty-seventh king in 755 A.D. invited many Indian Budhist Pundits and Sanskrit scholars, one of them was Padmasambhava (Panchen). Budhism in Tibet had come from both Chinese and Indian sources and both the schools were claiming mastery over the other country. In 792 A.D. a great debate ensued between the Indian school led by Padmasambhava and the Chinese school in which the Indian doctrine emerged victorious and the Chinese school was banished for ever from Tibet. Thereafter the Indian school remained supreme and Padmasambhava established the first monastery at Samye and ordained seven monks. Until nowy this exalted figure, Padmasambhava or Panchen, is known as the Guru Rimpoche of Tibet. Two other scholars, Sanatarakshita and Kamalashila, spread Indian thought on Budhism in Tibet.

After the death of Thi-Song-Deu-Tsen in 838 A.D., his successors could not reign over the extended boundaries, China and Nepal recaptured their land from the Tibetan. China too also faced internal political problems and could not retain control over the recaptured area of Tibet. By the end of 905 A.D., there was a large area of no-man's land between China and Tibet for which each of them claimed their right and later when one was stronger than the other and reclaimed control when political situation reversed. Tibet and China were two powers on an equal footing and Tibetans were generally the aggressors and had the upper hand. Budhism almost eclipsed during this period in Tibet but it was revived in 1055 A.D. by two scholars i.e. a Tibetan named Richen Sangpo and the other Atisa, a Bengali from the monastery of Nalanda. The present form of Buddhism in Tibet is mainly due to the Titanic efforts of these two scholars and not based on what was originally preached by Padmasambhava. Many monasteries flourished thereafter which spread their own ritual and practices thus creating different thought of school in this religion. Subsequently, these preachers were involve 3d in bitter rivalries which resulted in many feuds between the respective followers of these monasteries.

In the thirteenth century, the Mongols conquered China and Tibet and technically the first union between these two otherwise complexly independent countries under a foreign ruler took place. In 1338 A.D. the Chinese overthrew the alien Mongol ruler, Gusri Khan and Ghangclub Gyaltsen evicted the Mongols from Tibet and by 1350 A.D. he established himself as the real master of all Tibet and revived the traditions of the early Kings. Thus the link between Peking and Lhasa established only with the conquest of China by a foreign ruler, the Mongols, who were earlier accepted by the Tibetans as their overlord. Both China and Tibet regained their independence of the Mongols in their own way at different times, Tibet achieved it first and China afterwards. .

Dalai Lama Title

Tibet's religious linkage with Mongolia re-emerged when Sonam Gyatso, a brilliant scholar visited Mongolia in the year 1578 and converted into Budhism the leading prince Altan Khan together with a large number of his followers. Altan Khan gave Sonam Gyatso the tile of Dalai (meaning ocean of learning) and Sonam used this title retrospectively for his two predecessors Gedun Truppa and Gedun Gyatso and became the third Dalai Lama of the Gelupa sect. Many other Tibetan Lamas also visited Mongolia but none of them reached the eminence of Sonam Gyatso and in this way the foundations of the supremacy of Dalai Lama was established. Growing factionalism between various provinces was leading Tibet towards uncalled for destruction. At this juncture, the fifth Dalai Lama, Ngawang Lobsang Gyatso, invited the Mongol prince, Gusri Khan to put an end to the growing conflict. In 1642, Gusri Khan invaded Tibet, defeated and killed the Tsang king, displaced the Karmapa Lamas from the high estate and set up the Dalai Lama of the day as the religious head of the country. Gusri Khan assumed the title of the king of Tibet and the Dalai Lama became the religious head. The relationship between these two was that of a patron and a priest in which the temporal support of the lay power was given to the high priest in return for the spiritual support of the religious power to the ruler. Gusri Khan retired to Mongolia and left a Regent to look after the Tibetan kingdom. After the death of Gusri Khan in 1655, his successor showed little interest in Tibet as a result of which Dalai Lama concentrated all powers in himself and appointed his own spiritual son Sange Gyatso as the Regent. During this period Tibet recovered much of the lost territory up to Ladakh, finances of the State were put in order, census was held, penal laws were promulgated and ensured trade prosperity. He renewed contacts with India and translation of many Sanskrit and Pali books were undertaken. During this period of Tibetan history reunification of Tibet was brought under the rule of Dalai Lama and was thus termed as golden era of Tibetan history.

After the death of fifth Dalai Lama in 1682 A.D., his son Sange Gyatso challenged the overlordship of Lhabzang Khan the Khoshot Mongols the titular king of Tibet, a direct descendant of Gusri Khan and appointed a sixth Dalai Lama on his own. At this juncture in Peking, another branch of Mongols, the Manchus was ruling by defeating the Ming dynasty and Abahai was the Emperor of China who founded the Ching dynasty to rule China and never had any authority over Tibet. Even the then Dalai Lama was given extraordinary respect when he visited Peking at the invitation of the then Manchu Emperor Shunchih. Around this time, a new tribe Dzungars emerged as a new threat to the Khoshot of Mongols, Manchus of China and Tibet. Sagne Gyasto instead of maintaining a balance between these three tribes, wanted to overthrow the Khoshot Mongols with the help of Dzungars. Manchu rulers of Peking never wanted Dzungars to gain any foothold in Tibet sensing future invasion from them in their own territory. In this background, Lhabzang Khan, the Khoshot Mongol took the help of Chinese Emperor, a Manchu king , killed Regent Sange Gyatso, removed the sixth Dalai Lama and appointed a 21 year old monk as the seventh Dalai Lama.

Tibetans did not tolerate this replacement and they turned to the Dzungars of China for assistance who invaded Tibet and Killed Lhabzang Khan and deposed the seventh Dalai Lama. Dzungars started looting the monasteries of Tibet and the enraged Tibetans who had no other option except to seek the help of Manchu emperor of China who in 1720 captured Lhasa. Thus the Chinese Emperor achieved both big objectives i.e. a footing in Lhasa and the key to religious control over Mongolia which could be done through the Dalai Lama. This was the foundation of nearly two centuries of Manchu overlordship of Tibet who was not a Chinese emperor but a Mongol whose father had defeated the Chinese emperor and established the Manchu rule over the Chinese. He set up a Council of Ministers to advise the Dalai Lama and the post of the King and the office of the Regent was abolished. A Manchu Military Governor with 2,000 troops was appointed and garrisoned in Lhasa.

Soon a civil war erupted in Tibet and the Manchu troops again invaded Lhasa on the invitation of Tibetan. The Tibetan Council was reconstituted under the leadership of Phola Teji who ruled subsequently with great ability and he was given the title of Prince or King in 1740. He died in 1747 whose son Gyurme Namgyal succeeded him. He did not like the Chinese presence and revolted against the emperor. The Chinese representatives, the Ambans, murdered him treacherously to which the Tibetans repudiated by killing the Ambans and killed the remaining Chinese and other soldiers. Seventh Dalai Lama took control of Tibet at this stage and when the Chinese army arrived in Lhasa third time, peace was already restored. Again, Dalai Lama was given the power that had been exercised by his predecessor, the fifth Dalai Lama and religious supremacy re-emerged and Chinese started taking active interest in the running of the government through their representatives, the Ambans. Subsequently, five Dalai Lamas were not so effective and the political situation was in deep isolation under the leadership of the rigid monastic hierarchy which was now subject to foreign supervision.

Chinese Ousted

In 1788, the Hindu Gurkhas under Prithi Narayan who conquered Nepal from the Budhist Newars, invaded Tibet and occupied some of the frontier districts. The Tibetan and the Chinese Commanders entered into a truce with him promising him to pay a tribute which was not approved by the Dalai Lama and the Chinese Emperor. When the second instalment of the tribute was not paid, the Gurkhas again attacked Tibet in 1792 and sacked Shighatse and removed many of the precious pieces of art and treasure. The Chinese army intervened and chased the Gurkhas back to their country and nearly reached Kathmandu when on the request of Gurkhas an agreement was reached and the Nepalese agreed to pay a quin-quennial sum and the terms of the treaty were carved on a stone monument at Lhasa. This was the fourth time when the Chinese army came into Tibet but this time it came to protect it from an external enemy. This event had serious repercussions on Tibet because the power of the Chinese representatives were increased and the Lhasa Government became a shadow establishment carrying out orders of Peking.

Although, Chinese maintained their suzerainty over Tibet, their control on the internal affairs became feeble due to the factionalism in the Manchu dynasty and the encroachments by various European countries in China. The Anglo-Chinese war of 1840 further weakened the Manchus. When the Dogras invaded Western Tibet in 1841, Chinese help did not come and they were repelled by the Tibetans only. Again in 1855, when in violation of the treaty, the Gurkhas attacked Tibet, there was no Chinese army and Tibetans faced a humiliating treaty. Hence, in the middle of the nineteenth century the Manchu Emperors were unable to protect Tibet and lost control over it and the Regent ruled it independently. Then in 1876, the thirteenth Dalai Lama, Thupten Gyatso, the most notable figure in Tibet after the fifth Dalai Lama became the religious head in whose time Tibet started taking direct interest in international relations. He gave special emphasis on developing trade relations with India and Nepal. Large number of Buddhist pilgrims from Tibet used to visit their religious places in Bodh Gaya, Sarnath, Sanchi etc. whereas Hindus from India and Nepal started going to Kailash and Mansaraovar. Although, during the end of eighteenth century, Christianity tried to establish a foothold in Tibet but they did not succeed.

When the British established their foothold in India under the East India Company, they visualized that there could be prosperous trade with Tibet if facilities in this regard could be secured but the British representative in China, who did not know the conditions in Tibet, assuming that the Chinese exercised sovereignty in Tibet, gave suggestion that any negotiations for trade could only be processed through Peking. Even the British Foreign Office was working under the same impression. So all British efforts to get the Chinese agree to trade relations with Tibet were thwarted by the Chinese on one excuse or another. Chinese did not want any foreigners to develop relations with Tibet so that the later might not develop an independent outlook with the apparent motive that the nominal control on the internal affairs of Tibet is not exposed to the rest of the World. Later on weak China could not hold control on this theory and had to enter into an agreement in the Chefoo Convention in 1876 to provide facilities to a British mission for crossing Tibet either from India or China. Tibet was not a party to this agreement and Chinese had no power to make Tibet to do so. British sent a mission near the Indo-Tibetan border in Sikkim with a small military escort which was attacked by the Tibetan forces and occupied a portion of Sikkim. British sought help from China who was not in a position to exercise any influence on the Tibetan and could not provide any help to the British. Tibet also ignored the British ultimatum in 1888 and a clash took place which resulted in a stalemate but Chinese recognizing their weak position in this matter opened discussions with the British on the status of Sikkim and on the Indo-Tibet trade. Subsequently, an Anglo-Chinese Convention was signed in 1890 which fixed the boundary between Sikkim and Tibet and recognized Sikkim to be a Protectorate of Britain. A treaty of trade relation with Tibet was signed later on which was not accepted by Tibetans and Chinese had no power to make the Tibetans to accept it. This stalemate continued till Lord Curzon arrived as the Viceroy of India in 1899.

Curzon was aware that Chinese sovereignty over Tibet was a myth but fearing the Russian threat to her Indian empire and impending influence in

Tibet, the British found China's titular suzerainty over Tibet convenient and the shrewd British shut their eyes to the actual situation of independent Tibet and swallow the myth of Chinese suzerainty due to Russian threat. When British got the report that Dalai Lama was in contact with Czar of Russia, a mission with army support was sent into Tibet which was resisted by the Tibetan forces and more than 800 Tibetan soldiers were killed before the British mission reached Lhasa. Chinese were nowhere during these clashes. Dalai Lama fled to Mongolia leaving the authority to a Regent, Tri Rimpoche who obtained the authority of Tibetan assembly to conduct a treaty and as such an Anglo-Tibetan Convention was signed on September 7, 1904 in which mainly the reaffirmation of Tibetan-Sikkim defined in 1890 was confirmed. It also included opening of trade marts and posting of British Agents at Gyantse, Yatung and Gartok, provision for negotiating fresh trade relations and excluding any other foreign power from exerting influence in Tibet. This treaty proved that Chinese exercised no actual control over Tibet and Great Britain were in a special position as a kind of protector of Tibet. Again fearing the Russian expansionism, the British could not confront the make-believe Chinese suzerainty in Tibet and signed the Ango-Chinese Convention of 1906 by modifying the Tibetan Treaty of 1904 accepted the Chinese suzerainty and the onus of maintaining Tibet's integrity was given to China. This recognized the control of China over Tibet in the previous 30 to 40 years which never existed and the Tibetan were neither consulted nor informed about this Convention which was the unfortunate aspect of the British attitude toward Tibet. The privileged position of 1904 Convention with Tibet was further surrendered by the British when in the Anglo-Russian Convention of 1907, British agreed neither to negotiate with Tibet except through the Chinese nor sent a representative to Lhasa. Tibet was again not consulted. So in order to keep their own trade interests intact in China and Tibet, and in order to keep the Russian out, the British sacrificed the independence of Tibet though they knew fully well that the people of Tibet had no resemblance with the Chinese and were not ruled by them in any affairs of their independence.

Emboldened by these developments and fearing the British threat after their forces entered Lhasa, the Chinese reacted swiftly with unexpected speed and began to take military measures to restore their authority in Tibet. Although Tibetans violently opposed in the eastern forontier when the Manchu General, Chao Erh- feng, arrived on this frontier in 1905. By 1910 through ruthless use of force, whole of the eastern borderland was taken in possession by the Chinese. Since Dalai Lama was in exile, the new authority of China dismissed all the Tibetan ministers and direct contact between the British and the Tibetans was prohibited. The British were prevented from acquiring property. Chinese also sent feelers to Nepal and Bhutan to detach them from British influence who mildly protested in Peking. Due to persistent Tibetan opposition to the Chinese authority in Tibet, Chinese were forced to restore it to Dalai Lama who returned to Lhasa but never liked Chinese occupation. When Chinese threatened to march into Lhasa, Dalai Lama for the first time made appeal to Great Britain and other foreign powers for intervention to prevent the Chinese to do so. Ignoring this fact, the Chinese arrived in Lhasa with 2,000 troops. Dalai Lama fled to India and for all practical purpose Chinese were in control of Tibet despite the British protest but were never serious about the fate of three million Tibetans. The Chinese rulers for the last two centuries did nothing objectionable to spoil the peaceful relationship between the two countries. Chinese army was earlier sent only in case of any foreign intrusion but this time the Chinese army arrived in Lhasa against the will of the Tibetans. British did not respond to the appeal of Dalai Lama and rather used their influence to Dala Lama to accept Chinese suzerainty. British only woke up when the Chinese started intrigues in Bhutan and Nepal against their interest.

Tibetan resisted the Chinese subjugation tooth and nail and, made impossible for them to function. To the fate of the Tibetans, Chinese Empire started crumbling after the death of their Emperor in 1911. Chinese troops mutinied against their officers, some deserted and other took to looting and destructions which provoked the Tibetans to resort to furious counter-measures. The Tibetans set ablaze many Chinese garrisons and at several places these were completely annihilated. At Lhasa and Shighatse, fighting went on for a long time. When the Chinese totally lost control to the Tibetans, the British through Nepal Government in 1912 intervened and the remaining Chinese troops were removed from Tibet through India, disarmed and shipped back to China. In June, 1912, the Dalai Lama returned to Tibet and declare its independence. Thus, Tibet by physically throwing out the Chinese army asserted its independence and whatever might have been the status of Tibet before 1912, whether the Chinese were suzerain or sovereign, whether Tibet was an autonomous or a vassal state under China or was a part of China, it was clear that no vestige of Chinese control remained after 1912 when Tibet gained its complete independence. Thereafter the Tibetan Government did not make any concessions to the Chinese and took active measures to establish its own position. It sent strong reinforcements to the eastern front to meet the new threat from China and succeeded in establishing a strong line on the eastern front. For the next forty years thereafter there was no Chinese official in Tibet and no Chinese authority existed.

McMahon Line

In this region lot of political upheaval were taking place one of which was invasion of Mongolia by the Russian which frightened both the British and the China with regard to the fate of Tibet because Dalai Lama had in the past held secret parleys with Czar. Prior to the Tibetan declaring independence, the British could neither afford to make it her protectorate keeping in view the increasing trade ties with

China nor due to other political compulsions. They could, however, not undertake the duty to protect another 2,000 miles of difficult frontier and another area of 5,00,000 sq. miles of Tibet. British deliberately ignored the old relationship between the Chinese Emperor and the Dalai Lama which was personal one that of a Patron and a Priest and there was no political relationship between the Chinese and the Tibetan people as such. So, the British sent a message to Dalai Lama containing that Government of India had the desire to see that the internal autonomy of Tibet under Chinese suzerainty was maintained without Chinese interference so long as the treaty obligations were duly performed and cordial relations reserved between Tibet and India. British also wrote to the Chinese in 1912 and invited both China and Tibet for talks to define the status of Tibet. Keeping the Russian menace in mind, Chinese had no option but to agree for talks after much hesitation and evasive moves on the threat of the British inclination to hold direct negotiations with the Tibetans. Ultimately, the duly authorized representatives of Great Britain, China and Tibet met on equal terms at Simla on October 6, 1913. The British were represented by Sir Henry Mcmahon, China by Ivan Chen and Tibet by a leading Minister, Lonchu Satra.

In the ensuring negotiations, the Tibetans demanded for the recognition of their independence, abolition of the Anglo-Chinese Convention of 1906, revision of the trade regulations and acceptance of a frontier with China on eastern border. Chinese claimed sovereignty over Tibet tracing its origin from Chengis Khan. They claimed the right to post an Amban and 2,000 troops to control the foreign and military affairs of Tibet. They wanted a frontier with Tibet only 60 miles east of Lhasa which meant to include large parts of Tibet over which China had never exercised any type of authority except the conquest by Caho Erh-feng a few years earlier.

Acting as a mediator, McMahon tried to reduce the gap between the Tibetan claim of independence and Chinese claim of sovereignty and proposed the status before 1904 which would allow the development of a stable Tibet free from outside influence in close relation with the British. Under pressure, Tibetan agreed to accept the formal suzerainty of the Chinese as a part of bargain which would guarantee Tibet's freedom to conduct its internal affairs and put limits of Chinese suzerainty. Tibet was not to be a province of China and no Chinese officers or troops would be sent except one Chinese representative and his escort. Tibet also wanted to post a British officer in Lhasa which was not agreed as per the treaty obligation of Britain with Russia. There was strong disagreement on the question of Tibet's eastern boundary. Ultimately McMahon devised a plan of an Inner and Outer Tibet. Outer Tibet which bordered India and over which Lhasa had always exercised its full jurisdiction, would have its boundary up the upper waters of the Tangtse which existed since the time of Manchus. The Tibetan area to the east of that line would be called Inner Tibet which Dalai Lama would continue to exercise the customary religious authority over the monasteries but which for administrative purposes would be controlled by China. After negotiations lasting for six months a draft Tripartite Convention was prepared which is summarized as under:

1. Conventions of 1890, 1904 and 1906 were to stand except in so far that they might be modified by or be repugnant to the present Convention.
2. Britain and China to recognize that Tibet was under Chinese suzerainty and to recognize also the autonomy of Outer Tibet, to respect its integrity and to abstain from any interference in its internal affairs.
3. China not to send troops or station officers in Outer Tibet.
4. Britain to be similarly bound for the Trade Agents and their escorts.
5. China and Tibet not to negotiate with one another or with any other power except as provided in the 1904 and 1906 treaties.
6. Cancellation of Article 3 of 1906 Convention which virtually gave China a monopoly of all concessions over Tibet. But the Chinese position was safeguarded by not including China as a foreign power and, on the other hand, the British were to have the "most favoured nation" treatment in respect of trade.
7. New trade relations were to be negotiated between Great Britain and Outer Tibet.
8. The British Trade Agent at Gyantse might visit Lhasa as provided for in the 1904 Treaty.
9. The limits of Inner and Outer Tibet were defined in a map attached to the Convention.
10. Disputes arising from the Convention between China and Tibet would be referred to the British Government (This last provision was later removed in deference to Russian wishes)

A map showing the border of India and Tibet was attached to the Convention which later became the demarcation line and termed as McMahon Line. This map was treated as a part of the documents of this pact which was signed by all the representatives of three countries including China. Some features of this map were discussed between the British and Tibetan delegates. Chinese were however not included in these negotiations.

Since the Chinese Government participated in this Convention on the perceived British threat that this could be a unilateral agreement with Tibet denying China any political right in the affairs of Tibet, they deliberately did not ratify this Convention. In doing so, they deceitly kept the option in their right to deal with this issue in their favour when they would be in a position to do so. The British and the Tibetan representatives, although served proper notice to the Chinese, had no other option but to accept this Convention bilaterally.

The Chinese were thus barred to enjoy certain privileges as a result of their obstinate attitude to sign this Convention. In addition to other privileges, the vital issue of the recognition of the Chinese suzerainty over Tibet by the British was put on hold. Also the matter of Sino-Tibetan border was also left in the lurch and as such any right on the Inner Tibet was deprived as a result of the non-cooperation of the Chinese. On the other hand, the British got the freedom of direct negotiations with the Tibetans on political developments and improved the prospects of better commercial frade. The British thus established a properly defined frontier between Tibet and India, including Burma, along the crest of the Himalayas from the north cast corner of Bhutan to Isurazi Pass in North Burma.

In this impasse, due to Chinese non-cooperation, the eastern border issue remained desultory. Since the Chinese threat was loominy due to this impending problem, Tibet got some arms from the British which were much below British thwarted the Tibet move to yet arms from below their requirement. British thwarted the Tibet move to get arms from Japan. ammunition supply to Tibet was also very small, China by then had become politically weak due to their internal problems. Taking advantage of this situation, Tibetan forces got vacated vast area from the Chinese occupation by 1918. Subsequently, on British intervention, an armistice was signed in spite of a suggestion from the Chinese to make certain changes in 1914 convention to which the Tibetans did not concede at all. There was no mention of McMahon Line and the Indo-Tibet border demarcation in this istice. Subsequent efforts by the British to persuade China to join the tripartite agreement were parried by the Chinese on one plea or the other. hereafter. British Government supplied arms to Tibet for self-defence. Some officers of the Tibetan army were given military training. A telegraph line was constructed from Gyantse to Lhasa and geological survey was conducted in some parts of Tibet at the instance of Dalai Lama. British also helped Tibet to procure a hydro - electric plant at Lhasa and a Sikkimese Officer from Darjeeling was sent to Lhasa to train the police force. At this time, Dalai Lama was in a position to recover the territories which the Chinese Chao Erh-feng had occupied. He, however, stood by his commitment given to the Britishers and made no effort to recapture that area.

Independent Status

It would be pertinent to mention that the Chinese never questioned the delineation of the Indo-Tibet border defined as McMahon Line in the Simla Convention. They had their reservations only on the question of Tibet's eastern frontier. The Chinese sent two delegates between 1925 to 1930 to Lhasa to discuss these border issues with Dalai Lama who was firm that Tibet should be treated as an independent country having close diplomatic relations with China. This was not acceptable to the Chinese at any cost. Around this period, the Chinese had regained their military strength which was mightier than that of Tibetans. After the failure of diplomatic overtures, China attacked and captured the liberated area of Inner Tibet and also threatened to enter Outer Tibet. On British intervention again, Tibet had to give up everything to the east of Yangtze but kept possession of the entire area west of the river including the Yekalo district which for a long period had remained a Chinese enclave,

After the death of thirteenth Dalai Lama in 1933, China seized an opportunity to intervene in the affairs of Tibet and sent an armed delegation with wireless set under General Huang ostensibly to pay condolences. The Government of India got suspicious of this move and sent their officer from the Political Department to keep watch on the activities of Huang who later started discussions on the border dispute and demanded that Tibet dhe subordinate to China. The Tibetan Government agreed to the suzerainty on the conditions laid down in the 1914 Convention would continue to conduct their own foreign affairs and male relationship with the British Government. While departing Tibet, Huatia fed his two liaison officers with a wireless set. A Chinese mission was established in Tibet after a gap of over twenty years which started indulging in the internal affairs of Tibet. To counter this Chinese move and to allay fear of the Tibetans, the British sent a mission to Lhasa in 1935 under Sir Basil Gould who prior to his return to Sikkim left H.E. Richardson as a Liaison Officer with a wireless set. At this time, three independent countries, namely, Great Britain, China and Nepal had their diplomatic representatives at Lhasa.

After installation of a child Amdo as the fourteenth Dalai Lama in 1939, uneasy calm prevailed in Tibet. China too was fraught with internal dissensions. On the other hand, Japan was threatening to occupy the Chinese mainland which gave Chinese little time to intervene into Tibetan affairs. But that Tibet was effectively independent was proved by the fact during the Second World War when Japanese sealed off all the Chinese sea-ports, in spite of British persuasion, Tibet declared itself neutral in this war and did not allow the British or Chinese to use its mainland for transporting arms and ammunition sent by the Americans or British for China to protect it from Japan. British accepted this Tibetan stand and its Foreign Secretary Sir Anthony Eden wrote to the Chinese Foreign Minister in 1943 that Tibet had enjoyed de facto independence since 1911 and that the British Government was always prepared to recognize Chinese suzerainty over Tibet but only with an understanding that Tibet was regarded as an autonomous state. Even Shen Tsung- lien, adviser of Chiang Kai-shek wrote in his book that since 1911 Lhasa had enjoyed full independence for all practical purposes.

Subsequently, when the Britishers had decided for the independence of India, in July 1947, a formal information was sent to the Tibetan Government by them and the Indian Government over the impending issue to transfer of power in India. They were also given to understand that the Indian Government would exercise the right on the existing treaties which both Tibet and British Governments had entered into. Although the message was acknowledged but no formal reply was sent by them with regard to this new arrangement. When India became independent, the Tibetan Government unnecessarily raised a bogey of false and unfounded claim on the large territory of India ignoring the properly negotiated boundary McMahon Line. On Indian protest, the Tibetan Government eventually announced its agreement to the continuance of earlier relations and accepted the McMahon Line as accepted boundary between India and Tibet. But the previous illadvised and uncouth claim made by the Tibetans not only resulted in temporary low of a certain amount of Indian sympathy for them but also gave an excuse to China subsquently to bolster their claims on large parts of Indian Territory which ultimately proved the genesis of 162 war with China.

At this juncture, to other events took place which war important for the political status of Tibet. A Convention of the Asian Countries was held in Delhi in 1947 where Tibetan flag flew along with other countries was objected to by the China. Although, this flag was ultimately drawn yet the Tibetan delegation sat in the meeting as a token of their dependent status. Secondly, in 1948, a trade delegation of Tibet visited India, China, France, Italy, Great Britain and the USA where Tibetan passports issued to the delegates were accepted by the governments of these countries to allow these visits.

In view of these historical developments, it was quite evident that Tibet enjoyed a de facto independence from 1912 to 1950 when the Chinese Communists captured this country. This status was thoroughly examined by the International Commission of Jurists and in its report on 'The Question of Tibet and the Rule of Law' in 1959, the Commission came to the following conclusion which is reproduced verbatim:

"Tibet's position on the expulsion of the Chinese in 1912 can be fairly described as one of de facto independence and there are, as explained, strong legal grounds for thinking that any form of legal subservience to China had vanished. It is, therefore, submitted that the events of 1911-12 mark the re-emergence of Tibet as a fully sovereign State, independent in fact and in law of Chinese control."

Tibet as a nation had never been the territory of the Chinese which they forcibly occupied in 1950. Its existence could be seen in the history even before the B.C. era. Subsequent historical facts, however, amply prove that when China was strong, it invaded Tibet and annexed its territory but at the same time when Tibet was powerful, it not only recaptured its own homeland but also occupied the Chinese territory. This game of one-upmanship continued for decades between these two countries. Tibetans do not have any semblance of language, traditions, outlook and psychological make-up with the Chinese but in this regard they constitute India's entity of particularly for reasons of their spiritual creation of Buddhism from the soil of India. Thus, Tibet at no point of time was a Chinese territory but always enjoyed an independent stature which it disputed solely on the plea that they were captured and ruled by the Mongols as a result of which Tibet was part of China Might is right in this wishful thinking which no international power have dared to rebut except India who mildly protested and could not repudiate in view of its own weaker military strength compared to China. Tibet was annexed by force and made a part of Chinese territory throwing all historical facts of its independent status to the wind on the face of the debating forum of UNO.

After independence of India, the Nationalist Government of Chi Chiang Kai-shek rightly thought that British would no longer be in the Indo-Tibet borders. In 1948, they sent a letter to India to the presence of Indian officials in NEFA and suggested the res Tibetan Trade Regulations of 1908. While rejecting the claim of China NEFA, the Indian Government replied that these regulations were supersedes by the Shimla Convention of 1914. Although, the Nationalist Governme challenged the validity of Shimla Convention but the Communist forces of Mao had occupied Peking on January 31, 1949 and this issue was temporarily on hold due to political uncertainty in China. Soon large scale desertions from the Nationalist Government to the Communist forces resulted in the fall of Kuomintang Government of Chiang Kai-shek and its capital Nanking was occupied by the forces of Mao. Chiang Kai- shek and its loyal forces fled to Taiwan which is still an independent country for all practical purposes. It was then evident that Tibet would soon be the next target of China and would be invaded by the Communist forces in the near future.

In the changed political scenario of China, the Tibet, taking due security precaution, asked the Chinese mission and their traders to leave Tibet as it was possible that they would shift their allegiance to the new regime of Communists. Forces were mounted on the eastern border to defend the possible attack of Communist forces. On October 1, 1949, the establishment of People's Republic of China was formally proclaimed and on November 24, 1949, Mao Tse-tung appealed to the people of Tibet to overthrow the rule of Dalai Lama. Simultaneously, India formally recognized the Communist Government of China on December 30, 1949 after the Nationalist Government had moved in Taiwan. In May 1950, K M Panikkar took over as the Indian Ambassador in Communist China.

Tibet Invaded

Soon, the Communist Government started broadcast that the People's Liberation army was ready to liberate Tibet. Tibet Government sent their missions to India, Nepal, United Kingdom and United States to explain their case and to ask for help in case of Chinese invasion. The UK and USA did not receive the mission members. They also sent a mission to China but it was denied entry through Hong Kong due to visa denial by the British Govt. India's prompt recognition of Communist China was taken for granted by the Chinese and the subsequent anti-India tirade by radio broadcast and criticism of Pandit Nehru as stooge of imperialist forces was ample proof of the impending military occupation of Tibet in the near future.

In the North and South Korean clash in June, 1950, along the 38 parallel dividing line brought American intervention by the UNO which thwarted the North Korea attack and when UNO authorized the Allied forces to cross the 38th Parallel to bring the unification of Korea, Chinese moved their forces towards the Korean border. Pandit Nehru actively professed for the lasting peace in Korea to nullify the UN resolution autthorising US forces to cross the border of North Korea. Chou En-lai appreciated the efforts of Pandit Nehru to bring peace in this hostile region.

But Chinese had made preparations to invade Tibet for which behind the scene preparations were already in progress. In this pursuit, on October, 7, 1950, the Communist forces of China attacked the eastern Tibet and slaughtered the Tibet forces and arrested the Governor Ngapo Shape. Tibet asked the intervention of India as was asked from British in 1909 and 1931. Indian Government through her Ambassador made several verbal representations to the Chinese Government to settle the Tibetan question peacefully.

India formally protested to China on October, 21. 1950 and suggested that it would be against the interest of China to take military measures in Tibet since their entry in the United Nation was pending for consideration. To another protest of October, 28, 1950, Chinese Government replied that Tibet was an integral part of the Chinese territory and problem of Tibet was entirely the domestic problem of China and the Chinese forces would enter Tibet to defend the frontiers of China and no foreign interference would be tolerated. India again sent a note on October, 31, 1950 rebutting the charges of Indian interference into the Tibet affairs and stressed for the peaceful solution of the existing legitimate Tibetan autonomy within the framework of Chinese suzerainty. India also questioned the justification of the military operations because Tibet posed no military threat to China and was not guilty of any armed provocations. At the same time, India claimed that it had no political or territorial ambitions in Tibet nor did it seek any privileged position in that country but the recent developments are regrettable and prejudiced to the existing relations and for overall peace in the region. India again suggested for a peaceful solution of the matter. But the Chinese bluntly declared that unless India agreed to the Chinese Liberation Army entering and liberating Tibet, it would not consider India as a friendly country. At this juncture, the Chinese Ambassador in Delhi had, on behalf of his Government, refused to recognize the legitimacy of the Indian Mission in Lhasa and the Trade Agencies at Yatung and Gyantse and the existence of military escorts as these violated Chinese sovereignty in Tibet.

Exchange of notes between India and China did not yield any political solution of the autonomy of Tibet. When it became almost foregone conclusion that People's Army would enter Tibet any time, on November 7, 1950, a Tibetan delegation staying at Kalimpong sent a telegram to the United Nations for intervention against the armed invasion of Tibet by China on the basis of the historical background that racially, culturally and geographically they are far apart from the Chinese. Chinese invasion was an aggression of a stronger country on a weaker one. Tibetan requested for a civilized or judicial solution through the International Court of Law. International community reaction to this appeal was very cool except a small country El Salvador which wanted United Nations to take action against the act of unprovoked aggression of China in Tibet. Sensing that theTibetan issue if raked by India, would pose a hurdle in their UN entry, the Chinese forces halted their advance towards Tibet and maneuvered the UN by hoodwinking a show of settling the matter by negotiations. When the issue came up for discussion, the British argued that as the legal position of Tibet was not clear, the matter was allowed to wait till the Assembly had a better idea of the possibilities of a peaceful settlement. Indian delegation hoped that China would recognize the autonomy which Tibet had enjoyed for several decades. Both Russia and Nationalist China supported the British proposal and so the Assembly deferred any further discussion. Tibet was, therefore, left with no other alternative but to carry on direct negotiations with China and see what concessions it could get to ensure its autonomy. It was a negotiation between a helpless nation with a mighty aggressor and the result was a foregone conclusion. Thus a dictated Sino-Tibetan Agreement for the Peaceful Liberation of Tibet was signed on May, 23, 1951 which was based on the assumption that Tibet was a part of China and the People's Liberation Army of China, would march into Tibet " to eliminate the imperialist forces which were there for over hundred years". Thus Tibet lost the autonomy which she had enjoyed over centuries which was a slap on the face and big embarrassment for its neighbour India. Indian thought that this pact did not exclude the continuation of special contact between India and Tibet and would mean nothing more than the establishment of a Chinese protectorate of the kind which had existed before 1911. Even at this humiliating juncture, India was aimlessly working hard with the British Govt. and Afro-Asian group to secure a seat in United Nations and in Security Council for China. Such a weak and coward diplomacy by Indian policy makers proved disaster for the future generation of India which is still haunting in the guise of Jammu and Kashmir problem and territorial dispute with China.

Dictated Agreement

Thus a dictated Sino-Tibetan Agreement for the 'Peaceful Liberation' of Tibet was signed on May 23, 1951. Countrary to the political history regarding independence of Tibet, it was declared in this agreement that Tibet was a part of China and the PLA would march into Tibet to eliminate the imperialist forces stationed there for over hundered years. Thus, after singing this agreement, Tibet could not withstand its case of autonomy which it had enjoyed over centuries. This agreement was a big embarrassment and slap on the face India, its neighbour since the existence of McMahon Line was made open to its legitimacy. Indian diplomacy created a weird notion that this pact would continue to the legitimacy of the special relation with Tibet which wouldbe nothingmore than a protectorate of China which existed before 1911. Even at this humiliating juncture, India was aimlessly working hard with the British Government and other Afro-Asian nations to secure a seat in the United Nations and Security Council for China. Such a weak and cowardly diplomacy by Indian policy makers proved disaster for their future generation which is still haunting in the garb of Jammu and Kashmir imbroglio and its territorial dispute with China elsewhere.

In July, 1952, General Chang Ching-wu, the newly appointed Commissioner and Administrator of Civial and Military Affairs in Tibet swiftly carried out the occupation of Tibet with 3,000 strong Chinese army marching into Tibet without any resistance. More troops were stationed at vantage position all over Tibet. Work related to development of communication was undertaken up with greater speed and energy by the Chinese. While doing so, numerous Tibetans lost their lives when they resisted this long term planning of China to rule Tibet. Almost the whole World was a mute spectator on this tragic event wherein this cool-headed and God fearing inhabitants of Tibet were slaughtered by the mighty Chinese except India which protested in words otherwise had no option to intervene militarily against the powerful and well equipped Chinese army. Tibetan forces were destroyed completely to gauge the World reaction and resultant opinion of major countries in general and India in particular. China succeeded blatantly in its evil design to enslave this God-fearing community Everything turned out in China's favour. British who had traditional relations with Tibet did not show any intention to intervene in this matter even diplomatically. USA though intervened in Korea war did not show that anxiety in this affair. Russia supported its Communist brother and approved this illegal occupation of China as their legitimate right. UN position was reduced to a debating forum and the Tibetan issue was solved once for all in favour of the strong Chinese without any voice of resistance from any country.

In this show of strength displayed by the Chinese to whole of the World, they forced the Tibetans to come on negotiation table at Peking on their own terms and conditions. Tibetan delegation was forced to sign the dictated and dotted pact by the Chinese with a pistol directed at their head. According to this Pact, Tibet was made a province of China with no right whatsoever in any foreign affairs. In this manipulation, the Chinese could take all sort of measures to strengthen their defence forces in Tibet. In their evil design Chinese started planning to construct not only arterial roads from Sining and Formo to Lhasa but also from Khotan (Hotien) to Western Tibet and subsidiary roads to India's frontier. That also included the stockpiling of grains by levy from the people, requisitioning houses and lands for quartering Chinese troops and eliminating the Tibetan army as an independent force. Subsequently China increased its forces in Tibet by fourteen divisions in 1962. No country of the World protested to this illegal occupation by the Chinese in the United Nations and Tibet issue was conveniently forgotten for ever. Further stages of the sinister plan to subjugate Tibet also eliminate the Tibetan community before the World of today. Three million religious minded Tibetans were enslaved by Chinese at gun point and all powerful country were silent spectator on this dictatorial drama enacted at gun point.

Nehru Criticised

In addition to the diplomatic support at UN and other international forums, Indian Government considered supporting militarily the Tibetan people. After partition in 1947, Indian army got her share of less than 3,00,000 men comprising three divisions and twenty seven regiments besides about 18 regiments of artillery with almost obsolete arms and ammunition. This was much less in number compared to Chinese army of nearly 250 divisions which got all modern equipments from America during the regime of Chiang Kai-shek. Chinese army was well trained to fight in the cold weather in the hilly terrain whereas Indian army was not acclimatized in such warfare. At the same time Indian army was engaged in the internal problems of the country as a result of the partition. Also, the Communists were spearheading armed liberation struggle in Telegana and several other parts of the country where army was put on high alert. One third of the Indian army was stationed in Kashmir. East Pakistan communal riots further posed serious problems for the Indian army. In view of these internal problems and insufficient military strength forced the Indian government to abandon any military intervention in Tibet otherwise it was a matter which was debated at Government level at that time. In India at political and bureaucratic level, K M Pannikar, the then Indian ambassador in China tried to justify the Chinese occupation of Tibet as titular with internal autonomy which was his misguided version of the reality of the history. General Cariappa was forthright and realistic when he admitted that Indian army was not equipped or trained at large heights in cold weather and as such would be at a serious disadvantage against the two and half million Chinese army which was better acclimatized to such conditions than Indian army.

Any Indian army intervention in Tibet against the Chinese aggression would have proved not only utter failure but suicidal for the Indian Govt. although the then Director of Intelligence Bureau B N Mullick initially favoured such action but subsequently admitted his fault.

Some Politicians, academians and think-tank of that era, were critical of the soft policy of Nehru while handling this political crisis on its strategic border of 2,000 miles. There were schools of thought who opined that Nehru should have made conditional the recognition of Communist China in UNO seeking autonomy of Tibet and acceptance of the legality of the existence of McMahon line as frontier on the north-east border of India China border. Chiang Kai-Shek regime was sympathetic to the Indian cause of independence but on the question of autonomy, their attitude was identical to that of erstwhile Communist China. That sympathy was political in the background of his desire to secure full support of India in its war against Japan. Nehru justified the recognition on the ground that there was a change of Govt. in China which was a historical international event then and delay of recognition of powerful Communist regime would have deprived India all means of negotiation with them. This delay of recognition would not in any way had desisted Communist China in their plan to invade Tibet. Existence of a formidable Communist China on its North-East border was a cause of concern for India and this concern could not be deemed non-existent by pretending that it did not exist. Hence, Nehru's statesmanship that non-recognition of this new Communist China would pose more threat to India, was his intelligent format of Indian diplomacy of that period keeping in view that India was too weak for a military option in Tibet at that time. India had recently watched the military strength of China when it, challenged the mighty Americans in Korea. China' determination to annex all those territories which were either their part or not, this was beyond the unquestionable challenge for any weak country around China and India was one of them.

In the background of this historical reality, Nehru had no option but to engage in dialogues with the powerful Communist of China by getting its entry in UNO so that it too had no option but to declare India as a peaceful neighbour in the future to come and to deter its aggressive posture by engaging its in a big role in World diplomacy. This dialogue option was between two unequal parties and any hindrance on the part of India would have resulted the presence of a powerful hostile China on its frontiers and a real threat to annex its border of tribal areas wherein the British deliberately did not extend any effective administration prior to leaving India. The McMahan line did not exist as an administrative boundary because there was no Indian administrative personnel, troops or police permanently posted within 100 miles of that boundary and China could have exploited this vulnerable position of India in view of the fact that habitants of these areas had religious, ethnic, cultural and trade links with Tibet.

If in 1950, India were to take on China as was forced to do in 1962, there would have been a serious economic crisis and the Chinese could have extended their boundaries up to the foothills of NEFA and might have even driven out of India's influence Bhutan, Sikkim and Nepal. This could have posed serious threat to Indian position in Himachal Pradesh (Punjab then), Uttar Pradesh and even China capturing large portion of Ladakh because there was no road link at that time with Leh. Hence, Nehru's diplomacy to keep a friendly posture to continue dialogue with China at that time, allowed India considerable time to consolidate its hold in these poorly administered areas was of paramount importance and a master stroke to save any unforeseen danger to the Indian territory. Since India on its own had no particular option to save invasion of Tibet, the only sensible course was to secure as much autonomy for them as possible and also convince the World community that India had no hostile design in this area. This posture of Nehru made China to induce a moderate approach in Tibet and succeeded in disarming Chinese suspicion towards India and further consolidating its position in NEFA and other forward areas bordering Tibet up to 1959 is a fair amount of testimony to the farsightedness of his foreign policy which he adopted at that critical juncture. without any other options in hand.

Nehru never approved China's invasion of Tibet and was quite apprehensive of the expansionist posture of China. He advised IB that Pakistan and China are the two potent enemies of India, Pakistan would take shelter of Pan-Islamism for his support and China would utilize the international communism for its cause and they both should be the main target of Indian intelligence. Nehru was forthright in accepting the notion that when a country is weak militarily, it was always at disadvantageous position at the conference table. His support to China to get entry in UN was thus correct to that extent since he wanted that China should give up hostility and get involved more in the international affairs. He ordered IB to provide all possible help to the Tibetan refugees and suggested all sorts of initiatives to boost their morale because he opined that sooner or later Tibet would attain its independence with the high spirits of the Tibetan community. He did not announce these measures publicly since he did not want to lose India's position as a mediator and moderator in Tibet. He stressed the need to strengthen administration to the farthest end of the borders with China. NonCommunist Chinese owing allegiance to Taiwan were given full protection despite persistent protests by the Chinese diplomats.

Another feature of Nehru's statesmanship relates to forging long-term friendly relationship with Russia around this period. Nehru visited Russia in 1955 which was reciprocated by the two great Russian leaders Bulganin and Khrushchev. This exchange of visits changed the policy of Russian who accepted that two nations with different policies could also become friends in that post-second World War of NATO and Warsaw Pact. Russia admired the progress of India and ideal of democracy. Thereafter Russia dropped its animosity against the non-communist countries which was aimed at its ultimate rupture with China. Russian posture of neutrality between India and China added China's discomfiture further when their leaders Vorshilov, Kozlov and Madame Furtseva visited India in January, 1960. Subsequently, Khrushchev visited India a month later which was hailed by media as new era in the growing friendship between two countries. Thereafter, beleaguered China making anti-Russian rhetoric, claimed certain territories of Russia in Siberia, Kazakstan and Tadzhikstan which Russian repudiated and confrontation on their border started brewing. Hereinafter, Russia supported India in its major UNO decision when it supported India on Kashmir against Pakistan. In this stewardship of far-reaching consequences, Nehru not only neutralize the formidable communist duo of China- Russia in its neighbourhood but also earned unparallel friendship with Russia which is amply manifest in its excellent political, defence and trade relations. This was the astute diplomacy of Nehru due to which triggered India's growth in multiple areas.

In this hapless situation, the Indian Govt. swallowed this bitter pill with no option but to bow before the mighty while watching the treacherous act of Chinese in its neighbourhood knowing fully well that capture of Tibet would prove a forever political problem because Chinese would never allow India feel safe on this border. There was a widespread criticism of invasion of Tibet by Chinese in Indian newspapers, in public debates and in Parliament. Indian Prime Minister was evidently anguished at the Chinese perfidy while he narrated the events of past Indian diplomacy with regard to the historical relations of Tibet with China. Indian Government never thought that the hidden agenda of China was aimed against them while executing her sinister designs by capturing Tibet with perfectly executed political maneuvering in the United Nations where the big powers show little resistance against the almighty Chinese. Thus annexation of Tibet proved Water Lu for the Indian Government when Chinese refused to recognize the McMahon Line which was an accepted demarcation between India and Tibet as per the Shimla Convention of 1914 which China attended and negotiated but subsequently refused to sign. Had the Indian Government tried to convince the International Community at the United Nation to prevent China from taking any armed action for the occupation of Tibet, China would not have conveniently put forward her claim on Indian territories and attacked India in 1962 which brought the intolerable insult, shame and agony to this great country.

British Misadventure

While ruling India, British policy towards bet was circumscribed by the Russo-phobia because they feared Russian intervention in Tibet. In order to thwart this threat perception they accepted the Chinese sovereignty in Tibet despite objections of the Tibetans. It would be pertinent to mention here that the North-

West extremity of Kashmir State had a common boundary with Tajikistan of Soviet Russia. The British were so frightened of the might of Russia that their entire policy of Central Asian countries was concentrated to create wedge of some countries between their Indian empire and the Russian state. In this pursuit, they handed over large areas of North East part of India to Afghanistan and China across Karakoram range. Thus, the British were able to create a gulf between Russian and Indian territories by inducing Afghanistan and China in between implying therein that any incursion by Russia into the Indian territory would have to cross through these two independent nations which could be a difficult proposition for Russia. British too desired China to rule Tibet rather than see the presence of a strong Russia on the north border of Indian empire. Hence, due to the non-existent fear psychosis, the British sacrificed a large part of territory south of the Karakash valley to the Chinese on the platter and the Chinese entered this area for the first time and put a pillar on the Karakoram pass to mark the boundary. They further allowed the Chinese to enhance their jurisdiction fifty miles south in Aksai Chin area which emboldened the Chinese to put their claim over this territory in future. This political fiasco was a blunder on the part of the Britishers but they were aware that sooner or later India would attain its freedom from them and handing over its land to other country at that time would bring a temporary relief to them in this region. After India became independent, there was no alternative but to accept the legacy of the British and accepted this handover of territory to Afghanistan and China.

Dragon's Threat

While ruling India, British policy towards Tibet was circumscribed by the Russo-phobia because they feared Russian intervention in Tibet. In order to thwart this threat perception accepted the Chinese sovereignty in Tibet. Alarmed at the invasion of Tibet, Indian Govt. was naturally concerned about the impending infiltration of Communist China in the borders of Ladakh in Kashmir, Lahaul Spiti in Himachal Pradesh, entire hill area of Uttar Pradesh and in NEFA. There was about 16,000 Sq. Miles of uninhabited territory around Aksai Chin, Lingzi Tang and Soda plains in Ladakh and 35,000 Sq. Miles in the NEFA in the North East. China was not concerned about the boundary of Kashmir west of Karakoram because that area was under the control of Pakistan out of which 400 Sq. Miles of entire Shaksg fam valley was conceded to China. British were least concern to administer these tribal area considering it a waste of time and money and most of these areas were self governed by the tribal as per their own customs and as such slavery was dominated in these areas. There was no police or revenue administration leave aside the development of roads, communications and other basic amenities. British only intervened militarily in these areas when the tribal attacked population on the plains. There was no schools or hospitals in the entire Ladakh, NEFA and even in the hill areas of Uttar Pradesh and Punjab. There was a Patwari administration who worked as a revenue collector, magistrate and policeman and seldom visited the difficult terrain of the territory bordering Tibet and Sinkiang. In view of these geographical neglect by the British of these tribal area of India where erstwhile Tibet Govt. since decades claimed no territory, the Chinese Communist Govt. suddenly put their territorial claim which was non existent but treacherously made existent after the invasion of Tibet and declined to accept the McMahon line as the boundary which was a historical acceptance by British, Tibet and China as per the Shimla agreement.

Security Realignment

Prior to the invasion of Tibet by Communist Chinese forces when Sinkiang was captured by them on September, 26, 1949, Intelligence Bureau (IB), the newly born intelligence agency of India under its able Director B N Mullik, apprehending future infiltration inside India along the Sinkiang-Karakoram-Leb route by pro-Chinese elements, suggested several measures to the Govt. against this threat. IB suggested to open an intelligence-collecting centre at Leh which was declined by the Jammu and Kashmir Government due to paucity of funds and manpower. Since, IB was just established, Army help was sought and the first joint IB-Army check post was set up at Parnamik-Shyok to cover the route from Karakoram and an intelligence post was opened at Leh. IB also reported to the Government that in case of capture of Tibet by China, there was every possibility of sending infiltrators in the guise of Tibetans which would be difficult for the Indian authorities to identify and restrict their entry into Indian borders. There were three aspects to control these entries namely,. to prevent the infiltration of undesirable persons from Tibet, prevention of armed persons and introduction of a passport system and registration of Tibetans under the Foreigners Registration Act. Presence of large Tibet population on both sides of border of McMahon Line and in Sikkim, introduction of passport system seemed impracticable and in as a media it was decided that every Tibetan entering India would be given a permit by the check post on the basis of which the District Headquarters would issue a registration certificate which the person concerned would surrender while re-entering Tibet. In order to give this exercise a practical shape, IB sent a detailed proposal to open twenty one check posts to guard the passes on the Indo-Tibetan frontiers from Ladakh to NEFA in the north-east. One of these was to be in Ladakh in addition to one already established, one in Punjab, two in Himachal Pradesh, six in UP, five in North Bengal, three in Sikkim and three in NEFA. This proposal was accepted by the Government of India to guard the 2,000 miles of border of Tibet from infiltrators.

This action was initiated by the Government on the recommendation of Intelligence Bureau apprehending Chinese invasion of Tibet. When Chinese attached Tibet on October, 7, 1950, the Intelligence Bureau Chief B N Mullick again sent a detailed note to the Government on 3rd November, outlining the impending dangers on the frontier problems from Ladakh to NEFA in North East. He also emphasized the need to improve the administrative set up in the far flung areas of this region which was totally neglected by the British. There was no communications of any sort, no police, no schools, no hospitals and no other infrastructure which a civilized society needed to bank on their future development. Mullick had strong apprehension that the Chinese could exploit these weak points and infiltrate by one way or the other since there were no checkposts and other measures to counter their entry. He gave detailed picture of the internal Communist uprisings in various places in India which were a threat to the Indian sovereignty as a result of powerful China on its North East border. Mullick also emphasized the need to look into this threat perception in view of the changing World situation where India had no trustworthy friend for help in this scenario. Sardar Patel, the then powerful Home Minister visualized this impending danger from the Communist China after it captured Tibet and wrote a detailed letter to the Indian Prime Minister elaborating all points related to the Chinese threat on Indian border, Nepal, Sikkim, Bhutan and even in Burma. He also outlined all our weaknesses in the internal security and administrative revamping all along the border areas and in the Communist uprising region in other States.

Sardar Patel suggested in this letter that there should be an immediate meeting to discuss this imminent problem and suggest various measures to tackle these through the limited means of governance which were available to the newly independent India. There were criticism that Nehru did not give any credence to this letter of Sardar Patel and no Cabinet meeting was held thereafter on the suggestions mooted by Sardar Patel. But on the initiative of Nehru, within a week, all the concerned Ministries took various measures to tackle the issues raised by Intelligence Bureau and Sardar Patel which are detailed as under:

1. A small committee of military experts with a representative of IB in Shillong would visit the NEFA and suggest the placement of Assam Rifles at various entry points near the frontiers.
2. A high-powered Committee under the Chairman ship of the then Deputy Minister of Defence Major General Himmatsinghji with representative of Defence, Communications, Home, External Affairs and the Intelligence Bureau was constituted to study the impending problem created by the Chinese aggression in Tibet and make recommendations to improve administrative, defence, communications etc. in all the frontier areas.

3. The Government immediately sanctioned the Indo-Tibet checkpost staff and wireless communication for them.
4. The registration of Tibetans was also sanctioned as also the imposition of restrictions under the Foreigner's Registration Rules on the Chinese residents of India.
5. Intelligence Bureau and Home Ministry were authorized to expand the intelligence set-up in the frontier areas for which details were to be given to the Government.

Thereafter, IB opened its offices in Kalimpong, Darjeeling and Gangtok to check the espionage and subversive activities of the Communists and other foreign agents. Local police units of Assam and Bengal were also guided to improve counter measures in this regard to which they responded excellently in liaison with Intelligence Bureau. One Intelligence Bureau Deputy Director Waryam Singh was sent to Nepal who convinced the King about the threat on the borders of Nepal from Tibet. On his suggestion, King agreed to open checkposts on Nepal-Tibet border with the help of Indian Intelligence Bureau which operated with the stall of India and Nepal. These posts were further increased and the staff expanded at the time of the Koirala Government.

Major General Himmatsinghji Committee, termed as North and North-East Border Defence Committee submitted its report to the Government in September, 1951. This Committee thoroughly studied and analysed all boder problems in Ladakh, Punjab, NEFA, Sikkim, Bhutan, Nepal and even the Burma border. It made comprehensive analysis pertaining to administration, development, defance and security pertaining to army and air force, civil armed forces including Assam Rifles and other police units, communications and intelligence. Conclusion on the threat to Indian borders arising out of the capture of Tibet by Chinese of this Committee was almost identical as was perceived by IB Chief in October, 1950 and subsequently by Sardar Patel in his letter to Nehru in November thereafter.

Administrative Reforms

Recommendation of this Committee were fully accepted and put in place in letter and spirit and implemented for all round development in every field in all the tribal areas. As a result of this exercise, a monumental progress was envisaged in the specified areas in the coming ten years in every part of the administration. In NEFA alone, there were only three educational institution in 1947 which were increased to 211 including a teacher training institute, 6 higher secondary schools, 26 middle schools and 178 junior schools. In 1947, there was one doctor for a population of 43,000 and one hospital bed for a population 20,000 which was raised to one doctor for 2,800 and a bed for 370 people by 1962. Many health units and hospitals were opened in far flung areas. Government paid special attention to improve the standard of agriculture, animal husbandry, community development and cooperation, extraction of forest wealth and replanting of new forests and improving cottage industries.

In UP and Punjab, administration was extended to the frontier region. New Districts were created in the border areas and basic administration was restored in almost every village of the border. In Ladakh, police posts and administrative centres were opened in the deserted villages and development work started in all directions in the field of health, education, agriculture, animal husbandry, horticulture and cooperation. Communication development proved a serious problem in NEFA and Ladakh because of difficult hilly terrain in rainy season and cold weather. Subsequently, Border Roads Organisation was created which did a remarkable job and connected most of the vantage points to the control of the administration by road. First class airfields were constructed in Jammu, Srinagar and Ladakh and in particularly all the district Headquarterss in NEFA. Smaller landing strips were constructed at several places in the interior of NEFA where helicopters could land even at the most isolated places. Telegraph lines were put across to all the Base Headquarterss and Assam Rifles provided a line of communication by wireless.

The army strength was increased manifold in all the divisions i.e. infantry, armoured, paratroop, besides a large number of ancillary personnel. Twenty squadrons of jet fighters and fighter bombers and six squadrons of transport planes were stationed at various air force stations in these areas by the Indian Air Force. Defence expenditure from Rupees 168 crores in 1950 was increased to Rupees 400 crores annually by 1961.

IB Strengthened

In these difficult hill terrains of Ladakh and NEFA, IB, which too was in its offing stage, had to play a very significant role to secure the frontiers by establishing new check post all along the McMahon line whether delimited, demarcated or not. These check posts were to be opened at an average height from 12,000 to 15,000 feet in these areas. Not only the opening of these posts was a very difficult task, gathering of intelligence about China from the local sources in this area was too hard from the unfriendly inhabitants of these tribal areas who were kept isolated from the civilization for decades by the British. Presence of IB staff curtailed the liberty of these people which they strongly resented initially. There was paucity of trained and educated intelligence staff to work at these check posts where they had to cut off from all civilization for all particular purposes. If anybody fell ill, only God and nature could save him from the hand of death. Food supplies were scarce and even fuel was not available. The only means of communication with base camps was with old radio sets of the World War II vintage, pulled out of the army disposal stocks which too were in small numbers. In case of breakdown of these sets, repair work had to wait some time for more than a month. The post would then be without any reliable communication because couriers were available during good weather. Maintaining the food supplies and other mammoth paraphernalia was a colossal job not only for the IB but also for other government agencies which were put in service in the forward areas as a result of the recommendation of Himmat singh ji Committee.

During the British, responsibility of Intelligence Bureau was confined only to internal intelligence and all matter of foreign intelligence were handled by the Government of His Majesty in London. There used to be a representative of the Intelligence Bureau in London who used to get such external intelligence which could affect the internal security of India. After independence, task of external intelligence of IB was mainly to neutralize the threats to internal security arising out of the presence of hostile Pakistan and the emergence of a powerful China on its borders.

Communication between frontiers and base centres was a major problem for the IB. Due to bad weather conditions, IB couriers had to spend lot of time for comuting this distance. This problem was solved by IB through provision of wireless sets at the check-posts. The operatives for these wireless sets were trained not only for sending messages but also in repairing these sets in case of any breakdown. This two-fold task was very difficult because these check-posts had no electricity and the batteries of these sets were charged with gasoline and lubricating oil which had to be brought with the help of mules from the base camps. It took almost three years to fit the provision in place for the operation of wireless sets in all check-posts. Due to financial constraints, the government could not provide hand operated American or Japanese wireless sets and IB had to manage this task with heavy and crude World War II disposal stocks. A workshop was also established for training of operatives of this communication system. Most of the IB operatives were trained in Chinese and Tibetan languages with utmost difficulty due to non-availability of staff to train them for intercepting messages and send in their own codes to the respective head offices. This was an extremely difficult job because the Chinese language itself is a code which when intercepted turns into nuers and when it was further transferred in another code, it actually becomes a triple code. In order to overcome this difficulty,IB built up a big section of Chinese and Tibetan languages and also a very large cryptograpy section to decipher the huge number of messages intercepted by IB monitoring stations. Gradually, the reception, decoding and interpretation of these messages improved and it became the main foundation of intelligence network of IB at that time. It would be worthwhile to mention here that even today in R&AW, a Tibet Branch is functioning independently under the Chinese Section although this region is under China as its province.

Himmat singh ji committee recommended IB to be responsible for foreign strategic intelligence. Newly born IB did neither have trained intelligence operatives nor a training school to train the new recruits. Efforts were made to take police officials from various State police with liberal allowances but most of them were unwilling to sacrifice comfortable work in the plains and to go to the frontier where only blood and toil and ultimately ill-health and probably death awaited them. British Govt. helped in training some instructors in their country. Thereafter, IB opened their own training school in a old army barrack at Anand Prabat in Delhi to train the new recruits. Rigorous efforts were made by the then IB bosses to recruit physically and mentally fit youth particularly from NEFA who were willing to work in the difficult working conditions in frontiers. Three years training was imparted on this new cadre of IB institutionally and in the field before they were sent to guard the checkposts and collect intelligence. These cadre were also trained in the technical work of intelligence and in the language of the area where they were to be posted.

Most difficult problem at that time for IB was in telecommunication network. Since, weather condition in frontier could consume long time to reach the base camp for the couriers of IB, every checkposts had to be equipped with a wireless set. IB had to train its operative not only to operate the wireless set for sending messages but also they were trained to repair these sets in case of any breakdown. This two-fold task was too difficult because these check post had no electricity and batteries of these sets were recharged with gasoline and lubricating oil which had to be brought there with the help of mules from the plains. It took around three years to fit the provision in place for the operation of wireless sets in all check posts. Due to financial constrains, Government could not provide hand operated American or Japanese wireless sets, IB had to carry out this task with heavy and crude World War II disposal stocks. A workshop was established for training in this job. Most of the IB operatives were trained in Chinese and Tibet languages with utmost difficulty due to non-availability of staff to train them so that they could intercept messages of that language and sent in their own code to the respective head offices. There was extreme difficulty in this job because Chinese language is itself a code which was passed over the wireless in numbers and when that is put in another code, it really becomes a triple code. So in order to overcome this problem, IB build up a big language section of Chinese and Tibetan language but also a very large cryptography section to decipher the large number of messages intercepted by IB monitoring stations. Gradually, the reception, decoding and interpretation of these messages started improving and it became the main foundation of intelligence net-work of IB at that time. It would be worthwhile to mention here that even today in RAW, a Tibet branch is working under the Chinese section.

Under the guidance of Mullik, the then IB Chief, this extremely difficult task of opening checkposts along McMahon line and other parts of that region, was carried out from scratches and by 1960, 67 checkposts were opened for IB operatives despite non-availability of suitable staff in time. These were 9 in Ladakh, 9 in Himachal Pradesh-Punjab, 17 in UP, 10 in Sikkim and 22 in NEFA. Later the number of check posts mounted to 77 employing 1590 IB personnel which was around 50 percent of the total strength of IB, prior to Chinese attack on India. In any such venture all over the World, it takes almost 15 years to build up an intelligence organization but under the astute leadership of Mullick and able supporting-staff, this task was accomplished in just less than twelve years. As Mullik puts in his memoirs:

"There were many casualties in these checkpost due to unavailability of medical facilities. There were illness, deaths, family tragedies and even insanity due to loneliness for long time. But the IB men stood their ground and did not desert in those worse conditions. The country should give due recognition to these pioneers who surmounted all physical, climatic and environmental difficulties and worked singlemindedly for the security of the motherland. They were able to hold out because of their lofty sense of patriotism and high sense of duty. Hats off to these officers, who never worked in any intelligence organization prior to taking up this job in all difficult situation which arose due to the creation of a new country and presence of two hostile enemies on its long frontiers".

IB thus had no parallel in the modern history which expanded its area of operations in the extremely adverse conditions and financial constrains. Indian Government should recognize the sacrifice of these civil officials in a big way by collecting data of their achievements and build some monument in the memory of those who died for serving the motherland.

Uneasy Calm

After the invasion of Tibet, Chinese troops were stationed at all available areas in and around Lhasa causing obvious resentment among the Tibetans. This was further aggravated with these troops forcefully occupied houses of local population thus creating problems for them. There as already shortage of food for the people of this region and presence of these large troops further increased the scarcity of eatables for general public. Price of food items soared affecting the budget of poor people of Lhasa to which dissension against the Chinese started brewing. Dalai Lama's Prome Minister asked the suggested to shift them on the country side which was not acceptable to them. Contrary to this pleas of the Prime Minister, the Chinese put forward a false argument that these troops were in Lhasa to give protection to the Tibetans. When Tibetan ministers rebutted this plea and said that the Tibetans actually required protection from the Chinese themseles, there was no response from them.

Presence of troops caused serious repercussions in Lhasa and people demonstrated against them. When the Chinese banned these demonstrations, posters were displayed in Lhasa accusing the Chinese to cause misery to the local population. Soon, in a large gathering they demanded withdrawal of Chinese from Tibet which was considered a conspiracy by the Chinese at the behest of local inisters. Young Dalai Lama had to face rough weather both way by reasoning with the Chinese to keep restrain and forbid his ownpopulation not to create a situation which would give the Chinese excuse to resort to violent measures. However, relations between the Tibet Government and Chinese General were further worsened when the Chinese decided to absorb the Tibetan army in their fold as per the terms of Sino-Tibetan agreement. This action was unacceptable to the Tibetan ministers who opposed it tooth and nail. Chinese then demanded the removal of two trusted Prime Ministers of the cabinet. Dalai Lama could not muster courage in that situation and as a conciliatory approach, accepted the demand of Chinese General and asked his Prime Ministers to resign which was strongly resented by the Tibetan population.

In order to placate the hostile attitude of Tibetan people, in 1954, Chinese first invited a delegation of Tibetan officials, monks and merchants and subsequently Dalai Lama to visit various places in China with a view to portray a picture of the progress made under their regime. Dalai Lama attended the proceedings of Chinese Assembly. Mao Tse-tung tried to convince Dalai Lama that Chinese troops were sent to Tibet to help them rather then to rule there.

Thereafter, the Chinese set up a fifty-one Preparatory Committee of the Autonomous Region of Tibet under the Chairmanship of Dalai Lama with majority of their own representatives and he was reduced to a position of a figurehead instead of being a secular head of the entire Tibet which was an accepted clause of the Sino- Tibet agreement as he was now head of one of the three divisions of Tibet. Even the religious control of the monasteries was taken away from him and as such the Sino- Tibet agreement was thrown in the basket. Dalai Lama had no option but to accept this forcibly enacted arrangement for the sake of safety of his people as there were every chance of their being butchered by the Chinese army.

Without giving any credence to the Indian opposition of its invasion of Tibet, China mysteriously invited a pro-Chinese Indian delegation on May day celebration in 1951. This delegation of pro-Chinese elements was not invited through the Ministery of External Affairs. Indian Government protested to this undiplomatic Chinese action to which China sent an invitation for an official delegation from India. So, an official delegation led by Vijaya Lakshmi Pandit visited China which was accorded a rousing welcome by the Chinese. Thereafter, a Chinese cultural delegation visited India in 1952.

Panchsheel

In the changed political scenario on its north east border where mighty Chinese army captured Tibet, Indian ambassador to China suggested Indian Govt. to forgo extra-territorial rights extorted from Tibet by the British as its continuation could pose strong security and diplomatic problem for India and maintain only the economic and cultural relation with Tibet which was accepted by the Indian Govt. Subsequently, the political agency in Lhasa was converted to Indian Consulate and 12 rest housed were surrendered to the Chinese. Further, telegraph lines and military escort at Yatung were abolished and trade agents were brought into the framework of consulate relations thereby reducing India to a nonentity as far as its British period position was concerned. In exchange thereof, Chinese were allowed to open a Consulate in Bombay. It was important to mention here that neither side raised any question with regard to the legality of McMahon line as the line of control between India and Tibet.

After China eased out its military options in Korea, its posture suddenly took U-turn in 1953 when China objected to the dispatch of fresh Indian troops to replace the guards at Gyantse and Yatung, seized the wireless set of the Indian Trade Agent at Gartok and banned the entry of Political Officer, Sikkim to Lhasa without proper visa from the Chinese. In this new development, in August, 1953, Indian Prime Minister sent a message to Chou En-lai renouncing these action of China Government and suggested a solution of all these issues through negotiations. Chou En-lai replied to reframe the existing relations between the two countries in the changed political scenario and invited India for talks in Peking which started in December 1953. Hence, China was able to create a diplomatic situation suiting to their hidden cause. They unilaterally deprived India of all the privileges in Tibet which existed for nearly half a century. The Chinese strategy of creating a disadvantageous situation for its adversary first to which there was no self-acquired remedy and thus left no alternative but to accept the negotiated solution on their terms as was evident in this posture.

The Conference to the delegates of two countries started on December 31, 1953. While inaugurating the discussion, Chou En-lai straightaway asked the Indian delegation whether they accept the five principles of Co-existence (which was termed as Panchsheel) to which they replied that these principles had already been enunciated by the Indian Prime Minister Nehru and were acceptable. In the ensuing deliberations between the two countries suspicion and treachery was apparent but when the Indians insisting that all "pending questions" should be discussed and settled, the Chinese insisted that only "such questions as were ripe for discussions" should be discussed leaving the rest for future settlement. Precisely, Chinese wanted to keep the question of boundary open which in the opinion of Indian it did not exist. This issue was not discussed deliberately by the Chinese at that time with the intention to raise it subsequently on a suitable occasion.

After negotiations for four months, the Sino-Indian agreement of Panchsheel was signed on April 29, 1954. In this agreement five principles i.e. mutual respect for each other's territorial integrity and sovereignty, mutual non-aggression, mutual non-interference in each other's internal affairs, equality and mutual benefit and peaceful existence were agreed and signed. Hence, a new era in the relations of these two powers was launched in Peking. One of the basic features of this agreement was that pilgrims from India were allowed to go to Mount Kailash, Mansarovar and Lhasa and from Tibet to Benaras, Sarnath, Gaya and Sanchi. Most important point in this agreement was in the very preamble which mentioned Tibet as the Tibet Region of China and not as the Autonomous Region of Tibet, thus officially denying the the recognition of Tibet as a separate autonomous region thus, recognation of Tibet as an autonomous state was officially denied in this agreement which was a writing on the wall.

Subsequently in the month of October, 1954, a Trade Agreement was signed between the two countries at Delhi wherein China was allowed reasonable entry into Calcutta port to transport such commercial goods from outside which are not available in India and a branch of People's Bank of China was allowed to be opened in India. These developments were assessed and protested by the IB as a security concern and the most disturbing aspect of the second agreement was that the goods allowed to be taken from the Calcutta port were exclusively meant for Chinese forces in Tibet and there was every likelihood of the use of Chinese bank for dubious transactions not only by the Chinese living in India but also by the Chinese Government. As a reciprocity of this act, India did not get any such concession in Tibet. Supply of the goods from Calcutta port for the Chinese army rather helped them to suppress the Tibetan and also for aggressive posture to India itself. This was a self-inflicting blow to Indian diplomacy on these two concessions to Chinese. To the worst part, Chinese even did not allow the Indian Consulate even to make contacts with the Kashmiri Muslims who were residents of Lhasa. Rather Chinnese Consulate in India made contacts with groups who were hostile to India and the China Bank became a source for passing on funds to them. Recognition of Tibet as a province of China means surrender of all her extra-territorial rights in Tibet which they enjoyed since 1904 and further prevented India even to sympathize with the Tibetan and restricting India in raising any sort of support for these people at any International forum or against any repression. Renunciation of these rights were not to draw any favour for the weak Tibet but was abject surrender before mighty belligerent China which captured it by force and tightened further grip in the guise of this pact with India. Hence, it was a self-goal by India which paved the path for opening the border issue by the Chinese since they never recognized the McMahon line as frontier. Even the Tibetan, while denouncing this Indo-China pact, warned India that Chinese would certainly raise the question of boundary sooner or later at their convenience.

When the IB Director Mullik briefed Nehru about the impending boundary issue and other security threats arising after this pact with China, Nehru admitted to him that Tibetan had adequate grounds to criticize this pact but due to insufficient military power, India could not have done any better than this pact. He was rather hopeful that with the passage of time, suspicion in relations with China would be removed and they would adopt a reasonable approach to save the autonomy of Tibet and Indian interests would be safeguarded, which was a myth as was subsequently proved. It was a face saving reply by a weak in the vicinity of a mighty because if this pact had not materialized, India was too weak a power to resist China from closing its Trade Agencies and the Consulates by force. For IB, it was a blessing in disguise because in case of any confrontation with China at that juncture could have posed serious security and other problems of spying activities and false propaganda at international for a. In retaliation, Intelligence Bureau could have created such problems in Tibet but that would have aggravated the complex border issue. Under these circumstances, there was no other alternative buy to have a friendly approach because if we could not save Tibet, at least we could save our own frontiers. National interest was given the priority rather then creating a conflict in the neighbourhood at the cost of national exchequer which was not in good shape. In a nutshell, it was a meek surrender by a hapless country with no other alternative in hand.

Illusive Diplomacy

These two agreements brought the spirit of friendliness between two countries and the slogan of Hini-Chini-Bhai-Bhai was given prominance in all the future parleys. Immediately thereafter Coun En-lai visited India and was given warm welcome to which he promised eternal friedhsip with India. Even the critics of these agreement changed their opinion about China. Nehru responded with a visit to China. During the visit of Nehru, Mao Tse-tung gave hint to a future warning when he boasted before Nehru and said that China was not afraid of American atom bomb if used against them which could kill two to three million Chinese and enough would be left to capture USA. During this visit, Nehru talked to Chou En-lai about the circulation of Chinese maps in which some parts of India were shown as Chinese territory. Chou En-lai assured Nehru that these were old maps and the Chinese Government had no time to revise them. Krishna Menon later visited China and secured the release of some American soldiers which were taken as prisoners in Korea war. India also accepted the Chairmanship of the Neutral Nations Repatriation Committee for the repatriation of the war prisoners held by two sides in Korea to which she was later accused as siding with the American by the Chinese. Later in the Bandung Conference of Non-aligned countries in Indonesia, Chou en-lai tried to outwit Nehru on almost every issue and tried to portray as head of the most powerful country of the World. Later on, the Maha Bod Society invited Dalai Lama to participate in the 2500th birth anniversary of Gautama Budh which was inordinately delayed by the Chinese on plea or the other. He was allowed to visit India in the company of Panchen Lama who was their stooge. Chou En-lai deliberately visited India during this time to overshadow the presence of Dalai Lama.

Brother of Dalai Lama was in India as a guest. During the stay of Dalai Lama in India, he met the Director of IB, Mullick, and informed him that Dalai Lama had made up his mind not to return to Tibet and he would inform Nehru in this regard. When Mullick informed Nehru about this development, who opined that it would be against the interest of Tibetan people if Dalai Lama did not return to Tibet because he is the only dignitary around whom the whole of the Tibetan people would be united and his stay in India would demoralize them. He told Mullick further that he would talk to Chou En-lai so that the Chinese presence in Tibet was reduced in future. Mullick briefed brother of Dalai Lama about the views of Nehru and thereafter Dalai Lama dropped the idea of staying in India. He was assured on behalf of Nehru that in case of any exigencies in future, proper shelter would be given them in India at any time. Nehru did talk to Chou En-lai in this regard and after that the Chinese did go slow and a resolution was passed in the National Assembly not to introduce any reforms in Tibet for five years. Some troops were also withdrawn from the Central Tibet to reduce the economic hardship of the Tibetans.

During the visit of Chou En-lai, Nehru again raised the question of Chinese map which showed large part of Indian territory and certain parts of Sikkim and Bhutan in China. Prime Minister Nehru vide a note informed the Parliament as Premier Chou En-lai referred to the McMahon line and again said that he had never heard of this before although the then Chinese Government had dealt with this matter and not accepted this line. He had gone thoroughly in this matter in connection with the border dispute with Burma. Although, he thought this line, established by British Imperialism, was not fair. Nevertheless, it was an accomplished fact and because of the friendly relations which existed between China and the countries concerned, namely, India and Burma, the Chinese government were of the opinion that they should give recognition to the McMahon line. They had, however, not consulted the Tibetan authorities about it yet. They proposed to do so. With this, Nehru got the impression that there were no major border disputes and these could be settled through negotiation.

Throughout 1952-58, China-India maintained the friendship and India continued to support entry of China in the United Nations and did not recognize Taiwan. There were some border violations in UP, Punjab, Ladakh and NEFA which when reported to the Chinese Government were either denied or described as their territory. Uneasy calm prevailed on the borders but during this period Chinese built network of roads, both arterial and up to Indian frontiers, and consolidated its position in remote area of Tibet. Maps showing large part of Indian territory into China continued in circulation to which Chinese put up the same reply that these could be revised as they did not get time to do so.

IB's Heroics

After the capture of Tibet by the Chinese army, Prime Minister Nehru was deeply concerned about the security threat on the North East frontiers from Ladakh to NEFA. He advised Mullick, the able Intelligence Bureau Director, to take all possible steps on these border areas to strengthen the intelligence network to cope with all the future eventualities with regard to China. Mullick took this arduous task from scratch to open checkposts in the remotest inhabited area and by 1958 most of the villages from Karakoram in Ladakh in the north to Kibitoo in NEFA in north-east were under the control of the sleuths of Intelligence Bureau. With Sikkim Police and Nepal army, all the passes were covered by Intelligence Bureau. In Ladakh area of Lngzi Tang, Aksai Chin, Soda Plains and Depsang Plains were completely devoid of any population or even vegetation and not a single grass grew in these areas. These areas were located at the height of 15,000 feet and more which IB officials used to cross immediately after leaving Ladakh valley to reach these longitudinal flat valleys. These areas were easily accessible from Sinkiang in China. Army did not have any post outside Ladakh valley. Supplies were transported to Leh by air and by mules to the check posts upto 150 miles. There was no facility for making warm clothing in India to meet the requirement of IB sleuths in winter when temperature was less than 30 degrees in some areas. Kerosene oil was the only medium to meet the heating requirements. There were no reliable wireless sets and communication was done through runners who took more than two months to communicate to and fro and if by any chance, they could survive on the way, there was no communication from passes from October to middle of June due to winter. Helicopters were the only means of transport for IB officials which were always in short supply. Due to these persistent ground realities, it was impossible to open check posts in these uninhabited areas of Aksai Chin, Soda Plains etc. apart from the fact that these were of little use for most of the year.

In order to keep these areas under the control as part of Indian territory, an alternative plan was devised by the IB. Karam Singh, a diehard competent Deputy Central Intelligence Officer, was assigned the arduous task of extensive patrolling in the summer to lead trekking parties from Karakoram, the north-eastern route to Aksai Chin, Lingzi Tang etc. and the eastern route to Lanak La. Most of the maps were defective. Karam Singh and his staff deserved the highest credit for the pioneering job as they discovered new routes, scaled passes which did not exist on the available maps of the area accessed by them. These areas were surveyed up to 1910 with defective methods. Even today if India is claiming these parts as Indian territory, it was due to the commendable job of Karam Singh and his staff who rectified the old maps to add new areas. These patrol parties were incommunicado for over three months till they returned to Leh. Goat were the only animal to transport food and other articles of use. In order to reduce the burden of over load, the patrolling party did not carry any arms except a shotgun to kill a wild goat or duck for food which they hardly get. These brave civilian IB officer continued this job every year upto October, 1959.

Quite obviously, at the bureaucratic level at Delhi there was much wrangling among the officers of External Affairs, Army officers and Intelligence Bureau Director with regard to the opening of these new check posts because only IB knew the locations and other Ministries concern did not have any other source to counter the claims of IB. There were accusations of trespassing by the IB officials in Tibet or Sinkiang due to the faulty nature of maps but all the check posts were built inside the claimed territory of India. Prime Minister Nehru had given overall clearance to B N Mullick, Director IB, to open check posts all along the frontier as the responsibility for guarding these borders were in his charter of duties and as such IB was free to open any check post anywhere depending upon the security consideration and as such no formal clearance was required from any other authority. While opening these check posts other factors like the type of the land, its elevation, command of routs and availability of water and shelter were to be decided by the IB officials present on these borders and not by the Government officials present in other Ministries at Delhi. IB had clear instructions to open posts anywhere in our territory irrespective of the Chinese protesting and disputing our claims. Hence IB officials did not sometime bother in bureaucratic wrangling of Delhi and open the posts fearing the Chinese intervention to stall these openings. IB Director was confidant that these wrangling would be done away in their favour since Prime Minister Nehru had given clear instructions in this regard and objections of External Affair Ministry and Army Headquarters were ruled out by him. Nehru was more concerned that IB did not trespass into Chinese territory in any way be it opening of post or patrolling. Since the maps were defective and frontier was a vague line, sometime IB team trespassed into Chinese territory but when they realized the fact, they returned to their soil. In a particular case, Karam Singh entered Sinkiang area up to Malik Shah which was about 40 miles away from the border although this area was claimed as our boundary before 1937 which was reported to Nehru by the External Affair ministry but he ignored it by citing the availability of faulty maps. Prime Minister rather recognized the work of these patrols and his encouraging words spurred Karam Singh and his brave team on to more strenuous and daredevil efforts. He gave Karam Singh the medal for gallantry and, praising such difficult and hazardous undertakings, said that when an individual or a nation did not take risks, that individual or nation would start going down.

In addition to guarding frontiers, IB was asked to collect intelligence inside Tibet about the political, economic and military designs of China. Despite non-availability of modern equipments, IB sleuths by 1958, started monitoring operations in Tibet and Sinkiang with whatever sets were at their disposal. There was acute scarcity of Chinese and Tibetan translators and only twenty percent of the message were translated.

Mullik sought the help of some friendly countries to accomplish the task provided to him. IB penetrated into deep areas of Tibet through its sources and collected all sort of vital information about the activities of China in all fields be it political, economic or military. IB had accurate information about the Chinese position all over Tibet, the exact strength of their garrison and full details of their armament, stocks of ammunition and food, relationship with the people and communications and trade. There were difficulties in getting information through sources in time because the penetration of sources to far flung area some time took more than two months to procure a particular information. In winter season, intelligence operations were almost halted due to weather conditions. These intelligence reports were fully assessed, analysed and demarcated in maps before sending to Prime Minister Nehru and all concerned Ministries of the Government.

Road inside Aksai Chin in Indian Territory

There were some calumnies that IB failed to report the construction of 1,170 kilometer long Sinkiang-Western Tibet Highway which passed through 70 miles inside the Aksai Chin area in the territory of India. According to B N Mullick, IB Director, reports were sent as early as in October, 1951 when Chinese surveyors were noticed near Rudok in October, 1951 and again in November, 1952, it was reported by IB that China had engaged 2,000 labourers in this task. Indian Trade agent at Gartok had also reported in September, 1955 of the construction of this road. According to Mullick, regular source reports were sent to the Government on the basis of the information procured by the patrolling parties but Government officials of various ministries took no cognizance of this violation on one plea or the other. Last intrusion of Chinese in this regard was detected by the patrolling party in 1958 when IB sent a report to the Government to protest to the Chinese government in this regard. Ministry of External Affairs took the stand that this area had not yet been demarcated and infiltrations had been reported by over-zealous survey officers and since India was not in control of this area, it would be futile to protest to China. Army took the stand that they were in not in a position to militarily intervene because of the limited sources available to them in Leh. Army's response implied that they could not sustain the burden of maintaining any post on the border. They rather suggested to send only the patrolling party instead It was then decided that IB should increase their patrolling in these areas where Chinese could further move inside our territory. IB was also directed to try to open one post north of Phobrang at Tsogatasalu to check Chineseinfiltration. IB had theserious problem when their patrols starting from Leh had to cross three successive mountain ranges where passes did not open till July due to freezing conditions whereas the Chinese side had no snow clad passes to cross and they could enter the Indian territory and leave it after completing their assignment and could go back before the arrival of Indian patrols.

In the meantime, Indian Embassy from Peking also reported the completion of the Aksai Chin road in June, 1958 on the basis of which Foreign Secretary convened a meeting of the concerned Ministries wherein he maintained that neither the Embassy report nor the Intelligence report conclusively proved that the Sinkiang- Western Tibet highway actually passed through Indian territory and no Indian party had actually traversed this route and so therefore any protest was lodged we should be sure of our stand. It was decided that two patrol parties one of army and second of IB would be sent from two directions to confirm whether this road passed inside the Indian territory. Army patrol was led by Lt. Iyenger and IB by none other than the old fox Karam Singh. Army patrol was arrested by the Chinese but Karam Singh was able to detect that the Chinese had intruded inside Indian territory where he had left some articles as proof. The hazardous trip undertaken by Karam Singh confirmed without any doubt that the so-called Aksai Chin road did actually cut across Indian territory from Haji Langar in the north to Amtogar in the south. The Government of India then lodged a formal protest to China about this road and enquired if Lt. Iyenger was being held by them. Lt. Iyenger's party was then released but not at Haji Langar where it had been captured but at the Karakoram Pass which was the only point where there was no dispute about the lie of the frontier. The Chinese rejected the protest of the Indian Government about this road. Another patrol party of IB gave information to government about Chinese infiltration near Daulat Beg Oldi.

Thereafter, IB Director recommended the opening of new posts near this road which was summarily rejected both by the army and Ministry of External Affairs. While Ministry took the stand that this part of territory was of no use to India and even if the Chinese did not encroach into it, India could not make any use of it. General Thimayya played down the importance of this road and expressed doubts on intelligence reports about its existence basically of his own weakness to counter any sort of Chinese military challenge in this region to stop from constructing this road. His troops would have to suffer reverses if he was engaged in any sort of venture in Aksai Chin. Therefore, on one plea or other, he tried to focus on the lack of importance of this road to hide his own incompetence to meet the mighty Chinese army. At this Mullick, IB Director, erred when he did not report these repercussions to the Prime Minister himself because IB was the only organization which was having first hand knowledge about the encroachment of Indian territory but also the mass road construction programme by China inside Tibet. IB could better comprehend the security implication than the army which was nowhere near these developments. IB's suggestion would have forced the Prime Minister to have a new look to prevent the danger which was looming large on this border.

Thereafter, Chinese occupied additional Indian territory in the absence of any possible resistance from our side and at the same time built up a well planned road system in Tibet connecting all vantage points up to the border of India and Nepal, as a part of long terms commercial and military strategy against India. Its economy too was progressing well. Indian Government deliberately did not disclose the construction of road in Aksai and other intrusion by China to the Indian public so that there might not be any public reaction in India against China which ultimately put the Indian Government in a great deal of embarrassment both in Parliament and in media when these facts were disclosed.

Bloodbath in Tibet

After consolidating its control over Tibet, China focused on bringing its inhabitants into the mainstream of Chinese current policies coloured with communism. They tried to introduce land reforms and curtailed the powers of monasteries in Central Tibet area of Kham and Amdo. In this pursuit, they forcibly took possession of lands of some people of these areas. Residents of Kham, the Khampas were born warriors and Dalai Lama belonged to Amdo sect which were descendents from the Amodas tribe. Chinese tried to suppress these sects in the name of land reforms. These Khampas strongly resented the introduction of land reforms and revolted against the Chinese when they tried to keep around 300 village leaders as captive in a fort and to indoctrinate them politically. One night, all of them fled to the hills and a guerrilla warfare started. Thereafter, there was a large scale violence in which the Chinese unleashed all sorts of violent reprisals and mercilessly killed hundreds of helpless Khampa people. Khampas too retaliated and raided depots, attacked camps and disrupted communications. The Chinese blamed the Tibetan Government for fomenting this rebellion of Khampas and put pressure on Dalai Lama to quell it through his army which he refused. However, he sent al mission to pacify the violent guerrilla Khampas. This mission could produce Only a palliative result and there was an uneasy lull which later in orm when Chinese tried to prosecute the erstwhile rebels by sewing their.

All these violent activities took place when Dalai Lama was on a visit to landia in 1956 when the Chinese resorted to armed akression a nd the Khampas. Due to suppression by Chinese, a large number of Khampas left their places and took shelter in and around Lhasa, Tibetans took proper care of these refugees. When Dalai Lama returned to Tibet in February 1997, he found the population of Lhasa increased in big proportion due to arrival of Khampas. Nehru intervened after which Mao Tse- tung deferred these reforms for five years. After this declaration, the Chinese army suddenly turned conciliatory sensing a large scale rebellion all over Tibet.

After return from India, Dalai Lama was aghast to see the atrocities committed by the Chinese on the Khampas. He raised the demand of independence and declared that the Chinese were not the master of Tibetan destiny. The Chinese were oblivious to such utterances as a fallout of the atrocities on the Khampas but they were waiting for the right opportunity to react again. However, the overall situation aggravated and rebellion by Tibetans was unavoidable since distrust was continuously brewing among them against the Chinese occupation.

While in India, Dalai Lama had invited Nehru to visit Lhasa also during his forthcoming visit to China in July 1958. Nehru agreed to this proposal subject to Chou En-lai's consent for it. During the course of his stay in Peking thereafter when Nehru discussed this proposal with China Government, they put forth a plea that there was grave danger to his life while in Lhasa as a result of the presence of large scale of rebels there. In actuality, they deliberately did not allow Nehru to visit Lhasa so that he should not have a first hand view of the ground level situation there and secondly, they did not want his mediation on the Tibet matter at anycost. They were also apprehensive of large scale demonstrations against China by the Tibetan people during the presence of Nehru in Lhasa which they did not want him to witness.

Such a ploy of the Chinese was strongly resented to by the Tibetans as they hoped that after visiting Tibet, Nehru might put some pressure on the Chinese for some moderation after assessing the utter discontent among the local population in that area. Tibetans were extremely angry against the Chinese and their anger against the later was uncontrollable because by then they were of the firm opinion that they did not allow any outside intervention in Tibet for any of their cause. Now, Tibetans had formed opinion that they had only two options for them either to surrender meekly before the Chinese or aggressively revolt against them. Chinese suppression made them to choose for the second option.

Chinese unleashed their atrocities against the Khampas and Amodas which compelled its large population to take refuge in the November 1958, it rose twice in numbers. Tibetans forgot old time with Khampas and stood by them in their misery, Influx of Kham suspicion in Chinese army at Lhasa and they started house-to-house search for the refugees living there. This created panic among them and most them fled to the South Tibet along NEFA and floated their guerrilla Volunt National Defence Army to fight against the Chinese. Thereafter, the Kham rebels harassed the Chinese army continuously. There were some skirmishes near Lhasa also for which the Chinese blamed complicity of Tibetans with Khampas. They wanted to arrest large part of their population which forced them to flee Lhasa and join the Khampa rebels. These incidents were reported by IB sources in India because the Indian Consulate in Lhasa did not have any such information due to restriction on his movement imposed by the Chinese army. IB, however, was not aware of the actual magnitude and strength of the Khampa rebellion. Dalai Lama informed Nehru of this problem who discussed this issue with Chou En-lai. No action was taken by Chou En-lai in this regard. On the other hand, the Chinese accused Dalai Lama and his government for this revolt by the Khampas and brought more army to Lhasa which was nearly two lakh by February 1959.

Around this time, a rumour spread in Lhasa that Dalai Lama had been invited to Peking by the Chinese Government to attend the National Assembly. Tibetans thought it was a ploy of the Chinese to arrest Dalai Lama under this pretext at Peking and keep him a hostage indefinitely. This Chinese overture agitated them further. Thereafter, events took fast turn. In March, the Chinese Military Headquarterss at Lhasa invited Dalai Lama in their camp without his escorts to watch a theatre show which too was resented to by the tans as a trap to arrest him and fly him out to Peking. The Tibetans had formed an opinion that the Chinese would arrest Dalai Lama one day or the other. So, on March 10, 1959, around 10,000 Tibetans surrounded Norbu Linka in Lhasa where Dalai Lama was staying and did not allow him to go to the Chinese camp. There were some stray incidents of violence and crowd started shouting slogans asking Chinese to leave Tibet. When three ministers of Dalai Lama went to brief the Chinese Commander about the ongoing happenings, they were threatened by the Commander to face dire consequences since they thought that this agitation was instigated by them. Fearing capture of Dalai Lama by the Chinese, people formed voluntary squads and kept day and night vigil to protect him. On March 16, 1959, Tibetans got the information that artillery had reached Lhasa. They were certain that the Chinese army would arrest Dalai Lama, bombard Lhasa and unleash a reign of terror on the local population. Next day, two explosions near Norbu Linka further mounted suspicion in Tibetans that the Chinese would bombard that place any time.

During the course of this volatile situation in Lhasa, on the evening of March 17, 1959, Dalai Lama along with some family members, members of the Cabinet and some body guards left Lhasa in batches secretly. Actually! Dalai Lama had the intention to declare independence in Tibet territory itself! where the Chinese did not have any control. But, he abandoned this mowe since it was unsafe in view of the large presence of Chinese army in adjoining areas. The Tibetans were in utter confusion to know the whereabouts of Dalai Lama. When they did not get any exact news about Dalai Lama, they revolted in Lhasa on March 20. The Chinese army was eagerly awaiting for such a situation and they retaliated by bombing Norbu Linka, Potala and various places of resistance in Lhasa. After four days of military action about 4,000 Tibetans were killed and the same number were arrested. Repression of the Tibetans continued thereafter and life was not at all normal hereinafter in this part of the world.

Asylum to Dalai Lama

On March 31, Dalai Lama crossed Indian border near Khinzemane. Dalai Lama was given asylum by the Indian Government. He issued a statement at

Tezpur that he had voluntarily left Tibet which was countered by Chinese that this statement was issued at the behest of Indian Government. Prime Minister Nehru received him at Mussoorie where in a press conference he declared that he had voluntarily left Tibet. Disappearance of Dalai Lama gave Chinese the much awaited opportunity to destroy the last vestiges of the Tibetan Government and set up a Military dictatorship. They resorted to cruel genocide of Tibetan population which was done mercilessly with contempt. Chinese stooge Panchen Lama was appointed successor of Dalai Lama. Chinese army was deployed all over Tibet up to the border of India and Nepal and movement of every Tibetan was restricted at every place. Trade and communication with India was disrupted and even the pilgrimage to Kailash and Mansarovar was stopped. In order to crush the Tibet religion, unspeakable sacrileges were committed on the monasteries and monks were publicly beaten and humiliated due to which many committed suicide. All properties in the monasteries were destroyed and offerings were stopped as a result of which monks starved and most of them left Lhasa. Tibetans were taken as slave for road building and other menial jobs and large number of them died due to exhaustion or were beaten to death. They were deprived of their land and commune system was introduced.

International Jurists reported systematic genocide of Tibet population by the Chinese army. In India, except the Communist Party of India, every one deplored these Chinese atrocities. There was Worldwide condemnation of China. Indian Prime Minister Nehru declared that although India had no desire to interfere in Tibet but at the same time for the people of Tibet and the people of India were greatly distressed at their helpless plight. When a Communist leader of India questioned the propriety of the grant of asylum to Dalai Lama, Nehru not only asserted it as the wish of Indian people and assured that all the Tibetans who would enter as refugee in India would be granted asylum. He also repudiated the Chinese allegation that Kalimpong was used as a base for the rebellion activities in Tibet.

In UNO, the General Assembly passed a resolution on October, 21, 1959, calling for respect of the fundamental human rights of the Tibetan people and for their distinctive cultural and religious life. Large number of Tibetan refugees swelled in India through the borders of NEFA, Sikkim, Uttar Pradesh, Punjab, Ladakh and through Bhutan and Nepal. Indian Government not only welcomed these refugees but also took every steps to rehabilitate them. Buddhist population in India largely condemned Chinese reprisal and showed considerable sympathy to the Tibetan refugees.

Granting asylum to Dalai Lama and Tibetan refugees had strong anti-Indian reaction in China and government controlled newspapers poured venom against Nehru in particular and branded it as the internal interference of China and violation of Sino-India agreement. India was accused of fomenting all these problems in Tibet and rebellion was the cause of its internal policy. Even China warned India that in the troubled border with Pakistan, they would open another front on its northern frontier. IB had reports that the China-Pakistan nexus was in the offing. China's hostility with India was not due to these incidents in Tibet. It was a long conceived perception not only of Communists but was borrowed from the Nationalist government of Chiang Kai-shek which was aimed at expansion of its territory into many South-East Asian countries including India. In this pursuit China in its philosophy of enemy of enemy is my friend, found Pakistan as its ally on the western and eastern front of India. Tibet revolt invited all troubles from China which would have come sooner or later because China had already constructed a road in Aksai Chin area of India connecting Sinkiang with Western Tibet. They started questioning the validity of McMahon Line in order to bully India. Chinese map showing large area of Indian territory were never revised with the sole intention to keep as proof of confrontation in this regard. In the Sino-Indian agreement, Indian delegation wanted all pending matters to be settled whereas the Chinese wanted only those matters which were ripe for settlement. Hence, hidden agenda of China to keep the border issue alive was every time a writing on the wall when any sort of negotiation was conducted with the Chinese. When Nehru questioned the validity of Chinese map in circulation with Chou En-lai, he avoided the issue by saying that his government did not have time to revise these old maps but never accepted McMahon line as border. This was all treachery on his point because in July, 1958, a map was published in China officially which included whole of NEFA, large areas of Ladakh, UP, Himachal Pradesh and even major portion of eastern Bhutan as Chinese territory. Now it was clear that after consolidating its control in Tibet, China was vying to look beyond the McMahon line and questioned the entire boundary with India, Nepal, Bhutan, Sikkim and Burma which Chou En-lai earlier declined. There were exchange of protest notes between India and China followed by a personal letter of Nehru to Chou En-lai on December,

14, 1958 wherein he refuted the claims of this map. Chou En-lai on January 23, 1959, officially questioned the validity of McMahon line and suggested survey of it with mutual consultation and till then status quo to be maintained by both countries. It meant that China would be in control of illegally Akdai Chin area in Ladakh without Indian intervention. This was direct reprisal of China against India supporting Dalai Lama.

Indian Policemen Massacred

Nine days before Dalai Lama entered India, on March, 22, 1959, Nehru again wrote a detailed letter to Chou En-lai highlighting various treaties between two countries in the past wherein the territory of both countries were earmarked and henceforth no claim had ever been raised by either side on their legality. For the next six month no reply was received by India and in the meantime, China captured large part of north-east Ladakh. They occupied Khurnak fort and a hill overlooking Chushul and posted a picket at Rezang La. In some areas, they penetrated as deep as more than 30 miles in Indian territory. An Indian police patrol was captured in Ladakh near Khurnak Fort and was released after a month. In NEFA also they intrude and occupied some territory and when Assam Police resisted, they killed three policemen. Indian obviously could not retaliated as they were outnumbered by the Chinese. Acrimonious protest notes continued to exchange without any commitments. On September 8, 1959, Chou En-lai replied to Nehru's letter of March 22 and refuted all the arguments of Nehru point by point and rather blamed India for provocation on the entire border and accused India of imposing one-sided claims on the boundary question. He threatened that these attempt would never succeed and would impair the friendship of the two countries. Subsequently, Chinese Government repeated these charges. Hence, for the first time the entire Indo-Tibetan frontier was thrown in the melting pot by demanding negotiation over Indian territory of about 1,30,000 sq kms. This was beginning of an end.

In order to restrain China from capturing more territory in Ladakh, IB Director Mullick had suggested to open seven more checkposts near the Chinese occupied area. Chief of Army staff and Foreign Secretary, rather than accepting our own weaknesses, opined this as impractical, unnecessary and provocative. Subsequently, sanction was accorded to open two posts at Kongka La. Home Ministry there too put the cart before the horse and declined to give any CRPF force to complete this job. Mullick procured one company of CRPF from Jammu and Kashmir for this venture. Again brave Karam Singh was assigned this arduous job. Since winter was round the corner, this job had to be completed as early as in October. Karam Singh along with this CRPF company and his own IB personnel, opened the first post at Tsogatsalu on October 17 and the second at Hot Springs on 19th October, 1959. Karam Singh sent one patrol of one constable and one local man towards Kongka La where the next post was to be opened but this patrol did not return. In order to search this patrol, on October, 21, Karam Singh with twenty men and a small rear guard moved towards Kongka La. He found hoof marks on the way which gave indications that Chinese horsemen must have arrested the two patrol men. When this patrol party moved forward towards Kongka La, it was ambushed by two Chinese pickets near the bank of river Chang Chenmo which was two miles west of it. One Chinese picket was built on a hill top on the flank of the route by which the Indian party was advancing and other located in front on the other side of the river. In this ambush eight policemen were killed on the spot in few minutes by the Chinese. Rest of the soldiers retaliated and fired for their safety till their ammunition exhausted. In this encounter, one Chinese officer was also killed and some were injured by the Indian soldiers. Retrieval of Indian soldiers was cut off by the Chinese picket on the top of the hill. They could not escape along the river-bed as this was guarded by the Chinese picket on the other bank. Chinese further brought enforcement from Kongka La and arrested brutally injured twelve policemen including Karam Singh. One constable who was badly injured was left behind was later on killed by the Chinese. These arrested Indian soldiers were tortured at the prisoner camp at Kongka La on charges of trespassing the Chinese territory. This area was about 40 miles inside Indian territory from the traditional frontier at Lanak La which Karam Singh had trekked in June earlier and he did not find any Chinese then. Hence, Chinese intrusion inside Indian territory was more than 40 miles after June, 1959, where they killed these Indian policemen. Indian Government strongly protested and ultimately the Chinese released the prisoners and returned the dead bodies on November 14 on the bank of the Silung Barma river, which they claimed was the Western frontier of Tibet. If IB had opened these posts in June, intrusion of Chinese could have been forestalled. But they could do it by force. Thus they could not have claimed the absence of any Indian posts as evidence of their own possession over this territory as they did later.

This Kongka La incident was severely condemned by the Indian Parliament and by every Indian. Indian Communists instead of criticizing China for this dastardly act, simply deplored the shooting incident. This incident marked the end of an era of so-called friendship between India and China. these Indian policemen did not sacrifice their lives in vain as it warned India of the new sinister designs of China in the coming future. This incident opened the eyes of of the Indians in general and the Government in particular about the unscrupulous nature of the friend India had been dealing with henceforth and the nine dead policemen, whose ashes were enshrined at Hot Springs served as a writing on the wall for the future troubles from China. Thereafter October 21 each year is observed by the Police all over India as Remembrance Day to mark the sacrifice of these nine policemen for their country. On November 27, Indian Prime Minister said in the Parliament that this incident brought a tremendous reaction in India affecting every citizen and he was proud of that reaction.

This incident instead of making the Indian Government more active and alert on the border, made IB as scapegoat. Subsequently, in a meeting chaired by the Prime Minister, IB was made target by the Army Headquarterss and the External Affairs Ministry and accused of expansionism and causing provocations on the frontiers. This was totally untenable because this incident occurred more than thirty miles inside Indian territory where Karam Singh had visited in June earlier and no Chinese was found there by him at that time. Parliament and the people accused the Government of their inability to check the infiltration of Chinese rather than accused the IB whose officials were trying to fill the security gaps with inadequate facilities, of being aggressor and provocateurs. This was ridiculous since the Prime Minister had accorded his approval to open these posts.

In that meeting, Army demanded that no movements of armed police should take placed on the frontier without their concurrence which was accepted by the Prime Minister. Thereafter, protection of the border was handed over to Army. The Chief of the Army Staff demanded that all the Intelligence posts and their communications should be placed under his control which was opposed by Intelligence Bureau and External Affairs Ministry. When Prime Minister was properly briefed by Mullick, the IB Director, he declined the demand of Army. It was ultimately decided that all the Intelligence posts as well as the communications, which Army wanted to control, would remain with IB throughout the whole frontier and operation of the armed police from these posts would be controlled by the Army. Since, Army was in position to guard these posts due to concentration of sizeable Chinese presence in this area, the Army Chief for this reason had opposed the opening of these posts earlier. He was aware that if Police would be in trouble with the Chinese army, Indian army too was bound to be involved in that case for which they were ill-prepared at that time. Due to this reason, Army Chief wanted all disputes in these areas to be settled at diplomatic level rather than having confrontation and allowed the Chinese to occupy the territory up to their claimed frontier and then put up any armed opposition which they were unable to sustain.

Net result, thereafter was that IB did not open any new check posts in the forward areas along the Chinese frontier and Army too could not do so for some time. Security of the frontiers by the Army only remained on paper because no additional army units were moved to the frontier till a year later. Till then two borders were guarded by police and the Assam Rifles where over-zealous junior army officers tried to interfere with the intelligence people. All further consolidation of frontier which was started by IB in 1952 on the orders of Prime Minister Nehru was abruptly stopped after this incident of October 21, 1959 and the northern frontier of India was frozen at the points which had been secured by the Intelligence Bureau with the help of the CRPF, the State police units and the Assam Rifles with much difficulty against all odds of nature. Not one square mile of territory could be added to the effective control of IB possession after that date. In the absence of any hurdle which Intelligence Bureau tried to impose on the Chinese, they further occupied 8,000 sq. miles of our territory which Indian army could not stop. Though IB continued to brief Indian Government in this regard but it was helpless to take any practical action to recover this territory.

Thus a heroic approach adopted by IB under B N Mullick to take as much control as could be taken under extremely adverse conditions and circumstances, came to a grinding halt and the unwarraned acrimony heaped on IB by those who were least concerned about the Chinese intrusion in Ladakh proved fatal in future when India was humiliated by the Chinese in 1962. Could the bravery of a civilian officer like Karam Singh had any parallel in the army or other forces who dared the Chinese for eight years as a result of which thousands of kilometres of Indian territory was brought under its effective control. Hats off to Karam Singh and his team of policemen who brought laurels to IB which too was in its embryonic stage at that time with primitive intelligence gathering equipment and least training of any effective espionage.

Diplomacy amid Confrontation

Prior to the killing of these nine Indian policemen by the Chinese army, in September, 1959, there were exchange of letters between Nehru and Chou En-lai in which the later accused India of causing tension and trouble on the frontier and question the validity of McMahon line. He also challenged the right of India to talk about the frontier of Sikkim and Bhutan with Tibet. Nehru reiterated that in the erstwhile Sino-India agreement of 1954, it was apparently hoped that all problems which history had left behind had been peacefully and finally resolved and it was a shocking misadventure on the part of China to raise the border issue after five years of this agreement. Nehru suggested status quo or frontier pending discussion of border alignment. In November, Chou En-lai again wrote to Nehru and suggested the withdrawal of the army to a depth 20 ms from the line up to which each side exercised actual control implying that India should withdraw further 20 kms. in her own territory and China would withdraw in the territory captured from India. This would further strengthen the claim of China in Indian territory. Nehru rejected this suggestion and pointed out that entire territory in question was Indian where Civil administration was in force up to the frontier in question since long time back. He however agreed to stop forward patrolling and suggested a meeting between them which was accepted by Chou en Lai. Detailed notes were exchanged between the two sides claiming and counter-claiming their territories on the basis of their own facts and circumstances. Diplomatically, both countries did not agree to the positions of each other and hostility in their relations reached to the optimum level without any chance of resolution. In this scenario, on February 5, 1960, Nehru wrote a letter to Chou En-lai suggesting that although there was very little chance of an agreement on the frontier issues because the Chinese were contesting the historical facts yet a meeting between them might be helpful for which March, 1960 was given the option. He also attached a detailed note along with this letter in reply to previous claims of China. It was again reiterated in this note that although the boundary was not actually delimited or demarcated but its existence could not be contested in the background of historical facts, numerous treaties, customs, geography and international conventions.

During this period, China found Communists of India as their sympathizers who cited the landlords of Tibet as troublemaker for all problems in Tibet, supported China in their blame of engineering rebellion activities from Kalimpong inside Tibet by India and supported claim of China that the Sino-Indian border was not delimited and criticized the Indian Government for not agreeing to the just proposal of Chinese Government for a settlement by discussion. Nehru criticized Communists of India in the Parliament on their postures towards China. Referring to the forthcoming visit of Chou En-lai, he told the IB in a briefing that whatever might be the outcome of this visit, even if favourable, the fact would continue that this frontier had become a dangerous, live and explosive one. India could never go back to that period when it was a dead frontier by the mere fact that a strong, well armed State was standing on the other side. The frontier would remain dangerous unless China broke up, which not going to happen easily in the near future.

From 1959 onward, China apart from committing aggression on the frontier, occupied large part of Indian territory and disputed the entire Indo-Tibetan boundary. China further created trouble for India in Tibet and even inside India. This continued till Chou En-lai visited India in April, 1960. False allegation of land and air violation by Indian forces were hurled regularly. Indian Consulate was restricted in its movements beyond two kilometers. Working of Trade agencies at Gyantse, Yatung and Gartok was almost brought to standstill by various accusations. Indian traders were harassed. Newspapers wrote anti-India articles on regular basis. In India, China bank tried to capture the major Tibetan trade with the help of Chinese settled in Calcutta, Bombay and Assam. Chinese Consulate officials increased unlawful activities in Assam, Darjeeling and other parts of the country. They increased their hobnobbing with members of CPI and other opponents of Indian Government. Vilification campaign against India was started by the Chinese China Review in Calcutta. On the recommendation of Intelligence Bureau, Indian Government retaliated rather late but ultimately put restrictions on Chinese Trade Agency in Kalimpong, Chinese Press in India were warned, some trouble-creator Chinese were deported and the Reserve Bank of India put restrictions on the China Bank which was suspected to be involved in spending on espionage activities inside India. These were clear indications that friendship between two countries was almost over and confrontation was in full swing starting from petty issues to the larger border dispute. Chinese troops at this time were further making encroachments inside India. In this murky atmosphere of any rapprochement, visit of Chou En-lai in April, 1960, was to most likely not yield any success yet he wanted to score a diplomatic mileage and probably succeeded in doing so by portraying China' reasonableness and India's obduracy in the eyes of World community.

Chou En-lai and his deputy Marshal Chen Yi arrived Delhi on April 19, 1960. Prior to that China signed border agreements with Burma and Nepal create an impression in the world that China was reasonable towards som border disputes with neighbouring countries. China even recoge McMahon Line as border between Tibet and Burma which was disp hereinbefore. In order to reduce the Indian influence in Nepal, the chi proposed to roll out a number of economic aid programmes to Ne opened their Mission on reciprocal basis. China even agreed that is Everest was part of Nepal which it disputed in the past. All this generos heaped on Nepal to isolate India from the traditional decades-old relations between the two countries.

At Delhi airport itself, while receiving these leaders, Nehru referred to the bitterness arose between the two countries due to the aggressive approach of China in previous few months. There were demonstrations in Delhi by opposition parties to put pressure on Nehru not to budge to the demand of Chou En-lai to give an inch of Indian territory. Nehru personally appeared before the demonstrators and promised not to barter any territory of India while holding negotiations with Chou En-lai. During the course of negotiations, the Chinese too did not show customary courtesy of equality and stressed for the solutions which were suitable to their interest and neither showed any semblance of 'give and take nor talked about what was agreed in the Panchsheel of 1954.

In this untrustworthy atmosphere, the negotiations did not yield any success and miserably failed due to the obstinacy of Chinese leaders. It was evident from their attitude when Dr. Radhakrishnan cautioned Marshal Chen Yi during negotiations that he was behaving like a Marshal and not a Foreign Minister. As a face saving move, a joint communiqué was issued in which it was decided by both the Prime Ministers to set up a joint team of officials of two countries to examine all historical documents, records, accounts, maps and other material related to the boundary question. Both countries would put forward their claim on the basis of these evidences to their respective governments. Subsequently, in the press conference at Delhi on April 25, Chou En-lai in a written statement mentioned the existence of the border dispute and suggested to stop patrolling by both countries on border to avoid confrontation. Later, on his way back at Kathmandu, he criticized Indian Government for failure of negotiations. He also took exception to Nehru's reference in the Lok Sabha to Chinese occupation of area in Ladakh as an act of aggression. It was not understandable as to what was the motive of Chou En-lai to visit India knowing in advance that he would not yield any positive result. Probably, he wanted to create an impression among the world community that China was willing to resolve border dispute with India for which he did not get any co-operation from the latter. He tried to strengthen this analogy by signing such agreements with Nepal and Burma on this journey.

When the officials of both the countries met, there were differences of opinion between them about the modalities of discussions over the terms of reference. While the Indians maintained to discuss only the available material, the Chinese stressed to include the political aspects of the matter in the discussions. There was uncalled for wrangling in the negotiations which finally started only on the Indian assertions. After three rounds of meetings in Peking, Delhi and Rangoon, the Indian team submitted its report which was released by India in December 1960 whereas China released it in January 1962 after adding some references which were never discussed in the earlier negotiations. Evaluation of these reports by independent observers provedthat the type of evidence produced by India was stronger than that of India was utmost sure that the evidences given by China were much w and would not stand in any impartial judicial review. Indian Prime Minister even offered to refer the border dispute falsely created by the Chines to any international authority, including the International Court of Justice at Hague which was resisted by China since they were adamant to take any legal jurisdictional, administrative, traditional and geographical bases as solution but to settle it on the basis of politics and at the point of gun. During this period with the sole intention to humiliate India, China got over 2,000 sq. miles of territory of Jammu and Kashmir from Pakistan which was occupied illegally in 1948 aggression. China rejected all Indian protests in this regard as an unfriendly act.

Security Concerns

All these events further deteriorated relations between the two countries. Around this period, China stopped pilgrimage entry to Kailash Mansaroval when a Sadhu carrying Homoeopathic medicine for his use was stopped on the allegation that he was attempting to poison the Lake. Indian Government retaliated by imposing restrictions on Chinese Trade agency at Kalimpong and put stronger watch on the activities of Chinese Consulates in Calcutta and Bombay. Several Chinese involved in anti-India activities were deported forcibly across the Nathu La. Manager of China Bank too was deported for his connection with subversive groups in Calcutta. Editors of China Review in Calcutta was arrested for scurrilous anti-Indian articles. China too hurled false allegation of violations on border by Indian air and land forces. In the meantime vigorous activities were increased by China to build roads in occupied Ladakh area.

In a meeting with IB in March, 1961, Nehru discussed full implications of the on-going acrimonious activities inside two countries against each other. He realized the foolishness to rush headlong and get caught in a trap in the military confrontation with China. He clearly mentioned that while India should continue the political pressure for a settlement and in the meantime gain time to start preparation for a possible war with China. Thereafter, Government of India sanctioned the expansion of the army by two infantry divisions. In order to improve supplies to Ladakh frontier posts, the airfield in Leh and Chushul were improved and another laid at Koyal and a number of C-119 planes were purchased from Amercial and AN-12 from Russia. These purchases considerably improved the carrying capacity of the Indian Air Force. Several other measures were taken to make army self-sufficient in armaments. Although, Nehru stressed for strengthening the military force but he was oblivious of the fact that a war with China could last for years ruining the economy of India. At the same time. Pakistan was sharpening the new military aid against India to use it at opportune time. In view of these impending dangers, Nehru was right in his policy to engage China as much as if could be for political dialogure rather than headlong confrontation which would bring avoidable misery and disaster to the Indian population.

IB analysed the military potential in Tibet where China had enough stock-piling at bases near the frontiers to be able to carry on a war of couple of month's duration without depending on supplies from the mainland. Chinese army in Tibet was well conditioned as its communication with frontiers was good and it had sufficient strength to attack India from a place of their own choice. This was conveyed to the Prime Minister and Home Minister by IB. But the Army bosses had a different analysis of Chinese army and opined that the Chinese did not have the capacity to maintain more than five Divisions in Tibet in peacetime and not more than two Divisions during operations. Even these units would be poorly equipped and did not constitute any real danger to the security of India. Hence there was strong conflict of analysis about the military preparation of China in Tibet wherein Army held the opinion that IB was exaggerating the threat and Army Headquarters was discarding irrefutable evidence and deliberately underestimating the danger. In subsequent meetings, IB found that Army Headquarters continued to hold on to the belief that the Chinese military strength was of that mid-fifties and was slow to devise strategy and tactics to suit the situation and meet the threat as and where it developed. It was thus preposterous that IB reports were considered incredible by the army in order to hide their own incompetence.

In May, 1960, IB reported to the Government the evidence of continued Chinese activities of reconnaissance, probing, surveys and road-buildings much beyond the line claimed by them in 1956. IB reported the intention of Chinese to occupy the pastureland in the vicinity of Chusul region which was important for the inhabitants of this area. On the basis of this report, Prime Minister on May 26 convened a meeting of Chief of Army staff, Foreign and Defence Secretaries and ordered to open new posts to protect Indian territory around Chang Chenmo river valley and Pangong Lake. Protective steps like patrolling restarted in other forward areas. In September,

1960 another report was sent by IB wherein widespread Chinese activities all along the frontier in Tibet and many instances of fresh intrusions were informed to the Government and suggested to open more posts in Eastern Ladakh and movement of troops in forward areas. Additional intelligence posts were opened and our claimed frontier in South-East Ladakh which was the only inhabited area in the frontier region of this territory. In the North East the Chinese had already occupied nearly 7,000 sq. miles of our territory, which was bereft of any habitation or vegetation but between the Chinese and the Indian-occupied lines there existed nearly 3,000 sq. miles more of the same type of territory which was occupied by neither country.

After the retirement of Thimayya in March 1961, there was change guard in the army and General Thapar took over as Chief of Army Staff who took some resolute steps to strengthen army positions on the frontier Afterwards, there was considerable improvement in the coordination between the army and IB on the border areas which were never witnessed since 1948. But on one occasion in September 1961, army decided to withdraw some posts from Daulat Beg Oldi and Qizil Langar where it became difficult for the army to maintain supplies. IB discussed the serious implications of this withdrawal but the Army Headquarterss did not agree with the IB proposal. However, IB decided not to close these posts and functioned without any armed protection at the grave risk to its staff. With the change of events, army had to reverse its decision to withdraw from these posts when IB detected Chinese incursion nearly 30 miles inside Indian territory on the west side of Langar-Shamul road. They started construction of a fort about four miles east of Daulat Beg Oldi. In the wake of these developments, army not only decided to maintain these posts but also developed an air-strip a Daulat Beg Oldi for C-119 planes for supplies throughout the year.

In November, 1961, B N Mullik, briefed Prime Minister that there were some areas in our territory which were still not physically occupied by Indian security forces because they were difficult to access and were generally uninhabited. He pointed out to Nehru the danger that unless immediate steps were not taken to occupy them by the summer of 1962, there was every likelihood of these being occupied by the Chinese. Thereafter, Nehru ordered that Indian forces should remain in effective control of the whole frontier from NEFA to Ladakh and they should cover all gaps by setting up posts or by means of patrolling and Chinese encroachment or intrusion should be checked by Indian troops or police. He cautioned that the troops should not fire except in self-defence.

Thereafter, considerable efforts were made by the army and police to push forward to vacant areas both in Ladakh and in NEFA.

Hereinbefore, the attitude of the Army Headquarterss was cautious because there was no attempt to enter into any sort of confrontation with China. There was general perception that Indian Army was not attuned to take on the Chinese due to hilly terrain in this region which was unsuitable for the army to fight with the Chinese. Such mindset of the Army Generals was disgusting and worrisome for the security analysts in general and IB in general and IB bosses in particular because they were the only lot who were aware with the ground situation across the Indian borders. What was the option before the army when China was determined to enter into a conflict with India on one plea or the other. One could think of only retaliation and nothing else. Thus, IB was the only organization which was opposed to this weary approach of the army. According to Mullick, this was an uncouth assumption because battles are always fought on frontiers in absolutely adverse conditions. No country could allow it enemy to annex its territory without proper fight be the might of one i superior than the other. No army can choose a battle ground suitable to them t Fight even if it was hundreds of miles inside its own territory. Similarly, n country could afford to be subsumed by other despite its own weak position an nad to make incessant efforts to take on the enemy, Whatever might be its stror nd weak points. There is always possibility of a defeat of one side but t osition can be retrieved later and on that account no country give up contier without a fight on flimsy grounds and inane assumptions.

Prime Minister Nehru was criticized by some people for this policy. But there were no other options left for him by this time having exhausted all diplomatic efforts and peaceful methods of persuading Chinese to take a reasonable line. Chinese were determined to grab as much of the Indian territory in the garb of treachery, cajoling, threats, trespass, forcible occupation and even outright invasion, what other alternative was left than to confront them all along the frontier and not allow to transgress Indian territory any further? This was exactly the policy Nehru decided to follow and there was no other alternative left. If a country is militarily weak, does it mean that it shall not defend itself? Nehru was right in himself knowing fully well the armed strength of China but he was left with no other options but to assert and he was to defend the Indian frontiers at any cost. Militarily India would never be superior to China and if this criteria of numerical strength was the parameter of some critics to pick up confrontation, Nehru was right in logical conclusion to confront the Chinese even though the Indian Army was much inferior in its strength in comparison to the Chinese. According to Mullick, this policy was unfortunately delayed by Nehru with the honest intention to solve all pending disputes with China peacefully. Had it been implemented long back, much more Indian territory could have been saved from Chinese occupation?

Ultimate Debacle

At this crucial juncture, 1B was asked by the Prime Minister to give detailed information about the areas which were not till then guarded in the NEFA sector where army was to be deployed into all unoccupied territories after the decision was taken in the meeting in November 1961. It was not possible immediately to initiate action due to adverse winter season. In December, IB gave its assessment and informed the location of ten such unguarded gaps with a total area of around 5,500 sq. miles in NEFA which were still unoccupied due to sparse inhabitation and unreachable due to the absence of roads. IB, however, duly explained the location of nearest Indian posts and where the Chinese were establishing their posts across the border to capture these vacant areas. It was also informed by IB that the Chinese were spearheading strong propaganda in Tibet that they would liberate the remaining land of Tibet meaning NEFA from the Indian occupation. This propaganda was adversely affecting the morale of population of the frontier since there was no presence of Indian authorities with them.

With the beginning of summer, in April 1962, Indian Army started moving forward to open new posts in NEFA and Ladakh. Chinese protested to this movement of army which was rejected by Indian Government. In this volatile situation, relations between India and China were at its lowest ebb because of other stray incidents both in India and China when various steps were taken to deter the trade, diplomatic and other activities against each other. China in retaliation also opened new posts and surrounded the Indian position almost at every place where Indian Army had reached and further pushed forward in the vacant Indian territory. China recruited some NEFA tribal outlaws and trained them in violent activities. By September 1962, army of both the countries were standing guard face to face in hostility. On September 8, 1962, Chinese troops crossed into Indian territory and laid siege of a post in NEFA. Indian Government took the decision to get this area vacated from China. While doing so, expectedly, the Indian Government anticipating Chinese retaliation, enforced Indian troops on all the vantage positions in NEFA and Ladakh and made elaborate arrangements to thwart the possible Chinese attack. Even the Indian Air Chief proposed to bomb targets in Western Tibet, if necessary, to which resultant repercussions were discussed and decided to avoid at that time.

By the end of September 1962, full preparations were made by the Indian Army to get vacated the area forcibly occupied by China. Strangely, it was never assessed by their Commanders that they were not in the position to oust the Chinese. On October 9, the Indian Army started the operation and occupied the position adjacent to the Chinese occupation at Tsenjong in NEFA. Next day, the Chinese retaliated and fiercely attacked the indian position. This was the beginning of 1962 war with China. When the Indian troops repulsed the attack, Chinese after heavy death toll of their soldiers brought enforcement in large numbers. Indian troops relented due to the faulty planning of the Commanders in the field, no reinforcement to the Indian troops was made available to meet this eventuality whereas the Chinese were heavily equipped with artillery, mortars and MMGs. This failure on the part of the commanders to support a unit in distress was a monumental tragedy. Although the unit fought valiantly but they could not sustain the Chinese offensive without any back up by their Commanders. This inaction of officers lowered their estimation in the eyes of junior officers, NCOS and soldiers They themselves were also demoralized by their own mistakes and thereafter the lower cadre of army lost faith in the planning of the seniors in this region. B M Kaul, the Area Commander, sent a distressed message to Delhi explaining his inability to repulse the Chinese from Indian positions.

Obviously, Nehru was much perturbed person as a result of this tragic incident when the Indian soldiers were thrown into a hapless situation to face death at the hands of Chinese due to the inept handling by their seniors. He convened a meeting to take stock of the situation on October 11, 1962 midnight, which was attended by the Defence Minister Krishna Menon and Defence and Civil officers at his residence. Kaul explained his inability to hold fort end in the absence of proper logistical support, he was not in a position to drive the Chinese out of that area. After much wrangling and mudslinging, it was ultimately decided to hold the position in question and keep it in abeyance further offensive against the Chinese till adequate reinforcement was available in NEFA sector. On October 13, when press correspondents asked Nehru at Palam airport about the facts of the Chinese confrontation, he angrily replied that he had ordered the Army to push out Chinese from Indian territory for which he could not fix the date for the time being and it was for the army to decide further. Ostensibly, Nehru vented his anger in this manner because he was assured by the Army Generals in general and Lt. Gen. B M Kaul, the Area Commander of NEFA in particular that Chinese would be driven out from the territory where Indian troops were attacked on October 9. Kaul was with him at the airport when Nehru talked to the press. There were allegations from his political opponents and some writers that this statement of Nehru precipitated the prevalent situation on the border, which was far from truth because Chinese were continuously encroaching upon the Indian territory since the beginning of June and Indian patience was crossing the limits.

Chinese wanted a dialogue on this situation and fixed October 15, to discuss this matter at Peking to which India disagreed with precondition of withdrawal of Chinese troops. In the meantime, the Chinese brought heavy reinforcement at the area where troops clashed on October 9 in NEFA. Kaul cent another distressed telegram explaining his inability to hold position not only at the place of October 9 assault but from other places also. On October 17. the Defence Minister, Chief of Army Staff, all senior Army Officers of NEFA region, IB Chief and Assam Rifles Inspector-General assembled at Tezpur in view of Kaul's telegram and reviewed the situation on this front whether Indian Army should launch the assault to get vacated the territory occupied by China. Kaul reiterated his demand of withdrawal explaining the superiority of Chinese army in all respects quoting numbers, equipment, training, supply of weapons, including morale in his outbursts. IG of Assam Rifles too supported him to hold control of his posts in the winter but in real sense he was wary of any military support in the face of heavy deployment of Chinese army. Although, Army Officers were initially reluctant for an offensive due to the presence of large number of Chinese troops but when the matter was left on them to decide, they assured the Defence Minister in affirmative and it was a decision of army unfettered by any political and other considerations as the allegations were hurled by some army officers subsequently after the war. Had the Generals in this meeting decided that any offensive against the Chinese would be counter-productive, the government certainly would not have forced upon them this disaster which was later suffered at the hands of the Chinese army. Even the GOC, B M Kaul was actually bedridden on October 18 and had to be lifted by air from Tezpur for treatment in Delhi. Thereafter, there were false allegations against him that he was under house arrest as he fled from the war front after showing white flag to the Chinese army, which was a malicious rumour floated by some irresponsible elements against this brave and capable officer. Army bosses decided to replace Kaul due to his hospitalization but he was adamant to join at Tezpur after recoupment. Since the Chinese onslaught had already started, the NEFA sector had to be headed by another commander. After much wrangling, he was replaced by Maj. Gen. Harbaksh Singh during this conflict who joined at Tezpur on October 25 when war was in full swing.

China launched all-out attack in NEFA and Ladakh against Indian Army on October 20, 1962. At many places, Indian soldiers put up brave face but they were outnumbered by Chinese in all fields in this brief war which continued until October 28. Indian troops, particularly in NEFA, were too inferior to the Chinese both in numbers and in armaments. As a result of total lack of communication in NEFA, Indian forces suffered more casualties than in Ladakh. Indian Army put up better cohesion, resistance and valiance in Ladakh because it was deployed for quite some time there which made them acclimatize better with weather conditions and coordinated communication. Whereas, army in NEFA was positioned abruptly in unplanned manner with the result the soldiers fought the war without any coordination. In this sector, they had developed a phobia of 'can't be done because their field commanders had recommended withdrawal to safer places rather to put up resistance to the Chinese army. Probably, this was the main reason for the disaster in NEFA for which the junior cadre could not be blamed rather the seniors should bear the brunt. Moreover, the terrain of NEFA was far more difficult than Ladakh. Numerically, the Chinese were greater in their strength both in Ladakh and NEFA. In spite of all these odds, Indian soldiers heroically put up brave face and relentlessly made the Chinese feel the heat of battle although they were virtual winners due to their superiority in numbers and armaments. Up to October 28, the Chinese occupied that area which they were claiming as their territory both in NEFA and Ladakh. Tawang the strategic city in NEFA was also captured by Chinese. There was muffled criticism from the junior army men that they were let down by senior officers who claimed they were unprepared as they were expecting to be withdrawn from the forward areas. Although, Indian troops initially defended well but large presence of Chinese troops demoralized their cadre and they had no option but to retrieve. Heavy casualties were also inflicted on the Chinese too in this short war. In fact, in NEFA particularly the conditions were such that the senior army officers were reluctant to fight because they were infected with the spirit of pre-empted defeat which demoralized the junior cadre. Slogans of 'Hindi-Chini Bhai-Bhai' and go back from our territory propagated by Chinese made an adverse impact on their combating spirit because they were few yards away from them and were unable to retaliate to stop them. In these circumstances, it was not at all surprising that such a debacle was bound to happen. There were some individual gallantries in this war in the best tradition of the Indian Army but most of the Brigade was either annihilated or disappeared to save their lives.

After this debacle, Defence Minister Krishna Menon resigned on October 28 and Y B Chavan was given this portfolio. This resignation gave fuel to the fire that this defeat was due to the political interference in army affairs which was far from any truth. There was severe criticism of the government from all quarters for this debacle. Wild allegations were heaped that when government was aware of the paucity of essential arms and armaments for the war why the army was deliberately pushed in this holocaust in which thousands of soldiers were killed and morale of Indian Army was brought to its lowest ebb.

Nehru was extremely a distraught person because he was propagating policy of peace not only in his neighbourhood but was also trying to internationalize it through the non-alignment movement. His greatest shock was reflected in his speech on October 25 in the Parliament when he said "We were getting out of touch with reality in the modern world and were living in an artificial atmosphere of our own creation," implying that his peace policy was unsuited to China He further outlined his agony when he wrote a detailed letter on October 26 to the heads of friendly countries explaining the various parleys that took place with the Chinese Government prior to this war and the circumstances which were manoeuvred by China to launch this unjustified war and illegally occupied the Indian territory of more than 12,000 sq miles. Nehru called upon these heads of countries to pressurize China to retrieve to the position of September 1962. He also emphasized that this crisis was not only of India but whole of the world and would have far-reaching consequences on the standards of international behaviour and on the peace of the world. He also wrote to the Chinese Prime Minister on October 27 wherein he blamed him for the invasion which would result in further deterioration of relationship between India and China. In response to this letter to the head of states, the USA, Great Britain. Canada, Australia, New Zealand and other Afro-Asian countries not only sympathized with India but gave all sorts of equipment which were not available in India. America and Britain sent arms and ammunitions immediately thereafter which were sent to Leh and Tezpur with the help of American planes. Although, Russia did not send any military help to India but it stopped oil supplies to China and strongly criticized this conflict. Thus, China was made to realize in this gesture of foreign aid that in future India would not be alone in a long war. Since China was determined over its claim of territory in NEFA and Ladakh, it probably devised a short span war fearing American reprisal

After the October 1962 incidents, the moral of the Chinese forces were too high and additional reinforcements were ushered in NEFA. New roads were constructed at a fast pace for movement of big vehicles. Indian Army on the direction of Nehru retrieved at safe places and started making preparation to thwart the Chinese aggression in the days to come. Army Chief asked 13 Director to post IB staff in NEFA at the Headquarterss of each battalion and other places of army for better coordination. At some places, it proved of little consequence as the army officers did not like the guidance of civil operatives of IB but in some areas this move was quite productive. Prime Minister asked IB to give details of disposition of Chinese army on the border and in Tibet I reported the deployment of 14 Divisions for this war on the border along with reserve force in Tibet. Chinese army was increased to four Divisions in NEFA, two in Ladakh and one each in Sikkim and other border areas with a reserve of six Divisions in Tibet. While India had a Division in Ladakh two Divisions in Sikkim-Darjeeling and two in NEFA. Thus, Indian Army was fully outnumbered by Chinese at each place on border areas. In order to reinforce the army positions in NEFA, some formations from Punjab, Nagaland, Central and South India were moved to the borders. It was an arduous task which army officers carried with much alacrity and swiftness This reinforcement to some extent raised the strength of the units to counter the Chinese advances. These formations could have been better equipped if men and material would have reached there in time for which another seven days' time was required. But, alas this could not be done and the Chinese attacked prior to it. In Ladakh, the Indian Army formations were better placed than NEFA due to better terrain.

All-out Attack

The Chinese army finally attacked Indian forces at all places in NEFA on November 14, 1962 and in the next six days, one by one all defence positions of Indian army were overrun. Indian soldiers bravely fought with old .303 rifles and the Brens while Chinese were attacking with semi-automatic rifles. Indians fought hard and inflicted severe casualties to Chinese before succumbing to the presence of large number of Chinese soldiers comparatively. In Ladakh, the situation was not so easy for the Chinese where they wanted to capture Chushul which was strongly defended by a Company at Rezang La. In a fierce fighting on 17th November, 112 Ahir (Yadavs) soldiers lost their lives and succeeded in defending Chushul from the Chinese attack Their sacrifice is celebrated every year in Rewari, Haryana, as Shaheed Diwas on 18th November because they were natives of this region. Chinese casualties were much more in number in this face to face physical fight with these soldiers. Thereafter, Chinese did not dare to come down from their positions on the hill near to Chushul. The heroics of Indian soldiers at other places went unheard as most of them perished in the far flung areas and there was no one left to narrate the incidents. During this war, Indian positions were static whereas the Chinese displayed tremendous mobility in the difficult terrain which proved fatal for the Indian soldiers. They attacked all Indian positions from almost all directions and even did not allow to retreat. In these circumstances, the plight of Indian soldiers could be assessed while analyzing the strategy of both the countries in this war. In the utter confusion prevailed during this period, the Army evacuated from Tezpur leaving the civil population at the mercy of the Chinese. Indira Gandhi was there and she decided to be with the local population to boost their morale. There was nohint of ceasefire by Chinese while she was in Tezpur.

Ceasefire and Columbo Summit

Peking Radio announced unilateral ceasefire in the early hours of November 21, 1962 and announced that their forces would start withdrawal from December 1 to positions 20 kilometres behind the line of actual control which isted between China and India on November 7, 1959 implying that whole of NEFA and Ladakh would be evacuated and held positions north of McMahon Line. Both the governments would appoint officials to discuss matters relating to the 20 kms. withdrawal of the armed forces to form a demilitarized zone and the establishment of check-posts by each party on its side of the line of actual control as well as the return of the captured personnel. It was further declared that after the accomplishments of these assignments, Prime Ministers of both the countries could meet for discussion either in China or India. In a rare gesture, the Chinese offered that even if these proposals were unacceptable to India, China would unilaterally adhered to these measures.

Nehru did not accept these proposals after the ceasefire. He demanded withdrawal of the Chinese beyond the position of September 8, 1962 before holding any discussion on any of the suggestions made by China. Politically, every analyst was unmindful of the fact to justify the very purpose of this war wherein China was a victor but could not sustain its position and withdrew in a unilateral manner and left India aghast. Nehru rightly admitted after this war that psychologically China wanted to show to other countries that although India might be very big on the map yet it was no match to China and this humiliation of India was a warning to other neighbouring countries.

This unilateral ceasefire was not abruptly declared by China out of sheer mercy on India but out of a hidden fear that if this path was not immediately chosen then there was every likelihood in the coming days that countries like America, Great Britain and Australia etc., would increase their military support to India. Chinese apprehended the danger of deployment of American Air Force in India not only to attack from there but also from Taiwan and Okinawa and other Air Force bases from Pacific Ocean. Chinese were aware that in such an eventuality it would not be in a position to defend its military establishments and even their political status would be placed in a precarious situation in the presence of a hostile Taiwan. Therefore, a prolonged war could be of serious consequences to China. Hence, China wisely desisted from indulging in a long war with India and decided to pull out unilaterally in its own interest rather for any mercy upon India. At the same time, Chinese thought they would be able to dictate their terms and conditions on the negotiation table with India thereinafter as a result of this unilateral ceasefire. But Nehru was more defiant after this debacle and did not succumb to Chinese pressure for any negotiated settlement.

On December 10, 1962, at the initiative of Ceylonese Prime Minister Bandaranaike, representatives of six countries, i.e. Ceylon, Burma, Car Indonesia, UAR and Ghana met in Colombo and devised a peaceful on the ensuing Indo-China conflict which was termed as Colombo Proposals. In addition to proposing solution to each and every border conflict, the mai essence of this initiative was to maintain status quo by both the countri hereinafter. By April 1963 about 3,000 Indian soldiers were released by China.

In a nutshell, China was able to give a severe blow on the military pow and prestige of India which had been considered powerful till then in the Asian and African countries. Although it suffered a serious jolt but India was able to withhold all territories which were under its occupation prior to September 1962 except in North-East Ladakh which was occupied by the Chinese prior to the hostilities and lost only 2,500 sq. miles territory there. In real sense, while facing difficult terrain, the net material loss in territory was little but the humiliation suffered in this short war was unimaginable and unforgettable.

Intelligence Assessment

Government of India on the recommendation of the North and North-East Border Committee headed by Maj.-Gen Himmat Singhji, assigned the responsibility of military intelligence to Intelligence Bureau. In the dictionary of intelligence planning, military intelligence, comprises two different aspects i.e. strategic intelligence and operational intelligence. Strategic intelligence usually includes to assess the potential strength of the enemy, its preparations, communications, total strength, built-up, fortifications, armaments, morale, supplies and even political compulsions implying thereto as to what could be potential threat from the enemy country in case of aggression. It is usually further divided into collection and evaluation, collation and interpretation, assessment and dissemination. In the second aspect of military intelligence i.e. operational intelligence, when two countries are face to face for a war on the borders, the civil intelligence has no practical role to play since its presence is negligible because army has to deal with all its surroundings where enemy is at the front. Hence in that situation army has to collect intelligence through patrol, observers, air reconnaissance, interrogation of prisoners, and taking note of sounds, signs of movements, lights, smokes etc. This can be done by military units in forward area during the course of a war. This is the division of responsibility in all the intelligence agencies of the World about the military intelligence. Hence, in the war with China, Intelligence Bureau was responsible for strategic intelligence prior to the start of the conflict and it was the responsibility of the military to collect operational intelligence after the attack was launched by the Chinese on Indian military positions in NEFA and Ladakh. Regarding strategic intelligence, facts and circumstances in the following paragarphs would prove that IB provided all relevant information, deployment, strength and threat perception to the Government prior to the arms aggression.

In December, 1959, the IB sent a note to the Government pointing out that in NEFA there were ten sizeable gaps with an estimated area of 5,500 sq. miles remained unoccupied by Indian forces because these were thinly habitated and terrain was difficult. Positions of Chinese posts adjacent to our posts were indicated wherefrom Chinese could threaten vacant areas. Chinese propaganda in Tibet that liberation of NEFA was on the card was also informed to the Government. Four Divisions of Assam Rifles with Headquarters at Tezpur were stationed at Tawang, Dirang and Bomdila by the IB. In Ladakh, on this assessment, many army units were established in the Eastern region within couple of miles away of Chinese posts to block their intrusion. Obviously, Chinese violently protested to the opening of these posts and ordered re-patrolling in Ladakh. India rejected these protests and claimed that these were opened in Indian territory and the fact of the matter was that China had trespassed nearly 100 miles in Indian territory. IB again in May, 1962 informed Government that China had positioned nearly seven Divisions of army all along the border. Disposition chart of these positioning was also given to the Government. Another four to five Divisions of army units stationed as reserve was also informed by the IB. All other gaps inside our territory were also pin-pointed to the Government. On the basis of this review of IB, Defence Minister ordered the Army Headquarters to fill all these gaps by the army and in case any need help of police and Assam Rifles be taken. Prime Minister too reviewed the position along with Defence Minister and Chief of Army Staff and took strong exception to the delay in filling in these gaps. IB too opened some new checkposts to guard the border from its own point of view. Exchange of protest notes became order of the day between two countries thereafter accusing violation, aggression and occupation of each other's territory. There were some skirmish and violent activities also which were termed as localized.

Around this time, IB got two pieces of reliable information that Chinese Consulate in Calcutta was secretly propagating amongst the fellow travelers and other sympathizers that due to the adamant attitude of India, Chinese Government was going to adopt a new line of action towards India. The Consulate reportedly told that it was forewarning their friends in India as she had occupied certain posts within Chinese territory and China intended military action to remove these intrusions, so that they might not feel embarrassed in the wake of military action by China. It was further alleged that due to the provocative action of India, China had no other option except to act militarily to recapture its territory, which was wild and treacherous. Chinese press too solicited the support of Indian Communists in such eventuality. This authentic and sensitive report was personally passed on by the IB Director to the Prime Minister, the Home Minister and the Defence Minister. He apprehended that China was planning action soon thereafter next autumn. IB thereafter reported the movement of two Divisions of troops by China on borders. Indian Defence Minister Krishna Menon met his Chinese counterpart Chen Yi in Laos in June, 1962 and made last minute effort to avoid conflict without any result. Second information passed by IB to Government was that Pakistan's President Ayub Khan was prepared to attack India from west in case China attacked India from North and East. Thereafter, instead of disturbing the army units along Pakistan border, army units from South and Central India were deployed on Chinese border to counter the imminent danger.

In June-July, 1962, IB noticed movement of senior Army officers of China on the borders which was apprehended as future planning and tactics in case of war. Movement of some new troops were also noticed in Ladakh. These ominous signs confirmed that confrontation with China was round the corner. So again in IB, the situation was reviewed on August 31, 1962. IB reported to the Government that Chinese had opened thirty new posts in Ladakh and several new roads had been constructed. It was also reported that along NEFA border too Chinese were consolidating and strengthening their position in Tibet. Some NEFA Tribal were engaged by them to work as guide in case of war with India.

Immediately after apprehending the conflict, soon when weather conditions improves in September all along NEFA, IB again reviewed the border situation on September 7, 1962 and informed deployment of eight Division of Chinese troops and pointed out dispositions at every point from Ladakh to NEFA including Sikkim, Bhutan and Nepal. This estimate related to only deployment on border for offensive where as reserve force of three to four Divisions were kept elsewhere in Tibet which too could move to borders within two to seven days. Hence, total estimate strength with reserve force deployment along with dispositions were duly informed to the Government by IB in September, 1962. These details are sufficient to prove that strategic intelligence was up to mark and Government was informed immediately as and when IB got these from their sources after duly assessing its potentiality for security considerations. With regard to the Chinese Air strength, IB informed the Government that the Chinese were in possession of large number of Mig-17 and Mig-19 which are capable to attack even up to Madras without any hindrance. So, Air Force operations should not be enforced and restricted to only supply and transport only. IB Director himself gave a comprehensive assessment of the Chinese strength with tables and maps of dispositions on September 17 in the presence of Defence Minister Krishna Menon.

After the debacle of October-November, 1962, an Enquiry Committee of two officers Lt.Gen. Henderson Brooke and Maj.-Gen. P S Bhagat was appointed to investigate the causes of defeat of Indian Army in this short war with China. This Committee investigated basically the discrepancies in the army relating to training, equipments, system of command, physical fitness of the troops, capacity of the Commanders, staff-work procedure, higher direction of operations and Military Intelligence. All these findings of the Enquiry Committee were elaborated in detail by the then Defence Minister Y B Chavan in Parliament on September 2, 1963. Regarding Military Intelligence, he revealed that the Committee found that generally the collection of intelligence was not satisfactory and the acquisition of intelligence was slow and its reporting vague. Evaluation of intelligence reports was not accurate and assessment of the build-up of Chinese army was not made available. There was lack of co-ordination of new build-up of the Chinese army with the old deployment. There was no guidance with regard to the field formations due to this negligence. Dissemination of intelligence was slow and much faster methods to be enforced to send processed and significant information to field formations. The Defence Minister assured that the Military Intelligence had to be completely overhauled and he would personally look into it for improvement.

In so far as accountability of IB was concerned, it was not in the charter of this Committee headed by Henderson Brooke and Bhagat. This Committee never sought any documents or information from the Director of Intelligence Bureau to assess the role of intelligence in this war. So, there was no findings with regard to civil intelligence reports during this war by this Committee. However, the then Home Minister Lal Bahadur Shastri while replying to debate in the Parliament claimed that our intelligence though might not be perfect but in this war and prior to that had on the whole worked and functioned well. He further informed the House that he himself had seen the charts, assessments, facts, figure and details of Intelligence Bureau and he was quite satisfied with the findings. However, efforts would be made to reorganize it to the extent it required. Even the Prime Minister Jawahar Lal Nehru admitted in the Parliament on December, 10, 1962, that on the whole Indian intelligence had been first class. He rather admitted that in comparison to the revenue spending on intelligence of developed countries, Indian Government was spending far lesser amount. In comparison to expenditure, our resources were dismal but the intelligence out-put was far good. Hence, Government of India gave a clean chit to IB with regard to their inputs in India-China war of 1962 and the unfounded misgivings and allegations of its failure are far from any truth and the present generation of India should be made aware of it.

Author of this book had long discussions in this context with R N Kao, founder of Research and Analysis Wing (RAW) and K Sankaran Nair, his deputy. Both these legendary intelligence officers were of the opinion that overall intelligence with regard to the strength, armaments and potential threat was conveyed to the Army Headquarters. Army generals had morally lost the war before it actually started off with the Chinese army as reported by IB. There was complete lack of coordination to disseminate intelligence inputs in forward areas of Army operations. According to B N Mullik, when Lord Mountbatten, the then Head of the Joint of Staff in Great Britain visited India in May, 1963, he met him and showed him the intelligence report which IB had sent to the Government and Army in June, 1962 predicting Chinese Military action in coming autumn.

Lord Mountbatten, after going through the details, was of the opinion that this single reports was sufficient to prove that IB had informed the Government at right time of the impending danger and if he would have been the Chief of Staff, he would have moved troops forward to thwart the enemy. K.Sankaran Nair, the number two in RAW since its inception had also admitted that although B N Mullik was tremendous hard worker, committed and admired by Nehru but he had tendency to doctor reports. In that sense, there was every likelihood that some intelligence reports during 1962 war could be doctored by Mullik because he was autocratic to the extent that his orders had to be carried out at any cost. Thus, there was every possibility of exaggeration of the ground realities about the displacement of Chinese army on borders which Mullik had claimed in his assertion about the truth of IB reports in 1962 war. Overall, IB was in fact extremely heroic in its attempt under his leadership. It was because of Mullik's brave efforts that IB could open its posts at various locations along the border in extremely adverse conditions where no road connections were available, leave aside the routine daily-used requirements. A brave IB officer, Karam Singh, DCIO, put up unbelievable efforts to mount patrols in difficult terrains, made new maps of the areas of Indian territory, carved out large territory under his occupation and opened IB posts at such places which were never accessed by the Indian Army. This debacle of 1962 had nothing to do with any incompetence of IB but the entire blame had to be accepted by the Army Generals in right spirits because their mindset was against any war with China for which they had made comprehensive comparisons with their own army. This was a pessimistic approach because the war had to be fought at every cost without reaching any conclusion but they always apprehended defeat at the hand of strong Chinese army, which is inexcusable and IB should not be blamed for that self-inflicted fiasco. Mullik deserved full commendation for his valiant efforts to take IB to high spirits from its embryonic stage which was praised not only by his contemporaries but also by a renowned General of the stature of Lord Mountbatten.

❑

Pakistan War – 1965

Both India and Pakistan are schizophrenic towards the perennial Kashmir issue. This syndrome was further compounded with army coup in Pakistan under the leadership of General Ayub Khan in 1958. War monger, Ayub Khan was a self-proclaimed Field Marshal of Pakistan army. He was extremely jingoist, egoist and a power-groggy army officer who wanted to test fire his army and air strength against India in 1965 war. He was power-groggy in the sense that when he tried to infuse senseless fury in his army by inciting that they would have their breakfast at Amritsar, lunch at Ambala and dinner at Red fort in Delhi. His myth of jingoism about India was based on a slogan in Pakistan after the partition that "We have got Pakistan with a laugh and we will grab Hindustan with arms". Further Ayub's ego that "Hindu morale would not stand more than a couple of hard blows at the right time and place" backfired on him when an Indian Muslim soldier, Havaldar Abdul Hamid single-handedly made cremation ground of the lethal Patton tanks of Pakistan army on Bhikhwind road in the Khem Karan sector for which he was decorated with the highest gallantry award of Indian army, the Param Vir Chakra. So not only Hindus but Muslims of India also played a very significant role in 1965 war against the army of Ayub. He was also proved brainless by his own critics in Pakistan after this war who blamed Ayub Khan for raising high expectations among the people of Pakistan about the superiority of its armed forces which could not attain his aims and objectives in Hindu India and subsequently created a political liability for himself in Pakistan. Even the then Commander-in-Chief of PAF during the war, Nur Khan criticized Ayub Khan for starting war with unimaginative preparations. His stooge Z A Bhutto convinced Ayub that the Indian response to incursions in Jammu and Kashmir would not be across the international boundary and should be confined to Kashmir only which was militarily untenable and unwise instigation. Even the ISI and Military

Intelligence of Pakistan disagreed with Bhutto's assessment but were ignored by Ayub in jingoism.

Ayub himself was facing a rough weather in Pakistan during 1965. In 1964 elections, Fatima Jinnah, daughter of founder of Pakistan, M A Jinnah, contested election against Ayub Khan from Karachi. Although, Fatima had remote chances to win against Ayub but her presence frightened him and he ruthlessly rigged the elections fearing defeat from her. In the aftermath, two of his sons opened fire on demonstrators in Karachi killing thirty odd people and wounding more in frenzy to retaliate brutally. There were grave charges of corruption and nepotism against Ayub Khan around this period. In 1965, his another son kidnapped the daughter of the IG Police of West Pakistan, Anwar Ali. When Ayub Khan prevented his loyal minister, the Nawab of Kalabagh, from taking any action against his son in this kidnapping, he resigned in protest inciting undercurrent against him in his cabinet. Ayub had lost a lot of political grounds as a consequence of all these events. Ayub wanted to redeem his stature by portraying as the liberator of Kashmir and thus diverting the ongoing public outcry against his regime. He was ill-advised by his cronies that there was no doubt that in the course of a war with India, Pakistani people would stand united behind him and the prevalent political situation would take a U-turn for his long survival as dictator of Pakistan. A myth was generated among the forces that one Pakistani soldier was equivalent to three Indians in war. His gumption on the ground realities had overridden his military attuned head which ultimately lead to his own humiliation and abject failure in 1965 war.

Rann of Kutch Conflict

In this pursuit, Ayub Khan ventured into a skirmishes escalation of military conflicts in the Rann of Kutch in Gujarat in April, 1965. Pakistan was mysteriously given entry into SEATO and CENTO by western powers which authorized acquisition of large quantities of arms and ammunition from US and other countries under the Military Assistance Programme not to be used against India in any sort of conflict. These large scale modern military aid to Pakistan made Ayub to weirdly comprehend that India had not strengthened and modernized its army after humiliation by the Chinese in 1962 war and Pakistan should take advantage of that situation. At the same time, he devised a war scheme to test the water two-fold by deploying the US acquired tanks in Rann of Kutch. First, he deliberately focused in Rann of Kutch for an armoured conflict with the US arms and ammunition in clear violation of Pakistan's commitment to gauge US reaction which ultimately proved disastrous for Pakistan because US stopped all future military aid for violation of commitment by Pakistan. Secondly, Ayub thought that India would be enticed in this region for a limited war away from Kashmir where he had planned large scale intrusions later in that year.

In Rann of Kutch, the boundary dispute originated from the British days when Sindh province laid claim on certain areas inside Kutch region. After partition, Kutch acceded to India and Pakistan laid a claim of more than 3,500 sq. miles in this area. The disputed territory extending out from the old fort of Kanjarkot lies on the northern edge of the Rann of Kutch, a desolate area on the Arabian Sea. It is alternately salt flats and tidal basin. This area was admitted by India and Pakistan as disputed in their border negotiations of 1960. At that time, both sides agreed that validity of conflicting claims would be further examined pending which neither side would disturb the status quo.

Indian intelligence reported in January, 1965 that Pakistan forces were patrolling inside the Indian claimed territory and some posts were also established there. India, thus, accused Pakistan of violating the status quo by aggression. Soon thereafter, India moved large scale forces after this violation and established some posts in this area and built an airstrip near the border which brought the latent crisis head on. There were skirmishes armed conflicts between the forces of both sides which ended after Pakistan unilaterally declared ceasefire. On the intervention of British Prime Minister, both sides signed an agreement on June 30, 1960 at Karachi and later at New Delhi and this dispute was referred to a tribunal under the aegis of United Nations. However, USA stopped military aid to both Pakistan and India after this limited confrontation.

This short-term conflict was a prelude to the ill-devised sinister designs of Ayub Khan on Jammu and Kashmir which was created a disputed territory by Pakistan through distorted facts and fictions. The Rann of Kutch incident was assumed a victory by the Pak military leaders who turned their attention to ignite the Jammu and Kashmir dispute thereafter to alive it under the international fora so that a worldwide opinion could be mustered that Pakistan was the logical clamant of this region. Z A Bhutto, the then Pakistani Foreign Minister, declared in the Pakistan assembly that Pakistan would never be complete without the people of Jammu and Kashmir.

Salient features of 1965 war

Operation Gibraltar

After the stalemate and loss of some forward posts in the skirmishes of Rann of Kutch, general public of India was in a retaliatory mood and exerted enormous pressure to see redressal of this Pakistan sponsored dispute elsewhere. On the other hand, Pakistan had been preparing for a clandestine war against India since long by imparting training of guerilla warfare to Razakars and Mujahids in the Pakistan Occupied Kashmir(POK) to launch aggression in Jammu and Kashmir through their massive infiltration. Razakars force was a organization in POK created by army around August, 1962 wherein all eligible youths were forcibly recruited for guerilla training. Mujahids force was organized much later to work as porters with the Razakars. Pakistan army had planned to infiltrate these guerillas along with the main army soldiers in disguise and create disruption and sabotage in Jammu and Kashmir and incite the local population to revolt against the Indian government. After this initial thrust of infiltrators, regular army was to be put in action to capture the state of Jammu and Kashmir.

This task was planned meticulously by the army under the overall direction of dictator Ayub Khan who himself addressed the sector commanders and force commanders of these guerilla outfits at Murree in July, 1965. He emphasized the importance of this mission which was the last chance to liberate Kashmir. Subsequently, this guerilla infiltration was code-named as "Operation Gibraltar" and its constituents were named as Gibraltar force.

Gibraltar word was specifically used to boost the morale of this force because most of the Muslims were aware that a Muslim General Tariq Ziyad led a Islamic conquest in the Seventh century in Spain which gathered at the famous hill Gibraltar and captured the surrounding areas. So, Pakistan Generals had planned this operation in Kashmir on the pattern when Spain was defeated by the army of Tariq and took control of the local population.

Under this operation, a task force of more than 30,000 infiltrators was divided into ten divisions under an army major and comprising usually one Captain, three Junior Commissioned Officers, around six Non Commissioned Officers, 35 army personals from army, 3 or 4 Ranks from the Special Service Group and about 70 Razakars and Mujahids making a unit of about 120 guerillas. Each of these infiltrators were given large scale arms and ammunitions and civilian dress of green and Mazari shirts and Salwars along with jungle boots to portray as civilians. Command and Control of the operations were exercised by the Hq. Gibraltar Force in POK under Major General Akhtar Hussain Malik.

The plan of infiltration was conceptualized brilliantly by the Pakistani Generals. The infiltrators were asked to sneak inside the 750 kms long ceasefire line and the international border on August 5, 1965 from various points and mingle with thousands of people of Kashmir who were to congregate to celebrate the festival of Pir Dastagir Sahib on August 8, 1965. Next day, coincided with the anniversary of the first arrest of Sheikh Abdulla and the Action Committee of his party had organized procession and demonstration in Srinagar. It was planned that the Gibraltar Force raiders would sneak into this procession, stage an armed revolt and subsequently capture the Radio Station, Airfield and other vantage installations. Meanwhile, the other infiltrators would disrupt Srinagar-Jammu and Srinagar-Kargil roads to isolate Srinagar from rest of the valley. It was further planned that after this success, a "Revolutionary Council" would be constituted which would put forward a claim of lawful government and broadcast an appeal for recognition from all countries in general and Pakistan in particular. This would be a signal for the regular Pakistan army to launch further action in the valley to capture Kashmir by force.

In this pursuit, around 1500 infiltrators crossed surreptitiously inside Jammu and Kashmir on August 5 and concentrated at selected points to organize into larger groups. Some of these elements entered Srinagar in the vicinity of cantonment, the military deports, the radio station and the government secretariat. These infiltrators could not achieve any worthwhile success and in sheer disgust sniped the police lines. They failed to garner any local support and in retaliation resorted to arson and set afire about 300 houses of the congested Batamallu locality. This enraged the local population which chased these raiders and handed over many of them to the Indian security forces.

Elsewhere in the valley, situation was very alarming. However, on August 5, a Shepherd first reported the infiltration in Gulmarg area. The army immediately started its moping action and in the ensuing fight, the infiltrators ran away into forests leaving behind large scale arms and ammunitions. Subsequently, in a daring action, the army captured two Pakistani Captains near Srinagar. These officers were the first to spill beans about the elaborate details of whole operation. Meanwhile, Pakistan, through radio and press started a smear campaign against India citing the action of their infiltrators as the insurrection of the local population against India denying any sort of their involvement in this crisis. However, while whole of Jammu and Kashmir was deeply engaged in guerilla warfare by these infiltrators, they did not achieve any substantial success to capture any area. Neither they could manage to incite any public reaction against Indian government.

Indian army decided that this large scale infiltration by the Gibraltar Force of Pakistan could be neutralized by eliminating them. In this planning, army resorted to counter-offensive and crossed the cease-fire line to plug their entry points and destroy their sanctuaries inside the POK. Indian Parliament, in unanimity, demanded strong retaliation against Pakistan and leaders demanded army action inside Pakistan to dismantle the bases of infiltrators. Army reacted very swiftly after this Parliament decision. Three vital Pakistani posts were recaptured on the Kargil heights neutralizing the danger of cutting off the road between Srinagar and Leh. Subsequently, in Tithwal, several Pakistani posts were captured by the Indian forces giving a severe blow to the Pakistani plans of this operation. One of the most brilliant achievements of the army was capture of vital Haji Pir Pass which was beyond the imagination of the Pakistani Generals. Haji Pir, 8 kms inside Pakistan, a vital communication line which the infiltrators passed through was considered a lifeline for the saboteurs in Uri-Punch area. So, main entry position of the infiltrators was under the command of Indian army. The battle of Haji Pir was a very prestigious operation which was well planned and skillfully executed by the Commanders as well as the high morale of the soldiers ensured its success. Soon, in the moping operations, army totally wiped out the infiltrators from the Uri and Punch areas giving a fitting reply to the perpetrators of this crisis. On September 10, the Indian army sealed the Haji Pir sector and all enemy resistance ceased thereafter in this part of the valley.

Although, the Gibraltar Force partly succeeded in engaging the Indian army in the valley for quite some time which was a matter of grave concern but by and large they did not succeed to achieve any substantial success in Kashmir. Possibly, the Pakistani military junta misjudged the political situation of Jammu and Kashmir. They expected revolt from the Kiashmiri Muslims which did not erupt. The infiltrators did not get any support and sympathy from the local population except from some area near the ceasefire line. People of Kashmir defied the communal propaganda launched by the infiltrators and by the "Azad Kashmir" radio of Pakistan. Anti-Indian campaign by Pakistan had little impact on the Kashmiris and even the pro-Pakistani hardliners adopted a middle path and did not support the infiltrators. Even Pakistanis later on admitted that no Kashmiri leader was taken into confidence to preserve the secrecy of Operation Gibraltar fearing its disclosures to the Indian authorities by them. Even then, they wanted the Kashmiris to liberate even if they did not want it.

The guerilla force of Razakars and Mujahids were lacking determination in this warfare since they were forcibly engaged in this operation. Many of them deserted midway and run to their native places. Indian army sealed their entry points and most of them surrendered before them. Pakistani General had overestimated the capacity of the guerillas and underestimated the force and might of the Indian army. Guerilla operations can achieve success mainly with the local support which the Pakistanis could not muster in Kashmir. Moreover, they lacked motivation and grit due to forcible induction of unwilling cadres from the POK youths. However, the Pakistani guerillas achieved at least one indirect success. They got engaged about 4 Indian Divisions in Jammu and Kashmir in mopping up the infiltrators during the whole of September, 1965. Had these Indian Divisions been made available to fight the Pakistanis in the Punjab area, the fate of Pakistani army would have been really more destructive. In a nutshell, Operation Gibraltar was totally disastrous for the military authorities of Pakistan and yielded nothing in their long drawn ambitious to alienate the Kashmiri people from India and annex its territory with Pakistan. Ayub Khan and his advisors particularly, Z A Bhutto, were severely criticized after a post mortem of events which was later evaluated by the Pakistani defence strategist. This Operation ultimately thrust India into a full-fledged war with Pakistan in September, 1965 wherein all its calculations boomeranged that India would not cross the International Boundary and wage a war in Punjab and Rajasthan.

Operation Ablaze

It was not widely publicized that in April, 1965, while Pakistan attacked on some Indian posts in Rann of Kutch, Prime Minister Lal Bahadur Shastri had given instructions for military action against Pakistan. He directed General Chaudhuri to choose time and place according to his war preparations to which Chaudhuri had indicated to start offensive operation on May 10, 1965 on International border. Code-name of this retaliatory army offensive on western border in Punjab and elsewhere was chosen as "Operation Ablaze". After this approval of Prime Minister Shastri, the military formations in Punjab were put on "red alert" at Amritsar, Fazilka and Bhikhiwind. On May 6, all Divisions stationed in these areas were ordered to complete the defence preparations, including laying of defensive and tactical minefields. Working drawings of Ichhogil Canal were available with the army Corps Commander. Ichhogil Canal was divided into three parts for final assault by three Divisions of the army to open the Grand Trunk road axis from Wagah to Dograi. It was also emphasized to secure intact the road bridge over the Ichhogil Canal on GT Road, the railway bridge across the canal and the Jallo link bridge. Major General Niranjan Singh, General Office Commanding, undertook several ground and air reconnaissances of the area to take stock of the terrain of the operational area inside Pakistan. Surprisingly, the Corps Commander did not disclose the details of the Ichhogil Canal to his formation commanders and rather instructed them about their roles and to rehearse them accordingly.

However, by the middle of May, it was evident that any offensive against Pakistan would not take place since negotiations for cease-fire in the Rann of Kutch were in progress on the intervention of British Prime Minister. On June 30, 1965, an agreement was signed between India and Pakistan and Rann of Kutch dispute was referred to an arbitration under the UNO. After this agreement, troops of both the countries were withdrawn to the peace zone and further confrontation was timely averted. Thus, "Operation Ablaze" did not kick-start and ended in a damp squib. But while withdrawing from the border, Indian troops and civilians suffered a number of casualties due to explosions when mines were lifted by the army.

Operation Grand Slam of Pakistan

Operation Grand Slam was a contingency support to Operation Gibraltar in Kashmir. Although Pakistan army generals did not concede the disastrous failure of the large scale infiltrations and mounted large scale offensive operation to attack India in Chhamb and Jaurian area of Kashmir. This operation code-named "Operation Grand Slam" was four dimensional i.e. capturing of Chhamb, then crossing of river Tawi and consolidation, capturing of Akhnur and cutting of communication lines to reach Jammu. Had Jammu fallen to the Pakistani forces, the whole of Indian forces stationed inside the valley would have been isolated. Ayub had planned this meticulous operation to dictate his terms on India after Jammu was in his hand. Pakistan was aware that large number of infiltrators were still present in the Valley, on northern front and in Jammu. Indian forces were converging on Haji Pir Pass to forge a link between Punch and Uri. Pak Generals feared that after this link-up, the Indian army could push westward, endangering the capture of whole of POK. So, in order to divert the focus of this apprehension of India, the plan to attack Chhamb and Jaurian sector was conceived by Pakistani Generals. This plan was executed with utmost ferocity by launching a massive offensive with a powerful armoured-cum-infantry force in Chhamb-Jaurian sector on September 1, 1965.

It would be pertinent to mention here that this large scale military preparation in this sector and impending Pak attack was informed to the Indian authorities by the United Nations observers well in advance but it was not given due credence and no efforts were made to take counter offensive measures by army. The Indian army soldiers stationed in this sector were around 1000, mainly armed with light weapons. There were misconceptions even among the top army Generals about the actual strength of armour and soldiers of Pakistan in this region. While addressing top army commanders at Srinagar on August 31, 1965, the Chief of Army Staff had declared that although he was unaware of any offensive action by Pak army in this sector but if at all it started, would not go very far. One of his juniors countered it and said that Pakistan was bound to react to the capture of Haji Pir by Indian forces and would certainly attack some areas in this sector. Thus, Indian disposition in Chhamb-Jaurian sector was under-prepared to counter the offensive of Pak army.

So far, the Indian government had adopted a defensive policy towards Pakistan but after Operation Gibraltar, it was decided to resort to offensive hostilities aimed at both destroying the Pakistani forces and capturing its territory so that India would be in a dominating position to bargain. After due deliberations, any attack by China was ruled out but it was certain that they would help Pakistan in this war. So Indian forces were directed to defend Jammu and Kashmir, Punjab and Rajasthan against Pak army and also to defend Lakakh and Himachal from aggression with China and to launch offensive inside Pakistan. Army was also directed to ensure the security of Srinagar and the Valley, stop infiltration between Akhnur and Punch and to protect the line of communication between Pathankot-Udhampur-Srinagar-Leh. This decision was taken prior to the launch of Operation Grand Slam by Pakistan. However, in case of an aggression by Pakistan, all precautionary preparations were formulated to make offensive inside their territory from various positions in Punjab and Rajasthan.

In Chhamb and Jaurian sector, a new Indian Brigadier had taken over the command after the death of his predecessor in Pak shelling a few days earlier. The new Brigadier, after due diligence, had a plan to deploy the infantry battalions which could not be done due to paucity of required number of troops at his disposal. He further demanded anti-tank mines which never reached him. He sent reports about strong armour concentrations in the area by Pakistan but the Corps Headquarters did not believe him. While the Indian Commanders were discussing the ifs and buts of Pakistani intentions, its army attacked all the Indian posts in Chhamb and Jaurian sector at 0400 hours on September 1,1965 with intense artillery and mortar bombardment. Pakistani attack achieved remarkable success and Chhamb fell within an hour to them. Most of the Indian posts were overrun by the Pak soldiers with heavy armour. Pakistani tanks reached within 450 meters of the Brigade Headquarterss around noon. In this grim situation, the Brigade Commander sent an urgent request for air strikes by the IAF. The IAF sorties came at 1700 hrs. which while striking the Pak tanks also hit Indian gun positions and armour causing considerable damage to their own army soldiers and huge ammunitions. There was complete lack of proper wireless network co-ordination between the Army and Air Force which led to this fiasco. Many posts were abandoned by Indian soldiers fearing reprisal from Pak soldiers.

Pakistan offensive was successful on the basis of alacrity, speed and little reaction from Indian side which could be attributed to the slow decision taking attitude of the then authorities. Having captured Chhamb, Pakistani soldiers crossed Manawar Tawi river but remained inactive thereafter till September 3. However, to the good fortune of India, Pakistani intention to capture Akhnoor did not succeed due to a foolish decision inside the ongoing imbroglio in Pakistani army politics. Suddenly, on September 2, Major General Akhtar Malik who launched this offensive, was replaced by Yahya Khan whom Ayub Khan wanted to decorate with this success. But Indian army claimed that the stubborn resistance put up their soldiers forced Pakistan to delay the advance and decided to move more cautiously. There were allegations in Pakistan media that Yahya Khan lost considerable time to understand the ground situation which enabled the Indian forces to reinforce its army to retaliate and Pakistan's cherish dream to capture Akhnoor was never fulfilled. Subsequently, heavy fighting continued in the see-saw battle at almost every place in this sector where Pakistanis were certainly at vantage position and Indian army suffered heavy losses at some locations.

In the meantime, UNO made concerted efforts to bring ceasefire between India and Pakistan but all these efforts were thwarted by Pakistanis since their forces were in advantageous position in Chhamb-Jaurian sector. The Security Council called for an immediate cease-fire on September 4 which was not accepted by Pakistan who rather carried out air-raid on Amritsar on September 5. Pak army could never reach the Akhnour bridge and their outrageous plan to cut off line of communication of Kashmir from the rest of India remained a far cry. Thus, the four-phased Operation Grand Slam of Pakistan proved a death-knell for Ayub Khan and his forces were forced to run back to save Lahore being captured by the Indian army. However, Pakistanis claimed that this operation, to some extent, did succeed in releasing pressure on the troops which were defending the LOC in Kashmir area.

Attack Across International Border

In order to contain Pakistan in Chhamb sector, Indian forces mounted an all-out offensive towards Lahore, Ferozpur and Sialkot sectors on September 6. Pakistan Generals were taken aback at this attack and within hours most of the amour, artillery and brigade of infantry were withdrawn from Chhamb sector to safeguard other installations in the newly attacked area towards Punjab. In the wee hours on September 6, Indian army crossed International border and attacked Lahore sector in three axis and its formations reached up to Ichhogil Canal in the afternoon which was meant for the defence of Lahore. Pakistani Generals were caught unaware of this sudden attack of Indian army. According to Altaf Gauhar, who wrote biography of Ayub Khan, the "most surprised" man in Pakistan was Field Mashal Ayub Khan when Indian forces reached up to Ichhogil canal. Lahore airport was within the striking distance of Indian army. As a result of this development, the United States requested India for a temporary ceasefire to evacuate its nationals from Lahore. Important town of Dograi near Lahore was captured by Indian troops. Intense fighting continued on the bank of Ichhogil Canal where Indian forces fought valiantly till the cease fire.

However, it would be worthwhile to mention here that General Chaudhry, Indian Army Chief, did not seek IAF help for pre-emptive strike against Pakistan while launching formal war in this region. Had he got initiated air strike on important air fields of PAF, they would not have mounted air attack on Indian air bases which they actually did, causing a lot of destruction and damage to the Indian Air Force. Ultimately, IAF was brought in this war theatre which was a belated and unpardonable mistake.

Pakistani army too retaliated by launching massive armoured attack in Khem Karan area near Amritsar through the ultra modern Patton Tanks acquired from USA. This was an unimaginative action of the Pakistani Commanders without assessing the terrain situation of this area. In a fierce battle, Pak army faced one of the worst disasters in the tank battle after Second World War in Operation "Asal Uttar" (meaning Real Answer) wherein around 100 Patton tanks were destroyed by Indian soldiers. Company Quarter Master Havaldar Abdul Hamid of Indian army single-handedly destroyed seven of these tanks for which he was awarded with the highest gallantry award of Indian army the "Param Vir

Chakra" posthumously. Pakistan armoury was mauled by Indian soldiers and Madhupur canal was breached in Khem Karan sector submerging the movements of Pakistani tanks in large number which were subsequently captured by Indian army. For Pakistan, war was over that day.

This 22-day war continued till September 22 when United Nations Security Council unanimously passed a resolution wherein unconditional ceasefire was declared for both the countries. Since, Pakistani Generals had a strong feeling that if the war was prolonged further, Indian army would certainly inflict heavy losses of human life on Pakistani forces in addition to capturing sizeable Pakistani territory. On the other side, Indian Army was against this ceasefire since their forces were in full command and control and their momentum was gaining strength day by day. However, in democracy usually bitter pills are swallowed despite on strong footings and in this tradition, Indian army had to accept the ceasefire accepting by Indian leadership. Had Pakistan been on this advantageous position, they would have certainly prolonged this ceasefire demand. Indian leaders could not sustain the international pressure and accepted the ceasefire proposed by Security Council. The war ended next day.

In nutshell, it was a war to compare the strength of each by both the armies of Indian and Pakistan wherein India captured 3,885 kms of Pakistan territory and lost 648 kms India lost 3,000 of its soldiers while Pakistan lost 3800. About 200 Pakistani tanks were destroyed in comparison to 128 of India. Indian Air Force which was used belated suffered marginal losses more than Pakistan but it fought valiantly to the modern US Saber Jets of PAF with the old Russian aircrafts.

At the initiative of Soviet Union, both India and Pakistan signed a peace agreement on January 18, 1966 at Tashkent, now capital of Uzbekistan, to resolve their disputes. Indian Prime minister Lal Bahadur Shastri and Pakistan President Ayub Khan issued a joint communiqué which was declared as Tashkent Agreement wherein both the countries decided to resolve border disputes through peaceful negotiation. It was agreed by both the countries to withdraw their army to the pre-6 August, 1965 positions. In this bargain, Pakistan got upper hand. While India got its lost territory in Khem Karan and Chhamb but had to return Tithwal, Kargil and Haji Pir. Loss of Haji Pir and Kargil by India was very significant for Pakistan which was captured by Indian soldiers at a heavy loss of human lives and was strategically very vital for Indian security forces.

Allegation of Intelligence Failure and Factual Details

Intelligence in these conventional war is never fool-proof and as such some Army officers bitterly cried foul that reporting of IB was either inadequate or inaccurate. These allegations were bound to erupt to suppress their own failures when they could not fight this war in proper strategic planning which they did later in 1971 Bangladesh liberation war.

There were numerous instances when even the Army Chief General J.N.Chaudhuri was too cautious to mount offensive inside Pakistan across Internal border in Punjab and Rajasthan. One Indian journalist had pertinently pointed out this war as one of mutual incompetence because both General Chaudhuri and Ayub Khan studied in the same batch at Standhurst Military Academy in Britain. While the offensive against Pakistan was planned during the Rann of Kutch conflict, Gen. Chaudhury visited Amirtsar in the middle of June where he held a conference of Western Command officers. After the conference, he remarked that "All my experience teaches me never to start an operation with the crossing of an opposed water obstacle; as far as I am concerned, I have ruled out Lahore or a crossing at Dera Baba Nanak". Hence, Gen. Chaudhuri had a very defensive approach while launching offensive in Punjab sector without setting any target for the army.

According to Captain Amrinder Singh, former Chief Minister of Punjab, who was ADC to Lt. General Harbaksh Singh, the valiant Sikh GOC of Western Command, army in Khem Karan area got some documents from a slain brigadier of the Pak army which revealed movement of an armoured division from the direction of Khem Karan to cut off the Beas bridge. Soon thereafter the Pak army moved a new division of tanks that were hideden in the Changa-Manga forests. There was widespread panic initially in the units posted to defend that area but they fought with some exemplary courage and repulsed the attack. That night Lt. Gen. Harbaksh Singh was stationed in Ambala when Gen. Chaudhuri called him on phone in the early morning. According to Amrinder Singh, Lt. Gen. Harbaksh Singh was responding in monosyllables initially on phone but suddenly he resolutely countered and told Gen. Chaudhuri "Look Muchhoo, I will not do this. And if you still want it, then send it to me in writing". According to Amrinder Singh, General Harbaksh Singh confirmed to him later that General Chaudhuri wanted the whole of Indian army to withdraw from the entire Amritsar sector to hold a defence line on the Beas river while General Harbaksh Singh was not in favour of that. Decision of Harbaksh Singh proved monumental to change the ground situation next day when Indian forces reinforced their position in the whole of Amritsar sector.

General Chaudhuri had probably recollected two reporting of IB in his mind while conveying the decision to General Harbaksh Singh to withdraw behind Beas river. In June,1965, K Sankaran Nair, Deputy Director Pakistan Operation desk in IB sent a report to the Defence Minister, Y B Chavan that Pakistan had raised a second armoured division without the knowledge of the USA. This report indicated that the army had refused to accept this fact which was sent to them earlier. When the Defence Minister raised this issue with General Chaudhuri, he refuted that IB was exaggerating this report without any credible evidence. General Chaudhuri's lackadaisical attitude towards this IB report became evident when Pakistan sprang the surprise and 1st armoured division at Khem Karan and 6th armoured division at Sialkot were found to assault the Indian positions. Secondly, the Indian Army was surprised by the Pakistan's sudden appearance through various aqueducts under the Ichhogil canal. IB had already informed the army the entire intelligence details about these aqueducts well in advance since plans of the canal, including the aqueducts were obtained by their operatives from the World Bank and provided to the army. So, General Chaudhuri had these two intelligence inputs in his mind wherefrom he concluded that might of armoured division of Pakistan was much more than in size what he had assessed and thus thought of withdrawal beyond Beas river due to his own inborn speculations. It was the valour and skills of the officers and men of the brigade commanded by Brigadier Theograj which repulsed the Pakistani armoured attack under the able leadership of Generals G S Dhillon and Harbaksh Singh who defied General Chaudhuri in this war which brought honour to Indian Army otherwise General Chaudhuri had almost repeated the 1962 debacle.

Even Air Chief Marshal P C Lal indicted General Chaudhuri that he did not keep the IAF informed of his intending operation in the Lahore sector which found them off-guard and incurred avoidable losses of aircraft later on including the newly acquired MIG-21s. General Chaudhuri had his own exaggerated view on the size of aid which USA provided to Pakistan and acquired selt-possessed false assumption about the might of Pak army.

After the war, it was detected that Pakistan had only six weeks of war wastage of ammunition whereas India had some 90 days war wastage reserve. It was also found later that Indian Army had spent only eight to ten percent of the tanks and artillery ammunition. In this background, if the war had been continued for another week, Pakistan would have no option except to surrender before the Indian Army. Ignoring this glaring fact, General Chaudhuri advised the Prime Minister to accept the UN ceasefire proposal since he had wrong information that his army was running out of ammunition which was far from reality.

This fact was further elaborated by the post-war studies of Government of India which concluded that when the Indian Prime Minister enquired from General Chaudhuri whether India could win a spectacular victory if the war was prolonged for some days. The General had stated that most of India's frontline ammunition had been used up and there had been heavy tank losses also. It was later found that by September 22, the day of ceasefire, only about 14% of India's frontline ammunition had been fired and the number of tanks in the possession of India were more than double to that of Pakistan. According to these studies, indeed General Chaudhuri was a cautious General in this war and was perhaps afraid of the presence of much touted ultra modern Patton tanks with Pakistan army. However, General Chaudhuri should be praised for expanding the Indian Army, both qualitatively and quantitatively, after the humiliating defeat of 1962.

Many Army officers raised hue and cry that IB failed to provide proper intelligence about the disposition of Pakistani army starting from the skirmish war in April, 1965 in the Rann of Kutch to the ceasefire of September 22, 1965. The author had detailed discussion in this matter with former Secretary of R&AW, K Sankaran Nair, who was head of Pakistan desk in IB as Deputy Director during the 1965 war. In a tape-recorded interview, Sankaran Nair had revealed that in the beginning of 1965, he sent report to the army that Pakistani army had moved 10 Patton tanks on the border in the Rann of Kutch. Brigadier M M Batra who was head of Military Intelligence refused to accept the veracity of these reports and rejected outright claiming that these tanks could not operate in such sandy conditions in that area. Later on during the war in this area, Pakistan army used these Patton tanks much to the surprise of Field Commanders of Indian Army in the Rann of Kuch. Army authorities refused to accept the reports of IB about the presence of these tanks there leave aside sending any precautionary or advisory report to the Field Commanders in any case apprehending the use of Patton tanks in the conflict.

Sankaran Nair further disclosed that after the 1965 war, a two-men committee of then Home Secretary L P Singh and Defence Secretary P V R Rao was constituted by Indian Government to verify the allegations of Army that IB had not provided adequate intelligence in this war. S P Verma was then Director of IB and B N Mullick, former Director of IB was Director General of Security. Both these officers after a prolonged discussion decided to send Sankaran Nair to appear before this committee to produce all the reports that IB had sent to Army authorities about the various happenings in Pakistan before 1965 war. Sankaran Nair gave proof to this committee that 65 reports were sent to the Happenings Records of army pointing to the preparation of Pakistan for attacking India on the western border. Nair explained that he cited the example of Troginal Canal was spread to Italy as being one of the natural defences that Pakistan would use Ichhogil Canal and then attack our territory. Nair refuted the claim of Army that IB did not have operational plan of Ichhogil Canal which was constructed on the outskirts of Lahore for protection from Indian attack. He reiterated that leave aside the presence of this canal, even each and every dimension including depth and type of aqueducts in the canal were informed to the Army by IB. Nair blamed the Army Generals sitting in New Delhi for not disseminating these reports to the actual fighting formations because the reports were not received by the Commanders on the front. It was for the Army Intelligence where it was to be assessed and whom they had to disseminate which they never did with the result even the front formations did not know the existence of Ichhogil Canal. According to Sankaran Nair General Chaudhuri was a timid fellow who failed to capture Lahore which was within the reach of Indian army.

Since, the findings of this Committee have not been disclosed by the Government of India, Sankaran Nair's version about role of IB in providing adequate intelligence in the 1965 war is a clinching evidence since he was head of operation of Pakistan desk in IB at that time and he gave proof to this Committee of IB reporting on Pakistan. However, there were other circumstantial reasons to give credence to the version of Sankaran Nair.

In this war scenario, India was initially not prepared for counter offensive on the International border except to wipe out infiltrators from Jammu and Kashmir. Certainly there was no intelligence about the Operation Gibraltar with Army or IB with the result no army action was ever planned elsewhere. It was only after Pakistan launched Operation Grand Slam in Chhamb sector when Indian Army decided to attack in Punjab sector to detract Pakistan from the offensives in Chhamb. So, from the Indian side there was neither any strategic planning nor a strategic decision was taken prior to and after Operation Gibraltar in Jammu and Kashmir. Initially, this was a defensive war for India wherein decisions were taken by Western Command officers in general and Lt. General Harbaksh Singh in particular assessing the day to day situation. This brave officer took some bold decisions ignoring the Army Chief Chaudhuri which brought some glory to Indian Army otherwise it was another disaster like 1962 war if Indian Army had been retrieved beyond Beas river.

Indian Field Commanders were never clear about their aims and objectives in this war. These Commanders were unaware whether it was an all-out war, a limited war, a war to conquest enemy's territory or a war of attrition to reduce the striking power of Pakistan. In the absence of any of these objectives, they fought the war bravely as it was made to fight without any other options in their mind. Moreover, there was lack of co-ordination between the Front Commanders when the Divisional and Corps Commanders did not visit the frontline in order to control the situation with the result there was lack of aggressive spirit in some formations resulting in non-exploitation of favourable situations and sometimes collapse of defence. Thus ill-planned strategy and proper planning led to a sort of stalemate in this war.

Noted defence analyst K Subrahmanyam had time and again quoted certain evidences which proved what Sankaran Nair had claimed that IB gave credible reports in advance about Pak preparations for this war which was not disseminated to the Field Commanders by the Director of Military Intelligence of Army Headquarterss Thus, intelligence provided by IB was adequate to certain extent in this war which was not adequately utilized by Indian army top brasses and a false propaganda was launched from certain quarters that intelligence was not enough in this war.

❑

Libration of Bangladesh

Events Leading To Crisis

"Given peaceful conditions and the fullest co-operation from all sections of the people, we shall make this province i.e. East Pakistan, the most prosperous in Pakistan". This is what Jinnah, the founder of Pakistan, predicted immediately after independence. His successors, however, ignored this fact and exploited East Pakistan with iron hands as a colony of slaves which ultimately lead to Pakistan's separation from its western wing. Jinnah farsighted to instill the importance of secular nationality among his people when in one of his pronouncements he told to forget that they were Muslims, Hindus, Christians and Parsis and only think of themselves only as Pakistans. It was obviously a mature political and seasoned thinking because more than 15 million Hindus in the Eastern part were at the back of Bengali Muslims and to insist "We are Muslims first, Pakistans afterwards" would have jeopardized the position of these religious minorities in both the countries. Condition of Bengali Muslims was extremely pathetic prior to partition of 1947 in the sense that there was only one East Bengali Muslim in Indian Civil Service before independence and their incumbency was negligible in engineering, legal, medical and other professions. For most of the Hindus in East Pakistan, the partition was reckoned as a temporary phenomena as was told by Pandit Nehru to Leonard Mosley: "We expected that partition will be temporary and that Pakistan was bound to come back to us". That iw how in this background, the Hindus and Bengali Muslims started their life in East Pakistan after partition of the country.

Genesis of a "United Bengal" was mooted prior to 1947 by some big forces but it was turned down by majority of people of this region. Even H S Suhrawardy, Premier of Bengal during 1946-47 with the support of several

Congress leaders put forward the idea of a sovereign independent and undivided Bengal in a divided India during the time of partition talks in early 1947. So, it was in the mind of Bengali Muslims after the independence that at one time or other they would need a separate homeland for a number of reasons. Amongst which the most important being economic, political, historical, geographical and even biological which bring them no where near to their counterparts in Western part of Pakistan which was dominated by the Punjabi Muslims in all fields.

End of British Raj although cemented the two different cultures of Muslim religion into a country carved out of India which was separated more than 1100 miles by Indian territory between two wings of Pakistan. These two wings had nothing in common except two factors viz., a common religion and the fact that Pakistan achieved the independence by a common struggle; otherwise all other things like language, tradition, culture, dietary habits and calendar practically everything, were different. There was, in fact, nothing common in the two wings of Pakistan that constituted a nation. The people between these two wings speak and think differently. They not only eat and dress in their own distinctive styles but live different lives in entirely different environments. Even their sports were different. Football was the most popular game in East Pakistan which had a little liking in West Pakistan. Whereas in West, hockey and cricket dominated which had no following in trhe East. Both wings rarely had marriages within each other despite the fact the Government encouraged these marriages initially and offered booty of Rs. 500 to each married couple. Politically, both the wings have different ideology as West Pakistan considered it part of the Middle East Asia; because in 1958, the Pakistan Cabinet formally considered a proposal at the behest of President Iskander Mirza for confederation with Afghanistan and Iran to offset the intolerable political weight of the millions of Bengali Muslims. This ludicrous idea died a natural death due to unfavorable response from the leaders and political parties of the two wings of Pakistan. Likewise, the East Bengal was too much involved with its neighbours in South-East Asia, where it found a natural affinity and was never enthused by West Pakistan's international preoccupations.

"We are Muslim first, Pakistan afterwards" was the slogan which was the binding force at the time of partition in 1947 but subsequently after two decades of independence both wings of Pakistan and their entities began to seek separate channels of self-interest particularly when West began to dominate the naturally prosperous and more populous East. For its own survival, East Pakistan began to resist its domination and Islam, the common factor, took the back seat before the economic issues and the conflict of interest began to escalate since partition itself among the citizens of both sides. Although West always tried to unite Bengalis religiously by raising Kashmir issue but they were least concerned over this issue because they never had any family ties with them like the Punjabis and Pathans of West Pakistan. The Bengali leaders of East Pakistan ultimately realized and asserted that compulsions of economic development were too strong to be sidetracked by the slogan of Islamic solidarity and brotherhood because they had seen two decades of economic exploitation and backwardness in the name of Islam and religion bondage. It was a joke in East Pakistan that "you can see wings but not the bird".

First bitter taste of dishonest political domination by the West over East was diagnosed when Prime Minister Liaquat Ali Khan proposed a bicameral legislature at the centre in which East and West Pakistan would have 200 seats each in the lower house and 60 each in the upper house. Argument put forward in the favour of this formula was that the Hindu population of 15 million was a part of 56% population in the East and as such Bengali Muslims would be fewer in numbers in comparison to West if this population was ignored as voting community. This was strongly resisted by the Bengali population of East Pakistan and finally this proporsal was abandoned when Liaquat Ali Khan was assassinated at a public meeting in Rawallpindi under mysterious circumstances which was not adequeately explained by the official inquiry conducted thereafter. Two subsequent Prime Ministers tried to sort out this matter but it was ultimately settled through an agreement on representation on the basis of "Parity"– equal membership for east and west in a unicameral legislature in Pakistan. This formula was incorporated in the 1956 and 1962 constitutions but administratively the Bengali representation was negligible in various senior posts and was discriminated in every service in Pakistan. This would be evident from the following facts published by the Pakistan Government in its annual report of 1966-67

Services	**West Pakistan**	**East Pakistan**
Central Civil Service	84%	16%
Foreign Service	85%	15%
Foreign Heads of Mission	60	9
Army	95%	5%
Rank above Lt. Generals	16	1
Navy Technical	81%	19%
Navy Non Technical	91%	9%
Air Force Pilots	89%	11%
Armed Forces	5,00,000	20,000
Employees in Pakistan Airlines	7,000	280
PIA Directors	9	1
PIA Area Managers	5	None
Director, Railway Board	7	1

Pakistan had a parliamentary form of government from 1947 to 1958 but behind this façade of democracy, it was ruled by a small coterie of Punjabi dominated bureaucratic-military oligarchy which sidelined Bengali representation of East Pakistan in every walk of life, be it politics, bureaucracy, economy etc. These governments were in session for only 338 days during these 11 years and passed 160 laws whereas the Governor-General/President issued 376 major ordinances to rule Pakistan with iron hand. This was obviously resented by the Bengali Muslims of East. Although at later stage, Yahya Khan scrapped the parity formula and introduced popular representation on a numerical basis but by then the Bengali disenchantment in East had become pervasive in the face of economic strangulation and his efforts were overtaken by army's other more destructive action at national level.

Biologically, in West Pakistan nature had fostered energetic, aggressive people, hardy hill men and tribal farmers who have constantly to live in harsh conditions which was worldly apart from the gentle and dignified Bengalis of East Pakistan who were accustomed to the easy abundance of their delta homeland in the east. Even clothing in both the wings was different. In East the Muslim ladies used to wear sari which is usually a Hindu dress whereas in West their counterpart would wear salwar, kamiz and dopatta. In West they would wear ornaments and in East they would wear flowers. Even eating habits in both the wings were totally different. The Western part used meat and dairy products in abundance whereas in East rice, lentil and fish comprised the most popular food. Prohibition was enforced more rigidly in East Pakistan whereas off-licence liquor shops in Islamabad remained open and did brisk business even on Fridays, the Muslim Sabbath. Salacious films and carbaret acts flourished in Karachi and Lahore but were publically hated in Dacca and Chittagong. In Ramzan, fast were rigidly observed by the affluent in the urban areas of East Pakistan then by those in the West wing. Hence, nowhere these two sections of Muslims in Pakistan were anywhere near to any sort of daily habits leave aside the other political, economical and social issues.

Although, in Delhi Convention of Muslim League in 1946, Urdu was accepted as the official language of Pakistan but the intelligentia in East Pakistan and students demanded that Bengali should be made the official language of East Pakistan. This issue became a big law and order problem prior to the visit of Jinnah in March, 1948 to East Pakistan. The then Chief Minister of East Pakistan agreed to the demand of students that Bengali would be official language of East Pakistan and also the medium of instructions at all stages. However, Jinnah rejected this move and declared that "Urdu and Urdu only" would be the State language and the controversy was stalled for the moment. Subsequently, Liaquat Ali Kahn's assertion that Urdu was the language of the Muslim nation further betrayed the religious and language feelings of Bengali Muslims because Arabic, not Urdu, is the language of the Koran who felt that this anti-Muslim or Non-Muslim innuendo implicit in his statement, was directed against them and did not mean to Baluchi, Sindhi, Punjabi or Pashto spoken and taught in other provinces of West Pakistan. This was construed as an insult to their self respect for socio-cultural heritage. Some leaders further added fuel to this fire in this complicated matter. Malik Feroze Khan Noon, the Punjabi Governor of East Bengal in 1952 had remarked during a conversation in a press conference that the Bengalis were half Muslims as they do not halal (kosher) their chickens or meat. This insult heaped by him provoked every Bengali Muslim in East Pakistan. It was severely counterblasted by senior Bengali leader Maulana Bhashani who sarcastically said "Have we to lift our lungis (lion-cloth) to prove we were Muslims?".

This language controversy again exploded in 1952 when the Central government attempted to introduce Urdu script for the Bengali language. In Feb.1952 Khwaja Nazimuddin, The then Prime Minister declared in Dacca that Urdu would be the only State language to which students resorted to strikes in Universities and demonstrations against government continued for many days in whole of East Pakistan. Sheikh Mujibur Rahman got his first experience of jail in this language agitation. On 21st February,1952, four students were shot dead by the police during a demonstration. Law and order broke down in whole of East Pakistan and Army was called to restore peace. Although normalcy was restored with brutality but it left an unending effect on the agitation of language issue for the future. A "Shaheed Minar" was raised in the memory of those four students killed in the agitation, which became an emotional symbol of Bengali nationalism then. Most of the political parties extended full support to this movement which came to an end in 1954 when the Constituent Assembly accepted Bengali as one of the State languages. This boosted the morale of Bengali Muslims who were racially inferior by the rules of Pakistan whereas their level of education and intelligence was much higher in comparison to other constituents of Pakistan in West.

Gradually, the Muslim League was loosing its ground in East Pakistan because the Bengali Muslims were disillusioned considering it a party of West Pakistan and also due to the failure of their erstwhile rulers to ameliorate the economic conditions of their people Moreover, their racial discrimination made them skeptical towards their honest intention for development in all walks of life in East Pakistan. Since their level of education and general intelligence was much more higher than the people of other provinces of Pakistan, they felt discriminated and had to resort to violent means to get their initial barrier crossed in their achievement to get Bengali as State language. Thus, there was a general perception in their mind that they would get their demands fulfilled through these violent means only. The apathetic attitude of Muslim League was so indifferent in East Pakistan that from 1949 to 1954, only one by-election was held in the home district of the Chief Minister, in which a young student defeated the Muslim League candidate comprehensively buy huge margin. This outcome frightened the Provincial Government to such an extent that no by-election was held till 1954 although 34 seats were lying vacant at that time. This further contributed to the prevailing mistrust in Bengali Muslims and caused a great setback to the ruling Muslim League in East Pakistan.

On the economic front, East Pakistan was made to lag far behind comparatively due to partial planning of rulers of West Pakistan. Jute production from East Pakistan contributed towards 60% to 80% of the total foreign exchange earnings of Pakistan. A major portion of this earning was spent for establishing industries in West Pakistan to provide employment to refugees migrated from India after partition. According to rough estimate between 1947-48 and 1959-60, total government sector development outlay amounted to about Rs.2,750 million in East Pakistan and Rs.8,017 million in West Pakistan. In private sector only, less then 20% of developmental outlay took place in East Pakistan during this period. As such, upto 1960, the Central Government paid more attention towards the overall development of West Pakistan in comparison to its Eastern Wing. Other studies conducted on the economic front in relation to the two wings found startling revelations of disparity which could be seen from the following facts and figures:

1. Per capita income in West Pakistan in 1969-70 was 61 percent higher than in East Pakistan and double than what it was ten years ago.
2. Although East Pakistan comprised 54% of the total population but during 1950 - 55 only 20% of development expenditure was spent there in comparison to 80% of West Pakistan. Despite promises of parity, during 1965-70, East Pakistan got only 35% and West got 65%.
3. Prior to 1970, 40% to 50% of export surplus was dumped in East Pakistan for compulsory sale which was intentionally high-priced.
4. To meet the finance deficits of West Pakistan, export surplus of East Pakistan in the last 20 years ending 1968-69 to the tune of Rs.31 billion or 2100 million dollars was utilized at the open market exchange rate which was highly doctored in the economic reports.
5. Contrary to official arguments justifying a slower income growth rate for the East wing, West rulers devised a strange and dubious parameter i.e. East Pakistan had a slower rate of population growth than West Pakistan. East Pakistan's population rose from 41 million in 1949-50 to 53 million in 1959-60 and 69 million in 1969-70 which was 2.9% in the first decade and 3% in the second decade whereas in West Pakistan population increased from 32 million in 1949 - 50 million in 1959-60 and 59 million in 1969-70 which was an increase of 4% in the first decade and 3.1 in the second.

This disparity resulted in total collapse of economic condition of this region, where unemployment and poverty became rampant due to increased population and lack of resources for employment. Hence, a wrong message had gone in the mind of the Bengali Muslims that West Pakistan was exploiting the economy of their region and treating it as their colony because 22 families of West Pakistan were monopolizing the big business houses which were controlling 90% economy of Pakistan. They did major business in East Pakistan controlling factories, tea gardens, jute, media, imports and exports, banks and insurance and even car assembly plants. Colonialism is not the fit word for this exploitation because even thousands of statistical tables would not justify the Bengali frustration for this economic strangulation.

Communist leaders of East Pakistan also played a significant role at this juncture against this exploitation of Bengali Muslims by West Pakistan rulers. Although Communist Party was banned in East Pakistan; they found a leader of high repute in the form of Maulana Bhashani who was selfless and highly respected everywhere in every section of the society. It was in this scenario that the opposition parties jointly started challenging the Muslim League under the leadership of Suhrawardy of Awami League, Maulana Bhashmi and Krishak Sramak Party led by Fazl-ul-Haq. Surprisingly, at later stage Communists of East Pakistan became the core of Awami League on direction from Stalin.

By the end of 1953, all major political parties in East Pakistan, including the Communists united together against the Muslim League to fight the forthcoming provincial elections under one banner. This United Front presented a 21 point programme to the people of East Pakistan as a charter of freedom from all sorts of political and economic exploitation by West Pakistan rulers. This programme demanded complete Provincial Autonomy for East Pakistan, nationalization of jute trade, adoption of Bengali as the national language, fair return to jute growers, repeal of safety laws and release of political prisoners languishing in the prisons of East Pakistan. Out of total seats of 309, the Muslim League could win only 9 seats. Maulvi Fazl-ul-Haq became Chief Minister on 3rd April, 1954, on this 21 point programme of United Front. West Pakistan never liked this proposition and they dismissed this Government soon thereafter taking law and order as cue of dismissal. Iskinder Mirza who was appointed Governor of East Pakistan banned Communist Party, placed censor on newspapers and ordered large scale arrest of political opponents in whole of East Pakistan. This move further strengthened the belief of the people of East Pakistan that West Pakistan did not want a popular elected government. to rule this region and imposed a dictator nominee to rule with iron hand. They felt betrayed and wanted to get rid of this regime sooner or later.

When Ch. Muhammand Ali was appointed as Prime Minister of Pakistan in August, 1955, there was much resentment among the people of East Pakistan because both wings of Pakistan were ruled by West Pakistans which violated the established democratic tradition because one head should have been from East Pakistan. Upto 24th June, 1958, many ad-hoc governments. were installed to rule East Pakistan but were dismissed abruptly on one pretext or the other due to pressure from Western Wing and the political situation was created to such a limbo that President Rule was imposed on this day in East Pakistan. To further divide the United Front of East Pakistan, a puppet Awami League Government was installed in August 1958. During the session of Assembly in September 1958, there was a free fight and brawl in the Assembly between the members of Awami League and Krishak Sramak Party which resulted in the death of its Deputy Speaker Shahid Ali on the spot. Likewise, in West Pakistan, the Central Government. also did not function democratically and the constitutional machinery broke down due to political failure and Martial Law was imposed on the Country when army did a coup. General Ayub Khan became the President and Chief Martial Law Administrator. However, it would be pertinent to bring down the fate and records of every Prime Minister of Pakistan from independence in 1947 till Ayub imposed martial law in Pakistan in 1958.

When Jinnah became Governor-General, he put the stamp of his authority on the new state which was unchallengeable from any quarter because of the unassuming big political status of this towering political leader who was bestowed the title of Quaid-i-Azam. Jinnah was a dictator and considered all other political leaders as dwarf and naïve. Jinnah while ruling Pakistan, not only made Prime Minister and his cabinet ineffective, he also encouraged the bureaucracy and the army to bypass the ministers and report directly to him on various national issues. These precedents established the pattern of an expanding dictatorship and proved disasterous for Pakistan subsequently. Likewise, when Jinnah died in September 1948, others who succeeded him did not hesitate to impose the same autocratic authority politically and administratively. But while Jinnah exercised his authority selflessly, others had personal selfish motives. As such, in the next 11 years of so-called parliamentary government, Prime Ministers were removed from office either violently or by military-bureaucratic nexus and not by the electoral process.

The first Prime Minister, Liaquat Ali Khan was shot dead at a public meeting in Rawalpindi. It was rumoured that he was killed in a sinister plot of a Punjab politician which was never revealed in the resultant inquiry commission appointed to unravel the truth. Khwaja Nazimuddin, who succeeded him, was dismissed by the Punjabi Governor General Ghulam Mohammad. Next incumbent, Mohammd Ali Bogra a political naïve was Ambassador in USA prior to his appointment as Prime Minister. He had to constitute his cabinet on threat of dismissal and he termed his tenure as a "bastardly job" and was removed after few months and sent back as Ambassador again to his original post. Cauchy Mohammad Ali who was elected subsequently was to form a collation Government with Suhnawardy of East Pakistan but was sworn alone by Iskander Mirza to the utter dismay of Awami League leaders. He gave Pakistan its first constitution which was based on a political compromise with the Bengalis of East on the basis of "Parity" of representation which Bengali Muslims bitterly resented for the next 14 years. When he tried to assert his position for absolute power, his own colleagues revolted and forced him out in favour of Suhnawardy who by then had made peace with Iskander Mirza and the army. Since Awami League was in minority in the Assembly, Suhnawardy was a captive of the whims and fancies of Iskander Mirza and when he tried to assert himself he was shown the doors and a Bombay barrister was installed for only 40 days. He was succeeded by Malik Feroze Khan Noon who was a Punjabi feudal landlord and had spoiled his reputation while handling language crisis in East Pakistan in the early fifties. He survived for six months prior to elections of the National Assembly which were scheduled for 1959. He was overthrown by Ayub Khan, the Army Chief of Pakistan on 7th October, 1958, who became the first dictator of Pakistan and imposed martial law.

After the declaration of martial law, there was a general belief in East Pakistan that it was a conspiracy on the part of West to rule East Pakistan with the help of Army and bureaucracy. This belief was further gaining strength to this fact when Ayub did not visit East Pakistan for about a year after becoming President. They did not like the rule of Ayub who started advocating strong Centre whereas they had been clamoring for Provincial Autonomy. Ayub's dictatorial rule was further unacceptable to them when he appointed Zakir Hussain, a former Inspector-General of Police as Governor of East Pakistan. Zakir Hussain ruled East Pakistan ruthlessly and arrested large number of political workers and leaders and inflicted severe physical torture on them in police custory. Amongst the prominent personalities incarcerated and disgraced were Sheikh Mujib-ur-Rahman and Tafazzal Hussain, Editor of the daily Ittefaz. Mujib was a leader of the radical youth and Tafazzal Hussain was a close associate of the Awami League and preached Bengali nationalism which was unacceptable to Zakir Hussain who brutally tortured these two leaders during their arrest. Since, they were very popular among the masses, their arrest created unprecedented resentment among the people of East Pakistan.

Sheikh Mujib was so badly tortured physically in the jail at the behest of Zakir Hussain that he said to Bhutto in 1963 after his release that he was finished with politics. When Bhutto inquired the facts, Mujib with a bitter smile replied that this torture has taken the fire out of him. Apprehensively, Bhutto might have quoted these exaggerated facts but actually this torture unleashed on Mujib by Zakir Hussain for personal reasons, gave him enormous strength and vision which ultimately helped him to sustain the bigger political crisis during 1971.

Ayub Khan announced many economic packages to East Pakistan which were so small and too late that only a revolution in this field could have satisfied their people. In 1960, Ayub Khan made a practical experiment to bring the two significant political developments in services. In 1960, Ayub Khan in order to bring the two provinces together, made a practical attempt when he brought 100 agriculturist families from East Pakistan to settle in West Pakistan and allotted them land at Ghulam Mohammad Barrage. But due to some practical problems, this experiment did not succeed for one reason or other and all of them returned to East Pakistan after some time. This experiment instead of removing any parity gave another signal to the fact that these two provinces could no longer stay together because of much rooted hatred against each other. In services, the Bengali Muslims were ignored since independence which could be seen from the fact that upto 1965 there were two acting Secretaries in the government Secretariat and there was only one Major General out of seventeen in the Army. In other ranks, Bengalis constituted 5% in the Army and 11% in the Air Force. All these factors added fuel to the fire and the Bengali Muslims instead of many concessions offered by Ayub Khan regime tried to look for a separate State for themselves at any cost for which they were mentally and physically prepared. His policy of "Basic Democracies" created a class of loyalists for him which included powerful industrialists, pro-government politicians, bureaucrats who were considered his agents and were hated by common citizen. Due to these circumstances, demonstrations and agitations were hled against him sooner than expected in 1962. He appointed Monem Khan as the Governor of East Pakistan who resorted to ruthless measures to curb political agitation which was launched by the students of Dacca University. As a result of his oppressive attitude towards Bengali Muslims, he arrested Suhrawardy the most popular leader of East Pakistan for stemming the tide of political agitation. This action proved fatal for him in the years to come.

In 1962, Ayub Khan abrogated the 1956 Constitution and in the new constitution brought enormous dictatorial powers for him which was construed as a measure to rule East Pakistan in undemocratically because the 1956 Constitution was a balancing cord between East and West Pakistan. It had settled the core inter-regional issues such as problem of Parity, the system of Electorate etc., forever and also it was supported by the popular leaders of East Pakistan Suhrawardy and Fazl-ul-Haq. Legally Ayub had no authority to scrap the 1956 Constitution. Since, Ayub Khan had repeatedly postponed the National Elections, the Bengali Muslims thought it an ill-conceived devise to rule them with iron hand. Because of imposition of the new Constitution and arrest of Suhrawardy, the frustration which had already erupted among the masses of Bengali Muslims, touched the boiling point when unstoppable demonstrations and agitation were held in their support all over East Pakistan. There were allegations that even

American government tried to use this situation to restore democracy in this region. The CIA and Russian agents who were against Ayub for his pro-China policy became active and prepared a plan for a United Bengal comprising of East Pakistanistn, West Bengal, Sikkim, Bhutan, Nagaland etc. This idea of United Bengal was aggressively propagated amongst the students and masses through leaflets and pamphlets. One veteran leader, Khwaja Nazimuddin claimed in a press statement that the American Ambassador tried to persuade him to work for the secession of East Pakistan. Prior to the war of 1965 with India, Suhrawardy and Fazl- ul-Haq had died and the East Pakistans felt isolated and insecure in this war since there was no leader of comparative stature after them. Tashkent Declaration brought great disillusionment among them and even Ayub Khan did not visit this region for eight months after the war.

In this political vacuum in East Pakistan, Sheikh Mujib-ur-Rehman captured the high political status in East Pakistan politics due to his liberal attitude and radical past. He announced his Six Point formula as the political solution of East Pakistan. These points were:

1. The character of the government shall be federal and parliamentary, in which the election to the federal legislature and to the legislatures of the federating units shall be direct and on the basis of universal adult franchise. The representation in the federal legislature shall be on the basis of population
2. The federal government shall be responsible only for defence and foreign affairs and, subject to the conditions provided in (3) below.
3. There shall be two separate currencies mutually or freely convertible in each wing for each region or in the alternative a single currency, subject to the establishment of federal reserves systems in which there will be regional Federal Reserve banks which shall devise measures to prevent the transfer of resources and flight of capital from one region to another.
4. Fiscal policy shall be the responsibility of the federating units. The federal government shall be provided with requisite revenue resources for meeting the requirements of defence and foreign affairs, which revenue resources would be automatically appropriable by the federal government in the manner provided and on the basis of the ratio to be determined by the procedure laid down in the Constitution. Such constitutional provisions would ensure that the federal government's revenue requirements are met consistently with the objective of ensuring control over the fiscal policy by the governments of the federating units.
5. Constitutional provisions shall be made to enable separate accounts to be maintained of the foreign exchange earning of each of the federating units, under the control of the respective governments of the federating units.

The foreign exchange requirements of the federal government shall be met by the governments of the federating units on the basis of a ratio to be determined in accordance with procedure laid down in the Constitution. The Regional Governments shall have power under the Constitution to negotiate foreign trade and aid within the framework of the foreign policy of the country, which shall be the responsibility of the federal government.

6. The governments of the federating units shall be empowered to maintain a militia or para-military force in order to contribute effectively towards national security.

Sheikh Mujib received unprecedented support from all political leaders of East Pakistan. He went from town to town and was treated like a Messiah by the poverty-stricken people who felt their salvation lay in this new political structure. Pakistan government termed it as an Indian ploy and even went to the extent of accusing India that this draft of Six Point had been drafted by an officer of the External Affairs Ministry of India. Nonetheless, Mujib rose highly on his plank of Bengali nationalism and got unbelievable support from his people in the hope of their betterment. Internationally, foreign press hailed it as a signal of storm and supporting the formula and depicting Mujib as the hero of the nation. Bhutto described it as a veiled charter for a confederation which contained the genesis of constitutional secession. Ayub Khan did not give much importance to this formula and thought that it would die its natural death with the passage of time. Had he adopted a judicious approach and made peace with Mujib, this programme would have lost much of its efficacy. Contrarily, he tried to highlight this action of Mujib through his trusted papers so that he could be depicted as a secessionist and an Indian agent. It proved counter-productive and increased the popularity of Mujib to the maximum. In his campaign against the Centre and West Pakistan, he logically put before the people of East Pakistan figures of economic disparity in the pamphlets distributed in each and every town. Comparative prices of essential commodities such as rice, flour, meat, salt, cement, cloth, etc. which were three to four times higher in East Pakistan were displayed in each villages and town which certainly incited the inner feeling of every East Pakistan. In this political upstream of Bengali honour, the Pakistan government could not meet the challenge posed by the Awami league.

After the war of 1965 with India, Ayub's stability was questionable in Pakistan. The provincial government of Monem Khan had unleashed a reign of terror in East Pakistan which ultimately gave a major fillip to the movement of Mujib who was hailed as a savior of the poverty ridden people of this region. Mujib was arrested in April, 1966. East Pakistan press highlighted this arrest vociferously which provided great impetus to the movement of Mujib. He was released after few days after which he challenged the government everywhere in his rigorous tour of the province. East Pakistan government again arrested him in May in order to thwart his nationwide campaign. Awami League announced a public strike on June 7, 1966 to protest against the arrest of Mujib which was more successful than the expectations of the Awami League leaders. Processions were held all over East Pakistan, government offices were attacked, shops and cars bearing other than Bengali sign-boards and number plates were set on fire. This success united them against Ayub Khan. Six point formula was considered as their right to live honourably. Political situation was taking a dangerous turn against West Pakistan rule. Monem Khan in order to prove Mujib traitor, implicated him in the infamous Agartala Conspiracy when some officers of navy and civil services were arrested on charges of high treason and conspiracy. Mujib was named as an accomplice in this case while he was already in the prison. When general public raised a hue and cry against this incident and demanded publication of the details of conspiracy and wanted an open trial of the accused. There was a large demonstration of students all over East Pakistan against this trial. There was a strong apprehension among the masses that Monem Khan had deliberately involved Mujib on account of personal enmity. As the case prolonged, a favorable public opinion started building in favour of Mujib and other persons implicated in this case.

Agartala Conspiracy Case

Agartala Conspiracy case was discussed by the author with K Sankaran Nair who was the operational head and was handling these East Pakistan insurgents in the Intelligence Bureau, IB. Nair became Chief of R&AW in 1977 after serving in number two position under R N Kao from 1968 till 1977. Nair who was working under the cover as Col. Menon admitted that these East Pakistans were agents of Intelligence Bureau but Sheikh Mujibur Rahman was not their agent. If he was implicated in the Agartala Conspiracy case, it was done at the behest of Pakistan government under Yahya Khan. Nair confirmed that P N Ojha, a Deputy Central Intelligence Officer of IB was his junior who was interacting with these East Pakistans which included some Navy employees, Police officers and some political activists of Awami League party. Nair met these agents on border near Agartala few months prior to their arrest in East Pakistan. These agents were warned by Nair not to raid the armoury to capture arms from the Pakistan army, which they did after some time. Rather, Nair suggested to them that IB would send arms to them on a barge down the river from Agartala and they could collect these arms at suitable destinations for insurgency against Pakistan army. Nair also suggested them some separate ideas for their insurgent activities but they were aggressive and wanted some immediate action against the Pakistan army. They ignored the warning of Nair and raided the armoury which resulted in their subsequent arrest and this sedition case named as Agartala Conspiracy case was filed against them by the Pakistan government. Mujib was deliberately implicated in this case as agent of Indian intelligence which was emphatically denied by Nair in a recorded interview with the author on May 28, 2005. Nair further admitted to the author that prior to 1971 war of liberation of Bangladesh there was no mandate for the IB in East Pakistan except to supply arms to the agents and to train them on Indian territory to use these arms before launching them against the Pakistan army for insurgency. Nair also confirmed that there were some aberration in these operations but IB wanted to keep the pot boiling for the Pakistan army and the administration even before the war of 1971. In view of these disclosures of K S Nair, it is evidently true that Mujib was implicated in the Agartala Conspiracy case at the instance of Pakistan government. However, it is also true that other accused in this case were certainly agents of Intelligence Bureau of India but they were never instigated by IB to raid the armoury which they did on their own. This proved disastrous for them. So, IB was never a party to the raid of armoury by these agents which Pakistan government had done in the charge-sheet filed in this case in the court.

By the end of 1968, the political storm against Ayub regime gained momentum to oust him from power. His prolonged illness was the real cause of his lax control over the administration in general and amry in particular. The Presidential system, corruption and high-handedness in civil services, concentration of Pakistan economy in twenty two families, political suppression and alienation of people from political power were the main causes leading to unending demonstrations which ultimately became the reason for the downfall of Ayub. In East Pakistan, due to the absence of Mujib, Maulana Bhashani addressed public meetings at Dacca where one day he started a movement of "Gherao" and "Jalao" which got unprecedented support from the people of East Pakistan. By January, 1969, there were numerous cases of strikes, mass arrests and student-police clashes which took a heavy toll of human life. Law and order totally broke down and people demanded the Parliamentary form of government, direct elections on the bases of adult franchise, end of emergency, release of political prisoners and freedom of expression. The lava of independence was boiling underground since long and the inferno erupted with an unprecedented force which rocked the foundation of the misrule of West Pakistan. There was a situation of civil war due to violent clashes between the Bengalis and non-Bengalis. Ayub Khan had to release Mujib-ur-Rehman and other political prisoners due to the prevalent political compulsion.

Beginning of An End

After his release, Mujib addressed a mammoth public gathering at Paltan Maidan in Dacca and promised to launch an agitation for the acceptance of his Six Points. Mujib achieved so great popularity as a result of these political developments that he became the undisputed leader of East Pakistan. In order to find a way out from this political turmoil, Ayub Khan, Mujib and other political leaders met on a round table conference on February 26, 1969 which continued up to March with no result on Six Point formula of Mujib due to the stubborn attitude of Ayub Khan. Due to internal differences of opposition leaders and insistence of Mujib on Six Points and obviously resistance of Ayub, the Round Table Conference failed. Consequently, Ayub Khan resigned, abrogated the Constitution and handed over government to Yahya Khan, then Commander-in-Chief of the Pakistan army. On March 26, 1969, Yahya Khan became Chief Martial Law Administrator and President of Pakistan. According to 1962 Constitution of Pakistan, declaration of Martial Law was unconstitutional and the Governmentwas to be handed over to the Speaker in case of emergency and not to Commander-in-Chief which was done at that time by Ayub Khan. There were strong assumptions that Ayub was forced to hand over the command at the insistence of Yahya Kahn. Mujib was skeptical towards the new army rule but Yahya Khan adopted a placating approach towards him and other political leaders. Yahya Khan made three promises to the people of Pakistan i.e. a clean-up of the corrupt and inefficient administration, a general election at the earliest on the basis of adult franchise and transfer of power to the elected representatives of the people. Pakistans failed to realize that the new President was only repeating the promises traditionally made by military dictators the world over and that these had been universally betrayed in the due course of time. This was not for the first time that the people of Pakistan had allowed themselves to be so fooled into complacency. In so far as corruption was concerned, it had reached to such a phenomenal proportion during the regime of Ayub that any honest cleaning would entail almost the total replacement of the civil administration and of vast number in the military establishment. There was a general perception in the mind of some people who were close to Yahya Khan that he might be sincere to implement the first two promises but were skeptical about the third one. In their opinion, Yahya would hold the election and would delegate some authority to a civilian government with himself backed by the army, holding the whip in hand. There was a tacit understanding to this effect at army Headquarterss in Rawalpindi and the excuse as usual was the “National Interest”.

Yahya Khan was also convinced that Pakistans would not tolerate the denial of holding general elections for long. In this changed political atmosphere he wanted to manipulate his supremacy behind a façade of democracy. He had an inner coterie of advisors who were the virtual rulers of Pakistan. They were Gen. Hamid Khan, the Army Chief, Lt. Gen. Pirzada, his Principal Staff Officer, Lt. Gen. Tikka Khan, who ultimately received notoriety as the Butcher of Bengal, Maj. Gen. Akbar Kahn, the Director of ISI and Maj. Gen. Umar Khan, Chairman of National Security Committee besides two civilians Rizvi, the Director of

Civial Intelligence Bureau and M M Ahmad, the Economic Adviser. This junta briefed the President that as per intelligence reports Sheikh Mujib's party Awami League would not get more than 80 seats in East Pakistan and there would be a hung assembly. This junta was trying to influence the elections in favour of the Muslim League of Qayyum group in NWFP and for Jamat-i-Islami in Sindh and Punjab at the cost of government exchequer. This was resented by Khan Wali Khan who was leading the people of the North West Frontier and Baluchistan on a parallel course to Sheikh Mujib's autonomy demand. He publically supported the six-point demand of Sheikh Mujib. This junta was using Qayyum to break Wali Khan's strength in NWFP and Jamat-i-Islami to cut down Bhutto's influence in Sindh and Punjab. Bhutto even complained of being hounded by intelligence agents. Hence, Yahya and his junta wanted to rig the election results in favour of those who were loyal to them.

The clamping down of second Martial Law caused great disillusionment and consternation in East Pakistan because it was feared that it would curb their movement of autonomy and freedom. To prove his intention honest, Yahya Khan lifted ban on political activities on January 1, 1970 to enable political parties to campaign for the General Elections which were to be held by the end of the year. He announced the formation of Legal Framework Order in March, 1970, which enunciated five principles as the basis of coming elections and the Constitution was to be framed within 120 days with powers with him to authenticate or reject it. He also announced dismemberment of One Unit, the integrated province of West Pakistan, which was done in 1955 into its constituent parts, the separate provinces of Sindh, Punjab, Baluchistan and the North-West Frontier and the principle of "one man one vote" be substituted for parity in the elections which was widely applauded by the people of these provinces. This was a ploy because he was convinced that there were 36 political parties and groups in Pakistan at that time who would participate in the election and no one would get majority. In that situation he would dictate his own terms and form a constitution in that deadlock which would make his position safe for ruling further. He never foresaw that East Bengal's economic and political grievances arising from two decades of colonial exploitation would assume the proportions of a tidal wave during the elections which unassumingly proved his disaster and ultimately resulted in a political defeat for the West Pakistans in general and for Yahya Khan in particular. However, timely the people of Pakistan were jubilant that a firm date had at least been fixed for the general election and expected transfer of power but did not visualize the hidden agenda of Yahya which he unveiled through the Legal Framework Order on April 1, 1970 wherein he assumed all residuary political powers at his whims in case of a political stalemate or otherwise But it was too late for any political party to protest against the Legal Framework Order. To appease the Bengali Muslims, he appointed Admiral Ahsan as the Governor of East Pakistan who had a good reputation in that region.

Mujibur Rehman based his election campaign on his Six points to which he received unprecedented support from students, lawyers and working class. He asserted that he stood for provincial autonomy to safeguard the interest of East Pakistans and not for the disintegration of Pakistan. He presented Six Points to the people as a panacea of all their economic and political ills. Mujib exploited his inherent qualities of an unsurpassed agitator and excellent oration to the maximum extent and organized his party on systematic lines. By virtue of his fiery oratory, he convinced the poverty-stricken masses that they had been exploited for years and now it was the last chance for them to overcome this misery by voting him to power. He appealed to the people of East Pakistan to make the election a referendum on his party's manifesto which received unprecedented support from the whole of province. People of whole of East Pakistan rallied around him. Displaying a flamboyant posture in a public meeting he called upon the Bengali Muslims to rise to the occasion and completely eliminate the political Mir Jafars and parasites from the sacred soil of Bengal. His political strength increased to the extent that he was portrayed as the future Prime Minister of Pakistan and received all political support from bureaucracy, big bankers and business houses.

National Elections were scheduled in October 1970 but due to heavy floods which displaced millions of people from their homes and disrupted means of communications, postponed to December. Mujib blamed Pakistan rulers for this continuing disaster because they built big dams like Terbela and Mangla in West Pakistan whereas in East Pakistan they did not build a single one where flood situation was always alarming. This further had magical effect to his campaign. Further in the middle of November, 1970, cyclone disaster struck the coastal belt of East Pakistan which was the greatest natural calamity of the modern times. Mujib made an extensive visit to the cyclone affected area and launched scathing attack on Central Government for its apathy and callousness in dealing with the relief operations.

After these two unprecedented catastrophes and in the hatred against the West Pakistan among the Bnegali Muslims, the elections to the National and Provincial Assemblies were held in December, 1970. Awami League headed by Mujibur -Rehman emerged as the majority party of the country with 167 seats out of a total of 313 seats in the National Assembly. This was a referendum on Bengali nationalism. Bhutto's People Party won 88 seats and emerged as the largest party of West Pakistan. None of these parties won any seat in the other Provinces. The results had shown that the new generation of Pakistan which was literate enough not to be guided by the fundamentalists who were making political capital of the people's pity and ignorance. Religion would no longer serve as a rallying point in politics and the military-bureaucratic combine personified by the previous regime was rejected by the outcome of the results. But President Yahya Khan saw it as a personal disaster. The gambit of the Legal Framework Order, carefully tailored to ensure a manipulated deadlock in the assembly, had totally failed. His fear was strengthened by the announcement of Mujib on December 9 that the new Constitution would be based on the six-point autonomy demand of Awami League.

Yahya had only two options either to accept the verdict of the people and transfer power to Mujib or reject it, there was no third choice. In order to make way for the second choice he decided that the assembly would not meet unless the Awami League submitted in advance to the constitutional pattern they had in mind. Had he accepted the election verdict he would have saved the self-created political crisis which subsequently resulted in the death of one million people of East Bengal. Yahya Khan had no such intention. He wanted to forestall Mujib. Technique to do so was very simple-to create an East Pakistan and West Pakistan confrontation on constitutional issues before the assembly meet and the best actor to perform this role was none other than the highly ambitious and pliable Bhutto who was conveniently used by him for this sinister design. Since Awami League did not win a single seat in West Pakistan and likewise Bhutto failed to do so in East, this curious complexion gave Yahya an excellent opportunity for mischief to play against both the wings. Another mischief played by Maulana Bhashani and some others in East for independence in the middle of December 1970, to tarnish the image of Mujib, further strengthened the hidden agenda of Yahya Khan. He prompted some newspapers to spread the rumour that call for independence was not for two party system i.e. the Awami League and PPP but for two Pakistans. Hence the point was mooted that Bhutto-Mujib accord on an acceptable constitutional formula prior to the assembly meeting would be necessary to safeguard interests of Pakistan in the wake of the call of independence by some East Pakistan leaders. This ridiculous idea was moved to stall the democratic takeover in favour of Mujib because Bhutto himself did not get absolute majority in Punjab and Sindh in West Pakistan and had no following in the North-West and Baluchistan. Rather most prominent leaders among the Pathans and the Baluchis had thrown in their lot with Sheikh Mujib. Even some groups which were opposed to Bhutto in Sindh and Punjab were in favour of Sheikh Mujib to become head of the state. Hence, call of Bhutto-Mujib accord prior to the assembly meeting was a farce and raising the issue of independence was irrelevant to the fact that the Awami League had demanded autonomy and not independence which was mischievously raised at this juncture to degrade Mujib. Even government's own white paper issued on August 5, 1971 admitted this fact and as such the policies of Awami League were never a threat to the integrity of the state but were a deliberate attempt by Yahya Khan and his junta to thwart the take over of Mujib as the head of the state which was evident from the fact when he asked Mujib to come to an understanding with the PPP when he met him first time after the elections.

Hence, grounds were prepared by Yahya Khan and his junta to bypass the election results and to precipitate an East-West confrontation. Whole objective of this exercise was to create a political deadlock which would give Yahya Khan an opportunity to have a constitution that could guarantee his own supremacy and he meticulously manipulated it in the days to come. He was artfully and energetically converting this theory into a practical shape but publicly he did nothing to invite the ire of people and controversy in media. He deliberately did not set a date for the meeting of the assembly. Up to January 10, 1971 he was busy in game of shooting of ducks and partridges in Karachi, Lahore, Hyderabad, Bahawalpur and Larkhana, Bhutto's hometown where he was entertained by him in great style and reached a secret understanding with him in this game of far reaching consequences. He made Bhutto a tool to forestall Mujib. Bhutto was too ambitious to rule Pakistan and he realized that his interest was coinciding with those of Yahya. He foolishly did not realize that Yahya was using him against Mujib for his own political interest to rule Pakistan in his self-created stalemate.

During this era of political uncertainty, Sheikh Mujib in a rare political gambling sent an emissary to Bhutto. This emissary was a Bengali student leader from London who was having good relation with both these leaders. Mujib secretly conveyed to Bhutto that he was willing to give him big job if he was ready to accept his six points and asked to join hands with him in getting the army out of politics and back to the barracks. When this message was conveyed to him in Karachi, Bhutto overwhelmingly tried to contact Mujib to discuss it further but Mujib was not available on phone. Bhutto told the emissary that he was personally not against the six points but he could not ignore his party in this matter. He sent his confidant Mustapha Kaler to Dacca to meet Mujib. Although nothing came out of this parley but realizing that the ongoing confrontation would be disadvantageous to him, Mujib by joining hands with Bhutto would have turned the table on the General in case he tried to thwart the democratic process the way it was done against Ayub Khan. Hence it was a well conceived gambit to keep army out of politics but Bhutto was too shrewd and changed side towards the General because he had another plan in his mind.

In the meantime, to assert his political stature, Mujibur Rehman got the Awami League representatives public oath of unflinching adherence to the six points of his party manifesto which was perceived as a threat to the integrity of Pakistan in the mind of the people of Western wing. To complicate the matter further, some West Pakistan newspapers mischievously published report that Mujib would not call on Yahya Khan and would insist on the meeting at his residence to which Mujib had to issue a public denial. This was the first move to aggravate the ongoing political imbroglio. During the course of his meeting with Yahya Khan, Mujib tried to allay the misgivings about the position of the army in the projected provincial autonomy and gave him an understanding that the military budget would be intact for two years. Instead Yahya Khan did not spell out his ideas about the constitution and on six points manifesto of Awami League but emphasized the need to reach an understanding with Bhutto on the political structure of the new democracy. President Yahya Khan during an informal chat with media persons at Dacca airport before his departure to Rawallpindi declared that Mujib-ur-Rehman would be the future Prime Minister of Pakistan. This was a well conceived trap on the part of the General to create a confrontation between Mujib and Bhutto in which he succeeded.

Ultimetaly when Bhutto met Mujib on January 27, 1971, in Dacca, he did not probe the ideal of joining hands against the army and instead sought clarifications of the six point manifesto of his party. This was a secretly reached understanding of Yahya-Bhutto collusion to forestall Sheikh Mujib from becoming head of state. Bhutto exploited this situation to his political advantage and wanted to share power with the Awami League in the Central Government because he professed that the exclusive control of entire central administration, together with complete authority in East Pakistan, nobody could prevent Mujib from taking the final step to secession. Since, there was no Constitution; Bhutto presented the idea of two houses which was rejected by Mujib out-rightly. Bhutto wanted an outside assembly parley to evolve an agreed constitutional formula but Mujib wanted every solution on the floor of house. Bhutto feared that constitutional obligations would be imposed on him in the Assembly by Mujib because he had the majority to do so. Bhutto termed the Six point formula of Mujib as an end of Pakistan which was rejected by Mujib and as such the meetings between the two parties did not fructify in the form of any political and constitutional solution of the uncalled for impasse imposed by cunning Bhutto to incite the feelings of people of West Pakistan at this critical juncture in his favor. Consequently, a deadlock was reached due to the biased and malicious attitude of Bhutto because he was mainly interested in discussing the implications of Six points and no other brief was prepared by him or his advisers because this was a rallying point which could be extensively exploited by him in future to assuage the feelings of West Pakistan population who never wanted a Bengali Muslim to rule their country. Bhutto instead of bowing to the clear mandate given by the people of East Pakistan created an unwarranted volatile political situation and stalemate which caused great confusion and disillusionment among the people of East Pakistan who were hoping against hope to see Mujib as the ruler of Pakistan.

This outrageous political farce created by Yahya-Bhutto combine was evident from the following events:

- **January, 29:** Bhutto left Dacca after inconclusive meeting with Mujib with the understanding that he would further discuss the issue in the lobbies and committees of the national assembly.
- **February, 11:** After a two day meeting of his party representatives in Multan, he told the press that draft of the constitution was in its final stages.
- **February, 12:** Bhutto met Yahya Khan in Rawallpindi and changed his mind on the constitution draft.
- **February, 13:** Yahya Khan announced that national assembly would meet in Dacca on March.3, Bhutto in a party at Peshawar on this day declared that it had been decided that he would be the Prime Minister and Mujib was out.
- **February 14:** Bhutto met Wali Khan of the National Awami Party and sought his cooperation which he refused. Bhutto told confidentially to Wali Khan that he was not going to Dacca for the national assembly session which even his party did not know.
- **February, 15:** Bhutto addressed a press conference at Peshawar where he declared that he would boycott the assembly session unless he had an understanding with Mujib on the pattern of constitution which would safeguard the interest of West Pakistan. He threatened to "break the legs" of any member from West Pakistan who would try to attend the assembly session in Dacca.
- **February, 21:** Yahya Khan dissolved his civilian cabinet and convened a meeting of the military governors and martial law administrator at Rawallpindi for the impending action resulting from the ongoing political uncertainty.
- **February, 24-28:** Thirty six members of the assembly from West Pakistan booked their tickets for the inaugural session of assembly in Dacca despite threat of Bhutto to assault them. Bhutto publicly called for postponement of the assembly meeting.
- **March 1:** Yahya Khan postponed the inaugural meeting of the national assembly indefinitely citing East-West confrontation and boycott of the party of Bhutto which was termed as the gravest political crisis in Pakistan.

These developments clearly indicated a well conceived mischief on the part of Yahya Khan and Bhutto to postpone the inaugural meeting of the national assembly and its constitution-making purpose with the most blatant distortion of the truth. Mujib on this part insisted that the constitution should be debated and finalized in the national assembly and not in secret meetings outside its ambit and Bhutto's assertion that their draft constitution could not be altered one inch here or there was just a stumbling block deliberately created to do so which was evident as detailed here-in-above paragraph. Bhutto falsely spread rumours in

West Pakistan that Awami League leaders had demanded the imposition of an external debt of Rs.38,000 million out of a total of Rs.40,000 and an internal debt of Rs. 31,000 on West Pakistan through a constitutional provision. This rumour proved a master stroke for his ambition to become Prime Minister because army and politicians thought it a secession agenda to disintegrate Pakistan on the part of Awami League and their leaders. West Pakistan media also played a pivotal role by highlighting the impression that Mujib proposed to convert the National Assembly into a soverign body and by making the Legal Framework Order inoperative, wanted to impose a Six Point Constitution.

Mujibur Rehman committed a political blunder when he did not visit West Pakistan after winning the elections. Had he done so, he would have got support of many politicians like Khan Wali Khan and others who were against Bhutto and also could have undone the propaganda orchasterated against him by Bhutto and his party for political gains. He could have defended his Six Point Formula through public debates in West Pakistan and as such the wrong impression created by the media in this regard could have been cleared from the mind of general public of West Pakistan through this visit.

However, to allay misgiving in the World community, Yahya Khan announced on February 13, 1971, that the elected members of different parties would meet in the National Assembly in Dacca on March 3, 1971 to break the political deadlock. In order to exploit this political situation in their favour, Bhutto's Peoples Party had already threatened with dire consequences against convening the National Assembly session on the announced date. They took the plea that neither they had completed their consultations nor had taken the approval of the people of West Pakistan for a Constitution which was based on far-reaching concessions. On February 28, 1971, Bhutta addressed a public meeting at Lahore and launched a campaign of intimidation against all other parties of West Pakistan to prevent them from attending the session. As a result of this deliberate threat unleashed by Bhutto, Yahya Khan postponed the session of National Assembly sine die quoting that major parties from West Pakistan had announced their intention not to attend it. He obviously blamed India also for creating tension inside Pakistan. Yahya Khan's declaration in collusion with Bhutto was seen an attempt to frustrate the popular will of the people of East Pakistan to install a democratic government. Their general feeling reached to the conclusion that the rights of people of East Pakistan could never be realized within the framework of Parliament which was not a real source of power in Pakistan.

In the meantime, in order to curb the political activities in a well conceived treachery, Yahya appointed Tikka Khan, the butcher of Bluchistan, as Governor of East Pakistan. Mujib called for a general strike on March 2, 1971 and declared that it was the scared duty of each and every Bengali in every walk of life, including government employees, not to co-operate with anti-people forces and instead do everything in their power to foil the conspiracy against East Pakistan. On March 4, 1971, Mujib launched a civil disobedience movement throughout the province. Again on March 7, he announced his plan to run a parallel Government and formally issued a number of directives. These were a No-Tax campaign and closure of all educational institutions, courts and offices. Radio, Television and newspapers were directed to give full coverage to the campaign of Awami League. Inter-provincial telephone communication was dirupted and banks were directed to stop remittances to West Pakistan.

Yahya Khan detailed the reasons of postponing the assembly meeting in his broadcast on March 1, 1971 on the past concoctions and in order to divert political mood of people of Pakistan included India as the main villain for creating tension and complicating the whole situation. This speech was a turning point in the history of Pakistan. He cited the East-West confrontation without criticizing Bhutto on his boycott of the assembly. He did not care to inform the public that 36 members from West Pakistan were present in Dacca and more were expected to fly by March 3. Only People Party of Bhutto and Muslim League of Qayyum group, stooges of army, were absent whereas representatives from all the provinces including Sind and Punjab were present in Dacca. He could have used his military power to ensure smooth functioning of the assembly if he desired to do so but he deliberately swallowed the threat of leg breaking of Bhutto. He did not elaborate the provision of Legal Framework Order wherein it was enshrined that a member would be debarred of his seat if he absented himself for 15 days and if he did not take oath within 7 days from the date of the first meeting of the assembly. Bhutto would have fallen in line if Yahya Khan had enforced any of these provisions honestly but it was a pre-empted move staged with obvious understanding between Bhutto and the General. A prominent politician had disclosed that Yahya Khan had personally asked some representatives from Karachi, Peshawar and Lahore not to attend the assembly session. Yahya Khan's mention of tension created by India was probably the fall out from the hijacking of an Indian Airlines Fodder Friendship plane on January 29 by one Al Fateh militant of Pakistan occupied Kashmir and its subsequent destruction at Lahore and ultimately the ban imposed by India for the Pakistan over flights. Had he allowed the plane to return safely to India, there was no reason for India to ban the overflights. On the other hand, Pakistan declared the hijackers as freedom fighters of Kashmir and offered them asylum in Pakistan subsequently. This was criticized by Sheikh Mujib who was dubbed not only soft to India but also a dangerous man to have eyes at the helm of affairs. These excuses of forestalling him as head of state were only the self creation of Yahya-Bhutto nexus because they had decided the assembly would not meet unless the Awami League submitted in advance to their own formula for the constitution and they temporarily succeeding in their motive to stall it.

Clandestinely, prior to all these deliberations, Yahya Khan in order to keep secrecy for the impending military action convened a meeting of military governors, the martial law administrators and chiefs of defence establishments in the President's house at Rawalpindi in the first week of February. Responding to the future military action in East Pakistan, Admiral Ashan, the Governor of East Bengal resigned in the meeting but was prevailed upon not to do so because it would give a wrong signal to the military establishment. However, subsequently he and the martial law administrator of East Bengal were abruptly removed on March 2, 1971. Having secured his power base, Yahya Khan and his team began to move swiftly. Armed forced were put on high alert throughout the country on the plea of tension created by India. Ammunition and troops were loaded in darkness in a cargo vessel MV Swat which went to Chittagong via Ceylon. When this ship reached Chittagong, the writing on the wall was known to the Bengalis as to why long time was taken by Yahya Khan in the political parleys after the assembly elections. PIA commercial flights were used to airlift the West Pakistan soldiers via Ceylon to replace the Bengali units in East Pakistan. Ceylon authorities did not protest because all these solders numbering about 12,000 were shown as civilian passengers duly ticketed and manifested. All Bengalis serving in the Navy and Air Force were shifted to West Pakistan. Tanks deployed in defensive positions against India in the Rangpur district and in Mymensing were brought into Dacca. Families of West Pakistan military officers and civilians from all over East Bengal were brought to Dacca and later flown to Karachi on the same planes that brought the troops. Whole of this operation was finalized in the third week of February at the military conference in Rawalpindi but Yahya Khan shrewdly held numerous discussions with the politicians after that and disarmed suspicion while the army doubled up its strength in East Bengal. When on March 1, 1971 at Dacca, Yahya Khan announced on air the postponement of the session of national assembly, the whole of the Bengali community was stunned to hear it. Within minutes shops, offices, restaurants and bazaars were closed by the people themselves in Dacca. Long queues of angry crowd went towards the Paltan Maidan, the traditional venue for public debate. Abuses for Yahya Khan and Bhutto were at its high pitch and slogans of Joi Bangla and "Independence, yes, surrender, no" were shouted at full throat. Bangladesh was born that day in the hearts of its angry people. Sheikh Mujib was holding an emergency meeting along with his associates in the Purbani Hotel. The crowd was becoming impatient and looted and set fire the shops of West Pakistans at Jinnah Avenue. Pakistan flag was burnt. Mujib addressed the crowd from the balcony of the hotel and declared a general strike in Dacca on March 2 and a province wide strike the next day. He also announced that he would address a public meeting the next day at racecourse ground when he would unfold his programme of action for the achievement of self-determination. Mujib rebuked a section of crowd for riotous behaviour and ordered to return the stolen goods which some of them duly did. Although the angry people soon dispersed but there was total lawlessness in the city and the crowd went on rampage throughout the city.

Dacca was completely paralyzed on March 2, on the call of the general strike of Mujibur Rehman. In order to qualm the mounting trouble, a 12 hour curfew was imposed at 7 PM and the army moved in to restore normalcy and killed several people. They were attacked by the bare-handed Bengalis in every part of the city. A province-wide general strike, coupled with a non-violent, non-cooperation movement, engulfed the entire East Pakistan and forced the army back into barracks because it failed to stand up against the audacious defiance of the Bengalis.

On March 3, there was a total strike in whole of East Pakistan for a non-violent and non-cooperation movement. It was totally successful barring some sporadic incidents of violence. Troops were withdrawal from Dacca streets when they were denied foodstuffs on the orders of the Awami League. Mujib ordered to continue the strike in every walk of life. A daily shutdown was declared from 7 am. to 2 pm in the whole of East Pakistan when government offices were closed, banks bolted were shut and postal, telegraphs, telephone, airline and train services came to a standstill. In the army centers, foodstuffs were denied by the non-cooperating Bengalis. Arrival of Lt. Gen. Tikka Khan in place of Governor Ahsan did not improve the situation. government's writ had ceased to function in this region. Black flags replaced the Pakistan on government offices and other public buildings. The Bangladesh hymn was played instead of the national anthem over Dacca radio and television stations in compliance with Mujib's instructions, government employees were following the instructions of Awami League leaders. Demand for independence increased with the intensity of the movement. Despite the reinforcements flown from West Pakistan, the army was totally inadequate to deal with the upsurge. Fearing declaration of independence by Mujib, Yahya Khan opted the remedy in terms of applying brutal army action for a military solution to the political reprisal. In order to teach the Bengali leaders a lesson, Tikka Khan urged the President to give him enough force so that he could crush them in 48 hours.

In the meanwhile, the news of arrival of MV Swat in Chittagong with troops and a cargo of ammunition spread like fire. Brigadier Hari Ansari, a Bengali officer who was commanding the Chittagong garrison was abruptly replaced by a West Pakistan officer who instructed the local authorities to unload that ship. Unloading of this ship had been postponed for several days due to the non-co-operation of the duck workers. The dock workers spread the news that the local authorities were forcing them to unload the ship. More than one lakh people assembled in the streets of Chittagong. They were locked in battle with the West Pakistan army. Army resorted to massive firing on the innocent citizents. When

East Pakistan Rifles refused to fire on these Bengali demonstrators, seven Bengali army officers were issued court-martial orders and subsequently shot dead which gave a new dimension to this struggle of liberation. The tension caused by this event spread to sweep the entire East Pakistan.

On the afternoon of March 5, Yahya Khan was clear in his mind to provide the necessary force but time for the preparation and strike hard at the appropriate moment was inadequate. Accordingly, he ordered the massive airlift of army and contingency battle orders were enforced. Treacherously to achieve his sinister impending plan, he went on air and announced that due to misunderstanding the assembly meeting was postponed and to resolve the unfortunate impasse, assembly would meet on March 25, 1971. Apparently he was only trying to silence Sheikh Mujib on the eve of the Race Course meeting where he was expected to make a declaration of independence. This was a deliberate gamble which he did not miscalculate and duly trapped Mujibur Rehman and his political associates. Much to the dismay of people gathered on the Race Course ground, the much-desired declaration of independence was never made. Instead, Mujib launched a civil disobedience movement to achieve self-determination. This masterstroke of Yahya Khan gave him enough time for the military built-up.

On March 7, over a million people gathered at Race Course ground to hear declaration of independence instead of self-determination from Mujibur Rehman. Atmosphere was charged with utmost anger and anxiety because most of the people were carrying a variety of weapons like shot guns, swords, home-made spears, bamboo polls and iron rods etc. Not a single policeman or military person was to be seen around on the street of Dacca. Had Mujib been true to his deserved reputation as a revolutionary leader of the masses, he could have exploited this situation and led this strong crowd to the Eastern Command Headquarterss four miles away and got Tikka Khan surrendered for which a few hundred Bengali Muslims were willing to scarify their lives to get the army surrendered to them? Bangladesh could have achieved its freedom at a minimum number of lives and certainly a million would not have subsequently died and billion others made homeless by military brutality. Yahya's declaration to hold assembly on March 25 created confusion among the leaders and Mujib declared at Race Course ground that he would demand immediate repeal of martial law and withdrawal of all military personnel to their barracks. He also insisted for an inquiry into the loss of life and iinstant transfer of power to the elected representatives of the people before the Assembly meeting on March 25. These demands were a sort of compromise as the objective to achieve power non-violently. Awami League leadership, including Mujib misread the real intention of Yahya Khan. After this announcement, student leaders were dismayed and the general public did not respond enthusiastically in-between his speech. However, he gave a call for civil disobedience from the dais and issued following ten directives to the public :

1. No tax campaign would continue.
2. The Secretariat, government and semi-government offices, High Courts and other courts throughout East Pakistan would observe strike.
3. Railways and Ports would function but their employees would not cooperate if there was mobilization of forces for the repression of the people.
4. Radio, television and newspapers would give full coverage to the movement of the people otherwise Bengalis working there would not cooperate.
5. Only local and inter-district trunk telephone communication would function.
6. All educational institutions would remain close.
7. Banks would not effect remittance to the Western wing either through the State Bank or otherwise.
8. Black flags would be hoisted on all buildings every day.
9. Strike was withdrawn but could be declared at any moment depending on the situation.
10. A revolutionary council (Sangram Parishad) would be organized in each union, mohallah, Thana, sub-division and district under the leadership of local Awami League units.

After a few days, when people started complaining hardship in day-to-day life, some concessions were announced. These covered banking hours, operation of road and water transport, water, gas and electricity services, distribution of foodstuffs, rice and jute seeds, sanitation services and operation of Treasury office for payments to Bengalis. Post and telegraph officers were ordered to operate letter and telegram services only within East Pakistan. The only exception was made in the case of foreign press telegrams which was the only communication link with the outside world. The civil disobedience campaign was further tightened on March 15, when only tax collection started in the name of Awami League but also the whole machinery of central and provincial government was made operational by Awami League directives. Most of the West Pakistans were evacuated from East Pakistan via PIA flights which were carrying army personnel in the disguise of civilians through Ceylon airport. Army units from West Pakistan were denied foodstuffs and daily needs from the markets and food was flown from Karachi. Fear among the army was so intense that the officers had difficult time to contain the soldiers to avoid any uncontrollable situation.

One of the supreme Bengalis insult was delivered to Lt. General Tikka Khan when he arrived Dacca as Governor and Martial Law Administrator. He was not administered oath by the Chief Justice B A Siddiky and other Judges of Dacca High Court till March 27 when the army started its repression on the Bengalis. On March 15, Yahya Khan came to Dacca along with a team of officials for a "political settlement" with Mujib. In real sense, this was the last calculated move to trap Mujib and his associates to buy more time for the impending military action. Even Mujib was insulted when he found Rizvi, the Director of the Civil Intelligence Bureau and Lt. Col. Hassan in the meeting who involved him in the infamous Agartala Conspiracy case. The other person was the chief of ISI Maj. Gen. Akbar who was bitterly disliked by the Bengalis. This provocative group of officials met with a predictable reaction from Mujib whom he called monsters but in order to avoid the ostensible political impasse he sent Tajuddin, Dr. Rahman Sobhan his economy adviser and Dr. Kamal Hossain to hold negotiations with them and kept him reserve for summit meetings with the President in future.

As clandestinely preplanned, Bhutto accompanied with his aides also reached Dacca on March 21, 1971 to participate in the ongoing negotiations which continued upto March 25, 1971. All these negotiations were held under dishonest intentions on the part of Yahya Khan and Bhutto instead of leading to some compromise, generated further bitterness of feelings and widened the gulf that could never be bridged. What actually transpired in these meetings was never disclosed but according to Bhutto, Mujib demanded lifting of Martial Law, transfer of power to the people's representatives, division of the National Assembly into two committees, one for West Pakistan and the other for East Pakistan. The Committees were to meet in Islamabad and Dacca and prepare their reports formulating special provisions and requirements of each Province of Pakistan to be incorporated in the Constitution. This was also not accepted by Bhutto and he ridiculed it manifestly that it contained the seeds of two Pakistans. Diabolical attitude of Bhutto was apparent behind this stubbornness because his own guilt made him a pliant tool in the hands of the military junta and at the same time to use the junta for his selfish ends and then make them a scapegoat. This fragile background proved self-distructive to him ultimately when he himself ended up as a scapegoat at the hands of military junta and, thus, completed a full circle after sever years, with his execution in 1979. Bhutto had admitted in an interview in April, 1971 that Yahya Khan had a strong apprehension that if he went for a political settlement with Mujib, he would be immediately ousted by the Pakistan army's ruling-clique headed by General Hamid and thus was left with no option but to order army action in East Pakistan. Bhutto was certain in his calculations that if Yahya Khan would be ousted by General Hamid who had support of China, he would be installed in power at the instance of the army-lobby. The same thing happened but after nine months and in altogether different circumstances.

Ongoing negotiations for political settlement were in fact a farce which was never to be succeeded but curiously never broke down. Mujib probably could not understand or deliberately involved himself, with no other option left, in this stratagem which was giving Tikka Khan and the army the required time to bring in reinforcements from the Western wing. This sordid drama came to an end on

March 25 when Yahya Khan flew to Karachi after he was convinced that Tikka Khan had enough army and ammunition to teach the Bengalis lesson of their life. Even after his departure, Mujib issued a press release mentioning that we have reached an agreement on the transfer of power and the President would make a declaration soon in this regard. Foreign correspondents digested this declaration as piece of political naiveté because they had observed the army men sitting in their tanks and armoured cars and trucks ready for army action. It was a clear fact that Mujib and his associates were stupid enough to be befooled by Yahya Khan and his junta from March 15 to 25, 1971 and their blindness to the cruel reality of the awaiting disaster was unimaginable. They had seen PIA Boeings and Pakistan Air Force were flying round the clock with cargos and military personnel being carried from West Pakistan on their soil. Tanks and machine guns were brought to Dacca from other parts of the region. There was a constant movement of troops and Bengali army officials were either dismissed or sent to barracks with no work as they had become suspect for the Pakistan army. Mujib and his party men had seen a serious clash during this time between West Pakistan military men and the civilian people in Joydevpur, 22 miles from Dacca when they tried to disarm East Pakistan Rifles guarding the Chinese built ordinance factory. In this conflict, 120 innocent people were killed as a result of army firing. Mujib and his associates knew these developments but even then they engaged themselves in an endless series of talks with the Yahya Khan and his officers without the simple prudence of contingency planning. When war preparations were going on in the military cantonment five miles away, their civil disobedience campaign lacked the essential ingredient of success and their maximum pressure and minimum preparedness proved subsequently disastrous for the Bengali population when they were butchered like animals by the Pakistan army of Yahya Khan.

Outside East Pakistan, an application was sent by Awami League activists to the Secretary General of the United Nations for the admission of Bangladesh in U.N.O. Bengali Muslims held demonstrations in London and New York to show solidarity towards their oppressed people in East Pakistan. Pakistan flag was burnt outside the Headquarterss of the U.N.O. Some Bengali students also attempted to take over the possession of Pakistan Embassy in Washington. Obviously, every nationalist Bengali Muslim was contributing to the cause of liberating their country in every part of the world.

These facts were admission on the part of the rulers of Pakistan who created a situation for the Bengali Muslims since, 1947 that they were considered as second grade citizens in their own country. They usually highlighted their biological structure as "dark-skinned and short-built" people who would never be allowed to rule over them. This historical neglect of these intelligent people with rich culture ultimately led to the formation of their own country but only with the help of India.

Genocide

A senior Indian journalist while writing a book on 14 days of war between India and Pakistan made a very funny remark in the preface that this war was entirely the handiwork of General Yahya Khan and a wag in Delhi quipped that the Rashtriya Swamsevak Sangh i.e. RSS has planted him in Islamabad as their agent to undo the partition of Pakistan because he never digested the theory of two nations and had a strong feeling that sooner or later East Pakistan would be free from the clutches of Punjabi rulers of West Pakistan. Events leading to this truth are elaborated to prove that it was Yahya Khan and only Yahya Khan fully responsible for the creation of Bangladesh.

On Thursday the March 25, 1971 around 5 pm, Yahya Khan arrived at Dacca airport amid tight security to fly to Karachi for the 2000 mile journey vide the Indian peninsula and Ceylon. This day was the second anniversary of his elevation to the supreme power of Pakistan after Field Martial Ayub Khan stepped down as head of the country. To show the World community that he was serious for the solution of the ongoing political stalemate, he was in Dacca for ten days but in reality he was busy in planning the military strategy to wipe out every eligible Bengali citizen from the earth. The fact that talks with Mujib had failed was of no consequence because these were not intended to succeed at any cost as West Pakistans could never afford to be ruled by a Bengali Muslim. The hidden purpose of deliberations had been purely to buy time for preparedness and for a big strike by the army. Yahya Khan did not waste time at the Dacca airport for a big farewell because he had come after spending grueling eight hours with the top military hierarchy in the conference room of Eastern Command Headquarterss which was hardly one mile away from the airport. He had taken these long hours with the military officers for the impending military action on the innocent Bengalis who were demanding their democratic right to rule their country. The die had been cast for the worst genocide of the century after Second World War.

Yahya Khan was apprehensive that if the military action would start while he was In Dacca, there was every possibility of Indian intervention. He was briefed by the army officers that Research and Analysis Wing, R&AW, the Indian intelligence could play a mischief which would be dangerous to his life as well as Pakistan. A senior air force officer of Pakistan revealed that Yahya Khan did not want to risk being intercepted and forced landing in India by Indian air force at the behest of R&AW. So, the military action was planned to follow after his safe arrival at Karachi. After his plane landed at Karachi, massage of his safe arrival was flashed to Dacca by the army. Immediately after receiving the message, the order was out from Eastern Command Headquarterss in Dacca for butchering the Bengali community be it Hindu or Muslim, lady or children. Tanks and trucks with guns atop were rolled out in Dacca and Chittagong. The worst ever genocide of Bengalis had begun that night.

The army started its action about 11.30 pm after receiving the news of the safe arrival of Yahya Khan in Karachi. Prior to that at 8 pm, Sheikh Mujibur Rehman received a secret message through an agent of R&AW, at his house at 32 Dhanmandi that his house would be raided at night by the army personnel. After that Mujib told his political confidants to remain vigiant and go into hiding if army took any action in the night. However, he refused to leave his place and said if he would go, they would burn the whole of Dacca to trace him. After midnight, his telephone went dead. At about 1.30 am on March 26, 1971, two army jeeps with some trucks came to the residence of Mujib and arrested him in his night dress. He was taken away along with three servants, an aide and his bodyguard who was badly beaten up when he started to argue with the army men. Immediately afterwards, his wife and younger child fled the house and went into hiding. An hour later, another army truck arrived at his residence and fired from all available angles. His house was brutally ransacked thereafter. Subsequently, R&AW operatives monitored a transmission of army from Dacca to West Pakistan, shortly after the arrest of Mujib, that "the bird has been caged" which was flashed soon by the Indian media through radio broadcast all over the world. Foreign newspapers widely covered the arrest of Mujib the following day. House of Colonel Muhammed Ataul Ghani Osmany in Dacca was demolished during the sweeping moves of the Pakistan defence forces on the night of March 25. Osmany, who later on became head of Mukti Bahani, had earlier organized a convention of ex-army personnel to register their solid support to the freedom movement of Sheikh Mujib.

Brutality of West Pakistan Forces

Anthony Mascarenhas, a Goan Christian, who was Assistant Editor of the Morning News in Karachi, visited East Pakistan in April, 1971. After seeing the holocaust and hearing the mass destruction of human life there, he was so shocked and horrified that he flew to London in disgust along with his family and left Pakistan once for all. He was determined that "either I would write the full story of what I had seen or I would have to stop writng. I would never again be able to write with any integrity". He reported in detail the genocide in East Pakistan in Sunday Times on June 13, 1971, when the whole world came to know the actual facts about the heinous crime of West Pakistan army under General Tikka Khan. He later on wrote a book "THE RAPE OF BANGLADESH" in which he wrote the most terrifying event of the 20 Century after Second World War. Some of the details of Anthony Mascarenhas are elaborated in the following paragraphs.

At Dacca and other parts of the province, army intelligence had prepared the list of targets during the humiliating days prior to March 25, 1971. Targets of the systematic pattern of murders all over East Bengal was planned as per the following category of people:

1. Bengali Military men of the East Bengal Regiment, the East Pakistan Rifles, police and para-military Ansars and Mjuahids.
2. The Hindus who were considered as Indian agents were hunted from village to village and house to house all over the province.
3. The Awami Leaguers starting from the office bearers and volunteers down to the lowest link in the chain of command.
4. The Students of college and university including girls.
5. Bengali intellectuals such as professors and teachers whom the army considered as militants.

Prior to this planning, Pakistan army gave demonstration of the type of onslaught they had in their mind when innocent labourers were massacred outside Chittagong port without warning because there were no prohibitory orders to such assembly of people. More than 4,000 innocent were fired with automatic weapons and their dead bodies were thrown into the sea. Yahya Khan was present in Dacca at the time of this gruesome incident of innocent killings.

In this pursuit, the beginning was made in and around Dacca on the early morning of March 26, 1971. Some of the ghastly incidents of this genocide are as under:-

(a) The East Pakistan Rifles quarters at Peilkhana was attacked with tanks, bazookas and automatic rifles by the West Pakistan army. So was the Rajar Bagh police Headquarterss. Entire police revolted and fought for 18 hours. Unprepared Bengali soldiers at both these places were taken by surprise for this attack of West Pakistan army with vastly superior fire power but they put up a brave fight. Before they died, they gave the army hell of their life. More than 5,000 Bengali soldiers were brutally killed in this attack. Elsewhere in city columns of military men with bazookas, flame-throwers, machine guns and automatic rifles, sometimes supported by tanks, were attacking predetermined targets.

(b) One unit of army went to the offices of the pro-Awami League journal, "The People" which was witnessed by the horrified foreign correspondents from the terrace of the Intercontinental Hotel. The troops opened fire at point blank range in the narrow alley from where employees of this newspaper were trying to run but unfortunately none survived. Whole of the building was left with dead bodies which was subsequently set ablaze.

(c) In a mistaken identity, another prominent Bengali newspaper Daily Ithefaq was also attacked but when the mistake was detected, the premises were re-built and the paper was restarted with a second-hand machinery.

(d) In Shankaripati area in Tanti bazaar and in the clusters of houses built around two temples standing in a corner of the sprawling race-course ground which was Hindu dominated area, the army blocked both ends of the winding street and hunted down people from house to house and killed more than 8,000 men, women and children. Hindu population living in 5 villages within 30 miles of Dacca was massacred and their houses and markets were set ablaze. Hundreds of students and their teachers were killed in the university hostels and in staff quarters. With cold ferocity, Punjabi soldiers machine gunned clusters of citizens while others set afire 25 blocks of jam packed slum areas throughout Dacca. Over one thousand people were burnt in the inferno caused by the resultant fire. They were all Bengali Muslims.

(e) An army unit went to the house of Lt.Com Muazzam Hussain, a prominent Awami League leader and an ex-navy officer who was co-accused with Sheikh Mujibur Rahman in the Agartala Conspiracy trial in 1968. He was dragged from his house and brutally killed before his wife. Other prominent Awami League leaders and student leaders in the city met with the same fate.

(f) Iqbal Hall, the Muslim students hostel and the Jaganath Hall where the Hindu students lived, were surrounded by the army and within minutes these buildings were fired with bazookas and automatic weapons. Not a single student survived in this brutal killing. More than hundred Hindu students were buried in a hastily dug trench outside the hostel compound and bodies of Muslim students of Iqbal Hall were dragged away or left to rot on the roof of the building. Prominent professors killed in the attack were Dr G C Deb, head of the Department of the Philosophy, Dr. Mofizullah Kabir, head of the History Department, Dr. A N Maniruzzaman, head of the Statistics Department, Dr. M. Maniruzzaman, reader of the Bengali Department and Dr. Obinoser Chakrobhoti, reader of the English Department and Provost of Jagannath Hall. Dr. Innas Ali head of the Physics Department was seriously injured. Corroborative evidence from independent outsiders indicated that hundreds of professors, doctors and teachers, the cream of intellectuals, were taken for interrogation in the army area and systematically killed and never returned their home. Thousand of Bengali youth met the same fate in this dreadful cleansing process.

(g) 36 Bengali District Magistrates all over the province were either killed or fled to India. Selectively, more than 4,000 Doctors, Lawyers, Professors, Scientists, Journalists, respectable ladies and other intellectuals were taken to execution camps in corners of Dacca City and tortured with acid, knives, bayonets and other instruments and finally shot dead. Eyes of many were extracted from the sockets before execution.

(h) Initially, bloodbath continued in Dacca for 48 hours. In the first daylight hours of March 26, several hundred Bengalis were shot for “violating curfew” which was not publicly announced. When curfew was declared at 10 A.M. the pre-determined targets were raided and thousands brutally murdered in their home. Bengalis then only became aware that the West Pakistan army had launched a campaign of genocide in East Pakistan.

(i) Hindus were marked out because the regime considered them Indian agents who had subverted the Muslims of East Bengal. The Bengali military men and Police were selectively killed because they were the only trained groups who could offer any resistance to the army. Other targets were those who were thought to have political ambition which was a direct threat to the integrity of the state. Genocide was the "cleansing process" for the solution of the political problem whatever number of citizens were to be killed for that purpose. This was the final solution of East Bengal problem.

(j) In Chittagong town, on March 31 during day time, Pahartoli locality was attacked by the army in collaboration with Bihari refugees. More than 3,000 Bengalis were killed and all woman raped. About 500 beautiful girls were dragged to the Cantonment. These girls were subjected to rape regularly by the army men. The victims cried in pain and narrated that they could tolerate the pains of rape by so many beasts but it was impossible to bear the heat in body which resulted from excessive accumulation of semen.

According to an Australian Doctor, Geoffrey Davis, a Sydney Surgeon who spent six weeks in Bangladesh, the entire generation of women in Bangladesh was raped during the war by West Pakistan soldiers, suffered a lifetime of infertility and chronic diseases. He revealed in an interview in London later on that a high percentage of 4,00,000 women known to have been raped during the nine-month war, had either syphilis, gonorrhea or both venereal diseases. Many of them suffered complications arising from crudely performed abortions and became sterile or suffered from chronic debilitating diseases for the rest of their lives. Dr. Davis further divulged that majority of 2,00,000 women who fell pregnant to West Pakistan soldiers had been aborted by local village dais (midwives) or quacks in highly undesirable but unavoidable conditions before any aid arrived in the country. Dr. Davis arrived in Dacca when most of the pregnant women were already at least 10 weeks pregnant. He further revealed that in some areas girls of 12 and 13 were found naked stripped of their saris and raped together so that they could not run away or commit suicide. As soon as saris were given to these raped girls, many of them hanged themselves and other tied stones to themselves and jumped off bridges. Thousands of survivors were abandoned by their families because they were pregnant and were considered as "unclean".

A World Bank delegation reported that the population of Jassore town was reduced to 15,000 from 80,000 and that of Khshtia was down to 5,000 from 40,000. Ninety percent of the houses, shops, bank and other buildings were totally destroyed by the West Pakistan Air Force. The city looked like a World War II German town having undergone strategic bombing. It was like the morning after a nuclear attack. Thousands of other towns and villages met with the same fate.

On the night of March 25, Pakistan army attacked East Bengal Rifles Headquarterss in Chittagong and killed over one thousand Bengali soldiers who were under training at that time. In Sylhet, in a mosque few hundred Bengali Muslims were gunned down with the remarks that they were not true Muslims and hence not entitled to pray in mosque. In this town, houses were systematically looted and then burnt. All women, even some old ones, were raped in the presence of their men folks who were later shot. A Muslim engineer of Zikotala Mankeshwar was forcibly made to witness the rape of his mother, wife and sister-in-law by the Pakistaniast soldiers. On April 10, in a village called Naizirahat in Chittagong District, 200 presentable women were raped in the presence of their husbands and parents.

About forty per cent population of Dinajpur district comprised Hindus. Only a few could escape to India. The remainder were wiped out by the army. Some Hindus appealed for their conversion into Islam to escape the agony of torture to death. None was excused. All were shot dead and buried in a single pit. In Singia village about 1,500 Hindus were shot dead in about half an hour as this village was still hoisting the flag of Bangladesh. Their bodies were dumped in two large pits dug by Hindus themselves.

On April 5, Chittagong town was cordoned off by army. Houses were looted and after raping the women in the open, all the naked ladies tied like cattle, were marched to the River for a bath. About 50 girls were taken to Ramgarh military cantonment where each girl was raped daily by about 10 to 15 army men. At the time of rape, the Pakistani would shout "Jai Bangle" the war cry of freedom fighter and asked their miserable victims to shout for help to their father "Sheikh Mujib". These girls were brutally raped and tormented by the army who sermonized them that they had now received sacred Muslim semen so that they would give birth to true Muslims and not the bastards like Mujib. All those suffered in this ghastly and demeaning act were upper and middle class Bengali Muslim girls and ladies.

On April 26, Biharis, non-Bengalis, observed a "Revenge Day" in Mirpur and Samoli area of Dacca which was inhabited by upper and middle class Muslim government servants. Non-Bengalis were let loose to satisfy all their sadist tendencies. After loot and butchery, they raped every woman. About 3,000 Bengalis lost their lives and no one knew how many women lost their honour besides their lives.

There was another heinous cruelty practised by the Pakistan army which has no precedence in history. During curfew hours Pakistan soldiers used to blindfold all the young boys and took them to hospitals where their total blood used to be drained off for the injured Pakistan soldiers. After extracting full blood, their dead bodies were thrown in the river Buri Ganga. This ghastly act is reported to have been practised at many other places throughout East Pakistan by the Pakistan army.

In one of most horrifying act of brutality in Holati village under Sobar police station of Dacca District, on 1 April, the army along with Biharis armed with daggers and spears, set afire this pro-Awami League Hindu village where even the cattle and other animals were burnt alive. Those who ran out were machine-gunned as usual except some girls who were saved for sadistic pleasures. Small babies were snatched from their mothers and thrown up to fall on the pointed bayonets of their guns. The breasts of the ladies were chopped off and inserted into the mouths of the dead bodies. All those alive were asked to shout "Jai Pakistan but a six year old boy innocently said "Jai Bangla", the slogan he used to shout. The army men cut that boy into fifty pieces and gave one piece each to the Hindus still alive to eat and who so ever refused was shot dead to the glory of Pakistan.

On recapture of Maulvi Bazar, Sylhet district, in the third week of April, the town was looted and all suspects killed. All fair looking young girls were taken to army camp and raped. Next morning they were brought naked to the local playground and compelled to dance before the leaders of the Muslim League throughout the day. They were then taken to Shivpur army camp and nothing was heard of them again.

In another dastardly act, on April 27, a train derailed at Goal Tak which the army considered as an act of sabotage by the Mukti Bahini. Four Muslim villages in the vicinity i.e. Goal Tek, Morkon, Pagar and Abdulpur were charged with sheltering Mukti Bahini activitsts and the villages were set on fire while the villagers were asked to gather along with their families at selected places in batches of about thirty. Here fathers and brothers were asked to rape their own daughters and sisters in front of the gathering. On refusal, all of them were butchered including women and children. Some people were forced to jump into the fire and were roasted alive.

In the first week of May, about 200 Pakistan soldiers attacked a village in the police station Gazaria on the border of Dacca and killed hundreds of innocent villagers, looted their property and raped the women. These soldiers were given dinner by the Muslim League chairman of Gazzaria who was helping them all along. His daughter who served them dinner was taken away by the Company Commander to the military camp and never returned home.

Pakistan army fully exploited the services of Razakars, the local descendants of fanatic elements like the Jamaat-e-Islami and its military group Al Badr, a hoodlum organization meant to perpetrate barbarity over innocent unarmed Bengalis. Abdul Khalique, a political-science graduate who was heading this organisation mercilessly slaughtered hundreds of journalists and intellectuals in East Pakistan. Later, he was arrested with due process of law in independent Bangladesh for his crimes.

All over East Pakistan, the brutality of Pakistan army was appalling. Women and all young girls who had not even attained puberty were raped continuously for days and thereafter their breasts were torn out with specially manufactured knives. Children did not escape the horror. Lucky one were killed by the army with their parents. But many thousands of others went through what life remained for them with eyes gouged and limbs roughly amputated. Such heinous crime against this highly cultured Bengali community was much more grave than the Jews who did not face such slaughter in second World War.

Over 10 million of Bengali, Hindus and Muslims, saved their lives by fleeing in the borders states of India. There had been much cynicism in West where it was debated as to why India allowed so many refugees to enter their territory who could have been stopped at the border. It is worthwhile to mention that India has done no repeatedly. Right through the history, India has suffered from this "weakness". India welcomed waves of Jews fleeing from their persecutors in the Middle East a thousand years ago. It also offered shelter to the Parsis escaping the religious fury in Islamic Iran. In the late fifties, India gave asylum to Dalai Lama and thousands of Tibetans running away from the brutality of Chinese Army and for that it paid a heavy price in the 1962 when China attacked India and thousands of Indian soldiers died in this unprovoked war and every Indian felt humiliated.

For more than a thousand years, Hindu culture and influence dominated and permeated the entire region of South-East Asia from Burma and Ceylon to Vietnam and Indonesia. Indian brought the message of universal peace and goodwill in these region rather then unprovoked war unleashed by other cultures of the World. Once the former President of Vietnam, Ngo Din Diem while distinguishing the Indian and Chinese civilizations quoted the confrontation between the two and said that the one coming from the West i.e. India brought to them human and spiritual values and the other from North i.e. China came with blood and thunder.

Till the defeat of Pakistan army on December 16, 1971, over 3 million Bengalis, male, females and children were killed by the West Pakistan army. Commenting on the outcome of this war, one journalist wrote that "This was India's war of compassion; it would not have been fought without this element. Tactically, the destruction of Pakistan forces in Bangladesh could have been accomplished without entering that country. But the aim was to restore the country to the East Bengalis". We Indians are made that way. We can't help it.

Demeaning Role Of Richard Nixon, US President

American State Department was fully informed by their Embassy in Dacca of all these brutalities from the day Pakistan army started the genocide in Dacca on

March 25. A clandestine radio was maintained by the American Embassy which was sending all graphic reports during the early days of extermination. Even aides of Henry Kissinger were duly informed by one Archer Blood, the ranking Foreign Service Officer in Dacca of all the atrocities committed by Pakistan soldiers. But for President and his close confident Henry Kissinger, it was no issue of concern. Their Ambassador in India Kenneth Keating was the first to react when he expressed his shock and anger to the massacre of the Bengali community in East Pakistan. On March 29, he wrote to the Nixon administration to avoid association with the reign of military terror of Pakistan and recommended to deplore promptly, publicly and prominently this brutality.

While the slaughter of the Bengalis continued unabated and there seemed to be no reaction of such horrifying slaughter from the US Government, on April 6, twenty Americans working in the Embassy in Dacca sent a formal dissent from the American policy to the Secretary of State Rogers indicting their policy to fail to denounce the suppression of democracy in such atrocities committed against Bengali population in East Pakistan. They also urged their Governmentnot to bend backward to placate Yahya Khan. They as professional public servants expressed their dissent to the American policy makers of their current policy towards Pakistan asked them to redefine their policies in order to salvage the position of America as the moral leader of Free World. Around this time, Soviet Union sent a note to Yahya Khan defending democracy in East Pakistan and asked to end the bloodbath there. But all these reactions fell on deaf ears of Nixon and Kissinger because they had found a pliable conduit in Yahya Khan to reach China which would be a key in his re-election as President. This policy was conveniently rationalized as those against Yahya Khan were pro-India and pro-Soviet Union.

This was in fact the appalling ignorance of the ground realities of East Pakistan by the then clique ruling America which even took the risk of a World War in this region when their naval threat the Enterprise was sent for a showdown with Soviet Union. Had this happened, the Americans would have found themselves in a piqued situation because China was an ally of Pakistan in this war and Soviet Union was supporting India. This was the worst misjudgment of Nixon and Kissinger while trapped in ego of clashes with Indian Prime Minister Indira Gandhi whom Nixon hated to the core of his heart and at the same time she used to do that. Nixon hated Indira Gandhi and viewed her as deceitful "bitch" a view that Henry Kissinger was careful to emulate. Nixon had visited New Delhi in 1967 on his private tour whereupon he was not accorded the due ceremonial gesture by Indira Gandhi due to which he developed a strong disliking for her. He was invited on a dinner by the Socialist Party Member of Parliament, Piloo Mody, who was a teetotaler. On the other hand when Nixon went to Pakistan, Yahya Khan threw a very lavish party in his honour and treated him like the

President of America. Obviously, Nixon nused a strong grudge against Indira Gandhi. One of the close confidants of Yahya Khan conceded after the defeat of Pakistan forces in this war with India that had Nixon and Kissinger not pampered Yahya Khan which he calculated as the ally in war, he would have been more realistic. He admitted that Yahya Khan's decision to begin the attack in the East Pakistan was his own responsibility but there was a hope that the United States would bail him out if he did something stupid.

Nixon's much cherished dream to start political dialogue with China and to use Pakistan, who was a close ally of China as the appropriate channel, for initial communication was the main reason of willful ignorance of the political turmoil generating on the soil of East Pakistan. Even prior to the organized genocide started by the Pakistan army on March 25, a Senior Review Group of the National Security Council on March 6, smelt blood in the air and advised the American governmentto discourage Yahya Khan from using force against the Awami League in East Pakistan. Kissinger cautioned this committee about the special relationship which Nixon was maintaining with Yahya Khan. Hence, massive inaction was kept as the best policy of this crisis by Nixon and his administration. So, Nixon preferred a smooth link with China through Pakistan over the massacre of thousands of Bengalis in the most brutal ways by the Pakistan army.

In the middle of April, some South Asia interagency group along with the dissidents in State Department mooted a proposal that India was moving into a period of new political stability and was demonstrating a renewed willingness to develop a cooperative relationship with the United States. A group of State Department desk officers were also suggesting the White House to authorize an immediate embargo on the shipment of military arms and economic aid to Pakistan. This was ridiculed by the President who was on the breakthrough of his diplomacy with China. In this scenario, the ping-pong diplomacy of China prevailed with the help of Pakistan and the American table tennis on tour to Japan visited China too. Around this time, the Pakistan Ambassador in United States relayed a formal invitation of Chou En-lai for Kissinger or other envoy to visit Peking. So much was Nixon pleased with Yahya Khan that he made a gesture towards those who wanted strong stand against Pakistan terror in East Pakistan and sent a personal note in his handwriting that "To all hands. Don"t squeeze Yahya at this time. RN.." Such was the intensity of political selfishness of Nixon that he overlooked the butchering of Bengalis of East Pakistan in the wake of his opening dialogue with China by using Yahya Khan as conduit.

Deceptively, Kissinger visited India in July and held discussions with Indira Gandhi and other officials and misled them that USA would take a grave view of an provoked Chinese attack on India which he admitted in his memoirs as ruse. Rather he visited Peking via Pakistan and conceived a new power alignment of

US, Pakistan and China. India Ambassador to Washington, L K Jha informed the Indian Government that Kissinger had told him prior to his visiting New Delhi that in case of India Pakistan conflict, US would not be able to help India. Jha apprehended that US was bound help Pakistan in case of a war with India. These two conflicting incidents totally took a new turn in formulating the foreign policy of India towards United States. In order to counterbalance this new power alignment, Indian signed a 20 years friendship treaty with Soviet Union on August 9, which included a clause that the two powers would consult each other before going to war to remove a threat. It was in reality a defence treaty between the two powers. Kissinger described this treaty as the bombshell and a strategic victory of Soviet Union to get foothold in South Asia against China and US. He considered this treaty as a Soviet Union guarantee to India against Chinese intervention if India got involved in a war with Pakistan. India's strong decision was used by White House an attempt to silence the opposition from the bureaucracy and Congress to the policy of Nixon and Kissinger in South Asia.

Indian Ambassador played a very significant role during this period of crisis. He was closely working with Nixon's opponent Senator Kennedy who was Chairman of a Senate subcommittee on refugees. Jha was very active in media to bring the facts on prevailing situation of East Pakistan to public knowledge. In one private meeting Kissinger even warn Jha that President Nixon was angry against the attitude of the Indian Embassy with the Congress because many congressional leaders in order to support India were finding an excuse to attack the policy of Nixon in this region. Despite the warning of Kissinger, Jha and his associates continued their relentless efforts to brief their contacts in Capitol Hill.

In November, Indira Gandhi visited USA to convince Nixon that unless Yahya Khan changed his policies in East Pakistan, war was inevitable. One of the aides of Nixon remarked later that beneath the diplomatic smiles of Indira Gandhi, there was icy rage. She was there to tell Nixon and his bloody lackey Yahya Khan not to commit murder. Her retort was imminent when Nixon in his short welcoming speech referred sympathetically to recent floods which devastated some parts of India and she directly referred to the core problem. She emphasized to Nixon to take a deeper understanding of the situation because in addition to these natural calamities there was a man-made tragedy due the presence of millions of refugees on Indian soil. Nixon was rebuked politely and he knew it. He was indeed convinced that Indira Gandhi was fully prepared for a war with Pakistan not fearing any USA threat. On the second day of the visit of Indira Gandhi, Nixon repaid the perceived insult to her when he was not accorded the due diplomatic gesture during his past visit to India. He kept her waiting for forty five minutes for the scheduled meeting. One of the aides of Kissinger realized something was amiss when Kissinger didn't make his usual appearance just before the appointed schedule. In order to smoothen this untoward diplomatic insult, he took her to the Roosevelt Room upstairs in White House. No apology was rendered from any quarter to this indecency. Indira Gandhi later disclosed in an interview that in this meeting with Nixon she was talking more with Kissinger than with Nixon as he would pass the buck on to him at regular interval. Indira Gandh iconceded that he was unwilling to accept her assessment of any situation in this region. Nixon made a dramatic departure from the traditional US policy which, although allied to Pakistan, had sought to build up India as an Asiatic counterpoise to China. Kissinger in his memoirs admitted that he and Nixon were convinced that Indira Gandhi was not motivated primarily by conditions in East Pakistan but had decided sometime in mid-1971 to use the opportunity to settle accounts with Pakistan once for all. They were also fearing that Third World War was also not avoidable in this crisis. Nixon later conceded in 1975 during his secret grand jury testimony to the Watergate Special Prosecution Force that the United States had come close to nuclear war with Russians during India-Pakistan dispute.

Not only USA, some Arab countries like Jordan, Saudi Arabia, Libya, Algeria and Sudan were aggressively supporting Pakistan in the genocide of East Pakistan population. Egypt, friend of India, was neutral but did not speak against Pakistan. Only Palestinians openly sympathized with the Bangladesh cause while Lebanon and Iraq maintained neutral stance. Two Muslim nations of South East Asia, Indonesia and Malaysia did hide their pro-Pakistan sympathies. Nixon pressured CENTO members Turkey, Jordan and Iran to supply American military hardware to Pakistan. There were confirmed reports that Turkish aircraft did fly ammunition and other supplies to Pakistan at this insistence of Nixon.

When war between India and Pakistan started, by the end of first week of December, Congress and press were in an uproar over the continued tilt of USA towards Pakistan. In spite of these provocations against the policy of Nixon-Kissinger, licensing of arms shipments to India was suspended and export licenses for military goods were cancelled. Nixon blamed India for the war. US also falsely blamed that the Indians had attacked an American merchant vessel. Kissinger again deceptively mislead the World community by declaring in a press briefing that a negotiated settlement between the Pakistan authorities and the Awami League was on the card when India started war. This was all double talk by Nixon because the kind of settlement that Yahya Khan was prepared to accept would have been rejected out of hand by the Awami League leaders in Calcutta because they could not have acquiesced in any proposal without Sheikh Mujibur Rehman who was detained in the jail in West Pakistan. All available evidence indicated that Yahya Khan was not prepared to accept any settlement when his troops had built an unfordable moat filled with Bengali blood and corpses, between West Pakistan and East Bengal, in addition to the more than 1,100 miles geographical gap spreading the two States.

Nixon and Kissinger were so scared of every incident that they found additional dubious belief when US Secretary of State John Irwin requested Indian Ambassador Jha to give an assurance that India would not attack West Pakistan to which Jha also sought US guarantee on behalf of Pakistan that no Indian territory would be annexed if occupied by Pakistan. Any observer in New Delhi, journalist or diplomat with elementary knowledge of the working of the policy of Indian Government on Kashmir was aware that India was not interested in capturing the territory of Pakistan occupied Kashmir which was ethnically and geographically different from the rest of the State and of no strategic or economic value for the state of Jammu and Kashmir but on the other hand could be a strategic liability. India has only desired for a readjustment and rationalization of the cease-fire line so as to impart greater security to the adjacent Indian territory for the people of Jammu and Kashmir.

After this unilateral assurance was refused by India, Nixon ordered the Naval Task Group with the aircraft carrier Enterprise as its center to move towards Bay of Bengal. This Group had seven destroyers, a helicopter carrier and two companies of Marines. Chief of Naval Operations of this Group, Admiral Elmo Zumwalt had no advance notice of this deployment. He later revealed that the order of White House did not specify what the mission was, nor could anyone, including the Chairman of the Joint Chiefs told him what was the mission or they were sent to harm someone. Zumwalt later conceded that Nixon and Kissinger were perhaps frustrated by their inability to influence events in the subcontinent. So they Impulsively organized the Task Group and sent it on its way in a final effort to show the World that America was not to be taken lightly and portrayed as a military actor in every part of the World. He admitted that this action was untimely and futile. Soviet Union sent the naval war-ships, which were already stationed in Indian ocean, to counter the American Seventh Fleet. Nixon later claimed that he was successful to save West Pakistan from being captured by Indira Gandhi and also averted a nuclear war with Soviet Union in Indian Ocean. This was all concocted and humbug to save his face from public fury and humiliation.

Indira Gandhi sarcastically wrote a letter to Nixon wherein she cited the American Declaration of Independence with its call for man's right to life, liberty and the pursuit of happiness as a great moment of history which inspired millions of people to die for liberty. She then pointed towards the role of Nixon betraying the tenets of Declaration of Independence of his own country by supporting Yahya Khan in the genocide when their own people demanded the liberty. She bluntly wrote to Nixon that only lip service was paid to the need for a political solution but not a single worthwhile step was taken to bring the peace.

Deployment of Nuclear war ships in the Indian waters provided a much-needed support to those policy makers in India who were advocating nuclear development. They argued that the American Enterprise was equipped with nuclear weapons and had India had its own arsenal, Nixon would not have been so quick to deploy its warship at that time. Although, India under the dynamic leadership of Indira Gandhi had decided on developing nuclear options before this crisis but pro-Pakistan policy of Nixon expedited this process and India successfully conducted its first nuclear test on May 18, 1974 much against the wishes of USA.

Kao's Role

On March 27, 1971, Prime Minister Indira Gandhi declared in the Upper House of Parliament that it was not merely the suppression of movement but it was meeting an unarmed people with tanks. .We were fully alive to the situation and we shall keep constantly in touch with what is happening and what we needed to do. The Indian Parliament passed a historic resolution on March 31, 1971 that: "This House records its profound conviction that the historic upsurge of the 75 million people of East Bengal will triumph. The House wishes to assure them that their struggle and sacrifices will receive the whole-hearted sympathy and support of the people of India".

Ever since the confrontation between the East Pakistan politicians in general and Sheikh Mujibur Rehman in particular, Indian external intelligence, R&AW, gathered information from its sources of Pakistan origin in army, political and diplomatic circle about the impending action of the West Pakistan Government prior to the declaration of the election in Pakistan. One source from London in the mid 1970 reported that a Pakistan diplomat confirmed an impending military action in East Bengal. This report was subsequently sent to Joint Intelligence Committee by R&AW which was not given much credence. Kao briefed Indira Gandhi about it in a separate meeting wherein she reviewed the overall political situation. It was ultimately decided in this meeting that Kao would finalize a blue print for the insurgency activities inside East Pakistan to help the Bengali Muslims. Thereafter, Kao stepped up covert activities on the borders of East Pakistan. Many new check posts of R&AW were opened to penetrate into the army set up of Pakistan in those areas. Technical staff was also sent to these posts to monitor the wireless messages of Pakistan army from Eastern wing to the Western part and vice versa. By the time the elections were declared to be held in Pakistan, R&AW was fully in command to provide all internal assessment of the East Pakistan. Through a senior Pakistan officer in Dacca and from other various agents, R&AW sent assessment to the government that if at all elections were held in Pakistan, Awami Leage under Sheikh Mujibur Rehman would sweep the poll in this region. Only apprehension was that they would not install Mujib as the ruler of Pakistan. From intelligence point of view, R&AW was fully in command to provide all background information and assessment to the government from mid 1970 onwards. Indira Gandhi had planned to liberate East Pakistan from the clutches of the dictatorial rule of the military junta of West Pakistan in case Mujib was not allowed to become Prime Minister of Pakistan.

The first and foremost task Kao foresaw was to stop the overflight of Pakistan from West to East. Kao had planned other measures to stop these overflights when suddenly one Indian origin Pakistan agent of ISI was caught by the BSF while crossing inside India. In a swift intelligence operation, Kao used this agent in his planning to stop the overflights of Pakistan. Full details of this operation are as under:

Hijacking of Fokker Friendship plane, Ganga, of Indian Airlines by Hashim Qureshi

There was an agent of R&AW, Hashim Qureshi in Srinagar. He was working in league with BSF also at Jammu and Kashmir border. In Pakistan occupied Kashmir, a Pakistan sponsored terrorist organization, National Liberation Front was formed by one militant Mohammd Maqbool Butt for subversive activities in Jammu and Kashmir. This organization launched a movement Al Fatah for liberation of J&K from India and sent large number of its members for subversive activities there. Thirty six of their members were arrested by the J&K police with the help of intelligence agencies. In order to get the inside information about this movement, R&AW decided to infiltrate Qureshi into this organization since he was having full knowledge about the terrain of Pakistan occupied Kashmir and was also aware of the intelligence activities of Pakistan. But Qureshi changed his integrity when he was sent to Pakistan occupied Kashmir and subsequently won over by the Pakistan intelligence to work for them in J&K. Qureshi himself had admitted that he was trained in Pakistan Occupied Kashmir by ISI operatives at the instance of Maqbool Bhatt. He was given training of hijacking by a former pilot of Pakistan.

Qureshi was sent by Pakistan intelligence in J&K in the middle of January 1971 when he was arrested by BSF while he was crossing the border. When he was interrogated by the Indian intelligence agencies, he spilled the beans and revealed that he was sent by Pakistan intelligence to hijack an Indian Airlines plane from Srinagar airport. The plane was to be hijacked when it would be piloted by Rajiv Gandhi, son of Indira Gandhi, The then Prime Minister of India, who was a serving pilot in Indian Airlines. When this startling disclosure was reported to the head of BSF and R&AW, R N Kao devised a counter plan to defeat Pakistan intelligence on their own game through this hijacking. This was approved by Indira Gandhi.

R&AW and BSF, persuaded Hashim Qureshi to work for them in order to save him from prosecution by Indian authorities, to which he agreed. A plan was devised that Qureshi would be allowed to hijack an Indian Airlines plane from Srinagar airport to Lahore where he would demand the release of 36 members of Al Fatah who were in jail in India in lieu of the passengers on the plane. He was directed not to give the control of the plane to the Pakistan authorities until he was allowed to talk to Zulfiqar Ali Bhutto, Chairman of the Pakistan Peoples Party, who was the chief architect in instigating the political turmoil of Pakistan at that time. It was planned by Kao that he would blow up the plane after his meeting with Bhutto to prove his credentials for the cause of Al Fatah militants in jail, in the eyes of Pakistan authorities. In order to keep this operation a closely guarded secret, Qureshi was sent to a safe house of R&AW in Bangalore for security reasons till the finalization of the final plan. This was not disclosed to the J&K Government and other security agencies by R&AW.

After the plan was given final shape, on January 30, 1971 Hashim Qureshi along with another operative Ashraf Qureshi, his relative, was allowed to hijack a Fokker Friendship plane, Ganga, of Indian Airlines with 26 passengers on board from Srinagar airport and forced Captain Kachru, the pilot of the plane, to take the plane to Lahore airport. R&AW allowed him to carry a grenade and a toy pistol inside the plane. Pakistan authorities at Lahore airport allowed the plane to land when they were informed that it had been hijacked by National Liberation Front militants of Pakistan Occupied Kashmir. All India Radio soon made broadcast of this hijacking and whole of the World was informed that the Pakistan Government was behind this hijacking. Qureshi, as directed by R&AW, demanded the release of 36 Al Fatah members in custody of Indian government in lieu of the passengers on the plane and asked the Pakistan authorities to arrange his meeting with Bhutto at the airport. Indian government obviously refused to release the Al Fatah detainees. Qureshi was allowed to move freely at Lahore Airport by the Pakistan authorities where he used telephone and met media people while the second hijacker was guarding the passengers inside the plane. Bhutto met Qureshi on February 1, 1971 and they talked for sometime near the plane. Thereafter, the passengers were released and the plane was blown up. There are contradictory reports, but it was later confirmed that the plane was put on fire by the ISI operatives of Pakistan. This was admitted by Hashim Qureshi also after his release from jail. All passengers and crew members were sent back to India via Amritsar by Road.

Pakistan government initially gave him political asylum and hailed him freedom fighter. Most of the political leaders of Pakistan condemned this incident but Bhutto did not criticize this hijacking which further strengthens the claim of India that Pakistan was behind this hijacking with full knowledge of Bhutto. This was a master stroke planning by the Chief of R&AW, R N Kao, which brought international criticism of this hijacking. Indian government immediately banned the overflights of Pakistan from its territory.

In Pakistan, the truth behind this incident was known to general public that the hijackers did not belong to any freedom movement of Kashmir and, in fact, were agents of the Indian government. Even Sheikh Abdullah, who was released in 1964 because of the internal and external pressure, also denounced the hijackers as the Indian agents. Pakistan government appointed an Inquiry Commission in this case. The Commission came to the conclusion that the hijacking of the aircraft was arranged by the Indian Intelligence agencies as the culmination of a series of action taken by the Indian government to bring about a situation of confrontation between Pakistan and India. Taking advantage of this situation, the Indian government banned the flights of Pakistan aircraft over Indian territory in February 1971 and succeeded in its plans to create difficulties for overflights to East Pakistan and also to inflict financial loss because all flights from West to East Pakistan were enrooted via Srilanka.. Commission also gave opinion that the motive behind this conspiracy was to disrupt internal communications of Pakistan and to encourage separatist movements to disintegrate Pakistan.

This incident overtly gave India the right opportunity which was planned by Kao to cancel the flights of Pakistan over its territory which hampered the plan of Yahya Khan to send its troops by air to curb the political movement of Mujib in East Pakistan. Later on, the USA government clandestinely offered their planes to Pakistan to transport soldiers to Bangladesh via Sri Lanka and Himalaya range. This hijacking ultimately slowed down the arrival of Pakistan army through air route.

This was a master stroke of R&AW during the 1971 war for liberation of Bangladesh which Pakistan government did not apprehend and never denied the fact that Hashim Qureshi was not the member of Al Fatah terrorist organization. He was an Indian agent, who meticulously executed this top secret operation of R&AW which enabled the Indian government to create far reaching problems in the deployment of Pakistan army in East Pakistan due to the ban on oveflights from the Indian territory.

Hashim Qureshi and Ashraf Quresh along with four others were subsequently prosecuted in a Special Court of Pakistan under the charges of working for the Indian Intelligence services in this hijacking case. He was sentenced to nineteen years of imprisonment. He was released in 1980 by the Pakistan government. Hashim went to Netherlands after completing his sentence in Pakistan.

Thereafter, R&AW did not let down its important agent, Hashim. The Station Chief of R&AW in Netherlands was asked by the R&AW authorities to trace him there. He was duly traced and provided all sorts of help for his rehabilitation in Netherlands. Although R&AW used him as its agent in the hijacking in 1971 but the legal system in India did not pay any credence to that so-called secret operations and Hashim was arrested in December, 2000 when he was brought to India by R&AW authorities. He was also prosecuted in India for the Ganga hijacking case under various sections of the Indian Penal Code. In this double jeopardy case, because he had already been prosecuted by the Pakistan government in the Ganga hijacking case, Hashim is still facing prosecution on the same charges in Srinagar Court. R&AW authorities are still taking care of Hashim except for a brief period in May, 2008, when the then R&AW Secretary, Ashok Chaturvedi stopped his regular compensation but it was soon restored by the next Secretary of R&AW, when past facts were brought to his knowledge. He is presently involved in the political streamline of Jammu and Kashmir and doing social welfare programs for Kashmiri people.

Mukti Bahini – Brain Child of R N Kao

War with Pakistan to liberate East Pakistan at that juncture in March, 1971, was impossible for Indian government. Thus, R&AW had a big role to play prior to the entry of Indian army into the territory of enemy. Hence, a guerilla operation had to be planned to harass the Pakistan army. These operations are usually launched against the government which even after losing the confidence of their people, cling to power in utter disregard to the constitutional norms and practices. Such governments are never prepared to modify their policies to honour popular aspirations. So, the local population is left with no alternative but to resort to the guerilla activities to create all possible problems to replace a hated ruling junta with a popular government. Tyranny begets resistance in the natural scheme of things. Hence, the docile but oppressed people of Bengali origin got fuelled with patriotic ferver and were consumed by an avenging spirit. They were bent upon disproving the denigrating "libel in the field of action against those very traducers".

Unpopular Pakistan government after March 25, 1971, became the epitome of this outlook among the Bengali population of East Pakistan. In the case of this region, the right to have their own land and enjoyment of a fair social treatment motivated the Bengali population in one and sundry to rebel against the Pakistan army and to attain freedom was the sole aim of every class of the society. The motive of the movement was to conquer and destroy the oppressive oligarchy of Pakistan who exercised power through its agents and armed forces which were well equipped. Allied with it was the pampered bureaucracy which fulfilled the ambitions of the oligarchy. Bhutto in league with Yahya never wanted by puny Bengalis to rule Punjabis, Sindhis and Pathans etc. In his opinion, Bhutto's class had descended on earth to rule Bengalis and not to be ruled by them. With Hitlerits attitude and Nazi approach, he was determined to crush Bengalis. So, the Bengali honour took up arms against their own colonial rulers to drive them out of their motherland.

When the influx of refugees increased after the crackdown of Pakistan army on the innocent East Bengal people, Indira Gandhi called a meeting of Army Chief Sam Manekshaw and the R&AW Chief R N Kao in which she discussed the modus operandi to liberate this part of the land from West Pakistan army. She told General Manekshaw that she wanted to take military action against Pakistan army to liberate this wing of Pakistan. Manekshaw replied to her that Indian army had always been told by its political bosses that their role was defensive and meant to protect the territorial integrity. If Indian army was to put in action in East Pakistan, special riverine operation equipment and training was required for them wherein they were lacking. Manekshaw did not want a premature operation in this war and repeat the mistakes of 1962 and 1965. When Indira Gandhi asked the General as to how much time the Indian army would take for the offensive inside East Pakistan, he replied at least six months. She told Manekshaw to make preparation for the war and inform her when he was ready in his plan.

Since, the Indian army was not prepared and well equipped for an immediate army action at that point of time, it was planned to raise and train a guerrilla outfit of the Bengali refugees of East Pakistan by R&AW which would harass the Pakistan army till the Indian army would be ready for the final assault to the liberation of East Pakistan. She then asked R N Kao to prepare all possible grounds for the army for its final assault when the clearance from General Manekshaw was received for his readiness for the war. Kao submitted a full blue print soon afterward to form and train a guerilla outfit of the East Bengal national which would harass the Pakistan army prior to army action. After receiving nod from Indira Gandhi, training of the guerilla outfits by the R&AW operatives with the help of BSF and other police and para-military outfit started on all the borders of East Pakistan which was subsequently named as Mukti Bahini after initially termed as Mukti Fauj or Freedom Army.

After Yahya Khan flew back to Karachi on the evening of March 25, 1971, one Bengali source of R&AW came to the residence of Sheikh Mujib at 8 pm with a slip on which a message was given to him that his house by would be raided by Pakistan army that night. Mujib alerted his associates to go underground and chose to stay at his residence where he was arrested around 1.30 am in the night. His senior party men escaped to Calcutta under the guise of refugees. They were Syed Nazrul Islam, Vice President of the Awami League, Tajuddin Ahmed, Khondkar Moushtaq Ahmed, Qamaruzzaman, Mansur Ali etc. Youth Leaders like his nephew Sheikh Fazal-ul-Haq Moni, Tufail Ahmad, Shirazul Alam, Abdul Razak, Rab, Ashraf-son of Syed Nazrul Islam, Sheikh Zamal-the youngest son of Sheikh Mujib and hundred of other known and unknown leaders crossed over to Indian border after the crackdown of Pakistan army. Soon they were put under the command of R&AW at Calcutta. A provisional Bangladesh government in exile was formed at Calcutta at Theater Road on April 14, 1971 and name of the capital was given as Mujib Nagar. A Bangladesh Radio Station "Free Bengal Betal Kendra was established at Mujib Nagar for regular news to the people of East Bengal on impending plans of the Government in exile and to coordinate the other factions of the guerilla movement who for lack of communication were stranded in far flung areas of East Pakistan. Syed Nazrul Islam was named as Vice President and acting President in the absence of Sheikh Mujib and Tajuddin Ahmed was appointed as Prime Minister. P N Banerjee, Joint Director of R&AW at Calcutta was given the overall charge to look after this government in exile of Bangladesh and provide all sorts of other helps which they required for their covert and overt activities. Colonel M A G Osmany was made the provisional Chief of Staff of the Bangladesh Army and in that capacity, the Chief of all freedom fighters and head of Mukti Fauj which was renamed as Mukti Bahini by the end of April. Osmany was highly respected by Indian Intelligence and Army because of his high patriotic sense, his loyalty to Sheikh Mujib and commanded respect among all and sundry.

Deputy Chief of R&AW, Sankaran Nair who was in charge of Pakistan desk in R&AW, along with P N Banerjee head of Bangladesh operations in R&AW at Calcutta and Brig. M B K Nair, head of Technical division of R&AW made a hectic tour of all border check posts of R&AW. Commandos of Special Frontier Force, the paramilitary branch of R&AW, were deployed at many vital places near to these check posts to impart training on East Pakistan refugees. Brig. Nair opened many monitoring stations of R&AW in these check posts and inside Pakistan territory also to provide speedy information to Calcutta office of R&AW and to its Headquarterss in New Delhi about the training of Mukti Bahini cadres and movement and action of Pakistan army. R&AW prepared a technical network and encircled East Pakistan on all vantage points which proved of strategic importance for the phase one action, to train insurgents, of the Indian government and ultimately in the decisive liberation war of December, 1971.

At the time of indiscriminate genocide in East Pakistan, around 6,000 Bengali soldiers were serving in 6 battalions of East Bengal Rifles, about 15,000 in East Pakistan Rifles, more than 45,000 were serving in police and about 45,000 Razakars i.e. home guards in whole of East Pakistan. Most of these armed men were stripped off their arms on the eve of military crackdown. On March 25, 1971 most of police stations and police posts in urban areas were attacked by military and who so ever was sighted inside these places, was massacred. Third Battalion soldiers were slaughtered while asleep in Rangpur-Dinajpur area. First battalion also met the same fate at Jessore. However one Captain Hafizuddin along with 122 soldiers escaped under the cover of darkness. At Dacca's Rajar Bagh, armed police fought for four hours with one full Pakistan battalion supported with tanks but ultimately most of them were gunned down by the army. Some other Bengali army officers had to revolt to escape death during the genocide. One of them Major Khalid Musharraf who was posted at Dacca was sent on a patrol duty to Tripura border three days prior to army action on a false pretext of mounting tension with Indian army. When he did not find any untoward situation on border, he sought permission to return to Dacca but he was ordered to stay back there only. This aggravated his suspicion that his men might be disarmed during his absence from Dacca. He clandestinely returned to Dacca and along with other Bengali soldiers formed a rebel group of his unit and succeeded in outwitting the orders of surrender of his automatic weapons. When the genocide began and twenty thousand innocent civilians were killed, he hoodwinked his senior officers and overpowered three West Pakistan officers of his unit and escaped and formed a rebel set up near Sylhet. He himself assumed the charge of the Commander-in-Chief of those forces and raised the banner of revolt. He put up stiff resistance to Pakistan forces. His forces systematically destructed bridges, roads and rail tracks and successfully isolated Sylhet from Dacca for a considerable period of time. Another Bengali officer Major Shaffiullah was also conducting guerilla operation nearby and they converged into joint action against the army of Pakistan. Their forces thwarted the movement of Pakistan forces which were advancing from Dacca to Joydevpur to disarm their contingent.

Major Zia-ur-Rehman, another Bengali officer was informed in Chittagong of the dock worker's refusal to unload an arms cargo and also arrest of a Hindu officer of his regiment. He outwitted Pakistan army before the crackdown and controlled Chittagong and its radio station for some time with the help of other Bengali soldiers. He gave a call to all Bengali soldiers to revolt against Pakistan defence forces to avoid killing. He urged them to join the freedom movement of the Bengalis. Large contingent of East Bengal Rifles under Major Shaukat Ali was holding fort in Chittagong along with some fellow Bengali soldiers of the 8th battalion of East Pakistan Rifles. One Hindu officer, Major Chittaranjan Dutta was leading a small group of East Pakistan Rifles soldiers and armed police in Sylhet. Bengali soldiers, who were being deported from sea route from Chittagong became suspicious and took control of the ship and then forced the Captain at bayonet point to sail back to the port, revolted which sparked off Bengali nationalism in the Pakistan Defence Forces. All these splinter groups fought with Pakistan forces independently in far flung areas of East Pakistan for several days. Thereafter, operatives of R&AW, through their trained agents regrouped and re-equipped with arms, united these groups and brought them under the control of Mukti Bahini to fight a cohesive battle against Pakistan army along with the other trainees who were receiving training from R&AW agents and BSF and other paramilitary forces of India in and outside East Pakistan territory. Within two months after the military action R&AW was able to form a formidable guerilla outfit Mukti Bahini with the survivors of East Bengal

Rifles, the East Pakistan Rifles, young refugees, the police and some other army personnel and brought them under the command of Col. Osmany, Commander in Chief of the entire operation. People having different shades of opinion about the objectives and modus operandi of the struggle shed their difference, swallowed their pride and renounced prejudices in the wake of crackdown and to avenge the atrocities committed on Bengali population systematically by Pakistan army. They came forward to form a united front and forged a compact war-machine so that they could liberate their motherland from the murderous army of Pakistan.

R N Kao, his deputy K. Sankran Nair, P N Banerjee with the regional heads of Army, BSF, Col. Osmany and other senior ranks of Mukti Bahini, after long deliberations and planning, chalked out a full scale operation of this guerilla outfit for whole of East Pakistan by the middle of July, 1971. In the initial stages around 1000 trained guerillas of Mukti Bahini achieved minor success due to lack of vigorous arm training and no knowledge of specific objectives inside the territory. Initially they were sent in large batches of up to two hundred whom small villages could hardly feed and Pakistan army would detect arrival of such conspicuous batches. On their departure, Pakistan army would play havoc with villages which had provided them shelter. This made their visits unpopular and hence unfruitful. In order to overcome these initial problem, by the end of July, the actual operation started with long process of recruitment, training, type of utility of equipments, organizing them into effective guerrilla bands and then, allocating them their tasks and areas of operation with main constituents of this force comprising former soldiers, students, intellectuals and middle class youngsters both from Muslim and Hindu communities. Each of these volunteers was recommended by Members of the National Assembly deputed by Provisional government of Bangladesh in exile at Calcutta so that shady persons did not get entry into this outfit. Around 1,00,000 strong militia were recruited and trained for whole of East Pakistan with the help of R&AW which coordinated with other paramilitary outfits like BSF, CRPF, RAC of Rajasthan, Assam Rifles etc of India all along the Indian border and inside Pakistan territory. Prime Minister, Tajuddin Ahmed announced names of regional commanders and allocated their areas of operation as under:

(a) Major Khalid Musharraf was made in charge of Sylhet-Comilla sector;

(b) Major Zi-ur-Rehman assumed command of Chittagong-Noakhali area;

(c) Major Shaifulla was given charge of Mymensingh and Tangail sector;

(d) Major M A Usman to head South-West Sector; and

(e) Captain Hafizuddin to lead at Jessore area.

Mukti Bahini's land force was subsequently divided into two groups:

1. **The Niamit Bahini:** regular force which was assigned the task to wage guerrilla war against regular troops of enemy in the form of frontal attacks.

This force was trained by the paramilitary forces of India for this specific purpose.

2. **The Gona Bahini:** irregular force was entrusted clandestine tasks like laying mines, ambushes and sabotage operations such as blowing up bridges, culverts, powers houses and strategic nerve centers. They were trained by R&AW operatives for these covert operations.

Besides these two wings, Gram Parishads were formed in all 62,000 villages of East Pakistan which created insurgency units so that they could actively support the freedom struggle by limited guerrilla activity and provide information about Pakistan army to Mukti Bahini. Their main contribution was to help main forces of Mukti Bahini in organizing rural-guerrilla sanctuaries. This was a peaceful guerrilla activity which helped in recruitment and establishment of training centre in rural areas.

Mukti Bahini through its above components rendered several units of Pakistan army in absolute disarray in controlling their area of operation. From June onwards, it created a virtual hell for marauding Pakistan troops by launching raids in and around Dacca, knocking out power houses, raiding an ordnance factory and damaging beyond repair a plant which was converting motor launchers into gun boats meant for the use of Pakistan army. Tea processing units in an around Sylhet and a number of Jute mills in Narayanganj and the Nabarun jute mills in Dacca, Eastern oil refinery in Chittagong, Tita's Gas pipe line from Brahmanbaria to Dacca, three sugar mills of Pachagarh, Darsana and Thakurgaon, paper mills in Khulna, steel mills and fertilizer factories in Chittagong were thoroughly wrecked and brought to a grinding halt by the commandos of Mukti Bahini. Dacca plunged into darkness for several days because of the disrupted electric supply sabotaged by Mukti Bahini. Saboteurs wearing plain clothes and disguised as poor villagers carried out sabotage activities in rural areas due to strong security measures imposed by Pakistan army in these areas. As a result of this mounting guerrilla attacks of the Mukti Bahini all over East Bengal, all important government buildings like radio stations, national and state banks and the entire military-industrial complexes had to be protected by an eight meter high perimeter obstructions by the army. In one of the bravest operations, Mukti Bahini derailed a passenger train which was packed with Pakistan soldiers by bombarding it 2 kilometers away from Fulgazi railway station and killed most of them instantly. Pakistan soldiers in other areas were the main target of Mukti Bahini who were liquidated on mass scale in guerilla warfare of high intensity. By August,

1971 between 15,000 to 20,000 West Pakistan soldiers were killed by Mukti Bahini and several thousand were wounded seriously. Dacca military hospitals were so overcrowded with these seriously injured soldiers that the PIA cancelled several of its scheduled international flights, to transport the wounded soldiers from Dacca to Karachi.

Mukti Bahini expanded into an all-service structure which included among other technical wings, the elements of Navy and Air force operatives. Bengali naval and air-force personnel, who were stranded in West Pakistan had defected into India where they joined the liberation force. A viable naval wing was organized by R&AW to conduct maritime operations. They captured some Pakistan vessels in the Bay of Bengal. Under these vessels, the Mukti Bahini guerrillas succeeded in sinking a number of Pakistan vessels including coasters, oil tankers, barges, river steamers, boats and launches which included many American made barges and motor tugs. This ferocious menace of this wing of Mukti Bahani prevented many foreign ships from visiting the ports of East Pakistan thus resulting in short of supply of many important items for the Pakistan army. This also hampered the regular flow of essential commodities of day to day need to the Pakistan forces. By August, 1971, the Mukti Bahini naval wing had turned the East Pakistan waters into a zone of peril for hostile shipping which was ferrying war materials, especially to Chittagang and Chalna. Limpet mines had been planted in this area by these operatives. In September, two British ships, CHAKDINA, a 10,000 ton freighter and TEVIOT a 16,000 ton tanker, were badly damaged by the Mukti Bahini guerrillas. Many more ships were also damaged or sunk in Chittagong and Chalna ports. On 12 October, in a daring operation, a Mukti Bahini gunboat attacked a British cargo boat, the 7,000 ton CITY OF ST. ALBANS which was forced to go back to Calcutta.

Till the end of the monsoon, Pakistan troops remained closeted in the cantonments and towns and Yahya Khan had expected his troops to come out in full strength to crush the Mukti Bahini's strongholds which had reached to almost all the 62,000 villages of East Pakistan. This was almost impossible for the four and a half divisions of the Pakistan army. At the same time, strength of Mukti Bahini and its striking power had increased considerably during this period whereas the Pakistan army was tired since they had no break for over four months. Many a times, the Pakistan troops during encounters with the Mukti Bahini ran away and left behind large scale of arms and equipment. They left behind bodies of their soldiers which indicated their sagging morale. They went to the extent of looting ordinary provision stores and confectionary stuff in East Pakistan and departed with the compliment "Send the bill to Indira Gandhi".

In sharp contrast, the local Bengali populations always welcomed Mukti Bahini guerrillas when they appeared before the public and greeted with banners all over the East Bengal. Mujib's tape-recorded speeches were often played on such occasions. Bangladesh Radio Station operating from Calcutta delivered regular details of the success of Mukti Bahani which encouraged the morale of the local population and had worst demoralizing effect on the already harassed Pakistan forces. Bangladesh Friendship Society formed by Dr. Triguna Sen was one of the many organizations which organized funds and other arrangements for the Mukti Bahini. Special hospitals and convalescent homes were established around the border for the wounded soldiers of Mukti Bahini by this organization.

On the planning of R&AW, the operations of Mukti Bahini were initially restricted to hit-and-run raids on the military targets but subsequently it expended the scope and frequency of its hit-and-run raids, ambushes and attacks on small isolated enemy positions which resulted in liberating the occupied territory and bringing additional areas into the control of the Bangladesh government in exile. Many foreign correspondents and observers had confirmed that by mid-November, the Mukti Bahini had been able to liberate about one-third of Bangladesh and was dominating most of the remaining areas. Mukti Bahini's casualty ratio compared to the Pakistan army's was 1 to 4. Later it increased to a figure of as high as 1 to 15 and by the end of November more than 25,000 soldiers of Pakistan army were killed by them. In two separate operations, Mukti Bahini assassinated the former Governor, Abdul Monem Khan who was a collaborator of the oppressive regime. In another incident it made a fatal attack on Maulana Ishaque, a minister of East Pakistan government. These incidents brought many of the loyalists of Pakistan to the side of Mukti Bahini. Movement of the Pakistan troops was severely hampered not only by the rugged terrain but also with disrupted communications by R&AW operatives. Even local labourers refused to cooperate with the army fearing safety of life at the hands of Mukti Bahani. Lack of communication facilities made army soft targets of the Mukti Bahini. Guerrillas of Mukti Bahini increased bomb explosions and shooting incidents in Dacca intensively. An outstanding achievement in this regard was a raid on an army position near the railway station of Dacca wherein the guerrillas smashed 40 Pakistan bunkers and killed 30 Pakistan soldiers in broad day light. A correspondent reported that these guerrillas operated openly in Dacca whose eastern part had become a daily target of bombings and shootings. Green Road near Dhanmandi residential areas had become a "No Men's land" due to intense firing between the army and Mukti Bahini. A second year college girl from Pabna, Shirin Banu and her colleagues formed a guerrilla band and assaulted a contingent of the Punjab Regiment of Pakistan which was sent to capture the police line of that place. These girls killed many Pakistan soldiers in the ensuing fighting. These girls wore the Khaki outfits while fighting saying that Sarees would be worn only after the liberation of Bangladesh. Such was the morale of the local population of East Pakistan during those days. In a heart burning incident, Roshan Ara, a teenaged girl of Dacca University tied explosives around her body and leaped in front of the enemy tank brigade, blew herself in pieces but destroyed the first tank.

These daring incidents of the cadre of Mukti Bahini totally demoralized the confidence of the Pakistan army all over the Bangladesh and paved path for an easy access for the Indian army for a final assault in December, 1971. When Indian army sprang on the scene on December 3, the Mukti Bahini had prepared the ground for them through a lot of spade work. They received the army at various points on the border and guided them to the interior along the shortest routes, helped them with transportation, supplied valuable intelligence about enemy movements and positions, besides ambushing the enemy troops and cutting off their communication lines. All these invaluable services of Mukti Bahini provided a broad base for Indian army to achieve its military objective which was hurriedly launched. When final war started on December, 3, Mukti Bahini was working on every position on the flanks of the enemy and accompanying the formations of Indian army to guide them for assault on enemy stationed at vantage points.

R&AW operatives inside Mukti Bahini were so deeply penetrated into the Pakistan army establishment that their day to day planning was with R&AW Headquarterss in New Delhi. Gen. Niazi the military commander and Governor A N Malik could hardly keep any secret which did not reach R&AW through their agents in their camps. When in the last stages of war, a secret plan was devised by the Pakistan army officers in Dacca to evacuate their troops by sea route, R&AW agents sent this report to New Delhi and General Manekshaw immediately broadcast a warning to General Niazi to desist for any such action which would be futile and destructive. Gen. Manekshaw rather asked Niazi to surrender without further delay. After surrender on 16 December, Gen. Niazi rightly pointed out that they, R&AW operatives, made him blind and deaf throughout this war.

Mujeeb Bahini – R&AW Operated Special Frontier Force (SFF) in Chittagong Hill Tract

Special Frontier Force i.e., SFF, a commando task force was raised in 1962 by B N Mullik, the then Director of IB, after the Chinese invasion of India in 1962. This force was trained in guerilla warfare so that it could form a second line of defence behind army in case of of any future war with China. After the formation of R&AW in 1968, SFF was placed under its command. SFF was considered as an elite commando force prior to the formation of National Security Guard in 1984. Its commando possessed super quality of guerilla warfare since they were trained in difficult mountain terrain in Chakrata in Uttranchal. Amitabh Bachhan, the Indian superstar of the century of Indian cinema, might not be aware that when he became the Member of Parliament from Allahabad in 1984, his personal security officer, Tomar was a commando of SFF which was specially selected by R&AW for his security.

There was a group of youth Awami League student leaders who played a dominant role in ousting Ayub Khan from power. These student leaders were very loyal to Mujib. They fled Dacca after crackdown of the army. Prominent among them were Sheikh Fazal-ul-Haq Moni, Shiraz, Tufail Ahmad, Abdul Razak, Ashraf and Sheikh Jamal, the younger son of Sheikh Mujibur Rehamn. These youngsters selected and certified the genuineness of their own cadres who were their old colleagues from all over East Pakistan for training and insisted that they should have separate unconventional training as opposed to commando type training that Mukti Bahini was getting. They had their own political organization which had cells in every important town, tehsil and thana. They doubted the bonafides of certain elements which were getting training under the guise of Mukti Bahini. In their opinion, some of them had leftist inclination like the Naxalites of India, who were not loyal to their cause. According to them, a small faction inside Mukti Bahani had pro-Pakistan leaning and some criminals and bad characters were also getting training for their nefarious designs. Hence, they wanted their own guerrilla outfit so that information about their clandestine cells could be kept as guarded secret. This was not acceptable to the Provisional government in general and Tajuddin Ahmed in particular, who had old grouse against these leaders.

In order to sort out this matter, Kao placed this group under the command of Major General S S Uban, head of the SFF of R&AW after discussing this matter with General Manekshaw and the Minister in charge of this operation, D P Dhar. Uban was one of the founders of SFF when it was raised after the Chinese debacle of 1962. He was an astute soldier with high morality of his nationhood and dedicated to his duty to the utmost of his integrity and devotion. He was a trustworthy loyalist of R N Kao, the R&AW Chief. Kao was having detailed intelligence about the organization of these youth wing of Awami League and was convinced to impart independent training on them and subsequently sent them for insurgency against the Pakistan army. Kao was also convinced that some of the ministers in the provisional government were jealous of these young leaders as they were hot-headed and adamant but were true nationalist. This faction of this guerrilla movement was named as Mujeeb Bahini and given the Chittagong area to conduct its operations as the independent responsibility without the interference of Mukti Bahini and the provisional government. However, army, after initial hesitation for this outfit, agreed that the Army officers of SFF would work as Liaison Officers between the Mujeeb Bahini and the Army units to avoid any confusion with regard to Mukti Bahini. In addition to this task, SFF would independently work in the Chittagong Hill Tracts and its control would be directly under the Chief of Army Staff and not under the Eastern Army Commander.

A strong 10,000 force of youths was recruited by SFF and imparted guerrilla warfare training in various camps all along the hilly terrain around Chittagong District. Most of these youths were educated and many had left their degree, engineering and medical courses unfinished in their universities. Some were merely school boys. Most of them had seen the orgy of violence unleashed by Pakistan army on their nears and dears. Their vengeance could be observed in their eyes when they accustomed themselves in the guerilla training in record time in the chilly hill terrains where SFF was imparting them warfare of extreme physical strain. SFF Chief Major General Uban selected Demagiri, a check post in Mizoram on the border of East Pakistan as his Headquarters to launch guerilla warfare and harass Pakistan army up to Chittagong and Rangamati towns.

This force ultimately helped the SFF in capturing the Rangamati town where Mizo Commander Lal Denga was staying with his family. He was evacuated by the Pakistan army and taken towards south of Chittagong before the cadre of Mujeeb Bahani and SFF could have captured them. Two sons of Hindu Raja of Chakma community of this region, Tridip Roy, who was a minister in Pakistan government, were taken into protective custody by SFF because there was apprehension of their being lynched by the local Chakmas on whom they unleashed atrocities with the help of Pakistan soldiers. SFF with the help of Mujeeb Bahini killed hundreds of Mizo rebels who were working for the Pakistan army. Prior to war, many posts in the Chittagong hills like Dhanubak, Dighalchari and Baraital were captured from the Pakistan soldiers by the Mujeeb Bahini and the SFF. Many enemy soldiers were killed and others ran away for their life when Barkal and Subalong towns were captured by these insurgents. Huge arms and ammunition of Pakistan soldier came into the possession of SFF. Many other posts on Myanimukh-Khal junction like Mahamuam Rhlui, Masalang, Ganga Ram Rh, Tintillia and Mershiya fell to these guerillas of SFF and Mujeeb Bahani fighters prior to their movement for Chittagong.

Major General Uban, head of SFF, shifted his operational Headquarters at Rangamati inside Bangladesh after its capture by his commandos and young fighters of Mujeeb Bahani. General Manekshaw, when assured of SFF advancement inside Bangladesh territory, asserted the ferocity of this commando force and sent a urgent signal to its commander Uban. General Manekshaw's signal conveyed that interception of the wireless of Pakistan army indicated that they might withdraw from Dacca to Chittagong and then escape via Arakan Road into Burma. This was the only escape route for Pakistan army by road to Burma. Indian army chief ordered to move a strong commando force of SFF to block this road within two days. This most important task accomplished by the SFF commandos and the Mujeeb Bahini fighters with the destruction of Dohazari bridge over river Sangu in Bindraban area of Chittagong District within two days of the message of Indian army chief. All Pakistan soldiers defending this bridge were either killed by the SFF and Mujeeb Bahini or ran for their life towards Chittagong.

Incidentally, the large cache of arms and ammunition left by the fleeing Pakistan soldiers could not be transported by the SFF for want of air facilities which was not made available to them by the Indian Air Force for unknown reasons. Likewise, most of the soldiers of Pakistan army could have been taken as prisoners or those who wanted to surrender before SFF commander, could not be taken into custody due to lack of facility to accommodate them and were kept under vigil.

Some Mujeeb Bahini operatives infiltrated into Chittagong Port and City along with SFF commandos, captured the Chittagong radio station and announced surrender by Pakistan troops which demoralized a large number of army men of Pakistan present in that area. SFF commander was asked by the Army Headquarters not to enter Chittagong as two Indian Army brigades were on their way to accept surrender of Pakistan Army troops located at Chittagong. Although, the SFF Commander Major General Uban and leaders of Mujeeb Bahani were disappointed after they received this signal but it was obvious because they were not capable to handle the surrender of thousands of Pakistan soldiers in and around Chittagong area. But these Commandos of SFF alongwith the fighters of Mujeeb Bahani accomplished the most difficult task of driving out the powerful army of Pakistan from the hilly, marshy and flood ridden Chittagong tract as they were accustomed to the mountain guerilla warfare which Indian soldiers could have done with heavy human losses in the vicious terrain of this area. SFF deposited huge arms and ammunition which was sent to the army authorities in big plane AN 12 to Calcutta. Most of the officers and cadres of this force were duly decorated with honours by the Indian Government after the war. A total of 29 awards which included a Param Visisht Sewa Medal i.e PVSM to Major General Uban, one Ati Visisht Sewa Medal i.e. AVSM, six Visisht Sewa Medal i.e. VSM, six Vir Chakras, five Sena Medals and eleven Mention in Despatches were awarded to the SFF officers and Commandos for their gallantry in the war of liberation of Bangladesh. Kao, R&AW Chief personally honoured each and every SFF personnel who participated in this war. After surrender of Pakistan army, whole of the population of Chittagong town greeted the SFF Commander Major General S.S.Uban, his commandos and freedom fighters of Mujeeb Bahani in a public reception.

Kader Bahini, An Outfit Of Tiger Siddiqui (R&AW Operative)

Another guerrilla outfit trained by R&AW was named Kader Bahini after its leader Abdul Kader Siddiqui, nicknamed as Tiger Siddiqui. He was the main operative of R&AW in the most vital areas of strategic operation around Dacca. He was serving the Pakistan army when his brother brought him back to East Pakistan to complete his interrupted education just prior to the crackdown of the Pakistan army. Kader, the 23 years old charismatic, fearless and undaunted student of a local college was a revolutionary leader of guerrilla force of 16,000 local Bengalis. His force was in total control of over 70 miles of area between Dacca and Tangail. Kader was a self-styled Brigadier and was known as the "Tangail Tiger". Kader Bahini played havoc with the communication system of the army, ambushed enemy columns, blew up supply and ammunition dumps and assaulted a number of enemy convoys even beyond Tangail and up to Mymensingh district and some parts of Dacca. In this area, there were bridges on rivers which were flowing at an average area of six miles apart. Kader's guerrilla blew up each bridge in this area to disrupt the movement of the army. Kader was in full control of the Tangail District along with four thanas of Mymensing, five thanas of Dacca and three thanas of Pabna. He refused to work under the Mukti Bahini and in order to avoid confrontation, he was assigned this area for his operations by R&AW officers. His outfit had some former soldiers of the East Pakistan Rifles, East Bengal Rifles, farmers and the local students of this area. During the war on December 3, his guerillas proved of immense help to the Indian army in their smooth movement towards Dacca without any hindrance from the enemy.

During May and June, 1971, Kader Bahini had sunk one speed boat and sixteen plain boats. He also captured two speed boats and seventeen country boats in addition to fifty successful ambushes laid on the enemy in the Tangail area. Tiger Siddiqui personally lead his guerrillas to capture a triple-decker steamer at Matikta near Tangail. The steamer was loaded with thousand tons of ammunition for Pakistan army and it took ten hours to unload it and 99 boats were used to transship it to other places. Kader Bahini killed more than 3,000 Pakistan soldiers, including two Majors and captured alive 850 soldiers of Pakistan army including two Brigadiers, 4 Colonels and 18 Majors. Two days after surrender of the Pakistan army, Kader Bahini killed 3 Al-Badar pro-Pakistan activists in full public view. Some senior officers of the Indian army had frankly conceded after the surrender of Pakistan army that during the capture of Dacca, Kader Bahini had provided exemplary assistance to the Indian army by liquidating the enemy's small pocket of resistance while Indian troops were converging upon the capital.

All these three guerrilla outfits created by R&AW with the help of BSF and Army proved a vital force which provided an easy access for the Indian Army in the decisive 14 days war which has no parallel in educated guerrilla warfare force in the 20 century be it First World War, Second World War or Vietnam conflict. Indian Intelligence agency R&AW under the guidance of its founder R N Kao and his able and competent compatriots deserves full honour for such a well trained and educated guerrilla operation all over East Pakistan that Indian Army found very small resistance from the frightened Pakistan army which was harassed so badly by these guerrillas that they had confined themselves to cities and towns to guard them for their safety leave aside their capacity to face the brave Indian army. Kao worked out his plan with chess board precision which in the course of time checkmated the enemy. Presence of Seventh Fleet with the nuclear installed weapons, the Enterprise, did not bring any moral effect on the guerrilla operations and army action in Bangladesh. R&AW sources in the civil and army of Pakistan and some Pakistan diplomats on the pay roll of R&AW, provided invaluable information from Karachi, Rawalpindi, Peshawar, Dacca, Chittagong, London, Tehran, Kabul which was very vital in formulating the full fledged plan for liberation of Bangladesh. Pakistan Generals in East Pakistan were so scared of R&AW that they saw every civilian as R&AW operative be in hotels, banks, shops, foreign consulates business and even in government offices. There were impartial coverage of events by foreign correspondents that by November, 1971, Mukti Bahini and R&AW operatives were able to liberate about one-third of Bangladesh and was dominating most of the remaining areas during the hours of darkness. Total strength of Mukti Bahini had crossed over 1,00,000 by the end of November, 1971 and had their presence in every village and town.

General Niazi remarked about these guerrilla outfits of R&AW after his surrender at Dacca that "they made me blind and deaf". Another senior Indian Army officer conceded that without the support of these guerrillas they might have made a difference of two more weeks when time was a vital factor for the army and Indian government. When Lt. General J S Aurora, before whom the Pakistan Lt. General A A K Niazi surrendered on December 16, 1971, asked him when he was POW as to why he could not stop the Indian army approaching for Dacca when you were fully prepared in guarding the main approaches to which Niazi remained silent because Mukti Bahini had helped the Indian army to enter Dacca through the other routes without the knowledge of the Pakistan army. Niazi also wanted Lt. Gen. Aurora to issue a statement that he fought the war brilliantly which was not agreed to by Aurora.

14-Days War Of Indian Army For Liberation Of Bangladesh From Pakistan

According to K Sankaran Nair, deputy of R N Kao, Chief of R&AW, Indira Gandhi had asked Sam Manekshaw on March 25, 1971, "General I am afraid we will have to take strong military action against the army rule in East Pakistan, both in India's interest and to remove the dictatorial rule of the Pakistan army in its Eastern Wing". The General replied, "We were always told by the political bosses that the Indian Army's role was defensive and meant to protect our territorial integrity. To go into offensive mode in the East, requires special riverine operational equipment and training. We are lacking in both". "How long would you require to undertake such a campaign, then?", asked Indira Gandhi. "I shall require six months", replied Manekshaw. "All right General

Manekshaw, when you are ready please let me know" Indira.Gandhi told the Chief of Army Staff. She did not raise the question of readiness with the General until he himself went to her in October and told that he was then ready to attack in the East while holding the front in the West. She told him to hold his horses till she returned from a foreign tour she had planned to solicit the sympathy and support of Western countries like the UK and US for India in regard to the unbearable load of millions of Bengali refugees who had crossed over to the Eastern States of India following the brutal repression of Pakistan army. Indian army was fully deployed throughout the borders of East Pakistan soon afterwards for the imminent war of liberation. Some Mountain Divisions stood guard against a possible Chinese thrust across the Himalayas in case of their intervention in this conflict.

Prior to phase two of this operation i.e. military action, there was immaculate coordination among the rank and cadre of Indian government. D P Dhar designated as Chairman of the Planning Committee of Ministry of External Affairs, was inducted into the war council. He was the Minister-in-charge of Bangladesh war. On the military side, a Joint Intelligence Committee consisting of representatives of R&AW, the IB and the Directors of Intelligence of the three services, was formed under the Chairmanship of the Vice Chief of Army Staff. This ensured full co-ordination at the top. On the civil side, a Secretariat Committee consisting of the Secretaries of Defence, Home Finance, External Affairs with R N Kao, as Member Secretary, was set up to take executive decisions dealing with preparations for war and the execution thereof. The main direction, co-ordination and supervision remained with Dhar, Manekshaw and Kao. Prime Minister was in constant touch with each and every development. The decision making process was never allowed to get tangled in the bureaucratic red tape. Such was the friendly relationship between Gen. Manekshaw and Kao that both used to walk into their respective office rooms in South Block for on the spot discussion on vital matters. This co-ordination paid much dividend in the two week long war. So, by the beginning of November, Indian army was ready for final assault to liberate the East Bengal and to contain the West front from the Pakistan army.

In desperation, after nine months of constant harassment from the R&AW trained guerrilla outfits in East Pakistan where its army's morale was sagging and apprehending a coup de tat from within the Pakistan army by a coterie of army officers headed by General Hamid, Yahya Khan in order to get rid of the internal threat, attacked India on Friday, the holy day for Muslims, December 3 at 5.30 pm, Lt. General Jagjit Singh Aurora, GOC in C, Eastern Command was given direction to move its forces into East Bengal from all sides of the border. Indira Gandhi in a radio broadcast declared to the nation "Pakistan has launched a full scale war on us. We had no other option but to put our country on a war footing.

War in Bangladesh has become a war on India". Emergency was declared in the country.

R&AW operatives from Peshawar reported on December 2, the movement of the 7 Pakistan Division towards the Indian western sector in the Poonch and Chhamb areas. In East Pakistan, R&AW agents in Dacca and in other important cities, through their clandestine wireless sets started sending invaluable information with regard to the military installation and their movements so that the Indian army remained prepared in advance to counter all their moves. Hence, the final blow for this 14 Day war was in the offing and Indian army was impatient to avenge the last two wars of Pakistan.

Day To Day Account of the 14 Day War of 1971

December 3

Pakistan planes bombed Indian airfields at Amritsar, Pathankot, Srinagar, Avantipur, Uttarlai, Faridkot, Jodhpur, Sirsa, Halwara, Jamnagar, Chandigarh and Agra around 5.30 pm. This sudden attack was planned to cripple the Indian Air Force which was much superior to the Pakistan. India had long anticipated this action and dispersed planes to safer position about which advance intelligence information was given to the Air Force by R&AW. Yahya Khan had planned this air attack on the pattern of Israeli swoop over Egyptian airbases in June 1967 when at one stroke 400 planes of UAR's air force were destroyed. Pakistan attack made hardly any dent in the Indian Air Force apart from doing a minor damage to the runways at some airfields. In Eastern sector, Indian Air Force and Navy had sealed off the entire area of East Pakistan from the rest of the World. The air force had smashed the jet unways of Dacca at Tejgaon and Kurmitola and Navy laid a watertight blockade around all the ports. IAF destroyed 14 of the 19 Sabre jets based at Dacca. Indian aircraft carrier Vikrant struck heavy blows at the Chittagong harbor and Cox's Bazar and sank a number of gunboats, destroyed runways and hangars and set ablaze fuel dumps.

Pakistan army too attacked the western border in Fazilka, Khem Karan and Chhamb in Jammu. In the eastern sector, Agartala air base was bombarded with powerful rockets.

Around 2 a.m. on the morning of December 4, Indian Air Force retaliated and raided many air fields in West and East Pakistan. Around 1.30, a Pakistan Brigadier Abdul Rahman Siddiqui called a press conference at Army Headquarterss in Rawalpindi and declared that India had launched a land attack at five places from Poonch to Rajasthan. Minutes after this briefing, air-raid sirens screamed all over Pakistan after the attack of Indian air force planes. On the very first day, the Indian Air Force knocked out 33 planes of the Pakistan Air Force.

December 4

Indian Air Force retaliated with vengeance and by the end of the day, the Pakistan Air Force squadrons in East Pakistan had been decimated and left with only four Saber jets. Thereafter, Indian Air Force commanded total air supremacy in East Pakistan and flew 500 sorties on Dacca and Chittagong air bases and totally crippled them for air operations. In the Western sector, IAF retaliated with raids on Chanderi, Sherkot, Sargodha, Murid, Mianwali, Risalwala (near Rawalpindi) and Changa Manga (near Lahore). Several Pakistan aircrafts were destroyed on the ground. In a daylight raid on Musroor (near Karachi), nine Pakistan planes including one B57 bomber and eight fighter planes were destroyed. Air raids were conducted on Karachi for half an hour. The Pakistan radar station at Badin near Kutch was damaged. Pakistan Air Force too attacked Indian airfields in the Western Sector at Amritsar, Pathankot, Srinagar, Faridkot, Halwara, Ambala, Agra, Uttarlai, Jodhpur and Jamnagar. Indian troops on western sector captured a picket five miles in Tithwal and another between Uri and Haji Pir.

This day was a red letter day in the history of Indian Navy. At 2200 hours, the Indian Navy ventured into the Karachi waters and sank four Pakistan warships including two destroyers. It streamed inshore and then bombarded the harbour, blew up the port installations and set ablaze the oil storage tanks. There was no retaliation whatsoever from Pakistan side. Initial battle fought 25 miles of Karachi harbor and was conceded to be the largest naval action since second world war. Indian Navy sank the Pakistan battleclass destroyer Khaibar (2,325 tons), Shah Jehan (1,710 tons) besides two 335 tones minesweepers Tughril and Tipu Sultan.

Large area of Bevgram, Nurpur, Gangasagar, Imambari, Thakurgaon, Gopinathpur, Gazipur, Darshana (Kushtia district), Charkhai (Rangpur district), Phulbari (Dinajpur district), Mamalpur (Mymensingh district), Shamshernargar (Sylhet district) and Uthali (Jessore district) in Bangladesh territory were captured by Indian army in conjunction with Mukti Bahini. A naval blockade was imposed by Indian Navy on East Bengal ports. INS Vikrant caused heavy destruction to oil installation and docking facilities at Chittagong and Cox's Bazar ports.

Thirty three Pakistan aircrafts were shot down or destroyed on the ground (14 in the east and 19 in the west). Twelve Pak tanks were destroyed, 6 in the Ferozpur sector and 6 near Chhamb on this day at the battlefield.

December 5

This day belonged to Indian Navy. Admiral Nanda, Chief of the Naval Staff and his deputies Vice Admiral N Krishnan and Rear Admiral Sharma had planned the naval preparation prior to the war when it became inevitable due to political instability inside Pakistan. Indian Navy was keeping a close watch on the movement of Pakistan submarine Ghazi in the Bay of Bengal. Ghazi whose original name of DIABLO (Devil) was given on loan by US to Pakistan without due authorization. This 94 meter long, 2,400 ton and ten torpedo tubes submarines was given the task of immobilizing the naval base of Vishakhapatnam in India. Its mission was to keep the supply line smooth in Bay of Bengal from Karachi to Chittagong and other ports in East Pakistan. Ghazi had a speed of 20 knots on surface and 10 knots under water. It had a range of 14,000 miles, which meant that it could keep under sea for a month at a stretch. Ghazi was detected by Indian navy destroyer Rajput on December 3 night on the Sonar and was attacked by this Eastern fleet of Indian Navy. It was forced to surface by underwater projectiles and was re-attacked by gunfire when came on the surface and then dived for ever. Around midnight, there was underwater explosion when window panes were shattered in the harbour areas. On this day, two fishermen found a torn life-jacket with American markings in their net. A Daphone class submarine was to help Ghazi in a sneak attack to coincide with the Pakistan pre-emptive air strikes in the West but the whole mission misfired with the destruction of Ghazi. This submarine was the pride of Pakistan navy which was destroyed by Indian navy before it could do any harm to them. After this destruction, the Eastern Fleet pride INS Vikrant heavily attacked Chittagong and Cox's Bazar ports and destroyed oil dumps, gun positions and military targets. Vikrant detected another Pakistan submarine in this area and sunk it forever befor it could have retaliated. Sixteen Pakistan gun boats escaped ships at Chittagong were destroyed. Six Pakistan vessels were attacked with rockets and were immobilized. The airport installation, fuel dumps and wireless station in Cox's Bazar were put out of action. On the western side, Indian navy attacked few miles off Karachi harbour in the early hours and destroyed two Pakistan warships, the 2,500 ton battle class destroyer Khyber with 33 crew members and the second 177 ton destroyer Shah Jahan. Many defence installations near Karachi were destroyed despite heavy defence of the Pakistan navy.

Indian army with the help of Mukti Bahini moved close to Comilla in East Bengal and seized the key ferry point on the Meghna river about 22 miles from Dacca. Another Indian column moved from Agartala towards Ashuganj to capture a vital bridge which gave access to Dacca. In Jessore, where 6,000 Pakistan troops were deployed, Indian soldiers by passed the area in an outflanking operation with the maneuvering of Mukti Bahini to avoid head on collision with them and moved towards Dacca. Akhaura was captured and Indian troops were within 7 km. of Comilla. Six Pakistan officers and JCOs and 100 of 31 Baluch Battalion in Kamalpur surrendered before the Indian army.

On the western sector, Pakistan damaged a vital bridge in Hussainiwala and dropped bombs on Okha port in Gujarat.

The Soviet Union vetoed a US resolution in the UN Secuirty Council for a ceasefire and withdrawal of military from East Pakistan.

December 6

India recognized the new nation Gana Praja Tantri Bangladesh. Indira Gandhi declared in Parliament that the people of Bangladesh battling for their existence and the people of India fighting to defeat aggression now found themselves partisans in the same cause. She added that with the unanimous revolt of the entire people of Bangladesh and the success of their struggle, it had become increasingly apparent that the so-called mother state of Pakistan was totally incapable of bringing the people of Bangladesh under their control. Yahya Khan severed diplomatic relations with India. America announced the cancellation of all economic aid worth 87 million dollars to India to put political pressure for a ceasefire. The Soviet Union again vetoed a US sponsored resolution in the UN Security Council where its delegation led by George Bush and Chinese delegate Huang Hua branded India as the aggressor which was refuted by Indian delegate Samar Sen, Soviet Ambassador Yakov Malik and Polish Ambassador Kualaga.

In Bangladesh, Indian army liberated Brahamanbaria on the Comilla-Dacca road and Jamalpur in Mymensingh. It liberated Feni and Laksham in the south east and advanced in a flanking movement to isolate fortified towns and cities of Jessore, Sylhet and Lal Monirhat to move toward Dacca. Indian navy continued rocket attack on the harbours of Khulna, Chalna and Mongla.

On western sector, Indian army captured over 400 square miles of West Pakistan territory in the Barmer sector of Rajasthan. It also captured an enemy post of Ranhal in Bikaner sector. Indian troops fiercely fought with the six Pakistan infantry brigades supported by 150 tanks in Kashmir. The enemy attacked Fazilka and Hussainiwala. Indian troops advanced in Suchetgarh, Shakargarh and Dera Baba Nanak in Punjab. The Indian Air Force blasted the enemy positions including ammunition dumps in Kahuta on the Haji Pir area. On Kutch border, Indian army captured Chhad Bet. Enemy planes bombed Jamnagar and Okha where one Pakistan plane was shot down. IAF Hunters attacked the oil refinery at Attock where storage tanks kept on burning for hours. A gas plant at Sui was blasted and set ablaze. IAF Canberra attacked the Masrur airfield in the night and Hunters attacked during day in Karachi and left it stripped of its air cover.

Till this day, Pakistan lost 52 planes and India 19. They also lost 89 tanks.

December 7

On this day, the Indian army along with Mukti Bahini liberated Sylhet, Jessore, Meherpur, Jhenida, Sunamganj, Fenchuganag, Charkhal, Chhatak, Moulvi Bazar and Lalmunirghat in Bangladesh and were closing on the remaining Pakistan army strongholds in Dacca and Comilla. Indian navy captured six more coastal ships under charter to Pakistan.

In the western sector, Pakistan army was routed near Dera Baba Nanak and our troops captured Mahndro Ropar, Fetheropal Bagal, Mankau and Chachro in the Barmer sector. Thirty square miles of enemy territory was taken in control in the Chicken's Neck region of Kashmir. However, in Chhamb, the Indian forces had withdrawn to the east of Munnawar Tawi.

Indian Air force knocked out 49 Pakistan tanks on this day which brought the enemy tally to 118 and lost 15 in Chhamb sector and destroyed 53 Pakistan aircrafts and lost 22 on the end of this day.

On the political front, Bhutan recognized Bangladesh. Yahaya Khan invited Nurul Amin, the lone winner of a National Assembly seat from East Bengal beside Awami League to form a coalition government with Z.A.Bhutto to divert world opinion.

Senator Edward Kennedy, Muskie and other Democrats denounced the Nixon administration for branding India as aggressor. They remarked that the war did not begin then but started on the bloody night of March 25 with the brutal suppression of the Pakistan army after the results of a free election. United States took the posture that Yahya Khan had agreed it to negotiate with members of the Awami League but India insisted that she would negotiate only with Sheikh Mujibur Rahman. Again the resolution of the General Assembly of the UN was vetoed by Russia and ten other countries wherein Britain and France abstained during voting.

December 8

Chief of the Army Staff, Gen. Manekshaw gave a call to the Pakistan army from All India Radio to surrender or face certain death. He warned the Pakistan army that all their escape routes through sea and land had been blocked by navy and army of India. He, however, assured that they would be treated with dignity under the Geneva Convention after the surrender. This message was also dropped in the form of leaflets from air over the Pakistan military positions. This message worked like a psychological hammer blow to a crumbling morale and put the fear of God and Mukti Bahini in the Pakistan troops. This call had its desired effect. At Kalampur, 31 Baluch Regiment with 160 troops surrendered without any resistance. Near Comilla,100 soldiers of the 25 Frontier Force surrendered and Jessore airstrip was captured by the Indian army and Mukti Bahini. With the capture of Comilla, the biggest cantonment in Bangladesh, morale of Pakistan army was at its lowest ebb and with the fall of Brahmanbaria, an important junction to the north of Akhaura, Dacca was being surrounded for the final assault. Advance columns had reached Daudkhandi and were fighting the enemy at Chaura, a port near Meghna river. Magura and Satkhira towns were also liberated.

In the western sector, in Chhamb area fierce battle continued with Pakistan army. In Sind and Bahawalpur, more than 2,000 sq. kms of Pakistan territory was captured by the Indian forces. In Dera Baba Nanak and Chicken's Neck, Indian army repulsed the fresh Pakistan attack. Enemy troops were pushed back in Longewala in Jaisalmer. IAF Hunters destroyed 29 tanks besides crippling the regiment and their vehicles. IAF's attack on the oil installations off Karachi at Keamari left the area a blazing inferno which left Karach under a pall of smoke for some days and it was estimated that Pakistan had lost 50 per cent of its oil holdings in the Karachi area with this IAF attack.

December 9

Indian navy created havoc at Karachi harbour and reached within 8 km close to their defence. Four ships were sunk there. Naval fleet bombarded Gwadar and Jewani on the Makran cost, west of Karachi, and the sea war reached near the border of Iran. Like Bay of Bengal, the Indian Navy had established complete control in the Arabian Sea and any naval action of the enemy from sea was completely ruled out. Indian Navy suffered its biggest loss of war when when 1200-ton antisubmarine frigate Khukri was torpedoes by the Pakistan Navy. Captain Mahendra Nath Mulla in the highest tradition of the Navy, preferred to stand by his 18 officers and 176 soldiers who went down with the Khukri. Six officers and 61 sailors were the survivors left to tell the heroic story of their Captain. One shore-based aircraft Alize was also lost.

Indian army and the Mukti Bahini had tightened the noose around Dacca. The strategic inland river post of Chander, 64 km south of Dacca, Daudkhandi, 33 km east of Dacca, Ashuganj Ferryand Palasbari in Bangladesh were liberated by the Army and Mukti Bahini. Indian Army and Mukti Bahini were poised on the east bank of the Meghna river to attack Dacca. Three hundred Razakars were arrested in Ashuganj.

In the western sector, Pakistan domination of Leh-Srinagar Road was ended with the capture of 13,620 post in Kargil. In Kutch, Nagarparkar was seized. Fifteen Pakistan villages were captured by the Indian army.

Up to this day, Pakistan lost 73 aircrafts, 124 tanks, 3 warships, 9 gunboats and 2 submarines while India lost 31 aircrafts and 49 tanks.

December 10

Bangladesh forces were brought under the command of General J S Aurora and a unified command was announced. When the news that Indian Army was 40 miles away from Dacca reached there, 300 foreigners and 373 Pakistan sought shelter in Hotel Inter-Continental which was declared a neutral zone by the Red Cross. Noakhali town and the river port of Mangla were liberated by Mukti Bahini. A bridgehead was built by Indian army across the Meghna river for transporting the troops in Dacca. Two battalions of Indian soldiers were lifted across Meghna river by the IAF helicopters which outwitted the army stationed at Bhairab Bazar in Dacca. Biggest blow in the enemy defence was the capture of Jessore cantonment by the Indian forces. This Pakistan defence citadel had all modern fortifications and stocks capable of feeding any army of a division strength with arms and food for a considerable period. After this victory, Indian army found little resistance in reaching Dacca. After the call of Indian Army Chief General Manekshaw, panicked Pakistan soldiers preferred to flee towards Dacca to save their lives then to put up a fight. The Indian forces had placed themselves at vantage positions to strike Dacca if the Pakistan forces did not surrender to the call of the Indian Army Chief. Mukti Bahini smashed the Dacca radio station and put it out of commission when Indian forces virtually surrounded the city.

Indian Navy captured 8 Danish ships from Chalna and Chittagong which were chartered to the Gulf Shipping Corporation of Pakistan. Six coasters of 44 ton capacity and two 1,000 ton tankers were also captured. Clandestinely original names of these were painted and new names Guilt Trader, Gulf Zin, Gulf Crescent, Gulf Navigator and Gulf Princess were written there and these chips were carrying arms and reinforcements for Pakistan troops by displaying misleading boards "Carrying Humanitarian Relief " under United Nations. This was shown to the World media by Indian authorities. The Captain of one of the tankers, later told that his ship was hired by Pakistan from Singapore and on way to Chittagong it was intercepted by Indian Navy. Another vessel MY Orient Glory was captured with 3,500 tonnes of contraband items. Later custom authorities of India declared that out of the eight ships sailing under the guise of United Nation, detained by the India, were carrying about 3,000 tonnes of goods belonging to Pakistan. Some of the coastesr had empty holds and were possibly on a mission to evacuate the fleeing Pakistan army from Bangladesh to West Pakistan. In its decisive assault, Indian Air Force raided ships, steamers, barges, gunboats and Pakistan position in many part of Sylhet, Comilla, Rangpur and Khulna. Indian forces encircled the Kushtia district Headquarterss. Indian forces and Mukti Bahini liberated Lakshan, Bansult, Phulpur, Hajiganj, Chenutia, Harishanuara and Dangamara. For the first time in the history of Indian armed forces, Indian paratroopers were dropped in action on Tangail, 61 miles north of Dacca from 50 Dakotas, Packets and AN-12s. The drop was carried out with clock like precision and battalion was kept supplied on subsequent days first by paradrops and eventually by Carribou aircraft using an improvised strip.

Pakistan's 26 Infantry Division supported by two armoured regiments attacked Chhamb sector in the western front resulting in heavy casualties. Heavy fight continued in Uri, Kurail near Baramula, Poonch Naushera and Ranian. Gen Manekshaw expressed his inability to allow UN Military Observers to remain at the Jammu-Sialkot check post.

Diplomatically, Pakistan made another attempt in UN General Assembly by claiming that small country was being attacked by a large country to which Indira Gandhi rebuffed that she was willing to listen foreign advice but would not bow to any threat and would also not accept any resolution which was against its national interest.

December 11

Morale of Pakistan army in Bangladesh was sagging as an SOS was sent by the Chief Military Representative in East Pakistan, Major General Rao Farman Ali Khan to the UN Secretary General U Thant to send aid for evacuating his military and civilian personnel to West Pakistan. General Manekshaw waned Farman Ali against his attempt to escape. General Manekshaw sternly threatened the Pakistan army in Bangladesh on an air broadcast at 3 pm that he had intelligence reports that two coasters were ready at the Gupta Crossing and Indian Air Force would take action to destroy these vessels if any attempt was made to move into the sea. He further warned that he had instructed all his forces to destroy all the Pakistan merchant ships and armed forces if any attempt was made to flee in five of the disguised merchant ships. General Manekshaw cautioned that he wanted to spare military lives. When Security Council tried to consider the appeal of Farman Ali, Yahya Khan sent a message to ignore this appeal. Lt. Gen. A.A.K.Niazi as GOC of Eastern Command put Farman Ali under house arrest on order from Yahya Khan. Nevertheless, Yahya Khan kept exhorting General Niazi in Dacca to keep on fighting and promised him that "something big" was in the offing and hinted at a likely armed intervention by the Chinese from the north, and later, a rescue operation by the US Seventh Fleet task force speeding to the Bay of Bengal from the South-East Asian waters. Gen. Niazi appeared at the Inter-Continental Hotel and claimed that he had come here to command his forces and would never desert them. Indian Foreign Minister, Swaran Singh declared in London, on way to the United Nations, that it was unrealistic to talk of ceasefire at that stage when Pakistan themselves declared war and committed aggression. Eighteen hundred Pakistan soldiers were captured by the Indian soldiers in Bangladesh.

R&AW operatives gave assessment that at least 40,000 out of the total Pakistan troops had managed to make a series of strategic withdrawals towards Dacca. Aerial reconnaissance photographs indicated they were taking up positions in an area some eight miles outside the city and that all the heavy artillery they could muster had been set up behind them.It was apparent that few of them actually reached Dacca while many fled towards the river ports in the hope of escaping to the sea.

In their third attempt, the UN were refused permission by the Pakistan authorities to evacuate British nationals and UN personnel from Dacca when two planes sought permission to land in Dacca.

However fierce fighting continued in the western front in Jammu & Kashmir, Rajasthan and Gujarat.

December 12

The battle for capture of Dacca started on this day when Indian Air Force bombarded military installations. More than 200 Mukti Bahini guerrillas were severely ambushing the Pakistan military personnel on the outskirts of Dacca and inside the city. Indian forces advanced from Bhairab Bazar, Chandpur and Comilla through land and sea routes. Pakistan naval personnel closeted themselves inside the Chittagong and Daulatpur cantonment. Indian Air Force smashed hundreds of Pakistan tanks in the Chhamb-Jaurian sector at 5 am and Indian artillery damaged the defence along the Ichhogil canal near Lahore to capture the Lahore airport and to attack other military installations in the surrounding areas.

President Nixon called on India to halt the armed attack as he considered the occupation of East Pakistan as an attack on the existence of member state of the United Nations. Indira Gandhi refuted his charges and held the US responsible for the entire catastrophe because US helped Pakistan against Communism but instead misused the military aid to suppress the voice of people for freedom and justice. She called it a big hoax when US claimed that there were other agreements for this military aid.

Untill this day, Pakistan lost 80 aircrafts, 148 tanks, 3 warships, 2 submarines and 16 gunboats where as India lost 39 aircrafts, 54 tanks and one frigate.

December 13

Army Chief Gen. Manekshaw issued a third warning to Pakistan army that any further resistance was senseless because their garrison was within the artillery range of Indian forces. War in Bangladesh had then centered to Dacca where commando paratroopers were dropped by the Indian Air Force helicopters. Indian army had almost encircled Dacca and its fall was imminent. Indian soldiers were moving fast without resistance from the Pakistan forces from Bhairab Bazar, Mymensingh and Jaydevpur towards Dacca. Indian army strategically by-passed the resistance areas where Pakistan army was positioned to halt their movement towards Dacca. Subsequently these places were attacked and the enemy liquidated by detachments of the Indian Army with the support of Mukti Bahini, which had been trailing behind to contain the Pakistan army. These surprise attacks paralyzed the enemy and paved way for free movement of the advancing Indian Army which was converging upon Dacca much before the enemy could recover from the trauma.

The USA government tried to frighten the Indian government when seven ships task force was moving by the formidable nuclear-powered aircraft carrier Enterprise with 100 fighter bombers, reconnaissance planes and helicopters and a few bombs. At this point of time, the Soviet Union also sent its fleet with the addition of a guided missile warship and a destroyer in the Indian Ocean to help India in case of any American intervention in ongoing conflict which was on the verge of a humiliating defeat for Pakistan. Indira Gandhi wrote to U Thant, the Secretary General of UNO that she would declare cease-fire only if West Pakistan rulers withdrew their forces from Bangladesh and reached political settlement with the Bengali leaders. Bhutto desperately warned India that if necessary Pakistan would wage one thousand years war against the latter. When Bhutto warned Russia for its support to India then Uzbekistan and other Republics would demand secession if Moscow supported the cause of Bangledesh, Yakob Malik Soviet delegate in UNO rebuffed him by saying that he was talking everything except the root cause of the problem i.e. repression in Bangladesh by Pakistan army.

December 14

This was a red letter day in the history of Indian Intelligence R&AW. Through one of its operatives, a message was received at R&AW Headquarterss in New Delhi that East Pakistan Governor A M Malik and his other Cabinet colleagues would hold a meeting at 1200 hrs during the day at Government House at Dacca for a possible surrender before the Indian Army. This message was disseminated to the Army and Air Force by R&AW. Indian Air Force was unable to identify the location of the Government House which was to be air attacked by the Air Force. R&AW officers identified this single storey building near Paltan Maidan adjoining a huge mosque with a dark blue band running along with the top of the dome. This identification was conveyed to Indian Air Force by R&AW. Indian Air Force immediately sent the AN-12 bombers and at 1200 bombarded the Government House where the Pakistan had gathered for the meeting. Malik took refuge into the cellar and started praying to Allah to save his life. He and his colleagues resigned then and there in the Government House dissociating themselves from the regime of Yahya Khan. One UN official John Kelly and a journalist Gavin Young of the Sunday Observer, London, were also trapped with Malik during this air attack of IAF. Gavin Young reported in the Sunday Observer "Then the raid still seething round us, Malik, a devout Muslim, took off his shoes and socks, gracefully washed his feet in a small washroom opening into the bunker, spread a white handkerchief over his head and knelt down in a corner of the bunker and said his prayers. That was the end of Government House. That was the end of of the last Government of East Pakistan". Thereafter, they sought refuge at the Inter-continental Hotel which was under the Red Cross. Earlier 16 senior civil servants led by the Inspector General of Police M S Chaudhury had sought refuge in the Hotel Intercontinental.

The battle around Dacca was in full swing with artillery bombardments. Indian soldiers achieved the first big success when they routed the 03 Dacca Infantry Pakistan brigade on the outskirts of the capital. Brigadier Khader Kahn, Commander of the Brigade surrendered before the Indian army. This surrender did not deter Lt. Gen. Niazi who persisted on his fight to the last even if it was meant for the destruction of Dacca where he had two brigades with six to seven thousand soldiers along with other 15,000 to 20,000 who had retreated to Dacca. Since communication lines were totally disrupted by Mukti Bahini, Niazi was unaware about the position of his remaining army in the remaining part of Bangladesh.

Later in the same afternoon, Yahya Khan signaled to Niazi, giving his consent to a surrender by the Pakistan Army in Bangladesh, which he had refused it to General Farman Ali a few days earlier. The cable was jointly addressed to Gen. Niazi and Dr. Malik and enjoined: "You should now take all necessary measures to stop the fighting and preserve the lives of all armed forces personnel, all those from West Pakistan and all loyal elements".

December 15

After Dacca was surrounded by Indian forces along with Mukti Bahini, Indian Army Chief Gen. Manekshaw asked Niazi to stop fighting and set a deadline until 9 am on December 16 to surrender before the Indian army. In order to avoid unnecessary killing of Pakistan soliders, Gen. Manekshaw ordered that no air action should take place during this grace period but warned that the offensive would be mounted with utmost vigour if the surrender did not take place. Subsequently, Indian Air Force stopped attacks on military targets in Dacca at 5 pm on December 15 to give time to the Commander of Pakistan forces to surrender. General Niazi through American Embassy pressed for cease-fire which was not agreed to by Indian Army Chief. In a last ditched effort, Niazi sought facilities for repatriation of his forces to West Pakistan abroad vessels of the Seventh Fleet which was also rejected by India. Finding no option for a safe passage to leave East Pakistan, Niazi ultimately agreed to surrender his force before the Indian army General Manekshaw arranged a radio link with a special code to finalize surrender arrangements speedily with Niazi. In rest of Bangladesh, Indian Army and Mukti Bahini was in full control of other cities. SFF of R&AW

had surrounded Chittagong awaiting the final assault. Gen. Manekshaw assured Niazi that the wounded Pakistan troops would be taken full care of and the dead would be given a ritual burial. In the meanwhile, Pakistan rounded up more then 250 Bengali intellectuals, artists, professors and other intelligentsia and leaders to be used as hostages for negotiation with the Indian Army. All these were killed in cold blooded manner when their action was deplored by the Indian side.

Meanwhile, on the western front, Indian Navy totally destroyed the Karachi port. About 20 Soviet warships including missile cruiser and destroyers were heading for the Bay of Bengal to counter a possible attack of the Seventh Fleet and Enterprise of USA.

Bhutto made angry speeches in the U.N. abusing everybody. After calling on Muslim Bengalis to revolt against the Hindu army which was in occupation of East Pakistan, Bhutto tore a piece of paper to show his contempt for the Security Council and then walked out with the entire Pakistan delegation. Before boycott, he shouted that if the Security Council wanted an abject surrender, he would be under no circumstances a party to it.

December 16

This day was the historical day for the Indian Army. Lt. Gen. A A K Niazi was left with no option but to surrender his army and save it from destruction at the hands of Indian soldiers in case of refusal as warned by Gen. Manekshaw. At 1 pm Major Gen. JFR Jacob, Chief of Staff, Eastern Command, flew by helicopter to Dacca with the instrument of surrender. Major Gen. Gandharv Nagra of Indian Army, who went to discuss the terms of surrender with Niazi was surprised when the later told him that "the bastards sitting in Pindi have got US licked". At 2.45 pm Gen. Jacob signaled to say that the instrument of surrender had been accepted and initialed by Gen. Niazi. At 3.30 pm four more battalions of Indian Army and Mukti Bahini entered Dacca under the command of Major Gen. Nagra. Gen. Aurora, accompanied by Air and Naval Chiefs of the Eastern Command, Air Marshal Dewan and Vice Admiral Krishnan and Major Khondkar, Chief of Staff of Mukti Bahini, flew into Dacca by helicopter from Agartala, having got there from Calcutta by another plane.

Dacca's Ramna Race Course ground was packed with hundreds of thousand Bengalis carrying the gold, green and crimson flag of Bangladesh. Slogans of "Joi Bangla", "Joi India" and "Joi Indira" were continuously raised by the crowd. They lifted General Aurora on to their shoulders and hugged every Indian officer and jawan within reach. This was the same venue where nine months earlier Mujibur Rahman had defied the Military junta of West Pakistan. At 4.31 pm, Lt. Gen. Niazi divested himself of his epaulette of ranks, unloaded his revolver and finally pressed his forehand to that of Lt. Gen. Jagjit Singh Aurora,, GOC in C,

Eastern Command, as an act of submission and symbolic gesture of surrender which was the biggest since World War II. He was on the verge of tears, his face pale and haggard. Whole of Pakistan army of more than 93,000 soldiers with huge arms and ammunitions surrendered to the Indian army at Dacca and elsewhere in East Pakistan and sought protection from Mukhi Bahini and local population which had suffered atrocities at their hand. At the time of signing the document of surrender, two gold capped pens of foreign made were tried for signature but both did not work. Then General Niazi tried his own pen which also did not work. Then an ordinary pen of an Indian Air Force officer was used to sign the document of surrender.

Instrument of surrender signed by Gen. Niazi stated that his forces would lay down arms and surrender at the places where they were located to the nearest regular troops in the command of Lt. Gen. Aurora and Pakistan Eastern Command would come under the orders of Lt. Gen. Aurora after the instrument was signed. Disobedience of orders would be construed as breach of surrender terms and would be dealt with in accordance with the accepted laws and usages of war. This document further mentioned that Lt. Gen. Aurora had given his solemn assurance that personnel who surrender would be treated with dignity and respect which soldiers were entitled to in accordance with the provisions of Geneva Convention and guaranteed the safety and well-being of all Pakistan military and paramilitary forces who surrendered. Protection would be provided to foreign nationals, ethnic minorities and personnel of West Pakistan region by the forces in the command of Lt. Gen. Aurora.

That was the end of a brutal story of inhuman genocide of the Bengali population orchestrated by General Yahya Khan and executed by Lt. Gen. Niazi wherefrom the whole of map of East Pakistan was wiped out and Bangladesh was born on its ashes. Happy end of this story was prepared and enacted by the brave Prime Minister of India, Indira Gandhi amid threats hurled by Nixon and his coterie of evil advisors. After surrender Lt. Gen. Niazi confided with Maj. Gen. Jacob that he wanted to surrender at least seven days before he actually capitulated but Yahya Khan prevented him from doing so on the assurance that he and his army would be rescued either by the Chinese or by the US Seventh Fleet. More than estimated four and a half divisions of the Pakistan forces totaling more than 93,000 were rounded up by Indian soldiers all over Bangladesh.

Lt. Gen. Aurora while addressing a press conference in Calcutta the day after the surrender observed that individually Pakistan soldiers, units and sub-units fought extremely well with resolution and competence But their overall plan on how to fight the war was faulty. He opined that if Lt. Gen. Niazi could have concentrated his forces between the natural barriers of the rivers Meghna and Madhumati, they could have kept the war going for several months.

Gen. Aurora further observed that in many respects Pakistan had superior weapons. They had more automatic weapons and more recoilless anti-tank guns whereas Indian army had more tanks than Pakistan army. Gen. Aurora had great praise for the Russian amphibious PT 76 tanks which were ideal for the soft, paddy field covered terrain of Bangladesh in contrast to the American Chafees that Pakistan army used in the East. Gen. Aurora paid a glowing tribute to Mukti Bahini and said that his troops had the great advantage of the help rendered by Mukti Bahini. They gave valuable information and helped Indian forces to cross obstacles.

Soon after the surrender of Pakistan army in Bangladesh there were demonstrations all over Pakistan for this humiliating defeat because there was total censor on press and radio and general public was kept in dark by Yahya Khan and his cronies. Air Marshal Asgar Khan demanded the public trial of Yahya Khan and others responsible for this war debacle. Even General A A Niazi has admitted in his memoirs that there was no need of military action in East Pakistan at that time as handing over power to Sheikh Mujibur Rahman was the only solution.

Indian Prime Minister Indira Gandhi announced a unilateral ceasefire on both the fronts four hours later. Pakistan President although initially tried to soothe his wound by saying that in such a big war temporary defeat on one front did not mean end of war which would be continued till victory but subsequently declared ceasefire on pressure from USA.

In this war, 2,307 Indian soldiers died, 6,133 wounded and 2163 were missing. Pakistan casualties were much higher in proportion to India. Indian forces knocked out 244 Pakistan tanks, 94 aircrafts - about one third of its actual strength, 22 naval crafts, 4 warships, 16 gunboats, two submarines and many sailing crafts. India lost 45 aircrafts and 73 tanks.

India was now in possession of 3,600 sq kms of West Pakistan territory against 126 sq kms of Indian territory held by Pakistan. In the Kutch sector 850 square miles, 1,200 square miles of territory in Sindh along the Rajasthan border apart from penetrating 48 miles along the old Rajasthan-Sindh railway to Naya Chor, 830 sq. miles in the Shakargarh area, south-east of Sialkot, 30 sq. miles of the Khemkaran enclave on the Punjab border were captured by Indian army. In addition, India readjusted the cease-fire line so as to ensure the security of the Indian territory in Kashmir. Indian army captured as many as 36 posts in the Kargil region that dominatd the strategic Zojila-Leh road linking Srinagar with Ladakh. It also secured strategic positions in Gulmarg, Uri, the Lippa valley, south of Titwal, the Buina bulge north of Titwal, Gurais in northern Kashmir and the Tilel valley east of Gurias. Indian armed forces in conjunction with the Mukti Bahini liberated an area of 1,42,199 sq kms of Bangladesh from Pakistan army in this 14 days of war. At the end of this war, Pakistan found its armed forces in tatters being left with just 10 army divisions, including two armoured, out of a total of 14 divisions, less than half of its air force and a mere remnant of its navy. The army equipment captured by Indian army in Bangladesh were enough to equip two army divisions. Above all, Pakistan was reduced from one-fifth to one-tenth the size of India and also lost 54 per cent of its population.

General Niazi later in his memoirs "Betrayal of East Pakistan" blamed Indian General J S Aurora, before whom he surrendered in Dacca, for a series of blunders. He wrote that no military scholars would give the Indians the credit for victory which was obvious from the fact that most the Generals of Aurora's command were not considered for promotion or even retention in the post-war army because of their failure in East Pakistan. General .Aurora rubbished the charge of Niazi that he failed to analyse the terrain of East Pakistan. He lamented that Niazi's book would only appeal to those persons who did not know the methods of fighting. He mocked that he caught Niazi with his pants down since he had no imagination on how to fight the war. He agreed that the terrain was not suitable for the use of tanks as Indian army had to cross many water obstacles. Aurora claimed that his aim was to bypass the defences of enemy army and not to attack them head-on. General Aurora asked two questions to Niazi when he was taken as Prisoner of War that he had the prepared defences guarding the main approaches from the border but he could not do anything when Indian army bypassed his defences. Niazi told him that his plan was to attack from both the sides after the Indian army bypassed. When Aurora questioned why it didn't happen, Niazi was silent. According to Aurora, his imagination didn't work that Indian army was going to bypass them to proceed as far as Dacca. General Aurora further disclosed that while Niazi was a POW, he sent a message urging him to issue a statement that he had fought the war brilliantly but no notice was given to his request. However, General Aurora agreed that he would have been happy if Government would have appointed him as the Chief of Army Staff. Rueful General disclosed that while he was fighting in the east, General Cadeth, Commander of the Western Army Command was engaged with the Pakistan forces in the west. Surprisingly, Indian Government appointed the Commander of the Southern Command General G G Bewoor who had no direct role in the war of 1971, as the next Army Chief. Such manipulations are quite often prevalent in Indian bureaucracy who played a significant role in such policies and the political bosses seemed gutless to deprive the deserving ones their rights and left them recluse for the rest of life. Hats off- to- them.

After the 93,000 Pakistan army POWs were brought to India, R N Kao, the R&AW Chief planned another psychological combat operation for the generations to come. He directed Col. V.Longer, the head of Information wing of R&AW to prepare leaflets on regular basis about the democratic system in which Indians were living and circulate these leaflets among these POWs on regular basis. These POWs were bound to go back to their homeland one day or the other. So, prior to their departure, many leaflets outlining the Indian democratic system, Indian Judiciary, Indian culture and many other aspects of Indian society were distributed among these POWs so that they could go and preach these values among the coming generations of Pakistan.

After the two World Wars in the last century, world community witnessed many wars among various countries but this war was altogether different in which such a large number of soldiers, more than 93,000, surrendered within two weeks of time without offering much resistance to the Indian Army. This was all possible because Indian army and intelligence strategists had meticulously planned this war well in advance in two phases i.e. Phase I Guerrilla Operation and Phase II Army intervention. Kao, the R&AW Chief and General Manekshaw had excellent personal rapport which proved a masterstroke in this war. Both were having their offices in South Block next to Prime Minister Indira Gandhi and used to walk into each other's office without any prior appointment to discuss the on-going situation or to plan any strategy. Phase one belonged to the Indian Intelligence R&AW which with the help of paramilitary forces trained a guerrilla force of more than 1,00,000 Bengali population to harass the Pakistan Army before the final war was fought. This outfit Mukti Bahini fought with the Pakistan forces for eight months and totally demoralized them for a conventional war. Special Frontier Force of R&AW independently fought in the Chittagong Hill tract and on their own got vacated this region from the clutches of Pakistan army before actual surrender. This is the unique achievement of R&AW which has no parallel in the history of any other intelligence agency of any other country of the World. This happened only because of a very outstanding planning and execution of its plan by the first Chief of R&AW, R N Kao who had no equal in experience or intellect. R&AW was created three years ago and lacked in its strength, equipments etc. Even then Kao completed this memorable task with the vigour of his able officers. His competent team comprising his deputy K Sankaran Nair, who subsequently successfully organized Asian Games in 1982 in New Delhi and later became Indian Ambassador in Singapore, P N Banerjee, Joint Director in charge of the Eastern Sector of R&AW, Brigadier M B K Nair, head of technical wing of R&AW and other valiant officers who even penetrated deep inside East Pakistan to train the Mukti Bahini and snapped communication lines at various places in the western sector during this war. Recent US-Iraq war has proved that even CIA or KGB and even Mossad of Israel did not figure in any big war in comparison to the contribution and achievement of these unsung heroes of R&AW of India under the dynamic leadership of R N Kao in 1971 war for liberation of Bangladesh. Government of India conveniently forgot his contributions in this war and summarily removed him in 1977 when Indira Gandhi lost the election and he was unnecessarily blamed for being responsible for indulging in the internal affairs during Emergency of 1975-77. It was a ridiculous decision to malign such an upright, highly patriotic and daring Intelligence officer who was matchless to his rivals and had no parallel in the intelligence world. He was duly rehabilitated by Indira Gandhi when she returned to power in 1980 and was appointed her senior Advisor in policy planning and creation of LTTE in Srilanka for Tamilian cause and NSG to combat terrorism in Punjab, were his new brainchildren. It is high time the authorities should shed their political inhibitions and recognized his contribution in the Indian intelligence services. Such an act will not only revive the sagging morale of Indian intelligence but will also prop up the much needed strength for future.

❑

Merger of Sikkim

Operation Third Eye

"During the course of a discussion with R N Kao around the end of December, 2000, I enquired details of this bloodless coup d'etat of Sikkim which was engineered by him on the direction of Indira Gandhi, the Indian Prime Minister. He laughed and said that during the integration of princely states after the Indian independence from the British, was it possible for Sardar Vallabhbhai Patel to send army to annex Hyderabad and Junagarh without the uprising of local population against their respective Nawabs. I understood his reference. Then, I specifically asked him whether Indian intelligence had some role in that uprising of people of Hyderabad and Junagarh. He mysteriously smiled and closed his eyes for fair amount of time and I kept watching the reaction which was radiating from his calm poser indicating some thing was striking his mind and he was recalling some past events. I did not pursue further on that matter but there must be some undisclosed memory which was brainstorming him on the events of that integration. I could later guess that merger of Sikkim was a repeat of annexation of Hyderabad and Junagarh when I remembered what Kao told me instantly when I discussed Sikkim issue with him. Was Indian intelligence involved in the annexation of Hyderabad and Junagarh is still a mystery but Indian intelligence is responsible for the merger of Sikkim as an Indian state is a reality.

When I tried to discuss whatever knowledge about Sikkim merger was known to me through other sources of R&AW, Kao became little nostalgic but mysteriously smiled for a while. Since his memory was fading due to advancing age, he could not elaborate ex-tempore full facts of this operation of Sikkim. However, he revealed that this operation was personally conducted by him along with four or five selected officers of R&AW and nothing was known even to other high ranking officers. I corroborated this fact with his number two K.Sankaran Nair in 2008. Nair was shadow of Kao during their undisputed rule in R&AW from Sept 21, 1968 till 1977 when Morarji Desai, the Janta Party Prime Minister unceremoniously retired them from service. Nair confirmed to me that he never knew anything of this operation in spite of being in such a senior position at that time. On persistent requests on one plea or other, Kao revealed the name of those officers of R&AW who accomplished this assignment in the most secretive modus operandi wherein territory of more than 3,000 square miles of Sikkim was merged with India much to the challenge of two giant powers, China and U.S.A. Kao had written full details of this operation in his memoirs which are deposited with Nehru Memorial Museum and Library but these could be opened after 25 years of his death as per his wish along with two others i.e. "Bangladesh liberation" and "Assassination of Mrs. Indira Gandhi". I have tried my best to put a true picture of this operation from the available sources of R&AW, discussion with R N Kao and available written material on this subject but veracity of these details would be corroborated only when memoirs of Kao will become available for public consumption in 2027. In the meantime, let these known facts of this historical achievement of R&AW, authentic to certain extent, are known to public, which is unparallel in the history of any intelligence agency of the World be it CIA, MI6, Mossad or others. To say the least, this material ia a great tribute to the legendary Indian spy late Kao, a true Indian by heart and devotion. Kao told me that after the merger of Sikkim, he had a plan to disintegrate the Tarai area of Nepal because of increasing presence of China there much to the discomfiture of the Indian Prime Minister, Indira Gandhi. He foresaw the Maoist menace to India in 1975 which is now posing a serious security threat to India. However, merger of Tarai of Nepal was deferred in view of political turmoil in India when Indira Gandhi declared emergency in the country in June, 1975 just after merger of Sikkim with Inidan Union. Most of the opposition leaders were arrested by her and internal political storm hampered her in formulating other external planning of the region. Unfortunately, when elections were held in 1977, Indira Gandhi was defeated and her party did not come to power and Kao's operation of merging Tarai and other assignments, did not materialize".

(As per discussion with R N Kao)

Historical Bakground

The word, Sikkim, is derived from the Limbu words meaning "New Palace". The Tibetans called it Drend Zong i.e. the land of rice while the original inhabitants, Lepchas called it "Nye-ma-el" meaning heaven. It is divided into two geographical regions of north and south. The southern part comprises dense forests and precipitous hill. It is a sparsely populated area whereas the northern region is comparatively more open and undulated wherein good pastures and pine forests are found

Although, there are little facts known about the early history of Sikkim but the Lepchas were considered to be the original inhabitants of Sikkim and they rightly claimed to be natives of this region. It is believed that in the beginning of Seventeenth century, three Lamas came from Tibet to Sikkim to convert the people to their doctrines. At Gangtok, they found a young man by the name Penchu Namgyal who happened to be the great-grandson of a Tibetan noble, Guru Tashe. These Lamas installed him as the Gyalpo or the king of Sikkim. This was decided in 1641 at a place called Yoksam. Kingdom of Sikkim in those times which was very extensive and included Chumbi Valley of Tibet and Darjeeling districts of West Bengal.

Thereafter, Sikkim was ruled by succession from father to son. During the reign of third Gyalpo, Chador Namgyal, Sikkim was overrun by Burmese in 1706. Tibet came to the rescue of Sikkim and drove out Burmese. In this gratitude, the ruler of Sikkim founded the great monastery at Pemionchi. Due to weak monarchy in Sikkim, around this period, Nepal started usurping its territory and province of Limbuana was taken into its hold during the reign of Gyurma Namgyal in 1717-1734. Nepal again invaded Sikkim during the time of sixth Gyalpo in 1780-1790 and overran upto Tista river in the eastward. But soon there after Nepal was defeated by Tibet and this region was re-aligned. The Chola-Jelap range was made the northern and eastern boundary of Sikkim. Chumbi valley was taken by the Tibetan and the region west of the Tista was given to Nepal.

During this period, the princes and princesses of the dynasty generally contracted marriage alliance with the aristocratic families of Lhasa with the result Tibetan culture gained increasing influence in Sikkim, modifying the ways and modus operandi of the original indigenous Lepchas. The style of the Court became progressively Tibetan, although on a more modest scale, and the Nepalese influx was apprehended as an intrusion that might endanger and disrupt the established order.

There were some Sikkimese who favoured the settlement of Nepalese because they felt that Sikkim was an underpopulated country and manpower was needed for development of its resources. They professed that Nepalese were tough and industrious people who would bring the vast empty wastelands under cultivation and contribute to raising the economy of the country. Hence, in the nineteenth century, there were two factions among the Sikkimese, one pro-Nepalese and the other pro-Tibetan.

Like Nepal and Bhutan, Sikkim with around 3,000 sq. miles of area, was one of the most strategic territory for India due to its border on the North along side Tibet which was occupied by the Chinese in 1950. Except from south, it is separated by mountain ranges of Himalaya from Nepal on the west and Bhutan on the east. Some area on the east is bordering Tibet. These mountains of the height ranging from

10,000 to 28,000 ft. contain certain passes which are the travelling routes among these four parts of this region. Chola ranges on the eastern boundary with Tibet have two important passes of Nahu La, 15,512 ft. and Jelep La, 13,354 ft. Singalila range dividing it with Nepal contains Chiabhanjan, 10,320 ft., pass The highest peak, Kanchenjunga, 28,140 ft., according to Sikkimese belief, the most sacred treasures of the of land and considered to be the symbol of prosperity and destiny of its people.

Prior to its merger with India in 1975, total population of Sikkim was around 2 Lakh which comprised three main tribes namely, the Lepchas, Bhutias and Nepalese. Lepchas were the original inhabitants of the country and their numbers were about 17,000. There are different versions about the origin of Lepchas. According to one version, Lepcha is a Nepali word meaning 'vile speakers' and the second one compared it with a fish 'Lapcha" found in Nepal. This fish is stated to be of submissive nature like the Lepcha people. Lepchas were originally animists but later profess as Buddhism. They are known for their mild, quite and indolent disposition. Second tribe Bhutias were immigrants from Tibet and their population was about 16,000. They also professed Buddhism and are generally very strong, hardy and good tempered. The third tribe, the Nepalese are Hindus by religion and their population was more than 1,50,000 in numbers. They were considered steady, industrious and rich people.

British sojourn in Sikkim commenced in 1814-15 with the agenda to have communication with China and to neutralize the Nepalese and Bhutanese influence in the region. British were fighting a war with Nepal and they found an ally in Sikkim Raja whose territory was captured by Nepal in a previous overrun. British promised Raja to recover his territory from Nepal. The Nepal war came to an end in 1815 with the Treaty of Segauli between the two. The British handed over some territory to Sikkim and signed the Treaty of Titalia on February 10, 1817. Under this treaty, Sikkim lost its right of independent action in its dispute with Nepal and other neighbouring States. In 1835, it was forced by the British to "gift" Darjeeling to them. This act worsened the relations between Sikkim and the British. Although, there were some minor disputes related to criminals hereinbefore but in December, 1849, the arrest of Dr. Campbell, Superintendent of Darjeeling along with a renowned botanist Dr. Hooker during a tour by the Sikkim authorities enflamed the ongoing subtle storm into a full scale war. The British retaliated through a military expedition and annexed around 640 sq. miles of Sikkim territory bordering India.

The British could not annex the whole of Sikkim to the Indian territory due to the presence of considerable Tibetan faction in its territory. Though Tibet did not intervene on behalf of Sikkim directly but it granted the Raja an allowance of 6,000

Rupees per year which the British had stopped his Darjeeling grant. This gesture further enhanced the Tibetan influence in Sikkim in the next decade that the British in order to assert their position were forced to undertake another military expedition in to Sikkim towards the end of 1860. The military expedition attained unqualified success and the power of Majaraja was completely reduced and he submitted to the mercy of the British. But due to various political considerations like hostility with Tibet, China, Nepal and Bhutan and the future of tea trade in this region forced the British not to annex Sikkim during this expedition. 1857 mutiny in India was another factor to desist in this action. So, instead of annexing Sikkim, it was made de facto protectorate of the British under the Treaty of 1861 and the British gained substantial advantages without annexation.

In 1886, the Tibetans invaded 13 miles inside Sikkim and captured a place called Lingtu on the Darjeeling road. Maharaja of Sikkim, Thothab Namgyal supported the Tibetan action and declared that the land in occupation actually belonged to Tibet. In March, 1888, the British sent the forces and expelled the Tibetans from Lingtu. Maharaja of Sikkim and his family members were taken to Kalimpong and were kept under house arrest. Government of India under the British, appointed a political officer and entrusted the administration of Sikkim to him.

Defeat of Tibet forces by the British, alarmed the Chinese and convinced them that if they would not follow the dictated lines of the British, they would lose their influence in Tibet. So, in March, 1889, the Anglo-Chinese Convention was signed. Article Two of the Convention categorically admitted Sikkim as a protectorate of the Government of India. H M Durand, Secretary to the Government of India, emphasized this point in an Official Note (21 May, 1889):

"Sikkim is part of the Indian Empire.....It can have no dealings with foreign powers to whose eyes India should be all red from Himalayas to Cape Comerin."

This convention set aside all previous drawbacks of the Treaty of 1861 and once for all decided the status of Sikkim as "protectorate" of the Government of India. In the coming decade, Indian Government consolidated its authority in Sikkim and dictated with impunity its diktat not only in the royal affairs but in order to decontrol the Tibetan influence, encouraged the mass immigration of Nepalese population. The newly appointed Political Officer, Claude White, deliberately and actively encouraged the influx of Nepalese immigration into Sikkim to diminish the control of the Lepchas and Bhutias. The Nepalese were mostly Hindus and their language was Sanskrit-influenced. Their culture and way of life had closer affinity with India than with Tibet. British policy behind the settlement of large bulk of an Hindu-orientated population in Sikkim was to preclude the risk of its looking northwards in Tibet for direction and support. British wanted to wean away the ruler from Tibetan influence so as to bring him more securely under their own control and for that cause they gave support to the pro-Nepalese lobby. British never approved the royal subservience to the Tibetan authorities and to the Chinese Amban (representative) in Lhasa and on the refusal of the Maharaja to do so, did not hesitate to detain him in India from 1892 to 1896 and administered Sikkim freely.

In 1903, the Government of India opened the Tibet route for trade and sent Young Husband Expedition who signed Lhasa Convention on September 7, 1904 and resolved all the British difficulties regarding the status of Sikkim and boundary with Tibet. Through this Convention, Tibet not only recognized Sikkim as the protectorate of the Government of India but also confirmed the Sikkim-Tibet boundary as laid down in the Convention of 1890. China confirmed the Lhasa Convention by signing the Peking Convention with Britain in 1906. This Convention had far-reaching consequences about Sikkim wherefrom Sikkim was recognized as the protectorate of the Indian Government internationally. Government of India demonstrated its power in Tibet and consolidated its position in Sikkim. Thereafter, Sikkim no longer had any problem either from Maharaja or outside powers like Tibet and China, for remaining period of their rule in India.

British further demonstrated their absolute authority over Sikkim when after the death of Maharaja Thothab Namgyal on February 11, 1914, his second son Sidkeong Namgyal was chosen as successor ignoring the elder son Tchoda Namgyal who had pro-Tibetan leaning. He was groomed by the British for the throne in the expectation that he might be more amenable to their guidance. Although, he was brought up under monastic discipline as a reincarnate of a high lama in Tibet, he later went up for studies to Oxford for two years. British sent him on a world tour to visualize his worldwide outlook. However, he died under mysterious circumstances on December 5, 1914.

Sidkeong was succeeded by his younger brother, Tashi Namgyal as the new Maharaja. He studied in Mayo College, Ajmer, which housed mostly the children of Indian rulers. He was brought up in an atmosphere more suitable to the British culture and the British could safely count on him as a ruler who would raise no obstacle to their designs. Tashi was restored the powers that were withdrawn during the reign of his father. Tashi was a gentle, courteous ruler who wished well for whole of the World. He was revered and loved by his people as a father figure who would not wish to harm the slightest creature.

Tashi was a tolerant person by temperament and did not impose any restriction on the Nepalese influx which remained unabated during the authority of Political Officer, Claude White and his successors. Tashi considered the Nepalese as the

Protecting Power's problem. For thirty years up to 1944, when his son Thondup took over the reins as his principal adviser, the Nepalese were afforded every opportunity to get themselves firmly entrenched in Sikkim and established as the majority party. The course of Sikkim's subsequent history, including its merger with India and extinction as an independent entity, stems directly from Claude White's initiative in formulating the British stance vis-à-vis the settlement of Nepalese in Sikkim. Hindu Nepalese were in two third of the majority of population when the British left India in 1947. They did not mingle with the other minority of Lepchas and Bhutias and maintained their strong Hindu caste system. In spite of their majority, political power remained with the ruler and his principal advisers who were mainly from the traditional Bhutia-Lepcha families. Soon thereafter, a feeling was growing among a section of the Nepalese population that although they were a majority community but treated as second-class citizens and would never acquire highest offices of state under the existing ruling dynasty. With the imminence of independence of India where Congress party was leading agitation against the Princely States, they found opportunity to promote their own political interest of a state independent of a ruler. They found it the right time to transform the monarch Sikkim into a democratic state in India where Nepalese would be the ultimate political achievers.

Indian Independence and Voice for Democrat Sikkim

By the time, the British left India in 1947, the ethnic imbalance saw sea changes in Sikkim where the Nepalese population was around seventy-five percent, Lepchas were second to fourteen percent and the Bhutia community were third to eleven percent. This ethnic imbalance was shrewdly manipulated by the Maharaja by co-opting the ethnic notables from all communities in the economic, administrative and political fields. Among the Bhutias, new social class Kazis emerged as the power behind the ruler acquiring social and economic dominance. Lepchas were reduced to protégés of Bhutias with hardly any political or economic leverage. Except some elite from the Nepalese population, majority of Sikkim population were petty traders or labourers and often treated as second class citizens without any land rights. Main reason of the imbalance was due to the fact because more than half of the land of Sikkim was vested with the Maharaja and his family as private estates where cardamom growing and rich forests gave substantial income to them. This socio-economic imbalance opened its voice to the fore when other states within India rose against their princely rulers for democracy.

When India attained independence, Sikkimese people did not have any political party to ventilate their political demands. Rather some welfare bodies like Praja Sammelan, Praja Mandal, Praja Sudhar and Swatantra Dal were formed in different parts of the kingdom during the end of 1946. These bodies functioned without any policy, programme or ideology. Indian independence gave fillip to these bodies a sort of strength to rise against the autocratic regime of the Maharaja. Representatives of these bodies met at Gangtok on December 7, 1947 and unitedly formed a political party, the Sikkim State Congress. Tashi Tsering was elected President of the party and C.D.Rai as General Secretary. Other important leaders who took active part in the formation of this political party were Kazi Lhendup Dorji, Khangsarpa, Capt. Dimik Singh Lepcha, D D Gurung, Chandra Das and Senam Tsering. The Sikkim State Congress represented all the three ethnic communities of Sikkim with its programme and ideology of struggle against the exploitation by the rich landlords under a feudalistic system and setting up a democratic government. A delegation of this newly formed party met the Maharaja, Tashi Namgyal and presented a memorandum to him and demanded abolition of land-lordism, formation of an interim Government and accession of Sikkim to India.

Towards the end of 1948, two leaders of Sikkim State Congress, Tashi Tsering and C D Rai went to New Delhi and met Prime Minister, Jawaharlal Nehru. They apprised Nehru of the political situation of Sikkim and demanded representation of Sikkim in the Indian Parliament. Nehru highlighted the constitutional difficulties for this representation to which these leaders requested to remove these difficulties. These leaders were advised to keep the demand for accession with India in abeyance.

Maharaja of Sikkim obviously did not hesitate to counter the emergence of the Sikkim State Congress under his nose. Through his stooges, he launched his loyal political party, the Sikkim National Party which was composed mainly of the minority communities of Lepchas and Bhutias. This party opposed all popular demands of the Sikkim State Congress and passed a resolution on April 30, 1948 at the behest of Maharaja that Sikkim, under any circumstances would not accede to the dominion of India and its political relations with the Indian Union would be on the basis of equality. This resolution further emphasized that Sikkim was close to Tibet than to India due to historical, social, cultural and linguistic bondage. Geographically and ethnically, Sikkim is not a part of India and had only political relations which were imposed on it. Being lamaist, she is religiously distinct to India than Tibet. Warning India directly, the resolution concluded that a happy buffer Sikkim would be of great advantage than an unhappy Sikkim in India on one of its future international boundaries of great importance, which would be of disadvantage, indeed a danger to India. Maharaja played his card shrewdly throwing a direct warning to the newly independent India who could hardly take any retaliatory action at that time. Nehru's idealism decided the issue finally maintaining the status-quo with Sikkim.

On the other hand, within a short span of its formation, the Sikkim State Congress assumed significant power centre in Sikkim. Every section of the population including government officials joined the party. There was a growing demand for popular government. In February 1949, the Congress launched a statewide movement "No-rent campaign" demanding implementation of land reforms. When twelve leaders of the Congress were arrested, the Political officer of India in Sikkim intervened and persuaded to suspend this agitation. When the Maharaja did not implement the demand, the Congress on May 1 again launched Satyagraha movement for the establishment of responsible government in the State. More than 5,000 agitators besieged the Royal Palace when Maharaja did not heed to their demand. Indian army intervened and gave protection to the Maharaja in the Indian Residency. The Maharaja, in order to avert the grim situation, on the advice of the Political Officer of India, asked Tashi Tsering to form his own Ministry. First democratic Ministry was formed and Tashi Tsering was appointed as Chief Minister on May 9, 1949 along with four other Ministers.

Since its inception, this Ministry was never allowed to work by the Maharaja on one plea or the other like non-implementation of land reforms and accession with India. Since, there was no constitution defining the power of the Maharaja and the Ministry, each side tried to impose their respective diktat. The Maharaja exploited the prevalent imbroglio and invited the Indian government to intervene as the administration was getting out of control. Indian government was in a dilemma because its sympathies were with the Sikkim State Congress to run a democratic set up but at the same time could not force the Maharaja to work in tandem with them. The Maharaja exploited this dilemma and arbitrarily dismissed the popular Ministry on June 7, 1949 within one month of its formation. Government of India, with no option, took over the administration and ultimately India-Sikkim Peace Treaty was signed on December 5, 1950.

India-Sikkim Peace Treaty of 1950

When India became independent, a standstill agreement was signed with Sikkim on February 27, 1948 whereby "all agreements, relations and administrative arrangements as to the matter of common concern existing between the crown and the Sikkim State on August 14, 1947 were deemed to continue between the dominion of India and the Sikkim Darbar pending the conclusion of a new agreement or treaty". Subsequently the two governments resolved, in order to strengthen the good relations already existing between them, to enter into a new treaty with each other. Hence, the India-Sikkim Peace Treaty was signed at Gangtok on December 5, 1950. This was obligatory mandate which had to be accepted by both the parties without any ifs and buts at that time. Thirteen Articles of this Treaty elaborated matters related to, previous treaties like, autonomy, defence, external relations, trade, communications, citizen rights, extradition, privy purse, judicial remedy and appointment of representative.

This treaty betrayed the aspirations of the Sikkim State Congress Party which was raising the demand of merger of Sikkim within the Indian territory. Due to other international political considerations, India was helpless to accede to this demand because of many existing problems all over the country due to recent partition. Kashmir problem and Bengal communal riots were more important issues on the agenda of the then leadership. Integration of the princely states was another matter of paramount importance because of the challenge thrown by the Nawabs of Hyderabad and Junagarh. Refugees problem had affected most of the Indian states. The Maharaja of Sikkim fully exploited these grey areas of Indian politics at that time and in this dilemma, Indian Government had no other option except to sign this treaty. Since, Sikkim Congress leaders were advised previously by Indian government to keep the demand of accession to India "in abeyance", they were compensated to a small extent and a seat was allotted to Sikkim in the Council of State under the Government of India Act, 1935. This treaty also disappointed the National Party which had demanded political relations with India on the basis of equality because Sikkim was accepted as protectorate of India under the provisions of this Treaty. However, a press note issued prior to the signing of this treaty gave indication that Maharja of Sikkim as a non-Sovereign ruler admitted that Government of India is ultimately responsible for the establishment of a good and progressive government in its protectorate.

After the 1949 agitation of Sikkim State Congress against Maharaja brought significant change in the Sikkim politics. India took a stand thereafter that the posting of a Dewan as head of the administration would guarantee its de-facto control and signed the treaty in 1950 maintaining Sikkim as a protectorate. This decision proved fatal because it undermined the stature of the Political officer to administer the state of Sikkim. Henceforth, during British regime the Political Officer as Resident assumed more executive powers in Sikkim due to its being a border State of Tibet and the Maharaja was just a nominal head for all practical purposes. Induction of Dewan completely changed this equation and in the new arrangement, the Maharaja emerged as dominant power in the state. In the ensuing conflict of power sharing between the Dewan and the Political Officer, the status of the later was considered as India's diplomatic representative which boosted the morale of Maharaja in dictating other political aspirations at his will. This proved self-defeating move of the Indian diplomacy at that time. Dewan was supposed to check the abuse of power in the administration but his powers were devalued and the Political officer was reduced to the status as diplomatic representative, the Maharaja became the centre of power and Delhi lost its leverage to check this menace. In the coming period, he got appointed a Dewan who was friend of his son and soon the political scenario in Sikkim started taking new dimensions much to the discomfiture of Indian government and its people. Maharaja started manipulations in the elections to install his chosen men in power on one hand and started equating the status of Sikkim with Bhutan which brought him into conflict with his people and Indian government over the years. He deliberately neglected the majority Nepalese Hindu citizens of equal rights and opportunities and when he overstepped his external authority, these people started looking towards India for support.

Post-Treaty Farce Engineered By King

The Maharaja, keeping in mind the ongoing internal problem as a result of the partition of the country, asserted his dictated authority in the administration of Sikkim. He was supported by his second son Palden Thondup Namgyal who became the power centre of Sikkim politics after the Peace Treaty. Rather, he played significant role in the formulation of the text of the Treaty and became virtual ruler thereafter. The Sikkim State Congress raised the banner of revolt for popular reforms after the treaty. This forced the Maharaja to create a legislative body called the Sikkim State Council in 1953. It was given the power to enact laws for governance and law and order with the assent of the ruler. This body was not authorized to have any say in external relations and appointment of the Principal Administrative Officer. This body consisted of twenty four numbers, eighteen elected and six nominated by the ruler. Seven elected seats were reserved for Nepalese, seven for the Bhutias and Lepchas, one seat each for Sangha, the Chongs and the Scheduled Tribe. Distribution of these seats was not fair and equitable because the Nepalese who were seventy five percent of the total population were given the same number of seats as to the twenty five percent of the Bhutia-Lepcha communities.

In addition to this deliberate attempt to downsize the Nepalese Hindus in their representation, the Maharaja complicated the election process for them on the basis of parity and not one man one vote. A candidate after getting elected from his community, had to secure fifteen percent votes of the other community for which seats had been reserved to enable him to be elected. All political parties except the National party resented this process of election. This electoral anarchy was devised by royal house to cut across the growing influence of the Nepalese Hindus in dominating the Sikkim politics which the Indian Government saw as a sort of guarantee against the Tibetan influence in Sikkim. Ruler had no option but the Prince assumed the Nepalese Hindu presence not only a threat to his throne and to the age-old culture of the land but to the survival of Sikkim as an independent entity. His deep-felt nostalgia for the traditional values of the Sikkim of his ancestors gave rise to an apprehension amongst the Nepalese Hindus that they were pariahs and would be denied full citizen rights by the Palace.

Although, the Prince was convinced that it would be unjust and impracticable to evict the Nepalese Hindus who made Sikkim their home since the early years of the century. He thought to take firm action to stop further influx of the Nepalese but sensing the indignant outcry of a large population not only inside Sikkim but also in Nepal and India against such discrimination it would create unavoidable situation for the Palace. However, to allay the apprehension of the Lepchas and Bhutias that their culture was in danger, an Institute of Tibetology was established at Gangtok. There was another apprehension that with the capture of Tibet by the Chinese, invaluable Tibetan texts of historical, religious, literary and scientific importance would be destroyed or pillaged from Tibet's monastic libraries. The institute was set up as a focus for Tibetan-based research and was eventually inaugurated under the joint auspices of the Dalai Lama and Pandit Jawaharlal Nehru, the Indian Prime Minister. Indian government financed all the expenditure in this venture.

In 1953, first elections were held in Sikkim without any election laws. In these elections, the Hindu Nepalese filled nominations on the basis of the general election as in India. For the Bhutia-Lepcha seats, the candidate had to be elected in the primary election by these voters only. In order to finally get elected, these candidates had to be confirmed in the general election by all the voters including, Nepalese, Bhutia and Lepchas. So, Maharaja not only had his say in the State Council but also elected his own men in the executive council to further administer Sikkim on his terms. The second general election of 1958 were also conducted on this parity system and suitable candidates were forbidden to get elected. Even winning candidates were got defeated on account of communal voting and complicated counting arrangements. It would be pertinent to mention that the Prince had no statutory role in the administration as it was known and accepted that his was the ruling voice. His father was temperamentally not interested in attending to administrative details and the ruler's decisions were in fact the decisions of his son. He was averse to the cause of so-called economic development and democratic ideology because he saw grave danger to the disintegration of social structure of Sikkim in this process. He wrested all the administration powers in himself and wanted to deprive the politicians of Sikkim of their political desires since he saw a hidden threat to his monarchy in such a scenario.

In 1959, the Sikkim Election Tribunal, at the behest of the Darbar, disqualified three leaders, Sonam Tsring, Kashiraj Pradhan and Nahakul Pradhan for a period of six years from seeking election to the Sikkim Council. Subsequently, the Maharaja reduced the penalty of Kashiraj Pradhan and Nahakul Pradhan to six months but Sonam Tsring was barred for three years under the same section of penalty. This discrimination against the State Congress leader brought all leaders of different political parties to get united against the Maharaja. Kazi Lhendup Dorzi, President of the Swantantra Dal called a Joint Convention on September 23 and 24 which was presided over by Nahakul Pradhan. In this convention, many important resolutions i.e. introduction of joint electorate system based on universal and adult franchise as in India, establishment of a Legislative Assembly consisting of 24 seats, Dewan to be the Speaker with the right to casting vote etc. were passed.

In a significant development, in May, 1960, some dissident leaders of State Congress and National Party along with the Praja Sammelan and Swatantra Dal merged and formed a new political party the Sikkim National Congress. Kazi Lhendup Dorji was unanimously elected the first President of the new Party. The Party demanded a written constitution including fundamental rights, codification of laws and a High Court. Influx of 60000 Tibetan refugees along with Dalai Lama in India, increased tension on this border and Indian government's priority shifted to the security of the state and these legitimate demands of the Sikkimese were deferred and the maharaja found an opportunity to become hostile to these demands. Thereafter, the Maharaja denied some legitimate executive rights to the leader of this newly created political party in the legislative council in spite of it second largest in number. In July, 1961, the Maharaja promulgated the Sikkim Subjects Regulation without the consent of the State Council which provided citizenship to all Sikkim nationals even born before 1850 but excluded the Nepalese population which was more than 70 percent. The Nepalese Hindus, who were backbone of the Sikkim National Congress, were discriminated under this regulation. Taking advantage of the 1962 India-China war, the Maharaja postponed elections to the Council which were due in May of that year. The Council was replaced by an advisory consultative of thirty-one which comprised the stooges of the Maharaja much to the disliking of the SNC leaders.

Coronation of New King and His Marriage to an American Agent, Hope Cook – First Reason for Merger of Sikkim with India

Maharaja Sir Tashi Namgyal who ruled Sikkim since December 5, 1914, died on December 2, 1963. The Prince Palden Thondup Namgyal succeeded him as ruler. At the time of his coronation, he was a widower as his first wife died in June, 1957. He had two sons and a daughter from this wedlock. After her death, he became alcoholic. His general behavior became obstinate and his relations with the local politicians and with Government of India started worsening steadily.

On March 20, 1963, he married Hope Cooke, a resident of New York. Hope had a lonely and difficult childhood as her mother died when she was two years old. She developed respect for the Indian Prime Minister Jawaharlal Nehru whom she considered as a crusader for the freedom and dignity of people all over the World and a dedicated leader with profound wish for the physical and economic uplift of the Indian people. During her stay in the hill-station of Darjeeling, she met her husband to be, the heir to the Sikkim throne. He was then forty years old, just twice her age. He was in need of love and companionship since he started taking alcohol due to loneliness. Prince too had a lonely and difficult childhood and their common feeling of loneliness acted as a bond and drew them closer. For the Prince, love apart, the fascination of the white-skinned race was an equally compelling factor for this alliance.

When news of his proposed marriage to an American went around, most of the Sikkim population was against this proposal. There was an old tradition among the Sikkim rulers to marry into Tibetan clan. Prior to this, Prince's uncle Sidkeong Tulku, who was educated at Oxford, wanted to marry a Burmese princess which was opposed by the orthodox Sikkimese. In the case of Hope Cook too, the Council of Elders, by tradition, was summoned by the ruler, the proposal was accepted with some hesitation.

According to sources of R&AW, at the time of her marriage, there was no evidence of Hope's link with CIA or any American agency. But the scale and style of the celebrations of this marriage in Gangtok was so expensive that apprehension and implication of this alliance alarmed the Indian Government and IB. The guest list was indication enough of the new look this American bride was fast bringing to Sikkim in her brain. Sikkim was making her debut on world stage. This was first time in the history of Sikkim that foreigners from distant continents were invited to this royal wedding and arrangements were made awfully extravagant so that they should carry back the impression not of a medieval and feudal culture of Sikkim but of a progressive and enlightened country capable of standing on its own feet if given a chance to do so. The plethora of foreign diplomats and relatives wearing their old-world morning coats and western-style regalia, outnumbered the Sikkimese gentility who were relegated to the position of back stage observers. All these celebrations were at the expense of the resources of Government of India who had no option but to watch helplessly.

After this marriage, the Prince, who was even averse to marriages of Lepcha-Bhutia to Nepalese, was in a predicament that he had violated his own created ethics in this regard. Hope was aware of this embarrassment and as such she was determined to prove herself Sikkimese by adoption and took infinite pains to assimilate herself to the ways and habits of the traditional Bhutia and Lepcha communities. She started wearing Sikkimese dresses, served Sikkimese beer in rustic bamboo pipes at Palace functions, picked up the languages of these communities and conversed in scarcely audible whispers in the manner of high-ranking ladies of the Tibetan aristocracy. She started getting herself involved in the Sikkimese arts and crafts and traditional textile articles.

Hope's link with CIA were coming to surface and detected by the Indian intelligence when she frequented foreign visits with the King and in those foreign countries they portrayed themselves as the ruler of a country whose status was of an independent entity having special relations with India. The Prince professed to dispel the notion that Sikkim stood on the same constitutional footing as the erstwhile Princely state of India and could as summarily be absorbed by India whenever it chose. He equated Sikkim to Nepal and Bhutan although the treaty of Sikkim was not identical with Indian treaty with Bhutan. He did not explain the fact that India had the treaty for the specific responsibility for Sikkim's defence and foreign relations whereas Bhutan was only to be "guided by the advice of the Indian government". The Prince was provoked, under Hope's influence, to make demands to a degree he would not have ventured if left to his own judgment. From the Indian point of view, these foreign visits of the Prince were of negative value and damaging his image as a friend and ally upon whom India could rely and place trust. On the other hand, he had developed a strong feeling that Sikkim was more developed than Bhutan and should be treated with equal status but he too was aware that if he overstepped the mandate, Government of India's patience would get exhausted to Sikkim's ultimate detriment. However, Pandit Jawaharlal Nehru was too sympathetic to him.

This marriage brought a perceptible change in the style of functioning of the Prince. He started neglecting his Tibetan guests and even his officers were finding difficulty in obtaining access to him for discussing and obtaining orders on affairs of State. He became more interested in entertaining guests of Hope from her homeland and taking them on tour around his country and its institutions. Prior to this marriage he was freely accessible to the rural public but after this marriage they were totally neglected by him. While this marriage brought Sikkim into the limelight but it had the grave and harmful effect of creating a distance between the King and his people. King started neglecting not only his old and trusted advisers but also his own family members. The Prince had two sisters Princess Coocoola and Coola who due to sheer brilliance were of abundance support to him in his political affairs. Coocoola imbibed with all sophistication and culture of west, functioned as the Prince's roving ambassador be it in the corridors of power in New Delhi or socializing with the American President's aides in Washington. She was the chief hostess at State function as well as the chatelaine of his Palace. She had always kept her ears very close to the Sikkim politics and was forthright in her opinion on various subjects. In Hope, she saw a rival to her hold over the Prince and Hope, in her turn, made it clear subsequently that she was the queen. Coocoola's hold in the Palace and in Sikkim politics was reduced considerably after this marriage. She, with the help of some Indian officials, was running a very good business in Gangtok and Calcutta. In order to protect her business interest, she stopped criticizing the Indian government after the arrival of Hope Cook. Second sister of Chogyal Coola married an Indian and was stripped off her citizenship and right in property by him after the marriage because the Sikkimmese girl were deprived of these rights after marrying a foreigner.

For the Prince and Hope, the title of Maharaja and Maharani were not only inadequate but indicated a subservient status. According to them, if Sikkim had to become an independent kingdom, they had to be King and Queen. Hope was more aggressive in this venture. In this hidden pursuit, on March 16, 1965, the Prince, now Crown changed his Indian status of Maharaja to that of Tibetan sounding status of "Chogyal". Chogyal is a compound of Tibetan words — "Chos" denoting religion and "Gyalpo" means ruler or king. The word Chogyal, therefore, meant righteous ruler or the defender of faith. The status of the Maharani was changed to that of Gyalmo. On April 4, 1965, in a colourful ceremony, the Maharaja Kumar Palden Thoundup Namgyal was crowned as king of Sikkim. India was represented at the coronation ceremony by Indira Gandhi, then the Information and Broadcasting Minister of India. This ceremony was celebrated with great pomp and show wherein foreign dignitaries of the highest diplomatic level overshadowed the presence of local leaders and royals. In an emotional speech, Prince pledged to make Sikkim as a paradise on the earth. Indian government regarded this coronation as only religious function as it carried no implications touching Sikkim's international status as an independent entity. So it extended recognition to the new titles as a gesture of good will. Previously Indian government agreed to the ruler's request to double the strength of the Sikkim Guards, which was raised with Indian help. This was agreed to for the sake of good relations. But serious doubts were raised when these guards were made to play a "national anthem" while presenting the annual presentation of colours to the Guards. Hence, Chogyal under the influence of Hope was assembling the symbols of a nation state before making a final bid for his hidden agenda of an independent Sikkim which ultimately brought him in confrontation with India.

However, the "American Influence" was primarily working on Hope's mind and she tried to become the de-facto queen of a state. She started a plot for political and diplomatic manoeuvrings over Sikkim's identity and tried to redefine the new role of Prince, now as Chogyal, in a democratic set up for the world community. This American influence, made Hope to realize that unless public opinion within Sikkim itself could be effectively mobilized, there was little prospect of raising the status of Sikkim as defined in the Treaty. This tacit agenda of America played further on the mind of Hope and on this influence, she floated a so-called scholar body, the Youth Study Forum, which was aimed at highlighting the need for safe-guarding the identity of Sikkim and countering any move to bring the country under tighter control of the Protecting Power. Members of this Forum were financed by Hope and were awarded scholarship in her sinister design to downgrade the role of Indian government in the status of Sikkim abroad. Hope subtly advocated independence for Sikkim and also demanded to repeal the order wherein Darjeeling district was merged with the

West Bengal state. Prior to this, Hope personally wrote an article in the Bulletin of the Institute of Tibetology contesting the legality of the transfer of Darjeeling and Kalimpong to the British East India company and claimed Sikkim's sovereignty over that area. While working as Chairman of the Textbooks Committee for the schools, she deliberately introduced anti-Indian nuances to poison the mind of the coming generations against India. The Lepcha dialect, which was understood by a minuscule minority, was declared the official state language of Sikkim. This antagonized the majority Nepalese. Hope tried to make Chogyal a symbol of unity for his ethnically divided people, but he was portrayed as partisan of Bhutia-Lepcha minorities which further evoked a spirit of Hinduism among the Nepalese all over parts of Sikkim. Hence, Sikkim was divided on religious cards by Hope which Chogyal could not deter owing to her influence which he has to sustain owing to age difference and a white beauty in his palace. The aspirations of Sikkimese to have their own flag, their own system of government and separate identity were highlighted in a very subtle manner. Editors of local papers were compelled to refer the Chogyal and Hope, as Their Majesties and the heir apparent was called the Crown Prince. The address on Palace writing paper was given as Sikkim via India. Hope took the help of some foreign friends and diplomats to put pressure on India to bring Sikkim at par with Bhutan. Around this time an anti-India demonstration was organized on the India's national day with the tacit approval of Chogyal and Hope which was sufficient evidence of American influence over her.

The Youth Study Form was instigated to advocate the cause of Sikkim under the membership of Colombo plan so that it could attain an independent entity in this region. In May, 1967, the Chogyal under the influence of Hope, declared that the Treaty should be reviewed since it was signed in 1950 and thereafter Sikkim had made phenomenal progress. At the behest of the Palace, three Executive Councillors of Sikkim issued a blunt statement on June 15, 1967, declaring that Sikkim gained its sovereign status on August 15, 1947 when India achieved its independence from the British rule and Sikkim did not figure in the list of the Indian Union Territories under the Indian Constitution. They even suggested that a Round Table Conference between India and Sikkim should be held to assign new status to Sikkim as an independent country with India to look after only defence. Even Hope commenced a campaign for the admission of Sikkim into U.N.O. Youth Forum was propagating anti-India campaign. Hope also built up a small lobby in the United States and amongst a few other foreigners, specially diplomats, whose interests were anti-Indian because through her they found a ruler of a Himalayan kingdom bordering Tibet having anti-Indian postures. These moves by the Palace under the guidance of Hope, whom IB was keeping under high vigil, sent the obvious signal to Indian Government that the Americans through Hope were making all out efforts to take Sikkim out of the control of Indian government. In another anti-Indian incident, Chogyal created an "External Affairs Committee" in December, 1968 consisting of his Secretary Jigdal Densapa, the Finance Secretary, Khunjang Sherab and Madan Mohan Rasailly. These three persons were known for their anti-Indian tirade. They tried to emphasize that the 1950 Treaty had outlived its utility. They demanded that India should sponsor Sikkim for help from FAO, ECAFE and ILO and it should also associate with small developed countries with similar problems. This was done at the behest of Hope Cooke.

In another unconventional development, the Chogyal in 1970 wanted to attend the wedding of King of Nepal as an independent monarch but he was shocked when he was informed that he would be given the status of Head of the Government and not that of Head of State as he expected. He had to cancel his visit due to this reason but in diabolic intention sent his four councilors who were styled as "Ministers" to attend the function. When some Journalists questioned the Nepal Foreign Minister as to why these dignitaries were accepted as Ministers of Sikkim, he was shocked but made a diplomatic admission that their description was designated by Sikkim and Nepal was helpless about it. This was an open move of confrontation by Chogyal with Indian Government.

Arrival of this American lady on the political scene of Sikkim, was one of the main reasons, which forced Indian government to merge it with India. It would be pertinent to mention here that both the Chogyal and Hope Cooke were disloyal to each other. Chogyal was having an affair with a Belgian woman after his marriage with Hope which she disclosed in her memoirs after her divorce with Chogyal. Hope had also developed relations with an American whom she had known from her childhood and met him during a visit to USA after her marriage with Chogyal. Hope had a dual personality. In public, she displayed the Sikkimese culture in her wardrobes and behaviour but privately under the strain of this controlled behaviour, she became hostile to even Chogyal at times. Both were heavy drinkers and at times did not control emotions even in public life. When Sikkim population revolted against Chogyal, in 1973, she left Gangtok for good along with her two children. Subsequently, she divorced Chogyal some time in 1975 and finally settled in USA and later married that person. Her marriage to Chogyal was a marriage of convenience in which Hope, an ordinary citizen of America found an opportunity to become the queen of a princely state. She had nothing to lose because she never became Sikkemese by heart rather Chogyal was at the receiving end being the son of his soil. Hope had been successful in embarrassing Indian government and extracted some concessions for Chogyal which in ordinary course he would have never received. She provided all foreign support to Chogyal by building a lobby in the United States at the behest of CIA and was also helped by operatives of this agency from Calcutta and Delhi to nurture anti-Indian postures from the ruler of this princely state bordering Tibet.

Strategic Location of Sikkim and Chinese Intention - Second Reason for Merger with India

Although, as per the Chinese myth, Sikkim was one of the fingers of its palm, but Sikkim is the only State adjoining China on which it has never made any territorial claim either cartographically or by military action. In the Convention of 1890, China had duly recognized the boundary between Sikkim and Tibet. When Indian Prime Minister Jawaharlal Nehru passed through Nathu La during his visit to Sikkim and Bhutan in 1953, Chinese officials welcomed him and a tablet with the legend "Sikkim-Tibet border" was put up at the site where the 1895 demarcation line was crossed. Even in a note to the Government of India on June 4, 1963, Chinese accepted the boundary between Sikkim and Tibet as defined in the 1890 Convention.

Both, the Convention of 1890 and the Treaty of 1950 also accepted Sikkim as the protectorate of India with defence and external affairs its responsibility to govern. But as usual, the Chinese never digested this arrangement when Chinese Prime Minister Chou En-lai clearly stated on 25 April, 1960 in a press conference at New Delhi that China respects India's relationship with Bhutan and Sikkim but the official Chinese publication "Peking Review", very next day amended the statement by adding "proper" before "relations". Obliquely, it meant otherwise and indicated that China did not recognize India's responsibility for the defence of Sikkim. Obviously, Indian government vehemently protested to the Chinese provocation and expressed the hope that in the interest of Sino-India relations, in future such propaganda would be stopped.

The existing situation was further aggravated when in a letter in September, 1959, Chou En-lai wrote to Nehru that the question of boundary between China and Sikkim did not fall within the scope of discussions. Nehru duly defended the Indian stand in the Parliament and warned Chinese that if something happened on this border it would be construed as interference in the internal affairs of India. Even during three sessions of bilateral discussions with India between June and December, 1960, the Chinese officials also took the position that the boundary between Sikkim and Tibet did not fall within the agenda of their discussion which was clear indication that China did not recognize the special relation of India with Sikkim.

Soon after these political overtures, the Chinese on Sikkim-Tibet border began to intrude into Sikkim. Between 1960 and 1961, three incidents of intrusions were noticed by Indian security forces and the Chinese aircrafts violated the air space through reconnaissance flights. Chinese also indulged in the sinister propaganda that Sikkim and Bhutan were part of their territory and would be united with the mainland in the near future. Indian government defended its position and again warned that any aggression against Sikkm and Bhutan would be aggression against India.

Surprisingly, during the October-November, 1962 Chinese-India arms conflict, there was no military action on the Sikkim border from their base in the Chumbi valley. The Maharaja of Sikkim declared a state of emergency to coincide with a similar declaration by India. Trade with Tibet was stopped and the peaceful border became militarily sensitive where soldiers of both countries were ready to meet any conflict. The ruling clique of Sikkim began to assess the new circumstances an opportunity for their own aggrandizement and tried to play these two big countries against each other. In that context, they wanted to project Sikkim at par with Nepal in this region.

In the beginning of 1963, the Chinese increased the incidents of intrusions again and instead blamed India for creating tension on this border so as to impair the good neighbourly relations between China and Sikkim, thus making clear again that all previous arrangements with Sikkim by India were not acceptable to them. False allegations of violation of air space by Indian aircrafts and intrusions by Indian troops were also leveled by the Chinese to distract world opinion on this region. However, allegations and counters were continuously made by both the countries till December, 1964. On January 19, 1965, around 30 Chinese soldiers with wireless sets crossed more than two miles into Sikkim near Knogkra La to which the Indian government again strongly protested without any future assurance from China.

Although, the situation on the border after the January, 1965, remained relatively quiet but China tried to interfere in the internal affairs of Sikkim. When Palden Thondup Namgyal was crowned as Chogyal of Sikkim on April 4, 1965, at Gangtok, Liu Shao-Chi, the Chairman of the People's Republic of China sent a telegram of congratulations to the Chogyal. Government of India strongly protested to this move of Chinese government and again reiterated that the external relations of Sikkim were the responsibility of Indian government and any communication, formal or informal, to the Sikkim government or the Chogyal should be routed through Indian government.

During the war of September, 1965 between India and Pakistan, activities of Chinese on this border again became serious and threatening. Asserting solidarity of China with Pakistan, Marshal Chen Yi China's foreign minister openly declared that Sikkim-Tibet border did not come within the scope of the Sino-Indian border question. On September 17, 1965, Chinese sent a 72 hour ultimatum asking India to dismantle defence structures which were built on Tibetan side of the border. In fact, these structures were non-existent which Chinese falsely propagated. The ultimatum also demanded India to return 4 Chinese inhabitants and 59 yaks and 800 sheep purportedly captured by Indian forces. India refuted the ultimatum which was further extended by 3 days by Chinese. On September 21, Indian and Chinese troops were engaged in an arm conflict across Nathu La. This was first arm conflict since the Indo-China war of 1962. Surprisingly, as usual, the Chinese withdrew their forces to their side of border on September 24, vacating the 800 yards intrusion made by them inside the Sikkim border. They also declared that Indian forces had removed the offending border installations. On the midnight of October 10-11, Chinese forces again fired across Nathu La which was retaliated by Indian troops. Next day, three companies of Chinese troops, using Nahhu La firing as a ruse, intruded into North Sikkim across Sesa La where Indian forces challenged them and in the battle which continued for four hours, two Indian and thirty Chinese soldiers were killed.

Year 1966 was relatively quiet as there was no major intrusion by the Chinese. But in the guise of graziers, a number of Chinese infiltrated into Sikkim from the Tibet border. In August, 1967, the Chinese again tried to stretch their line of communications into the India side which was thwarted by Indian troops. Indian troops laid a barbed wire fence inside their territory to mark the border line and also to check the intrusions. This job was completed by Indian forces on September

6. Next day, the Chinese intruded over the fence and stayed for some time into the Sikkim territory. Suddenly, on September 11, the Chinese started firing with 76 mm. guns on the Indian troops which was retaliated by them. This was the most serious firing since the 1962 Sino-Indian conflict. The Chinese action coincided with the visit of the Chogyal to New Delhi. India proposed cease-fire to China which was rejected as a deception but on September 16, the China agreed to exchange dead and wounded soldiers to which India agreed. Peking Radio announced this as a gesture to preserve the Sino-Indian friendship. After the exchange of dead and wounded bodies, there was a virtual cessation of hostile activities for about two weeks. This lull was broken on October 1, when the Chinese troops fired on the Indian soldiers across the Cho La about 3 miles north-west of Nathu La. Indian government again protested to China against its activities on the Sikkim border and warned to repel any aggression in future. Thereafter, till January, 1971, there was no major clash between the Chinese and the Indian troops and the Sikkim-Tibet border was relatively quiet.

As early as in 1962, there were reports in the British press that China had made efforts to make alliance with Sikkim and Bhutan but the Indian Prime Minister Nehru disclaimed any knowledge of such a move by the Chinese. He however acceded that the Chinese had not recognized the existing Convention and Treaty with Sikkim wherein it is protectorate of India and responsibility of external affairs were wrested with them.

Indira Gandhi, The Iron-Willed Lady – Third and Major Factor for Merger

These skirmish activities of the Chinese on the Sikkim-Tibet border after the death of Jawaharlal Nehru were taken seriously by his daughter Indira Gandhi who became Prime Minister in January, 1966. Although, the Indian officials considered these exchange of fire between the Indian and Chinese soldiers as not so serious but a design to keep the pot boiling on this border much to the discomfiture of the Indian government. It was evident that the Chinese tried to drive a wedge between India and Sikkim by exploiting the ambitions of the Chogyal to become an independent monarch. Indira Gandhi was fully aware of this hidden agenda of both the China and the Chogyal.

Indira Gandhi had been closely associated with Prime Minister Nehru since 1947 being the host of her father Jawaharlal Nehru, the first Indian Prime Minister. She had watched the humiliation of India when China insulted her father in the 1962 conflict. She was witness to the agony and trauma of Nehru after this war. She was also closely associated with the affairs of 1965 war with Pakistan. India's military reverses in the 1962 border war with China had lowered her prestige in the minds of the Himalaya kingdoms including Sikkim. The so-called Chinese success had lent some credibility to their anti-Indian propaganda. India had become a soft state in the mind of these kingdoms. In these adverse circumstances, the ruling group in Sikkim saw an opportunity to upgrade their autonomous status to that of an independent nation. They were further encouraged in view of the repeated attempts by China to create tension on Sikkim border and the advisors of Chogyal interpreted it as a signal to contest the special relationship treaty with India. After Indira Gandhi became Prime Minister in 1966, humiliation of these two wars were raising a revenge in her mind which she drafted in the foreign policy of the country. First of all, she wanted to get rid of the dual military pressure of Pakistan from east and west. She not only helped the Bengali Muslim when a genocide was unleashed by Pakistan on them in 1971, but travelled worldwide to form political opinion in favour of India in that conflict.

Indira Gandhi, after the victory of Indian forces in Bangladesh in December, 1971, had properly assessed the role of China in that war. Pakistan was hopeful that China would play a major role on the northern border of India in that war but the Chinese betrayed them and did not engage in any sort of confrontation with the Indian forces. Indira Gandhi explored these previous Chinese in the ensuing Sikkim merger with India and was quite confident that China would never dare to interfere in this affairs of India. However, she decided not to take any chance in the matter of security on this border with China. The defence of Sikkim was a strategic compulsion for India as it provided the shortest route from Tibet to the Gangetic plains. Its passes could be crossed even in winters without any difficulty. Nathu La was the vantage place from the point of defence to India. Moreover, barring some officials of Chogyal and a few Bhutia landlords, the majority of the Sikkim people were not interested in the ambition of the Chogyal for an autonomy. All they wanted was transfer of power to their elected representatives and faster economic progress. For all these reasons, the defence of Sikkim was of paramount importance to India vis-à-vis China. Hence, Indira Gandhi was determined to merge Sikkim with India in view of the ongoing Chinese intrusions for years on this border so that in future it could take China politically and militarily with impunity after Sikkim become part of the Indian territory. So, the unprovoked regular firings by the Chinese since 1963 on the Sikkim border was the second reason for the merger of Sikkim with India by the then Indian Prime Minister, Indira Gandhi.

As detailed hereinbefore, the accession of Sikkim was raised by a section of Sikkim politicians immediately after the British left India in August, 1947. This plea of accession had the support of Sardar Vallabbhai Patel, the then Indian Home Minister but was rejected by Prime Minister Jawaharlal Nehru. Again in December, 1948, these leaders met Nehru who assured them that the voice of the people of Sikkim would be regarded as the supreme authority in shaping destiny of Sikkim. Maharaja was never receptive to these demands and started repression against these leaders. Subsequently, Government of India made various ad-hoc arrangements to keep Sikkim in its fold as a protectorate State much against the desire of majority of Sikkim population.

When Indira Gandhi became Prime Minister in 1966 and she had to go through the dramatic changes in the security of Sikkim due to China and Chogyal, she confided with one of her aides that her father Jawaharlal Nehru had made a mistake by not heeding to the Sikkimese demand for accession to India in 1947. She admitted that she never asked Nehru about his decision in the matter but her guess was that he had assumed that China would leave Tibet's autonomy undisturbed and, in anticipation of this, he had perhaps thought it fit to do nothing in Sikkim that would provoke them. She had no hesitation to admit that in retrospect Sardar Patel's instinctive reaction seemed correct. Conclusion emerged in the discussion was that India should undo the earlier mistake and support the people of Sikkim in their struggle against Chogyal.

It would be pertinent to admit here that Indira Gandhi did have a soft corner for Chogyal. She inherited this favourable opinion from her father who looked upon him as a young man of promise, a potential dynamic leader who would lead Sikkim out of its medieval outlook. Father of Chogyal requested Nehru to groom him under his guidance so that he could shoulder his responsibility in future. According to R N Kao, who was then Security Officer of Nehru, the suggestion was accepted by Nehru and Chogyal spent several months at Teen Murti, the official residence of Prime Minister Nehru, as a member of the Nehru family. Indira Gandhi developed personal respect for him due to this gesture of Nehru. She had met him earlier in his own habitat in 1952 and again in 1958 when she accompanied her father on his visit to Sikkim. She also attended his Coronation and was impressed by the speech of Chogyal, delivered on that occasion. In this speech he had recalled with sincere affection his memory of Jawaharlal Nehru and referred to India's assistance in extremely laudatory manner. He had also tried to retain an element of personal warmth in his relationship with Indira Gandhi. He profousely welcomed her on her first official visit to Sikkim and said that she was not only welcomed as Prime Minister of India but the protecting power and more so as a very dear friend of Sikkim.

Indira Gandhi's disappointment with Chogyal began when she found him too weak to resist the blatant anti-Indian posture of Hope Cooke. She believed that in view of the sullied relation with the USA which began in Bangladesh war, the Chogyal would be honest enough to be sensitive to Indian concerns. In view of the visit of President Nixon to China in 1972, Hope Cooke, whose American connections encouraged Chogyal to develop active anti-Indian lobby. Chogyal's proximity to US through Cooke and their activities were in Indira Gandhi's full knowledge through R&AW.

In late sixties, Indira Gandhi overcame internal problems of the Congress Party when she overthrew the old hawks and with new blend of leaders became undisputed authority in the new-look Congress Party. She took certain bold steps on economic front and nationalized fourteen banks. She stopped privy purses of erstwhile rulers of princely states and their integration with India. On the international front, she emerged as an undisputed iron lady in the sub-continent when Indian army defeated Pakistan in East Pakistan and Bangladesh was carved out in December, 1971. In order to assert militarily in this region, she signed a military pact with Russia in September, 1971 to contain the arch enemies Pakistan and China. After 1971 war with Pakistan, when US President sent Seventh Fleet in Bay of Bengal to threaten India, Indira Gandhi decided to make India a nuclear country and in that process she authorized her scientists to work relentlessly and India went nuclear in May,

1974. All these events and developments made Indira Gandhi more assertive and imaginative with regard to the security of the country. Around this period, she had a blend of able, competent and forthright team of officers of Kashmiri Pandit origin. D P Dhar was Chairman of the Policy Planning Committee during the Bangladesh war, P N Haksar was her Principal Secretary, T N Kaul was the architect of Foreign Affairs and R N Kao one of the most enterprising Intelligence Officer of the World was head of R&AW, which played a pivotal role in the liberation of Bangladesh. This lobby of Kashmiri Pandit officers were jealously quoted as "Turmeric Diplomacy" among the Indian bureaucracy during that period. This lobby of officers had outwitted the Nixon-Kissinger duo during Bangladesh war on all political fronts. Subsequently, another Kashmiri Pandit officer, P N Dhar became her Principal Secretary.

R&AW was closely keeping tab on the activities of Hope Cook and Chogyal in their sinister designs to attain an autonomous status for Sikkim. When Indian government protested to Chogyal on the activities of his associates who were authors of the statement and publicly stated that they had crossed the jurisdiction. This was a ploy because anti-Indian activities of his stooges continued to develop directly under his inspiration. During 1970 elections in Sikkim, this anti-India tirade reached unacceptable proportion for the Indian government. The pro-Chogyal party Sikkim National Party again raised issue of revision of Treaty and even the Sikkim State Congress which was earlier in favour of merger with India, was prevailed upon by Chogyal to support this demand. Chogyal was making anti-India postures under the impression that India was too frightened of China to take any stringent action against him. He was also encouraged by some Indian officials who were pampered by him at Gangtok. These officials instigated him to make demand for United Nations membership for Sikkim by Chogyal which he thought India was too weak to resist. He was briefed by these officials that Government of India was indeed a weak minority Government in Delhi, pre-occupied with its own problems of day-to-day existence.

Indira Gandhi was buying time to take appropriate action in Sikkim because during the whole of 1971, she was engaged in bitter problems of Bangladeshi refugees who fled to India due to the genocide by Pakistan army in East Pakistan. After Pakistan Army was defeated and 93,000 of its soldiers surrendered in Dhaka on December 16, 1971 before Lt. Gen. J.S. Aurora, her moral was at the zenith. She was received in a rousing reception in Dacca in March, 1972 and was hailed as savior of Bengali Muslim community. After this significant development, Indira Gandhi had secured the eastern borders of India for the coming generations. Her attention then shifted to securing the Indian borders with China and her first attempt was to secure the Sikkim border. Hence, she was now convinced that the volatile border of Sikkim along China should not be the border of her protectorate but should become the border of India for all political and diplomatic consequences.

Indira Gandhi Ushered R&AW for the Merger

Pro-merger leaders of Sikkim were henceforth convinced that Indian government would never endorse their demand in view of the policy adopted by officials of the Ministry of External Affairs of India. Their experience in this regard was not out of any imagination but with past reasonings because every time their movement had gathered strength, Government of India had intervened and helped Chogyal to suppress it. These leaders were rightly distrustful to officials of External Affairs Ministry. Indira Gandhi too was convinced, not without reason, that some of our problems in Sikkim had been aggravated by our own officials. She was tired of the fruitless discussion which the officials of Ministry of External Affairs were holding with Chogyal to be more reasonable to the political aspiration of the people of Sikkim and more friendly in his relation with India. These tedious and endless discussion yielded nothing, rather made Chogyal more intransigent. In comparison to the confusing and conflicting reports of Ministry of External Affairs, the internal assessment of Sikkim projected by R&AW to the Prime Minister was more accurate and meaningful. On the basis of these reports, Indira Gandhi was convinced that R&AW had established extensive contacts with the people of Sikkim and proper understanding of their political aspirations. She was aware that Sikkimese leaders had arrived at a conclusion that only through R&AW they could achieve success of their merger movement with India. Indira Gandhi had clear understanding that diplomats and the intelligence officers had vast difference in their style of working. While the diplomats were more suave, the intelligence people were better informed and more effective on the ground level with local population.

In view of the above assessment, in September, 1972, Indira Gandhi called P.N.Haksar, her Principal Secretary and R N Kao, Secretary of R&AW and discussed the internal situation of Sikkim with them at length with special reference to the continued anti-Indian activities of Chogyal at the behest of Hope Cooke. She asked Kao to come out with the suggestion whether he would be able to manage this situation for the subsequent merger of Sikkim with India. Kao as dutiful as ever sought a fortnight's time to come out with the blue print of this assignment.

In R&AW at that time the eastern part of India including Sikkim, were under the command of one Bengali IPS officer P N Banerjee, Joint Director at Calcutta. Banerji had played a very important role during the Bangladesh war and was even a close confidant of Sheikh Mujibur Rahman. He was treated like a family member by Mujib and his family. This brilliant officer had accurate knowledge of each and every events of his region. Due to his utmost sincerity and devotion, he was one of the blue-eyed boys of Kao in R&AW. Kao had fully recognized the excellent work of this highly decorated officer in training Mukti Bahini. Banerjee possessed the highest sense of friendly disposition which made him a projection of faith and belief among the persons he ever met.

At Gangtok, A S Syali, another IPS officer was posted as Officer on Special Duty among the staff which was administering the affairs of Sikkim. After R&AW came into existence on September 21, 1968, Kao opened various Foreign Intelligence Posts inside Sikkim and on borders of Nathu La and other passes. While these posts were working as administrative offices of the Government of India but in fact were the field offices of R&AW in Sikkim. Syali too was not designated on the regular ranks of R&AW but was working on a cover job under the rank of OSD. This Sikh officer was earlier groomed by Kao in the China desk of RAW and had full and comprehensive knowledge and account of not only Sikkim but also other adjoining countries in general and China in particular. He had established his network in whole of the Sikkim population through his junior officers posted at all the Foreign Intelligence Posts (FIPs). He was assisted by two Sikkim and Nepali origin Senior Field Officers, equivalent to DSP of police, These officers were assisted by junior officers of RAW on these posts, who were mostly of Nepali, Sikkimese and Tibetan origin.

India, Kao called both P N Banerjee and A S Syali to Delhi for dicussions. At his office, Kao briefed both these officers to send their assessment for the proposed assignment given to him by the Prime Minister. After a fortnight, Banerji and Syali in consultation with other R&AW operatives prepared a comprehensive assessment of the prevailing political situation and submitted full facts of Sikkim to Kao and discussed all pros and cons of modus operandi of merger through this Operation. Next day, Kao accompanied by Haksar, met Indira Gandhi in her South Block office and submitted blue print of this operation much to the satisfaction of Indira Gandhi and she immediately ordered action on the proposed merger of Sikkim. Banerji and Syali were authorized by Kao to start this operation with utmost secrecy and not to disclose it to even other higher officers in R&AW Headquarters. So, this big operation was launched and handled directly by Kao with these two senior officers of R&AW in the field at Calcutta and Gangtok respectively.

Kao was fully conversant with the prevailing one-upmanship attitude between the Indian diplomats and the intelligence operatives in the foreign missions. This harmful tendency in the bureaucracy was responsible for many flaws in shaping the foreign policy everywhere and in Sikkim it was particular. Kao discussed this problem with Indira Gandhi and soon appointed Kewal Singh as the Foreign Secretary with whom Kao was having excellent rapport. So, both the diplomats and R&AW officials developed a sense of different responsibility with Kao as R&AW head and Kewal Singh as Foreign Secretary. Prime Minister Office too was quick to clear all policy matter on the direction of Prime Minister, Indira Gandh, who was personally in touch with Sikkim affairs.

Kazi Lhendup Dorzi Roped in By R&AW for Merger

Kazi Lhendup Dorzi belonged to a highly respected Lepcha-Bhutia family of the Land owning class, known as Kazi. When he was young, he was removed from the headship of the monastery of Rumtek, one of the most prestigious place in the whole state. There were allegations of corruption and defalcation of funds against him which Kazi claimed were concocted against him at the behest of the Palace. He harboured a deep grudge against the King due to this reason and was determined to retrieve his reputation. He was otherwise a man of quiet and shy disposition and tolerated this insult and could not made much headway to redeem his honour. This was one of the reasons when he participated in the formation of a political party, the Sikkim State Congress in December, 1947 and demanded the accession of Sikkim with India.

Kazi was an upcoming and important politician in Sikkim since India's independence. In New Delhi, he met a high profile Belgian lady Elisa Maria who claimed her friendship with Turkish Prime Ministr Kemal Ataturk and Chou En-lai of China. She probably put these claims to cultivate influential people and Indian politicians in New Delhi. However, she came to India to teach French in Delhi where she started building up her social status. She was very talkative and did not succeed beyond a limit in the political circle. However, through a small time politician in Congress, she came into contact with Kazi. In her company with Kazi, she found a person who could listen to her sermons in English without any hindrance because Kazi lacked knowledge of English and was a low profile politician with subdued nature.

In Kazi, Maria found an opportunity she was seeking for herself to secure a position of power and eminence and in Maria Kazi found a white skinned consort with brilliant mind which could match his arch foe Chogyal and his American wife Hope. Two leading personalities of Sikkim, Chogyal and Kazi mortgaged their destiny to these foreign wives for all sorts of political collusion in the state. Both these foreigners, obviously, were envious of each other and developed instant hate and jealousy because of their dominant and ambitious character to overpower the wills and personality of their weak natured husbands. Kazini, the title bestowed on Maria after her marriage with Kazi, was appalled by the poverty of the Sikkimese people regardless of their ethnic origin. Maria fully studied the mood of Sikkim politics and was determined to secure her right by actively participating in the political struggle against Chogyal led by Kazi, the only potent rival to confront the Palace in this ambition. She foresaw future of Sikkim being in the hand of Kazi wherein she would be first lady of the state be it an independent entity or merged within India. In that pursuit, she worked hard to mobilize public opinion against the ruler. Maria was a moving force behind Kazi and in order to bring majority Nepalese population in his fold, she cleverly adopted a young Nepalese upcoming leader, Narbahadur Khatiwala as her son which gave her a strong political weight in Sikkim politics. She was intelligent enough to exploit every possible device to elevate her husband to the seat of power. Maria was careful to remain behind the scene and acted through her husband and son in political manipulations. She viewed the royal pretensions of Hope with disdain and used her talents for organization and publicity on behalf of the Sikkim National Congress. With her husband from minority tribe of Bhutia and adopted-son from Nepalese majority population, she tilted power centre of Sikkim politics in favour of Kazi much to the discomfort of Chogyal and Hope.

At later stage when Chogyal started his vicious anti-Indian campaign with the help of his American wife, Maria found an excellent opportunity to get raised a banner of revolt against him through pro-Indian democratic leaders with Kazi leading from the front. Subsequently, when she was debarred by Chogyal from

Sikkim, Maria started operating her campaign from Kalimpong and made it a hub of anti-Chogyal activities. R&AW was providing all sorts of help to Maria while she was in exile at Kalimpong and rather found her easily accessible there in comparison to Gangtok. She was a compulsive and impulsive asset of R&AW against Chogyal and his wife to block entry of any pro-Chogyal in the household of Kazi so that he could work relentlessly against the ruler and bring Sikkim in the fold of India.

Kazi too was an old friend of Indian intelligence from the early days of his political career but due to lack of mandate, intelligence operators of IB could not openly support him for independence of Sikkim from present monarchy. MEA officials of India had made mess of the internal affairs of Sikkim wherein every political leader was too scared to come out openly against the whims of the Palace. When R N Kao, R&AW Chief was authorized by Indira Gandhi to go ahead with the merger plan, he sent P N Banerjee and A S Syali to meet Kazi and asked them to make him mentally reconciled to work in line with R&AW for future course of action for merger of Sikkim. In a clandestine meeting with Kazi at Kalimpong in the first week of October,

1972, Banerjee and Syali outlined plan of R&AW for the merger of Sikkim. Kazi was initially hesitant because of his past experience with officials of Ministry of External Affairs but when he was convinced that R&AW would now take care of this plan and Government of India had decided to implement it, he was persuaded to agree to work for the proposal by none other than Elisa Maria who was present at that place and was not initially involved in these discussions. Kazi, however, sought an appointment with R N Kao for his personal satisfaction which Banerji agreed to arrange in near future.

Kao met Kazi in the second week of October at Calcutta and assured him that Indira Gandhi had given R&AW full authority to work for the merger of Sikkim within the territory of India. Kao also briefed Kazi that full details of this entire game plan had been devised and would be executed in phases with the guidance of P N Banerjee from Calcutta and under the direct supervision of A S Syali in-charge of R&AW at Gangtok. Kao also emphasized that utmost secrecy would be maintained in this top secret operation and full proof steps had been taken so that no suspicion would ever develop among the Sikkim population that he was working in league with R&AW in this operation. Kao also made Kazi assertive that full financial and other logistic support would be provided by Indian Government to meet all sorts of consequences not only at Gangtok but in other far flung areas of Sikkim, particularly on borders alongside Tibet. After this long meeting with Kao, Kazi was mentally prepared that it was the right opportunity to take revenge from Chogyal and to teach him a lesson of his life and also to become the head of Sikkim state in the near future. Maria too became more than confident after Kazi briefed her the outcome of his meeting with Kao and she was the only effective catalyst which made a weak Kazi to take head on the mighty Chogyal henceforth. So, the die was cast and future of Sikkim was summarily drafted on the red crossed file of R&AW "TO BE SEEN BY THE ADDRESSEE ONLY" by R N Kao for the knowledge of Indian Prime Minister, Indira Gandhi narrating outcome of his meeting with Kazi. Indira Gandhi was too pleased on this achievement of Kao and actual operation of R&AW started thereafter.

Three-phased Strategy of R&AW For the Merger

First Phase - Kao Tested Water to Boost Confidence of Sikkimese for Confrontation With Ghogyal

After Kazi Lhendup Dorji was persuaded by Banerjee and Syali to build political opinion against Chogyal, every precaution was taken by Kao to tread a cautious path while achieving his goal particularly in view of the presence of China's threat on the north side. On the other hand Bhutan-Nepal diplomacy, who were bound to be critical of merger of Sikkim with India, had to be taken care of simultaneously. Initially, R&AW operatives were assigned the task to unify anit-Chogyal elements for merger and test their strength. In November, 1972, Syali in consultation with Kazi, directed all the junior officers of R&AW posted in various FIPs in Sikkim to provide all financial helps to the cadre of Sikkim National Congress. They were also instructed to maintain excellent relations with these cadres and made them mentally prepared for the cause of getting rid off Chogyal and his tyrannical regime. Pro-Chogyal people were identified by RAW officials all over Sikkim and all measures were taken to take care of them in all respect. Chogyal was informed by his people about these activities of R&AW. Since, R&AW officials were working under cover of Indian government, Chogyal did not dare to blame them due to this bureaucratic hiccup. Syali was designated as Officer on Special Duty. On the contrary, Chogyal blamed IB for interfering in the affairs of Sikkim. He protested to Indian government and asked to withdraw its head Tejpal Singh from Gangtok. Indian Government accepted his demand and retrieved Tejpal Singh to India.

Syali had watched the election scenario of April, 1970 election manipulations of Chogyal wherein he imposed his own henchmen to win the rigged elections. Nominations of some eligible candidates were arbitrarily rejected and names of anti-Chogyal voters were deleted from the electoral list by the ad-hoc committee which conducted these elections. Chogyal declared Sikkim as a Buddhist State. Thereafter, a large number of Tibetan refugees were granted citizenship whereas thousands of Nepalese living in Sikkim for several years were denied this privilege.

Chogyal was more interested in curbing the voice of those people who were espousing for the cause of liberation of Sikkim from his clutches rather than make any progress towards the economic upliftment of the poor population of Sikkim. Grievances of students and Government employees were ignored. He had decided to swim against the progressive tide and appointed most of the anti-Indian elements in top positions to administer the Government. In June 1972, he assumed all executive powers which were exercised by the Indian Dewan hereinbefore. On the advice of Hope, Chogyal through National Party released election manifesto wherein it was declared that it would strive for a status for Sikkim equal to that of neighbouring Nepal and Bhutan which were members of the UNO.

Since, November, 1972, R&AW officials all over Sikkim were keeping tab on these activities and had started making preparation to put up an effective political force under Kazi to counter all these manoeuvres of Chogyal. Syali with the guidance of Banerjee from Calcutta was working tirelessly to get united all anti-Chogyal leaders and bring them under one umbrella in the coming elections of February, 1973. He and Kazi drafted the 13 point manifesto of the National Congress. Some salient features of this manifesto were abolition of communal pattern of voting, fundamental rights, constitution for Sikkimese people, elected government and friendly relations with India.

Hope Cook directly involved CIA in the forthcoming elections in Sikkim so that an anti-India mandate could be secured through legitimate elections to prove at world forum that the people of Sikkim were disillusioned with the present political arrangements with India and Sikkim should get its autonomy for all practical purposes. Holbrook Bradley, Director of the U.S.I.S., a CIA front organization, was in Gangtok before elections to provide all sort of help to Chogyal and his party, the National Party. After the election results were declared, Peter Buleigh, a CIA operative working under cover as Political Officer of the U.S. Consulate in Calcutta, visited Gangtok and met Chogyal and Hope in a close door meeting. Involvement of these two CIA officers in Sikkim affairs around the period when elections were to be held in Sikkim, was ample proof for R&AW to inform Indian Government that Hope Cook, with CIA' guidance, was making all out efforts to bring legitimacy of the demand of Chogyal for an autonomous status in world arena.

Election results of February, 1973, proved the focal point in the political evolution of Sikkim. Subsequent events continued to rock it for the next two years wherein R&AW proved a consistent catalyst to decide fate of the local population. Sikkim National Party of Chogyal emerged victorious due to inequities of the electoral system. The National Congress of Kazi and Janta Congress alleged that elections were rigged in favour of the National Party. These allegations were not without foundation because during the counting of votes, hundreds of bogus votes were found in the boxes of National Party candidates. Despite protests by the National Congress workers for aiding and abetting the National Party to rig the elections, no action was taken by the Returning Officer. Even, the counting agents of National Congress were physically assaulted by the followers of Chogyal in the very presence of the government officials who were guarding the counting centre. On February 4, the National Congress and Janta Congress took out a procession in Gangtok to protest against this blatant oppression and injustice but they were not allowed to use any mike to make public aware of these atrocities committed by the people of Chogyal. All these oppressions on the Sikkim leaders and general public, developed strong resentment against Chogyal which gave R&AW fair chance to further strengthen the movement all over Sikkim. Syali tightened his noose through all his available sources around Chogyal and his cohorts. Pro-democracy leaders all over Sikkim were provided all sorts of financial and other help to build up their organization and infuse the spirit of revolt against Chogyal operatives by Syali and his men.

This was first phase of the planning of R N Kao wherein he tested water at the ground level and was more than satisfied with the performance of Banerjee and Syali who in the last four months were able to awaken Sikkim population to believe that they could not breathe in an atmosphere free from the anarchy of Chogyal. Political leaders against Chogyal who by then were distrustful of Indian diplomats changed their attitude and made assertive by R&AW that Government of India was determined to do away the hierarchy of the ruler and bring rule of democracy in Sikkim. R&AW further proved this disposition meaningful when on March 26, 1973, the newly appointed Executive Committee, wherein two members were nominated from National Congress and Janata Congress, boycotted the swearing-in ceremony. This was the biggest shock of life which RAW inflicted on Chogyal and Hope. R&AW operatives under Syali became more active and assertive all over Sikkim hereinafter to boost morale of general public. Elisa Maria was a compulsive force of R&AW at Kalimpong wherefrom she was working with new vigour and velocity for her hostility towards Chogyal in general and Hope in particular. R&AW was able to infiltrate thousands of Nepalese youth, including ladies through her efforts in and around Gangtok for future course of action in last week of March. Maria got opportunity of her life to avenge her inborn hatred against Chogyal and Hope which R&AW fully exploited.

Second Phase – Direct Intervention by R&AW to Get Elected Assembly for Sikkim

In last week of March, 1973, R N Kao along with Haksar met Indira Gandhi and discussed his impending operation wherein he outlined that initially India should not declare openly merger of Sikkim as its policy and rather propagate for cause of the democratic autonomy by elected people under Chogyal as head of state. Implementation of merger plan had to be done systematically with caution and legitimate means. This diplomatic deception was of paramount importance to check foreign reaction and to keep hostility of neighbor countries under control. In a nutshell, it was finalized to get elected an assembly of pro-democracy leaders at initial stage which would demand the status of Sikkim as "associate" in stead of a "protectorate" state. The initiative had to come from the people whom the assembly represented and India, with mandate under its authority, was then to react. It would be important to mention here that even highest policy makers of the Ministry of External Affairs were aware of this move of R&AW that India would go beyond "associate" status and merge it thereafter as Indian territory. Indian Prime Minister, Indira Gandhi approved the proposal submitted by Kao and gave him free hand to implement this plan in minimum possible period. Kao immediately gave go-ahead signals to Banerjee in Calcutta and Syali in Gangtok to fire their cylinders at utmost speed with fair amount of caution.

After boycott of the Executive Council on March 26, two main opposition parties, the National Congress of Dorji and the Janta Congress intensified their agitation for electoral reforms on the basis of one man one vote. Chogyal through one of his trusted supporter of Sikkim Youth Study Form tried to woo the Janta Congress leader to raise demand for revision of 1950 Treaty. Pradhan disclosed this agenda of Chogyal to other opposition leaders who were certain that any move hostile to India would result in perpetuating the authoritarian rule of Chogyal for all time to come. They rejected this attempt of Chogyal and denounced it as an attempt to distract them from their original demand. This infuriated the Chogyal who resorted to strong measures and on March 27, 1973 arrested K C Pradhan under the Sikkim Security Act for sedition. This fatal mistake to arrest Pradhan was the milestone in writing political history in future.

Arrest of Pradhan was not out of any instant conclusion but was a long standing belief in the mind of Chogyal that moral values of India since Nehru ear and sensitivity to any international criticism would prevent India from taking any hard posture against him. He was living in a fool's paradise that with help from Hope he would ensure all support from America and hostility of China towards India would ensure that one of the fingers of its palm could never be cut by India. He never visualized the magnitude of the agitation and hostility of his Nepalese and Lepchas tribes which were totally under the command of political leaders who were now fully pampered by R&AW. He was under grave misconception that he would retrieve the situation through international reaction and would engineer a revolt within the Sikkim Congress. His own stubborn nature was supplemented by the ill-advise of his own family members and a small coterie of officers around him made him assertive to put up a fight rather to agree the four inconsequential demands of the opposition leaders. To his misfortune, he misjudged the determination and strength of Indira Gandhi, the iron lady of India, at that stage. His own brand of secret agents were never able to detect the network created by Syali and his junior officers of R&AW all over the Sikkim territories among anti-Chogyal factions.

When news of arrest of Pradhan was disseminated by R&AW sources all over Sikkim, it had strong reactions from the anti-Chogyal Sikkim population. On March

28, a big demonstration was organized in Gangtok protesting the dictatorial approach of Chogyal to unleash a reign of terror against the just demands of opposition leaders. Both the National Congress and the Janta Congress formed a Joint Action Committee in consultation with Syali to fight against the tyranny regime of Chogyal. The JAC declared that they would soon submit a charter demands for the future of Sikkim to Chogyal very shortly. In the meanwhile, thousands of Nepalese population, including ladies were dispatched by R&AW operatives to Gangtok from Darjeeling, Kalimpong and other areas. Maria and overenthusiastic Narbahadur Khatiwada played a very significant role to help R&AW to send these volunteers to help JAC leaders against their forthcoming confrontation with Chogyal in and around Gangtok.

Next day, a large number of people started agitation all over Sikkim at the behest of JAC which issued a clear call to fight against the oppression and exploitation of Chogyal. Students and government employees were forced to join the agitation. Situation was becoming uncontrollable for Chogyal and his coterie although they continued their violent measures to overcome the ongoing violent situation. The anti-government demonstrators captured eight police posts and divested the policemen of the arms and ammunition. Wireless sets were taken away.

Kao was burning midnight oil during this crisis in his South Block office. He and Banerjee roped in some reputed legal experts and hurriedly drafted a 16 point charter demands for new form of political set up in Sikkim. Since most of the opposition leaders were semi-literate, this task had to be completed by R&AW secretly. These demands were abdication of the Chogyal, repoll on the basis of one man one vote, reformation of a democratic government, written constitution incorporating fundamental rights, independent judiciary for justice and codification of law, revision of Indo-Sikkim Treaty to ensure steady friendship, streamline the citizenship rights, Advisory Council of people, inquiry into misuse of Indian aid funds and police excesses during recent agitation, externment of Tibetan refugees who helped Chogyal in the atrocities against Sikkimese people. This R&AW dictated charter of demand was issued by JAC the very next day.

These demands had far reaching consequences among the Sikkimmese people and the agitation was intensified more vigorously thereafter. All three important leaders of JAC, Kazi Lhendup Dorji, Nahakul Pradhan and Bim Bahadur Gurung were given shelter in the office of Indian Political Officer by Syali fearing liquidation by Chogyal. Their captivity proved another factor to turn the agitation violent and repressive against Chogyal by JAC volunteers.

Chogyal's response to the movement of JAC was stubborn rather than conciliatory. His confrontational attitude polarized the ground realities against him. Part of the reason for the new vigour of the JAC volunteers was the belief of its leaders that India would not let down them as had been done earlier. In the past, every time their movement had gathered strength, the Government of India had intervened and helped Chogyal to suppress it. This was done as a matter of obligation under the treaty. But this time, Kazi and his confidants were convinced that Government of India was determined to ensure democratic rights for the people of Sikkim but the shapes of things to come was uncertain till then.

Situation became out of control that day when in an unprovoked incident Tenzing son of Chogyal was personally involved in the riot. Few miles on the outskirts of Gangtok, he along with his arm guards forcibly tried to stop the demonstrators from surging into the capital. When the people resisted his violent attempts, he tried to flee back to the Palace and his armed guard fired at the demonstrators in self defence wounding two in the melee. This incident added fuel to the fire and exacerbated the already explosive situation. R&AW operatives found right opportunity to retaliate and spread this news vigorously all along Sikkim. Infuriated mob started moving toward the Palace to lay siege around it.

After the JAC issued its charter of demand, law and order problem all over Sikkim in general and in Gangtok became a matter of serious concern. Around 15,000 people had reached Gangtok in the agitation. Narbahadur Khatiwada with the help of R&AW operatives managed to infiltrate thousands of anti-Chogyal demonstrators from Darjeeling, Kalimpong and other areas of Sikkim. All the four administrative districts in Sikkim were virtually captured by the agitators. Local students were actively dictating as policemen. Administration had totally collapsed. All the government offices, shops and schools were voluntarily closed by the local public. The police had deserted their posts and with all their firearms and wireless sets looted. A number of government offices were burnt and valuable revenue records destroyed. In Gangtok, the Police had been disarmed and confined to their barracks for fear of retaliation by the agitators who assembled in thousands from all areas of Sikkim. Chogyal took refuge in his palace under the strict vigil of his guards. As a measure of precaution, Indian army blocked all entry points to the palace for safety of Chogyal and his family.

Elsewhere in other areas of Sikkim, situation was explosive and completely out of control of the Sikkimese officers who were demoralized and sharply divided on ethnic lines. Even administration of jails was taken over by pro-JAC agitators and old scores were settled with their opponents by confining them with brutality. Food supplies were cut off and total anarchy prevailed all over Sikkim. However, the JAC volunteers provided food and shelters to their fellow agitators all over Sikkim with the help of R&AW operatives.

At Gangtok, senior Nepali officers suggested Chogyal to accept demands of the JAC but he was adamant to bow before his people whom he considered slaves.

Kazi Lhendup Dorji openly declared that the stage for negotiations between Chogyal and the JAC for any negotiated solution has passed and Government of India should take over the administration of Sikkim.

JAC agitation assumed a menacing form on April 4, the day on which special festivities were arranged to celebrate the fiftieth birthday of Chogyal at the Palace. The police opened fire on demonstrators at a place and injured several agitators. This infuriated the volunteers of the JAC who then attacked and took control of many police stations. Next day, Chogyal issued warrants of arrest against Dorji and other JAC leaders. In response to these retaliatory repression by Chogyal, JAC volunteers started marching towards Gangtok from all other far flung areas. Chogyal was taken aback at the turn of the events. It was feared that more than 15,000 volunteers of JAC would lay siege of the Palace and force him to abdicate. Initially, he requested Government of India to send army to maintain law and order but when the administration completely collapsed, he requested to take over the administration of the whole of Sikkim.

Kao was constantly sending briefings to Indira Gandhi on the grim situation of Sikkim. She was more than convinced to take over the administration of Sikkim which had collapsed completely but she was awaiting to see the Chogyal demoralized and come with a request to save him from his own people. K S Bajpai, the political officer, corroborated reports of Kao. Indian Government sent Secretary in External Affairs Ministry to April 5 to assess the situation. He too confirmed the same day that he along with Bajpai and the officer commanding the Indian troops met Chogyal and found him in a desperate state of mind and his control had slipped out of his hands.

Such was the influence of Kao on Prime Minister, Indira Gandhi on this affair that Foreign Secretary, Kewal Singh and even her Principal Secretary had to eat a humble pie when they met her on April 6 to brief on the situation and to seek her instructions. That meeting lasted only about half an hour. They both were surprised to find that she had already made up her mind before listening what they had to say. Kao had already informed her about the demands of JAC leaders. Indira Gandhi briefly advised the Foreign Secretary that she would accept request of Chogyal for help as soon as it came.

R&AW played havoc with Chogyal because within a week the political scenario underwent a dramatic change and he was then convinced that it was impossible for him to hold his people back. Although, he tried to counter attack by mobilizing the Bhutia community in the North to hold pro-Chogyal demonstration and assembled at Gangtok in his favour. Such situation could have resulted in serious communal clashes because the majority Nepalese population had already laid siege of Gangtok. Chogyal was warned by Indian officials of serious consequences if that stage was created by his henchmen and he had no option but to relent. He, after consultation with his own officials and colleagues held a meeting with Avtar Singh, Secretary MEA, and formally asked for Indian help to restore law and order situation in his state. He sent a letter to this effect on the evening of April 7 to the Indian Political Officer. This was followed by a telegram by the leaders of the JAC to the Indian Prime Minister, Indira Gandhi, appealing her to help in saving the innocent people of Sikkim from the ruthless repression unleashed by Chogyal to perpetuate his feudal privilege against the demand for democratic rights. The telegram also highlighted reference to misuse of India aid and concluded with a renewed appeal to intervene to save lives and secure democratic rights of the people of Sikkim. Even on 8 April, Dorji openly declared that Indian Government should not support Chogyal whose hands were stained with the blood of unarmed people who were demanding democratic reforms.

Indian Government acted swiftly on April 8 after the request of Chogyal for help was received. Army was asked to take control of the law and order situation of Sikkim. This was restored immediately without difficulty. B S Das who had served as head of diplomatic mission in Bhutan was appointed Chief Executive to administer Sikkim. Next day, Indian Government made a comprehensive statement in Parliament elaborating the circumstances due to which India had to take control of the administration of Sikkim. The statement emphatically assured Sikkim people that India would make every effort to ensure that the interest of the people were served and safeguarded and the state marches on the road to political stability, security and economic prosperity. This statement had an profound impact on the leaders of JAC who suspended their protest movement on April 9. Kazi Lhendup Dorzi while briefing the press openly declared that the JAC had called off agitation in view of the promise of Indian Government to meet the legitimate demands of the people of Sikkim. He made it clear that JAC was not prepared to have useless, infructuous and bipartite parleys with the discredited Dhogyal. R&AW was playing its cards close to the chest.

Hereinafter, India had to shoulder the dual responsibility to safeguarding the legitimate interests of the Sikkim people vis-à-vis obligation of internal and external security of the state under 1950 Treaty. This agitation proved that India had reluctantly overrated Chogyal's local importance and unnecessarily catered to his whims and fancies which stood exposed and reality of hollowness of his pride was unearthed. This was further strengthened from the fact that he had to be saved from the wrath of his own people. Kewal Singh and other Indian officials met Chogyal and persuaded him to agree to political and administrative reforms. Reluctantly, he agreed to call an all party conference to produce a set of agreed reforms. However, Chogyal did not appreciate the swiftness which rescued him in this political crisis. He too did not speak against the vicious propaganda launched by China but admitted that the movement in Sikkim was neither directed by India nor any of its agencies. Notwithstanding this, Indian Government remained unconcerned about the Chinese propaganda because its indifference to any such accusation would at least give China the message that India was no longer worried about its hostility.

The people and leaders of Sikkim expressed a sense of relief when India took over administration of Sikkim. But some members of Chogyal family and his henchmen tried to rake up this matter at international fora with the help of anti-Indian forces. Pheunkane, sister of Chogyal, alleged in a press conference at Hongkong that India unconstitutionally resorted to impose constitutional reforms in Sikkim. She alleged that India hired peasants from Darjeeling who created unrest in Sikkim. His half-sister Semla alleged that women among the anti-Chogyal demonstrations were non-Sikkimese. In a long distance interview, his Secretary described the demonstrators as Sikkimese of Nepalese origin and characterized their leaders as undesirable elements. China initially did not make any comments on this development but after a fortnight the New China News Agency, NCNA deplored this take over and quoted that since Chogyal was asserting to develop an identity for Sikkim which irked Indian Prime Minister Indira Gandhi. NCNA further said that Chogyal wanted to get one of the division of Indian soldiers withdrawn and as a retaliation India had forcibly taken over the administration of Sikkim. India too took note of this Chinese reaction but in order to sidetrack this mischief, thought of making an agreement which satisfied the aspirations of the people of Sikkim and at the same time give due credence to the 1950 Treaty.

In Delhi, Kao held meetings with officials of the Prime Minister office and Ministry of External Affairs to finalize the modalities of agreement to be executed between Chogyal and political leaders of JAC with India dominating as facilitator. When Indian Foreign Secretary Kewal Singh met Chogyal in the second week of April, he was as usual stubborn in his approach and accused India of instigating the hooligans who looted innocent people and demanded criminal action against Kazi, his wife and his son Narbahadur Khatiwada whom he called Communists and a danger to both India and Sikkim. He tried to emphasize to Kewal Singh that any change in the political structure would be a breach of faith on the part of India since Sikkim had a separate identity under the 1950 Treaty. When Chogyal did not relent, Kewal Singh took serious exception to his insinuations and warned him to read the writing on the wall. He reiterated that he could only function as a constitutional head, the power being vested with the people. Syali, the R&AW head in Gangtok was in constant deliberations with the JAC leaders and ensured that they did not accept anything but elected government of the people with India as dominant power above Chogyal.

After Kewal Singh returned to Delhi without any negotiated settlement of the ongoing crisis, Chogyal saw a ray of hope in the position being restored to status quo ante with minor changes. This was a political blunder because when India was requested for intervention in the wake of agitation by Chogyal, he was too weak to refuse any sort of political settlement and all pre-conditions should have been imposed by him. But the Indian Government wanted a negotiated settlement with him to set up an elected government of people of Sikkim. But Chogyal was dishonest in his intentions and wanted to wriggle out of his earlier commitments. Powerful Tibetan lobby at the behest of China and American foreign agents advised him not to surrender before India. R&AW operatives instigated the Youth Congress volunteers to again raise banner of revolt against Chogyal. They demanded abolition of monarchy. Indian Political Officer again warned him to go by his earlier commitment failing which there would be dire consequences. Kewal Singh again came to Gangtok on April 22 with a draft agreement. It was a bilateral understanding to work out tripartite arrangements between Indian Government, Chogyal and the political parties for final agreement. Chogyal again raised lot of hue and cry but finally agreed on these lines.

Finally, Kewal Singh returned with a new draft agreement on May 7 to Gangtok with minor changes on the one discussed on April 23. Chogyal again sought explicit assurance on the continuation of 1950 Treaty which was not accepted. The famous May 8 Agreement was signed at 9 P.M. in the Palace. Some dramatic happenings took place prior to the signing of this agreement. At first, Kazi and his group refused to go to the Palace. K C Pradhan and B B Gurung, other leaders of JAC expressed fear that Chogyal would poison their liquor. Narbahadur Khatiwada gave a very balanced opinion that Chogyal should come to the India House to sign the agreement. After great persuasion by Syali, they were taken to the Palace. Chogyal was heavily drunk at that time and accused the leaders of betrayal and treachery to the Sikkimese in this sell-out to India. Soon thereafter, all the political leaders, Chogyal and Kewal Singh signed the tripartite agreement on terms accepted by them. Kewal Singh swallowed all the insults, the political leaders went through in the Palace.

This agreement was a virtual stamp on the charter of JAC dictated by R&AW during the time of agitation excluding the demand of abdication of Chogyal which was vociferously got raised through leaders at that time. It contained eleven articles with several sub-clauses. Some of the salient features of this agreement were i.e. provision of a Legislative assembly for Sikkim elected on the basis of adult franchise for a period of four years, an Executive Council responsible to the assembly and safeguards for minorities and appointment of a Chief Executive to administer Sikkim. Assembly was given powers to propose laws and adopt resolutions on fourteen subjects including finance, economic and social planning, education and agriculture. No power was given on four topics i.e. the Chogyal and his family, matters before Court and appointment of Chief Executive and members of Judiciary and issues which were the responsibility of Indian Government. Chogyal was to administer the Palace and the Sikkim guards. Police was kept under control of Indian Government.

In New Delhi, the Indian press, by and large, hailed the May Agreement as a major development for the upliftment of Sikkimese population. Kazi and his collegues celebrated this achievement as a major victory against the tyranny rule of Chogyal and his henchmen, particulary his highly ambitious American wife, Cooke. Chogyal was still skeptical to the final success of this agreement and chose to remain silent on this issue.

In June, 1973, an advisory council was constituted by the Chief Executive pending the election and framing of a new constitution under the May agreement. This council had five members of each of the three parties i.e. National Congress, Janta Congress and National Party of Chogyal. This too was resented by Chogyal who wanted direct control of administration through Chief Executive which was not allowed. Chogyal wanted to interfere because he was aware that except Kazi, Narbahadur Khatiwada and K C Pradhan, most of other members of this council did not possess any aptitude and calibre to rule Sikkim. He was aware that integrity was also not a virtue amongst them barring three or four because corruption was a way of life in Sikkim at that time since he had centralized all financial powers under him before May agreement.

Chogyal became restless after these events and in order to divert the hostile political scenario in his favour, he planned to visit all parts of Sikkim. In order to frustrate him further, R&AW operatives through their local contacts, which by then had made up a firm belief that it was now or never to get rid of Chogyal and his henchmen, instigated the local population to boycott meetings of Chogyal. When Chogyal sent his trusted persons in advance to prepare for his visit in West and South Sikkim, they were almost lynched and were saved with the help of police. When Chogyal visited some areas to solicit public support, he met hostile crowds shouting slogans against him and abusive placards with shoes hung as buntings. No one came to pay homage to him as per past custom. This made him demoralized and his confidence started crumbling beyond repair. Indian Government began consolidating the administration of Sikkim and R&AW in its operational planning got engaged in encouraging the Sikkim population to get a democratically elected government suitable to New Delhi.

In view of the April, 1973 agitation, Hope Cook was so terribly frightened of the past events that she decided to leave Sikkim for good. When the Palace was surrounded by mobs shouting anti-Chogyal slogans, her protégés, most members of the Youth Study Form, who received her patronage and financial support, deserted her. Her efforts to bring the Sikkim imbroglio at the United Nations proved futile. She was more worried about the safety of her two children in Sikkim hereinafter. While Chogyal was hopeful to retrieve the situation with his past experience of an uncertain Delhi, Hope Cook had no such illusions and did not want to take the chances. She knew Chogyal would not leave Sikkim at any cost as it was his first and only true love and she was young enough to make a new beginning in U.S.A. and he was old enough to lead a recluse life in Sikkim. She declined the request of Chogyal to stay with him at that crucial juncture foreseeing danger to the life of her children. Although, Indian Government was committed for their protection but her dreams to become the queen of a sovereign country were shattered after the agitation. She left Sikkim on August 16, 1973 and finally divorced Chogyal in 1979. This American lady, who was to a larger extent responsible in influencing the mind and actions of Chogyal that ultimately resulted in the disastrous events led to the agitation and ultimate merger of Sikkim with the Indian territory, went off the Sikkimese political scene for ever.

In this second phase of this operation, Kao succeeded on two important counts. First, Assembly of the people was got constituted to elect their own representatives and rule Sikkim democratically with due political process and not at the diktat of Chogyal. Secondly, it frustrated Chogyal and his American-controlled wife, Hope Cooke, to make Sikkim a sovereign state on the map of the World. The May Agreement not only reiterated control of India over the defence and foreign relations of Sikkim but also made the Chogyal a subordinate of Indian Government reducing him to merely as the constitutional head of Sikkim without any powers. He sought guarantee from Indira Gandhi assuring of its separate identity under the Treaty to which no written assurance was given by her on advice of Kao. Further, there were specific provisions in this agreement wherein if a dispute erupted between him and the Indian nominated Chief Executive, ruling of New Delhi would be the supreme and had to be accepted by him. These provisions gave Kao a blank cheque to encash on the third phase of his merger plan. This Assembly would provide him the desired platform for his operational requirement so that R&AW operatives in Sikkim could send persons of their choice in the Assembly.

Phase Three – Elections in Sikkim to Make it "Associate State" and Ultimate Merger

A S Syali, the RAW head in Sikkim had completed his tenure and was selected for another special assignment for which he had to be relieved from Gangtok. Visionary, R N Kao selected another IPS officer from U P cadre, G B S Sidhu to replace Syali. Sidhu happened to be the son-in-law of then Indian Foreign Minister, Sardar Swaran Singh. Kao personally told the author that this selection of Sidhu was deliberately done by him with the imagination that in case of any political wrangling with regard to Sikkim operation, Sardar Swarn Singh would manage the situation due to presence of his own son-in-law on the scene at Gangtok. Sidhu, the burly towering Sikh, took control of this operation in August, 1973 when the pot was boiling too hot for Chogyal. In comparison to

Syali, Sidhu was more aggressive and imaginative under the astute command of Banerjee at Calcutta. Soon, their operational working became so trustworthy which once Banerjee told Kao that due to bad weather and heavy rains, personal wireless connection between him and Sidhu became in- operational at times. Sidhu complained to Banerjee that if some important and immediate decision had to be taken with consent from Banerji, he was at a loss to do that due to wireless glitch. Banerjee authorized Sidhu to take whatever decision he wanted to take be it right or wrong. If right, he would appreciate Sidhu and if wrong he would admit that Sidhu had not done that. That was the type of trust and working relationship prevailing among R&AW officers during that period.

Sidhu had an arduous task of making all preparations to put up a strong political front against Chogyal forces in the forthcoming elections of Sikkim assembly. First and foremost task, he managed was to get two important constituents of JAC united into a single political party. In this pursuit, he got the National Congressof Kazi Lhendup Dorzi and Janta Congress of K C Pradhan formally merged and a new party, Sikkim Congress was formed to contest the 1974 elections. Kazi was elected President and K C Pradhan as Vice President of this party. Like Congress party of India, Sikkim Congress too decided to have a tricolor with blue star in the centre as its flag and ladder as election symbol. leaders of the United Sikkim Congress declared that they would soon release its election manifesto protecting the privileges of the minority communities of Lepchas, Bhutias and other backward classes of Sikkim.

It would be worth mentioning here that R&AW worked for total independence of Sikkim without any interference either from other Indian officials administering there prior to the May, 1973 agreement or even thereafter when Chief Executive was appointed by India to work under the titular head of Chogyal. Even the new Chief Executive admitted that Indian intelligence agencies refused to assist him as these were doing earlier before to the Dewans. He conceded that his repeated requests for assistance were turned down in spite of the fact that everyone was aware that they were in constant touch with all the political elements. This was a policy decision of Kao because he apprehended that this top secret operation should be kept as a shrouded entity because it would have severe repercussions if a whiff of its actual planning went outside R&AW. Sidhu although designated as Officer on Special Duty, was administratively an Indian officer working independently without any indulgence of Chief Executive or other Indian officials. His first priority was to monitor and enlist the prospective candidates of Sikkim Congress in coming elections and make them psychologically strong and financially secured to outclass Chogyal and his henchmen. Sidhu had two local R&AW officers of Sikkim ethnic tribes who along with several other junior officials made extensive tour of far flung areas and on their recommendation a roster of such candidates was prepared. Most of these political leaders barring few, were educated and they were encouraged against Chogyal by every means suitable to them. Kao had authorized Sidhu to pump as much money as required to the Sikkim Congress candidates so that they could win elections at any cost since it was a now or never situation for R&AW.

Since, in the May agreement, 30 seats were proposed for the assembly, delimitation of these seats was to be done by the Chief Election Commissioner of India. Till December, 1973, Indian officials in Sikkim were consolidating the law and order situation. Indian Government then sent the Chief Election Commissioner, T Swaminathan to Sikkim who discussed ways and means to conduct elections with Chogyal and other political leaders. Although, Chogyal wanted a Sikkimese as election commissioner but ultimately an Indian R N Sengupta was selected to conduct these elections. Other major issue of separate seat for monks and scheduled caste, was resolved after prolonged discussions among all these warring factions and ultimately it was agreed by all the parties to have thirty two seats. The new Assembly was to be elected on a one man one vote franchise. Subsequently, after obvious wrangling with Chogyal, deadlock was resolved by a compromise scheme according to which 32 seats were divided on ethnic basis. 15 seats were reserved for Nepalese and Bhutia/Lepchas each, 1 for monastic community (the Sangh) and 1 for the Scheduled Caste. In communal terms, the Sangh seat was for the Bhutias and the Scheduled Caste seat was for Nepalese. This composition was more favourable to Chogyal.

In the delimitation process of these 32 seats, the election commission with much difficulties adjusted the 75% Nepalese and 25% of Lepcha/Bhutia population in their respective 15 seats. It was also decided to conduct elections with the help of Indian officials. Sidhu was certain to put up winning candidates in all the 15

Nepalese seats in consultation with Kazi in general and his brain trust Elisa Maria Kazini along with the young firebrand Narbahadur with great organizational capacity were the formidable trio who were determined to crush Chogyal in these election. His dilemma was to find winnable candidates in other 17 seats. He with the help of this trio and K C Pradhan found formidable candidates from Lepcha/ Bhutia and other two reserved seats and soon provided them all required help prior to the declaration of elections. Nepalese population in the minority seats were encouraged through all possible means to help the candidates selected to contest under the banner of Sikkim Congress. R&AW sought the help of some influential leaders of these minority tribes resorting to all sort of means and practices in order to create winnable situation for Sikkim Congress.

Sidhu played another havoc to Chogyal. He purchased loyalty of some influential leaders of the National Party of Chogyal and this news too was conveyed to him deliberately through his sources. These leaders had retired from active politics but commanded respect of all important segments of Sikkim population. They had mutual respect for Kazi. As is a saying that in times of adversity, the mind and body sometimes creates a situation of not only self-destruction for an individual but make him victim of his own deeds. Chogyal became target of this myth prior to the 1974 elections. When he was made suspicious of his own henchmen on the disinformation of R&AW, he disbanded all old guards of his National Party and created a youth wing of his party called the Youth Pioneers under the leadership of his niece Sodanla, daughter of his sister Coocola. These youths were bunch of discredited hoodlums even in the eyes of National Party supporters. Most of them were young Bhutias who were either taxi drivers or petty shopkeepers. When they indulged in strong arms tactics and unsocial activities, workers of National Party were disillusioned with Chogyal in this new venture of political jugglary. Subsequently Chogyal realized his mistake of pampering Youth Pioneers and in another gamble, he set up a new party called the People's Democratic Party which was lead by some dissipated inconsequential Bhutias and Nepalese. He made Sonam Gyatso to whom his second sister was married, as head of this party. He was a reluctant choice for this job because basically he was a businessman without any political base. He privately admitted that he had been forced in that embarrassing situation by Chogyal to be associated with most undesirable elements in the new party. Sidhu then created a political atmosphere of suspicion and uncertainty for Chogyal wherein he started doubting credentials of even his nearest and dearest being on the pay roll of R&AW. Kazi and his party were more emboldened on all these developments around Chogyal.

Sidhu in consultation with educated leaders of Sikkim Congress prepared a draft manifesto of their party which was ultimately finalized by Banerjee in Calcutta and approved by R&AW Headquarterss at Delhi from legal point of view. The manifesto made special reference to land reforms for Sikkimese population by abolishing the private estates of Chogyal and his cohorts and demarcation of untitled land. Special references were made by R&AW in this manifesto for Sikkim Congress towards its future attitude with India. It was envisaged that Sikkim Congress would strengthen the already existed bonds with Indian Government and it was aware that the democratic developments of Sikkim would be benefitted from the interest shown by the Government and people of India. Further, it was stressed that for historical reasons, progress towards democracy had been inadequate and in order to make it more progressive towards democratic rights and institutions, concerted steps would be taken henceforth like the people of India. These were significant clauses inserted by R&AW towards its operational designs. It was a clear writing on the wall by Sikkim Congress for Chogyal, at the behest of R&AW.

Sidhu along with Kazi, Elisa Maria and Narbahadur Khatiwada shortlisted candidates in all the 32 seats in the forthcoming elections around January, 1974. Special care was taken to choose such candidates from 15 minority seats of Lepchas and Bhutias with consent from majority of Nepalese population in those constituencies. Junior R&AW officers posted in the foreign intelligence posts in these areas were asked to crosscheck the credentials and winnable chances of these candidates. Soon, the posters and leaflets for each candidate of these 32 candidates and manifesto of Sikkim Congress were prepared by Sidhu and his R&AW operatives in Gangtok and then got published in Calcutta under the supervision of Banerjee. Truck loads of these printed materials were sent to various parts of Sikkim by R&AW operatives and distributed among the general public by budding politicians. Thousands of small hand-operated loud speakers were supplied to these politicians and political workers for campaigning to create public awareness about the misrule of Chogyal and atrocities unleashed by his paid-men for the past many years. Chogyal and his henchmen were caught unaware of these developments. Kazi Lhendup Dorzi was projected as the undisputed leader to counter Chogyal in posters and leaflets. Elisa Maria proved the most prized asset for R&AW as she did not allow a single pro-Chogyal person to enter house of Kazi. Sidhu was aware of her intellect and dominance over Kazi. She was a non-stop speaker. Sidhu told Kao, as the author learnt from the later, in a meeting wherein Kazi once laughed and told him to use one ear to listen her and second to relieve that burden because he would be tired of listening to her and she would never stop talking once started. But she was ruthless in her denunciation of Chogyal and his misrule because of the old grudge and mutual hatred. She never forgot the raids conducted by Chogyal's police at her residence in Gangtok prior to agitation and humiliation heaped on her by banishing her from Sikkim to Kalimpong. She was determined to crush Chogyal politically and R&AW exploited this desire to its maximum. Narbahadur in his usual aggressive postures, exhorted the Nepalese sentiments to his community and worked tirelessly to make them anti-Chogyal in almost all the 32 constituencies of Sikkim. He had theinherent wish to be undisputed leader of the Nepalese community in the coming future exercising all powers which would be possible only when Sikkim would become part of India. In this resurgent political pursuit, he was top R&AW asset in Sikkim after Kazi and Maria in the coming elections.

Chief Election Commissioner of India conducted assembly elections of Sikkim from April 15 to 19, 1974. On the polling day, each booth was guarded and taken control by R&AW operatives all over Sikkim to stop any untoward infiltration for bogus polling by Chogyal's henchmen. Instead, Sikkim Congress workers were brought in large number for voting. Sikkim Congress contested all the 32 seats. Old National Party of Chogyal contested only 5 seats since his old guards chose to be neutral in these election fearing reprisals from the Sikkim population after election results as they had apprehended the pro-Kazi and anti-Chogyal wave. The newly sponsored party of Chogyal, the People's Democratic Party contested 26 seats although they were cited as Independent candidates by him and his cronies.

Election results of the Assembly surprised everybody including Kazi but not Sidhu, the RAW supremo in Sikkim, who had already sent his assessment to Kao about the outcome of results prior to the elections. Sikkim Congress won 31 seats polling, more than 70 percent of votes and the other single seat was won by National Party. Kazi won his Tashiding constituency unopposed. Most notable victory of Kazi's party was the Sangha, monasteries seat, stated to be stronghold of 57 recognized monasteries, controlled by Chogyal. This was a mandate for 75 percent of Nepalese Hindu population which overwhelmingly voted for their future survival with India. All Chogyal candidates were defeated with large margin of votes in each constituency. There were no allegations of rigging even by Chogyal. Press from India and abroad covered these elections and gave their fair assessment of its results. Indian Election Commission was complimented by press and even by Chogyal to the smooth conducting of election in spite of difficult terrain in most of the areas. Not a single case of malpractice in the polling was either alleged or brought to the notice of Election Commissioner. People of Sikkim decided the battle of one-upmanship between Kazi and Chogyal who were instinctively gravitated with the former knowing well that Chogyal was politically diminished permanently in his own kingdom. Propaganda of R&AW that the Government of India had overcome its excessive regards for the sensitivity of Chogyal and were then more supportive to the demand of people, proved final blow to Chogyal in the elections. Even the monks ditched him and elected Sikkim Congress candidate from their traditional seat. Fence- sitter voters saw Kazi destined to rule Sikkim and voted for him overwhelmingly.

For Chogyal, elections results proved the most humiliating event of his life inflicted by his own people, who out of respect considered him both secular and religious head. Even this humiliation did not make him wiser due to his inherent weakness of not to accept the ground realities. He portrayed himself to be reconciled to the new developments but behind the scenes he began subverting the loyalty of

Kazi's supporters in his favour. R&AW was keeping strict vigil on these dirty tricks of Chogyal and Sidhu properly guarded them through his operatives in all parts of Sikkim. Still he was living in his bizarre frame of mind, unaware of the facts that his confrontation was not with Kazi but hereinafter with Indian Government which was determined to install a people elected government in Sikkim at any cost and was ready to confront all challenges, be it regional or international. He had some misconception that some pliable Indian officers who had done so in the past, would discreetly help in his future fight with Delhi, unaware of the ground realities created by Kao and his juniors around him. R&AW brought Elisa Maria, now respected Kazini of Sikkim, to Gangtok from Kalimpong in a triumphant welcome by Sikkim Congress supporters. Chogyal in this hour of defeat did not forget his graces and invited newly elected members of the assembly for a generous feast and even hugged and kissed Kazini, his mortal enemy, in full public view to project a different personality of tolerance. This was a ploy of Chogyal because he wanted to disrupt the functioning of the assembly and for that he had hatched a discreet plan of which R&AW was aware in advance.

Final Legitimate Blow

After the election results, followers of Kazi demanded the abdication of Chogyal from all the constitutional responsibilities and wanted inauguration of new assembly by Chief Justice of India or Chief Executive which was legally not feasible in view of the position that Chogyal was head of state on that date in the absence of any rules or constitutional obligations. Even the venue of oath had to be shifted from the Palace to the precincts of assembly on persistent demands of Sikkim Congress volunteers. After much persuasion, an agreement was reached that Chogyal would inaugurate the assembly but leave immediately thereafter and elected members would then debate the address and move a vote of thanks. Such was the depth of hatred among Sikkim population against him on that occasion. On May 10, 1974, Chogyal inaugurated the new assembly with a brief speech. Kazi Lhendup Dorji was unanimously elected Leader of the House. Kazi moved a resolution vetted by R&AW on future political events in Sikkim. This resolution declared that assembly was empowered and thereupon appealed to Government of India to give a legal and constitutional framework for the objectives of this resolution, to define powers of Chogyal and to recommend specific proposals for future strengthening the Indo- Sikkim relationship and for participation in the political and economic institutions of India for all practical purposes as envisaged in May 8, 1973 agreement. Even most of the members of assembly, for lack of education, were unaware of the hidden agenda of R&AW in this resolution. This was the masterstroke of R&AW wherein political and economic institutions of Sikkim were made part and parcel of the Indian subject and a direct challenge to the protectorate status of Sikkim.

This resolution was passed unanimously by all 32 elected members of assembly, including the lone opposition member, Kalzang Gyasto of National Party of Chogyal who later on complained that he voted in favour of it due to his lack of English language knowledge. Government of India was requested to depute a constitutional expert to finalize a legal and constitutional framework to the objectives of the resolution. Most of these members of assembly were of same stature like the lone opposition and never understood the real implication of part three of the resolution pertaining to participation in economic and political institutions of India.

It would be pertinent to elaborate R&AW sponsored participation of Sikkim in the economic and political institution of India. Obviously, it could only be

Planning Commission on the economic matters and the Parliament on political issues. Participation too had different connotation on economic issues where Planning Commission was already involved in the formulation of Sikkim plan and allocation of funds. But participation in the political process could be attained through membership of the highest legislative body of India i.e. the Parliament. This was not possible unless Sikkim was listed amongst the Indian States under the Constitution which was not so at that time. Hence, such participation could be possible only if Sikkim was designated with a different constitutional status. Chogyal was thus convinced that all this was a preclude to ultimate merger of Sikkim with Indian union. Leaving him aside, even the highest echelons of Foreign Affairs ministry of India were unaware of such an intelligence planning and manoeuvring of Kao. Elisa Maria Kazini was on top of the world because this resolution was cleared by her in the presence of her son Narbahadur Khatiwada. Subsequently, this was approved by elected members and Kazi was authorized to move it before the Assembly. Having found entangled in this web of Kao, Chogyal in his last ditched effort of reprieve, sought to meet the mentor of whole of this drama, Indira Gandhi, the Indian Prime Minister. He was not honest in his intentions because he tried to divide Sikkim Congress on this issue and sought tacit support among the officers and students. R&AW was keeping tab on all such activity of Chogyal and Indira Gandhi was aware of it.

In response to demand of the Assembly, Government of India deputed a constitutional expert to Gangtok with a draft constitution which was not in consonance with the voice of elected members who wanted a constitution in which all powers would vest in representatives of the people. After discussion with Kazi, his colleagues and with Indian Government, the draft was amended to the satisfaction of the assembly. This draft was made the basis of the constitution bill which was to be presented before the Assembly on June 20 to promulgate a constitutional framework for Sikkim.

Since beginning. Chogyal had challenged the legality of this resolution. Having realized grave implications of this resolution and draft constitution bill that emerged from it, he resorted to physical tactics to prevent it from adoption. The Assembly was scheduled to meet on June 20 when Chogyal declined to deliver his customary address. He succeeded to certain extent in creating dissension among Sikkim Congress and two of its elected leaders opposed the proposed draft constitution. In the morning, he succeeded in mobilizing local officers of his community to his side who tried to force their entry into the Assembly premises to disrupt the proceedings. Their family members and a number of students were also forced to join them. Several hundred demonstrators from all sides of Gangtok tried to move towards the Assembly venue. When the mob tried to approach the entrance of the venue of assembly, they were dispersed by using tear gas and physical intervention by police in self-protection. R&AW took control of the two dissident leaders of Sikkim Congress who initially opposed the resolution and they apologized to Kazi in the evening. Most of the protestors and officers in particular, were also made to realize their mistake by R&AW operatives and sought mercy in writing to save them from future consequences. The irate Sikkim Congress wanted to retaliate to bring thousands of its own supporters for a confrontation but were persuaded with great difficulty since situation started moving to their side. When total normalcy returned in the evening, the Assembly met at 10'O clock in the night and unanimously adopted the resolution with some amendments, endorsing the Government of Sikkim Bill, 1974.

When political situation was becoming suitable to the largest extent to R&AW operatives in Gangtok, Kao in Delhi informed Indira Gandhi that Chogyal was adopting delaying tactics to give his assent to the new bill and was bent upon dividing the elected members of Sikkim Congress. She was also informed that Chogyal would come to Delhi with an alternative constitution maintaining therein his monarchical rule in constitutional garb. Kao also briefed that his son Tenzing through a London paper tried to embarrass India that Sikkim was in danger of being annexed with India by destroying its status of protectorate. Indira Gandhi was thus convinced by Kao that Chogyal was attempting to garner support from outside and was resorting to delay his consent to the proposed bill in the Assembly.

In the meantime, volunteers of Sikkim Congress were "pressed" into political upsurge by Sidhu and demonstrations started in Gangtok and elsewhere in Sikkim condemning undemocratic attitude of Chogyal. Sikkim Congress volunteers started marching towards Gangtok to protest against Chogyal who was admant to adopt the constitution. The crowd in the streets of the capital began to assemble and soon swelled over twenty thousand in number when a public meeting was held by leaders of Sikkim Congress. At this meeting, a resolution was passed that Chogyal should be abdicated forthwith as constitutional head as he was responsible for the happenings from June 20 onwards and his activities were prejudicial to the peace and security of Sikkim. He was also accused of creating communal discord and dissent among Sikkimese population due to his anti-people and anti-democracy stance. He was warned that the people would overthrow him if he would use power to suppress the will of the people. Sikkim Congress declared that either Chogyal should work according to provisions of May 8, 1973 Agreement or quit political scene lest he would be sacked. Kazi and other leaders declared in Gangtok and elsewhere that the frame-work of the Constitution as "drafted" was the best for the people of Sikkim since it protected the interest of all section of its society. R&AW was thus complimented by these leaders indirectly from their fora.

R&AW was aware that while in Delhi, Chogyal would spill venom and project his case while highlighting the then obsolete provisions of 1950 Treaty besides other international repercussions on the present state of affairs in Sikkim.

In order to counter that apprehension, Assembly met on June 28 and took up the reading of the Bill clause by clause. All members expressed their views on issues which required clarification and were duly recorded in the proceedings. The Bill was unanimously approved by the Assembly since all pro-merger members were adopting the line suggested by R&AW. The lone opposition leader was absent on counting. Assembly adopted another resolution which was passed for seeking representation for the people of Sikkim in the Parliament system of India. Kazi Lhendup Dorji sent a telegram to Indian Government to enact the Bill if Chogyal failed to give his assent within 48 hours. Dorji endorsed a copy of this telegram to Chogyal also to mend his ways. He warned Chogyal that Assembly members were shocked that he was obstructing the enactment of the constitutional frame work which was in adherence to May 8, 1973 Agreement wherein he was a signatory. Further, on June 30, Kazi declared that people of Sikkim would determine their destiny without Chogyal if he failed to respond to 48 hours ultimatum for the promulgation of the Sikkim Government Bill, 1974. He warned Chogyal to assist in fulfilling the aspirations of the people of Sikkim in establishing a democratic form of Government failing which people would not tolerate him any more. Sidhu was burning midnight oil along with all his staff members in Gangtok. Assembly members were provided all sort of physical support against possible oppression by Chogyal's henchmen. Banerjee too was desperate in Calcutta but confidant of the ability and strength of Sidhu and his operatives. Elisa Maria was too ecstatic since she was calling all the shots along with her son Nar Bahadur Khatiwada who was an important asset of R&AW in this cause. Kao was composed in Delhi prior to the scheduled visit of Chogyal to meet Indira Gandhi, who was already briefed by him on events of Gangtok where democratic process was in the final stage of its completion but for the stubborn attitude of Chogyal.

Chogyal rushed to Delhi to persuade the Indian Government to undo the irreversible political process when whole of the Sikkim population stood against him. After meeting Foreign Affairs Minister, Sardar Swarn Singh, he called on Indira Gandhi on June 30. He tried to emphasize that constitution bill was in violation of the treaty of 1950. He also sought to project that Sikkim Congress leaders were unreliable and untrustworthy Communists and he was the true friend of India. Irony of this situation for Chogyal was that Indira Gandhi was fully briefed by Kao on the prevalent situation of Sikkim and hostile overtures of Chogyal. Thus, she was brief and almost curt to Chogyal and stressed that the politicians he was referring to, were the chosen representatives of the people of Sikkim and advised him not to go against their wishes for a democratic government. Chogyal wanted to prolong the deliberations but Indira Gandhi, as usual felt silent and looked aloof to give feeling him of her negative response. Feeling ignored, Chogyal left the meeting and Indira Gandhi bade him farewell with folded hands in enigmatic smile without any assurance to him on public postures. Kao as usual proved his mettle to politically frustrate him both in Delhi and Gangtok.

After Chogyal failed to get any favour from Indira Gandhi, he gave the impression in Delhi that he had decided to give his assent to the constitution bill in the assembly. But when he returned to Gangtok on July 1, his attitude was still obstinate and uncompromising although he declared to pressmen at Calcutta airport that he was not contemplating abdication and would comment on the proposed bill after its clause by clause consideration by the Assembly. While in Delhi, where he was staying at Ashoka Hotel, he was swayed by another charming lady, Bhuvaneshwari Devi alias Princess Leena of the erstwhile Patiala state, who was a lawyer by profession. This ambitious lady convinced Chogyal that through her numerous political contacts at high level in Delhi, she would ensure to redress his legitimate demands by Government of India. Intentionally, Princess Leena wanted to attain glory by portraying herself as savior of Sikkim and thus become lasting companion of Chogyal, if she succeeded in this imaginary and futile attempt. Chogyal, being a desperate man found Princess Leena as last hope to retrieve him from that deteriorating situation. Both were engrossed in weird state of mind in spite of the fact that Chogyal was briefed about Indian Government policy by one of his friends. The dye was already cast by Kao and his R&AW operatives everywhere be it Delhi or Gangtok. Chogyal was under the strict surveillance of R&AW in Delhi and Bhuvaneshwari was no exception thereafter.

Chogyal returned to Gangtok as a bitter man since all his efforts to maintain status quo did not yield any result. A companion like Bhuvaneshwari encouraged him to leave the legacy of a fighter who fought for autonomy of Sikkim to his last- ditched efforts. In this scenario, Bhuvaneshwari prepared a detailed speech wherein he tried to highlight all legal and moral issues before the Assembly to retrieve some of the past glory of Sikkim. Main focus was on the autonomous status of Sikkim as per Treaty of 1950. The Assembly was summoned on July 3 wherein Chogyal wanted to deliver his speech personally which was resented to by the elected members who wanted his consent first and speech thereafter. His speech was read by the Chief Executive which was rejected by the Assembly suo moto. All the 30 of the 32 members who were present, voted for the adoption of the bill. Finally, the cornered Chogyal reconciled to the new situation and gave his consent to the Bill on July 4, 1974. Hence, fate of Sikkim as a separate entity was sealed to the larger extent by Kao but his job had not been fully accomplished on this outcome. He had planned another strategy to nip this evil in the bud for ever.

China responded to this political development in a subtle manner although one of the five fingers of the Chinese palm had been cut off by Indian intelligence

R&AW. They obviously reiterated that India had designed to overthrow Chogyal and annex Sikkim in its territory. Hope Cooke in USA might be celebrating this day, July 4 as Independence Day of her native country but must be remorseful of the shapes of things that had taken place after her departure from Gangtok. She was the inventor of this destiny of Chogyal who had to give up his kingdom while pampering this beauty of white origin for a short span in his life which proved disastrous to him.

Status of "Associate State" for Sikkim – Decision of Kao

Kazi hailed July 4 as a red letter day in the history of Sikkim. After the promulgation of the Government of Sikkim Act, he was sworn in as the first Chief Minister of Sikkim and a popular Ministry with five Ministers was installed on July 23, 1974. This was the end of a 300 year old feudal rule of dynasty in Sikkim.

Soon after Kazi became Chief Minister of Sikkim, on instructions from Kao, Sidhu met him and as decided earlier asked him to send a formal request to Indian Government to take action on clause 30 of the constitution relating to the association of Sikkim with Government of India in participation and representation for the people of Sikkim in the political institution of India. Kazi made this formal request as planned by Kao. It would be pertinent to mention here that matter of "Associate" state of Sikkim with India was the brainchild of R N Kao and his R&AW officers and Foreign Affairs Ministry or the Prime Minister Office had no opinion whatsoever in it. Indira Gandhi had given blanket approval to Kao in Sikkim affairs to give it merger shape at the earliest possible since she was facing heat in view of the May 18, 1974, nuclear explosion from most of the major powers of the World. Sikkim was also a hot potato for her and she did not want to waste much time to decide its fate once for all.

In view of this background, just after taking oath, on recommendation of Sidhu, Kazi sent a formal request to Government of India on July 24 to take such steps as may be legally or constitutionally necessary to approve the Government of Sikkim Act, 1974 and the resolutions passed by the Assembly to providing representation for the people of Sikkim in Parliament. Government of India, in consultation with Kao, constituted a committee of officials of Law Ministry, Attorney General and Foreign Affairs officials to prepare a draft for enactment of Sikkim as "Associate State" of India. R&AW asked Kazi to send another reminder to expedite this matter. To put another political pressure, a letter was sent the following day on behalf of S K Rai, general secretary of the Sikkim Congress Party requesting Government of India to take early decision on the request of the Chief Minister of Sikkim regarding representation in Parliament. Kazi again sent a letter to Indian Government for taking an early decision on his July 24 recommendations. Indian Government had decided to respond positively as a consequence to the constitutional obligation. The Constitution of India had therefore to be amended accordingly to incorporate the aforesaid demand of Sikkim Chief Minister.

On the recommendation of the committee constituted for this purpose, the draft amendment bill was prepared and circulated among Members of Parliament on August 31, 1974 wherein provisions were made to declare Sikkim as associate state of India and election of two members by its assembly for Rajya Sabha and Lok Sabha respectively. In Parliament, there were some opposition from the Communists and Congress(O) on this bill. Indian Foreign Minister, Sardar Swaran Singh defended the bill and assured the house that amendment was not against any party i.e. the Chogyal and for the wishes of the people of Sikkim. Atal Bihari Vajpayee, the Jan Sangh leader, wanted to make Sikkim 22nd State of India instead of conferring only associate status to which Sardar Swaran Singh appealed not to hasten the pace as Indian Government was going to the point up to which Sikkim was prepared to go. Most of the members hailed it as a historic development though belated. On September 4, the Lok Sabha passed the bill with an overwhelming majority of 310 against 7. Replying to discussion in Rajya Sabha, Sardar Swaran Singh allayed fear of some members about hostile world opinion and affirmed that Nepal had termed it as bilateral matter and there was complete understanding in Bhutan and Bangladesh on this issue. The Rajya Sabha passed the bill on September 8 with a majority of 168 votes for and 8 against.

Thus, the 35th Constitution Amendment Bill was passed in the Indian Parliament and Sikkim was accorded the position of an "associate state" of India. The Chogyal was reduced just as the titular head with no powers to interfere in the day to day administration of Sikkim. Kao was, thus, nearing the final stage of his Sikkim operation because such an amendment of "associate state" was his brainchild and even during the annexation of princely states after independence no such vocabulary was enacted for constitutional obligations as was done in Sikkim by him. Foreign affairs officials and Law Ministry were hesitant to such amendment but diktat of Indira Gandhi on the advice of Kao prevailed and rarest of rare amendment was made by Indian Government in the Constitution for operational requirement of R&AW.

Neighbouring Sri Lanka and Burma did not say a word of criticism of what was done in Sikkim. As the Indian Foreign Minister declared there was complete understanding in Bhutan and Bangladesh on this matter. In Nepal, there were some anti-Indian demonstrations outside the Indian Embassy. Some newspapers of Nepal criticized the Indian action while others hailed this decision as pro-Nepalese since more than 75 percent of the population in Sikkim was migrated Nepalese who would be master of their destiny. Nepal ultimately declared that developments in Sikkim were a bilateral matter between India and Sikkim and Nepal had nothing to do with it. Obviously, China and Pakistan bitterly criticized this development. Pakistan accused India of swallowing up Sikkim and argued with United States to resume arms assistance. Chinese reacted and said it did not recognize India's illegal annexation of Sikkim as an associate state and that it supported the people of Sikkim in their struggle for independence against Indian expansionism. China also criticized Russia for supporting Indian action in Sikkim and asserted that India would not have taken that action without tacit support of Russia which was also accused as the ferocious enemy of the people of this region. USA was closely watching all these developments of Sikkim and refrained to comment on this issue since Sikkim had no international status and according to them it reflected the will of the Nepali majority. Rest of the world did not give any importance to this event.

Chogyal's Retaliation

In the beginning of September, 1974, Chief Minister of Sikkim, Kazi Lhendup had informed Indian Government about the nefarious attitude of Chogyal towards the elected Assembly. On advice from R&AW, he sent written letter to abdicate him as head of state. However, Indian Government advised him to exercise restraint with expectation that Chogyal had no option but to reconcile with his constitutional role and adopt constructive approach. This opinion was derived when he assured Indian Prime Minister, Indira Gandhi on September 17 that he accepted India's right to accede to Sikkim Government plea for representation in Parliament to which she assured him that status and privileges would be unaffected by the 35th Constitutional amendments.

Unfortunately, Chogyal did not recognize the rising tide of democracy and tried to reverse the will of the people. In October 1974, he deputed his younger brother abroad to contact certain elements in foreign countries in an attempt to internationalize this issue through U.N.O. These elements sent an appeal to the UN Secretary General to intervene in this alleged aggression of India. Chinese delegation also made allegations that India had annexed Sikkim. Indian representative in UNO refuted Chinese allegation that Sikkim was a princely state under the British protection like other 500 odd princely states. Immediately, thereafter, Chogyal communicated to Government of India contesting the statement of Indian representative and asserted that Sikkim had never been a part of India, geographically, ethnically and racially. Chogyal further claimed that Sikkim did not sign any instrument of accession in any covenant under which the Indian princely states lost their sovereignty and identity. He tried to interpret that Indo-Sikkim Treaty of 1950 did not mean that Sikkim surrendered its sovereignty and international autonomy or that India was granting Sikkim a special status. He opted to confront Indian Government instead of what he accepted to Indian Prime Minister, Indira Gandhi on September 17.

These facts confirmed that Chogyal did not take into his strides that odds had gone against his extravagant ambitions and he did not reconcile to his status as constitutional head of his state and let Sikkim become stable for its future political status. Instead he continued his tirade against Chief Minister Kazi and his colleagues and never adopted a working relationship with them. He realized that unless he would weaken the new power centre that was ruling Sikkim, no foreign powers would come forward to help him. He started creating dissensions among the Sikkim Congress leader through all deceitful means. R&AW was keeping tab on all these activities of Chogyal in Sikkim and abroad and Indira Gandhi was regularly briefed of his impending actions. Bhuvaneshari Devi, his new companion, his sister Coocoola and all his close advisors were under the scanner of R&AW and Indian Government was convinced that Chogyal was bent upon for a fight against further merger of Sikkim. Elements against Kazini started raising dissent against the working pattern of Sikkim Government. K C Pradhan, number two in Kazi cabinet was dismissed for pro-Chogyal stance and R&AW had to resort to other measures to counter-check anti-Indian Chogyal and his cronies.

In February, 1975, Chogyal himself gave the right opportunity to the Indian Government which was much awaited by R&AW for a final show down in this political imbroglio. Chogyal was invited by Nepal Government as a private guest to attend the coronation ceremony of the King. Probably, he was deliberately allowed to visit Kathmandu to display his true colours before hostile elements of India. He went out of way and met the Pakistan Ambassador and the Chinese vice-premier, Chin-his Liu.. They capitalized this opportunity and promised support to Chogyal if he were to raise this matter at the United Nations. Although, he approached the US Senator Charles Percy but he did not lend any support to him. On March 1, 1975, in a press conference, he criticized the motive of Indian Government and legality of Sikkim's new status. He declared that Sikkim wanted to achieve separate identity and preserve its international status and he had written to the Indian Government in this regard. He reiterated that he would also approach the United Nation in this regard. This was an open revolt of Chogyal against India.

On the basis of detailed reports of R&AW officers from Kathmandu, R N Kao briefed Indira Gandhi of each and every meeting of Chogyal with hostile elements and details of his outburst before media community against India. Around this time Hope Cooke, his estranged wife became active in United States to raise this issue through India-baiters. His sister Coocoola raised the same bogey at Hong Kong where he made frequent visits during this period. R&AW had a tough time to counter these ladies in their respective places but were able to contain them subsequently. In view of these developments on foreign soil, R&AW prepared its ground for a showdown with Chogyal in Sikkim.

Indian Government in general and Kazi in particular were upset on Chogyal's statement in Kathmandu that there was no responsible democratic government in Sikkim. He also made a false allegation there that a bomb had been thrown on his car while he was coming to Nepal. Later on, this allegation was found as mischief and no marks of any bomb attack were found on the car. Kazi counter-attacked Chogyal that he had not reconciled himself to the democratic aspirations of his people and rather playing a destructive role by raising false rumours. Sikkim Congress leaders too reacted to the false propaganda of Chogyal in defaming his elected ministry. Sikkim Youth Congress too was provoked and they jointly issued a statement that Chogyal had lost confidence of the people and demanded his immediate abdication. Demonstrations were planned against him all over Sikkim on arrival from Nepal. Sidhu and his RAW operatives were fighting their last ditched battle against that monster.

When Chogyal entered Sikkim, demonstrators of Sikkim Congress had violent clashes with his guards at the border town of Rangpo. R C Paudhiyal, a prominent Sikkim Congress leader, was injured by his guards and had to be moved to the hospital in a serious condition. R&AW had completely overshadowed the Palace and through its sources found that Chogyal had decided to use the Palace Guards to assassinate prominent Sikkim Congress leaders. It was also confirmed that Chogyal was bent upon to terrorize and physically harm common people in a bid to disrupt law and order situation, obstruct functioning of the government and subvert the democratic institution. A member of Assembly was stabbed by a Palace guard in his presence. A bomb was found planted in the car of Chief Minister. All these incidents were duly taken care of by R&AW.

On April 7, 1975, one Sonam Tshering was arrested by R&AW and handed over to police custody where on interrogation he admitted that he had been paid huge amount and arms by Captain Sonam Yongda, ADC to Chogyal, to kill some prominent Sikkim Congress leaders. He also revealed that this conspiracy was hatched two months ago to create disturbances in Sikkim by planting bombs, looting and arson. Police arrested Captain Sonam Yongda while he was trying to flee towards North Sikkim, a few kilometers away from Gangtok. He admitted that this conspiracy was planned by Chogyal to assassinate top Sikkim Congress leader and some civil servants to create a situation of chaos in Sikkim. Yongda also alleged that Madan Mohan Rasaily, Auditor General and Capt. Raolland Chettri, Adjutant, Sikkim Guards were entrusted the job for execution of this plot. He also admitted that some agents were also recruited and given training of arms and explosives to create law and order situation in other parts of Sikkim. During interrogation he figured out that these arms and explosives were received by Rasaily from some outside destinations. These agents were provided with false documents to flee Sikkim in case of their being apprehended by Government.

After Captain Sonam Yongda gave a statement to the police on the conspiracy, a large deposit of arms and ammunition meant for arson was recovered by

R&AW in the backyard of the Palace and handed over to the police. These arms and ammunitions were found removed from the main armoury of Sikkim Guard which were meant for the security of Chogyal. Although, Chogyal tried to defend that arms were hidden to ensure that some unscrupulous persons might not loot them, this was absurd since further interrogation of Sonam Yongda confirmed that Chogyal had planned to deliver these to the conspirators to use against Sikkim Congress leaders and general public. R&AW operative unearthed the plot masterminded by Chogyal to kill few Sikkimese for his sinister designs. Captain Yongda also revealed during interrogation that at Kathmandu, the Chinese Deputy Premier, Pakistan Envoy and even King Birendra had advised Chogyal not to return to Sikkim as they had a separate plan for Sikkim's independent existence but it was rejected by him with the belief that India would never merge Sikkim.

Soon thereafter, the Indian Government dispatched army units to the Palace and disarmed the guards and took control of the premises and its surrounding area. Sikkim Guards tried to retaliate but Indian army but when one guard was killed in cross firing, the Guards surrendered and within 30 minutes, the army took full control of the Palace and arrested 243 guards. Demonstrators assembled all over Gangtok were taken under control by 5,000 strong Indian army so that they might not attack Chogyal in retaliation to his anti-people destructive activities. Chogyal was put under house arrest by the security forces. All communication lines of the Palace were cut. Indian tri-colour replaced the Sikkimese flag at the Palace where the12th King of the Namgyal dynasty was held "captive" by Indian army to save from the wrath of his own people.

Final stage of the third phase of operation Sikkim of Kao had reached the finishing line of its victory. Sikkim Assembly unanimously adopted a resolution on April 10, 1975 which abolished the institution of the Chogyal and declared Sikkim as a constituent state of India enjoying a democratic and fully responsible Government. Chief Minister Dorji described this resolution as historic since the only opposition representative also voted in favour of Sikkim Congress. He hailed the struggle of population of Sikkim against the oppressive rule of autocratic Chogyal who tried to put all sorts of obstacles to deprive any sort of opportunity to the democratically elected representatives of people to rule Sikkim. A copy of the resolution of merger was sent to Indian Government to complete constitutional formalities. This was the final blow to Chogyal by Dorji and his family to retrieve any effort by Chogyal to save his kingdom from being transferred from anarchy to the wishes of the people.

Referendum

After the Sikkim Assembly declared the merger of Sikkim with India as its unified territory on April 10, 1975, T N Kaul, the Indian Ambassador to USA spoke to R N Kao and suggested him to go for referendum in favour of this resolution before the Sikkim population. Kao discussed this suggestion with Indira Gandhi who enquired him whether he would be able to ensure the positive results. Kao smiled and asked for her consent which she gave immediately. Kao conveyed decision of Indira Gandhi to Banerjee in Calcutta and Sidhu in Gangtok who had already made preparation for such an eventuality. Not to take any chances, Kao dispatched three senior most officers of R&AW, Sardar I S Hassanwalia, Shiv Raj Bahadur, Additional Directors and N C Bhatnagar, Director, to assist Sidhu in the proposed referendum. All sort of logistic support were placed at the disposal of these officers of R&AW at Gangtok by Kao for smooth conduct of this last phase of operation.

Government of Sikkim conducted a special opinion poll at 57 stations on April 14, 1975 before the Sikkim population to give their personal opinion for the merger of Sikkim with India. While 59,637 votes were polled in favour of the Resolution,

1496 voted against it. The resolution was approved by an overwhelming majority. All three ethnic groups voted in favour of the merger. Nepalese considered Chogyal as their oppressor and were convinced that merger with India would give them full-fledged democracy and expand their economic opportunities. Bhutia also ensured that their future in Nepalese domination would be safer in Sikkim as an Indian state. The down trodden Lepchas also opted for merger for their economic development with India. For the first time in the history of Sikkim, all these three ethnic communities found common solution of their political and economic interest in merger with India. However, there were allegations at later stage in 2007 even by K C Pradhan, the then Minister of Agriculture that referendum was nothing but a charade because Indian soldiers rigged the polls by pointing rifles at the hapless voters. This disclosure by a prominent Minister of that regime confirmed the fact that R&AW sponsored referendum was an eyewash to bolster the image of Indian diplomacy at international fora.

Just after the declaration of the result of the referendum, Sidhu informed Kao of this historical achievement which was conveyed to Indira Gandhi by him immediately. Chief Minister Dorji and his colleagues visited Delhi on April 16 and met Indira Gandhi and requested her to accept the decision of the Sikkim Assembly and subsequent referendum of the people of Sikkim. Thus, Government of India decided to implement the resolution of Sikkim Assembly by amending the Constitution and accord the status of full statehood to Sikkim. The referendum in Sikkim was thus put to the due parliamentary process. Accordingly, the 38th amendment bill was moved in Lok Sabha on April 23, 1975 by Y B Chavan who had succeeded Sardar Sawarn Singh as Foreign Minister. The passage of bill, making Sikkim as the twenty second state of Indian Union was passed the same day with 299 members voted in favour and 11 against. The Rajya Sabha passed it on April 26, with 157 members voted in favour and 3 against. President of

India put his seal on this act on May 16, 1975 and Palden Thendup Namgyal, the Chogyal of Sikkim ceased to be the ruler of the Namgyal dynasty which ruled Sikkim for 333 years.

This was the second biggest operation of R&AW under Kao which was meticulously implemented by him along with three senior officers of R&AW, P N Banerjee, Joint Director of Eastern region at Calcutta, Ajit Singh Syali and G B S Sidhu both Sikh officers and a few junior officers of R&AW. Kao revealed to the author that after the completion of constitutional requirements of this operation, he called on Sardar Sawarn Singh and complimented him that he gave his son-in-law G B S Sidhu to him and he gave Sikkim to India. Operationally, no single agency of the world be it CIA, Mossad etc. no such big territory of more than 3,000 square miles had ever been merged by any intelligence agency to any country. Most hailing feature of this operation was the utmost secrecy that was maintained even within R&AW by Kao and these officers. As far as the burden of Indian exchequers was concerned, this whole operation was conducted with a very meager amount.

However, full credit of the Sikkim merger certainly goes to the resolute leadership of Indira Gandhi, the Indian Prime Minister. Since the agitation of 1973 till merger in

1975, she herself monitored the formulation and execution of the policy on Sikkim. She was hailed for her exceptional management of Bangladesh war but merger of Sikkim was another feather in her cap. In her political career, these two events were different in their magnitude and consequences wherein she was able to change the political map of this region with the emergence of an independent Bangladesh from the clutches of Pakistan and with the peaceful merger of Sikkim with India, a dangerous gap on the northern and easters borders of India was permanently sealed. It was discussed in R&AW later that the circumstances were less favourable for her in the merger of Sikkim. In Bangladesh war of 1971, Indira Gandhi was undisputed leader of the country and world opinion was in favour of India after the genocide unleashed by Pakistan army in East Pakistan and India faced the worst refugee problem. By 1974, India was in the midst of grave economic crisis and a political turmoil against Indira Gandhi was at its peak as a result of the call of JP movement to oust her from power. China and Pakistan were hostile to her at the international fora. Other countries in this region were suspicious of her intentions since they had denied democratic rights to their own population and were afraid of the same crisis as faced by the people of Sikkim. Against this background, it was the strong will and determination of Indira Gandhi which steered her through in this achievement of merger of Sikkim in spite of presence of large Chinese army on this border and hostile diplomacy of USA leadership at that time.

❑

Assassination of Sheikh Mujib

Sheikh Mujib-ur-Rahman was not a witness to the mass killings of his people Pakistani army during 1971 Bangladesh war of liberation. He was imprisoned in a Pakistani jail. He got the true account of genocide of his countrymen when he was released by Pakistan government in January, 1972. All sections of people, including defence forces who participated in this war against Pakistan wanted a total change in the character of new ruling regime. But to their utter dismay, they found Mujib, who portrayed himself as a Messiah of his people, altogether a different politician when he released anti-independence folks and pro-Pakistani traitors, the Jamai-i-Islam, Muslim League, Al Badr and Al Shams collaborators from jail unconditionally and granted them amnesty.

Mujib in Jail

During repression of Pakistani army in East Pakistan from March 25, 1971, there was no news about the fate of Sheikh Mujib-ur-Rahman. Indian intelligence outfit RAW intercepted a message "Chiriya Ko Pakar Liya Hai" during the day indicating that Mujib had been taken prisoner by Pakistan army. He was then taken to West Pakistan. On December 22, 1971 i.e. six days after the surrender of Pakistan army, the whole of World was informed by Pakistani government that Mujib was safe in a jail. This was disclosed two days after Z A Bhutto had taken over as President from Yahya Khan. Prior to his ousting from the office, Yahya Khan had signed the death warrant of Mujib leaving for his successor to execute it. Bhutto, however, did not act on this warrant fearing a backlash for more than 93,000 Pakistani prisoners of war at the hand of Bangladesh population. This execution by Bhutto was bound to face the wrath of people for his own survival. Bhutto went to meet Mujib in the jail and presented a him a transistor set to listen as to what was happening in Bangladesh and elsewhere. He also told Mujib that he was the President and Chief Martial Law Administrator of Pakistan. Mujib asked him who made him a General of the army. On January 3, 1971, Pakistan government announced that in deference to the world opinion, they had decided to release Sheikh Mujibur Rahman from Pakistan. On January 8, 1971, Mujib was released and flown out of Rawalpindi in a chartered PIA plane to London owing to political compulsion as Bangladesh was not given the recognition by Pakistan by that time.

Magnanimity

A few hours after the departure of PIA flight, Bhutto made the cryptic announcement: "The bird has flown." This metaphor was deliberately used by him because when Mujib was arrested on the night of March 25, 1971, the Pakistani army wireless message intercepted by the Indian intelligence RAW which contained the words "the bird is caged", the Indian government had used to convey the world that Mujib had been arrested by Pakistan government. While addressing his first press briefing at the conference room of the Claridges Hotel in London, Mujib announced that he had nothing against the people of Pakistan for what they did to him or his people in the past few year. This was the first signal of his magnanimity which ultimately proved disastrous for him in the coming years. From his London hotel, he telephoned to the Indian Prime Minister Indira Gandhi and expressed his gratitude for the help she extended for the liberation of Bangladesh to which Indira Gandhi thanked him and wished him to return to his country for changing the course of history after a bad period of 25 years during which his people suffered immensely.

Why Mujib chose to be get himself arrested on the night of March 25, 1971, remained a mystery. RAW offered him a safe passage to India but he declined. He never left his residence when RAW operatives informed him in advance that he would be arrested in the night by the Pakistan army. According to Matiur Rahman, subsequently a Minister in Mujib Government, Joseph Farland, the American Ambassador from Pakistan had flown to Dacca and had a closed-door meeting with Mujib in March, 1971 prior to the crackdown of Pakistan army. Despite stiff resistance from senior leaders of his own party, Mujib was in favour of a compromise with Yahya Khan after his talks with Farmland. R N Kao, the RAW Chief, had apprised General Osmany of this development in Dacca and also warned in advance about the impending crackdown of Pakistan army in East Pakistan. General Osmany, taking cognizance of this fact, personally visited to Mujib and talked of several options including going underground or escaping to India along with Mujib. But when Tajuddin came to Sheikh Mujib, he told Tajuddin that he would stay back and court arrest to the Pakistan army.

Apparently, that decision was the result of his briefing with Farland because according to reliable sources, American policy at that time was to have two friendly client states on either side of India with Mujib heading Bangladesh in east and Pakistan already existing on west. Mujib was asked to comment on this issue by a journalist to which he replied that if Pakistani army would not have found him that evening, it would have destroyed the whole of Dacca and as such he risked his life so that other innocent citizens could escape for safety to India and elsewhere. Some contemporaries felt that it was unfair to say that he stayed at home on that night because he felt he would be safe in Dacca after his meeting with U.S. Ambassador prior to crackdown of Pakistani army. However, this was a mystery and would continue to be a matter of discussion in the history but the obvious reason was to save as many people as possible due to his arrest to Pakistan army. Mujib was portrayed as fatherly figure by the Bangladeshi population which made him to act as a ruler by his heart than his head. Mukti Bahini cadres were in militant mood and determined to deal summarily with those who had collaborated in genocide with Pakistan army but Mujib, in spite of resistance from this cadre, pardoned many of them who also helped Pakistani army in liberation struggle. He even gave amnesty to those who deposed against him in the concocted Agartala Conspiracy case wherein he was arrested and imprisoned by Pakistan government for months together. Mujib was blackmailed sentimentally and emotionally by many such elements by sending their wives and sisters weeping before him to get released some hardened anti-liberation persons which Mujib did not realized at that time that how much harm he was going for the future of his country in general and to him and his family in particular.

RAW's Support

Soon after the formation of his cabinet, Sheikh Mujib requested Indira Gandhi to help in organizing his intelligence service and to rehabilitate the youth cadre which fought war of liberation in Mukti Bahini, Mujib Bahini and other militant outfits. R N Kao, who played a pivotal role in training all these guerilla outfits, was sent by Indira Gandhi to Dacca to meet Sheikh Mujibur Rahman and help him in this matter. After discussing the prevalent uneasy situation in Bangladesh, Kao returned to Delhi and briefed Indira Gandhi about his meeting with Mujib. She accorded the permission to depute two officers of RAW, P.N.Banerjee and Major General S.S. Uban to help the Bangaladesh government in this matter. P N Banerji was then a Joint Director in RAW, in-charge of eastern sector with Headquarterss at Calcutta. Previously, he was assigned the task to take care of the Bangladesh Cabinet in exile and as such he was close to almost every Bangladesh political figure of that time. He was also aware of the ground level realities of Bangladesh at that time. Banerjee was asked the job to organize the intelligence department of Bangladesh. Another intelligence officer, Major General S S Uban, the towering Sikh, head of Special Frontier Force, armed wing of RAW, was assigned the job to rehabilitate the youth leaders of Mukti and Mujib Bahini along with other militant outfit cadres, who were euphoric to find suitable place in the new country which got independence through their struggle against the Pakistani army. Most of these youths were imparted training by the SFF operatives of Ubarn in their fight with Pakistan army and as such they had highest regards for him due to their past association. So, Uban was the most acceptable person to these cadres.

Major Problems

At the infant stage of its liberation, Bangladesh was facing three major problems on its domestic front which was worrying Mujib to run a smooth democracy. The first and foremost difficulty was the non-surrender of arms by certain groups of people who could use them against the government when they could find an opportunity. Lot of arms caches taken from the Pakistani armory during liberation war, were in the custody of these so-called freedom fighters and criminal elements which could prove dangerous for the security of the newly formed government. Second problem was the question of rehabilitation of genuine youth cadres of the country who were trained by the Indian intelligence, RAW and were still unemployed. Disorganized Bangladesh army had no trained establishment to absorb them permanently and the Government did not have any concrete plan for their rehabilitation in other departments. The third major task was the smuggling of various commodities across the border with India by unscrupulous elements from both sides which was adversely affecting the economy of Bangladesh.

In consultation with Banerjee, the RAW officer, Sheikh Mujib agreed and ordered the formation of Jatiya Rakhkhy Bahini (JRB) or National Security Force of around

12,000 cadre of all patriotic youth of Mukti and Mujib Bahinis and other cadres to reconstruct the shattered economy of the country as also to establish law and order framework. These cadres were capable enough to unearth the arms caches within the country and bring to book all elements who were working against the national interest of Bangladesh. This cadre was to be used for anti-smuggling operations across the borders and ultimately for reconstruction purposes in the agricultural and other fields. This force was to work under the direct control of Sheikh Mjibur Rahman and Colonel Nuruzaman was appointed as the Commander of the force which was garrisoned at Dacca. Selected cadre of this force was sent to India for practical training at the establishments of RAW. This force played an important role in the formative period after independence and won the confidence of the people of its country. When Indira Gandhi visited

Dacca after the liberation of Bangladesh, there was absolutely no law and order in that country but with the help of this force, security arrangement during her visit were so water tight that her visit went without any untoward incident. There were stray incidents when these security men caught seven persons in different places carrying grenades in their pockets and behaved in abnormal manner.

Prior to the coup in Bangladesh on August 15, 1975, P N Banerjee was mysteriously found dead in his room at night in hotel Intercontinental where he was staying after his duties with the Government of Bangladesh. There was a lot of hue and cry that he was poisoned by the agents of ISI and CIA but on post mortem it was found that he died due to cardiac failure and there was no outside hand for this death. R N Kao also confirmed this fact of his natural death to the author that no other force was involved in it. Major General Uban too was subsequently repatriated to India after he completed the initial training of Jatiya Rakhkhy Bahini cadre. Mujib wanted his son Jamal to be trained at the Indian Military Academy but due to bureaucratic red tapism about his educational qualification, he could not be trained in India and Marshal Tito of Yugoslavia took him to his country where he could not accommodate himself due to language problem. Subsequently, he completed his training at Sandhurst Academy in England and joined the Bangladesh army as a commissioned officer.

Industries Nationalized

During the liberation war, economy of Bangladesh was totally ruined. Finding no way out, Mujib nationalized jute, cotton, textiles, banking and insurance sectors. He formally took over all Pakistani assets of 511 enterprises abandoned by the Pakistanis. 111 units, each with an asset of over 1.5 million, were nationalized. Even the industries of Bengali enterprises having assets of over 1.5 million Takas were also nationalized which resulted in resentment among the local industrial houses who expected liberalized economic policies from their new government. Taking over of so many industries, imposed a severe managerial burden on the government. Benefits of state ownership and trading were cornered by the intermediaries which triggered corruption in all walks of life resulting in deterioration in public life in Bangladesh.

Expectation that the newly elected Awami League with a fresh and massive mandate from the people would be able to tackle the situation more effectively, withered away. Rice, the staple food of the Bangladesh population, disappeared from the market. Rice was sold at 100 Taka or more per seer whereas Mujib had promised to sell it at 2 to 3 Ttaka per seer. The situation further worsened in the beginning of 1973. Incorrect decision and delayed action on procurement of food created further distortions in the economy. Nixon and Kissinger, who were known opponents of Mujib, not only manipulated the blocking of food sale to Bangladesh from USA but also used their influence to other non-government agencies not to sell any food to Bangladesh. Mujib appealed to the UN and other nations at a very late stage when prices rose more than double which put huge pressure on the foreign exchange reserves of the country. Despite repeated calls from Mujib, large scale hoarding and black marketing continued inside Bangladesh. News of starvation deaths starting pouring from all parts of the country. Hence, Mujib government miserably failed to handle the economic situation of the country and the people wanted to get rid to of this administration.

Relatives Favoured

It was universally believed in Bangladesh that Mujib was building a family fortune and a family-centered dynasty. Sheikh Abu Nasser, only brother of Mujib who was living in a poor state in 1971 became the largest contractor in Khulna district by 1975. He was reported to have increased his wealth by two-way trade network, in which he exchanged Bangladesh jute in India for consumer goods, alcoholic beverages, cigarettes and drugs for sale in Bangladesh often in violation of trade agreements that had been signed by Mujib. He became very rich overnight to own two Mercedes Benz cars and two luxurious homes and frequently traveled between Dacca and London. There were also allegations that some of the army officers who engineered coup, had been demoted or dismissed by Mujib government when they alleged to have intercepted the illegal shipments of jute and other contraband items of Sheikh Nasser to India.

Sheikh Fazlul Huque Moni, who was a trained guerilla warrior of liberation war of Mujib Bahini of RAW, was the son of one of the four sisters of Mujib and was commonly known as "nephew of the nation". He was the most confidant advisor of Mujib. In 1970, he was small time press reporter at with a salary of 275 Taka per month. After liberation, he took over the Pusban Press and the Pusban Building in the Motijheel commercial section of Dacca and began publishing newspapers and magazines. He also controlled a number of agents and firms that imported relief goods into Bangladesh, primarily through permits and licenses and accumulated huge personal wealth, including several cars and two homes in the posh residential area of Dacca. Abdul Rab Serneabad, husband of one of the sisters of Mujib who was a Minister in the Mujib cabinet enjoyed good reputation of honesty and integrity but his son Abdul Hasnat ran his own private army to intimidate political opponents in Barisal area where he owned several cars and homes. Another son of Mujib's sister, Sheikh Sahidul Islam was made the youngest Minister by him. There were allegations that he was involved in a bank robbery and scandal in 1972 and in the killing of seven Dacca University students in 1974. It was also alleged that Mujib's sons, Jamal and Kamal were also in the 1972 scandal and even Kamal suffered bullet wounds in a shoot-out at the scene of the crime. Another husband of his sister, A T M Syed Hossain was a small time officer in 1971 but within three years he was elevated to the post of Additional Secretary.

Mujib ignored this indiscipline among his family members and close associates, who had acquired political and financial favours from him with the result this national hero, became unpopular all over the country. When Mujib's Awami League won 307 of 315 parliamentary seats in the 1973 election, some political opponents dubbed this as blatant and violently rigged by his supporters. Thereafter, violent attacks against his party men and government officials mounted all over the country. In 1974 six members of the Bangladesh parliament were killed by unknown assailants who resulted in the murder of more than 6,000 Awami League members. Arson, looting and bombings became order of the day in 1974.

Emergency Clamped

With the Bangladesh economy deteriorating rapidly as a result of floods and famines in 1974 and failure of the administration to tackle the grim situation, Mujib declared a state of emergency on December 28, 1974. He assumed all powers to arrest and curtailed freedom associated with the courts and the press. All political meetings, demonstrations, strikes and lockouts were banned. On January 25, 1975, Parliament amended the 1972 constitution, and made Mujib the President of the country. The voting was 294-0 and Members of Parliament were given copies of the amendment only after they had entered the halls of Parliament. Mujib was vested with all executive powers and authorized to declare Bangladesh a one-party state. Subsequently, he abolished all opposition political parties, stripped the supreme court of its powers to enforce fundamental rights, created special courts and tribunals directly answerable to him and closed down all but four daily newspapers, two in English and two in Bengali. Only Government and party controlled newspapers were allowed to function. When emergency was clamped, only two Members of Parliament resigned in protest. One of them was General M A G Osmany, the war-time Commander-in-Chief without whom the army could not have been organized around the seventeen hundred miles border nor brought under the unified command of the political leadership. When Mujib was going to amend the Constitution and take all powers in his hand dissolving the political parties to make one, General Osmany had said in meeting of the Parliamentary Party: "Look Sheikh Mujib is a very dear name for Bengalis but they will never tolerate a Mujib Khan" (meaning Mujib following the footsteps of Ayub Khan or Yahya Khan or Tikka Khan). In reply, Mujib had shown the door to the General. The other Member of Parliament who resigned was a young Barrister, Moinul Hossain, son of late Tofajial Hossain, popularly known as Manik Main whose mighty pen as Editor of the daily Ittefaq had deeply influenced people's opinion. This autocratic behaviour and political attitude of Mujib made him head strong with power that he forgot the sacrifices of a liberation time General Osmany who was respected by all the Bengalis of that country.

On June 7, 1975, Mujib announced a new regime in which the entire government was to be merged with his single political party, the Bangladesh Krishak Sramic Awami League (BAKSHAL) which was headed by a 15 member national executive consisting of four relatives of Mujib and ten of his close associates and Mujib himself. A 115 member central committee representing various segments of society, including the military was made a subordinate organization th this national executive. No one was allowed to serve in the government without becoming a member of BAKSHAL and everyone of any consequence was required to seek membership in BASKHAL lest they be charged with being anti-national. By mid-June his party men had begun to move into offices in the central secretariat ousting bureaucratic officials and plans were launched for expanding the numbers of districts in Bangladesh from 19 to 61 where governors from among political friends and associates of Mujib were chosen.

Radical Groups Formed

In this political scenario, many Mukti Bahini fighters who suffered, sacrificed and won independence, in utter frustration withdrew their support to Mujib and formed radical political parties and groups all over Bangladesh. Among them, one of the stalwart of Mukti Bahini, Major Jalil formed Jatiyo Samajtantric Dal (JSD) which got 8% votes in the 1973 elections. Siraj Sikdar a house-hold name from the Pakistan days, whom few had seen as he had been underground for most of his life, formed a militant group, Purba Bangla Sarbohara Party. Many of the well-known leftist political activists including Mohammed Toaha of Noakhali Abdul Matin of Pabna and others had gone underground and sniped at police outposts thus declaring a war against Mujb government. Lt. Colonel Ziauddin who was a hero during the liberation struggle, a Commander of Dacca Brigade of Mukti Bahini was dismissed from the Bangladesh army. He had joined these militant outfits. JSD of Jamil held a rally against starvation at Paltan Maidan on March, 17, 1974, highlighting the government apathy to stop smuggling and provide safety and security to people all over the country. This rally was fired by the police wherein more than 30 persons died instantly. This was known as Minto Road Massacre. Leaders of JSD were arrested and many went underground. Its paper Ganokantho and offices were burnt down.

Siraj Sikdar's Sarbohara Party was highly militant which led people to seize of Government stores from where grains were distributed to the people. Police outposts were attacked. In a hunt out, the underground leader, Siraj Sikdar was caught and was shot dead by the Bangladesh police. Some of the underground militants who were legendary and were true soldiers of freedom, were against the exploitation and repression and wanted to rebuild the society free from communal and call-distinctions ethos, were either killed in encounters or fled to unknown destination for their safety.

Mushtaque Ahmed, Minister in Mujib Cabinet was CIA agent since the liberation government formed in Calcutta in April, 1971 and was removed from the post of Foreign Minister when RAW found him in league with a CIA operative in one hotel at Calcutta. He along with Taheruddin Thakur, the known pro-Pakistani collaborators, became stronger and meaningful in police and other department and got preference over the nationalist elements. Some military officers were dismissed from service on false charges at the behest of the confidants of Mujib, which brought discontentment among the rank and file of army.

RAW's Warnings Ignored

RAW was closely keeping tab on all these developments in Bangladesh through its sources in various departments. RAW received advance information of the conspiracy against Sheikh Mujibur Rahman which was hatched by some disgruntled junior officers in the units of artillery and cavalry. R N Kao personally informed this fact to the Prime Minister, Indira Gandhi and mentioned that these reports had been received through a very delicately placed source whose identity had to be kept secret at all cost. With her approval, Kao personally went to Dacca in December, 1974. He met Sheikh Mujibur Rahman at the Banga Bhavan and requested him to come out for a little stroll on the garden. When they were out of ear-shot, Kao conveyed to him the information which RAW had received about the danger to his life. Sheikh Mujib was euphoric at that time and waving his arms said, "These are my own children, they will not harm me". R N Kao did not enter into any argument with Mujib beyond saying that the information was reliable and that he would send him more details of the conspiracy in the future. As a follow up of the previous meeting in December,

1974, Kao sent one of his trusted RAW officers in March, 1975 to Dacca. This officer gave him exact details of the units and ranks of the serving and dismissed officers who were planning a coup against him but Mujib ignored all these warnings of RAW conveyed personally by Kao in December, 1974 and again in March, 1975 by his trusted RAW officer.

Mujib Killed

In the early hours of 15 August, 1975, four Majors of the Bangladesh army, Farooq Rehman and Khondkar Abdul Rasheed, related to one another as brother-in-laws and ex-Majors Shamshul Islam Noor and Shafiquer Rahman Dalim, both of whom had been dismissed from military service more than a year prior to the coup, with the help of some junior ranks of army numbering 47 killed Sheikh Mujib, 14 members of his family and 46 in total including relatives and friends in less than one hour. Around 30 tanks were deployed at vantage spots in the streets of Dacca to create fear psychosis among the residents to avoid any repercussions in the aftermath of the coup. Although, CIA was not directly involved in this coup but some members of the coup were certainly had the blessings of CIA operatives at American embassy in Dacca. This truth could be attributed to the fact when Eugene Boster, Deputy Chief of American Embassy tried to locate the American Ambassador at 6 A.M. next day, he was found driving his car in Dacca city to assess the prevalent situation after coup. When Major Rashid, one of the coup leaders informed CIA linked man Mushtaq Khondkar that the mission was completed, he enquired as if he was sure that Mujib was killed that night. Khondkar was made President of Bangladesh in the afternoon.

Surprisingly, after the news of coup was announced on radio, senior officers of the armed forces debated at the GHQ as to how they should deal with the Majors who had not only staged a coup but brazenly announced that armed forces had taken over in Bangladesh, which was actually not true. A couple of officers demanded immediate action against the Majors but majority of them dithered and were in favour of waiting till the picture become clearer. They did not risk their jobs because army chief Major-General Shafiullah was a man without any initiative and his authority was always challenged by his deputy, Major-General Ziaur Rahman which further proved beneficial for the coup leaders since no action was taken by these army officers against them. In this confused political scenario, all the service chiefs pledged their support to the new regime – a question which has remained unanswered in the political history of Bangladesh till now.

Allegations Unfounded

There were allegations that RAW had no advance information about this coup. These allegations are totally unfounded and untrue. Sheikh Mujib had acquired such a big political stature in Bangladesh at that time that he ignored the warning of RAW Chief R N Kao in December, 1974 and again in March, 1975 that there was no one in Bangladesh who would harm him. This illusion proved fatal for Mujib and he paid the price of ignoring the advance warning of RAW on two occasions.

❑

Emergency and R&AW

Emergency was imposed in India on June 25, 1975 by Indira Gandhi after she was disqualified by the Allahabad High Court for malpractices in the Lok Sabha election on the petition filed by her opponent Raj Narayan. She ruled the country with iron hand and proved herself as the biggest dictator of India during this period. Thousands of people were put behind bars without any charges of criminal conduct. Almost all political opponents were detained under Maintenance of Security Act (MISA) on frivolous charges. Excepting Chandrasekhar, there was not a single leader in the Congress Party, who opposed her for this draconian act of political vendetta.

Sanjay Power

Sanjay, Indira Gandhi's younger son created his own power centre in the country and dictated the entire administration with his whims and fancies. He had a blend of aggressive and motivated youth congress workers who created total chaos and malfunctioning of the Indian government. The Youth Congress workers resorted to extortion, looting and committing atrocities against general public and their political rivals. Sanjay's coterie was ruling in almost every state at the back of Indira Gandhi. Tyranny hatched out at the behest of selected cronies of Congress Party with vested interest, who had their own axe to grind and had nothing to do with the welfare of Congress Party or for Indira Gandhi, turned out to be a blunder for her political career. Imposition of such a barbaric rule saw total censorship of press in the country. All the news reports were censored and unfortunately the whole fourth estate community, except for a selected few, bowed to her diktat. Ram Nath Goenka of Indian Express was one of them who swam against the tide and had to face a lot of music and considerable heat for his newspaper. Indian judiciary was made to crawl as per the orders dictated by her or her stooges. There was only a single Judge, Justice H R Khanna, among the full Constitutional bench of Supreme Court of India, who dissented while justifying the proclamation of Emergency in the country. Other Judges acted like municipality clerks and favoured this darkest chapter of Indian independence. This period of Emergency is the biggest stigma on this largest democracy of the World which new generation of this country is hardly aware of.

Kao Blamed

R N Kao, head of R&AW, was one of the bureaucrats who was blamed for interfering in the internal affairs of the country during Emergency. Media reports after his retirement blamed that he overstepped his foreign affairs brief, interfered in domestic policy and supported the Emergency. It was also alleged that Kao took over as intelligence overlord overseeing domestic security operations on order from Indira Gandhi. The author personally discussed this subject with Kao who vehemently refuted all these unfounded allegations. Although, there were no specific cases wherein RAW was found involved in the internal affairs of the country during Emergency excepting creation of a special desk, namely, Front Organizations (Fo) in June, 1975 to keep a tab on the movement of political opponents of Indira Gandhi outside India. This fact is known to the author being a former RAW official. Telephone calls and postal letters of all these opponents were monitored by RAW operatives. Movements of these opponents and their family members were tracked outside India by RAW officers posted in foreign missions abroad. Laila, wife of George Fernandes, a bitter critic of Emergency, was suspected to have taken asylum in France with their Socialist Party. An enquiry was conducted by RAW in France but she was not traced there. Likewise, postal letters of Ram Jethmalani were censored at New Delhi by RAW during Emergency. This Front Organizations Desk was subsequently dismantled and its records were destroyed on the eve of Janta Party coming to power in March, 1977.

Kickback

The author came across only one instance of RAW's involvement in internal affairs of the country when Sankaran Nair, the then number two in the organization disclosed that a six million dollars kick-back payment was deposited in Swiss bank by Government of India through this agency. Nair was, however, ignorant about the source and reasons of this kickback. According to him, Kao was asked by Indira Gandhi to deposit this money through his trusted man in order to maintain the secrecy. Kao called Nair and said "Look they have requirement, so, will you talk to Gopi Kaul, the Finance Secretary about it". Gopi Kaul wanted

Nair to take this amount in foreign currency notes to Swiss bank in Geneva. Nair told Kaul that he would take some time to agree to it. He consulted one of his friends in Bank of Tokyo and enquired as to how many boxes he would require to carry these six million dollars, in highest denominations. His friend replied that five largest size of Samsonite cases would be required to carry this amount of currency. Nair returned to Gopi Kaul and said "I believe, this is the amount, this is how it has to be taken. I do no mind if government's money is gone but I do not want to be killed for this". Kaul was upset on this reply of Nair and then asked him to go to Bombay where he would order the Reserve Bank to authorize payment to him in Geneva by City Bank, their corresponding bank. Nair collected the cheque from Reserve Bank Governor in Bombay and deposited it at City Bank in Geneva where a numbered account was known to them and receipt was given to him.

When Janata Party came to power in 1977, Morarji Desai, the then Prime Minister, ordered the Reserve Bank Governor to enquire whether Six million dollars of money was deposited in the account of Sanjay Gandhi, younger son of Indira Gandhi, during Emergency. This enquiry related to the amount which Nair had deposited in Swiss Bank in Geneva. Reserve Bank Governor made enquiries in his bank and found that Morarji Desai wanted to sack a Deputy Governor, Luther, who was appointed during Emergency on the recommendation of Sanjay Gandhi. Luther knew about this transaction and he gave the telex copy to Morarji and told him that this money belonged to Sanjay Gandhi.

A detailed investigation was conducted in this transaction by the government. Subsequently, it was found that after Indira Gandhi conducted the Nuclear Test in May, 1974, USA government through its lobby of Nuclear Power monopolized countries imposed various economic sanctions against the Indian Government. These sanctions resulted into foreign exchange crunch in India adversely affecting the economy of the country. The Shah of Iran, though having soft corner for Pakistan, started developing respect for Indira Gandhi, the Indian Prime minister, after this nuclear explosion which was considered a bold step in breaking the monopoly of mighty powers in nuclear embargo, in the opinion of Shah. At this juncture of acute financial crisis, Hinduja brothers, the known wheeler dealers of that period were close to Sanjay Gandhi and offered to bail out the Government from the crunch by procuring help from Iran.

Against this background, Government of India requested the Shah of Iran for loan on soft terms for one of its industrial project, Kudremukh iron ore project. When Gopi Kaul, the Finance Secretary of India, went to negotiate the loan in Iran, he was helped to broker this deal by Hinduja brothers. After this loan was sanctioned by Iran with the help of Hinduja brothers, Kaul requested the Iranian government to give another 250 million dollars as straight loan to tide over sever foreign exchange problem, particularly to make payment for the outstanding dues of crude oil of Gulf countries. The Iranian Finance Minister who was against India, refused to give this additional loan to India. Hinduja brothers used their clouts and contacts in Iran successfully and through one Rashidyan, a local financier and close friend of Ashraf Pehlawi, the favourite sister of Shah of Iran got finalized this loan. Ashraf persuaded his brother, the Shah of Iran to sanction this additional loan to India on soft terms.

Hinduja brothers brokered a kick-back of Six Million Dollars from Government of India in the name of Ashraf Pehlawi and Rashidyan. Obviously, Indira Gandhi gave her consent to this transaction at the suggestion of Hinduja brothers, which was to be deposited in Swiss Bank at Geneva. This payment of kick-back in Geneva was to be deposited by the Ministry of External Affairs on behalf of Ministry of Finance. Since, Indira Gandhi wanted this sensitive kick-back transaction to be treated a closely guarded secret, she did not involve any foreign affairs officer and asked R N Kao to complete the transaction which he got executed through Nair. Reserve Bank Governor briefed Morarji Desai about this transaction which was not meant for Sanjay Gandhi but was deposited as kick-back in lieu of the loan got sanctioned through sister of Shah of Iran.

This kick-back controversy subsequently embarrassed both the ruling Janta Party and the Congress Party in 1977. Congress moved a no confidence motion in the Parliament against Morarji Desai Government over this payment and accused the then Foreign Affairs Minister, Atal Bihari Vajpayee, for lying in the Parliament that this kick-back was meant for a foreign agent who helped in procurement of much needed crude oil from the Middle East where Pakistan was instrumental to scuttle this supply to India by playing the Muslim card. Congress members waived copy of telex message to Geneva Bank from Reserve Bank of India and demanded to know how "Nair" mentioned in telex could be a foreigner and an oil broker. Vajpayee was either not properly briefed by Prime Minister Office or these facts were made known to the newly appointed staff in that office subsequent to the change of government after the Emergency. Sankaran Nair was watching these Parliament proceedings from the official's gallery enjoying the fake drama enacted by both the ruling and opposition parties on this no-confidence motion. This motion was, however, disallowed by the Speaker of Lok Sabha and the ruling Janta Party escaped from the embarrassment as Nair had given his consent to Congress to depose against Morarji Desai due to his past misbehavior with him. This was the only known incident when R&AW was found involved in the internal affairs during the Emergency. This was perhaps a single case in the history of independent India when a kick-back was officially sanctioned by the Prime Minister, Indira Gandhi to the so-called foreign agent through the Hinduja brothers. It is still a mystery whether the numbered account in which Sankaran Nair deposited the money belonged to the so-called foreign agent or to Hinduja brothers or Sanjay Gandhi.

Misconception About RAW

Morarji Desai who became Prime Minister after the 1977 general elections was put in jail by Indira Gandhi for the entire duration of emergency - from 25 June, 1975 to March, 1977. In his memoirs, he wrote that in any democratic country, no Prime Minister keeps all the intelligence agencies under his or her control but Indira Gandhi kept all these organizations whether belonging to the Home, Finance or Defence Ministries, under her control. He blamed her that R&AW, under a Kashmiri officer of her own choice, was created in 1967-68 for her personal gains. While agreeing to the creation of this agency as Finance Minister, Morarji claimed that he could not forgive himself for his stupidity in not seeing the possible implication of that seemingly innocent action. This was the instrument of coercion which Indira Gandhi used against all who came under her surveillance including member of her own Cabinet. These were the views of Morarji Desai about R&AW when he took over as the Prime Minister during Janta Party regime in 1977. Although no documentary evidence was found regarding involvement of RAW in the internal affairs of the country during Emergency or working at the behest of Gandhi against her political opponents but there was a general apprehension in public mind and in political circle that it was done so. However, it is on record that the then Information and Broadcasting Minister during Emergency, V C Shukla was accused of imposing censorship on press in this era. He took away two of his friends from IB and R&AW, K N Prasad and A K Verma on deputation in the I&B Ministry for this purpose. It was alleged that they were building dossiers not only on Journalists and their own officers but also creating a large scale network to spy on every high-ups in the government. Sophisticated electronic gadgets for bugging were imported in I&B Ministry for espionage activities. It was alleged that they were working in close association with R N Kao. These two officers were allegedly converting the entire Central Information Service into a gigantic intelligence organization They wanted to take 14 IPS Officers on deputation to I&B Ministry for this purpose.

Ill-treated

After Morarji became Prime Minister, he called R N Kao for a meeting in his South Block office. This was told to the author by Kao that when he went to meet Morarji Desai, a man in the late twenties or early thirties was sitting with the personal staff of Morarji Desai. He was bearded wearing a kurta over the pant. As soon as, Kao entered room of Personal Secretary to Morarji Desai, the same person pounced upon him and shouted that he was the killer of Emergency. Kao somehow managed to escape that assault and went into the room of Morarji Desai who was furious about the fact that R&AW was misused by Indira Gandhi during Emergency for her personal gains. He asked Kao details about it to which he denied that R&AW was misused against anyone during Emergency. When

Morarji Desai persisted with the enquiry, Kao requested him to conduct an inquiry in this regard so that real facts could emerge. He asked Kao to proceed on leave for the remaining period of his service. He also asked him to meet Chaudhry Charan Singh who was the Home Minister for further details in this context. Kao complained to Morarji that a man sitting in the room of his Personal Secretary tried to assault him. Morarji avoided the subject and his ignorance made Kao to believe that this assault was preplanned and he was aware of it. When Kao left Moraji's room, the man who tried to assault him was still sitting there and murmured the same words. Kao told the author that it was a deliberate ploy in the room of Morarji's PA to which whosoever may be responsible but silence of Morarji Desai on this incident definitely hurt him throughout his life.

Charan Singh too was furious with Kao when he met him in his North Block office and he also enquired about the involvement of R&AW for personal aims of Indira Gandhi during Emergency to which Kao repeated the same reply as he did with Morarji Desai. When Kao asked Charan Singh to appoint a Committee to inquire about any such involvement, Charan Singh told him that he was doing the same to get the truth. He appointed a one-man Committee headed by S P Singh, an IPS Officer of Maharashtra cadre, who was his son-in-law, to ascertain facts as to what extent RAW was misused by Indira Gandhi during Emergency to settle score with her political rivals.

After the exit of Kao, K Sankaran Nair, number two in RAW was appointed as Secretary. Nair an upright, flamboyant and plain-speaking fearless officer was called by Morarji Desai whom he repeated same questions which he asked Kao earlier. When Morarji asked to reduce the strength of R&AW to its half and stop all "immoral" operations inside and outside the country, Nair bluntly refused to do so. He tried to convince Morarji Desai that such government action would not only demoralize the cadre of R&AW but also severely affect the credibility of RAW towards its paid agents who were providing legal information through illegal means. When Morarji again told that he was downgrading the post of Secretary of R&AW to that of Additional Secretary, there was a high-pitched discussion between Nair and Morarji. Nair questioned Morarji that three months earlier, the Government appointed him as Secretary of R&AW and now he was downgrading him which he would not accept and rather prefer to take retirement. Nair immediately put up his resignation in the presence of Principal Secretary of Morarji, V Shankar. He was sent to the post of Secretary, Minority Commission to complete his term of retirement till December, 1978. These facts have been confirmed by Sankaran Nair in a tape-recorded interview to the author.

Stalwarts Out

That was the end of an era in Indian Intelligence when two of its top ranking officers who had acclaimed international reputation and were respected in other intelligence agencies of the World, had to make an unceremonious exit merely on suspicion. Their past contribution and sacrifice towards the benefit of Nation i.e. creation of Bangladesh, merger of Sikkim in a bloodless coup to the Indian State etc. were not given any credence while judging the spontaneous reaction of the Emergency period by Morarji Desai. Although, Kao returned to an advisory post during the comeback of Indira Gandhi in 1980 but thereafter from 1984 till his death, he lead a reclusive life. Nobody in the ruling circle even thought of recognizing his contribution to the Country by presenting him with a suitable award which many officers of very low caliber capability got due to sheer flattery. Shankaran Nair is still alive and living a retired life in London and Bangalore. The author found these two icons of Indian intelligence fraternity to be ill-treated by political bosses. Had they been in any other country, their contribution would have been properly recognized, but alas this was not done to them here. There was a big vacuum in the intelligence circle after these two stalwarts were shown door by Morarji Desai and no suitable replacement was available with the government. Some bureaucrats wanted to bring a few IPS officers from State services but ultimately N F Suntook, who was Chairman of Joint Intelligence Committee at that time, was appointed Chief of RAW to a lower rank as Director equivalent to that of Additional Secretary. He was only a matriculate and was nominated to North East Frontier Service which was created after independence. He was a very ineffective and timid person who totally depended on the advice of his juniors and was nowhere near his predecessors.

Operations Scuttled

Suntook could not resist the whims and fancies of Morarji Desai. RAW was reduced to two-third of its actual strength. All re-employed defence officers were removed from their services. Many directly recruited operatives, who were groomed as the future core of intelligence community by imparting training for two to three years, were dismissed from service. Among the dismissed staff were, field officers, economists, scientists, cipher and crypto officers. Some of them subsequently joined journalism and did substantial harm to the RAW authorities by exposing their working and internal secrets. In addition to the internal frustration which imbibed after the slashing of staff in RAW, there were many top secret operations inside India and in the foreign countries where large sum of amount was involved for the future policy planning. These operations were scuttled in the middle of their accomplishments and severely affected the morale of the operatives and operators. They felt themselves betrayed and cheated because they were caught in such a mess around them that when they were asked to stop the work they were assigned, they had to face the ire of other fellows with whom they were working in far flung areas. It was a state of limbo in RAW at that time because all the operational work came to a grinding halt abruptly irrespective of the fact that huge amount was already spent on these special operations. It would not be possible to evaluate the whole list of these small and big operations but some of them which were vital for the security and benefit of the country, need to be brought to the knowledge of the general public.

In Bangladesh, after the assassination of Sheikh Mujibur Rehman on 15 August, 1975, Khanodakar Mushtaq Ahmed was installed as President who too was overthrown by General Zia-ur-Rehman in a coup later. Zia-ur-Rahman got a referendum in his favour from the public with army support soon afterward. His army started persecuting the Mukti Bahini activists who did a Herculean task during the freedom struggle against Pakistan in 1971 war. It was a known fact that Mukti Bahini was the brainchild of R N Kao during the liberation of Bangladesh and most of them were in close contacts with the RAW operatives. More than 2,500 such Mukti Bahini activists under the leadership of Tiger Siddiqi crossed over to India to save their life from army. Tiger Siddiqi was the General of a faction of Mukti Bahini during the Bangladesh war of freedom and played a very vital and decisive role in that war. They wanted protection and help from the Indian government which was decided to be given unofficially when Kao was head during Emergency.

Tiger Siddiqi along with his followers was given shelter inside India and it was decided to give them funds to work against the undemocratic government of the dictator, Zia-ur-Rehman. They were asked to operate inside Bangladesh but in case of any danger from the Bangladesh security forces, BSF was instructed to allow them to cross inside the Indian territory so that their life could be saved. After Morarji Desai stopped all such operations, this operation was also dropped by RAW. After that 200 of these Mukti Bahini activists who had entered inside Indian territory when they were driven out by Bangladesh security forces, were handed over back to Bangladesh at the instance of Morarji Government. Most of these activists were killed by Bangladesh security forces instantly on Indian border. Luckily, Tiger Siddiqi their leader was not handed over to the security forces at the instance of Sankaran Nair who was handling this operation because he doubted the intention of Bangladesh government in this regard which ultimately proved him right. This was the biggest betrayal of Morarji government to the liberation war heroes of Bangladesh, who were working with the help of RAW, which resulted in mass killing.

In another identical case, some Chakma male refugees, who were persecuted by local Muslim population and the Mizo rebels who were trained inside Bangladesh by the Chinese to work against India, fled inside India. Muslim population wanted to dispossess them of their land with the help of Bangladesh security forces. They wanted help from the Indian Government to settle near

Agartala because they were provided all facilities by R&AW for their struggle against the Mizos, prior to the liberation of Bangladesh. They wanted to bring their families back to India which came to the knowledge of Bangladesh security forces through the Mizo rebels. Manabendra Larma, the Chakma leader with help from R&AW, was given asylum in India with the purpose only to organize refugee camps for these innocent Chakma community from oppression in Bangladesh. Sankaran Nair, the new Chief of R&AW, explained this position to Morarji Desai and wanted this help to be continued for the innocent Chakma population. Initially Morarji did not agree but when Nair put his foot down, he made him agree to continue this help to Chakmas. Thousands of their ladies and children were saved by R&AW from the clutches of Bangladesh security forces and were called in refugee camps inside India through clandestine routes. They were later on settled in the hilly terrain around Agartala. Had Nair not taken this tough stand before Morarji Desai, thousands of this Chakma population would have been butchered by Bangladesh security forces and Mizo rebels.

In addition to the above operations, Morarji Desai Govt. stopped payment without assigning any reasons to the R&AW agents who worked for the bloodless coup in the merger of Sikkim to Indian State. There were unconfirmed media reports that in another such operation, large amount of money was funded to Wali Khan a prominent North-West Frontier leader who had sought asylum in Afghanistan after the persecution of political opponents of General Zia ul Haq who in a coup overthrew Bhutto. It is alleged that, after Morarji Desai stopped further financial help to Wali Khan, he used the money already given to him for the cause of working against Zia ul Haq Govt;, for his personal aims and did not work for Indian Govt. thereafter. Sankaran Nair confirmed to the author that Wali Khan wanted Indian help for his political cause against the Bhutto government which was given with the consent of Indira Gandhi. But Morarji stopped this abruptly when he became Prime Minister in 1977.

These were the few cases where RAW had to stop all help to their agents who were working for them inside India and some other neighbouring countries. In addition to these, some operations in Western and South East Asian countries were dropped, which were planned to combat insurgencies in North East region of the country. This menace is still haunting the Indian security system. The present government instead of containing or countering it, has announced to talk with the leaders of insurgents to solve the problem of North East and other Naxal infested areas of Andhra and West Bengal. Hence, Morarji Desai government did irreparable damage to R&AW after the Emergency which is still haunting RA&W and adversely affected the morale of the agency to the extent that intelligence has failed everywhere after that. Our Prime Minister, Indira Gandhi was killed in her office and a former Prime Minister, Rajiv Gandhi too paid the price primarily due to the failure of Indian intelligence.

Parting Gift

After about six months, when Charan Singh appointed a Committee to ascertain facts about RAW's involvement in the internal affairs of the country during Emergency, S.P.Singh, his son-in-law gave his report to the government. This report totally exonerated R N Kao and Sankaran Nair who were number one and two in R&AW during Emergency. However, when Kao went to meet Morarji Desai after completion of his service on retirement in April, 1978, Morarji Desai told him that although nothing was found against him on record to prove indulgence of R&AW in the internal affairs during Emergency, yet he was still a suspicious officer in his eyes. However, Charan Singh, Home Minister, told Kao that he got the report of the committee and did not find any adverse facts against him and R&AW during Emergency. Kao overwhelmingly told Charan Singh that it was the best parting gift which he got from Indian Home Minister. Charan Singh then gave him a warm farewell. Although, after the inquiry about involvement of R&AW during Emergency, nothing indiscriminate was found against R N Kao and any other officer of R&AW yet Sankaran Nair during discussion with the author admitted that in some cases Indira Gandhi took the help of R&AW on some irregular and internal work which was given to them. This he admitted to Morarji Desai tacitly. Nair told Morarji that they were bureaucrats and had to work within a certain frame of policy on the wishes of the political rulers to whom they could not resist. Therefore, if Indira Gandhi used them against him, he could use them against Indira Gandhi to which Morarji Desai remained silent Hence, RAW was certainly used by Indira Gandhi selectively in the internal affair of the country during Emergency although there was nothing found no record to prove this fact because intelligence officers are not fool enough to leave any loose thread which will flap in the wind which could hit them back.

Shah Commission

Morarji government appointed Shah Commission to look into the circumstances leading to the imposition of Emergency in the country and the atrocities committed by the leaders of Congress party during this period. CBI case was registered against Indira Gandhi for imposing Emergency for internal disturbances in the country. Fearing venom, Indira Gandhi was determined to send her son Rajiv and his family to Kathmandu because King of Nepal had offered her asylum in his country in view of the changed political scenario in India. She consulted R N Kao in this regard who advised her not to accept this asylum because in case this news was leaked out, the general public might not resort to violence at the behest of new regime. He also gave his opinion that although Morarji Desai was a bitter opponent of her but he would provide all sort of protection to her family. She accepted this advice of Kao and remained in India. However, Yunus

Khan, a close associate of Indira Gandhi, wrote in a book that Kao took away the passports of Indira Gandhi family to give to Morarji Desai for cancellation which was highly motivated, false and mischievous since he was envious of his being very close to Indira Gandhi.

Nagarwala Case

Although not related to Emergency matter but the Nagarwala case related to the internal interference of R&AW in 1971 and as such required certain clarifications. On 24 May, 1971, V P Malhotra, Chief Cashier of State Bank of India, Parliament Street, New Delhi, received a telephone call introducing himself to be P N Haksar, Principal Secretary to Prime Minister, Indira Gandhi. He then asked that she required Rs. 60 Lacs for Bangladesh and he should make arrangement for that amount. He was instructed to treat this matter as "Top Secret" and should bring the amount himself. The caller then asked Malhotra to talk to the Prime Minister herself for further clarification. Thereafter, a female voice purporting to be that of Indira Gandhi, Prime Minister of India, told him to bring the money out of bank himself and hand over to a courier who should be recognized by the exchange of code words divulged to Malhotra. She assured Malhotra that he should collect the necessary voucher and receipt of this amount from her office after making the delivery. Malhotra was met by R S Nagarwala near Bible House on Parliament Street and was represented himself to be the courier sent by the Prime Minister. He also gave the code words to ensure Malhotra that he was the right person. Thereafter, Malhotra handed over the amount to Nagarwala.

Malhotra went to the Prime Minister's residence and failing to meet her there, he went to the Parliament House where he met P N Haksar, her Principal Secretary. Malhotra asked Haksar to give him receipt for the payment made to Nagarwala to which he was informed that no such demand was made either by the Prime Minister or any one else on her behalf. Malhotra immediately reported this matter to the police authorities as to how he was cheated in this case. Nagarwala was immediately arrested from a Parsee Dharamshala near Delhi Gate and entire amount was recovered from his friend's house at Defence Colony. Later on, there was uproar in the Parliament in this matter and government had to face a rough weather. Subsequently, Nagarwala was imprisoned for four years in this cheating case. He died in a mysterious condition inside jail but the medical report confirmed a cardiac arrest.

Stigma Hounds

There were numerous unconfirmed press reports that this money was withdrawn at the behest of RAW for the Bangladesh operations and Nagarwala was got killed by R&AW inside jail so that the real facts of this transaction remained an unresolved mystery. These two details were discussed by the author with R N Kao and K Sankaran Nair, his deputy in R&AW. Both emphatically denied that R&AW was ever involved in this case and had nothing to do with the death of Nagarwala inside jail. Nair had admitted in a tape recorded interview with the author that charges of Nagarwala that he was working for R&AW were rubbish and no money was deposited in the State Bank or anywhere for operations in Bangladesh. He affirmed that there was no dearth of funds for operational purposes in Bangladesh and as such where was the need for R&AW to indulge in this fruitless exercise knowing fairly well that this cheating case would be unearthed in the shortest possible time. Although, there was another angle to this mysterious transaction when Malhotra left his job from State Bank of India, he was rehabilitated as Chief Accounts Officer in Maruti Udyog, a dream automobile company of Sanjay Gandhi, the younger son of Indira Gandhi. Such immature political actions certainly bring stigma to these rulers of the country which certainly hound them till they were alive and these intelligence agencies are made target by media without any reason to explain.

❑

12

Revolt in R&AW

After the Emergency era of 1975-77, when general elections were held, Congress Party under the leadership of Indira Gandhi was swept away from power. In North India it lost miserably where only one Member of Parliament won his seat. Indira Gandhi too and her son Sanjay lost from Rae Barelly and Amethi in U P Morarji Desai who was in jail during whole of the Emergency period, became Prime Minister of the country. There was a general apprehension among political circle that R&AW, which was supposed to look after the external intelligence only, interfered in the internal affair of the country during Emergency and was misused by Indira Gandhi against her political opponents. Morarji Desai, a staunch opponent of Indira Gandhi, after assuming the charge of Prime Minister made his first bureaucratic targets of R&AW officers. After its head R N Kao and his deputy K Sankaran Nair were given marching orders, Morarji Desai ordered the new Chief of R&AW, N F Suntook to reduce strength of this agency to its two third of the existing size. Many young R&AW officers were dismissed from service and others on deputation from various departments, were reverted to their parent cares. Among the dismissed staff were Field Officers, Technical Experts, Economists, Scientists, Crypto, Secretarial and Cipher trained officials. Some of these sacked officers later joined journalism and did enormous harm to R&AW by exposing various internal secrets in the media.

In 1979, there was unrest among the police cadres of many states in India. Bihar and Punjab policemen went on unprovoked strike. Sensing the extent of indiscipline which was creeping in among the police staff of many other States, Government of India started some reconciliatory measures for police. Staff Councils were formed for Police in many other states. Discontentment was brewing in the Intelligence Organizations since there was no platform to take care of the grievances of the staff. There too, these Councils were recommended to solve administrative grievances of these agencies by the authorities concerned and their employees while sitting on one forum. In R&AW and IB, Staff Councils were appointed by the middle of 1979. These Staff Councils were supposed to meet every three months to review the past progress and worked out new agenda for the future course of action. But in R&AW, they met only once in 8 months. The then hierarchy of R&AW took this exercise as a stumbling block in their autocratic working culture. It would be pertinent to state that most of the senior officers of R&AW comprised of police officers which was against the formation of these councils.

However, Morarji Government could not complete its terms of five years due to internal squabbling among various factions of Janta Party during that period and mid term poll were announced in the end of 1979. Congress Party under Indira Gandhi again came to power in 1980 in a paper thin majority. In the meantime, R&AW authorities did nothing meaningful to boost the morale of the then depleted R&AW cadres as a result of the flogging given by Morarji's Government. The Staff Councils appointed to redress the administrative grievances, proved utter failure and subsequently made defunct by the Police hierarchy sitting on top level at R&AW. During the course of one such meeting, one senior R&AW officer belonging to IPS cadre made a sarcastic remark that due to his misfortune he was made to sit with these elements. The staff body took these uncalled for verbal attack as an insult and boycotted the Staff Council. Thereafter, some activists met at various places in New Delhi and decided to form their own Association which was duly registered on June 30, 1980 with the Delhi Government. R&AW authorities could not have any knowledge of this clandestine activity of the employees and big manhunt was launched thereafter to get the Association de-register with the concerned authority. Author was one of the leading force behind the formation of this Association in R&AW. Similar association was also formed and registered in the Intelligence Bureau at Delhi, where the employees were also facing this identical problem.

After three months of its formation, about 90 percent employees of R&AW became member of this Association at Delhi Headquarterss and in various outstation officers all over the country. Managing Committee of this Association sought recognition from the Government and wrote a comprehensive letter in this regard to the then Prime Minister of India, Indira Gandhi, under whom this department was functioning. This Association although not recognized by the Government, used to have regular meetings with the authorities to settle various administrative grievances of R&AW employees. Leaflets and posters were regularly distributed among the employees highlighting the motives of the Association on various demands. However, R&AW authorities never digested the formation of this Association and started making dissention among the activists by hook and crook. Some of these were lured for foreign postings and in turn they started hostility towards the cause of this Association. Authorities never wanted the emergence of a new power centre to counter their monopolistic functioning which was working unhindered henceforth.

In the beginning of October,1980, employees of Administrative wings of R&AW raised the demand of payment of security duty allowance to them at par with the other cadres. They had been discriminated for this allowance since the inception of R&AW which was never considered favourably by the authorities. One morning, they refused to dR&AW the keys of their respective rooms to open their offices and whole of the Headquarterss at Lodhi Road remained closed till afternoon when an urgent meeting was held by senior officers of R&AW with the author and another colleagues. It was agreed in this meeting to take up this matter with the Government of India. Soon thereafter, the branches at Headquarters start functioning in routine manner when the authorities realized the writing on the wall. Prior to this incident, around 100 sweepers who were working on daily wages were permanently absorbed in R&AW with the efforts of the Association. Soon thereafter, the author asked the employees to resume their duties and all branches at Headquarterss started functioning in routine manner.

Prior to this incident, around 100 sweepers of R&AW were working on daily wages basis for the last so many years. Since they were not on the regular roll of R&AW, some of them could be security hazard which authorities never realized. Author discussed this matter with the concerned officers and asked them to make permanent in their cadre. When these officers started dilly-dallying in this matter, the Association asked these sweepers to start a relay hunger strike in front of the R&AW Headquarterss. Soon, this strike started in a tent where large crowd gathered to watch this unprecedented incident in R&AW. When the strike reached seventh day and the R&AW authorities did not relent, the Association asked these employees to demonstrate with their family members including ladies and children from the next day. The author was again asked to intervene in this matter by the authorities to which he sought assurance that these employees would be regularized within two days. When the Author got assurance in this regard, he asked the sweepers to postpone the demonstration for two days to which they agreed. Next day, 85 sweepers of R&AW got regularization orders anbd made permanent in the organization. Similarly, most of the canteen staff was also functioning on ad-hoc basis. They also approached the author to get them absorbed in permanent posts. The author took up this issue also with the authorities to give these employees permanent status. Better sense prevailed in this regard and R&AW authorities accepted the proposal of the author and gave permanent job to all the canteen staff.

While an uneasy peace was prevalent in R&AW Headquarterss at Lodhi Road due to these two incidents, on a fateful day i.e. on 25 Nov., 1980, a senior officer of the rank of a Colonel of R&AW slapped a Scheduled Caste employee publicly due to some altercation while shifting the furniture of his room. This incident was spontaneously protested by the members of the Association with the authorities and demanded disciplinary action against that officer. Next day, R&AW authorities issued a draconian order that forbade the movement of R&AW employees at its Headquarterss from room to room and floor to floor basis so that employees could not assemble for their Association activities. Counter Intelligence and Security (CIS) staff was stationed outside every room on each floor of this 11 storey building to monitor the movement of the employees. This action caused uncontrollable resentment among the rank and file of the cadre working in this building. Curfew like situation was deliberately created by the authorities for confrontation with Association. It was now and never opportunity for them to settle score with the employees.

Next day, on 27 November, 1980, office bearers of the Association went to meet the head of CIS unit at R&AW Headquarterss to withdraw this nasty order which would hamper their routine working due to this uncalled for restriction imposed on the movement of employees on floor to floor basis. When the concerned officer refused to relent on this issue, there were allegations and counter-allegations among those who were present at the scene. Situation became explosive when authorities threatened to resort to strict action against the office bearers of the Association. This news spread like fire in the building and whole of the employees at R&AW Headquarterss stopped their work and assembled in open area of the building to protest against that autocratic action of the authorities. Three officers of R&AW were Gheraoed and confined into one room. This incident started at 11 in the morning and continued till evening when R&AW Chief Suntook, who used to sit in South Block office, came to the Headquarterss personally to meet the office bearers of the Association to break the deadlock. He was misguided by a coterie of IPS officers who frightened him that his life would be in danger if he would go to the place where R&AW staff had assembled. Instead, they had made preparations for a police action and sought assistance from Delhi police and thereafter R&AW Headquarterss was cordoned off by several hundred of policemen of Delhi police. Around 7 in the evening, a senior officer came to the site of agitation, fully drunk, and warned those present there that if they would not relent, they would be taught the lesson of their life. This provocation added fuel to the fire and the employees became more rigid in this confrontation.

When all negotiations to sort out a possible solution to this ugly situation did not materialize, Delhi Police along with 25 trucks of CRPF soldiers stormed into the eleven storey R&AW Headquarterss building around 8 at night. All the employees, including ladies, who were present in the building were severely beaten and 33 were taken into police custody. All the office bearers were arrested on the spot and taken to three police stations, Lodhi Road, Nizamuddin and Defence Colony of South Delhi. On direction from R&AW authorities, all these arrested employees were subjected to inhuman torture in these police stations and later on taken for medical treatment in a local Government hospital. Author was given special treatment by the police officials at Lodhi Road police station where a team of R&AW officers was specially deputed by the authorites for this dastardly act. Next day, on 28 November, whole of the staff of R&AW at Delhi and in other cities all over India, went on strike voluntarily to show solidarity to their fellow employees who were got arrested by R&AW authorities. All the arrested employees were granted bail by a Delhi Court at Patiala House where thousands of employees had assembled to stand surety for the arrested office bearers of the Association and other colleagues. All these 33 employees were suspended from service the same day by the authorities.

On 29 November, 1980, whole of the staff of R&AW at Delhi and other outstation offices all over the country, went on an indefinite strike to demand withdrawal of police cases and reinstatement of the suspended employees. All the 33 suspended employees were debarred to enter the building of the Headquarters. So, an indefinite relay hunger strike by the suspended employees was started outside the entry gate of Headquarters. Delhi police took control of safety outside the building and policemen were deployed on main gate and other vital position outside the complex of Headquarters. When the deadlock for reconciliation was not broken for few days, on 4 December, 1980, several hundred lady employees of R&AW met Indira Gandhi, the then Prime Minister, at her residence and narrated their woes to her. They requested her intervention in this matter to which she was sympathetic. She did not take any action in spite of the assurance she gave to these lady employees that she would personally call the Association office bearers and listen to their grievances. Even thereafter, R&AW authorities suspended 19 more employees, including a lady, in Delhi and elsewhere in India. An internal effort was made by some senior officers on 6 December, 1980, to settle the matter but this move was also thwarted by a senior lobby of IPS officers who had sinister designs to defame the then head of R&AW, Suntook, who was a non IPS officer.

This agitation ultimately intensified in the branches of R&AW all over the country. After two weeks, when there was no indication of an end to this agitation to diffuse, R&AW authorities took the extreme step and dismissed 8 employees, including a lady, at Delhi Headquarters and 2 at Lucknow office, from service without assigning the reason of their dismissal. Fearing more such dismissal all over India, the Association at once, called off the strike on 8 December evening and again requested the Govt. to intervene in this matter but nothing was done. There was uproar in the Parliament on 11 December against the atrocities in R&AW but the then Government did not relent to resolve the matter. After that, the Association filed writ petition against these dismissal in Delhi High Court, which intervened and issued directions to R&AW authorities not to dismiss any more employees hereinafter in that situation. Subsequently, confidential reports of more than 2,500 employees were given adverse remarks by the authorities all over the country as a result of this agitation and ruined their future prospects in promotion and other benefits.

This Revolt in R&AW certainly became stigmatic and tarnished the image of the organization because most of the Indian and foreign press covered this happening in details. In order to redeem some favour from the media, in the middle of December, 1980, A K Verma, a Joint Secretary in R&AW, through a senior journalist of Blitz, a weekly Bombay magazine, invited some prominent media persons, for a cocktail party in a five star hotel in New Delhi. Verma gave a briefing about the ongoing revolt inside R&AW and put the blame on a foreign agency for this agitation. One journalist Patwardhan of a weekly, the Current, asked Verma if this uprising was engineered by CIA. Initially Verma gave assent to this reply but when Patwardhan further probed that if CIA could penetrate inside R&AW and was responsible for the uprising then it was capable enough to even dislodge the Indian Government. Verma had no answer to this observation and the press briefing was abruptly wounded up and the host and his cohorts realized the mistake to mislead the media persons present in that party.

In this two week of turmoil in R&AW, 52 employees were suspended and 10 dismissed from service. Among these was a Scientist of Science and Technical Division of R&AW. This brilliant officer was instrumental in detecting the location of a nuclear plant at Kahuta in Pakistan in 1978 and presented proof whereupon the Morarji Desai Government raked up this issue before the World. This officer was decorated with a reward by Government of India for this achievement. There was another senior field operative who worked in Kashmir in the difficult days during IB and was decorated with many awards. Besides these two, there were many competent officers from Language Division, Economic Division, Field officers and good number of Secretarial officials among these suspended and dismissed from service. Two ladies were specifically suspended and dismissed because they had gone to meet the Indian Prime Minister, Indira Gandhi and narrated the inside misery of their working to her. This was done deliberately to deter the ladies of R&AW to work for the Association in future.

While this untoward incident was raking up in R&AW, three office bearers of IB employees Association, were dismissed on 27 December, 1980 by IB authorities falsely invoking article 311(2(c) of the Constitution and as such backbone of that Association was broken by these dismissal. Intelligence Bureau too was apprehensive that this agitation of R&AW might not spread in their organization and as such in preemptive action, these employees were dismissed which produced desired result and the activities of IB Association became standstill thereafter. Most of their activists were transferred in far flung areas and strict discipline code was imposed at various offices in and around Delhi. This agitation of R&AW proved disastrous to the demands of IB employees who could never raised their voice after the happenings of R&AW. Their fire-brand President, B B Rawal, who was one of the dismissed employees, later started his career as a Lawyer in Delhi and was elected President of the Central Administrative Tribunal Bar Association. He filed many cases in various courts to highlight the prevalent corruption in IB and R&AW. He died of a heart attack in 2013.

In January, 1981, the author sought an appointment with R N Kao, the founder of R&AW, who was appointed as Senior Advisor by Indira Gandhi, the Prime Minister. Kao met the author in his Rashtrapati Bhavan office and a long meeting of more than two hour took place wherein full details of this agitation was discussed in a very cordial environment. In the end, Kao assured the author of a positive solution of this problem. At the end of the meeting, Kao stood up and escorted the author to the gate of his office and shook hands with him to the utter astonishment of the author since no such treatment he had ever received from other senior officers of R&AW. The author discovered the highest sense of sincerity and dignity from this icon of Indian intelligence. Since then meeting with Kao, a permanent relationship to be compared to a father and son, developed between him and the author which continued till the death of Kao. Further incidents would reveal that Kao did not care to the rank which author held but maintained a family like relation with him for the reasons best known to him.

Kao discussed this matter with Suntook in January itself and soon the author was called by Suntook to his South Block office to break the deadlock. Since, the pot was still boiling hot due to media hype and political uproar in Parliament, Suntook was little aggressive in that meeting. Presumably, young age of the author seemed to be the reason for this aggression because most of those R&AW officers present in that meeting were quite senior to him in rank and bigger in age. He accused the author of inciting the cadre of R&AW in the agitation to which he agreed on the plea that situation was made to go out of hand by a coterie of some officers of R&AW at the Headquarters on that day of incident. Suntook wanted an unconditional apology from all and sundry, which the author refused and suggested a face-saving solution in a dignified manner for both, the authorities and the employees. Suntook did not relent on his demand to which the author politely refused. While departing from his room, the author warned Suntook that 62 employees roaming on the streets of the capital of India, would damage the already sagging reputation of the organization and he should not be blamed for that by the future generation of R&AW. Suntook replied that he would meet all the consequences be it at any cost. The author never took the opportunity to again approach Suntook in this case. For the first time since its inception in 1968, Indian public became aware that a secret organization with the name of R&AW had been functioning under the Government and much more to know about its internal affaairs became a sense of curiousity thereafter.

Author briefed Kao about his discussion with Suntook in his office. But he got the impression that Suntook too had already given the details of the meeting to Kao prior to author. The meeting arranged by Kao did not yield any fruitful results but, Kao and the author developed a sense of deep mutual respect for each other probably on the frank and forthright stand taken by the author with Suntook which was conveyed to Kao by him. Probably, Suntook might have exaggerated the aggressive postures which happened with him in his office in the presence of other R&AW officers. Kao did not utter any dissenting opinion on that matter and rather assured the author that he would find out a solution to this problem at the appropriate time in the future. This meeting with Kao too lasted for more than an hour and the eminent journalist, Patwant Singh, was made to sit for long to meet Kao. He again came to the door of his office to take leave of the author and sought assurance from him to continue their relations in the future whatever might be the outcome of official matter. B K Ratnakar Rao, who later retired as Special Secretary of R&AW, was Staff officer of Kao and escorted the author to the outer gate of his Rashtrapati Bhavan office.

After this strike, N F Suntook ordered embargo to post competent officers of R&AW in foreign missions after this strike so that they should take stock of the murky situation inside R&AW and take suitable measures to boost the sagging moral of the cadre. A number of mediocre IPS officers who were instrumental for this fiasco, were sent abroad to keep them away from the activists of Association. These included A K Verma, Joint Secretary, M D Dittia, Director and U N B Rao, Assistant Director, who were shunted out abroad to soothe the growing anger against them among the employees. One traitor, A I Vasavada who was the founder member of this Association and was made to defect to work for the authorities clandestinely, was also given a foreign posting much to the resentment of the employees. Rakesh Mittal another IPS officer who was inquiry officer against 19 employees and got them dismissed or punished with major penalties, was rewarded with a foreign posting in London and then Islamabad where he was severely beaten by ISI and had to be brought to India in a special plane for medical treatment. Besides these, some middle rank officials who used to feed malicious information against the Association, were also rewarded with posting in foreign missions. These arbitrary decisions of Suntook further damaged the internal situation of R&AW.

These 62 suspended and dismissed employees used to meet regularly at various places in New Delhi to chalk out strategy to get away from that intolerable situation. In order to ventilate their grievances, they used to meet several political leaders of various political parties including Atal Bihari Vajpayee, Chaudhry

Charan Singh, Chandershekhar, H N Bahuguna, Chanderjit Yadav, Madhu Dandwate, Som Nath Chaterji, Shahbuddin etc. Most of these leaders took up the cause of these employees with Indira Gandhi but did not yield to any favourable result due to her obstinate attitude. In the Parliament, the Government had to face rough weather while defending questions pertaining to the ongoing problems of R&AW employees. Every time false and misleading replies were put before the Parliament members instead of taking some wise steps to resolve the matter. However, the author developed a good personal rapport with some of the leading politicians of that era and Atal Bhihari Vajpayee was one of them.

Suntook had to face a torrid time in R&AW due to his stubborn behavior he portrayed to the author after his meeting arranged by Kao to resolve this matter. In the 1980-81 winter, all the outside walls of R&AW Headquarterss were painted with oil paints by these employees with slogans around 7 in the evening. Next day, special chemicals were researched to wash away these slogans and thereafter lot of armed SSB personnel were deployed around R&AW Headquarters to counter such move of the Association in future. But the employees, most of them of young age, did not relent and resorted to trade unionism on parallel line with politicians to get their demand resolved at any cost. Regular posters about misrule of R&AW authorities were got painted on the walls in Parliament Street opposite Parliament House, PTI, UNI and other press offices on Bahadur Shah Zafar Marg. CIS unit of R&AW deployed its operatives who used to take hired labourer in government vehicles and get removed these posters in the early morning to escapte the knowledge of media and politicians. A special team of officers was created in CIS unit who used to patrol in night at various vantage points in the capital of Delhi to search for such posters pasted by R&AW employees Association and get those removed before the next morning. This exercise continued for many months and hide-seek between the R&AW sleuths and Association activists in the streets of New Delhi. R&AW authorities under Suntook preferred to resort to these undignified practices rather and wise sense never prevailed upon their mind to find out a face saving formula for the ongoing problems. Numerous articles appeared in the press about these happenings and other internal functioning of R&AW. A section of some senior officers wanted this game to continue for their personal benefit.

Suntook retired on 31 March, 1983 amid a controversy that he along with his wife discreetly fled the country on 30 March, one day prior to his retirement. A leading Bombay newspaper published a cover story in this regard with a banner "India's Top Spy Missing. Biggest escape since Philby-US suspected destination, panic in ruling party". It reported that N F Suntook, head of R&AW had defected to US with sensitive documents. Later on, another R&AW officer wrote in a book on this matter that this news was planted some activists of the Association of R&AW at that time. However, Government issued a clarification later in this regard that he had gone on a mission in a friendly country in Indian ocean. The author was informed by a senior R&AW officer much later that Indira Gandhi got a SOS call from the Prime Minister of Mauritius that his Government was suspecting a coup at the behest of certain foreign power and he required her help since he lost faith in his own intelligence. So, Suntook was sent to Mauritius to render his advice to their Prime Minister. He returned to India on 12 April and the controversy was diffused. How far it was true, could not be corroborated but the fact remained that Suntook in spite of what he did towards the R&AW Association, could never be blamed for any activity detrimental to the security of the country. He was a true nationalist. Unfortunately, his post-retirement life was full of pain and agony till his death although R&AW took proper care of him.

G C Saxena succeeded Suntook and became fourth head of R&AW in April, 1983. He was the guiding force to Indira Gandhi on terrorism which was spreading its wings in Punjab and other parts of North India. She gave a statement on advice of Saxena that intelligence had failed in Punjab because some trade unionist and casteist were recruited during the regime of Janta Party. Her indication towards casteist word was for Sikh officers working in R&AW. The author, in his capacity as General Secretary of the R&AW Association, issued a clarification that during Janata Party Government, Morarji Desai slashed the strength of R&AW to its two-third and as such there was no recruitment during that period and question of any trade-unionist or casteist joining R&AW during Janta regime did not arise. It was also clarified that either she was grossly misguided by her advisors or words had been put in her mouth to sidetrack their inefficiency to tackle the terrorist problem in Punjab. G C Saxena issued a charge-sheet against the author on this clarification in press. The author got reprieve from the Court. Later, he summoned the author for solution of the ongoing problem after assassination of Indira Gandhi amid the election campaign of Rajiv Gandhi. The author found him totally unaware of the outcome of the election results because he was worried about his fate if opposition would come to power. He tape-recorded the conversation with him and put permanently in the archives of R&AW because it was used by a subsequent R&AW Chief against the author. Such so-called stalwarts were responsible for the Blue Star operation after which Indira Gandhi perished and Rajiv Gandhi got the thumping majority in the 1984 general election due to her death.

Some time after operation Blue Star, a middle-rug level Congress leader arranged meeting of the author with R K Dhawan, the powerful Private Secretary of Indira Gandhi, in the Parliament House office of the Prime Minister. Author briefed Dhawan in detail about the root cause of many problems inside R&AW as a result of which such big revolt erupted in November, 1980. He also apprised Dhawan of the growing danger which these employees were spreading in press and with political leaders which would haunt the working condition of R&AW

in the coming future. Some issued related to Punjab were also discussed because intelligence failed there due to this agitation in R&AW. Dhawan assured the author that he would soon discuss this matter with the Prime Minister whereupon he would call him for a one to one meeting with her. The author apprised Kao of this development who was then sitting in Bikaner House. Kao assured the author that this positive development could ensure a settlement but when author insisted that he too should talk to Indira Gandhi first, Kao replied that on his own he would not talk on this matter to the Prime Minister but if she would seek his opinion, he would certainly help to get it resolved. However, due to the tragic death of Indira Gandhi on October 31, 1984, this issue again remained unresolved and legal cases of these employee continued to hang in various Courts in Delhi and Lucknow.

After the retirement of G C Saxena another IPS officer S E Joshi succeeded him as head of R&AW. The author had a brief encounter with Joshi in July, 1980 when he met him in his R K Puram office after the formation of Association of employees in R&AW. Joshi told author that he was in dark about these developments and thereafter a long discussion took place on the internal affairs of R&AW. Author found Joshi quite reasonable and forthright in his approach towards the problems of employees.

S E Joshi, who was expert of Pakistan, had very excellent rapport with the then Prime Minister, Rajiv Gandhi. Joshi was averse to the media hype about R&AW. Soon after his taking over as R&AW Chief, one newspaper published his rare photograph which disturbed him and he scolded the branch head of CIS unit for this publication. Author was given to understand by a senior R&AW officer that Joshi was fed up with the confrontation of the authorities with the employees and wanted to break the stalemate.

One fine morning, an emissary of R&AW came to the residence of the author and informed him that Joshi wanted to settle the suspension and dismissed cases of 62 employees which were languishing in various courts at New Delhi. The author enquired as to why he had the hitch to do so. He informed that Joshi wanted the initiative should come from the author. This was crosschecked by author through his sources inside R&AW. He consulted his colleagues in this regard who impressed upon him to call for a meeting with Joshi. Some time in August, 1986, the author telephoned S E Joshi and sought appointment with him which was immediatley granted. The meeting took place in his office at R&AW Headquarters in the evening. This one to one meeting lasted more than one hour wherein most of the issued related to the court case of 62 employees were discussed. Both Josh and the author made up their mind to get these resolved at the earliest. However, Joshi told the author that he would need the consent of the Prime Minister in this regard. He assured that he would again call him after three days for further discussion if Prime Minister agreed to this parley.

After three days, Joshi again called the author in his office and informed him that the Prime Minister had given his consent to break the ongoing stalemate. Joshi gave one page third person note to the author outlining some pre-conditions to settle this issue. He, however, gave an optimistic assurance that if they disagreed on a particular point, they should not hamper the big problem and settle the other issues before returning to the original point in future. The author gave assurance of a positive approach and sought some time to take decision on the proposal of Joshi.

After some protracted deliberations among his colleagues and thereafter with Joshi, a framework for the withdrawal of all the court cases was devised by Joshi and the author. Subsequently, all cases against these 62 employees were withdrawal and they were reinstated in R&AW from 1 March, 1987 onward in batches. There was a humorous discussion with Joshi when author asked him about the placement of these employees in Delhi or elsewhere. Joshi told that this was his prerogative as to he would keep all in Delhi, or send some outside or transfer everyone out of Delhi. Author told Joshi frankly that since they had clear opinion on each and every issue, there should be no confusion on this point to which Joshi was hesitant to accept. Then author told Joshi that if he could not say no on this matter then say yes to which he laughed loudly.

All 33 employees who were implicated in criminal cases, were reinstated and joined back in R&AW on 1 March, 1987 in the same rank and on the same pay. Other 29 were also taken back one by one depending upon the nature of case and time to complete the proceedings. Both ladies were subsequently reinstated along with other employees.

This strike in R&AW and further developments of intelligence failures, were regularly reported by the print media during the eighties. Had the current pro-active electronic media been available during that period of agitation in R&AW in 1980, situation would have been totally different and the ugly confrontation between the authorities and employees which was diffused after 7 years in 1987, could have been sorted out instantly in December, 1980 itself. Although, many national newspapers covered this event regularly but Government did not react so promptly due to lack of private electronic media at that time. BBC covered this event in its radio and TV news on one or two occasions. Reuters too published a story on it.

This uncalled event in R&AW, directly affected more than 3,000 employees out of the total strength of 5,000 in 1980. One could very well imagine the internal mismanagement in R&AW at that time whose seeds were sown on Novt. 1980 which had become a tree later on. These employees on roads of New Delhi, used to ventilate their grievances to many political leaders and in the press but the massive majority in 1984 elections which the Congress Party got after the assassination of Indira Gandhi, further blinded the eyes of the then ruling Government. At the behest of G.C.Saxena, Government passed another draconian Act i.e. Intelligence Organisations (Restriction of Rights) Act, 1985, and banned union activities in R&AW and IB and made it a cognizable criminal offence for the employees to even meet the media people.

That ghost of November 1980 agitation of R&AW is still hounding the working culture inside R&AW because those 3,000 employees, who were directly affected at that time, are still serving in R&AW but their attitude of self belonging was swept away and they are still disgruntled because they did not get their promotion and other benefits in time which affected their morale and mental make up. They all have been superseded in promotion and treated step-motherly in comparison with other fellow employees. To cite a practical example of this anomaly, most of the Secretaries of R&AW during their span of service for the last 25 years, have earned minimum six promotions whereas a constable, a clerk, a field Officer and other junior rank officers have got maximum two promotions in this period. Such big anomaly in senior and junior cadres in R&AW would never bring the effective and disciplined working conditions among the junior cadres which is the backbone of this premier intelligence agency of the country and the Government is still not taking seriously this matter. Accountability of R&AW had never been taken seriously by any Government at the centre.

❑

Morarji Desai–CIA Agent and Indira Gandhi Bitch- American Deception

An investigative USA journalist Seymour Hersh, has written a book "THE PRICE OF POWER" in which he elaborately wrote a chapter on the India-Pakistan war of

1971 when Bangladesh was carved out of Pakistan. In this book, he made two derogatory, unfounded and insulting references against two former Indian Prime Ministers – Indira Gandhi and Morarji Desai. His first reference related to Indira Gandhi in which he mentioned that Nixon had hated Indira Gandh and viewed her as a deceitful "Bitch", a view that Henry Kissinger was careful to emulate. Nixon visited New Delhi in 1967, during a private tour around the world, when he was not given a ceremonious treatment by Indira Gandhi for which he was unhappy with her. He vividly remembered a dinner with a leading Indian politician, Piloo Mody, who was a vegetarian and did not drink. In Pakistan, the treatment was much better. Yahya Khan, with his aristocracy and military pomp and show, honoured Nixon as the future President of US with a sumptuous dinner with a variety of scotch.

Deceitful Bitch

In early November, 1971, Indira Gandhi visited Washington for a meeting with President Nixon to apprise him that unless Yahya Khan was warned to modify his policies, war was inevitable in the region. On the second day of her meeting with Nixon, he unfolded the perceived insult of his 1967 visit to India by making her wait for forty-five minutes before final encounter. One of Kissinger's aides realized some thing unusual when Kissinger didn't show up before the appointed time. In order to avoid further embarrassment to her, he took Indira Gandhi upstairs in the Roosevelt Room to save the ugly situation. No apology was given to her for this pedestrian behavior of treating a state head that too the largest democracy of the world. This was a deliberate attempt on the part of Nixon but to quote Indira Gandhi a deceitful bitch is a graver insult not only for her but to every Indian. Surprisingly, either this book has never been read or scrutinized by any Indian official in the Ministry of External Affairs or this fact has been foolishly overlooked for more than three decades of its publication.

CIA Agent

The second reference concerning another Indian Prime minister, Morarji Desai, related to their hard line attitude towards India. Seymour Hersh wrote that both Nixon and Kissinger justified this approach on the basis of a "reliable source" who was reporting from India through CIA. This source was never named for obvious reasons. According to Hersh, Nixon and Kissinger might have been honourable in protecting the man but few in the American government who knew his identity must also had known that his information was highly biased. The informant was undoubtedly described by Hersh as Morarji Desai, a prominent Indian politician who was fired from the post of Deputy Prime Minister by Indira Gandhi in 1969 – but stayed in her cabinet – after a bitter political dispute. According to Hersh, Desai was a paid informer for the CIA and was considered one of the Agency's most important "asset". He had been in public life since the late 1940s, serving as Chief Minister of the state of Bombay, India's Finance Minister, and briefly, as Deputy Prime Minister. He was a political reactionary and a bitter opponent of Prime Minister Gandhi; his hostility showed repeatedly in his book "The Story of My Life." He further wrote that former American intelligence officials recalled that Desai was a star performer who was paid $20,000 a year by the CIA during the Johnson Administration through the 303 Committee, the covert intelligence group that was replaced by the 40 Committee under Nixon and Kissinger.

He further added that one official of CIA remembered that Desai continued to report after Nixon's election, much of his information having to do with contacts between the Indian Government and the Soviet Union. According to this official, Kissinger was "very impressed with the asset. He couldn't believe it was really in the bag." During meetings with CIA and other officials dealing with international crisis, he would occasionally smile knowingly and say to Helms, the CIA Chief, or one of his deputies, "Why can't you have a source in the cabinet."

In the footnote Seymour Hersh quoted "I have been able to establish firmly that Desai was reporting through 1970. After that year, the officials who were willing to discuss Desai's information with me were no longer in position to see his reports, which presumably continued to flow to Washington. American officials inadvertently provided another hint that the reports were continuing by stressing the high position and proven reliability of the source they used in late 1971 to try to justify the administration's policy in the war against Pakistan. Desai became Prime Minister in March, 1977. Indira. Gandhi returned to office in July, 1979." This fact is far from any truth since Morarji Desai never worked in the Cabinet of Mrs. Gandhi after the bifurcation of Congress in 1969. After a gap of eight years of political oblivion, he became Prime Minister of India in 1977 when Indira Gandhi and her party lost the General Election.

Concocted facts

Seymour Hersh further wrote a totally false and concocted fact in this book that CIA received a report, allegedly from inside the Cabinet of New Delhi contact, during the India-Pakistan war in the first week of December, 1971 which was full of tough talk from Prime Minister Indira Gandhi. The source, as described by Kissinger, could only have been Morarji Desai. "A report reached us from a source whose reliability we had never had any reason to doubt and which I do not question today to the effect that Prime Minister Gandhi was determined to reduce even West Pakistan to impotence" Kissinger said. He was of the opinion that the intelligence showed that Indira Gandhi would proceed with the liberation of the southern part of the Pakistani province of Kashmir long an area of dispute between India and Pakistan and continued fighting until the Pakistani army and air force were wiped out. The report handed directly to Kissinger without any evaluation, was seized by the White House to justify its policies. Nixon and Kissinger relied heavily on it in their memoirs. According to Hersh they did it knowingly that the information turned out to be incorrect because India did not invade West Pakistan. There was another flaw in the intelligence. According to Indian Ambassador L K Jha and other officials, the Indian cabinet as a whole did not discuss sensitive military issues. Indira Gandhi instead relied on a small sub-cabinet committee in which the CIA was not likely to penetrate. This fact is self contradictory because Morarji Desai was not in the Cabinet of Indira Gandhi at that time and was an opposition leader. Secondly, after the liberation of Bangladesh Mrs. Gandhi offered a unilateral cease fire on the western border which was accepted by Yahya Khan. Hence, facts of this report are either self invented by CIA or the CIA was grossly misguided by their agent, if any, because he could never be Morarji Desai, former Indian Prime Minister.

These remarks by an American writer about the two former Indian Prime Ministers i.e. calling Indira Gandhi a "bitch" and Morarji Desai as 'CIA agent" is a direct insult to this biggest democracy of the World. Seymour Hersh had no business to quote the personal remarks of Nixon about Indira Gandhi which could not be substantiated in the absence of any documentary evidence. This was highly derogatory, irresponsible and insulting not only to Indira Gandhi but also to entire India. Strangely, no upright Congressman of the party of Indira Gandhi who is highly respected till today, has not found enough courage to take Seymour Hersh in any Court of Law anywhere in India or in USA for these unsavoury remarks in his book.

Hersh Challanged

As regards the fact about Morarji Desai being tainted as CIA agent by Seymour Hersh, a Chicago based organization of Indians Abroad For Truth (IAFT) filed a case against him where some misleading instructions and information were given to the court which resulted in the acquittal of Seymour Hersh. It was pleaded by Seymour Hersh that he sent the transcript of the chapter "Indian and Pakistan war" , in which the allegations against Desai appeared, to the Indian Embassy in Washington for a review before its inclusion in the book. This fact was confirmed by the lawyer of Morarji Desai Cyriac Kappil, who contested his case against Seymour Hersh that he had in his possession a copy of the manuscript of author Seymour Hersh's book which contained notes of comments made by an Indian official of Indian Embassy in Washington during that period whom Hersh claimed as a diplomat in Indian Embassy at Washington during 1981-82. Kappil further said that he spoke in this regard to Indian Ambassador K.Shankar Bajpai in 1983, a day before he was to return to India after his term was over, for help from the Embassy by providing files that would provide samples of the handwriting of the concerned diplomat, but he did not cooperate in this matter. He made the same request to his successor P K Kaul who also did not give any help to him. In 1986, Kappil visited India and met several officials of External Affairs Ministery in New Delhi in this regard but got no response to get at the root of the matter. He sought cooperation from the Indian Government in this case but no one helped him. He wanted the deposition of Jagjivjan Ram, a prominent politician, in this case too no avail. He met former ambassador L K Jha who according to Kappil was very courteous and supportive but he was also tightlipped in this case. Kappil further said that Hersh testified during the trial that he was very friendly with Indian Ambassador K R Narayanan in 1981-82 while he was his neighbour, during the period in which he was helped by the Indian diplomat in his manuscript.

Strangely, neither the Indian External Affair Ministry nor the Indian Govt. or any retired Ambassador from Washington or any Indian leader made any attempt to verify the fact as to which Indian diplomat gave his consent to the manuscript of Seymour Hersh in which he quoted Morarji Desai as CIA agent. On the other hand, the lawyer of Desai was in possession of the handwriting of that official which could very well be identified by the officials of External Affair Ministry as to who were there to whom Seymour Hersh gave the manuscript and who gave his approval to it. This was not a long or complicated investigative exercise but a simple verification of the facts which, for reasons best known to the Indian Government, is still not been probed which could clear the name of a leader of high moral values and a true nationalist. This uncalled for reference is still haunting him as a stigmatic Indian Prime Minister in Hersh book.

Suspicion on Y B Chavan

On October 19, 1989, an Indian daily "The Independent" published a story from Bombay on this subject in which it was alleged that Morarji Desai was not the CIA agent as quoted by Seymour Hersh but the needle of suspicion as quoted by Hersh that he was Chief Minister in Bombay, Finance Minister of India and Deputy Prime Minister was pointed towards another leader of Maharashtra, Y B Chavan who also held these political positions at one time or the other and was contemporary of Morarji Desai. It was also mentioned in this story that Chavan was having intimate relations with a lady official Jane Abel of American Counsel in Bombay during 1960 - 62 when he was Chief Minister of Maharashtra. After he was appointed in the Indian Cabinet posy India-China war of 1962, this lady official was also transferred by the US Government from Bombay to New Delhi where she stayed till 1964. It was further alleged in this story that the sleuths of Intelligence Bureau in New Delhi, while putting this lady on surveillance, found Chavan visiting her residence secretly during late evenings in private taxi with his cap tucked under his arm prior to entering his house at 1 Race Course Road. The fact that Jane Abel was in Bombay from 1960 to 1962 and moved to Delhi in 1962 when Chavan was also in Delhi as Defence Minister was even admitted by a leading magazine of India at that time. It would be pertinent to add here that Additional Private Secretary of Chavan was also caught by the Indian counter espionage agency, IB, during emergency for passing classified information to CIA which was not supposed to be in his possession as reported in a leading weekly in 1982. It should however not be construed that Chavan too was aware of this clandestine activities of his Private Secretary or was a party to it.

It was further revealed in this story that a former diplomat, A K Verma, who later became Chief of RAW, was posted in Washington during the period this manuscript was stated to have been shown to a diplomat in the Indian Embassey. Verma was accused of imposing censorship during Emergency in 1975-77 being friend of V C Shukla, the then Information and Broadcasting Minister. When Morarji Desai Government came to power in 1977, L K Advani, the Information and Broadcasting Minister shunted him out of this Ministry, Thus Verma had a malice against Morarji Desai, and he deliberately agreed his name being tagged CIA agent by Seymour Hersh when he gave the relevant manuscript in the Indian Embassy in Washington in 1981-82. Verma being Secretary of RAW was free to give his explanation in this regard which he never did.

Uproar Started

When this story published in the "Independent" newspaper, there was spontaneous uproar in the media and among a small section of workers of a union of Bombay Port Trust. These Mathadi (headload) workers were one of the strongest sections of the Congress Party led labour force in Bombay which was patronized by some prominent leaders of this party. About 300 workers of this union held demonstration or made to do itt by a section of Congress leaders, against the publication of this report outside the office of Times of India newspaper in Bombay. They demanded instant apology from the editor failing which they threatened to blaze up this office.

Some prominent Maratha editors came heavily on this news item and wrote counter editorials in their newspapers and magazines against tht story trying to using the harshest possible language as they had in their mind, to protect Y B Chavan, a Maratha by caste, against whom the needle of suspicion was directed by that national daily. These editors never tried to come forward or say anything in defence of Morarji Desai, a Gujarati, They also did not ask for a probe in the matter to the fact as the diplomat who cleared the name of Morarji Desai was the Secretary of RAW, A K Verma, whose name was mentioned in the story as a possible person because all circumstantial evidences were pointed towards him in the article. One editor Gadkari of Loksatta went an extra mile to give it another political colour directly hinting that Morarji himself was instrumental in planting this story by utilizing the services of his trusted follower Subramaniam Swamy.

These eminent journalists tried to portray the manifestation of regional bias by highlighting the national achievements of Chavan and sidetracking Morarji Desai rather than putting forward strong Indian sentiments to prosecute Seymour Hersh in their individual or collective capacity. Strange are Indian sentiments when regionalism upstages the inner conscious of even those who are at prominent stature to keep a balanced approach for national cause. But in this case, Maratha regionalism tried to outclass in one-upmanship to the Gujarati cause who were comparatively courageous enough to file a libel suit against Hersh in a court at Chicago for that publication.

This news published by "The Independent" though unsubstantiated, was not the story of a day dreamer but certainly emanated from Horse's mouth inside RAW where some old IB sleuths were discussing their younger days spying adventures of Delhi rendezvous which included this fact vis-à-vis others like capture of Maqbool Bhatt, a Pakistani terrorists of JKLF in the Sixties in Kashmir by a daring IB young officer, arrest of Sheikh Abdullah by an old fox, Bangladesh infiltrations etc. These old genius of this espionage world were neither against Chavan nor in favour of Morarji Desai but the fact remains that an old operative of IB, in his mid seventies, is still privy to this information of

Chavan's misdemeanour with Jane Abel, though it might not be for any exchange of official information between them but may be for some other reasons. He was a witness to Chavan's visit to her residence and not to what transpired inside the house. He gave only this information of Chavan's visit to his bosses and never said that he was a CIA agent. Needle of suspicion was his relations beyond the official mandate with Jane Abel which Chavan maintained with her which Morarji Desai never had with any American diplomat if insiders of IB and RAW are to be believed. So, the description published by Hersh that the so-called CIA agent was Chief Minister of Maharashtra, Finance Minister of India and briefly as Deputy Prime Minister of India applied to both Chavan and Morarji Desai and based on the fact that Chavan had intimate relation with the lady diplomat, shifted the balance of suspicion to him rather then Morarji Desai. Now, it is up to the Indian Government to pitch in with whatever clarification they have in their intelligence archives.

Destroying Pakistan

However, assertion of Seymour Hersh that India had plans to destroy Pakistan forces in West Pakistan and CIA obtained this information from a Cabinet level source in India was pure invention of either by Henry Kissinger or the CIA or by both. Even in the Annual Report of the Defence Ministry of India pertaining to 1971-72, the Director of Military Operations had admitted that directive to Indian army was to seize as much territory in East Pakistan as possible and fight a defensive battle in Pakistan territory on Western front. This amply denounced the theory floated by Kissinger and CIA. According to papers of the Washington Special Action Group released by Jack Anderson on December 6, 1971, General Westmoreland reported to Kissinger that the Pakistanis might hold out in East Pakistan for as long as three weeks. There was no mention of any Indian plan vis-à-vis West Pakistan in this report. Even on December 21, 1971, the Enterprise mission was justified by the State Department spokesman on the ground that Americans were to be evacuated from East Pakistan whereas Kissinger in his book "The White House" had written that by December 7, 1971, he had information obtained from a source at Cabinet level in India that the Indian Army had plans to destroy the Pakistan army. The Enterprise mission was ordered on December 8, 1971. Were there any changes on the ground on the western border to give credence to such fear of Kissinger? Even George Bush, the then US Ambassador in UN did make persistent queries to Sardar Swaran Singh, Indian Foreign Minister, who then attending the UN about Indian intentions in western sector, were the self contradictory assessments of US Government which were blown up beyond proportion by Kissinger because Indian Government had no such plans to destroy Pakistan army on western front.

Deceitful Practices

US administration have attained the notoriety of have indulged in such deceptive practices as done by Kissinger to justify their foreign and military policies to Congress. The most notorious was the Tonkin Bay incident. Seymour Hersh himself had written how the US administration suppressed the information that the Soviet Union shot down the KAL007 without knowing it was a civilian jet airliner. President Reagon ordered air attack on Tripoli and Bengazi on the basis that he had reliable proof of Gaddafi's complicity in the Berlin disco bombing in which a US servicemen was killed. The US administration was reported to have convinced its allies of Gaddafi's involvement by producing intercepts of decoded messages passed between Berlin and Tripoli. Subsequently, the West Germans arrested the woman who planted the bomb and her interrogation revealed her connection not with Libya but Syria. Richard Helmes, the CIA Director, asserted before the Senate hearings that the US administration had nothing to do with the toppling of the Allende Government in Chile. Later, he was convicted for perjury on this false deposition. In the Iran-Contra affairs, a former National Security Advisor also faced trial for perjury for giving false information to the Congress. Last but not the least, President George Bush Junior gave false information to his allies purported to be obtained by CIA that Saddam Hussain was in possession of Weapons of Mass Destruction. He convinced the allies in this regard who helped him in his attack on Iraq and subsequent killing of Saddam Hussain. It was later made public that the report of CIA were doctored at the behest of Bush and Tony Blair, the British Prime Minister criticized Bush for this fiasco. The US intelligence, CIA usually found working on apprehensive theories and made its government to resort to arbitrary military actions against small countries. It could not dare to do so against India in 1971 and mislead that the Enterprise was sent to evacuate the Americans from West Pakistan but it was an indirect threat to bully India which was bound to be repulsed with USSR aid, which Nixon and Kissinger had assessed and in their face saving attempt gave a distorted theory to the factual position.

Immature Investigation

Seymour Hersh had been critical of Nixon-Kissinger- duo policies and politics of that era. When he was made aware that Kissinger referred to a Cabinet level source in India in the Washington Special Action Group meetings and the source was identified none other than the former Indian Prime Minister, Morarji Desai, he should have made more serious research on this delusion because Morarji was not in the Cabinet in 1971. If he had further pursued his investigation, he might have stumbled on the fact that there was no information of any Indian plan to destroy the Pakistan army in West and this was manufactured in Washington by Kissinger at the behest of CIA. Hersh's immature investigation was in accepting first that there was a Cabinet level source in India and second, never corroborated from elsewhere, was that he was Morarji Desai. One accept such fatal flaw from India-biased Nixon- Kissinger format, who could make such terrible assessment, out of sheer disliking to Indira Gandhi that referring to Morarji as a Cabinet level source when he had been out of her Cabinet for more than two years and was an opposition leader, was their gravest mistake. Hersh claimed that he had some six sources in the CIA to confirm that Morarji was the CIA agent. While testifying in the Court, Hersh disclosed out of these six sources, two were out of Government, one was in the CIA, one was in the world of the NSA, National Security Agency, which is the communications wing of intelligence people and two were working in the White House. Two of these sources he characterized as "active sources" who "were telling him lot of details". At one point, during his testimony, Hersh stated that he thought the most important thing was to know that the sources upon which he was relying were sources that he had the utmost confidence in and that was the driving forces of what he wrote. It was ridiculous. He should have ascertained the basic discrepancy, which he could not do due to his lack of proper knowledge, as to how a Cabinet level source as described by Kissinger in December, 1971, could have been Morarji Desai who was not in the Indira Gandhi Cabinet and how he could have access to information which was privy only to the Cabinet Committee on Political Affairs. These CIA sources must be working in air rather at grounds on the factual fallacy of their disinformation. CIA could never cultivate a good connection in India till the last century excepting that in 1986, one R&AW officer Unnikrishan was apprehended just on his induction in their net and the other Rabinder Singh was whisked away by them when he was about to be arrested. CIA never had the guts to get up to any political leader of India and Kissinger, out of malice against India, made the mistake of his life in insulting Morarji Desai by implicating him as CIA agent.

Mystery

With these facts, it is still a mystery whether a nationalist to the stature of Morarji Desai who is mentioned as a CIA spy in his book by Seymour Hersh, was in reality so or his name was implicated with personal bias, is probe worthy. Since Indian intelligence is found involved on two counts here i.e. one for surveillance of Intelligence Bureau on the American lady diplomat Jane Abel whom Chavan used to meet clandestinely in Delhi and the second about former Secretary of RAW, A K Verma for his alleged clearance of the manuscript of Seymour Hersh wherein name of Morarji Desai was mentioned as a CIA agent, government had to come out with whatever information is in their possession. More so, the derogatory and abusive remarks about Indira Gandhi in this book needs the attention of the Indian Government to be taken as a serious matter and legal action whatever possible should be taken. Hersh had no business to cast aspersion on the patriotic honour of the nation while publishing such malicious fiction and a slanderous attack on a patriot none other than the true Gandhian, Morarji Desai, a man of dignity and honour.

❑

Vanished R&AW Spies

There were two incidents in R&AW, when two of its senior officers were won over by CIA to get inside information. These officers were K V Unnikrishnan, a Director level IPS officer, who was arrested in June 1987 for giving classified information to CIA. He was put under in prison under National Security Act for one year and was released subsequently when Rajiv Gandhi, the Indian Prime Minister, let him off for further prosecution. In second case, Rabinder Singh, an ex-army Major, who was working as Joint Secretary in R&AW, fled USA via Nepal in 2004, with the help of CIA. Both these officers were, however, dismissed from service.

CIA was found involved directly in these two incidents but there were other instances when R&AW officers managed their settlement in foreign countries like USA and Canada with the help of the sleuths of these countries and abruptly left their job in R&AW. Some of these officers were working on sensitive posts in R&AW before their disappearance to these countries. They defected on legal documents and R&AW hierarchy in particular and Government of India in general watched these incidents haplessly without getting involved in any controversy to expedite them from these governments. But, the extent of damage and level of its magnitude would never be known to R&AW in view of their working on sensitive desks.

In this regard, the author made detailed enquiries from some former officers of R&AW and found following spies vanishing from India in foreign countries.

Sikander Lal Malik (Personal Secretary of R N Kao)

Defection of Sikander Lal Malik, Personal Secretary of R N Kao to USA is one of the most sensitive cases in the history of R&AW. Malik joined as personal assistant of Kao in 1958 during Intelligence Bureau. After the formation of R&AW in 1968, Malik too was transferred as personal secretary of Kao. Malik was arrogant while serving with Kao and some senior officers were behind his blood due to this reason. There were some incidents of indiscipline which made him unpopular among his colleague. Due to his proximity with Kao, no one dare to take any sort of action against him although Sanakaran Nair, number two of Kao had developed a strong disliking for him due to his rustic behaviour. Nair, with a lady in a safe house of R&AW. Nair wanted to sack him from service after this incident but generosity of Kao prevailed upon him to take a lenient view due to his long association with Kao. Malik was sent on a foreign posting to USA in the Indian Mission at New York, with the blessings of Kao.

After completion of three years of his tenure at New York, Malik was supposed to return to India but he managed his stay in USA by getting extension of for a year twice citing personal problems. According to US laws, a person is automatically entitled to get green card – a work permit for an indefinite period of time, when he stays for five year there regardless of the status of stay, legal or illegal. Malik returned to India and sought retirement from service.

Malik settled in USA permanently after his retirement from R&AW. It was ridiculous on the part of Indian government to allow him to return to USA knowing fully well that he was personal secretary of Kao for seventeen years and was in the know of so many sensitive information about R&AW. It is beyond imagination how much damaged he could have done to the country.

M S Sehgal (Senior Field Officer)

M S Sehgal was a head constable in Delhi Police prior to joining IB. He was subsequently transferred to R&AW on the recommendation of G C Saxena, who later on became R&AW head. Saigal used to work for the household activities of Saxena due to which he got rapid promotions and became Senior Field Officer in R&AW. Saxena was on a foreign assignment in Indian Mission at London in the earlier eighties. On his recommendation, Sehgal too was sent there over the seniority of many capable officers.

While serving at London, Sehgal was involved in many unethical activities like womanizing and gambling. He was spending his salary at racecourse as a result of which he was in heavy debts. He paid these loans after he received money from an insurance company following the death of his wife. However, there were rumours inside R&AW that his wife died in mysterious circumstances which was made to look like an accident.

He returned to R&AW Headquarterss after completion of his assignment in London when G C Saxena was Chief of R&AW in 1983. Suddenly, Sehgal disappeared from his duties and was never traced thereafter. He was spotted in London afterwards where he was found living in a comfortable manner. He neither resigned his job nor sought retirement but vanished from R&AW as a serving officer. R&AW too did not make efforts to extradite him from London probably at the instance of G C Saxena.

Major R S Soni (Assistant Director)

This was one of the most intriguing case of neglect and suspicion in R&AW. Major R S Soni was a former defence officer. He was working as Assistant Diretor on the sensitive Pakistan desk for quite some time after resigning from army. During the course of surveillance by the Counter Intelligence branch of R&AW, Soni was suspecting of passing classified information to ISI agents in New Delhi. While R&AW sleuths wanted to arrest him red-handed, he became suspicious and disappeared from his residence and was never traced thereafter.

Subsequently, it was discovered after thorough investigation that Soni had migrated to Canada without resigning and taking prior permission of R&AW. There was no inkling of his migration to Canada in R&AW because accounts section kept depositing his salary at least for three months even after he was absent from his duties.

Ashok Sathe (Senior Field Officer)

CIA recruited him while Ashok Sathe was on two foreign assignments from R&AW. He was working on China desk prior to his first posting in Indian Mission at Ulan Bator in Mongolia from where he was covering China operations. Later on, he was transferred to Khorremshahr in Iran.

While in Iran, Ashok Sathe's senior at Tehran found him embezzling secret fund by footing bills of fake agents and entertainment activities. When he was confronted on this account, he had a brawl with his senior at Tehran Mission. He was recalled prematurely to R&AW Headquarterss for this act of indiscipline. But prior to his departure from Khorremshahr, he set his office on fire and sent a report that due to short circuit, all his records had been engulfed in fire.

After his return to R&AW Headquarterss, Sathe was subjected to a departmental enquiry for his acts of indiscipline in Iran. He confronted to the authorities and resigned from post portraying as if it was a protest. Subsequently, R&AW authorities discovered that while serving in Iran, he was in league with CIA counterparts. Soon after his seeking retirement, Sathe was found having a greed card for himself and got settled in California. This was the first known case wherein a R&AW officer was settled by CIA in USA.

Shamsher Singh Maharajkumar (IPS Officer)

Although, this case was not of any defection to a foreign country but it was the one of the first of its kind when a senior IPS officer that too from a former princely family of India resigned abruptly from the coveted post of a Director. Shamsher Singh was a 1957 batch IPS officer serving on deputation in R&AW. He was a former scion of royal family of Nabha state in Punjab.

He was first posted at Islamabad in Pakistan as R&AW head in Indian High Commission. Subsequently, he got assignment in Bangkok before he was sent to Canada for another foreign posting. While in Canada, he managed to procure an international passport for himself. He did not inform the R&AW authorities about this passport. Shamsher Singh quietly returned to India in October, 1976 and resigned from his service at a very young age. He slipped back to Canada and settled there.

M I Bhaskar (Senior Field Officer)

Bhaskar was sent on a foreign posting to Tokyo in Japan. Curiously, he managed another assignment to Washington concurrently without coming to R&AW Headquarterss. Normally, a three years tenure was fixed for such foreign postings after that one had to service in India for quite some time. But in the case of Bhaskar, this practice was overlooked or managed since he joined Washington posting direct from Tokyo. Bhaskar too managed a green card for himself while serving in the Indian Mission. After completion of his terms in US, he returned to India, resigned from service before settling down in Washington.

B R Vaccher (Senior Field Officer)

Vachher was the younger brother of a former Inspector General of Punjab Police. Due to his high level connections, first he got a foreign posting in Nepal and later served in USA. Curiously, Vachher was a bachelor who were barred for any foreign assignment in R&AW for security considerations. But this condition was waived in the case of Vachher and he was sent on two such assignment. Vachher too managed a green card of US. He came to India in 1977, resigned from his job and managed to settle in America.

R J Khurana (Additional Secretary)

Khurana was posted as Counselor in Indian Embassy at Washington in USA. He was working on sensitive Pakistan desk of R&AW prior to this stint. After completion of his tenure, he returned alone to Delhi in R&AW but did not bring his family members from USA. When this fact came to the knowledge of R&AW authorities, he was asked to clarify the reasons thereof. He put forward some flimsy excuses which did not satisfy the authorities. Although, he was kept away from the R&AW Headquarterss to an obscure posting but no disciplinary action was taken against him since he was retiring after some months. Khurana migrated to USA after retirement from R&AW. It was later discovered that he and his family members were given card holders of USA which he managed while posted in the Indian Embassy at Washington. There were rumours in R&AW that CIA managed his migration to USA. R&AW could not keep tab on his activities while in USA but it was a matter of serious concern that such a senior officer of this agency was got settled in USA and Indian Government remained silent on such a sensitive matter.

❑

CIA Trapped Rattan Sehgal

CIA Trapped Rattan Sehgal

Some time in January, 1997, R&AW Chief sent a note to Government of India suggesting to bar IB from interacting with foreign intelligence agencies. This was done, keeping in view the ongoing turmoil in IB, when a senior level officer was under cloud of suspicion of being a CIA agent. The note put forward four ways which can be taken to prevent embarrassment to the government following the forced resignation of Rattan Sehgal, the said officer, for his alleged proximity with some officials of American mission in Delhi. Other two recommendations of R&AW included detailed account of foreign connections of IB officials and, freezing of interactions between the intelligence agencies and apex business chambers like, FICCI, CCI etc. This note was a sort of warning to Government following this incident of a CIA mole in IB. It was a strange caution by R&AW, particularly when media reported several stories of placement of lot of kiths and kins of their own officers in foreign countries and mostly in the USA. When such an incident is detected, Indian Intelligence hawks are strange geniuses to go to any extent to score a point over the other to prove their one-upmanship. IB had used the same weapon when a CIA mole Unnikrishan, a R&AW officer, was got arrested to the Special Branch of Delhi Police. In real sense, they clamour for other's blood in the garb of such national disaster in Indian spying community,There are no suggestions whatsoever to weed out the rot, which is still haunting these agencies awaiting another such a disaster to surface.

CIA Lady

Rattan Sehgalwas working as Additional Director of the Counter Intelligence desk of IB. He was first detected by the IB counter intelligence team itself, meeting a lady official of the US Embassy who was under their surveillance for quite some time. This lady was August, the Deputy Station Chief of CIA in the US Embassy. When this fact of Sehgal's connection, was brought to the notice of the then acting Director, IB, Abhijit Mitra, he mounted day-and-night surveillance on Rattan Sehgal because this liaison with the CIA operative was clandestine and without the approval of the Director of IB.

Prior to the appointment of Additional Director in IB, Rattan Sehgal had dubiously been able to get himself appointed as Joint Secretary (Personnel) in the External Affairs Ministry through Rajiv Gandhi due to his Doon school connections. Since the formation of R&AW, this post was continuously held by their officer who had to liaise with the Ministry of External Affairs (MEA) and RAW officials posted in Indian Missions abroad. There was a considerable resentment in RAW as a result of Sehgal's appointment on this post since IB had no business to work in the MEA. It was subsequently found that many sensitive posts in various missions abroad were usurped from R&AW and a number terrorists sneaked into India due to inadequate information in those Missions, Possibly, Rattan Sehgal while working on this post in MEA could not properly coordinate the diplomatic and intelligence channels for which R&AW had to encounter many unwanted controversies at later stage.

Unauthorized Liaison

In 1994, when Rattan Sehgal was trying to get an extension on this post, the then Cabinet Secretary Zafar Saifullah became suspicious of this extension and sought meeting with Sehgal. When Saifullah inquired about his past achievements, Rattan Sehgal claimed that he made a breakthrough in the 1993 Bombay bomb blast case and played an audio tapes of conversations with some suspects purported to be from the Gulf. After this meeting Saifullah suspected that Rattan Sehgal might have unauthorized liaison with some foreign intelligence agency since it was not his mandate to keep such a audio. He did not record these developments anywhere but recommended reversion of Sehgal to his parent cadre of IPS in Madhya Pradesh instead of retaining in IB. Saifullah retired soon theereafter and Rattan Sehgal managed to come back to IB as Additional Director through his clouts in New Delhi bureaucracy. It was speculated in the intelligence circle that Rattan Sehgal could have been recruited by CIA when he was working in the MEA where he used to visit various missions abroad and was to liaise with the foreign agencies in his capacity as MEA official. He used to boast among his colleagues that at one point of time, at least 12 ambassadors used to sit in his room. IB should have taken note of this uncalled for disclosure by him which smacked of something bizarre.

There was another allegation against Rattan Sehgal that during the last visit of Indira Gandhi as Prime Minister to USA in 1983, he accompanied her as a security cover. While coming back, he did not accompany her but sent seven suitcases full of personal luggage in the VIP plane in which she traveled from USA to India contrary to the blue book regulations. He sought the help of P C Halder, the then IB officer responsible for security at airport to clear that luggage but he declined to do it. Although heavy customs duty was imposed on this luggage but Rattan Sehgal used his clout in the PMO and got it exempted and paid nothing to the custom authorities. Strange are the ways of selection of such dubious officers to another sensitive posts like appointment of Sehgal in MEA subsequently, knowing fully well of his past misdemeanor of corrupt practices.

Surveillance

Dubbed as fun loving "Golden Boy" in IB, there was a sufficient evidence in the organization which warranted scrutiny of Sehgal's activity but was never done due to reasons beyond imagination. On subsequent surveillance by IB, it was detected in May, 1996 that he used to meet two lady diplomats of American embassy in luxurious hotel Ambassador where he was videotaped while receiving two packets from them. Later on, he was again detected with another male diplomat and these two ladies in a meeting late in the night at his residence for about three hours. Overall, ten such meetings were reported by the surveillance team of IB to its Director, Arun Bhagat, out of which two were "friendly encounters". Sehgal was never warned of these meetings as there was no concrete evidence of his being passing any document or information except for his meeting and receiving packets. When August, was transferred out of US mission in New Delhi and was replaced by another lady diplomat, Rattan Sehgal ordered his juniors not to put surveillance on her since she was new in the city and was unaware of the topography and as such no worthwhile achievement would be made in the surveillance on her. This was, however, ignored by the juniors.

In another suspicious development, Sehgal accompanied the then Prime Minister H.D. Deve Gowda during his visit to Italy in October, 1996. Although, he was supposed to accompany the Prime Minister, being head of securityon whole of the tour but he stayed back in Rome when Gowda was visiting Venice along with other security personnel. He alleged to have met the CIA Station Officer in Rome clandestinely.

Arun Bhagat in Langley

These charges were sufficient enough to get him prosecuted but for reasons unknown till date, no action was taken against him till Arun Bhagat, DIB, visited USA in October to attend the meeting of the International Association of the Chiefs of Police at Phoenix in Arizona. After attending this meeting, Arun Bhagat sought permission from the then Home Secretary K. Padmanabhaiah to meet the CIA Chief in Washington which was denied to him as he did not disclose the agenda to the Home Secretary. Moreover, the IB chief was not supposed to meet CIA officials but to liaise with FBI officials only. Presumably, Arun Bhagat had briefed Home Minister, Indrajit Gupta about involvement of Rattan Sehgal with CIA and he overstepped Home Secretary and sought permission from Home Minister which was granted to him. Arun Bhagat spent the whole day at Langley, Headquarterss of CIA, holding deliberations with the top officials obviously on Rattan Sehgal.

It was reported in a leading daily in London that a Russian mole in CIA had tipped the Indian Government in the middle of 1996 that Rattan Sehgal was being recruited by CIA through two lady diplomats working on cover of CIA at US embassy in New Delhi. Hence, it was a mystery whether IB put surveillance on Rattan Sehgal on the tip of Russian intelligence or it was on their own suspicion.

It was learnt that in the beginning of December, 1996, Arun Bhagat called Rattan Sehgal in his room and inquired as to why he was meeting the CIA officials which he denied accepting only chance meetings at social functions. When Rattan Sehgal was shown the films and photographs of his meeting with CIA officials, he claimed these as part of his official assignments which he was authorized by the department. When further grilled on the two packets he received from them, Sehgal claimed these as golfballs and wine bottles. He was further questioned regarding the place of his meetings, self driven cars, suspicious turns and parking of vehicles, dinners and hotel meetings. Rattan Sehgal was reported to have broken down thereafter. When Arun Bhagat asked him to resign or face prosecution, he put in his papers for voluntary retirement because evidence against him were skimpy and sketchy. It would be pertinent to mention here that search of his house did not yield any incriminating evidence against him. Indrajit Gupta, the then Home Minister, confirmed that Rattan Sehgal had been asked to resign. If he had refused, he would have been prosecuted but his passport was seized by the IB. He however admitted that no serious damage was done in this case. He also confirmed that the two officials of the US embassy in New Delhi, who were undercover of the CIA, had been asked to leave the country.

This was supposedly done to put a lid on the controversy as prosecution of Rattan Sehgal could have brought so many disturbing facts to the knowledge of the press and public which would have affected the Indo-US relations. Prior to this, there had been explicit understanding to share intelligence on many vital problems which two countries were facing due to Islamic fundamentalism and the militancy in Kashmir. However, had such a bungling occurred in USA, person like Rattan Sehgal could not have escaped prosecution whatever might be the consequences of these mutual political relations.

Tata Tea Case

Later on, Rattan Sehgal again came under cloud in October, 1997, when his name figured in the Tata Tea and ULFA case, the insurgency and business conglomeration, wherein it was alleged that he was aware of the meeting which

Tata Tea executive held with ULFA leaders in Bangkok. He did not reveal the facts of the meeting to the government and Assam police. When the then Home Secretary prepared a note for CBI inquiry, he elicited views of Rattan Sehgal and Arun Bhagat the then DIB, Sehgal was said to have taken the defence that he was introduced to the Tatas by M K Narayanan, former DIB. He claimed that he informed the then DIB, D C Pathak about his meetings with company officials and documents of these meetings were picked up by IB when his house was searched by them. However. Arun Bhagat, the former DIB, claimed that not a scrap of paper on this matter was available in the IB This mystery has since remained unveiled.

Recluse

Rattan Sehgal in IB escaped prosecution in this CIA-linked case in 1996 but prior to that Unnikrishnan, a RAW officer, in a similar case with CIA operatives at Chennai was got arrested by the then RAW Secretary, S E Joshi. However, Arun Bhagat, the Director of IB, in this case took a contrary view of the identical situation and asked Sehgal to put in his paper for voluntary retirement. Why Government of India allowed such controversies to persist and did not intervene to overrule the decision of Arun Bhagat. Why Unnikrishnan was arrested under the National Security Act for such identical charges? These were unanswered questions which were put under carpet the mystery whether charges against Rattan Sehgal were not so grave. Was it a short term sex encounter with a white skinned ladywhich is general weakness of Indian diplomats? Sehgal had reportedly handled many sensitive desks in IB and most of his contemporaries believed that he could be everything but a spy of CIA. This stigma made this career sleuth, a recluse for the rest of his life

❑

16

Purulia Arms Mystery

For the past two decades, the author has raised many voices on various platforms to make RAW, like the CIA and other intelligence agencies of the World, accountable to Indian Parliament. But all his efforts have proved futile and fell on deaf ears of our politicians to whom detailed notes were regularly sent on this subject. There are many other instances of R&AW's failure to guard India from external terrorism, last is 26/11 Mumbai attack by Pakistan trained terrorists. In 1990, Jaswant Singh, Chairman of Estimate Committee mooted the idea to bring R&AW and IB under the purview of Parliament. When the author discussed this matter with the then Chief of R&AW, G S Bajpai, he laughed it away saying that he would see how it would be through in Parliament. Surprisingly, there was no discussion on this move of Jaswant Singh at any quarter thereafter. When I met Bajpai sometime later, he again laughed mysteriously and said that he got it thwarted. This is how R&AW is a Government within the Government, immune from any accountability, be of any nature.

But now, the cat is out of the bag once again. Kim Davy, the prime conspirator in the sensational arms drop case in Purulia in West Bengal in 1995, revealed in a TV channel that R&AW was involved in this arms drops in December, 1995 with the approval of Indian government.. It is not the first time confession in this case. This fact was disclosed by Peter Bleach, the other accused in this case when interrogated by CBI while in custody after his arrest.

This is not the isolated case when there were allegations of involvement of R&AW in the internal matters of the country. In 1989, there were media reports that R&AW supplied arms and imparted training in Bodoland for separatists of Bodo tribe to create a situation which could warrant the Central Government to impose President rule in Assam after dismissing the duly elected state government of Prafulla Kumar Mahant, citing uncontrollable law and order situation in the state. These are two glaring examples of the alleged involvement of R&AW at the behest of Central Government in clandestine operations to dislodge the legally elected opposition led governments in the states.

There is past history of Central Government when it had used the hand-picked Governors to oust the duly elected opposition governments in various States of India. In 1980, Bhajan Lal hijacked the majority of MLAs of Janta Party and merged with

Congress with the full backing of Sanjay Gandhi. Tapase, the Governor of Haryana thwarted the attempt of Ch. Devi Lal to swear as Chief Minister and forcibly installed Bhajan Lal as Chief Minister of Haryana who was having the backing of much less MLAs than Devi Lal. Tradition of Aya Ram Gaya Ram of shifting loyalities three times in a day by MLAs in Haryana, started after this incident. Bhajan Lal by hook and crook managed to prove his majority on the floor of house making mockery of the Indian democracy. There were reports that Tapase was duly rewarded by Bhajan Lal by giving Petrol Pump and other benefits to his kin. Ram Lal, another Governor of Andhra Pradesh, who was branded Lakdi Chor (Wooden Thief) by the Telgu Desham Party in Andhra Pradesh, when he toppled the duly elected N T Rama Rao government at the behest of Rajiv Gandhi and Arun Nehru. Buta Singh displayed this notoriety in Bihar and more efficiently Romesh Bhandari installed such government of Jagdambika Pal in UP for a day during election time to facilitate his protégés to win election. There are many other examples of such sordid display of misuse of official machinery by stooges of Central government i.e. Governors to oust the legally elected opposition parties in many states in India. This trend was conceived by Indira Gandhi and adopted by his son Rajiv Gandhi also.

Installing their own government by forcibly dislodging the legally elected government in the States is the familiar practice in this country. Hence, to take a different mode of using its intelligence agencies to create a fictitious and self-imposed law and order situation and to dismiss the duly elected opposition governments under this garb, must be invented by the ruling party with the connivance of then Chief of RAW. Prima facie, it could also not be ruled out since circumstantial evidence in Purulia arms drop in West Bengal and Bodoland militancy, ostensibly created by alleged involvement of R&AW at that time, are ample proof to put needle the suspicion of its involvement for such a venture of Central government of those time.

In the instant revelation of Kim Davy in the Purulia arms drop case in face to face interview on news channel with anchor, has clearly raised certain serious and sensitive questions which still have remained a mystery and need thorough investigation by the Indian Parliament. Government has obviously denied ambiguously these new revelations and CBI has also clarified that no intelligence agency was involved in the arm drops. CBI has its own dubious track record in such cases when there was admission in a case pertaining to R&AW that the concerned file investigated by them about involvement of a former R&AW Chief in disproportionate asset case, is missing from their Headquarterss.

Some of these circumstantial evidences about involvement of R&AW and other Indian agencies in Purulia arms drop case, are questionable and need thorough re-investigation if the government has the will and desire.

Prior to arms drop in Purulia on December, 17, 1995, Kim Davy, purported as a New Zealand national on a fake passport which was obtained in the name of a child who died 33 years ago, along with 7 other Russian associates landed in Varanasi on November, 23, 1995 in a Latvian aircraft AN 26YLLVV and stayed in Bharat Hotel. Owner of this hotel Jawaahar Jaiswal was a former MP who was very closed to the then Congress President Sita Ram Kesari, Ghulam Nabi Azad and other prominent Congress leaders. Curiously, there were much better hotels in Varanasi but their stay in this small one with frugal facilities. He stayed there for four days and was in contact with local police, ATC, custom officials and local kingpins. They used to visit the airport daily to inspect the aircraft where one of their associates was present whole time. From the hotel they made several international telephone calls in Hong Kong, Britain, Singapore, Pakistan, Indonesia, Burma, Bangladesh, USA and East Germany. On November, 27, 1995, this aircraft flew back to Karachi with five persons. It was suspected that Kim Davy along with two other associates stayed back in India. There was every suspicion that he had some other assignments in India to carry out thereafter. When and wherefrom Davy left abroad after straying in Indian, is still a mystery. These facts give credence to the doubt that December 1995 mission of Kim Davy was accomplished after a thorough surveillance and proper rehearsal of executing the plan to drop the arms at the destinations assigned to them. Why, the local police, IB and for all practical purpose R&AW, were not unaware of this sojourn of Kim Davy in Varanasi particularly when it was known that plane flew from Karachi and returned there without these three persons? This is the first and foremost lapse of security breach, to be looked into.

Director General Civil Aviation i.e. DGCA, gave clearance to AN-26 Latvian aircraft to land at Varanasi on December,17, 1995 from Karachi and and then to overfly Calcutta to Rangoon. When the flight landed at Varanasi on the scheduled day, the crew renewed the demand to DGCA to land in Calcutta, which was duly granted on the ground that "no adverse information about the flight" was available with them. After taking off from there on December 17, 1995, the aircraft dropped 240 AK 47 rifles, 10 rocket launchers and 81 anti-tank grenades over Purulia in West Bengal. Now according to the mastermind of this operation, Kim Davy, R&AW had ensured that the Air Force's radar in this area was switched off so that the aircraft was not traced up when it flew in to drop the arms. This is the biggest revelation in this case. If Davy is to be believed, then the government should check the record of the IAF radar system of that day and if this system is found switched off, involvement of R&AW, in this arms drop, is the ample proof to nail the lies in this case investigated by CBI.

Kim Davy further claimed that the Indian authorities knew the flight plan, the number of people on board, the cargo, the drop zone and everything was known well in advance and approved by the concerned authorities before landing at Varanasi. He further alleged that it was a matter of record that R&AW was informed on three defined dates by MI5 about the arms drop, likely number of people on board in the plane and drop zone in India. In spite of these details, Davy further disclosed that there was a British former intelligence officer on board in the plane. His assertion is further proved when he asked who "in their right mind would fly a plane from arch enemy of Pakistan into Indian air-space with a load of clandestine weapons without having it cleared by the Indian authorities". Davy's disclosure was further affirmed by the visiting British Home Secretary Michal Howard in India later in a press conference that the British Government had warned the Indian Government about the arms drops. This assertion of Kim Davy and British Home Secretary carries a lot of weight in the sense that two years back Dawood Ibrahim, masterminded bomb attacks in Mumbai killing hundreds of innocent Indian citizens. Indian intelligence agencies in general and R&AW in particular knew that ISI had given him shelter in Karachi and he was engaged in a hidden war against India. So DGCA's clearance to this aircraft is questionable and if R&AW had the smallest inkling of MI5 about this aircraft carrying arms in India which British Home Secretary admitted in New Delhi, this AN-26 craft should have been properly searched at Varanasi airport. This failure of other security agencies in particular and R&AW in general, raises further eyebrows in this arm drops and need proper investigation of its involvement since needle of suspicion is against them.

There were media reports that R&AW informed government on November, 15, 1995 that a small aircraft would go from Karachi en route to Daaca carrying arms and ammunition. If those reports are taken into cognizance, then indictment of R&AW is further proved to the fact that Kim Davy visited Varanasi on November 23, 1995 in this plane and later on dropped arms on December 17, after taking off from Varanasi at 10 PM. Mysteriously, landing permission at Calcutta was granted on that very day at Varanasi airport by DGCA. If R&AW was at all in the know of this plan, how the other agencies of the government like IB, local police, custom etc. did not search this aircraft at Varanasi, These lapses further proved the surmises in the credibility of any report of R&AW in this case.

To the ill luck of the occupants of this plane, while returning from Phuket in Thailand where it landed because Rangoon did not permit the landing, bad weather in Bay of Bengal, forced it to take permission from Madras Air Traffic

Control for "technical purpose" due to bad weather in Calcutta. Had the weather in Calcutta been landing-worthy, this plane would have reached Karachi safely and whole of this mysterious mission of arms drops would have died a natural death. However, it was made to die such death by the Indian law enforcing agencies thereafter due to patchy investigations. When a lot of hue and cry was made in the media after the arms drop on December, 17, in Purulia, the Home Ministry started picking the threads of this incident and the needle of suspicion zeroed on AN 26 Latvian aircraft which by then had taken off for Karachi from Madras. The Indian Air force was pushed in action to intercept this plane which forced it to land in Bombay. Air Vice-Marshal V.G.Kumar of Indian Air Force claimed that he instructed the airport authorities to quarantine the force-landed aircraft and asked them to put a vehicle in front of it to prevent the aircraft's get-away attempt. Deliberately, the aircraft was parked 6 kms. away from the airport building and when officials of the security and intelligence agencies reached the tarmac, they found the door of the plane opened, the kingpin Kim Davy was driven off in the official air-port vehicle and was made to flee the airport without custom and immigration checks and clearances. How this Hollywood movie type drama was got enacted at the Bombay airport and by whom when Davy ran away from there under the nose of the security and intelligence agencies? This is the most intriguing and questionable act of Indian security and intelligence agencies which needs a thorough probe and accountability of all the agencies involved in this fiasco, by the Indian Parliament. Had this happened in any other country, so many heads of these agencies would have faced severe punishments but in India no one has ever been questioned till date. Hats off to their cover up operation in this case of international conspiracy to befool the Indian politicians.

Kim Davy openly admitted in the TV interview that Pappu Yadav a RJD MP of the party of Lalu Yadav helped him escape from India. If this fact has an iota of truth, then there is a deep routed conspiracy in this whole game plan because party of Lalu Yadav was an ally of P V Narasimha Rao government at that time. Pappu Yadav was lodged in a jail in Patna and was readily available to questioning in this regard if the government wanted to threadbare truth on the claim of Kim Davy.

These facts and circumstances are the inexplicably evidences that almost all the government agencies involved in this sordid drama, failed to various lapses be it at Varanasi, at Madras, at Bombay airport or at Home Ministry, at IB or at R&AW Headquarterss. It rather gives credence to the claim of Kim Davy that R&AW was directly involved in this arms drop case to supply these arms and ammunition to some rebel groups in India. The then government at centre openly admitted in Parliament that there was total lapses in the security and intelligence system in this case and had convinced the opposition parties that many heads of these agencies would roll but nothing happened thereafter and no one was neither blamed nor indicted. Strange are the working of Indian government dominated by bureaucrats, if such a heinous crime of breach of national security is gone without a logical conclusion.

Prior to this Purulia arms drops in a similar incident, the Sunday Observer Correspondent from Guwahati reported on August, 6, 1989, involvement of R&AW in the guerilla training of BODO extremists. This was reaffirmed by this newspaper a week later also. According to these news reports, the then government at centre was using R&AW to enflame BODO agitation by imparting mercenary training for its cadre to create chaos and confusion in Assam so that taking the cue of failure of law and order situation, the duly elected government of Praffula Kumar Mahant was dislodged. Some questionable activities of RAW at the behest of the then Chief A K Verma were reported in this scenario.

Assam government security officers, through their sources, claimed that Central forces of Special Security Bureau and Special Frontier Force, two armed wing of R&AW, were training BODO extremists at Chaprakata near Bongaigaon in Goalpara District, Kokraijhar and in the jungle of Barpeta Districts. It is pertinent to mention here that SSB and SFF have their field training centre in these districts. A forester of the royal government of Bhutan was killed by the BODO extremists when he stumbled on one such training camp north of Manas tiger sanctuary. This training of field craft, ambush and firearms, was further extended to the north of Brahamputra river in the dense forests of Assam, Arunachal Pradesh and Bhutan. This LTTE type guerrilla training gave credence to the claim of Assam government when these BODO extremists used command detonated landmines to blow up six police vehicles killing more than 20 policemen.

According to the admission of a junior level officer of SSB, BODO youths were trained by their organization to manufacture crude but highly explosive devices using commonly available substances like detergent powder, NPK fertilizers and charcoal. These explosive were used in mines, booby traps, time bombs and hand grenades by BODO extremists from January to July, 1989 in various part of Assam claiming life of more than 300 innocent citizens. It is noteworthy that this region does not have its border with any enemy or hostile country where government can put claim that these arms and ammunitions were smuggled from the other countries. Magnitude of this high quality guerrilla warfare training by R&AW operatives could be gauged from the fact when these extremists blew up a ultra modern bridge with these devices on national highway which an enemy country could do so only with a tank. Hence, it was ample proof to prove that no outside terror outfit was involved in such training and it was a home invented extremist mission.

Assam government duly sent a strong letter of protest to the Central Government quoting names of more than six senior officers of various Central forces who were having free excess in this terror infested area whereas the Assam policemen were the selected targets of the BODO extremists. It was also reported that Upendra Brahma faction group of All Bodo Student Union was the main beneficiary in terms of money and arms training from these forces of Central Government. There were reports of visit of Upendra Brahma, the main extremist leader and other prominent leaders of BODO agitation, in Calcutta and Delhi offices of these Central agencies for future planning.

These press reports further give brief details of various high ranking R&AW officers frequently visiting in ARC planes to various parts of Assam and Arunachal Pradesh. In one such incident, a high ranking official visited Tezpur in September, 1988, next day of his visit, there were explosion of bombs in various parts of Assam and buses were looted near Tezpur. In addition to these details, other officers of R&AW reportedly made several sorties in the BODO extremists areas. According to another press reports, several safe houses were hired for these extremists for briefing and de-briefing by junior officers of R&AW. Significantly, not a single operative of R&AW, IB or Central forces was ever attacked by these extremists except the selected Assam policemen or officials.

After these reports appeared in the media, there was uproar in the Parliament by the opposition parties. L K Advani of BJP and P Upendra of Telgu Desham Party raised this matter at Zero hour. AGP MP Nagen Saikia sought reply from the Home Minister about involvement of R&AW in the training of BODO extremists. As always, the government denied involvement of any of its agency in the training of BODO extremists.

But the pertinent development which took place, after this issue was raised in the Parliament, was that the activities of BODO extremists immediately fizzled out and there was total lull in this worst terrorist infested area for the next one year. This fact of alleged involvement of R&AW, duly corroborated the claim that Central agencies were certainly involved in this mission because there was no proof of involvement of any foreign outfit. Secondly, fizzling out of the agitation of grave nature when it was disclosed in the Parliament, were circumstantial evidence of of allegation of R&AW sponsored training to extremists.

These two major incidents of involvement of R&AW, further strengthened the claim of the author for the past two decades that intelligence agencies should be brought under the umbrella of Parliament for its financial and operational accountabilities. Due to utter incompetence of R&AW, one Prime Minister Indira Gandhi was killed at her residence, one former Prime Minister Rajiv Gandhi was blown up by LTTE suicide cadre, Punjab Chief Minister Beant Singh was assassinated, one former Army Chief General Vaidya and many leading politicians were killed by terrorists. Terrorism of Punjab and Jammu and Kashmir is still in our memory for the last three decades. LTTE, the brainchild of R&AW retaliated to the Indian Peace Keeping Force and killed 1,155 Indian commandos including 5 Colonels and crippled more than 3,000 soldiers. Such high casualties did not take place in three wars with Pakistan Jammu &Kashmir assembly and Indian Parliament were attacked due to lack of proper intelligence. No one has forgotten the Kargil war where a shepherd gave intrusion information and no R&AW report was available. And the last and the least, wounds of 26/11 attack in Mumbai by Pakistan trained terrorist are still green in the heart of every Indian when there was not proper intelligence reports from R&AW to take precautionary measures.

Being a former employee of this prestigious and once one of the best intelligence out fit of the World under R N Kao which played a pivotal role in the liberation of Bangladesh and subsequently in the merger of Sikkim with India, the author has thorough knowledge that top hierarchy of R&AW, since the last two decades was found involved in one-up-manship, lacking sense of belonging, indulging in corruption and total lack of devotion and sincerity. It is high time the government of India should wake up and make corrective measures to make this agency accountable to Indian Parliament.

❑

Rabinder Singh—CIA Agent

Alarmed at the United States unilateralism in the wake of the brutal hanging of Saddam Hussain, more than 70 countries took initiative to seek moratorium on executions. This was done as a step to ward off death penalty, which at times does not justify legal endorsements due to political or personal obligations and motives of a head of state as was evident in this case of US President George Bush. A resolution in this regard was moved at the UNO which got momentum and its final outcome warranted priorities of every country with proper assessment of internal political situation particularly, due to escalation of global terrorism. Although, extradition of persons accused of heinous crimes is not an automatic process but most of the countries have signed the extradition treaties to bring back such person for trial and punishment in their respective countries. Even assistance of Interpol is taken to arrest such delinquents and extradite them to the country of their domicle for legal trial. Hence, criminal act of a particular person committed in any part of the world is under the global purview and does not immunize to give him any escape route. Particularly, U.S.A. and India are two biggest democracies who are prominent flag bearers in getting these by-laws implemented to keep tab on the global terrorism and other criminal activities. But surprisingly, in the case of Rabinder Singh, a Joint Secretary level officer of R&AW, who was spying for CIA and reported to have escaped to USA via Nepal, both countries are mysteriously silent on his extradition to India. Since, connivance of CIA to deliberately defect Rabinder Singh from India is on record of R&AW, big brother USA never consciously thought of this matter serious enough owing to weak presentation of this case by Indian government. When C D Sahay, the then Secretary of R&AW, summoned the CIA station head in US Embassy at Delhi and gave proof of his arrival in USA, he pleaded ignorance to this fact. Although, he promised to brief Sahay after checking details with CIA

Headquarterss, a week later he reported that CIA had absolutely no information about Rabinder Singh's defection. He also tried to convince Sahay that no such person had ever entered into USA as per records of their immigration authorities. This was a blatant lie and misuse of super power tactics to which India protested mildly keeping in view the prevalent Indo-US strategic relationship. So, when USA has its own axe to grind, it never gives credence to any such relationship which India could never dare to retaliate. Thus, the global norms for extradition are enforced only on small countries and USA is too big to be questioned when such incidents take place there and Rabinder Singh's episode is true example of it.

US Government is very particular in resolving such grave matters if their interest is paramount but due to India's weak foreign policy with regard to the US, the Indian Government does not seem to be serious and bold enough to take up extradition of Rabiner Singh resolutely. Even, the Indian Prime Minister Manmohan Singh has visited USA many times after this incident but the matter was never considered and given any priority on the agenda of important diplomatic deliberations. M K Narayanan, the then National Security Advisor, who was instrumental in clinching the Indo-US Nuclear deal, did not take any concrete action in this regard although he openly admitted in the media reports that Rabinder Singh was in USA but he was non-committal for his extradition. This lackadaisical attitude of Indian government is highly questionable and requires proper legal action on the part of the concerned court in New Delhi where this matter is getting dust for the last so many years.

Disappearance of Rabinder Singh from India to USA is not only sensational, mysterious and probe worthy, but his induction in R&AW too by A K Verma, the then Secretary of R&AW, from army in 1987 is equally questionable. Rabinder Singh, a clean-shave Sikh, belonged to a middle class family of Amritsar. His father was a retired Lt. Col. of Indian Army who was re-employed in Information & Broadcasting Ministry in the seventies. A K Verma, an IPS officer of MP cadre was serving on deputation as Deputy Director in R&AW during this period. A K Verma was a childhood friend of V C Shukla, who was appointed Information & Broadcasting Minister at the behest of Sanjay Gandhi, younger son of Prime Minister, Indira Gandhi, during Emergency i.e. 1975-77 to handle press in favour of the government. V C Shukla, for this particular reason, brought A K Verma on deputation from R&AW to I&B Ministry during Emergency and both were blamed for clamping censorship on print media from June, 1975 to March, 1977. While serving in this ministry, A K Verma and father of Rabinder Singh became friends and their family relations continued thereafter. When Janta Party formed government in 1977, A K Verma was reverted from I&B Ministry to MP Police by L K Advani, the then Minister of Information and Broadcasting for gagging media but he managed his stay in R&AW through his bureaucratic clouts.

Prior to this, in 1972, Rosy, sister of Rabinder Singh, migrated to USA and got employment in CIA front organization, US Agency for International Development (USAID). His elder brother Jagjit Singh also shifted to USA subsequently with the help of Rosy, followed by his parents. Rabinder Singh joined Indian Army through Indian Military Academy in June, 1970 and got promotion up to the rank of Major in the mid eighties in Gorkha Regiment. Thereafter, he was ignored for promotion to Lt. Col. because of his mediocre caliber. This further developed a sense of frustration into him towards his service career in army.

In early eighties, A K Verma became Joint Secretary in R&AW and later on posted as Counselor at Indian Embassy, Washington, USA, in 1983. Since A K Verma had relations with Rabinder Singh's family since 1975, his posting to Washington further strengthened their family ties which A K Verma fully exploited during his stay in US. It is reliably learnt from the contacts within R&AW that during this period a few Sikh groups in USA were sympathetic to the Sikh militants in India who were involved in Pakistan sponsored terrorist movement for the creation of Khalistan in Punjab. These Sikh groups were providing financial help to the Sikh militants in Punjab through clandestine channels. In order to get inside information of these Sikh groups in USA, A K Verma recruited Jagjit Singh his source and infiltrated him into these Sikh groups to get inside information which was later on found useful for R&AW in India. It is also learnt that while serving in the Indian Embassy in USA, A K Verma through Rosy got employment for his son Deepak Verma in Digital Equipments Company Ltd., which was also a CIA sponsored outfit working in many parts of the World for their espionage activities.

A K Verma came to India in the end of 1986 after completion of his tenure at Indian Embassy in Washington and was promoted as Additional Secretary in R&AW. Subsequently, he maneuvered his promotion as Secretary of R&AW in July, 1987 by superseding his senior R Govindarajan. Thereafter, he brought Rabinder Singh on deputation from Army to R&AW. That is how Rabinder Singh was inducted in R&AW by A K Verma knowing the fact that he was ignored in the Army for promotion to the rank of Lt. Col. During this period, militancy in Punjab was at its peak and Amritsar area was hub of these militant activities. A K Verma posted Rabinder Singh to Amritsar in 1989 because during his service in army he took part in operation Blue Star at Golden Temple in Amritsar in May, 1984 and was thus considered competent by Verma to work for R&AW at Amritsar.

When Rabinder Singh was posted at Amritsar as Deputy Commissioner, in-charge of R&AW office, maternal uncle of his wife was posted as a senior police officer at Amritsar. According to insiders in R&AW, Rabinder Singh got all sort of police assistance through this blood relation in his nefarious activities inside and across the border. He got involved with many leading Sikh militants stationed in Pakistan through certain sources who were recruited by R&AW operatives in border area. IB authorities had confirmed reports and informed government also that he was possibly on the talent hunt list of ISI through these militants. They provided all details of vulnerable life style of Rabinder Singh to ISI which were probably given to CIA since both these agency were in league at that time.

Rabinder Singh attained notoriety in Amritsar while working like an autocrat due to his proximity with the local police officers. His mischievous and destructive mindset made him supercilious and over-enthusiastic in his working behaviour and he overstepped his official mandate while conducting top secret trans-border operations on the border area of Pakistan. There were rumours that he got killed some Sikh militants in connivance with his Punjab police connections, to gain confidence of his senior officers at R&AW headquarterss. Some of these militants were also working for the IB officers in this region at that time. This matter was reported by these militants to the then IB in charge of Amritsar who sent a detailed report to his seniors in Delhi. Since, Rabinder Singh was blue-eyed boy of A K Verma, all these complaints of IB were put in the dustbin. This fact was known to Rabinder Singh which further emboldened his notoriety and he captured many disputed properties, including several acres of agricultural land in Punjab, Haryana and Rajasthan, through these Sikh militants. Another section of these militants, who were working for IB, were behind his blood for the killing of some of their colleagues. His car was later on ambushed by these militants near Amritsar but he fortunately escaped unhurt. Even this incident did not open the eyes of the R&AW authorities at Delhi and they continued with his stint at Amritsar instead of taking cognizance of this serious matter. IB also reported that he was throwing lavish parties at Amritsar to the police, army and civilian bureaucrats where all unethical and shameless acts of indecency were reported to have been seen by some insiders of R&AW. It was also reliably learnt that senior officers of R&AW who used to visit Amritsar for official duties were found involved in these activities and Rabinder Singh used their weaknesses in future at Delhi Headquarterss of R&AW for his evil designs and he collected classified information for CIA from these officers.

Inside R&AW, there were confirmed reports that Rabinder Singh was involved in huge embezzlement of Secret Service Fund during his posting at Amritsar in the name of clandestine operations in Pakistan. He used to claim money from Secret Fund for information supplied to him by non-existent militants who were already killed but he claimed them his operational sources. He used to send ISI sponsored fake and fabricated reports to the R&AW headquarterss which were never corroborated by any other sources due to the intense terrorist activities in border areas at that time. No one in R&AW had the courage to rein him or question him due to the backing of senior hierarchy of R&AW knowing fully well that he was a corrupt officer suspecting him of being a double agent and not at all trustworthy. Even then, he was allowed to work at Amritsar at his own whims and fancies. His Robin Hood style of working emboldened him to do all the misdeeds in the garb of secret operations which he ultimately maneuvered in future to spy for CIA for which he utilized his past connections fully well and in perfect modus.

There was a strong belief among a section of senior officers of R&AW that ISI, through their trained militants and other operatives who were apparently working for Rabinder Singh, used to send doctored reports to R&AW headquarterss. Operations based on these reports resulted in many disasters and caused huge casualties to civilian and security forces in the border areas of Amristar, Gurdaspur, Taran Taaran and Ferozpur Districts. It was also reliably learnt that ISI fully exploited his vulnerability through militants and made him to function on their dictated lines. There was firm belief among the staff of R&AW at Amritsar during that period that he was on the pay roll of ISI which could not be substantiated due to lack of direct evidences. There were also reports that Pakistan trained Sikh militants, working for him, used to stay at his official residence at times which was the biggest security hazard. He claimed these militants as his informers. This fact too was also reported by the IB office of Amritsar to Home Ministry but to no avail. Some of the senior officers of R&AW at that time had strong belief due to his lavish living style and link with doubtful Sikh militants that he was directly or indirectly working for ISI. They warned the top hierarchy in this regard but to their utter dismay they did not take proper action to contain him.

Controversial Stint in Damascus

After completion of his normal tenure in Amritsar in 1991, he had a brief stint at R&AW headquarterss. Soon thereafter, Rabinder Singh was sent to Indian embassy at Damascus in Syria. He was in charge of Visa section in the embassy. There were indications that he was deliberately posted in this country by the R&AW authorities with the motive that he would be kept away from the Sikh militant groups which were active against India in US, Canada, UK and other European and Asian countries. There was a strong apprehension against him that if he was kept in R&AW headquarters at New Delhi, there was every likelihood of his getting involved with these Sikh militants who were working for ISI in Pakistan. Thus, he was posted to this station so that he would cool his heels in this non-descript place.

According to sources in R&AW, there was corroborative evidence that some Islamic militants wanted to infiltrate into India through some missions in Gulf countries and Damascus was one of them. In view of this information, specific instructions were issued to all the Embassies of these countries either to deny Visa to the doubtful persons and if there was some recommendation for some political reasons, that could be entertained only after getting clearance from R&AW Headquarters. For diabolic intention, Rabinder Singh deliberately withheld these instructions of R&AW to himself and issued Visas to some Islamic militants which was brought to the notice of the Indian Ambassador in the Embassy by one junior officer of R&AW posted in the Visa desk. It was also learnt that in Damascus, Rabinder Singh, developed friendly relations with Murtaza Bhutto, the estranged son of Z A Bhutto, who sought asylum in Syria due to political compulsions of Pakistani politics. He did not seek clearance from R&AW authorities for this uncalled for liaison. This fact was also known to the Indian Ambassador, who brought it to the notice of Ministry of External Affairs which in turn informed R&AW about this liaison. R&AW authorities duly cautioned him to keep away from Murtaza Bhutto but he defied these instructions and secretly continued his relation with him.

When the Ambassador became suspicious of the scandalous and dubious working of Rabinder Singh, he denied all his approvals for issuing Visas to some unwarranted persons which were recommended by him. He could not tolerate the dictum of the Ambassador and misbehaved with him. He physically manhandled him in the presence of Embassy staff. This incident was reported by the Ambassador to the Ministry of External Affairs which after consultation with the R&AW authorities, reverted Rabinder Singh prematurely to New Delhi at R&AW. Rabinder Singh completed only one year at Damascus but no disciplinary action was taken against him by R&AW authorities for his unruly behaviour with the Ambassador. In normal practice, such indiscipline is never tolerated in R&AW but he cooked up a cock and bull story against the Ambassador to satisfy the R&AW bosses. A section of senior lobby of R&AW authorities wanted to take strict disciplinary action against Rabinder Singh on this charge of indiscipline but another lobby with whom Rabinder Singh maintained dubious relations, prevailed upon them and this matter was buried under the carpet and he was given benefit of doubt. Even the Ministry of External Affairs was projected with the wrong picture of this case by R&AW authorities and the concerned Ambassador was rather implicated for that incident. In normal course, Rabinder Singh should have been punished for this indiscipline but he got scot-free due to his high connections in R&AW. This incident further emboldened him to commit such offences in his official duties inside R&AW.

In the meantime, as a rule to serve in R&AW after the completion of deputation period of more than 4 years, Rabinder Singh resigned from his Army service and opted for absorption in R&AW in its cadre R&AW Administrative Service (RAS). He manipulated this induction through his clout at higher level. He was assigned the seniority of the year 1977 with the result he was promoted as Joint Secretary after return from Damascus. Thereafter, he was posted to insignificant post of Administrative Section of R&AW. There were allegations against him there too that there, he earned lot of money fraudulently in purchases of various equipments and other administrative purchases meant at all India level for R&AW staff. These facts were known to the then Secretary of R&AW but he did not take any action against him due to his past proximity. Although, three were no concrete evidence that Rabinder Singh was recruited by CIA for spying around this period but there were ample reasons to keep tab on his questionable activities which were prejudicial to the security of sensitive organization like R&AW. He used to through lavish dinner parties to senior officers including the Chief of R&AW at his residence, five star hotels and at his farmhouse. Everybody in R&AW knew that he had acquired disproportionate assets to his known sources of income but no one dared to take any action against him due to his allegiance with a coterie of senior officers who were favoured by him at times in the past. He openly used to claim in cocktail circles that he was the richest bureaucrat of India but no one in R&AW had the guts to question the source of his richness and lavish style of living.

Counselor At Hague

R&AW authorities should have become suspicious of the activities of Rabinder Singh, had they properly visualized his anxiety to get proximity with the US authorities. After return from Damascus, he planted a story to the hierarchy of R&AW that he could infiltrate into the US State Department through his sister Rosy who was working for the USAID. To prove his credibility, he even carried out an operation for the collection of intelligence about US Government activities in South Asia through his sister. Initially, R&AW authorities got some valuable information through Rabinder Singh about USA but subsequently there were apprehensions that CIA might be using his sister to plant disinformation in R&AW through him. One such disinformation which CIA tried to plant through him was that the US embassy in New Delhi had reported to the State Department in the late eighties that the then Chief of Army Staff was planning a coup against Rajiv Gandhi, which was totally false and untrustworthy. This disinformation cropped up suspicion in R&AW authorities and his credentials, which were already questionable, further strengthened the fact that he was in one way or other, was involved with the CIA. R&AW did not take any corrective action to contain this errant officer of doubtful integrity.

In the mid-nineties, Rabinder Singh tried to get him posted in the Indian Embassy at Washington in USA through the then Minister of State for External Affairs, R.L. Bhatia who represented Amritsar Lok Sabha seat in Punjab which was also the home town of Rabinder Singh. Such recommendations and interferences of politicians and bureaucrats is quite common in R&AW. Rabinder

Singh was aware of such manipulation in R&AW and he approached Bhatia through two businessmen of Amritsar to get him posted in the Indian mission at Washington on compassionate grounds to get medical treatment of his injured daughter. Bhatia subsequently admitted that he made no effort to ascertain integrity of Rabinder Singh and took up his case solely on humanitarian grounds on the recommendation of his two friends of Amritsar. Ministry of External Affairs put its foot down and did not allow him to go to Washington due to his past behaviour in Damascus in Syria where he assaulted the Ambassador and his dubious links with some Islamic militants including Murtaza Bhutta of Pakistan.

However, in the middle of 1999, Rabinder Singh through his clout in R&AW, managed to get the plump post of Counselor in Indian Embassy at Hague in Netherlands. This was again strongly resented by the Ministry of External Affairs due to Damascus incident. The then Secretary of R&AW through his connections with the PMO, got his posting approved and he was sent to Hague despite the disapproval of Ministry of External Affairs. This was the turning point where from he got free hand in his nefarious activities because there was no authority to check his activities at Hague. According to the information gathered by the author through his contacts in R&AW, Rabinder Singh was formally recruited by CIA at Hague for spying in R&AW with the help of his sister Rosy who was already working for CIA through its front organization, USAID.

Passport Scandal

Although, there were no confirmed report as to what nature of information Rabinder Singh supplied to CIA while posted at Hague. After his defection to USA, R&AW collated some reports which disclosed that through his friend Gurinder Singh, another senior officer of R&AW, who was posted in Indian Embassy at London as Minister during this period, several Sikh militants were sent to India through Indian Consulate at Birmingham on fake passports and visas. These Sikhs had deserted India during militancy in Punjab in the eighties and nineties when Rabinder Singh was posted at Amritsar and he knew most of them. They got his assistance from Hague to gain entry inside India on fake passports and visas. This fact was revealed by B.B.Nandi, a former Additional Secretary of R&AW in a news article highlighting the involvement of some R&AW officers posted at Indian Consulate in Birmingham in issuing passports and visas to these miscreants, which was under the direct administrative control of Gurinder Singh from London. There were reports in R&AW that Rabinder Singh started using R&AW officers for his spying activities and his old friend Gurinder Singh was the first person used by him when he infiltrated hundreds of black listed miscreants in India from Birmingham. These miltants were stranded in U.K., Netherlands and many other European countries since operation Blue Star in Golden Temple at Amritsar in Punjab in May, 1984.

This "Passport scandal of Birmingham" took place during 1999 to 2001 when Rabinder Singh was posted in Hague and Gurinder Singh was in London as reported by Nandi. R&AW authorities tried to hush up this case but the British Home Department reported it to the Indian Government after that an inquiry was conducted By the Ministry of External Affairs and it was found that G.S.Bora, First Secretary and K.C.Sharma, Assistant, both R&AW officers, posted at Birmingham Consulate office, issued several hundred of fake passports to illegal migrants at the behest of Gurinder Singh. They earned millions of rupees through this racket. After reversion to India, these officers acquired properties worth more than their known sources of income but no action was taken against them by R&AW authorities due to high political links of Gurinder Singh. Rather Gurinder Singh managed to send G.S.Bora to another foreign posting at Bir Ganj in Nepal to keep him away from investigation by any agency. It was learnt that Gurinder Singh invested huge amount of money in properties at Chandigarh and Noida and Bora also purchased properties in Vasant Kunj at Delhi and Haldwani in Uttrakhand. It was further understood that Gurinder Singh through his CIA counterpart in London got his son recruited in CITI Bank at London during his tenure as Minister in Indian High Commission at London. Although, Rabinder Singh was not directly involved in this case but his share in this racket could not be ruled out due to his close relation with Gurinder Singh.

According to the information of the author if telephone conversation records of Rabinder Singh from Hague with Gurinder Singh in London during their posting in 1999 to 2001 are traced by any investigating agency, it would be revealed that they contacted each other hundreds of time, which was never in their protocol. So, Gurinder Singh was the first senior officer of R&AW who was used by Rabinder Singh to work for him while serving in Hague.

Why CIA Wanted Spies from R&AW ?

The author investigated through his sources in R&AW to ascertain as to why CIA wanted a mole in R&AW to spy for them particularly at that time when heat of Indo-US strategic relations was in the embryonic stage. CIA had a dubious past of planting frivolous information on brownie conception to which it was ridiculed in the past by even US politicians. New stories were floated by overenthusiastic operatives about the existence of illegal nuclear capabilities by their detractors in this part of the world, much to the discomfiture of US in general and CIA too, in particular. However, CIA could not penetrate into these countries to get first hand reports about such existence. R&AW had its own credibility of being one of the best intelligence agencies of the world, particularly in this region, and CIA had comprehensive details in this regard. So, CIA wanted to recruit an insider of R&AW, who could provide details, if any, available in R&AW about the nuclear capability of Iraq, Iran, North Korea or any other country of this region. Such unauthorized capability could legitimize the unilateral action of USA in UNO or at any other international fora to substantiate their stand that these countries were in possession of nuclear capabilities which could be detrimental to World peace. This investigation was initiated by the author after news appeared in media that R&AW authorities had filed charge sheet against Rabinder Singh in a Delhi Court for spying. There were two major international incidents which propped up CIA to recruit a human intelligence source inside R&AW as well as in other strategic departments of Government of India. First incident was its failure to detect the Pokhran II nuclear blast by the Indian scientists and the second was conclusion of US Senate on the manipulated reports of CIA on Weapons of Mass Destruction, WMD, acquired by Iraq.

CIA Failed To Detect Nuclear Test at Pokhran in 1998

US media lambasted CIA for its failure to anticipate and forecast India's nuclear test at Pokhran in May, 1998 which was successfully exploded despite the fact that US was apprehensive of it. US Government even appointed a Committee under retired Admiral David Jeremiah to inquire into the failure by CIA to predict the Indian nuclear tests after Atal Bihari Vajpayee became Prime Minister, who had given such an indication in their election manifesto. This inquiry found out that CIA's record of human intelligence in India was abysmally worse and it had no spies worth the name in India. The agency had miserably failed to penetrate the Indian nuclear programme in comparison to its success in other neighbouring countries like Pakistan and China. According to this committee, there was only one analyst in CIA to study satellite pictures of important nuclear and missile sites of India which was highly incompatible to the logistic demand. The Committee comprehensively concluded that there were insufficient personnel to study the data available on India and whatever staff was available, had little experience and India was a forgotten case and there was such apprehension worth the name in the mandate of CIA.

In the past, CIA had adopted a practice to provide intelligence information to its diplomats to issue demarches relating to the clandestine nuclear activities, gathered through their satellite monitoring or through other sources for a particular country. These diplomats warned the concerned head of that country about their impending nuclear designs to forbid them from any future development in this field or face the sanctions in that case in future. In this routine exercise during 1995, then US Ambassador in India Frank Wisner met Indian Prime Minister Narsimha Rao and showed him some photographs of US satellites which detected that India was preparing for a nuclear test which would harm the Indo-US relations if India would not abandon its plan to conduct such test. These details were revealed by media subsequently. Hence, while conducting the nuclear blast at Pokhran in 1998, Indian scientists were wary of this US warning of 1995 and as such took all possible security measures to conduct the nuclear test in utmost secrecy so that US Government should not have a wind of it.

When Pakistan test-fired the Ghauri missiles, CIA analysts believed that Indian retaliation to this action would be a similar missile test and no imminent nuclear test by the Indian Government was on their agenda. Since the BJP led Indian Government had promised in its election manifesto to introduce nuclear weapons programme, US Government had ordered CIA to intercept communications on India's nuclear test sites through satellite monitoring. Indian Scientists out-manoeuvred CIA by choosing the summer season for this test when lot of dust flew in deserts of Rajasthan and visibility at ground level was out of reach of any satellite. US satellite system failed to detect nothing extraordinary in the desert and the Indian coverage was lessened and collection of nuclear intelligence switched to priority targets in Pakistan, Central Asian states and elsewhere in Asia. These satellites were taking photographs of the Indian missile test sites once in three days instead of daily basis as per the existing system in CIA.

Politically, the Indian Government outwitted the Americans when Indian Prime Minister Vajpayee was called on by the US Ambassador Bill Richardson followed by the US National Security Adviser, Sandy Berger, for routine courtesy meetings after formation of his government. Vajpayee did not give any impression that he would exercise any nuclear option at that juncture. US strategic policy makers believed that India wanted to improve trade relations with USA and any such test would prove deterrent in their political state of affairs. Covert silence on the impending nuclear plan by Vajpayee was part of a sophisticated disinformation campaign of the Indian Government which CIA failed to apprehend during the prevalent political parleys between the two countries.

After the Admiral Jeremiah panel indicted CIA for its failure to anticipate and forewarn the US Government on Indian nuclear test at Pokhran, American media openly published reports that after this fiasco, CIA had planned to detach its staff from the US embassy in New Delhi and other organizations in India. CIA decided to work on its own, abandoning the traditional practice of posting CIA staff in the guise of defence attaches, commercial or tourism specialists in the Embassy and other missions elsewhere in India. After this incident, CIA wanted to operate independently in India and cultivate its agents like it had done in Pakistan and Afghanistan in the past when they raised Talibani militants against the Soviet army in 1979 onwards. As a prelude to the existing system of CIA operations and in their new plans, it decided to revert to the basics of old fashioned spying using "Human Intelligence" inside all sectors of India be it intelligence, scientific, defence, political or diplomatic establishments. The then CIA Director, George Tenet, after testifying before the Senate Intelligence Committee, openly declared before media persons that he would directly examine as to how CIA was collecting intelligence in India and how collection and analysis of such intelligence reports was properly utilized to ensure that such a failure like the detection of that nuclear test, did not occur in future. Thereafter, CIA started intense recruitment drive for engineers, scientists, IT specialists, linguists and other professionals with higher perks and salaries to work in various desks of CIA against India besides recruiting moles in Indian establishments at exorbitant cost and they succeeded to some extent in that venture.

The disclosures of US media regarding CIA's manifestation to infiltrate in the Indian establishments were a clear signal and sufficient ground for R&AW to ensure protection of its pliable officers of doubtful integrity from the clutches of CIA. This was intrinsic when in another case it had already been detected in its Chennai office during 1986-87 when Unnikrishnan was caught spying for CIA. Rabinder Singh's doubtful integrity was known to each and everybody in R&AW from his initial posting in Amritsar where he not only amassed huge money and property but also became suspected target of ISI. His stint in Damascus was another pointer to keep him at bay and divested him from any sensitive assignment particularly abroad. From 1993 till his detection and subsequent disappearance to USA with the help of CIA, every R&AW Chief was aware of his lavish style of living, acquiring of disproportionate assets to his known sources of income and his tendency of entertaining senior and junior officers of R&AW by throwing parties at his home, farm houses and at Five Star hotels but no action was taken by any body to keep tab on these activities nor any efforts were made to find out his discreet connection with foreign agencies particularly, the CIA. It was known to everybody in R&AW that he was always interested to know the details of desks of his acquaintances which was highly questionable. This was either a deliberate attempt or utmost failure of R&AW authorities by ignoring these facts when one of its officers publically acclaimed to be the richest bureaucrat of India. Earlier, Rabinder Singh himself provided disinformation about US State Department which he got through his sister who was known to be working for CIA sponsored NGO, USAID. This was ample pointer to the fact that Rabinder Singh was a dubious character whose style of living and working was dubious and required thorough verification but his vulnerability was not taken into account mysteriously by anyone in R&AW, which was probe worthy. CIA needed another Unnikrishnan who was honey-trapped by them which was readily available as Rabinder Singh who was money-trapped and fully exploited to hapless R&AW.

Reports Fabricated To Justify Iraq Invasion

Most of the intelligence failures of CIA were deliberately covered with doctored reports or apprehensive warnings for the US government. This was subsequently proved to be totally false and fabricated which was found later in the manipulated intelligence to justify invasion of Iraq. One such identical incident took place on August 4, 1964 when CIA deliberately supplied skewed evidence that the North Vietnamese ships attacked American destroyers in the Gulf of Tonkin in the Pacific. On the basis of this information, the then President of USA Lyndon Johnson got the carte blanche and ordered air strikes on North Vietnam after the recommendation of the US Congress which passed a broad resolution for military action based on these manipulated reports of CIA while no such attack took place on the American warships. This ultimately resulted in a full-scale war in which thousands of innocent Vietnamese were brutally killed with no fault of their government. These facts were revealed by the US National Security department after more than 40 years of this happening when these documents were made public. At that time world opinion was formulated in favour of USA by its government to justify the attack on Vietnam on the basis of these fake and doctored reports of CIA. This was a blatant misuse of military power by a powerful country against a poor nation merely on apprehension.

As far as Iraq invasion of USA is concerned, CIA did not have any concrete and authenticated intelligence reports regarding possession of Weapons of Mass Destruction (WMD) by Saddam Hussein which could justify the US attack on Iraq. After his election as President of USA, George Bush Jr. had made up his mind to take revenge against Saddam Hussein for the insult and humiliation he heaped on his father who was President during the invasion of Kuwait by Iraq in 1991. Terrorist attack of 9/11 by Al Qaida on the World Trade Center of USA, gave him open option to further increase his political activities on this pretext for which he ordered air attacks on hide outs of Taliban terrorists in Afghanistan and subsequently made a hue and cry that President Saddam Hussein was is possession of WMD which could be detrimental to the security of the World peace. He linked this attack with the worldwide battle against Islamic terrorism and Iraq was the hub of these activities as per the credible evidence supplied by CIA to US government.

According to media reports published prior and after the Iraq war, CIA tried to get rid of Saddam Hussein through the ethnic Kurds under a political opponent Ahmad Chalabi an Irani national. He happened to be a double agent simultaneously working for the Iranian Revolutionary Guards intelligence which hated Saddam Hussein for the prolonged Iran-Iraq war of the eighties. There were reports that Iran used Chalabi, who was a paid CIA agent, against Saddam Hussein and passed bogus intelligence to the CIA through him that Saddam was in possession of WMD so that USA would attack Iraq and Iran get rid of its hostile neighbour. It was reported that CIA built up case of war against Iraq on the basis of these bogus and exaggerated reports on nuclear weapons supplied by Chalabi at the behest of Iran.

Senate Intelligence Committee appointed to look into the lapses of CIA committed prior to Iraq war, denounced its performance when media reports indicted it for preparing doctored reports against Iraq. Both the Democrats and Republicans, who supported President Bush to take military action against Iraq for possession of banned biological and chemical weapons, subsequently admitted that the law makers would not have voted in favour of the war if the CIA had given them correct intelligence about the Iraqi threat of possession of WMD. The then Director of CIA, George Tenet, resigned prematurely, owing moral responsibility. It was found that sustained media campaign consisting of planted stories and orchestrated pronouncements created by CIA operatives, ensured in a climate of opinion, in favour of possession of WMD stockpiles in Iraq. Actually, CIA built up a self-created fear psychosis through false and concocted propaganda that these lethal and banned weapons could be transferred to the Islamic terrorists any where in the world for which USA should stop Iraq by destroying these weapons which was subsequently found far from any truth. This was all humbug on the part of President Bush since he had asked his Defence Secretary Rumsfeld to start preparing for the Iraq war in November 2001 itself for which every member of the National Security Council except Collin Powell, Secretary of State, gave their consent. It was concluded in the findings of the report of the Senate Intelligence Committee that intelligence assessors of CIA succumbed to the pressure of the US Government and provided them manipulated intelligence reports suited to them to form world opinion in their favour to attack Iraq for possession of WMD. CIA was thus exposed for this misdemeanor.

In this background of US invasion of Iraq when CIA on their own could not find any concrete evidence against Iraq for possession of WMD, their operatives tried to infiltrate R&AW whether they had any information about Iraq on its nuclear capabilities. Their reliance on R&AW could be contributed to the fact that R&AW in the late seventies successfully infiltrated into the Kahuta nuclear enrichment plant of

Pakistan through its sources and whole of the world came to know about the future nuclear programme of Pakistan. Even Israel Government sought Indian Government assistance to air attack this plant but due to its own political compulsions, Indian Government declined such cooperation. At that time, there were media reports that Moshe Dayan, the then Israeli Defence Minister, clandestinely visited India and held secret meeting with the Indian Prime Minister Morarji Desai in this regard but Morarji Desai refused to cooperate with his Israel counter part and attack on Kahuta by Israel did not materialize as the Israel air force did not have any other refueling arrangements for their aircrafts in this region except in India. So, CIA contrived to seek their affirmation about WMD from the cupboards of R&AW.

According to the information gathered by the author, CIA through Rabinder Singh wanted to have corroborative evidence from R&AW so that they could get an independent and unbiased intelligence assessment about Iraq, which could strengthen their case for world opinion in attacking Iraq for possession of WMD. Rabinder Singh on his part tried to get such reports from his connections in R&AW. According to the findings of investigating team of R&AW, he got several top secret files from S.K.Gupta, head of Science and Technology desk and after taking photocopies of the relevant reports, sent these documents to CIA for their consumption. This desk of R&AW had detected the Kahuta nuclear plant in Pakistan in 1978. However, there were no corroborative evidence in R&AW to prove that CIA used these reports in formulating their assessment of WMD with Iraq.

Hence, after the successful nuclear test at Pokharan by Indian Government which CIA failed to forecast or detect and then publically declaring that they would recruit agents in every fields and departments in the Indian government, they successfully snared Rabinder Singh inside R&AW. CIA provided him huge financial help in this bargain from which he acquired several properties in Delhi and in other parts of the country and recruited more than 57 officers of R&AW to work for him. Rabinder Singh purchased 11 properties in and around Delhi worth millions of rupees. Besides details of agriculture land and other assets outside Delhi which he built up prior to his defection, are a matter of investigation Subsequently, prior and after the Iraq attack, CIA through Rabinder Singh tried to get as much evidence and proof as R&AW was having on the nuclear capabilities of Iraq. Hence, due to these political compulsions, CIA wanted a spy in R&AW, which they successfully got in Rabinder Singh.

It was a well known fact that prior to this foray inside R&AW, there were attempts by CIA to infiltrate into other offices of Government of India through their friendly countries. In the past CIA, through the French external intelligence agency, was getting copies of reports from their agents on regular basis which were sent to PM office by the IB and the R&AW. French Agency was procuring these reports from its source in the office of the then Principal Secretary to the Prime Minister. This fact further corroborated that CIA successfully planted a mole in Indian Prime Minister office as a part of its earlier announcement on recruiting agents in India like it did in R&AW.

Rabinder Singh Suspected As Foreign Agent

There were two conflicting versions in R&AW to show how Rabinder Singh became suspicious of being working for some foreign agency. Rabinder Singh's activities were first detected by a middle rank officer S.Chandershekhar who was asked by Rabinder Singh to give such information of his desk which was not in his sphere of working. Rabinder Singh's persistence invoked suspicion in his mind and out of panic he decided to report it to head of Counter Intelligence and Security i.e. CIS unit of R&AW. When this fact was brought to the notice of CIS by Chandershekhar, in order to ascertain his motive, Rabinder Singh was provided genuine reports of the US mission in Islamabad which were intercepted by R&AW. Rabinder Singh promptly asked for more information in this regard which confirmed the suspicion reported by Chandershekhar to the R&AW authorities. Moreover, he had often expressed interest in the activities of others with whom he had little concern or connection. His other routine activities were dubious but no one took cognizance of these acts which normally should have been taken seriously by R&AW.

According to another version that he first came under suspicion after a slip made by an American diplomat to the officers of Intelligence Bureau in Delhi during a routine meeting in December, 2003. This intelligence operative of CIA was working under cover at the American embassy in New Delhi who used to meet the IB officials for routine anti-terrorism briefings and exchange of information in this regard. After

9/11 attack on World Trade Tower in USA and terrorist attack on Indian Parliament, a joint mechanism was evolved by the US and Indian Government to share their information with regard to terrorist activities and for which regular meetings were held by the intelligence officers of both the countries in New Delhi and in Washington. In one such routine meeting in New Delhi with IB and R&AW officers, this officer dropped name of Rabinder Singh which confirmed the suspicion of Chandershekhar. The author confirmed from his own sources in R&AW about these two versions, which were found correct.

Initially, CIS unit was in dilemma whether to start discreet inquiry or put him on regular surveillance since Rabinder Singh was holding a senior status in R&AW. Moreover, there was lack of legitimate resources in R&AW to track such criminal offence against their own officer for prosecution in the court of law. However, hesitantly from January, 2004, Rabinder Singh was put under surveillance by R&AW authorities after suspicion arose against him on the basis of these two incidents. For some time, the intensity of surveillance was low but subsequently it was decided to mount it aggressively in view of his interaction with colleagues in expensive restaurants and five star hotels which aroused more suspicion on the gravity of the situation. The CIS unit of R&AW tapped all his landline telephones including his mobile number and opened a mini control room for audio and video coverage of bugged devices. His room at R&AW Headquarterss was fully bugged with audio and video coverage of each and every happenings on day-to-day basis. His Defence Colony residence too was bugged and similar micro cameras for video recording of the visitors and their subsequent conversation was clandestinely installed there by CIS unit of R&AW.

His movements were closely monitored and more than 20 R&AW sleuths were on his surveillance at his residence and office.

It is pointed out here that at this juncture, there was intense internal squabbling among three seniormost officers of R&AW i.e. C D Sahay, Secretary, his deputy J K Sinha and next senior Amar Bhushan. These three IPS officers belonged to the same year of induction in service in IPS and Amar Bhushan was seniormost among them in the initial ranking of IPS officers of Home Ministry but he joined R&AW at a later stage after C D Sahay and J K Sinha and as such given seniority junior to them in the R&AW Administrative Service (RAS). Amar Bhushan represented against this anomaly to the Government but did not get any reprieve in this regard. He also filed a case in the Central Administrative Tribunal but did not succeed in getting any favourable justice from CAT. Hence, all these officers were hell bent to outwit and let down each other in their day to day working which meek Sahay could not control. This squabbling helped Rabinder Singh to escape India when he became sure that he might be arrested very soon after he was searched on April 19, 2004 by CIS unit of R&AW.

Amar Bhushan, Special Secretary, was in charge of CIS unit of R&AW which was keeping surveillance on Rabinder Singh. N K Sharma Director in this unit, was his deputy. It was learnt that Amar Bhushan used to send half baked information about Rabinder Singh to C D Sahay to settle his old score of seniority. When C D Sahay came to know of this fact, he directed N K Sharma to report him directly about the activities of Rabinder Singh by ignoring Amar Bhushan.

Rabinder Singh Hounded By R&AW

According to details gathered by the author, on the basis of the audio and video bugging of Rabinder Singh from Jan. 2004 to April 19, 2004, 57 officers of R&AW, serving and retired, were identified for supplying information and documents to him. One of the most prominent among them was A K Verma, former Secretary of R&AW, who was seen exchanging some documents with Rabinder Singh in the videotape installed secretly at his residence. Verma's lust for money and dubious past could be a clear signal of his appearance on secret tapes of R&AW when he was detected exchanging documents with Rabinder Singh at his residence. There was strong apprehension among officers of R&AW who conducted investigation in this case that Rabinder Singh recruited A K Verma to work for him. This was corroborative since both were found exchanging documents in the videotapes procured from the secret cameras installed at the residence of Rabinder Singh. Since the investigation in this case was not done by any independent agency like CBI or Special Branch of Delhi Police, this fact could not be ascertained and still remains a mystery. But prima facie there was strong evidence of video recording to prove that A K Verma was actively instrumental in providing some vital information to Rabinder Singh for CIA.

Second important person who was found supplying documents to Rabinder Singh in the videotapes was another former Secretary of R&AW, Vikram Sood predecessor of C D Sahay. Vikram Sood had been regularly writing editorials in newspapers which could prove his inclination to highlight many regional issues in favour of US Government. These editorials were based on the material and information he gathered while serving as Secretary of R&AW. These articles mainly focused on the pro-USA policies in Iran, Iraq, Afghanistan and Pakistan which justified that his brain and body were still working for Amercians. He was thus helping Rabinder Singh in one way or other while supplying some documents on the video tapes. Vikram Sood was second former Secretary of R&AW found working for Rabinder Singh in the video tapes.

In these secret audio and video tapes procured by R&AW authorities, Rabinder Singh procured sensitive information and documents from 57 officers of R&AW and took photocopies of these reports from the photocopy machine installed in his room. Being Joint Secretary of R&AW, he was attending all weekly meeting of R&AW which was headed by its Secretary where desk officer of every branch used to brief on the development of various countries. There was every likelihood that Rabinder Singh had tape recorded and video-recorded all these conversations and passed on to CIA regularly while giving other reports of his collaborators.

According to reliable source of R&AW, sometime in the beginning of April, Rabinder Singh was cautioned by another Joint Secretary of R&AW S.B.S.Tomar that he was under surveillance by CIS unit of R&AW. He informed him that there was a suspicion of his being working for some foreign agency. Tomar was the first officer detected in the bugging device to warn Rabinder Singh. Thereafter, Rabinder Singh made up his mind to flee India and applied for leave to visit USA on the pretext of attending the engagement ceremony of his daughter which was declined to him. This refusal of leave by R&AW authorities to him further confirmed the information of S.B.S.Tomar which was vital for his escape from India. Contents of video tape installed in his room at R&AW Headquarterss, would prove that after this disclosure of Tomar, he became so alert that he was seen inspecting each and every article of his office room to find out whether some spy camera was installed there for secret video recording. He was seen standing on his table and trying to trace this camera even in the bulb of lamp which was hanging over his table to increase electrical visibility.

On the morning of April 19, 2004, in the secret video recording, found Rabinder Singh collecting files from the cupboards and making bundles to take out of his room. It was apprehended by the detector of this recording that he might take these files out of building of R&AW Headquarterss that day. When this fact was informed to Amar Bhushan, he informed Sahay accordingly and it was decided that each and every employee of R&AW should be frisked that evening before living leaving office so that Rabinder Singh should be assured that it was a routine checking. Since this was done first time in R&AW, it further gave credence to the information of Tomar to Rabinder Singh that he was under surveillance of CIS unit. Rabinder Singh was caught with 13 bundles of secret files in this frisking. During this frisking another Joint Secretary of R&AW Bhaskar Roy was caught with a pen drive which had secret details of more than 100 files of China desk where he was working but no action was taken against him. Hundreds of classified documents were seized from senior and middle level officers of R&AW who were being taken out of Headquarterss. Large numbers of pornographic materials, pen drives, CDs and DVDs were found in the possession of R&AW employees during this search. Subsequently, R&AW Chief warned in his weekly briefing with senior officers that such searches would be a regular feature in future. Although, this ploy to downplay the singular activity of Rabinder Singh did not work and rather confirmed to him that he could be arrested any time hereinafter.

After this surprise check, Rabinder Singh became absolutely certain that the information given to him by S B S Tomar was correct. In order to crosscheck, he deliberately outwitted the surveillance team in April end to further strengthen this apprehension. He went to Delhi airport purportedly to catch a flight for his home town Amritsar. When surveillance team was exposed by him, surprisingly even then R&AW authorities did not arrest him since it was amply evident by then that Rabinder Singh was aware of his being under watch by R&AW authorities.

According to another reliable source of R&AW, in the end of April, 2004, his immediate boss S K Tripathi, Additional Secretary, whose documents he was seen photocopying in the video tape, deliberately cautioned him as to why he was having liaison with certain person of US embassy with whom he had no business. Rabinder Singh had reportedly brought to the notice of Tripathi a noting by former Secretary Arvind Dave in one of the operational Branches, wherein he had given in writing that liaison with previous agents should be regularly maintained by the running officers of R&AW. Tripathi under whom Rabinder Singh was working, precisely made this disclosure to Rabinder Singh at the behest of his seniors that his involvement with the CIA officer was in the knowledge of R&AW authorities which further confirmed the information of Tomar to him. Tripathi was mysteriously silenced thereafter. All these inputs, alarmed Rabinder Singh of his exposure to R&AW authorities. He thereafter worked on his plans meticulously to flee India with the connivance of CIA. All these disclosures to Rabinder Singh were known to the higher echelons of R&AW but they did not apprehend him intentionally probably fearing their own miseries in the aftermath of that action. S.K.Tripathi purposely informed him of his being in contact with CIA operatives in US embassy at New Delhi. This fact was in the knowledge of R&AW authorities because Trpathi would be involved in numerous legal problems being his immediate boss, if Rabinder Singh was arrested. So, in order to save his own impending problems in future, Tripathi cautioned Rabinder Singh so that he could escape the country to avoid all legal implications. Subsequent bugging interceptions revealed that Rabinder Singh had sought permission from Tripathi that he wanted to visit Nepal during that weekend along with one of his friends which was granted to him by Tripath secretly. These facts were clear indication that Tripathi was one of the main conspirators in defection of Rabinder Singh.

Later on, media reports claimed that there had been privileged information in their possession that Rabinder Singh was forewarned by a senior officer of R&AW that he was under cloud of suspicion for maintaining links with and parting with classified information to a foreign intelligence agency. This officer was certainly none other than S K Tripathi. Hence, it was a known fact not only inside R&AW but in the media also that a certain section of senior officers wanted Rabinder Singh to perish from India so that no direct proof for investigation was left for the government to bring other conspirators to the rule of law. There were strong apprehension inside R&AW that Rabinder Singh was directly briefed by some seniors to do so to avoid all possible future troubles for other conspirators arising out of his impending arrest.

According to latest revelation by the then head of CIS unit of R&AW, a digital photocopier was clandestinely installed in the room of Rabinder Singh at R&AW Headquarterss to take print of the documents through its memory which he photocopied for himself during the day. Prior to the installation of this digital machine, in 22 days bugging, Rabinder Singh was detected through video recording taking photocopies of more than 350 documents, contents of those were not known to the CIS sleuths. In the next 16 days, when digital photocopies was installed, he took away photocopies of more than 210 reports, copies of those were also taken as proof by CIS unit. R&AW watchers were aware that he was taking these reports to his residence where a shredder was available with him. This was amply evident that he was sending the contents of these reports to his handler and thereafter destroying them in the shredder. Rabinder Singh was caught taking away 13 bundles of files from his cupboard and he stopped taking photocopies further from the digital machine. Later on, he became cautious till he escaped and took photocopies of only 16 documents, that too he did not dare to take to his residence. All these reports, whose proof were gathered by R&AW, were classified and contained sensitive information relating to various desks of R&AW. These reports precisely covered the operational activities of not only all neighboring countries but were also concerned with other intelligence inroads devised for foreign policies with many countries of Europe, South East Asia and CIS region. Some of these reports included R&AW's assessment in Afghanistan about Taliban-Pakistan nexus, ISI-Military concerted designs for terrorism in J&K and Security situation therein, Chinese military incursions on borders, Maoist menace in Nepal, US activities in CIS countries and support to Pakistan, political developments in Bangladesh, outcome of Sri Lanka elections and its consequences to India, Science and Technology wing reports of R&AW on various nuclear programmes, support of R&AW to various NGOs, lobbyists, journalists etc. at various places. These details were collected from the desk officers of these branches on old photocopier and taken to his home. When digital photocopier was installed, Rabinder Singh photocopies reports related to latest status of nuclear power plants in Pakistan, Nepal Marxists' nexus with Naxalites in Andhra, Bihar, Jharkhand, Orissa and Chhattisgarh, Bangladesh army's role in domestic affairs, Indian influence in the aftermath of elections in Sri Lanka, R&AW's assessment on security in the Valley, NSCS's tasking of intelligence requirements for Islamic terrorism, drug trafficking on Myanmar border, disappearance of a R&AW mole in North Korean nuclear plant, sectarian violence in Pakistan and dissension in Pak Army over handling of insurgency in the FATA area, IB's report on foreigners activities in India, LTTE' latest procurements, Bhutan-US relations, Norway's perception of peace process in Sri Lanka.

Brijesh Mishra Dragged Arrest

C D Sahay did not disclose this matter to Brijesh Mishra, National Security Advisor and Principal Secretary to the Prime Minister, Atal Bihari Vajpayee, obviously till Rabinder Singh was found working for a particular intelligence agency. CIS head, Amar Bhushan was averse to this decision till investigation were completed by his team and prevailed upon Sahay to keep this matter within the walls of R&AW. However, after some time Sahay brief NSA on this development who cautioned him not to have dragged this case so far. NSA's main focus was its impending implications on the strategic Indo-US relationship for which he was going to make a presentation before the Cabinet Committee on Foreign Policy in the near future. However, Brijesh Mishra did not ask Sahay to arrest Rabinder Singh since voting for the last phase of general elections was round the corner and this disclosure in media would have dampened the chance of NDA government to retain power. So, the spy was allowed to mushroom with his adventure in the guise of political compulsion which was far more paramount for the rulers because once he was out of box, a fall out could have resulted in the political fiasco for ruling NDA. In subsequent meetings with R&AW Chief, Brijesh Mishra wanted to buy time to take some stringent action in this case due to his own vulnerable position since within party, dissension was brewing for his head. Delay to arrest was deliberately dragged fearing adverse publicity.

Rabinder Singh continued his spying spree and took photocopies of reports related to government formation in Sri Lanka, ongoing fighting between insurgents and Myanmar forces, latest round up of Indo-Nepal relations, seizures of arms from ULFA insurgents inside Bangladesh, deployment of coalition forces in Afghanistan, Chinese supply of arms and communications equipment to Myanmar, factional clashes within LTTE etc. In addition to these documents, he was getting weekly reports of R&AW's assessment with most of the neighbouring countries and source reports on various operational functioning elsewhere. All these reports were sensitive and classified.

These revelations by the head of CIS unit of R&AW, were sensational proof of taking photocopies of classified documents of almost all the desks of R&AW and there was little ground left to its authorities to question Rabinder Singh as to why and for whom he was getting these reports. He was allowed to dabble when time was running too fast for R&AW authorities who were bent upon to find so called clinching evidences, which were available in abundance with them as documentary proof. But what for and whom so far, they were waiting, was a mystery. C D Sahay confided with one of his confidants at a later stage that Brijesh Mishra wanted this case to be handled by the next government since results of the general elections were round the corner. So, Rabinder Singh was allowed to merrily take safety route to USA through CIA operatives and with the connivance of big wigs of R&AW. Investigation records gave proof that prior to his defection, his driver warned him that he was under surveillance, the fact which not one but two of his senior colleagues corroborated day after in his office. These bugging reports were available with the R&AW authorities which were clear indication of their obsession to get away with this troublesome creature out of their sight for ever. Even he was found using different SIM cards purchased from various locations in Delhi, Mumbai and Chennai, which too was never questioned by R&AW authorities. Moreover, Home Ministry permission to officially monitor these mobile numbers was never sought so that legal transcriptions of the conversations could have been made available as prosecution evidence. Rabinder Singh perished to the full knowledge of R&AW Chief C D Sahay which subsequently brought reprieve to the 57 collaborators who parted with sensitive information to him. 19 of them, who were over enthusiastic and colluded to provide sensitive operational disclosures to him, were never prosecuted and rather rewarded to lucrative foreign assignments to USA, European and Asian countries. Even, the investigating officer, A.K.Sinha, who hushed up this case legally, was assigned the prize posting in Mauritius. Although, N K Sharma, Director of CIS, who was quite often ridiculed by C D Sahay for his over-zealous investigation, was made to sulk initially but he disclosed the veracity of this investigation to M K Narayanan, National Security Advisor, putting blame on C D Sahay for the defection of Rabinder Singh. Sharma was, however, rewarded by Narayanan for a posting in Canada, after which he retired.

There is a strong Indian myth that crow never bites a crow. This myth was fully made proverbial by a team spies of R&AW which was captained by C D

Sahay, who saved 57 of the collaborators in this dirty games of espionage by manipulating the legal system of this country. It was further revealed by the head of CIS unit of R&AW that it was detected from the hard disc of the two laptops that Rabinder Singh was imparted training by his handler to take pictures of the documents using the cameras and string them in the external flash memory. This was probably done since he was not proficient in typing. Over 23,000 files had their imprints on the hard disc which were transmitted by him to his handlers. These pictures were transmitted after porting the flash memory on the laptop using as a docking station. The images of documents were transmitted using a secure file transfer internet protocol. After transmitting the files, the data was regularly deleted by him. So, a fictitious drama was enacted to prolong this case when there were more than a dozen evidences to arrest Rabinder Singh. Moreover, R&AW authorities were aware that Nepal was his favourtie sojourn, where he used to vist at least once every six months, even without seeking permission from the higher ups. Even then R&AW authorities did not take notice of these dubious activities of Rabinder Singh who could be meeting his handlers there incognito.

PIL In High Court Against Co-accused

The author tried to nail this case relentlessly and also filed a Public Interest Litigation in Delhi High Court for legal action but the Hon'ble Judges found it a hot potato. Instead of getting it to some logical legal action, the Judges tried to coerce the author to file an affidavit as to how he got the names of these collaborators. The author readily agreed to disclose his sources in the chamber of Chief Justice which was declined. Even then, the author was prepared to reveal the truth had the Chief Justice given guarantee to the security of their service in R&AW which he was not obliged to grant. However, the Court opined that since the matter was under investigation in another court, their indulgence at that juncture was uncalled for. These strange legal wrangling give credence to the faith of ordinary citizen of this country that to extract justice at the cost of their life and financial resources, is a far cry and so-called activists are made to shut their mouth to let these sordid events happen unabetting in this country, which no one can dare to rein. The author subsequently appealed in Supreme Court against this order but there too this case was not considered fit for legal consumption. While coming out of the Supreme Court, the author duly saluted the Indian judicial system out of sheer desperation since he had no axe to grind except bringing the conspirators of this espionage case to legal prosecution. A lot of money was lost in this misadventure which these legal luminaries should understand that to approach higher courts is not an easy affair now a days. Author had certainly a point for public interest in this case, which was not given any credence.

The Secretary of State of the United States of America hereby requests all whom it may concern to permit the citizen/national of the United States named herein to pass without delay or hindrance and in case of need to give all lawful aid and protection.

Le Secrétaire d'Etat des Etats-Unis d'Amérique prie par les présentes toutes autorités compétentes de laisser passer le citoyen ou ressortissant des Etats-Unis titulaire du présent passeport, sans délai ni difficulté et, en cas de besoin, de lui accorder toute aide et protection légitimes.

El Secretario de Estado de los Estados Unidos de América, por el presente solicita a las autoridades competentes permitir el paso del ciudadano o nacional de los Estados Unidos aquí nombrado, sin demora ni dificultades, y en caso de necesidad, prestarle toda ayuda y protección lícitas.

R. K. Sharma

SIGNATURE OF BEARER/SIGNATURE DU TITULAIRE/FIRMA DEL TITULAR

NOT VALID UNTIL SIGNED

PASSPORT
PASSEPORT
PASAPORTE

USA

UNITED STATES OF AMERICA

SHARMA

RAJPAL PRASAD

UNITED STATES OF AMERICA

Washington

Passport Agency

...SHARMA<<RAJPAL<PRASAD<<<<<<<<<<<<<<<

017384251 9USA4808101M1404063<<<<<<<<<<<<<04

(Typed Copy of Passport)

The Secretary of States of the United States of America
Hereby requests all whom it may concern to permit the citizen/national
Of the United States named herein to pass without delay or hindrance
and in case of need to give all lawful aid and protection

R.K.Sharma

SIGNATURE OF BEARER / SIGNATURE DU TITULAIR/FIRMA DEL TITULAR

NOT VALID UNTIL SIGNED

UNITED STATES OF AMERICA

PASSPORT

Type
P

Code
USA

Passport No.
017384251

Surname
SHARMA

Name
RAJPAL PRASAD

Nationality
UNITED STATES OF AMERICA

Date of birth
10 Aug 1948

Sex
M

Place of birth
INDIA

Date of Issue
07 Apr. 2004

Washington
Passport Agency

Date of Expiration
06 Apr. 2014

USASHARMA<< RAJPAL<<PRASAD<<<<<<<<<<<<<<<<<<<<<<<
0173842519 USA 4808101M1404063<<<<<<<<<<<<<<<<<<<<<<04

No.______

EMBARKATION CARD
(DEPARTURE)

Please write in Block letters, Do not FOLD

Family Name	First Name	M. Name
SHARMA	RAJPAL	PRASAD.

Sex : Male ☑ Female ☐	Nationality: U.S.A.

Passport No.	Date of Issue	Date of Expiry
017384251	08 Apr 2004 (Day/Month/Year)	06 Apr 2014 (Day/Month/Year)
Entry Visa No.	**Place of Issue**	**Visa Expiry**
5421	TIA	07/05/2004 (Day/Month/Year)

Mode of Exit	Departure Date
By Air ☑ By Land ☐	07/05/2004 (Day/Month/Year)
Flight No. 05 032	Exit Point TIA.

Place(s) Visited in Nepal

- ☐ Everest Area
- ☐ Lumbini
- ☐ Annapurna Area
- ☐ Chitwan
- ☐ Pokhara
- ☐ Ilam & Surroundings
- ☐ Bardia National Park
- ☐ Langtang Area
- ☑ Others

R. Sharma

Signature

EMBARKATION CARD
(DEPARTURE)

Family Name	First Name	M.Name
Sharma	Rajpal	Prasad
Sex M/F - M	Nationality – U.S.A.	
Passport No.	Date of issue	Date of expiry
017384251	7th April, 2004	6th April, 2014
Entry Visa No.	Place of issue	Visa expiry
5421	TIA	07.05.2004
Mode of exit	Departure Date	
By Air - By land	07.05.2004	
Flight No.	Exit Point	
5032	TIA	

Place visited in Nepal

Others

Sd/- Signature

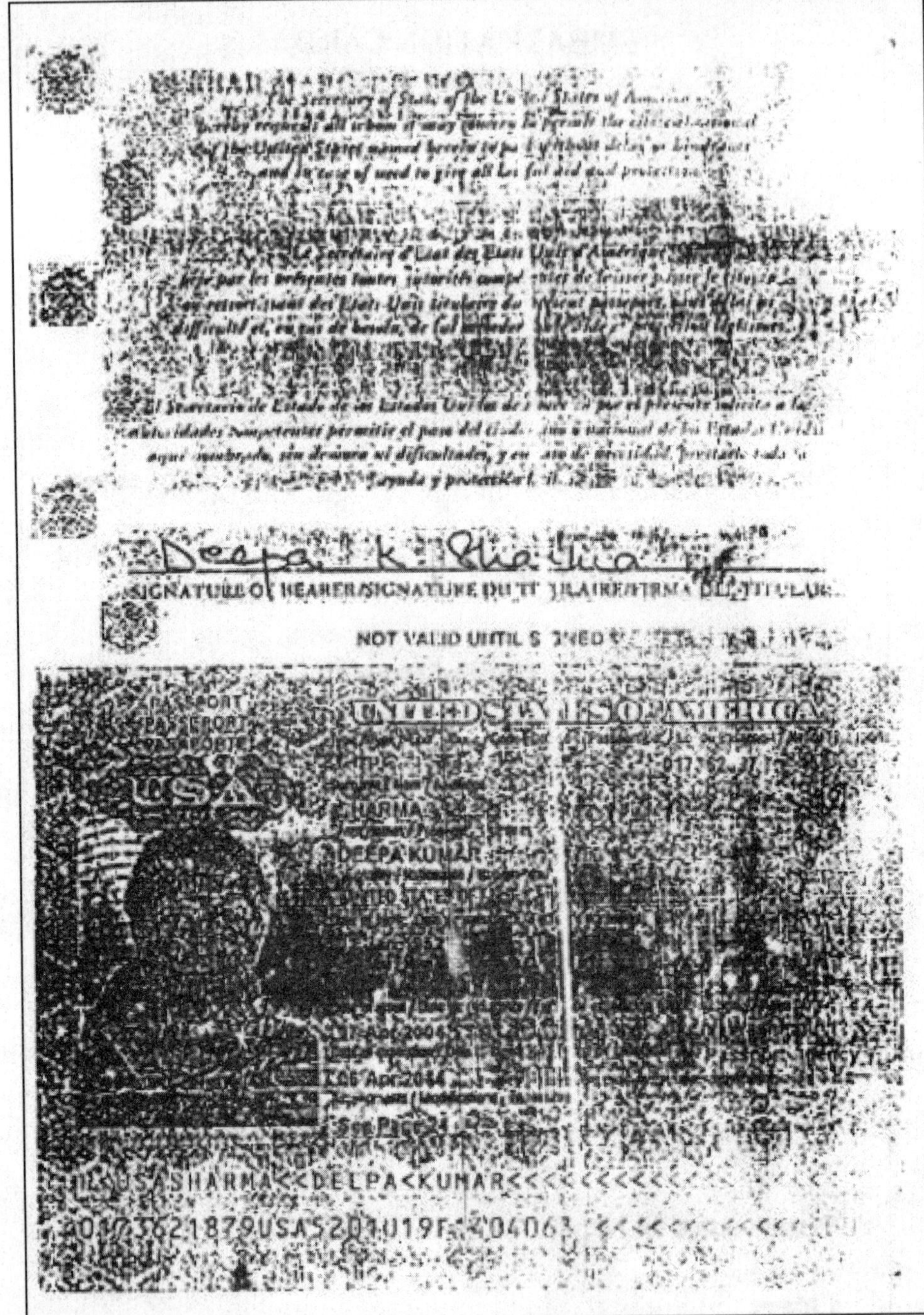

The Secretary of State of the United States of America hereby requests all whom it may concern to permit the citizen/national of the United States named herein to pass without delay or hindrance and in case of need to give all lawful aid and protection.

Le Secrétaire d'Etat des Etats-Unis d'Amérique prie par les présentes toutes autorités compétentes de laisser passer le citoyen ou ressortissant des Etats-Unis titulaire du présent passeport, sans délai ni difficulté et, en cas de besoin, de lui accorder toute aide et protection légitimes.

El Secretario de Estado de los Estados Unidos de América por el presente solicita a las autoridades competentes permitir el paso del ciudadano o nacional de los Estados Unidos aquí nombrado, sin demora ni dificultades, y en caso de necesidad, prestarle toda la ayuda y protección lícitas.

SIGNATURE OF BEARER/SIGNATURE DU TITULAIRE/FIRMA DEL TITULAR

NOT VALID UNTIL SIGNED

PASSPORT
PASSEPORT
PASAPORTE

USA

UNITED STATES OF AMERICA

SHARMA

DEEPA KUMAR

UNITED STATES OF AMERICA

17 Apr 2004

06 Apr 2014

See Page 24

USASHARMA<<DELPA<KUMAR<<<<<<<<<<

0173621879USA5201019F1404063<<<<<<<<<<<<

(Typed Copy of Passport)

The Secretary of States of the United States of America
Hereby requests all whom it may concern to permit the citizen/national
Of the United States named herein to pass without delay or bindings
and in case of need to give all lawful aid and protection

Deepa K.Sharma

SIGNATURE OF BEARER / SIGNATURE DU TITULAIR/FIRMA DEL TITULAR

NOT VALID UNTIL SIGNED

UNITED STATES OF AMERICA

PASSPORT

Type
P

Code
USA

Passport No.
017362187

Surname
SHARMA

Name
DEEPA KUMAR

Nationality
UNITED STATES OF AMERICA

Date of birth
10 Jan 1952

Sex
F

Place of birth
INDIA

Date of Issue
07 Apr. 2004

Washington
Passport Agency

Date of Expiration
06 Apr. 2014

<USASHARMA<< DEEPA< KUMAR<<<<<<<<<<<<<<<<<<<<<
0173621879 USA 5201019F1404063<<<<<<<<<<<<<<<<<<<<<

No.________

EMBARKATION CARD
[DEPARTURE]

Please write in Block letters, Do not FOLD

Family Name	First Name	M. Name
SHARMA	DEEPA	KUMAR

Sex: Male ☐ Female ☑

Nationality: U.S.A

Passport No.	Date of Issue	Date of Expiry
Z17362187	7 APR 2004 (Day / Month / Year)	6 APR 2014 (Day / Month / Year)

Entry Visa No.	Place of Issue	Visa Expiry
5422	TIA	07 MAY 2004 (Day / Month / Year)

Mode of Exit	Departure Date
By Air ☑ By Land ☐	07 MAY 2004 (Day / Month / Year)
Flight No. OS032	Exit Point TIA

Place(s) Visited in Nepal

☐ Everest Area ☐ Lumbini

☐ Annapurna Area ☐ Chitwan

☐ Pokhara ☐ Ilam & Surroundings

☐ Bardia National Park ☐ Langtang Area

☑ Others

Deepa K. Sharma

Signature

EMBARKATION CARD
(DEPARTURE)

Family Name	First Name	Name
Sharma	Deepa	Kumar
Sex M/F	Nationality	
Female	U.S.A.	
Passport No.	Date of issue	Date of expiry
017362187	7th April, 2004	6th April, 2014
Entry Visa No.	Place of Issue	Visa Expiry
5422	TIA	7th May, 2004
Mode of exit	Departure Date	
By Air__By land__	7th May, 2004	
Flight No. 5032	Exit point TIA	
Place visited in Nepal		
Others		
		Sd/- Signature

Defection Orchestrated

According to sources of the author, in a deep routed conspiracy, C D Sahay, Secretary of R&AW, called the Director of CIS N K Sharma in his room on April 30, 2004, and asked him to withdraw surveillance on Rabinder Singh. He told that since nothing extraordinary was being found thereinafter in the ongoing repetitive surveillance, hence it was now wastage of time and energy. Sahay also created misconception in the mind of N K Sharma that due to differences among senior officers of R&AW about what kind of legal action to be taken against Rabinder Singh and therefore further surveillance was a futile exercise. N K Sharma had no option but to stop surveillance forthwith. After the surveillance of Rabinder Singh was abruptly stopped on the direction of C D Sahay, as a part of this conspiracy, Kishan Verma, Joint Secretary, in charge of Control Room of R&AW, instructed the staff posted therein, not to deliver any letter at the residence of Rabinder Singh till further orders. This was planned with the motive because if any employee of R&AW would go to his residence and found him missing, he would reveal this fact to senior officers and other employees of R&AW and the whole conspiracy to allow him to flee the country, would be unraveled. For this connivance, Kishan Verma was rewarded for a prize posting of Counselor in Washington.

In the subsequent part of this conspiracy, when it was known to other officers of R&AW that Rabinder Singh had disappeared from his residence on May, 1, 2004, a core committee meeting was hurriedly convened by C D Sahay to assess the emergency situation and to take future course of action in this fall out. Primarily, it was decided to inform the IB initially verbally at once. Thereafter, a formal request was to be sent for a Look Out notice against Rabinder Singh so that IB and local police could search him on the borders of India, airports, bus stops, railway stations. prominent hotels and other hide outs across the country. This task was assigned to the Joint Secretary of this desk Niraj Srivastava. Investigation team found that mysteriously, Niraj Srivastava neither informed verbally nor sent a formal request to IB for a Look Out notice in this matter. He rather misinformed his senior Amar Bhushan that he had done so. This fact was confirmed by the IB officials who deposed before the investigation team of R&AW. These startling revelations of sources of R&AW give credence to the fact that C D Sahay with the help of his junior officers deliberately and successfully allowed Rabinder Singh to cross inside Nepal to further flee to USA with the help of CIA operatives at Kathmandu.

When on May 1, 2004, Rabinder Singh became certain that his surveillance was completely withdrawn, he and his wife Parvinder Kaur travelled in the car of his co-brother who dropped them on the Indian side of the Indo-Nepal border. On May 2, both of them crossed over to Nepal and arrived at Nepalganj where they were received by David M Vacala, First Secretary in the American Embassy who was a CIA operative. All of them stayed that night at Hotel Sneha in Nepalganj. Next day, on May 3, they took a local flight in the morning from Nepalganj and reached Katmandu where they stayed in the guest house of American Embassy. David Vacala was previously posted in US Consulate at Mumbai from 1997 to 2003 before he was transferred to Washington where he worked in CIA Headquarterss up to May, 2003. He was involved in Afghan affairs during this stint at Washington and made several visits to Kabul. He was then transferred to US Embassy in Kathmandu in June, 2003. He was an old hand of CIA in this region. There were circumstantial reasons to believe that Vacala could be one of the handlers of Rabinder Singh because frequencies of his visit to Kathmandu were abnormal during 2003 to 2004.

Rabinder Singh was issued a passport by the US embassy of Kathmandu in the name of Ram Prasad Sharma bearing number 0173842519 dated April 7, 2004 which was valid for 10 years. His date of birth was shown as August 10, 1948. His wife, shown as Deepa Kumar Sharma, was issued a passport bearing no. 017362189 dated April 7, 2004 also for 10 years. Her date birth was shown as January, 10 1952. Both of them boarded flight no.5032 from Tribhuvan International Airport on May, 7, 2004 as per the details given in embarkation card of their departure. Rabinder Singh and his wife were boarded in this Austrian flight for Vienna for USA from Kathmandu around 11 PM in the night. This was a bi-weekly flight from Kathmandu to Vienna.

Rabinder Singh Fled To USA

When Rabinder Singh safely boarded the plane on the night of May 7, 2004, for his destination to USA, on May 8, at 5 in the morning, C D Sahay, R&AW Chief, telephoned the station in-charge of R&AW in the Indian Embassy at Kathmandu and informed him that Rabinder Singh was in Kathmandu. He asked him to trace him there. R&AW operatives immediately mounted surveillance on the airport and other vantage points like the office and residences of US Embassy officials and leading hotels. Finally, on May 10, they detected that Rabinder Singh and his wife had already fled on the night of May 7 by the Austrian flight. Subsequently, the investigation team which conducted inquiries in this case, detected that prior to boarding the Austrian flight on May 7, a call from the mobile phone of Rabinder Singh to C D Sahay, R&AW Chief, was traced from Kathmandu to New Delhi. This call from Rabinder Singh to Sahay proved the fact that he was fully aware of each and every movement of Rabinder Singh till he boarded the flight to USA. Sahay deliberately telephoned the R&AW station chief at Kathmandu on May 8, knowing that he had already fled on May 7, to locate Rabinder Singh in Nepal to cover up the whole mishap so that subsequent inquiry into this case of his disappearance from Kathmandu would find nothing indiscriminate of his involvement in the conspiracy. According to investigation report, there was nothing on record of R&AW to prove that any one in R&AW informed Sahay that Rabinder Singh was in Nepal from May 3, to 7. Had it been so, and proper action taken in time, R&AW operatives at Kathmandu would never have allowed him to defect due to their strong presence at that station. There had been numerous cases when R&AW whisked away many terrorists from Kathmandu to India in their plane with the tacit permission of Nepalese government without completion of diplomatic formalities. So, Sahay cautioned R&AW station chief on May 8 after Rabinder Singh had escaped from there only as a cover up exercise. These startling disclosures were available with the investigation team but in order to put a lid on the factual conspiracy to save the collaborators, a cock and bull story was built up and presented in a Delhi Court as eyewash. These facts were known to M.K.Narayanan, the then National Security Advisor but he too remained silent on the prosecution of these conspirators who conspicuously allowed Rabinder Singh to defect to USA. It is learnt that the court has consigned this file to record in the absence of main culprits Rabinder Singh and his wife, who would never be brought for prosecution.

Main Conspirators

Nineteen officers were indicted by the investigation team for criminal offence for giving classified information and documents to Rabinder Singh and with conspiracy to defect to US. Details of these officers are given below:

Helped In Fleeing

1. C D Sahay, Secretary of R&AW.
2. S.K.Tripathi, the then Additional Secretary.
3. Niraj Srivastava, Joint Secretary.
4. Kishan Verma, Joint Secretary.
5. S.B.S.Tomar, Joint Secretary.

Suppliers of Documents and Information

1. Vikram Sood, former Secretary. He was found supplying documents to Rabinder Singh in his car and at his residence in the video tapes of surveillance team and spy camera installed at his residence.
2. A K Verma, former Secretary. He was also found supplying documents in his car and at his residence in the video tapes of the surveillance team and spy camera. Rabinder Singh visited his residence regularly empty handed and found returning with bags full of documents. He was supplying defence canteen whisky while visiting his house in NOIDA.

3. Gurinder Singh, former Special Secretary. He was found on spy camera having sex with a lady at the residence of Rabinder Singh.
4. Amitabh Mathur
5. Major General Mattoo, Joint Secretary.
6. Balaji Srivastava, Director.
7. Ilango, Director.
8. Bigadier Dasgupta, Director. In another spying case he was arrested by Delhi Police when he was found with a lady CIA operative.
9. Rajiv Sinha, Director.
10. Brigadier Budhiraja, Director.
11. S.K.Gupta, Director.
12. Vakil Ramdass, Deputy Secretary.
13. K.V.Reddy, Deputy Secretary.
14. Ashok Bajpai, Deputy Secretary. He was son of former Secretary of R&AW, G.S.Bajpayee. When he was interrogated by the investigation team, out of fear of his arrest, he resigned from R&AW and fled to a foreign country.

Subversion of Legal System

In normal circumstances, this spying case should have been handed over to the CBI or Special Branch of Delhi Police for investigation as was done in the previous case of Unnikrishnan. But since R&AW authorities had confirmed that two former Secretaries of R&AW A K Verma and Vikram Sood were detected in the secret spy camera exchanging documents with Rabinder Singh and his mobile call on the phone of the then Secretary C D Sahay on May 7, 2004 from Katmandu prior to his escape to Vienna and USA, was traced by the investigating team and 57 senior and middle level officers of R&AW were found hand in glove with Rabinder Singh who provided all the sensitive information and documents to him, they were in dilemma to wriggle out of the web. It was, therefore, devised to file a Luke warm complaint absolving all these officers of the serious charges. Most of these officers supplied secret information of their desk but surprisingly the investigating team had left out many of them and indicted only 19 officers of R&AW whose charges were found too grave for which criminal action was to be taken against them. However, they too were not made co-accused in the final charge sheet filed in the court.

Involvement of these officers with Rabinder Singh was detected on the basis of conversation of tapped telephones and mobile phone of Rabinder Singh and secret videotapes collected from the spying cameras installed in the room of his office and at his residence in Defence Colony. Had this case been investigated by the CBI or Special Branch of Delhi Police, most of these officers of R&AW whose involvement with Rabinder Singh was on record, would have been arrested and put behind bars for their connivance in this criminal act. In yet another identical case of this nature, one senior officer of R&AW Brig. Ujjal Dasgupta, Director of Computer Division was found supplying computer data base of National Security Council Headquarters to Rosanna Minchew a lady of US Embassy in New Delhi who was a CIA officer. Dasgupta was arrested by Special Branch of Delhi Police along with three other officers of National Security Council and languished in Tihar jail before he was granted bail. But keeping all legal procedures out of place, all these officers of R&AW found involved with Rabinder Singh, were not charged for their connivance in this criminal offence because this case had been investigated by a team of R&AW officers after taking special permission from the Home Ministry which is not the normal legal practice in Government of India till date. Thus, involvement of CBI or Special Branch in such cases had been outmaneuvered by R&AW to save these 57 officers from being prosecuted at the hand of law enforcing agencies.

Conspirators Rewarded

Instead of taking any criminal action against these 19 officers, even some of them were sent on foreign assignments in Indian Missions abroad. Lackadaisical attitude of R&AW authorities in this manner could be assessed from the fact that one such officer Kishan Verma, who was conspirator in Rabinder Singh's defection, was posted in Indian Mission at Washington, USA, where Rabinder Singh had allegedly been given shelter by CIA. This grave security lapse was known to every body in R&AW. According to reliable sources, it was also known to R&AW authorities that Kishan Verma was stated to be spending more than his salary in USA for the education of his two daughters. Probably, he was still getting money and supplying information from some outside sources who could be none other than Rabinder Singh in Washington, where he could not be crosschecked by the R&AW authorities for such misadventure. Another such dubious officer Vakil Ramdass was sent to Johannesburg in South Africa. There was a strong apprehension in R&AW that he not only supplied information and documents to Rabinder Singh but was also a double agent of ISI while serving in Islamabad. Such officers who were rewarded in this manner include Rajiv Sinha and S.B.S Tomar who were posted in Moscow and Washington respectively. Tomar was the first person who informed Rabinder Singh that he was under the scanner of surveillance of R&AW authorities.

R&AW authorities devised a novel procedure which was illegal to save these officers who were found involved with Rabinder Singh and supplied vital and secret information to him. R&AW authorities keeping all legal norms on tenterhook, manipulated in the name of secrecy and sensitiveness of this case and got approval from the Home Ministry for constituting a team of their own Investigation officers, who would investigate this case and submit a charge sheet in the criminal court which was motivated and unethical. According to legal provisions prevalent in various departments and ministries of Government of India, in such cases investigation is conducted by the CBI or by the Special Branches of the Police of the respective State. Moreover, R&AW does not exist as an independent Ministry or Department in Government of India according to the Constitution but function as a wing of Cabinet Secretariat with no legal authority to conduct such investigations. R&AW even dors not have legal powers to tape the telephones or mobiles of any person and in case of any such necessity, they take the help of IB who gets permission from the Home Ministry in this regard. Even Intelligence Bureau does not have any legal power to conduct such investigations for their own employees which is conducted by CBI or Special Branch of Police.

Even if findings of this team of investigating officers of R&AW, headed by one Director, A.K.Sinha was given the credence, 57 officers of R&AW were contacted by Rabinder Singh to gather information and documents from them, out of which 19 were actually indicted by this team for supplying secret and sensitive information. This included three former Secretaries of R&AW, two serving Special Secretaries, five serving Joint Secretaries and others were middle level officers from the rank of Under Secretaries to Directors. Even these officers were not made co-accused in the charge sheet and only a case against Rabinder Singh and his wfie was filed in the Court at Delhi.

This spying case is far more serious in magnitude in comparison to the infamous Samba Spying case of Army of 1975 wherein more than 50 army officials up to the rank of Major were arrested and put under Court Martial. R&AW authorities filed charge sheet against Rabinder Singh under Officials Secret Act only and these 57 officers who were conspirators with him, were not included in the charge sheet for obvious reasons. Even 19 officers who were indicted by the investigating team were also excluded from any criminal action by the R&AW authorities to avoid their own problems arising out adverse media attention. Even trial in this case was being conducted in camera to keep media away from the actual facts.

In Navy War Room Leak case, the then Chief of Navy Arun Prakash found his own relative R Sankaran involved along with other officers of Navy and some civilians for spying in some navy arms purchases. Navy Chief had powers to prosecute these officials under the Defence Act but in order to bring transparency in the investigation, he referred this case for investigation to the CBI. Even the Court refused in-camera trial in this case. CBI pursued this case and a red corner notice had been issued against Sanakaran who was absconding and stated to be hiding somewhere in United Kingdom or any other European country. He has since been detected and is being extradited for prosecution in India.

In another spying case of 2006, when some computer analysts of National Security Council Secretariat (NSCS) were found supplying secret data of more than 7,000 pages to an American lady diplomat Rosanna Minchew who was a CIA operative, they were arrested by Special Branch of Delhi Police and languished in Tihar jail for aconsiderable period. Among these NSCS officers, one Brigadier Ujjal Dasgupta was a R&AW officer who was arrested by the Special Branch and now released on bail. Hence, in the Rabinder Singh Spying case different legal yardsticks had been adopted by the R&AW authorities to avoid arrest of their accused officers and Government of India was deliberately befooled or they too wanted it to happen like that.

In a very recent case of R&AW, one of its former officer Maj. Gen. V K Singh wrote a book entitled "India's External Intelligence — Secrets of R&AW" wherein he exposed the prevalent corruption inside R&AW at senior level. R&AW authorities filed a complaint against V K Singh in CBI to register a case against him under the Official Secret Act, which was duly registered but the CBI Court granted him bail and the matter is still under investigation by CBI. Rabinder Singh Spying case was graver and more sensitive in nature in comparison to V K Singh but R&AW authorities for obvious reasons did not refer this case to CBI and got it investigated through its own mechanism. This is not only injudicious but mysterious and is probe worthy.

Legal Status of Case

According to media reports, Rabinder Singh was dismissed from service under article 311(2)© of the Constitution. R&AW authorities recommended that Rabinder Singh be charged under Section 8 of the Officials Secret Act so that he was declared proclaimed offender. According to media reports, Home Ministry had subsequently granted such permission and accordingly a charge sheet was filed in the court of law. Rabinder Singh was stated to have been located in USA for which a 30-page complaint was filed by the Investigating Officer in the court where it was reported that efforts are in progress for his extradition from USA. Government of India invoked National Security Act to arrest Rabinder Singh and attachment of his property under sections 82 and 83 of the Criminal Procedure Code.

After obtaining a non-bailable arrest warrant in February, 2007 against Rabinder Singh, R&AW authorities approached CBI to make a case against him with Interpol to secure a Red Corner Notice as he was stated to be living in Jackson Height area of New York in USA. On February, 3, 2007 i.e. after around three years of his defection, CBI approached the Interpol Headquarterss in Lyons, France in this regard to which Interpol sent a questionnaire in which certain other queries were raised including the nature of secret information gathered by Rabinder Singh and why a delay of around three years was caused by Indian Government to secure this notice. Surprisingly R&AW refused to reply the queries raised in the aforesaid questionnaire and stick to their own stand that they would supply only the information given in the charge sheet in the Chief Metropolitan Magistrate, Court. Since, R&AW authorities were not co-operating with the Interpol on the contents of this questionnaire, there is absolutely no chance to secure a Red Corner Notice against Rabinder Singh and as such Interpol on August, 14, 2007 refuses to publish Red Corner Notices against Rabinder Singh and his wife Parminder Kaur. In view of this anomaly, he could not be arrested even if he openly detected in USA or elsewhere in the world. This is highly deplorable and questionable.

Extradition Thwarted

CBI also forwarded a formal request on February, 2 2007 for provisional arrest of Rabinder Singh and his wife as per Article 12 of Indo-US Extradition Treaty to the Ministry of External Affairs. It was communicated therein that concerned investigating agency had confirmed therein that request for extradition as per Article 9 of Indo-US Extradition Treaty would be forwarded within time period prescribed in the Treaty after confirmation of the detection of the couple. However, the Ministry of External Affairs informed on 30.11.1977 that the US Department of State had declined the request for provisional arrest of Rabinder Singh and Parminder Kaur. In view of these developments, the extradition proceedings could not be initiated. So, US government put their foot down to extradite him to India and Indian government did not think proper to take any more provocative action in this case. Even if Rabinder Singh is apprehended in USA or somewhere else, there is every likelihood that R&AW authorities would get him eliminated because in case he is extradited, 57 officers of R&AW would be arrested and put in jail for trial along with him for their connivance in this espionage case which the authorities would never like to happen. Absence of Rabinder Singh from the scene of criminal trial for whole of his life, would give the escape route to these officers for scuttling the prosecution under Officials Secret Act.

Rabinder Singh espionage case is altogether different from other prominent spying cases of the country because in most of the cases, the perpetrators were caught and on their interrogation, connivance of other accused were detected. In this case, since Rabinder Singh was deliberately allowed to escape the country with the help of the then Secretary of R&AW C D Sahay. The charge sheet was prepared on the basis of the statement of 57 officers of R&AW who were questioned by the investing team on the basis of their being caught on the tape recording of phones or being found exchanging documents on video tapes of spy cameras. Since there would be no corroboration of these facts from the chief architect of whole of this spying episode, Rabinder Singh, credibility of the statement of these officers could be questionable because they were aware that Rabinder Singh had been deliberately allowed to flee to save the fate of all these officers from being convicted as co-accused. Had an independent inquiry from CBI or Special Branch of Police been done, truth of the matter would have been different as presented in the Court by the R&AW authorities. Due to this lack of evidence, R&AW authorities have failed to put up proper reply to the questionnaire of the Interpol with the result, chances of Rabinder Singh being caught in USA and extradited to India are very remote. Politically, Indian Government would not make any resolute demand to the US Government because he was escorted by CIA operatives from the Indian border on May 3, 2004 and given shelter in USA.

❑

Bizarre R&AW Incidents

K Sankaran Nair, Former R&AW Chief Caught On Wrong Foot K.Sankaran Nair, the flamboyant and mercurial intelligence officer usually nom- de-plumes as Col. Menon as operational code throughout his life in R&AW. Usually, such a cover name had to be adopted for operational and bureaucratic safety in spying world. Till the end of eighties, many R&AW officers were sent on pseudonymous names. Once a very senior officer, H N Kak had to face many problems in India after his return from a cosy foreign assignment where he was working on a different cover name. Thereafter, this practice was discontinued, except in some extraneous circumstances. However, even now R&AW officers are working on cover name in their operational duties, be it in India or elsewhere in any part of the world. How and wherefrom R N Kao either borrowed or invented such a practice for his officers is still a mystery.

Prior to 1971 war, the Defence Minister, Jagjiven Ram called R N Kao in his South Block office where Chief of Naval Staff was also sitting with him. The Defence Minister told Kao that he himself had been reporting that war clouds were gathering. If that hostilities would start with Pakistan, Indian Navy should attack Karachi harbor as pre-emptive measure so that the enemy's navy be bottled up from harassing our ship movement in the Arabian Sea. He further told Kao that the Naval Chief had information that the enemy had put in new defences to guard the entrance of the harbor on the nearby cliffs and Navy had no intelligence at all. He asked Kao if could get full intelligence of this area. Kao promised to do his best and withdrew. He called his number two K.Sankaran Nair and told him the requirement of Navy. Nair bowed in acknowledgement of the assignment and left. Later, he rang up one of the R&AW officers in Bombay and gave him his task.

A few days later, the Bombay operative rang back and gave his plan. Nair then sent for Rao his naval assistant and Murty, the specialist from the photo laboratory of R&AW. Later, the three of them flew to Bombay and met the R&AW officer who planned this operation. He told them that a Parsi doctor on a B.I. ship that periodically sailed from Bombay to Kuwait and back via Karachi port, was prepared to help them. In return, we had to get him off the customs hook on which he was caught for trying to smuggle in electronic goods on one of his voyages. Nair then called on the Collector of Customs, an old college mate of his. He fixed up with him to drop the case against the doctor by paying a heavy fine, with money from the secret funds of R&AW. After this manipulation, Nair met the doctor under his nom-de-guerre Cdr. Menon of the Navy. It was arranged that the two R&AW officers Rao and Murty, cover names Rod and Moriarty respectively sailed two days later on the doctor's ship. Before the ship entered Karachi harbour, the doctor arranged for Rod and Moriarty to take their equipments and get admitted in the ship's sick bay as patients. The two got under bed sheets with the photographic equipment.

At the entrance to the harbour, the pilot boat brought the Karachi CID personnel on board. They ordered the Captain to bring all Indian passengers, with their passports, before them. The passengers were asked to sit in front of the CID men, who kept their passports until the ship left harboor the next day. The CID Deputy Superintendent scrutinized the passenger manifest and cursed when he found that two passengers were missing. When the Captain told that the two were ill and were in the sick bay, the CID officer said he would see them there. But he beat a hasty retreat when the Parsi doctor said they were down with chicken pox.

The pilot, thereafter, took the ship between the two cliffs of the entry point which guarded the narrow entrance to the harbour. The two patients got busy photographing the cliff side on the port, in sequential frames. Rod pointed out the fortification and gun mountings while Moriary clicked away furiously with powerful telephoto lenses. While going in, the sick bay was on the port side. The next day, sailing out of the harbour, the sick bay was on the side of the other cliff, which was also fully photographed.

Once in the Arabian Sea, the ship sailed to Kuwait, where two R&AW passengers, now recovered miraculously from chicken pox, got off the ship and booked into a hotel. They unloaded the films and put them in tamper-proof covers. The next day, they went to the Indian Embassy and met the R&AW officers working there under cover, who had been told in advance about the impending arrival of Rod and Mariarty. They handed over the films which were sent by diplomatic pouch to Delhi. Rod and Mariarty, then left by plane to Delhi.

At Headquarterss, the photo lab developed the films under Mariarty's expert eyes. When the films were ready, R N Kao asked the Defence Minister to ready his war room and came with his Naval brass for a projection of the films of harbor. Mariarty projected the films panel by panel through a high magnification projector. The Naval Chief and his aides were as much amazed as satisfied with the projection and the intelligence there from. The Defence Minister thanked Kao, who later thanked the two officers who had carried out this fine operation.

Some months later, when war broke out, Indian Naval Missile boats blew the hell out of the fortifications of the harbour and bottled the enemy's Navy.

There was a funny sequel to these doings, when the Parsi doctor arrived in Delhi and traced Nair's residence. When he rang the bell, the lady of the house came out. The doctor asked to see Cdr. Menon and was told that it was the house of Nair. Not satisfied, the doctor went to the neighbouring house and asked who stayed next door and was told it was Nair. The doctor then went to Naval Headquarterss and spotted the board of Cdr. Menon. He barged in and seeing the officer sitting there shouted 'you are not Cdr. Menon'. The officer said 'of course not. Cdr. Menon is out of sea and I am officiating here at his desk. Now get out before I boot you out'. The doctor's next part of call was at General Manekshaw's office. The General rang up Kao and told him that his boys seems to have been playing some mischief with the doctor who was claiming a National Award for his alleged services to the Nation. He suggested that the Doctor's mouth could possibly be shut if a decent sum of money was given to him. When Kao rang up Nair, he told him that doctor had been got off the Customs hook as well as greased reasonably well.

R&AW – Relatives and Associates Wing

During Emergency era, Sanjay Gandhi, the younger son of Indira Gandhi, was calling shots in the government functioning and he taunted to someone about R&AW that it is "Relatives And Associates Wing". It was correct to certain extent when the author too joined it in 1973.

After bifurcation from IB, R&AW did not get adequate staff due to stiff resistance put up by IB bosses in its formation and smooth functioning. Kao got a skeleton of around 250 employees to start this organization. Many divisions like language, crypto etc., which were exclusively meant for external intelligence, were not transferred to R&AW. Soon, a large expansion was the emergent need to establish its offices all over the country. In order to break the red-tape barrier of government procedures in recruitment, Kao got free hand for recruitment from Indira Gandhi and sought Union Public Service Commission exemption which was granted to him. Recruitments up to class II non-gazetted officers was decentralized and heads of regional offices were empowered to recruit staff for their respective requirement. Many IPS and Defence officers and other Cadres were taken on deputation for various wings of R&AW.

In this emergent recruitment drive all over the country, mostly relatives and other known persons of those who were serving in R&AW were given appointment to various posts. Some unscrupulous officers had allegedly taken money in these recruitments when some complaints were received at R&AW Headquarterss in this regard. Obviously, this have to happen in this corruption ridden country and R&AW was no exception.

Kao had planned to make R&AW a non-Police organization unlike IB which was dominated by IPS officers at the top level. He started a separate cadre of Class I service on the pattern of Indian Foreign Service. First recruitment in this regard was made in 1971 when four directly recruited officers were appointed as Class I officers. Surprisingly, all these four officers were kins of either those who were in R&AW or other influential persons in services elsewhere. This trend started in 1971 is still continuing. Taking cue from this trend, most of the junior cadre comprised either sons and daughters of junior officers or their known associates. Nowadays, a large scale bungling in these recruitments has been detected wherein millions of Rupees are being minted by senior officers. During Ashok Chaturvedi's tenure, this bungling crossed all corruption barriers. Three daughters of his Personal Attendant, Kapoor were given appointment in R&AW on various posts without any proper examination. It was revealed by a senior officers who was on the recruitment board that their recommendation was overlooked and persons with different criteria were given appointment. The List is quite long and some of them appointed in Class I posts, known as BDS i.e. Back Door Service in R&AW, are given as under:

1. N. Ramani. He was the first direct recruits of R&AW in Class I post of Under Secretary rank in 1971. He was the son of one Deputy Secretary of R&AW, Subramanym. He retired as Joint Secretary.
2. P.V.Kumar. He was also appointed in 1971. He was son of Lt. Gen. Kumarmanglam who was a friend of K.Sankaran Nair. He was aspiring to become R&AW Chief after Ashok Chaturvedi but was overlooked by the government due to his mediocrity. However, he managed to get into NTRO as post retirement gift due to the recommendation of his IAS wife who is a leading lady in New Delhi bureaucracy.
3. Atul Razdan. He was nephew of T.N.Kaul, a former Foreign Secretary of India. He retired as Joint Secretary.
4. Raja Sagar. He was the last among these four recruited in 1971. He was son of former Lt. Gen. Moti Sagar.
5. P.M.Heblikar. He was the son of former IG of Police, Karnataka. He too was ignored for R&AW chief after K.C.Verma. He retired recently from the rank of Additional Secretary.
6. J.Ranade. He was son of a former Director General of Shipping Ministry. He was forced to resign from R&AW when he was found guilty of

suppressing some facts about the job of his wife which she did in USA when Ranade was posted in Indian Embassy at Washington. Had he not done so, he was likely to be terminated from the service on this count.

7. B.G.Rawal. He was son of a former Central Intelligence Officer of IB. He too retired as Joint Secretary.
8. C.K.Sinha. He was son of former IG of Police M.K.Sinha and brother of Lt. Gen. S.K.Sinha, former Governor of Jammu and Kashmir. He too could not succeed to become R&AW chief and retired as Additional Secretary due to allegation of corruption.
9. Raksha Ramachanran. She was the daughter of former Chairman of Railway Board.
10. R.N.Nair. He was son of former Lt. Gen. Nair, a distant relative of Sankaran Nair. He had a dubious past in R&AW while serving in Indian missions at Islamabad, Hong Kong and Colombo. There were charges of corruption in secret fund against him. He was recently found involved with a lady suspected to be working for the Chinese. He was compulsorily retired by the authorities on this charge.
11. M.R.Bhalla. He was brother in law of Arun Bhagat former Commissioner, Delhi Police and Director, IB. He got appointed when Bhagat was serving as Director in R&AW. He did not continue in R&AW longer and left after a few years.
12. Sharad Kumar. He was the nephew of the then Director of CBI, D.Sen.
13. M.J.Abraham. He was the son of former Joint Director of R&AW, J.Abraham.
14. C.K.Devars. He was son of F.S.Devars, IPS, former Joint Director of IB.
15. Alka Pande. She was daughter of former Director of R&AW, J.C.Pande.
16. Captain K.S.Mirchandani. He was son of former Joint Director of R&AW, S.Mirchandani.
17. Ashok Bajpayi. He was son of former Secretary of R&AW, G.S.Bajpayi. He resigned out of fear and left India when he was found involved in passing some information to Rabinder Singh, a CIA agent in R&AW.
18. Anita Kumar. She is the daughter of a former Joint Director of R&AW, S.M.Warty.
19. Neeraj Srivastava. He is nephew of G.C.Saxena, former Secretary of R&AW. He is working as Additional Secretary and would retire from this post.
20. Madita Mishra. She is niece of Brajesh Mishra, First National Security Advisor and former Principal Secretary to Prime Minister Atal Bihari Vajpayee.

21. Jaydeep Nair. He is the son of P.P.R.Nair, former Additional Secretary of R&AW. He was recruited in 1992 when Nair was in service. Presently, working in the rank of Joint Secretary.
22. Abhijit Halder. His father was pilot of Rajiv Gandhi. He was recruited when A K Verma was Secretary.
23. Deepak Kaul. His father was friend of A K Verma and was the station chief of Air India at Abu Dhabi. He was president of Abu Dhabi Circket Association also. He was also recruited by A K Verma
24. Anshul Sharma. He is son in law of Sunder Kumar, a former Additional Secretary of R&AW.
25. R.P.Singh. He is son of a former IAS who was Election Commissioner of Punjab and a batch mate of C D Sahay, former Secretary.
26. Shrila Dutta Kumar. She is daughter of Shymal Dutta, former Director of Intelligence Bureau.

Most of these officers appointed in Class I service were mediocre but some were quite brilliant to become R&AW chief. These officers along with the IPS cadre were amalgamated into R&AW Administrative Service i.e. R.A.S. after the recommendation of K.Sankaran Nair Cadre Review Committee in 1986. In spite of formation of R.A.S., the ongoing confrontation between the IPS and non-IPS persist in R&AW and the IPS lobby merged in R&AW did not allow some competent officers to become chief either by spoiling or down-grading the annual confidential reports of these officers. Most glaring example of this rivalry was denying this privilege to Rana Banerjee, an IAS, the most competent expert on Pakistan affairs in R&AW. Prime Minister Manmohan Singh used to address Banerjee as a Pakistani Pandit due to his enormous knowledge and operational capability inside Pakistan. Banerjee was vocal to criticize Ashok Chaturvedi for the fiasco of 26/11 in Mumbai and he paid the price for that. M.K.Narayanan, the then NSA, got appointed an IB man, K.C.Verma as R&AW chief and Banerjee was sidelined as the first IAS to become head of R&AW.

Now, R&AW is totally an IPS dominated organization. Even, the present chief Alok Joshi, an IPS of Haryana cadre, joined R&AW in 2008. He does not belong to R.A.S. thus superseding the other officers in this cadre. There was strong resentment in the higher cadre to his appointment of his being a non-R.A.S. man. But the most devastating matter of concern is that most of these IPS joins R&AW for a brief period and after taking one or two foreign assignments, prefer to revert to their parent cadre of state police. It indicates that they do no have the sense of belonging to R&AW and after earning hefty amount, they leave it on their own choice. This constitutes complete chaos in R&AW and R&AW Administrative Service has almost become defunct. Government should take note of this anomaly and disallow deputationists to go back to their state cadres since their expertise of long stint in R&AW is of paramount importance in operational matters which is of no use in state police.

Ram Jethmalani (Lawyer And Leader Of BJP) Nailed By R&AW In London For His Link With An Alleged Indian Origin Smuggler

One Dalem Chand Baid of Bombay with a Maldive passport was detained at Heathrow airport in London on June, 1, 1981, for seeking entry into U.K. He was a suspect of the then notorious Choraria gang of smugglers operating in Hong Kong, Nepal, India, UK, USA and West Asia. This gang was involved in numerous smuggling activities, including foreign currency in these countries. During interrogation by the Customs authorities at Heathrow, an amount of around $2,25,000 currency wrapped in old newspapers, was recovered from him. Since, there was no restriction on import and export of foreign currency in UK, no criminal case was registered against him. However, the Immigration authorities refused entry to him into UK but Baid challenged his deportation in a Court in London. He was, therefore, held in temporary detention by Immigration officers pending the decision of court.

R&AW operatives in London were keeping track of this case. During there trail, it was detected by them that within a couple of days of this incident, Ram Jethmalani arrived in London and contacted Baid in detention through a local lawyer, Handa. After Handa established links with Baid, he asked the immigration authorities to hand over $2,25,000 to Handa and rest of his belongings be kept there. Since, no criminal offence about this currency was committed by Baid as per UK laws, this amount of money was handed over to Handa by the immigration staff. It was later on found by the R&AW operatives that Jethmalani collected this money and left for USA immediately thereafter.

This report was sent to R&AW Headquarterss at New Delhi by their counterparts in the London Mission. R&AW authorities asked to conduct discreet enquiries and get authentic details of this affair and also about the nature and extent of Ram Jethmalani's involvement in it. On further investigation by R&AW, it was found that Dalam Chand Baid, according to his passport, was a resident of Happy House Apartments, 28A, Nepean Sea Road, Bombay-36. His passport No. L-218551 was issued on March, 5, 1981 at Male, the Maldive Islands. He was a conduit of the infamous Choraria smuggling gang and the currency recovered from them was a dubious transaction which he wanted to smuggle someone in London. Jethmalani's role was limited to transfer this money to USA as the reports of R&AW. However, Baid's passport was cancelled by the Indian High Commission on instruction from R&AW Headquarterss from New Delhi. Enforcement Directorate of India entered the arena to get Baid deported for this offence.

N F Suntook, R&AW Chief Was On A Secret Mission When Indian Press Dubbed Him As Absconder

In the second weak of April, 1983, a sensational news was published in a leading daily in Bombay that the then R&AW Chief, N F Suntook and his wife left India on March 30, 1983 without the permission of Indian government. He was suspected to have fled to USA where he was likely to get a job. Suntook was set to retire on March, 31, 1983 i.e. one day after this disappearance. Although, the Indian Home Minister clarified that there was more to it than met the eyes but rumour mongers in the capital were on rampage. B.Raman in his book "The Kaoboys of R&AW" put blame for this publication on an employee of R&AW against whom Suntook had supposedly taken action during 1980 strike in R&AW. This allegation was far from truth and wishful thinking of Raman. Suntook went abroad on March 30, and the news was published on April 9 i.e. 11 days after the incident. Every R&AW employee, including the union activists, were aware of this happening. Had the union activists decided to leak this matter in the press this could had been done the very next day instead of keeping it to wait for 11 days. Raman had a pathological phobia to tarnish the image of those activities since his service days which he reflected in his book by giving false and unfounded facts which was unfortunate. Every one in R&AW was aware that farewell party of Suntook was postponed due to some emergency which could have been a front page news for any newspaper in the capital had the unionist desired so. However, Suntook returned to India on April 10, and handed over his charge to the next incumbent G.C.Saxena. Government of India issued a notification to extend his service beyond March 31, granting him 10 days of extension in service.

This mysterious mission of R&AW Chief was planned after the Indian Prime Minister, Indira Gandhi received an emergency message from the Mauritian Prime Minister, Anerood Jugnauth to intervene in view of an impending coup by his political rivals headed by one Paul Berenger. Since, Jugnauth was undisputed leader of the migrated Indian majority population and had Intimate relations with Indira Gandhi, she decided to help him out in this imbroglio. There had been media reports that Indira Gandhi planned military and navy operation to bail out Jugnauth which was a weird imagination. On the advice of Kao, Indira Gandhi sent Suntook to Mauritius to diffuse the situation in favour of Jugnauth. Suntook stayed in Mauritius for ten days and with the help of other R&AW operatives and though his own sources achieved a remarkable success to subdue the radical rival Paul Berenger and his coterie with the result Jugnauth continued to stay as Prime Minister for another ten years.

R&AW had been an excellent organization till the Janta Party slashed its staff to two third and pruned the operational expenditure. This left its staff in a state of uncertainty for their future and inside situation was volatile. This state of affair was further aggravated by some officers which resulted in the formation of a union and an all India level strike took place and haunted the smooth functioning of R&AW for many years. Suntook shunted out all these mediocre officers out of India in 1981 onward to smoothen the internal rivalry among various R&AW cadres which were agitated after the police atrocities on unionists.

Bhajan Lal, Haryana, Chief Minister, Saved in New York By R&AW Operative Who Lost His Job For This Charity

While Rajiv Gandhi was Prime Minister of India, Haryana Chief Minister sought permission from him for medical treatment in New York. Rajiv Gandhi was initially hesitant to this permission in view of threat to his life from the Sikh militants in USA but when Bhajan Lal insisted, Rajiv Gandhi agreed but he cautioned R&AW about his safety in the US. In New York. While Bhajan Lal was staying in a hotel, the R&AW operative in the Indian embassy, Mirchandani, was assigned the job to handle his security.

One afternoon when Mrchandani noticed five Sikhs assembling in mysterious situation a few yards away from the hotel. Mirchandani immediately went to the nearest police station and reported this matter to the concerned police officer. Soon, the New York police swooped on those Sikhs and ultimately unearthed a plot wherein it was found that they had gone to assassinate Bhajan Lal outside the hotel premises. A total of six Sikh terrorists were arrested from outside and inside the hotel. Automatic weapons, photographs of Bhajan Lal, his room numbers of the hotel, details of the Hospital where he had been operated upon for eye surgery and lay out of the plan of hospital and hotel were recovered from the arrested terrorists.

After these arrests, the USA government further intensified the security of Bhajan Lal till he stayed there. Delhi government was informed about this abortive plan of terrorists to assassinate Bhajan Lal. Rajiv Gandhi informed Bhajan lal on telephone of this incident since he was unaware of what was happening during his stay in USA.

Mirchandani returned to India after completing his three years tenure in the Indian embassy in New York. While he was serving in R&AW at New Delhi Headquarterss, Ministry of External Affairs sent a summon from the Court of New York wherein Mirchandani was asked to depose as prosecution witness against those Sikhs who were arrested in the plot to kill Bhajan Lal. Mirchandani was asked by R&AW Chief to go to New York and give evidence in that case to which he refused fearing threat to his own life. When R&AW Chief persisted, Mirchandani sought guarantee from him for the safety of his life in New York to which the Chief did not want to commit. Ultimately, Mirchandani was asked to resign from his post for refusal to comply with this delicate dictum. He had a quite number of years of service before him in R&AW but due to this piquant situation wherein the authorities were unable to protect him of any untoward happening but forced him to leave his job abruptly.

Although R&AW hierarchy expects such dangerous performance from their operatives at every place of their postings but when the need to protect them arises, they shrugged away with lame excuses and this example of Mirchandani is fair enough to prove it. They could not provide adequate answer to the logic of the delinquent officer of R&AW and was made a scapegoat to sacrifice his lucrative job and made to live the life of a recluse.

R&AW Officers Floated Private Limited Firm To Swindle Secret Fund

In a rare clandestine operation, rather foolishly, two Joint Secretaries of R&AW, B Raman and V Balachandran, floated a private limited firm "Piyush Investment and Finance Pvt. Ltd." which was duly registered with the Registrar of Companies, Delhi in 1988. Addresses of these officers were shown from the safe houses of R&AW located in South Delhi area. This novel method was devised by the then Secretary of R&AW, A K Verma to divest secret fund for personal benefits. At initial stages after launch of this firm, 90 Lakh of rupees were withdrawn from the secret fund under "Operation Retreat". This company purchased three flats i.e. two in Gauri Sadan apartments on Hailey road in the posh Connaught Place area and the second at Taj apartments near Safdarjang hospital on ring road. Promoters of these properties were made payments through cash and cheques in the name of Raman and Balachandran.

However, the author investigated this fictitious operation and discovered that A K Verma had acquired many properties in the garb of this operation. These properties were purchased in and around New Delhi in his name and in the name of his family members.

The author filed a criminal case in the CBI court on the basis of the documents of this finance company. The court has ordered CBI enquiry on the basis of the facts against A K Verma. Fate of the two Joint Secretary, B Raman and V Balachandran is also hanging in this dubious transaction wherein they floated a Private Limited firm while serving in R&AW.

Such fictitious operations are usually generated by R&AW officers on papers to swindle secret fund to which government has no legal machinery to check this corruption. Many futile attempts were made by some politicians to make this agency accountable but these were thwarted by R&AW hierarchy in the name of manipulated secrecy. First of such an attempt was made by Jaswant Singh, Chairman of Estimate Committee, in 1990 to bring IB and R&AW under his purview. The author vividly remembers that G S Bajpai, the then R&AW Chief, laughed away on this statement of Jaswant Singh and asserted that he would ensure that such move be scuttled in due course, which he strangely manipulated through the then Prime Minister V P Singh. Since then, no attempt has been made by any one at any quarter and this agency is acting like a bull in China's shop much to the chagrin of some defence analysts.

How A K Verma, R&AW Chief, Sent Manufactured Reports to Prime Minister V P Singh About Pakistan After Kidnapping Of Rubaiya Saeed Daughter of Then Home Minister Mufti Mohammand Sayeed in 1989 To Get Extension In Service

During the regime of Rajiv Gandhi from 1984 to 1989 some bureaucrats became very powerful in view of their close proximity to him since he was naïve in the politics and depended much on these babus. The then R&AW Chief, A K Verma was one of them. Verma was handling the most sensitive operation of LTTE in Sri Lanka and Rajiv Gandhi formulated his policy on this issue on his advice although it proved disastrous for himself and he got killed in this imbroglio. Since Rajiv Gandhi got the unimaginable majority in 1984, these bureaucrats never thought that he would lose elections in 1989. So, Verma was the brain behind Rajiv Gandhi in his policy towards the neighbouring countries, particularly Sri Lanka and Pakistan.

A K Verma was accused by opposition parties for fomenting militancy in Assam by giving aids to Bodo extremists to create law and order problem for the AGP government of Prafulla Mahant in Assam. There were allegations that Rajiv Gandhi wanted to get rid of this ruling government and Bodo agitation was given momentum by R&AW at the behest of A K Verma. This issue was raised in the Parliament by senior leaders like L K Advani of BJP and P Upendra of the Telgu Desam Party when media exposed this conspiracy. Some evidences were highlighted by the media when R&AW was found abetting insurgency in this part of Assam. Although, government declined the truth of these reports but the opposition parties were gunning for Verma's head.

Rajiv Gandhi lost the general election in November, 1989 and V P Singh became Prime Minister of India on December, 3, 1989. He appointed Mufti Mohammand Sayeed, the first Muslim Home Minister of this country. Just after days of change of guards in Indian Parliament, Rubaiya Sayeed, the 23 year old, doctor daughter of Mufti was kidnapped about 500 meters from her house in Srinagar while she was returning from her college. Four militants belonging to Jammu and Kashmir Liberation Front i.e. JKLF, abducted her in a maruti car and kept her hostages in Sopore at two different places. These kidnappers demanded the release of five of their comrades in lieu of her release. Although, the then J&K Chief Minister, Farooq Abdullah was averse to the release of these militants but due to threat from the Central government to dismiss his government, these five militants were got exchanged for the release of Rubaiya Sayeed.

Soon thereafter, V P Singh was under tremendous pressure from his own party men to oust the favourite babus of Rajiv Gandhi and A K Verma was the foremost. But after this kidnapping incident, Verma devised a novel modus to outwit the beleaguered V P Singh. He sent numerous exaggerating reports about the Pakistan sponsored terrorist preparations to V P Singh. It was reliably learnt that V P Singh made up his mind to wage a formal war with Pakistan on the basis of these reports. There were demonstrations in Delhi and in Islamabad after this kidnapping and relations between India and Pakistan were at its lowest ebb.

While, all these incidents were in full swing, number two in R&AW R Balakrishnan through one of his confidante sent a message to the author that A K Verma was deliberately sending exaggerated reports to V P Singh to spoil the India's prevalent political relations with Pakistan and get extension of his service which was left for two-three months. The author, through a senior journalist Ram Bahadur Rai, met Rajmohan Ganhi who was very close to V P Singh and conveyed to him the details as to how A K Verma was cooking up false R&AW reports for his personal benefits. Rajmohan Gandhi had unsuccessfully contested elections against Rajiv Gandhi and was a known favourite of V.P.Singh. In the evening, Rajmohan Gandhi discussed this matter with V.P.Singh and the ongoing bitterness with regard to Pakistan was subsided and favourable signals of normalcy were exchanged between both nation and no untoward incidents happened.

After one month of this happening, P.Upendra, the then Railway Minister, conveyed to the author that A K Verma through V C Pande, Principal Secretary of V P Singh, was again trying to get his extension in service. The author conveyed this fact to L K Advani who became uncomfortable about V P Singh on this issue. However, Madan Lal Khurana raised this issue at Zero hour in Parliament that the controversial R&AW Chief was being given extension in spite of his past dubious activities. While V P Singh sitting in the Prime Minister chair remained silent on this question but L K Advani told Khurana that no extension was being given to Verma. There was a laughter in the house when Advani replied on behalf of Prime Minister. This issue was closed thereafter and Verma retired thereafter.

Strange are the manipulations these bureaucrats fabricate on the vulnerable position of the politicians. V P Singh was given support by Left and BJP to keep Rajiv Gandhi out of power. A K Verma tried to capitalize this opportunity and misused his sensitive position and started sending exaggerated reports to V P Singh on Pakistan for his personal gains which no one in the government tried to verify and rather a fire was generated to be head on with Pakistan

Author Got G S Bajpai Appointed As R&AW Chief On Kao's Advice Whom Bajpai Betrayed Subsequently

After V P Singh became Prime Minister of India, search for new R&AW Chief had already started due to change of government since the then incumbent, A K Verma, was bound to be sacked. The author consulted R N Kao in this regard and sought his opinion in this regard since he had groomed the then corps of intelligence officers. Kao told that G S Bajpai was the only suitable officer for that post. Since, Bajpai was already appointed as Secretary of Security by Rajiv Gandhi, his re-induction into R&AW was remotely possible. When the author further persisted of second choice in this regard, Kao strongly advocated the name of Bajpai, as best choice for that post.

Bajpai and Verma were at loggerheads since their younger days in R&AW. There was another drawback in the selection of Bajpai. He was on deputation in the Ministry of External Affairs for a number of years, which was although a R&AW post but operationally he was cut off from his original department. Rajiv Gandhi deliberately appointed him Secretary of Security because in case of his reversion to R&AW where A K Verma was head, they would have fought owing to their past animosity which was dangerous for smooth functioning of R&AW. Thus, there was almost negligible chance of Bajpai becoming head of R&AW.

When Kao reaffirmed Bajpai's candidature as the best possible option, author became serious to lobby for him through his political and media friends who had close proximity with V P Singh. His two prominent journalist friends and one eminent lawyer who later on became an important minister in Atal Bihari government, persuaded V P Singh to appoint G S Bajpai as the next R&AW head. Meanwhile, Kao asked Bajpai to meet the author. The meeting took place at his residence wherein Bajpai gave author the warmest of regards. His whole family seemed to be aware of this lobbying and their gesture of welcome was absolutely a symbol of gratitude.

On lobbying by the author with his close friends, Bajpai was appointed head of R&AW in June, 1990. Sometime, in the month of July, the author met R N Kao in his routine manner. Kao enquired as to how Bajpai was performing his job as R&AW Chief. Author replied that he was bogged down with a heap of files sent by various desks of R&AW since some seniors were against his re-entry in R&AW. Kao spontaneously replied that Bajpai would prove disastrous in his job if he got himself engaged in file business. Then he revealed a closely guarded secret that while he was head of R&AW, he never saw any file before lunch hours. He used to devote his pre-lunch hours to monitor various happenings in and outside India. After giving a proper thought and assessing the impending outcome of these events, he would dictate advisory notes to the concerned operatives so that they could tab on all the activities which could have any sort of implications for the country. He reiterated that fortunately he had a very capable number two

K Sankaran Nair as his deputy who would handle all the residuary working of R&AW and he was giving maximum possible time for his operational work. Kao was sad that Bajpai had not been on those yardsticks which he had in his mind.

Later on, Sankaran Nair with whom the author developed a very close relationship, visited Delhi in July, 1990. He and the author used to go to his favourite destination in Delhi, Delhi Golf Club where he used to be its President in the past. The author had a personal case which Bajpai had promised that he would get it resolved. Sankaran Nair personally came from Bangalore in this regard. Next day, Nair told the author that Bada Saheb i.e. R N Kao had called Bajpai and his wife for lunch for his case. After that lunch meeting, Nair conveyed to the author that Bajpai duly touched the feet of Kao and promised that he would get resolved the case of the author.

Thereafter, the author had number of meetings with Bajpai in this regard and on his advice got some politicians involved to put pressure on V P Singh, which was a motive to drag on the issue. Ultimately, V P Singh government resigned due to Mandal commission agitation and Bajpai got the excuse on that plea. Later on, Subodh Kant Sahay, the Internal Security Minister, in Chandershekhar government also asked Bajpai to get that matter resolved to which he tried to build up cock and bull stories to gain time.

It sounds highly disgraceful that these treacherous, selfish and rudderless bureaucrats would go to any length and eat the worst of garbage when their own vested interest is involved. Kao, the genius and a fatherly figure of whole of R&AW, would have never approached to such a gutless creature as Bajpai, but some how he did it and was shamelessly betrayed by Bajpai. Thereafter, Kao told the author that he never imagined that a person like Bajpai whom he groomed for this coveted post would put up such devilish behaviour. Such incidents are quite common in R&AW where human approach is put on tenterhook when personal benefits are seen in the offing. Bajpai was no exception. Later on, when Narsimha Rao became Prime Minister in 1992, Bajpai wanted extension which was denied to him. He tried to become Governor of a state or Ambassador in a Mission. He was not considered for these assignments also. Bajpai never knew why he did not get these post-retirement benefits, the author was instrumental in averting these decisions and he conveyed this fact to Kao for which he gave a mysterious smile.

Mohammad Hamid Ansari, Indian Ambassador In Iran, The Present Vice-President of India, Manhandled By Wives Of Mission Staff For His Inaction To Get Released A R&AW Operative Kidnapped By The Iranian Intelligence

M H Ansari was one of the few Muslim diplomats in the Ministry of External Affairs. He was posted Ambassador to Tehran in late 1990. After few months of Ansari's taking over this assignment, one Personal Assistant, Kapoor was kidnapped from the Tehran International Airport by the Iranian Intelligence officials while he was returning from leave in India. This young official was tortured for three days and his whereabouts were never informed to the Indian Embassy by the Iranian government. He was continuously drugged and given inhuman treatment during all these days before he was thrown on a lonely road in Tehran. Ansari did not pursue this matter with the Iranian government much to the discomfiture of the staff posted in the Mission.

The Shia Kashmiris from India were imparted religious preaching at a religious centre at Qom near to Tehran by the religious clergy of the Iranian counterpart. R&AW officers posted in the Mission were monitoring the activities of these trainees and reporting to their Headquarterss with information to Ansari who was against some of these reports. One R&AW officer D B Mathur had developed his contacts in this religious centre and used to procure inside information through his sources which was known to Ansari. One morning, when Mathur was on his way to the Embassy, he was kidnapped by the Iranian Intelligence officials and taken to some unknown destination. When Mathur did not report for his duties, his colleagues made efforts to trace him in Tehran.

Ansari sent a casual report on Mathur's disappearance to the Ministry of External Affairs and did not take up this matter seriously with the Iranian government. Staff inside Mission was agitated on the lackadaisical attitude of Ansari in this serious matter. Finally, after two days of this incident, all the wives of the staff members of the Mission, numbering more than 30, assembled outside the gate of the Embassy to protest to Ansari for his inaction in getting released Mathur. Initially, these ladies were not allowed to enter the Mission premises but on intervention by some senior officials, they were sent into the building. Ansari refused to meet these ladies in spite of their repeated efforts through his personal staff. When the situation reached to the boiling point, wife of Mathur along with some other ladies barged into the room of Ansari and rebuked him for his inaction to trace his staff member. Ansari was caught on wrong foot and faced this ugly situation without any provocation.

In the meantime, one of the staff members of R&AW, N K Sood, telephoned the author and gave details of this incidents to take up this matter with the Indian government. Next day, the author met Atal Bihari Vajpayee, who was leader of opposition when Narsimha Rao was the Prime Minister. Author briefed Vajpayee about this incident of Tehran. Vajpayee immediately talked to Narsimha Rao in this regard who promised a prompt action in this matter. Within few hours, Mathur was released by the Iranian Intelligence officials when PMO intervened and took up this matter with the Iranian government. Mathur was subjected to third degree torture by the Iranians to get inside information of R&AW agents in Iran which he refused to divulge. Later on, Mathur was prematurely withdrawn from Tehran and ordered to leave within 72 hours to India. It was most unfortunate incident when Ansari did not get it resolved at his own level and the Indian government had to intervene to get released its official from the Iranian Intelligence officials. Most of the operations of R&AW received set back after this incident since its operatives became insecure due to inaction of Ansari. R&AW operatives had penetrated inside the Qom religious centre to monitor the activities of some Kashmiri elements whose activities were detrimental to the security situation in Jammu and Kashmir but this incident made them to abort further infiltration inside that centre at that juncture. Later on, a senior R&AW officer was sent to get the factual details of this matter. That officer also indicted Ansari in his assessment to the R&AW Secretary, Narsimhan, who chose not to rake up this matter with the government in view of his own incapabilities.

Later, one Security Official, Mohammand Umar, posted at the Embassy was approached by the Iranian Intelligence officials to work for them. Umar refused to oblige them and informed his senior in the Embassy who in turn briefed Ansari that Umar could be targeted after his denial to Iranian Intelligence officials. Few weeks thereafter, Umar was also kidnapped by the Intelligence officials of Iran and severely beaten up and thrown on a secluded place outside Tehran. Ansari again did not protest to the Iranian government on the torture of Umar and rather asked him to remain silent. When Umar wanted to take up this matter with the Indian government, Ansari with the help of R&AW Station Chief, Venugaopal, wanted to excruciate him and deport to India on flimsy ground. When this fact was known to other R&AW operatives, they protested to their Station Chief Venugopal and asked him not to make that poor employee a scapegoat at the behest of Ansari. Venugopal relented and refused to cooperate with Ansari in this matter.

It would be pertinent to mention here that M H Ansari developed very good personal relations within the Iranian government but did not want to rake up these kidnapping issues to bring any sort of bitterness for his own benefit. His son was got married in a highly connected Iranian family which was a questionable alliance in view of his own sect.

The prevalent egoistic approach by Indian diplomats to downplay the functioning of R&AW officials in their Mission has been a worrisome cause of affair for the Indian government because the diplomats have a pathological feeling that the posts grabbed by R&AW were their ancestral decree. They forget that these R&AW officials provide aggressive inputs to the government to formulate its foreign policy based on the best interest of the country rather than the suave approach by these diplomats to portray their personal disposition having no relation to the national cause. They should mend their approach to be in league with the R&AW operatives for concerted approach for the sake of the country.

Five Bureaucrats, Including R&AW Chief G.S.Bajpai And IB Director, M.K. Narayanan Indicted by Verma Commission For Lapses in Rajiv Gandhi Assassination Escaped Through Their Own Manipulations

After the Verma Commission submitted its report on the lapses leading to the assassination of Rajiv Gandhi by LTTE cadre, the Indian government of P V Narsimha Rao appointed a committee of four member group of Ministers comprising of S B Chavan, Home Minister, Ghulam Nabi Azad, the Civil Aviation Minister, Satish Sharma, Petroleum Minister and Hans Raj Bhardwaj, the Law Minister to examine and suggest follow up action on the report. This group of Ministers, submitted their report to the Prime Minister and indicted five senior bureaucrats Vinod Pande, Cabinet Secretary and Shiromani Sharma, Home Secretary in the V P Singh government, Raj Bhargava, Home Secretary in Chandra Shekhar government, former R&AW Chief, G S Bajpai and former Director of Intelligence Bureau, M.K.Narayanan for dereliction of their duties which caused the assassination of Rajiv Gandhi.

This report put blame on Vinod Pande, Shriromani Sharma and G.S.Bajpai for withdrawing the SPG cover and not providing adequate security to Rajiv Gandhi when he was not holding the post of Prime Minister. There were allegations that IB did not provide inputs about the infiltration of LTTE cadre in the gathering where Rajiv Gandhi was to address a public rally. M K Narayanan, the then Director of IB was severely indicted for this fiasco.

There was reliable information that two cadre of LTTE along with a senior journalist met Rajiv Gandhi in the beginning of March, 1991 and sought his assistance for the cause of Tamils in Sri Lanka in case he returns to power as Prime Minister of India. Rajiv Gandhi had reportedly denied to give any assurance to them in this regard. One of these cadres was a R&AW source who later on gave details of this deliberation with Rajiv Gandhi to his R&AW handler in Chennai. According to insiders in R&AW, G.S.Bajpai did not send details of this source meeting to the government and also to the security apparatus responsible for Rajiv's security during the election campaign which he was carrying in South India.

However, no action was taken against these bureaucrats and they retired merrily with all post-retirement benefits leave aside any criminal action against them for this national tragedy. M.K.Narayan was rather rewarded with his appointment as National Security Advisor when Manmohan Singh became Prime Minister in 2004 and continued with this post till he was elevated as Governor of West Bengal after he was again indicted for the 26/11 terrorist attack in Mumbai. These Indian bureaucrats enjoy all sort of immunities for their lapses since the political leadership in this country is rudderless and lacks guts and determination to catch hold of these culprits who were responsible for many of such tragedies. Could any one give an example when a senior bureaucrat was ever prosecuted and sent behind bars for such serious dereliction of his duties? Hats off to the Indian bureaucracy who are the virtual ruler and these politicians are titular head since most of them lack the proper education to take stringent action in such serious lapses of national catastrophe.

Narsimha Rao Delayed Permission To R&AW To Free Foreign Tourists From The Clutches Al Fahran Militants

Six foreign tourists were kidnapped by militants on 4 July, 1995 from the Lidderwat area of Pahalgam in Anantnag district of Jammu and Kashmir. This kidnapping was claimed by one Al Fahran group an outfit of Pakistan militant group Harkat-ul-Ansar. These six included, two British, two Americans, a German and a Norwegian. On 13 August, they beheaded the Norwegian tourist which was found near Pahalgam. The kidnappers demanded the release of Maulana Masood Azhar and twenty other prisoners in lieu of these foreign hostages. Azhar was the same militant who was released after the hijacking of IC 814 Air India flight from Kathmandu. One American ran away from the captives and later on sent to USA.

Most of the foreign sleuths of FBI, Scotland Yard, MI6, CIA, US Special Forces were sent by their respective governments to include them in the investigation to get safe release of the hostages. A R&AW plane was flown to Srinagar Airport with all sort of monitoring facilities into it. R&AW operatives involved these foreign sleuths in listening to the transcript of the conversations of the kidnappers and the hostages. Pakistan government tried to project that these kidnapped persons had stage managed their kidnapping to defame Pakistan. These sleuths denounced Pakistan government for spreading false propaganda when kidnapping was done at their behest. Even the Germans offered their services to get released the kidnappers which was denied by R&AW.

Around one month after this kidnapping, these hostages and the militants were traced twice during the reconnaissance of the Aviation Research Plane i.e. ARC of R&AW. Location of the place where they were hiding, was cross-checked by R&AW operatives and a crack commando team of its SFF unit were stationed at Srinagar for final assault on the hideouts of the militants. Secretary, R&AW, sent a detailed note in this regard to the Prime Minister office to seek approval of Narasimha Rao, the then Indian Prime Minister. He was on a tour to the southern states of India at that time. For two days, this permission was not given to R&AW to attack the area where hostages were kept. Narsimha Rao returned the third day and gave his consent to this operation. After that the ARC planes were again sent to reconfirm the presence of the militants and the hostages in that area. By then, they had left that location and disappeared in the dense forests and could not be relocated again.

This operation of R&AW was foiled due to the lackadaisical attitude of those who were managing the Prime Minister office of Narasimha Rao. Some detractors of Narsimha Rao considered it as a part of Rao's Doctrine to frame Pakistan as a state sponsor of terror in Jammu and Kashmir which the western powers till then considered as a soft human rights issue. According to them, Rao used this Pakistan perpetrated act of terror to expose its proclivity for de-stabilizing Kashmir. Whatever might be the truth, five innocent citizens lost their lives in this game of attrition among the hostile neighbours.

Manu Chhabaria, Dubai Based businessman, Employed Two Former R&AW Chiefs A K Verma and N.Narasimhan and 15 former officers of R&AW and CBI To Help Him In his Dubious Business Activities In India

Sometime in 1996, Manu Chhabaria, the controversial Dubai based businessman of Jumbo Group, was found involved in a seventy crores hawala transaction by the ED Directorate. Income Tax authorities and Enforcement Directorate raided his business establishment all over India. Some of his near relatives and business executives were arrested by ED officials. A number criminal cases under the Customs Act were pending against him in Bombay Courts. Since, Chhabaria was not in India, Enforcement Directorate sought CBI assistance to get him extradited from abroad for interrogation. There were news reports that most of the business activities of Chhabaria were in the tax heaven countries, details of which were in possession of the Enforcement Directorate.

Chhabaria devised a sinister plan to infiltrate into all these Economic Enforcement agencies through former intelligence officers of R&AW and investigation officers of CBI. He recruited A K Verma as head of this venture at a very hefty monthly salary and rented out a portion of his residence to run his office from there. A monthly rent of 65,000 rupees per month and a deposit of 15 lakh of rupees were paid to Verma.

Verma expanded this dubious network of Chhabaria by recruiting former R&AW and CBI officers almost in all major cities of India where government offices, courts and other business activities of his companies were taking place. He recruited N.Narasimhan former R&AW Chief to work on a monthly salary of 10,000 rupees. Beside him, he gave employment to a former Joint Secretary, two former Deputy Secretaries of R&AW and six former Deputy Superintendents of CBI including some junior rank officials. A total number of 17 such former officers of R&AW and CBI were employed all over India to work for Chhabaria.

The author filed a PIL in the Supreme Court against these dubious appointments by A K Verma for safeguarding the clandestine business activities of Mannu Chhabaria in India. Doubts were raised about Chhabaria's working as a front man for some foreign agency in India and utilizing the services of these former intelligence officers for nefarious activities. The author apprehended before the Court that all these officers by the very nature of their duties and responsibilities were in the know of and in possession of sensitive secret information relating to the country in almost all fields. It was elaborated that these officers could lay their hands to the information relating to various political parties or members thereof conducted themselves both in public and otherwise, information of economic activities of industrial houses and of the Government in market deals relating to purchase and supply of defence goods and pay offs and commissions in that regard. The Court was informed that these officers could procure information for Chhabaria relating to modern equipment purchased for defence services including missiles, war planes, tanks etc. They could gather details of atomic energy programmes, satellite monitoring and placement, Space related policy decisions, Science and Technology planning, commercial and economic espionage, dossiers of international arms dealers and hawala payments of militants.

Author appealed the Court to get this matter investigated through CBI and asked to frame rules to regulate the procedure of such dubious employment of former intelligence officers. Although, the Court did not interfere but ruled that the author could take up the matter with the Home Ministry to frame appropriate rules in this regard. The author took up this matter further with the Home Minister of India but unfortunately, the then weak government of United Front did not initiate any action in this matter in spite of the observation of the Supreme Court. However, all the seventeen officers including Verma vanished from the scene and Chhabaria was hounded by Indian agencies.

I.K.Gujral Escaped Terrorist Attack on Report of R&AW

Even after becoming the Prime Minister, I.K.Gujral, due to his diplomatic background, did not forgo the pathological hatred against R&AW. He was also part of this misconceived notion that R&AW was sitting on some important posts of diplomats in foreign Missions which was considered as paternal inheritance by them. Gujral was patronized by Indira Gandhi in this culture of diplomacy although he was never a qualified incumbent in this field. Some of the Indian press persons used to dubb him Indian Lenin for his resemblance of beard to that great Communist leader although he was no where near to his stature. People like Gujral never confronted Indira Gandhi or his son Sanjay when Emergency was imposed in India and rather toed their line of dictatorship to survive for their benefit.

When a minority government of Deve Gowda was brought down by then Congress President, Sita Ram Kesri, there was no potential candidate to succeed him. In that political imbroglio, Gujral was spotted to fill up the stop gap arrangement much to his own disbelief since he never thought to get this post during his life time. Soon thereafter, he tried to portray himself as the greatest friend of Pakistan and started new initiatives to improve bilateral relations under his self-proclaimed diplomacy of Gujral Doctrine.

In this pursuit, he ordered R&AW Chief to abandon all offensive operations inside Pakistan which were aggressively gaining momentum on pre-planned manner. An important unit of R&AW which was the brainchild of all such operations was closed down which had serious implications on the security considerations much to the chagrin of its mentors. Lot of aggressive trans-border operations came to standstill and enormous amount of money was wasted in this unimaginative misadventure. This was the time when Punjab militancy sponsored by Pakistan was crushed and Kashmir terrorism was being abetted by Pakistan to replace it in lieu of Punjab. Fickle minded Gujral never foresaw this hidden agenda of Pakistan and being a refugee from that area developed emotional psychosis toward his native homeland in his over enthusiasm but myopic approach to handle trans-border terrorism.

Gujral got elected to Lok Sabha by the alligance of BJP-Akali from the Jalandhar seat. Around this time, some Sikh separatist militants in London planned his assassination in Jalandhar where he used to visit frequently. R&AW Station Chief in London was maintaining close watch on the activities of these elements. He got information that four militants had been sneaked into India and would be camping in Jalandhar to assassinate Gujral with the help of their local contacts. This information was sent to the Intelligence Bureau who trailed these militants in a Gurudwara at Jalandhar. IB mounted a very close watch on the activities of these militants and when they got the supply of arms and ammunition from their local contacts, they were nabbed by the teams of local police with the help of IB sleuths. Gujral called R&AW Chief and showered praises for him for saving his life. But much damage to the operational preparedness of R&AW inside Pakistan was already done by him. How these people are so naïve to handle such sensitive matters when they got these coveted posts which seemed to be immature and ridiculous.

R&AW Officer Who Got Killed Around 40 Pak Trained Militants Denied His Due Credits During Service Career

Some time in 1997 a middle level R&AW officer developed two important sources while posted at Kupwara in Jammu and Kashmir. This area was the hub of militancy and a number of youths from here escaped to Pakistan where they were getting training in terrorist camps at various places. This R&AW officer developed an educated lady who was teaching in an institution at Kupwara as one of his source.

This lady was very popular among her lady students. Militants getting training in Pakistan used to send letters through Couriers. These Couriers were illiterate persons who were working for these militants across border to collect information and other materials from these militants in Pakistan and sending to their family in Kashmir. They used to carry letters in the name of their family members and to their girl friends. Some militants used to send their photographs also wherein they photographed themselves with various weapons given to them in the course of their training.

These girl friends of the militants used to share the contents of the letter with this lady because most of them were semi-literate and usually went to her to read these letters. These militants used to disclose the tentative dates of their entry inside Jammu and Kashmir through particular routes.

This R&AW officer cultivated a postman of Kupwara also who used to deliver letters to the families of these militants. This postman started giving these letters to this R&AW officer. On the basis of the information gathered from the lady teacher and the Postman, this R&AW officer used to collate all sorts of details of these militants and send to his office as well as to the army. His station chief at Kupwara authorized him to meet the GOC of army of that area. This R&AW officer started giving these details to Maj. Gen. V G Patnankar who was GOC of 28 Infantry Division, Kupwara. On the basis of the information of this R&AW officer, army became more vigilant on the routes described by him and tentative date of return of the militants from Pakistan. In a span of about one year 40 hardcore militants were killed by the army while they were crossing inside Jammu and Kashmir from various entry point in this area. Maj. Gen. Patnankar used to send a certificate to his Headquarterss clearly mentioning the details of each and every militant killed by army personnel on the basis of the information supplied to him by this R&AW officer.

In R&AW, this officer was treated shabbily. He was an upright, die-hard honest but a little obstinate in his style of working. His officer-in-charge from Srinagar recommended a reward of twenty thousand rupees and a foreign assignment. A senior desk officer at R&AW Headquarterss also endorsed the recommendations of Srinagar office and approved him for a posting at London. The then R&AW Secretary, Arvind Dave, who had developed a personal bias against this officer some years ago, declined him not only the foreign assignment but also refused a reward of Twenty thousand rupees. This brilliant officer became remorseful thereafter. His other colleagues got four foreign postings during their service career but he got one and that too at an insignificant place. Some R&AW officers display their personal animosity above the national interest which not only harms the organization but leaves some individuals as recluse. These individuals devote their personal energy to demoralize this department rather than utilizing their talent for a better cause.

R&AW Station Chief In London Was Frightened To Send Report Of An Indian Arms Dealers To His Delhi Headquarterss

Some time in 1998, a high profile source, who was a prominent arms dealer in London gave a report to the R&AW Station Chief. This report contained extensive details about the involvement of two prominent leaders of Indian Parliament who were instrumental in arms dealing in India. This report was immediately forwarded by the Station Chief to Delhi Headquarterss with proper grading of the source.

The same source met the R&AW Station Chief after some period of time and gave another report wherein a very senior Congress leader was also shown working as a big arms dealer in India. Station Chief discussed the contents telephonically with R&AW Chief and sought his permission to send full report of the source report. Details of this report were never sent to Headquarterss on the direction of R&AW Chief but the Station Chief sent a small note to Him quoting the name of the Congress leader dealing in arms. Station Chief in London was vying to become R&AW head in future and sensing that disclosure of the name of this Congress leader as arms dealer at some later stage, would jeopardize his chances of getting that post. Atal Bihari Vajpayee was Prime Minister at that time.

It is reliably learnt that Atal Bihari Vajpayee utilized the services of these two politicians to scuttle the efforts of Sonia Gandhi to become Prime Minister after his government was reduced to minority ending his 13 months rule. Such serious charges would be never revealed by these R&AW bureaucrats who want to retire peacefully after superannuation to keep such controversies at bay. May God let these pusillanimous creature die in peace killing their inner conscious which had already withered away to certain extent. Certainly, this gentleman became R&AW Chief subsequently and proved disastrous when Rabinder Singh was hoodwinked by CIA.

Inaction of R&AW Diplomat, Boomerang, On Himself In The IC-814

Hijacking Of Air India Plane From Kathmandu

Prior to the hijacking of IC-814 Air India flight by Jaish-e-Mohammand terrorist from Tribhuvan International Airport at Kathmandu, a junior R&AW operative U.V. Singh, Second Secretary, informed his Counselor, S B S Tomar, a senior officer of R&AW in Indian Embassy, that according to information of his source there was apprehension about the hijacking of plane by Pakistani terrorists. Singh was asked by Tomar to furnish the veracity of this report. When he revealed that his source was a responsible officer at the airport, Tomar rebuked him and warned him not to spread such rumours. This report was never sent by Tomar to R&AW Headquarterss and he suppressed it without crosschecking.

A Few days later, IC-814, the Air India flight was hijacked by the Jaish-e-Mohammand terrorists and whole of the country watched this sordid drama as a mute and helpless spectator. Three dreaded terrorists included Maulana Masood Azhar were forced to be released as a bargain to get this plane and the passengers who were kept hostages at Kandhar for many days.

To his fate, S.B.S.Tomar, was also travelling in this flight and was held as captive in the plane along with other travelers in Kandhar. Had his identity been known to the hijackers, there was every possibility of his being killed in place of an innocent passenger Rupen Bajaj who was killed by the terrorists to frighten the fellow passengers. This errant R&AW officer was never reprimanded for this grave lapse by the R&AW authorities. Since, he was a near relation of a senior officer in the Prime Minister office, he was rather rewarded with a lucrative foreign assignment to USA instead of punishment r negligence which resulted in such big fiasco. These senior officers of R&AW enjoy all sort of immunities under the veil of secrecy and sensitive working of this organization and even the Chief is scared of such elements who have links in the Prime Minister Office or to the politicians.

PAK Sponsored Attack On The Meeting Of Prime Minister Manmohran Singh Thwarted At Srinagar On the Information of R&AW Officer Who Was Then Hounded By The Authorities

After the UPA government came into power in May, 2004, the Indian Prime Minister, Manmohan Singh was to visit Srinagar on 17 November, 2004. This was the first visit of a Congress Prime Minister after 17 years and assumed much significance for the Pakistani General Pravez Mushraff in general and his intelligence outfit ISI in particular. When the schedule of this visit of Manmohan Singh was known to ISI, R&AW intercepted a message from Pakistan wherein it was mentioned that "send a SALAM to Indian Prime Minister". This message was a clear indication that some Pakistani outfit would certainly try to sabotage the visit of Indian Prime Minister by indulging in some terrorist activity.

A middle level R&AW officer at Srinagar got information through his source that two militants were hiding in a house located about 200 meters away from the venue where Prime Minister was to address a public meeting at Shere-e-Kashmir cricket stadium. He gave this report to his seniors at Srinagar who instead of taking action on it asked the officer concerned to re-check the veracity of the report. Next day, he crosschecked this information from his source and informed his seniors that the information was credible and militants would attack near the public meeting of the Prime Minister. These seniors of R&AW did not give credence to information of their junior and did not inform R&AW Headquarterss in this regard as a precautionary measure.

However, one of his seniors advised this officer, S.K.Sinha to pass on the information to the Army Commander of that area. That R&AW officer met the concerned Military Commander and briefed him about his information of a possible militant attack on the venue where the Prime Minister was to address a public meeting at Shere-e-Kashmir Cricket stadium on 17 November, 2004. On the basis of this information, the Military Commander started his search operations and on the morning of 17 November i.e. two hours before the Prime Minister's scheduled meeting, killed two militants in a semi-gutted cafeteria in the Shankaracharya Mountains overlooking the Cricket stadium. Due to this fierce encounter with the militants, the public meeting of Prime Minister was re-scheduled and started few hours after the original timings.

When this incident was reported to the Army Headquarterss by the Commander of Srinagar, the Army officers disclosed in a joint meeting with the intelligence officers that this incident was taken control of on the basis of the report of the R&AW officer at Srinagar. R&AW officer present in the meeting denied that there was no such information available with them at their Headquarterss. S.K.Sinha, R&AW operative, was then approached by the SPG to disclose his source of the report which he refused to divulge.

After this incident, the R&AW authorities took strong exception to the reporting of that R&AW officer directly to Army and made his life miserable. He was severely reprimanded and transferred to a remote area as punishment and made him to lead the life of a recluse. Had that operative not informed the Army in time, there was every chance of a militant attack on the public meeting of the Prime Minister and gravity of human losses would have been in numbers. It is ridiculous that instead of rewarding this officer for saving the life of number of innocent citizens and possibly the life of the Prime Minister, he was reprimanded and punished for this information to the army. This is the state of affairs prevailing in this premier intelligence agency of the country which the Prime Minister needs to restructure and reorganize.

US Court Raised Questions On The Existence Of R&AW

One Surender Jeet Singh tried to seek asylum in USA in 2004 proclaiming himself as R&AW agent who supposedly worked for thirteen years in India during which he recruited more than thirty persons in his adventure. He claimed that he quit to work further for R&AW when he was asked to aid in the assassination of religious person who was working for him. He entered USA through his own passport and sought asylum on the plea that he would be killed by R&AW if he ever returned to India. He testified before the Court that R&AW is an organ of government of India and functions under the office of the Prime Minister. Its primary working resembles with CIA of USA. The Judge found his arguments incredible and rejected his appeal.

He preferred an appeal against the Judge to the Board of Immigration Appeals of USA to review the order to grant him asylum. This Board while affirming the decision of the immigration judge gave a strange ruling questioning the existence of R&AW as an intelligence agency of India. It gave judgment that he did not present corroborative evidence whatsoever of the existence of this Indian government agency that was similar to the CIA and operating internationally. Further, the Board said that despite the secrecy surrounding the operations of the CIA and other security agencies worldwide, it was not difficult to find evidence of their existence. It also upheld that the respondent did not produce evidence about the existence of R&AW, an organization that spies on and assassinate religious minorities, perhaps worldwide, and the asylum sought simply on his own made stories could not be granted.

Surender Jeet Singh appealed to the United State Court of Appeals against this judgment. This Court decided that the asylum sought was not a statutory bar but focused on the absence of proof of the existence of the R&AW as necessary corroboration of Singh's story. The "tale", the Board said lacked corroboration. The Board did not acknowledge that the R&AW existed.

The Court ultimately ruled that it was nonsense to suppose that they were so cabined and confined that they could not exercise the ordinary power of any court to take notice of facts that were beyond dispute. Court further affirmed that they can notice that the government of India exists. They can notice that the office of the Prime Minister of India exists. They can too take notice that a part of of the Prime Minister of India's office is the R&AW. The Court lamented that a simple Lexis search could reveal over 1,500 articles on the R&AW from reputable international media sources including the BBC. Its situation in the office of the Prime Minister was a matter of common knowledge. Even the Encyclopedia Britannica acknowledges the existence of R&AW: "India's most important intelligence agency is a civilian service, the Research and Analysis Wing (R&AW). The R&AW's operations are primarily aimed at the Indian subcontinent, though it also has directed efforts in the United States aimed at influencing that government's foreign policy". (21 Encyclopaedia Britannica 787 15th ed.2003). The Court reversed the adverse credibility finding by the Board whose centerpiece was lack of evidence of the existence of the R&AW.

Ashok Chaturvedi, Controversial R&AW Chief, Planted Misleading Reports To Clean His Name In 26/11 Terrorist Attack

In the aftermath of 26/11 terrorist attack of Lashker-e-Taiba in Mumbai, there was wide spread criticism of intelligence agencies, particularly of R&AW in their utter failure to forewarn the security agencies in this national catastrophe. Every citizen of this country was behind the blood of these intelligence outfit after the killing of hundreds of innocent people in Mumbai.

The then Secretary of R&AW, Ashok Chatuvedi, who was branded as the most incapable, destructive and dishonest Chief that has ever ruled in its 45 years of history, devised a novel way out to clear his name in this tragedy rather to concede his incompetence. He asked his crony A K Arni, the Joint Secretary, to plant a false story in the media. On December, 2, 2008, Vir Sanghvi published a lead story in the Hindustan Times captioned "26/11 could have been stopped". It was falsely mentioned in this report that R&AW sent three interceptions i.e. on September18, 24 and November 19 to the security forces about the possibility of terrorist attack on some hotels and other places in Mumbai through sea route.

This news report was a twisted version of the actual facts available with R&AW. According to sources of the author, September reports were not intercepted by R&AW operatives but were provided by the US government which were intercepted by their agency in Pakistan. The report of November was intercepted by R&AW operatives in Mumbai which was sent to M K Narayanan, National Security Advisor and all concerned security agencies including the Director General of Coast Guard. However, it could not be corroborated whether M K Narayanan duly coordinated with other security agencies to take some pre-emptive measures to this sensitive disclosure of R&AW.

After the revelation of Chaturvedi in the media, Home Minister Chidambram snubbed Chatuvedi for manipulating this false disclosure in the press to cover up the ghastly tragedy when whole of the nation was in a state of shock and agony. Chidambram warned Chaturvedi of serious consequences and even threatened to sack him had he not been retiring in two months from then. Chaturvedi was aghast of this rebuking of the Home Minister and in the weekly meeting next day cautioned his senior officers that IB might keep a tab on them and they should keep away from media as a precautionary measure.

Quite often, R&AW officers have been using their media contacts to highlight their performance to send a signal to the government to hide their incompetence. This trend has been prevalent for the last twenty years when the efficiency in their operational working has considerably reached to its lowest ebb. Gone are the days when even the name of head of R&AW was known to the media. Even photograph of R N Kao was rarely found in the press leave aside any details about the inside working of R&AW. Falling standard of intelligence production in R&AW caused such disclosure to distract the attention of government and public which is a pathetic state of affair in any intelligence organization and R&AW is no exception.

Former R&AW Chief G S Bajpai Professed In 2009 That, He Would Get Appointed His Son-In-Law S K Tripathi in 2011, Which He Manipulated

The most controversial R&AW Chief Ashok Chaturvedi was to retire on January, 31, 2009. This was the time when country was facing the worst ever heat of controversies with regard to the failure of intelligence apparatus in the wake of 25/11 terrorist attack in Mumbai. There was a strong need to replace him through a competent R&AW head who could deliver good in the future.

There were three officers in R&AW i.e. P V Kumar, Rana Banerji and S K Tripathi in queue to succeed Chaturvedi. Since Kumar was left with two month service, there were strong apprehensions that Rana Banerji, who was the best choice and an expert on Pakistan affairs, to succeed in view of the recent Pakistan sponsored attack by Lashkar terrorists in Mumbai. However, when the Appointment Committee of the Cabinet was about to finalize his successor, Chaturvedi sent a very critical and misleading confidential report to the Prime Minister Office giving adverse remarks against these two officers. He wanted his protégé S.K.Tripathi to become the next Chief so that he would cover up all his misdeeds and irregularities in Secret Fund from scrutiny and possible retribution. There were reports that Chaturvedi twice took Tripathi to Sonia Gandhi so that he should be properly introduced to her. Even G S Bajpai, father in law of S K Tripathi extensively lobbied through this political and bureaucrat connections to put forward his claim for this post.

However, M K Narayanan, the National Security Advisor, found this opportunity to settle his old scores with R&AW hierarchy and through Chidambram got his aide K C Verma appointed as R&AW Chief, a day prior to Prime Minister Manmohan Singh was to undergo for a heart by-pass operation pm January 24, 2009.

When K C Verma was appointed for two years as R&AW head, his tenure was to expire on January 31, 2011 and S K Tripathi was due to retire on December 31, 2010 i.e. one month prior to retirement of Verma. G S Bajpai openly declared after the appointment of Verma that he would manage that he demit his office one month in advance to pave way for Tripathi to succeed him as R&AW Chief.

True to this declaration of Bajpai, K C Verma wrote to the Prime Minister in the middle of December, 2010 that he should be relieved of his duties immediately on health grounds. There were rumours inside R&AW that a hefty amount was paid to K C Verma to seek retirement early so that Tripathi could be appointed as R&AW Chief before his retirement date of December, 31, 2010. Mysteriously, Verma demit office of R&AW head one week earlier to the retirement of Tripathi and he was appointed to this post for two years.

It would be pertinent to mention that S K Tripathi was under cloud for the $350 million deal with the Israeli manufacturer ELTA for the purchase of airborne electronic surveillance systems which were procured without trials and competitive bidding. Subsequently, the Prime Minister ordered review of this deal by High-Powered Committee under the Defence Secretary, comprising a retired Air Chief and a senior official from the Finance Minister. Despite this corruption charge, Tripathi was selected to head R&AW under which this purchase was done and as such he was made Judge of his own cause. This was ridiculous.

Salute to G S Bajpai that he catapulted his forecast of January, 2009 when he declared that he would get cut short tenure of K C Verma to appoint his son in law S K Tripathi as the next R&AW Chief. Baipai should be hailed as winner who outwitted whole of the bureaucracy and manipulated even the Appointment Committee of the Cabinet to get this coveted post for his son in law. Although, he himself was disastrous as R&AW Chief since Rajiv Gandhi was assassinated when he was holding this post. Perhaps, Sonia Gandhi was not aware of this fact or she was grossly misguided by her advisors otherwise had she known this fact, Tripathi would have never become R&AW Chief.

S K Tripathi, R&AW Chief, Was Guest Of Dawood Aide In Kathmandu, During 2007

S K Tripathi as Special Secretary of R&AW and his family visited Kathmandu on a private visit to Kathmandu on August, 19, 2007 and stayed there up to August 21 in a Five Star Hotel Yak and Yet. This tour was sponsored by one Rakesh Wadhwa at the behest of R&AW Joint Secretary, M K Pyasi who had earlier been posted at Kathmandu as R&AW operative. Rakesh Wadhwa was a known aide of Dawood Ibrahim. He was taking care of various business activities of Dawood including many Casinos. Pyasi had been hand in glove with Wadhwa in many nefarious activities and even rented out his house to Wadhwa in Gurgaon while serving in R&AW. It is learnt that after retirement, Pyasi has been working for Wadhwa and looking after his business in Goa including a Casino.

R&AW authorities are aware of all these activities but rarely take any action against such errant officers. Every one in the Indian Embassy at Kathmandu was aware that S K Tripathi was guest of Dawood man Wadhwa during that Kathmandu and what transpired among them for three days was a mystery. Government of India seems to have been working on the whims and fancies of these bureaucrats who later on allowed Tripathi to head R&AW in spite of his dubious connections.

Kargil Fiasco

R&AW operative from Srinagar sent a report in October, 1998, that one of its sources had revealed that around 100 militants were trained in POK to sabotage the Srinagar-Leh highway. This report reached the Home Ministry on May, 26 1999 i.e. seven months after its original dispatch. This was never disseminated to the concerned army and security agencies. Similarly, in October, 1998, the Pakistan army conducted a survey of Kargil area using Remotely Piloted Vehicles i.e. RPVs for reconnaissance which was known to the intelligence agencies but never visualized the importance of this uncalled for activity of Pakistan.

Prior to these lapses, the army placed an order of snow boots from a firm of Brussels. R&AW officer posted in that Mission informed that the Pakistani army had already procured 50,000 such pairs and there was no chance to get this consignment for Indian soldiers in the near future. Even, this report was not properly analyzed as to why Pakistan purchased such high number of snow boots for its army. So, lack of intelligence coordination lead to this intrusion in Kargil.

When this intrusion was detected by a Budhist shepherd, there were no exact location of the intruded places. Ultimately, ARC Chief R S Bedi, withdrew the ARC planes from the Chinese borders and placed them on hills of Kargil and detected the exact locations of the intruders. Army and Air Force swung in action but in the ensuing 74 days war, 527 young Indian soldiers lost their lives with a burden of around 1,500 crores on the Indian exchequer.

R&AW has not been functioning on the way it was groomed by R N Kao who made the hell for Pakistan army in Bangladesh in 1971 which ultimately surrendered before Indian army taking their 93,000 soldiers as Prisoners of War. Government has to take initiative to get it geared up for all such eventualities.

R&AW Officers A K Verma, Secretary, S Chandershekhran and B Raman, Additional Secretaries Launched Website Wherein They Disclosed Sensational Operational Activities of R&AW During Their Service Career

R&AW Secretary Ashok Chaturvedi filed a criminal case under the Officials Secret Act against Maj. Gen. V.K.Singh a former R&AW officer when he wrote a book on R&AW. That case is still languishing in the Court causing unwarranted harassment to an upright officer who tried to expose corruption inside R&AW in this book.

Making mockery of the Officials Secret Act, in 2004 A K Verma, S.Chandershekhran and B Raman launched a website http//www.saag.org under the name of an organization South Asia Academic Group. This website displays numerous information about the policy planning of R&AW which these officers have disclosed in various reports and articles. Millions have viewed the contents of these reports.

On perusal of the articles under various heads of this website, it is revealed that these officers have disclosed the classified material which they acquired while serving on various sensitive desks of R&AW prior to their retirement. This includes R&AW's planning to its neighbouring and Islamic countries, terrorism and counter terrorism, LTTE, Maoist movement and shortcomings of Indian intelligence agencies including Defence. Many top secret details of R&AW and ARC and their functioning in India and abroad were also put up for public view.

These officers are not scholars who got these information through any research work or database or libraries, where such sensitive details could not be found, but simply used the information from the U.O. Notes of R&AW which were in their possession.

In an identical case, one former lady officer of R&AW, Nisha Sahai wrote a book on Afghanistan affairs for which she sought official permission from the Government to publish it. This permission was denied to her on the plea that the book contained details of operation R&AW which she was handling while serving on the desk of Afghanistan in R&AW.

Soon, this website came to the knowledge of the author and he made a complaint to the Prime Minister to take criminal action against these R&AW officers under the Official Secret Act for disclosing secrets of R&AW. The author gave elaborate details of these strategist and sensitive disclosures which were summarized as under:

1. Report of Lord Franks appointed by the Government of India in 1983 which recommended two decisions to strengthen the Joint Intelligence Committee. This revelation was never known even to the higher hierarchy of R&AW.
2. Details related to the failure of IB in Mumbai and R&AW in Dubai to give advance information about 1993 Mumbai Bomb blasts which was termed as Zero Intelligence.
3. A K Verma's disclosure about no intelligence report prior to the dropping of IPKF soldiers in Jaffna University in Sri Lanka which resulted in heavy army casualties and other details related to technical intelligence interception of LTTE connection and no IB and R&AW corroboration in LTTE operations. Use of intelligence by the then Indian government in 1982 in Indo-US relations was also revealed in the reports.
4. Details pertaining to the training of Naga insurgents in Yunnan in Kachin state of Myanmar.

5. Revelation of clandestine operation when conversation of General Pravez Mushraff with Lt. Gen. Aziz Khan were intercepted by R&AW during the Kargil conflict.
6. Disclosure of formation of National Technical Research Organisation i.e. NTRO bifurcating from R&AW under R.S.Bedi, a former R&AW officer wherein he was denied TECHINT and SIGINT specialist and equipments by R&AW Chief C D Sahay and ARC Director, Amar Bhushn from their respective departments.
7. A K Verma's disclosure that in 1990 ARC could not arrange a plane for R&AW in an important operation because all its planes were grounded for want of spares and pilots.
8. Information about ARC's failure to reconnaissance over Kargil area when Pakistani troops were infiltrating into Indian territory and instead offering a plane to a Cabinet Minister to fly him and his girl friend for a pleasure trip.
9. Revelation that Arvind Dave, Secretary of R&AW during Kargil conflict misused ARC planes to airlift Burmese teak from Arunachal to Udaipur and Delhi where he was constructing a house and a farm house respectively. It was also alleged that Dave got set up a telemetry station at Udaipur for smoothening the long flight operation especially for ARC planes for this purpose.

The author wrote to the Prime Minister that some of these revelations which were available on the files of R&AW could be of strategic importance to various terrorist groups operating against India from Pakistan and other countries. Many reports pertaining to the strategic affairs and security, China, Iraq, Islamic affairs etc. could prove vital for these countries and other militant groups to formulate their defence and intelligence policies towards India because these reports reflect the political viewpoint of India on the assessment prepared by R&AW. The author stressed that these startling revelations could do irreparable damage to the defence and security of India. Since, these officers did not seek any government permission to write these articles, sources of their information were none other than the material available with R&AW. So, these officers were liable for prosecution under the Officials Secret Act as was done in the case of Maj. Gen. V K Singh and denial of permission to Nisha Sahai to publish a book based on material of R&AW.

Two Brothers J K Sinha, Special Secretary and C K Sinha, Joint Secretary, Swallowed Rupees 100 Crore of R&AW's Secret Fund

There was a press report in October 2004, that rupees 100 crore was swindled from the secret fund by some officers of R&AW. It was alleged that rupees 132 crore was earmarked for a particular party in the general elections of Bangladesh in 2004. When the victorious Prime Minister of Bangladesh visited India, she had a meeting with the officers of Ministry of External Affairs in New Delhi. During the course of this meeting, the MEA officers enquired from her whether she received the said money prior to the election. When she nodded in affirmation, one of the officers enquired how much she got. She replied rupees 32 Cr. All the officers, who were aware that 132 Crores were sent prior to the elections, were stunned to listen that rupees 100 Crores of secret fund was not delivered to her and was swindled by R&AW officers. MEA officials informed their Minister who brought this matter to the knowledge of the Prime Minister. M.K.Narayanan, the then National Security Advisor, was asked to conduct investigation into this embezzlement.

The author conducted his an enquiry through his own sources in R&AW as to who were responsible for siphoning off this huge amount of money from the secret fund. It was detected that J.K.Sinha, Special Secretary, in-charge of this operation at R&AW Headquarterss in collusion with his younger brother C.K.Sinha also a Joint Secretary in R&AW, misappropriated this amount. C.K.Sinha at that time was posted in Dacca and was supervising the elections. He was personally responsible for disbursement of the amount in question. Both these brothers were found involved in this embezzlement of rupees 100 Crore and who had paid only rupees 32 Crore to the concerned party in Bangladesh. It is pertinent to mention that these two officers happened to be younger brothers of the former Governor of Jammu and Kashmir, General S.K.Sinha. While J.K.Sinha was a former IPS officer who joined R&AW on deputation, C.K.Sinha was given appointment in R&AW as Class I officer through back door on the recommendation of S.K.Sinha in 1973.

On a further enquiry by the author, it was revealed that R&AW had also conducted its own investigation on this large scale swindling of secret fund by these two officers. The author also sought details through right to information act from R&AW to send the information pertaining to this embezzlement of secret fund but the R&AW authorities in the garb of secrecy, refused to divulge the facts to the author when he particularly quoted the names of these two officers in this embezzlement. Undeterred, the author brought this matter to the knowledge of the Indian Prime Minister Manmohan Singh but no one intervened and this case was merrily put under the carpet by the bureaucrats. Later, the author brought this embezzlement case to the knowledge of Delhi High Court and Supreme Court through a Public Interest Litigation matter but nothing came out of it despite wasting lot of time and money. Sandip Joshi, a R&AW operative who worked in Indian High Commission at Colombo, also accused J.K.Sinha of siphoning off Crores of Rupees in Sri Lanka elections but no one dared to take any action on the accusation of Sandip Joshi.

Embezzlement of R&AW's secret fund has been a common practice for quite some time since there is no government machinery to put check on these huge money transactions. It is high time that the Government of India should devise a mechanism to put cog in this money spiraling activities in R&AW by these unscrupulous officers.

National Security Advisors Are Damaging R&AW Maximum

During the course of a meeting at R&AW Headquarters, one senior ARC officer was narrating his past experiences in the room of a senior R&AW officer where author was happened to be a part of their discussions concerning R N Kao, the founder of this prestigious agency. The ARC officer mentioned that after the liberation of Bangladesh, Kao had called all the senior cadres in batches at his South Block office over tea to share their experiences of the war. While this ARC officer along with others was having tea, Kao received a call from PMO office on his secraphone that Prime Minister Indira Gandhi wanted him in an urgent meeting. Since tea was yet to be served to ARC officers, Kao told the caller that he would come after some time. After a gap of five minutes, the PMO again called up Kao to which he replied that he was still busy with his guests and would reach her soon after the meeting was over. When the PMO telephoned for third time, Kao asked the caller to wait for a moment and disconnected the phone. Kao then rang directly to Indira Gandhi and said, "Priyadrashniji I am busy with some guests and will be with you shortly". Tea session lasted for another ten minutes because the participants realized the urgency of PM's message and gulped the hot tea in that excited atmosphere. Such was the wave length of a respectful understanding between the R&AW Chief and the Indian Prime Minister and that too of a stature of Indira Gandhi who had to wait for half an hour at the insistence of Kao for that meeting. Nowadays this proximity has eroded for which both the Prime Minister and the subsequent R&AW Chiefs are responsible. This proximity has been further diminished by a new toothless authority, the National Security Advisor, newly invented sanctuary for a retired babu.

R&AW Chiefs were directly accountable to the Prime Minister till 1998. In November, 1998, the Atal Bihari government created the post of National Security Advisor (NSA) on the pattern of USA where it was functional since 1953. This was probably devised for himself by Brijesh Mishra, the Principal Secretary of Atal Bihari Vajpayee. This post was made equivalent to the level of State Minister in the Union Cabinet. Mishra was appointed the first incumbent to this post. Although, the sphere of duties of this post are advisory in nature but owing to close proximity of Brijesh Mishra to Atal Bihari, this post assumed unassailable authority at that time. This was a non-political power centre much more decisive not only on security matters but also in major political decision making. By the time, NDA government was on the verge of completion of its tenure in 2004,

Brijesh Mishra had become more controversial not only within the ruling cliques but made R&AW his own fiefdom. Most of the policy decisions pertaining to the operational planning of R&AW were scuttled without any planning and the intelligence production came to standstill. No worthwhile defence, security and intelligence functional infrastructure was created with the result that there was no intelligence worth the name during the Kargil conflict. Rather, Arvind Dave, R&AW Chief was appointed Governor of Arunachal Pradesh on Mishra's advice to keep him away from the purview of the Subramanyam Committee which was enquiring the Kargil debacle.

The then R&AW hierarchy usually termed this NSA barrier between the Prime Minister as Dwarpal i.e. the gatekeeper who would not allow any one to enter without frisking. Mishra's worst decision in the interference of R&AW came when he brought A.S.Dulat, a novice of external intelligence, as its Chief. This was a terrible blunder to encroach upon the basic structure of R&AW. Like the appointment of Chief Justice of Supreme Court or the seniority pattern prevalent in the defence forces, in R&AW also a cadre was prepared 1983 onwards to draw the future line of succession for its Chiefs at the behest of the then Prime Minister, Indira Gandhi. In view of the strategic requirements of India, it was then decided to make R&AW a self-contained organization exclusively to specialize in the collection, collation, analysis and reporting on foreign intelligence vital to the security interests of the country on a long term basis. Thus, a cadre was created comprising officers from the police, armed forces, science and technology and other fields of service to train them on long terms basis to make R&AW a specialized institution of international significance. This organization is not like other ministries of the government where any IAS officer can become its secretary but requires an altogether different frame of mind, capability and specialized training. Intelligence fraternity of R&AW, like the armed forces, are imbibed with impeccable loyalty and highly disciplined to their job. So, its head has to lead by proven professional competence in its specialized functioning so that he could create exemplary model to work with respect and dignity along with his juniors. Hence, a Tom or Jerry, imported from outside to head this esoteric institution, would adversely affect efficiency, discipline and loyalty of the cadre of R&AW and its consequential impact would be horrendous.

First time in the history of R&AW, an outsider A.S. Dulat assumed this such an uncalled for honour resulting into a number of horrific terrorist activities like attack on Indian Parliament and IC-814 hijacking during his tenure. While demitting his office, Dulat had purportedly advised the Prime Minister not to appoint non-R&AW officials to this post hereinafter since he was unable to perceive R&AW's operational functioning in foreign countries till his retirement. Mishra too was too naïve to understand its nuances, being a foreign service man with no intelligence background. It would be pertinent to mention here that NSA in US never has any say in CIA or FBI's internal functioning and only coordinates with all security and intelligence agencies to brief the US President. His role is defined as only advisory and not supervisory. Whereas in India, both R&AW and IB are put under the supervisory charge of these foreign affairs babus who are neither trained in the field of intelligence to advise these agencies nor suggest any meaningful operational planning. Thus, both these agencies R&AW and IB are still in a state of limbo ever since the NSA was heaped on them.

When UPA government assumed power in 2004, a new tribe of two retired bureaucrats i.e. J.N.Dixit, a foreign service expert for external and M.K.Narayanan, former Director, IB for internal matters, were appointed as National Security Advisors. M.K.Narayanan was Director of Intelligence Bureau when Rajiv Gandhi was assassinated by LTTE in 1991 and was indicted by Verma Commission for his failure to protect the life of the former Indian Prime Minister. How he managed to get this coveted appointment is intriguing in intelligence circle till date? Due to the sudden death of Dixit, Narayanan assumed charge of both these factions.

M K Narayanan had pathological animosity towards R&AW cadre because they usually dubbed him incompetent as Director, IB, due to his mediocrity which resulted in the death of Rajiv Gandhi. However, he surfaced from hibernation again in New Delhi bureaucracy due to his close proximity with Chidambram. His invidious internal ire towards R&AW came to the fore when he again brought another outsider P.K.H.Tharakan in 2005 as its head from the state police. He faced stiff internal rivalry from the senior R&AW officers who were vying for this post. After Tharakan, Narayanan got appointed Ashok Chaturvedi, a relative of the then Principal Secretary of Prime Minister, who proved most disastrous for the organization. Pakistan trained terrorists attacked Mumbai on November 26, 2008 due to the utter failure of R&AW during his regime. Again, in 2009, he brought a former IB man, K.C.Verma who sat like a parasite on this sensitive organization and retired as a non-entity worth to be remembered. So, M.K. Narayanan as National Security Advisor damaged R&AW to the maximum extent due to his evil approach in its operational functioning with the result that till now this agency has not positioned itself to its original hunting grounds and its state of affairs are in the hands of amateur officials who are only serving and not working.

Present, NSA, Shiv Shankar Menon too had a controversial stint in Ministry of External Affairs when he superseded more than a dozen IFS officers and got himself appointed as Foreign Secretary by M.K.Narayanan. After 26/11 terrorists attack in Mumbai, Narayanan was on a shaky wicket and he managed to get Menon as his successor so that he would be indirectly interfering in the security and intelligence affairs, which he did for quite some time even after becoming the Governor.

These retired species i.e. National Security Advisors are placed as barriers between the Prime Minister and the R&AW Chief for the past 15 years. Since then, these creatures have dismantled the basic fabric of the working conditions of R&AW as a result thereof rampant corruption has risen since there is no political authority to put cog in this corruption infested machinery. There were rumours inside R&AW that Brijesh Mishra and M.K.Narayanan were duly taken care of by the respective R&AW chiefs for their smooth survival. Let the good sense prevail and the political bosses should realize to do away with these creatures who are intelligence baiters but authoritatively intervened in the affairs of R&AW. These politicians should directly supervise the functioning of R&AW otherwise there would be more of 26/11s in India and this agency would become a laughing stock in future.

R&AW Kins Settled In USA

R&AW postings of senior officers in Indian missions at Washington and New York are considered prized one not on the criteria of money but a chance to help them settled their kins in the cozy atmosphere of that country. Usually, most of them arrange green cards and other visas for their children by using their diplomatic connections and that too with the help of their CIA counterparts.

During the regime of Narsimha Rao, it was revealed that two US banks i.e. Citi Bank and Bank of America, were found involved in the Security Scam of India. Personnel Department of Union Government, while investigating this scam, found some sensitive US connections and sent a detailed report about the kins of R&AW officers who were given employment in USA.

According to this report A K Verma's son Deepak got appointment in the CIA sponsored business establishment the Digital Equipment Corporation. Later on, it was learnt that he joined Clinton Foundation. Verma was posted in Washington in the eighties and since then his son is residing there. His successor, G.S.Bajpai also secured Green Card for his son Ashok Bajpai.

N Narasimhan, another Secretary outclassed all other officers and got settled his three kins in USA while he was posted in Washington. R. Balakrishnan and S Chandershekhran, A.Arjunan former Additional Secretaries also managed Green Cards for their children while serving in the mission in USA.

But the most curious is the case of R.J.Khurana, a former Additional Secretary of R&AW who was posted in USA. His entire family procured Green Cards when he was posted there. He did not bring his family back after completion of his tenure in USA in spite of the direction by R&AW authorities. After retirement, he too shifted there on USA Visa.

Although, every Indian citizen is free to serve and settle in any part of the World in the democratic system of this country. But there had been numerous cases when CIA was found involved in luring the Indians serving in strategic positions in various departments in Indian government. R&AW Joint Secretary Rabinder Singh was backed by CIA and clandestinely flown to USA and given citizenship there when he was likely to be arrested for espionage. In 2006, a CIA sponsored spying network trapped three top officials of National Security Council Secretariat out of which one was head of R&AW's computer division. Mukesh Saini, former Coordinator of Indo-US Cyber Security Forum, S.S.Paul, NSC Security Systems Analyst and Brig. U. Dasgupta, R&AW Director were honey-trapped individually by CIA operative Rosanna Minchew at various places in New Delhi. They were all arrested for spying and sent to jail. These are some known cases where CIA penetrated to secure sensitive information. There is every likelihood that CIA must be acquiring such information which could not be detected by the Indian intelligence agencies.

In view of these activities of CIA in India, these kins of senior R&AW officers are quite vulnerable to CIA in their own country. These children did not get employment on the basis of their qualifications but were got placed there with the due permission of US government. This favour is not given to the counterparts of Foreign Affairs ministry officers by the US government but specially targeted the R&AW officers. Government should take a serious view of this sensitive matter and impose certain restrictions, particularly on R&AW officers which they did in 1985 and passed the Intelligence Agencies, Restriction of Rights Act, which forbid intelligence officials to interact with press and media.

Bizarre R&Aw Incidents - From 2013 Onwards

One R&AW Chief was victim of his own deeds

One R&AW Secretary got information that another intelligence agency of India had hacked the official data of National Database and Registration Authority (NADRA) of Pakistan. NADRA is Pakistan agency like Indian Unique Identification Authority of India (UIDAI) which provides Aadhaar Cards to every Indian citizen. NADRA was stated to be fool-proof, comprehensive and highly sophisticated computerized system where civil registration of all Pakistanis was secured in the centralized data warehouse, network infrastructure and interactive data acquisition system to issue National Identity Cards (NIC) to Pakistani population. However, despite such impregnable disposition of NADRA, officers of Indian intelligence did excellent operation to hack NADRA and procured details of all the National Identity Cards of Pakistani citizens.

In order to update data of R&AW about NADRA, this R&AW Chief illegally procured this data through two officials of that intelligence agency. At a later stage in the change of events, this R&AW Chief became head of that intelligence agency. Thereafter, these two officials tried to exert unwarranted pressure on this head due to their past illegitimate help to him. Some seniors of the agency were aware of this action of this head of department. In order to nip the evil in bud for ever, whole of this unit was dismantled by him and concerned staff was posted to unwarranted positions due to which uneasy situation was created in the department.

Later on, this head of department devised a dubious method to collect classified information through private agencies who are engaged in hacking business in various part of India. Huge amount was spent on this working structure which was never accountable. Allegations of misappropriation of money were leveled against him in this process.

Sikh Couple Arrested in Germany Purported as R&AW Agents

Two Sikhs, a couple, were arrested by the German authorities on charges of spying for R&AW officials purported to be posted at the Indian Consulate in Frankfurt city of Germany. Media reports revealed that this couple was suspected to be gathering information on Kashmiri separatists and Sikh groups operating in Germany and passed on to R&AW officials for which they were paid USD 7974. This matter was progressing in the Court of Law and if these charges were proved, this couple could be imprisoned for 10 years prison.

Prime facie, this case was handiwork of Pakistani intelligence officials in connivance with some German officials to implicate and defame the Indian intelligence agency R&AW in such shoddy affairs inside Germany.

In brevity, it is pertinent to mention that there is no official postings of any R&AW official in any Mission as per the official records of Indian Embassy in Germany or Consulate. No name of such official was mentioned in court case. German police committed diplomatic perjury by claiming so in this case. German Government should have been protested to get release this couple who would not have been targeted and shown as taken petty amount of USD 7974 for such spying activity. This legal loophole should be investigated and anti-Indian elements involved in this case should be booked by German authorities.

No Compensation to R&AW Agents who Languished in Pakistan Jails

There were numerous media reports for decades that many Indian citizens claiming as agents of R&AW and other Indian Intelligence/Security agencies were arrested inside Pakistan on spying charges and got imprisoned for several years. Subsequently, they were released by Pakistani authorities on completion of their jail terms and returned to India. These Indian citizens were subject of the worst inhuman trauma and torture by the Pakistan military first and subsequently going through the inhuman conditions of Pakistani jails. Despite such barbaric tortures, if they remained alive and returned India, is not only divine gift but their heart-felt determination for the cause they were sent to Pakistan.

Some time back, I was called on a Tv channel propagating a film on R&AW fictions where some of these persons were also participants to reveal their life stores. I had no option but to defend them for what they did for the country. Thereafter, these persons narrated their miserable stories of torture in Pakistan and later their pathetic life conditions in India due to extreme poverty and no compensation by the Indian Intelligence/Security agencies which sent them for any sort of mission in Pakistan.

These persons were determined to raise their plight by sitting on fast unto death at Jantar Mantar near Indian Parliament. They had met many Indian politicians in this case but nothing was done to them. They were also planning to contact various media and human right commissions which would have nationwide and international repercussions. I requested them to postpone this action and assured them that I would take up their cause with the Government. They agreed to my suggestion.

I referred their cause to the Government around two years back but so far nothing has been done to help them. I am also given to understand that many such Indian citizens are still languishing in Pakistani jails. As a goodwill gesture, Indian Government should exchange these citizens with those Pakistanis who are in Indian jails on such identical charges. This human act would save many families from further humiliation and pathetic conditions.

Mumbai Attack of 26/11 & Misleading Report in Book "The Siege"

In the book "The Siege" authored by Adrian Levy and Cathy Clark-Scott mentioned that CIA sent first report about the impending attack in August, 2006 and thereafter 25 more alerts were sent to R&AW and IB. There is no truth in this book about the first report of August, 2006 that the Muslim insurgents fighting in Kashmir were "making preparations" for a major assault in Mumbai to target several Five Star Hotels.

This was totally misleading revelation in this book. Mumbai attack was actually planned by Lashkar-e-Tayyaba few months prior to the actual execution in November, 2008. Hence, such report sent by CIA in August,2006 to Indian Intelligence agencies i.e. two years prior to 26.11.2008 attack is imaginary and deliberately planted insignificantly.

Soon after 26/11 attack, a leading Indian daily published lead news at the behest of the then R&AW Chief that "26/11 could have been stopped". This was a ploy to cover up his own failure in 26/11 mishap. It was reported in this news that R&AW sent three interceptions of September 18, September 24 and November 19 to all security forces including Navy about the possible attack of terrorists through sea routes on some hotels and other places in Mumbai.

According to actual handlers of R&AW, CIA certainly sent two reports in September, 2008 but November 19 report was intercepted by R&AW operatives in Mumbai which was sent to M.K.Narayanan, the NSA and other security agencies including Director General of Coast Guard about possible sea route terrorist attack in Mumbai. In view of these facts, there is no truth in the weirdly disclosure in the book "The Siege" that 25 reports were sent by CIA to R&AW and IB in August, 2006 about 26/11 Mumbai attack.

Intelligence Goof-up on ISI Plant

Some photographs of Pakistani were sent to the Multi Agency Centre (MAC) as possible terrorist attack like 26/11. These photographs were procured by R&AW from a reliable source in Pakistan. These photographs were mocked by Pakistani media as of non-entity still living in Lahore. MAC issued terror alert and passed on these photographs to various intelligence agencies and four state security agencies. High alert was ordered in these states considering it as high terror plan particularly to the refineries in Gujarat and Punjab. In the blame game, R&AW clarified its stand that no intelligence agency could afford to sit on such vital intelligence input and would definitely share it with the concerned counterparts. R&AW report was limited to infiltration of these persons and did not elaborate their action plan. MAC did not verify and cross-checked the veracity with other intelligence agencies and state security departments and issued this alert which was blown out of proportion. It is pertinent to mention that all R&AW reports are not perfect when procured from sources abroad. Their veracity has to be done after due corroboration with relevant facts. But R&AW has its duty to send all such reports to MAC which has to verify the facts with other 14 intelligence departments and state police authorities to devise the actual action plan. So, it was MAC which was responsible for this goof-up and blaming R&AW would be incorrect and implausible.

Ganga Hijacker Case Against Author Boomeranged

In this book, the author first time revealed that one Hashim Qureshi along with one of his relatives hijacked Ganga Fokker Friendship Plane of Indian Airlines from Srinagar to Lahore as part of an operation of R&AW. This plane was hijacked on 30 January 1971 to Lahore and wab blown up on 2 February as planned by R&AW. Pakistan over-flights to East Pakistan were banned by India after this incident. Qureshi was jailed in Pakistan and later migrated to a European country wherefrom he was brought to India by Indian Government.

Qureshi issued a legal notice and then filed a suit for damages against the author in a Srinagar Court on this revelation. The author sought two clarifications from the advocate of Qureshi on his legal notice whether he is the same person who hijacked the plane and if so what was his motive behind the hijacking. These facts were never clarified. Later, the author informed the Srinagar court that locus of such libel is in Delhi and none where else. The author never heard of anything thereafter in this regard. Such incidents usually occurs if you write on serious issues.

Controversy of R&AW Chief visit to Nepal

In third week of October, 2020, there were media reports that R&AW Chief Samant Goel and some other officers visited Nepal and met Prime Minister Oli and some other politicians of Nepal. There was lot of hue and cry in political circle and media of Nepal about this visit and meetings.

There had been some bitterness between India and Nepal when this year Indian Defence Minister Rajnath Singh inaugurated a strategically crucial road connecting the Lipulekh pass with Dharchula in Uttarakhand. Nepal protested in this regard claiming this road was passing their territory and subsequently published a new map claiming these areas as its territories.

Political relations between two countries were at its lowest ebb thereafter. Thaw in these relations was apparently broken when Nepal initiated various diplomatic, social and political overtures to restore normalcy.

Although, this high profile visit of R&AW Chief should have been a closely guarded affair but it should not be construed as default line to create any other political rumbling there. R&AW has to tackle and discuss some security related matters with its friendly neighbouring countries and Nepal is one of them. Lot of Madarsas have been established in Nepal bordering UP and Bihar where anti-Indian activities are mushrooming at the behest of ISI of Pakistan. So, there could be such pertinent issues which were on the agenda of R&AW Chief in this visit to Nepal. There should not be any political tremors or hullabaloo in this regard.

Why NTRO is Headed by Police Officers

There is a misconception in Media and Bureaucratic circle as to why the Intelligence Agency, National Technical Research Organization (NTRO) is headed by Police Officers for the last few years. According to some higher sources, the Scientists who are involved in various research in technical and cyber sectors are perfect in their research but they lack the killing instinct of cross border terrorism operations.

Initially NTRO was headed by these scientists but subsequently this patron was analyzed and it was decided that in order to use NTRO for trans-border operations, IPS officers are operationally more capable than the scientists. Hence NTRO is now headed by police officers.

❑

R&AW Chiefs Since 1968

When one enters the room of R&AW chief at the extreme east corner on eleventh floor of its Headquarterss, just near the door on left hand side, portraits of every chief, starting from R N Kao, who was number one to S K Tripathi who retired as nineteenth, are displayed in the memory of all retired heads of this organisation. Kao and Sankaran Nair never sat in this room since they retired in 1977 and this building was inaugurated in 1979. I saw eight hangings on the wall. When I met the ninth one i.e. J S Bedi, sitting in this room, I could visualize that legacy of Kao was still alive in R&AW, the way Bedi was looking energetic to carry it on. But alas, he had only five months to go for his retirement and this bigger than life's image of Kao had to end. At that time, I never thought that R&AW had slumped eight steps down to what Kao built it since 1968 because Bedi was groomed under the nose of Kao and a ray of hope was visible in his personality. Halcyon days of Kao are passé. Nowadays, this agency has been made a laughing stock by the subsequent incumbents. Probably, the degradation in its operational capability has come about due to incompetence, sycophancy and short-sightedness which started to dominate number 10 and reduced it to a non-entity, particularly when number 19 retired in December, 2012. Corruption is rampant at all levels in its cadres. Discipline and sense of belonging has evaporated. Kao had only one house which he got built by taking loan from Life Insurance Corporation of India. He helmed R&AW for more than eight years during which he was involved in the biggest operation of Bangladesh liberation wherein billions of rupees were spent by him. Even currency notes were dropped in bags from helicopters for Mukti Bahini operators in far flung areas of difficult terrain. If he had the will to siphon off even the fraction of this amount, he would have built up a huge empire for himself. He was a diehard nationalist and an epitome of probity. Now, I see most of the other heads have acquired innumerable assets from the secret fund of R&AW. Even ARC planes have been used to transport construction material to build the house by a former chief. Such a retrogression at top of this agency is sending wrong signals among the junior cadres who too are following in their footsteps. Moral and character have become a thing of the past. In this messy scenario of R&AW which is completely devoid of any sense of honesty and dignity of its cadre, this agency warrants a massive overhaul. I am doubtful, if the political bosses would have the guts to do anything to improve the situation. I have made numerous attempts with these politicians to make this agency accountable to the Parliament but most of them were frightened even to talk about on this subject. Existence of this agency was diminished to a big void after bringing the National Security Advisors i.e. NSAs between R&AW and the Prime Minister. These NSAs are retired foreign service officers who had no knowledge of intelligence tradecraft but tried to intervene in affairs of R&AW with general experience in this field. In this uncalled for process, they create more problems for the organization than making things better. Thus, the basic structure of R&AW has been distorted by these retired professionals of foreign affairs. Now only a divine force can save this organization. We can only pray now. In this chapter, I have tried to portray a true picture of each and every R&AW chief, twentieth of which is in the chair now. I and R&AW as a whole, are least concerned about their professional achievements but we are certainly determined to expose their undoings which would hurt some of them but these are the real facts and not written with any malice. The revelations given hereinunder not only reflect my sentiments but represent the feelings of R&AW as a whole.

1. R N Kao – From September 21, 1968 to March, 1977 – The Longest Stint

R&AW was a brainchild of Kao. His stint is reckoned as golden era during the 45 years of its existence. Kao, the suave, erudite and legendary founding father of R&AW was a devout Hindu with staunch religious background. He inherited these moorings from his mother who brought him up in a strict discipline due to the untimely death of his father at the tender age of five. According to Sankaran Nair, deputy to Kao through out his career as head of R&AW, he was a finest human being he ever met. Due to his education in Allahabad and Lucknow, he imbibed the gracious Nawabi culture and would never use harsh words even while ticking off someone. According to Nair, he was never angry on wrong actions but when upset he would say "well, that is a very excellent mistake you have made, do not repeat it". Nair admitted that although he was his number two, Kao was his boss but he always treated him like his younger brother. Nair remembered him as an excellent sculptor and showed his bust sculpted by Kao.

I have never seen a perfect gentle bureaucrat like Kao who was meticulously dressed through all seasons. His favourite shopping destination for dresses was London. After retirement, I also found him in nicely dressed Khadi Kurta Pajama although he usually wore suit with tie. Sankaran Nair recalled an incident when Kao went to a very famous London tailor and got stitched a Bandh Gala suit which was delivered to him at the London airport while he was returning to India. When Kao tried it at Delhi, he was disappointed to find it tight under the arms. Next time, when he visited London, he went to the same tailor and said that he was pretty disappointed that such a famous name like him should give him a suit that did not fit him well. The tailor requested him to wear the suit and found it really tight. He asked him to take it off. After that the tailor took a big scissor and rant it through the suit, made all strips of cloth and put in the dustbin and said that he would make a new suit for him free of charge and requested Kao to select whatever cloth he wanted. According to Nair, he was so impeccably dressed that other seniors in the Indian bureaucracy who could not dress like him at that time, used to make fun of him by calling the best dressed man in whole of the Government of India, which he literally was. He was very particular about the clothes and matching things.

Kao never believed in half-measures and was always looking towards the age old problems of Indian government, particularly after the independence. At the young age of 37 in 1955, he unfolded the conspiracy of Farmosa, now Taiwan, agents who sabotaged an Air India plane, the Kashmir Princess, wherein the Chinese Prime Minister, Chou En Lai was destined to travel to Indonesia. Kao personally convinced Chou En Lai about the perpetrators of this air crash and absolved all fears of British connivance in this sabotage. This was his first major international mission wherein he proved his intellect not only to the Chinese diplomacy but got all sorts of kudos from the Indian intelligence fraternity in general and Pandit Jawahar Lal Nehru in particular.

Kao was always an innovator. After the debacle of 1962 conflict with China, he realized the need for aviation related intelligence and created Aviation Research Centre (ARC) in IB. Although, this is the domain of Indian Air Force but it never occurred to them to have such an organization. Ultimately Kao worked on this venture which is proving as asset for the Indian security apparatus. Kao tried to put tab on the Chinese nuclear and air preparations and in 1965 planted a nuclear device on Nanda Devi mountain along with CIA. This was a joint operation of IB and CIA to keep track of the Chinese nuclear plans. Kao also mooted the idea of formation of an Economic Intelligence branch in the IB to monitor Pakistan's expenditure on military preparedness so that India could effectively counter it. This was opposed by some seniors but he created an Economic wing in R&AW under Dr. S K Chaturvedi, an Economist of Planning Commission of India. This was a new pattern based on many foreign agencies. At later stage, this wing played a very vital role in its assessment towards Pakistan and China on defence related matters.

I was reading an article on Kao by a Pakistani journalist about his plans in Pakistan. Some false and concocted words were used against Kao by him obviously out of malice. Kao unleashed a rein of terror on the Pakistani forces after March 25, 1971, through the Mukti Bahini, a guerilla outfit, trained by his operatives all along the borders of East Pakistan. A part of the Pakistani army was made to suffer major causalities through the guerillas of Mukti Bahini and rest were made to run for their lives. When the decisive war broke out on December 3, Indian army found a smooth sailing in East Pakistan and within two weeks 93,000 Pakistani soldiers were made to bite the dust and taken into custody by Indian military. So, Pakistani press is obviously envious of this landmark achievement of Kao and I don't blame them for their discomfort with this icon of Indian intelligence who played a major role to cut Pakistan to a small size. Kao was ruthless in his approach when it comes to a national cause and he proved his mettle in this historical triumph of Indian army with the help of R&AW. He told me that he had been working on another operation inside Pakistan in Sindh province. Jiye-Sindh movement was gaining momentum during his tenure and there was a strong undercurrent for a separate Sindh for the Sindhi population which were persecuted by the ruling clique of Punjabis. Kao had planned a strategic operation for this Sindhi cause in Pakistan when separate flags were usually hoisted on top of houses by the Sindhis on the independence day of Pakistan. This beginning was abruptly stopped when he was unceremoniously removed by Morarji Desai in 1977. His planning to cut Pakistan to size further died a premature death after his departure from R&AW.

After teaching Pakistan a lesson of their life, Indira Gandhi wanted to confront China since she watched the humiliation of her father Jawahar Lal Nehru in 1962 conflict with China. She roped in Kao in this endeavour to merge Sikkim with Indian territory under the nose of China. Kao devised a secret plan and with the help of three top senior officers and a few R&AW operatives, merged about 3,000 sq. miles of this region with India. This was a bloodless coup wherein the Chogyal, ruler of Sikkim, was made to surrender his kingdom to Indian sovereignty. No intelligence agency in the world be it CIA or Mossad, has ever achieved such a major historical event which R&AW under Kao did in 1975. Kao told me that only three to four senior officers were involved in this operation. This fact was admitted by his number two K.Sankaran Nair to me that even he was never aware anything about this operation. Such a top secret working prevailed at that time in R&AW which is elusive now a days.

When Indira Gandhi became Prime Minister again in 1980, he appointed Kao as her senior advisor. She formed a policy planning committee on major national and international issues which comprised G.Parthasarthy along with Kao. This committee was the brainchild behind the creation of Hindu Tamil population outfit LTTE. Kao confirmed to me that Indira Gandhi had decided to carve a separate autonomous homeland for the Tamilians who were suppressed by the majority Sinhalese for ages. Although, the political agenda for an independent status for this homeland of Tamils was not determined but Indira Gandhi had authorized Kao to make a blue print for it. In this pursuit, the Tamil youths of Sri Lanka were imparted guerilla training at Chakrata in the R&AW field station and V Prabhakaran, the founder of LTTE, was one among the first batch of this training. Subsequent events in this matter are now a history because when Rajiv Gandhi became Prime Minister, he scrapped this committee and his group of advisors turned the table on this Hindu cause which ultimately finished with the killing of Rajiv Gandhi.

At the later stage of his stint as Senior Advisor to Indira Gandhi in 1980, on the suggestion of Kao, Siachin glacier was captured by Indian army which dealt a severe blow to Pakistan in particular and China in general. National Security Guards, the elite commando force was also the brainchild of Kao to counter Punjab terrorism.

When Allahabad High Court set aside the election of Indira Gandhi in 1975, she clamped emergency in India curtailing all fundamental rights of Indian citizens. Millions of people were put in prison without legal trial and atrocities were committed on the innocents. When Morarji Desai became Prime Minister in 1977, he unceremoniously removed Kao from R&AW, on false allegations that he interfered during emergency in the internal affairs at the behest of Indira Gandhi. Although, absolved of this charge by a committee, he was made to retire ignoring all his past achievements.

I met Kao after the country wide strike in R&AW in November, 1980. He was senior advisor to Indira Gandhi at that time and I was leading the agitation of R&AW employees. Since then, we developed a very close relationship which continued till his death. During the course of our regular meetings some interesting events took place which would throw a transparent light on our relationship.

M V Kotnis, the first German language expert of IB, was posted as R&AW head in Bern, the capital of Switzerland sometime in the late eighties. He was a good friend of mine and knew my relations with Kao. Kotnis requested me to arrange his meeting with Kao so that he could take his blessings prior to going to Bern. I requested Kao in this regard to which he promptly replied that Ho Chi Minh i.e. Kotnis. I appreciated Kao's memory because Kotnis used to keep beard resembling to the great leader of Vietnam, Ho Chi Minh. When we met Kao, he told Kotnis that Bern is a small but a beautiful place where one would find the best stationery items. Kao gave name of a particular shop to Kotnis. Kotnis promised to visit that shop and bring some stationery items for Kao. Such immaculate was his memory and his affection to his juniors was beyond imagination.

Ram Bahadur Rai, a senior Hindi journalist working with Jansatta a leading Hindi daily, asked me to arrange a meeting with Kao after the assassination of Rajiv Gandhi. Although, Kao used to avoid meeting media people but on my request, he agreed to meet Ram Bahadur Rai for whom I have great respect. During the course of a casual discussion, Ram Bahadur Rai asked Kao whether the reputation of R&AW was tarnished after the assassination of Rajiv Gandhi to which he said "yes". Next day, a front page news item appeared in Jansatta wherein it was quoted that according to Kao, the image of R&AW suffered due to the assassination of Rajiv Gandhi. R&AW authorities sent that news clipping to Kao who telephoned me to come to his residence. When Kao asked me why that story was published without his approval, I was embarrassed. However, he did not persist on that issue further.

My journalist friend Rajat Sharma, now owner of India TV, had ventured into electronic media in 1993 and was working with the first private channel, ZEE TV. He started a famous interview programme, Aap Ki Adalat, sometime in 1993. I was also associated with him for some time in this venture. Rajat used to interview the prominent persons from various fields in this TV show. One day, Rajat requested me to bring Kao on this programme. I requested Kao hesitantly to meet Rajat in this regard. Kao agreed to meet Rajat after my persistent persuasion. I asked Rajat to bring some tapes of his past programmes so that Kao could make up his mind after watching these. Rajat had a very cordial meeting with Kao who told him that he would convey his decision of participation in this programme through me. After few days, I asked Kao in this regard who replied that he discussed this matter with T N Kaul, former Indian Foreign Secretary and P N Dhar, former Principal Secretary to Indira Gandhi and both of them advised him to keep away from media at that age. Kao asked me to convey his reservation in this regard to Rajat which I did.

Sometime in the beginning of 1989, while I was posted at Amritsar, I was asked to come to Jammu in connection with an enquiry. Since terrorism in Punjab was at its peak at that time, I avoided for security consideration to travel to Delhi on return journey by train. I did not get a birth in Indian Airlines plane but got a seat in Pawan Hans Dornier, a small plane. While landing at much lesser speed than larger plane, the Dornier was slowly going towards Palam Airport at Delhi. When this plane passed over few yards over the house of Kao in Vasant Vihar. I noticed from the window of the plane that roof of his house was fully covered with medium size earthen pots kept upside down. A few days later, when I met Kao, I asked him why these earthen pots were kept upside down on the roof of his house. Kao quipped when I dared to go on the roof. I replied that I watched it from the window of that small plane. He said that these pots keep the room temperature normal. When I tried to probe some religious reasons behind this exercise, he laughed it away to give me signal not to go further on this matter.

This year, on the anniversary of liberation of Bangladesh, many Indians who played some role in that event were honoured by their government. When I found Kao's name missing for this honour, I wrote a letter to Bangladesh Prime Minister, Sheikh Hasina Wazed, who happens to be daughter of Sheikh Mujibur Rahman with whom Kao had very good relations, to honour Kao posthumously also since he played a pivotal role in that liberation war. A copy of this letter was sent to the Indian Prime Minister, Manmohan Singh, also. But to my utter dismay, both the governments ignored my suggestion and honoured even those who had no contribution worth the name in this war. This was a grave insult by the Bangladesh government to this brilliant and intrepid intelligence head of R&AW.

Kao had the longest stint of almost a decade as head of R&AW. Till date, nineteen more officers got appointed to this coveted post of Chief of R&AW but no one could ever claim a fraction to what Kao had done for the country. I sometime feel rather disappointed as to where such genius personalities have vanished. Kao was too religious but ruthless in his action when the country's interest was concerned.

He was teetotaler but took care of all sorts of people. He loved Urdu poetry and usually cited some templates while in humorous mood but was very good in English language. His juniors regarded him like a God since he cared for them like his children. No congenial atmosphere was ever found in R&AW which prevailed when Kao was at its helm. He never harmed even the worst offender for which he was sometimes criticized by some of his detractors. Kao was honest to the core. He was controlling billions of rupees while handling the operations during the Bangladesh war. Anyone in his place could have made huge assets but he owned a single house in Delhi which he built on a land purchased from a private developer by taking loan from the Life Insurance Corporation of India. Later, he was advisor for a company from where he was getting some amount as fee.

Kao was the most outstanding intelligence head of R&AW who had no equal in other agencies of the world. His achievements are unparallel in intelligence history be it CIA, Mossad, MI6 etc. Such geniuses are rarely born and we have still to see even his shadow. These words could be a small tribute to this legendary personality.

2. K. Sankaran Nair – From March, 1977 to June 1977 – Shortest stint.

Sankaran Nair was the shadow of Kao till he headed R&AW. Nair was like younger brother to Kao and never a junior colleague. Nair too was a brilliant but temperamental genius who believed in work and no excuses whatsoever.

His flamboyance and matchless competence made him so horrific among R&AW staff that even senior officers used to hide themselves behind pillars while he was entering his R.K.Puram office. Kao once told me that he was fortunate to have a very capable number two in Nair who was instrumental in handling all administrative affairs meticulously with the result he was devoting his major time in operational planning and execution. This duo of Kao and Nair made R&AW so efficient that it was considered a terror outfit in Pakistan and other neighbouring countries were fully taken care of by R&AW operatives to toe Indian policy in the region.

In the liberation war of Bangladesh, Sankaran Nair was executing the planning of Kao all along the borders. Nair was instrumental in opening many monitoring stations on the borders. He planned training of Mukti Bahini through various security outfits in West Bengal, Assam, Tripura and other North East states. He toured extensively from March, 1971 on borders and even inside East Pakistan till the surrender of Pakistan army. He was duly rewarded by the Indian government for his valiant contribution after this war.

Nair was appointed Secretary of R&AW by Morarji Desai after the departure of Kao in March, 1977. In June, 1977, Morarji Desai wanted to degrade this post of R&AW to that of Director which was resented by Nair. There were heated arguments between the two in the presence of the then Cabinet Secretary. Nair refused to work in a junior rank and offered his resignation. He was ultimately shifted as Secretary, Minority Commission from where he retired in December, 1978.

I met Sankaran Nair through Kao in 1981 when he was made the Secretary General of Asian Games of 1982. He was having his office in Pragati Maidan complex which I found unworthy to work for a person of his stature. I asked him during my first encounter with him as to how he was working in this unfurnished small office. Nair usually never smiled but on my questioning he retorted that these bastard babus i.e. the bureaucrats, were putting up all sorts of problems for him since his appointment because he was a retired person and they wanted some serving officer to head this post. Although, Nair was very close to Rajiv Gandhi, who was personally supervising these games but Nair told me that he could not complain for all petty things to him since national prestige was at stake in these games. He talked for some time on the prevalent R&AW affairs and assured me to do something for the welfare of R&AW employees after the closing of Asian Games.

After successfully organizing the Asian Games, Nair was awarded Padam Bhushan by the Indian government. Later, he was appointed as Indian Ambassador to Singapore where he served from 1986 to 1988. Prior to this appointment, Nair was given the responsibility of Cadre Review of R&AW which he completed in a short span of time because of his association with the agency since its inception.

He chalked out a plan according to which R&AW officers were placed on seniority basis to head the agency as per their turn. He sought my opinion on the cadre review to which I sent a detailed suggestion to him in my capacity as the founder of R&AW union. This practice was scuttled by the NSAs which proved detrimental to the working of this organization.

I had regular meetings with Nair when he visited Delhi. He was based in Bangalore and also owns a flat in London where he used to go for short vacations. In Delhi too, he acquired a flat in the society of R&AW officers. I was his regular companion in Delhi since 1988 after his return from Singapore. His favourite place to meet his acquaintances was Delhi Gold Club. He was President of this prestigious Club during his R&AW days. We usually met at the residence of Kao and thereafter planned other outings in Delhi. Once, I gave him a detailed questionnaire about the achievements of Kao in IB and R&AW to which he briefed me parawise. He wanted that somebody should write on the achievements of Kao so that a detailed history of Indian intelligence is preserved for future generation.

After the demise of Kao in 2002, I planned to work for this cause to bring the achievements of IB and R&AW in general and R N Kao in particular to the knowledge of the younger generation of this country. I started on this venture and initially it was decided to make TV programmes to highlight particular achievements. I selected 20 subjects for this programme and commenced my research work. In this pursuit, I thought to take help of Sankaran Nair who was residing at London those days. On August 5, 2004, I wrote a letter to him outlining my planning and sought his participation in these programmes. He replied on August, 19 and conveyed his consent to participate in this venture. I had requested him to allow me to come to London for this job to which he also agreed. When I planned to go to London in October, I wrote another letter to him on September 18 for seeking his approval to which he replied on September 28 saying that he was returning to Bangalore in November and I should meet him there. These letters are kept as record for the memory of this outstanding Intelligence icon.

However, Nair could return to Bangalore in March, 2005 from London. When I telephoned to him for my coming to Bangalore, he told me that he was pre-occupied with some other work to attend at Bangalore which was pending due to his long absence to London and advised me to come to Bangalore sometime in May. I went to Bangalore in the last week of May after completing my research work on the subjects relating to Indian intelligence.

When I met Nair at his residence in Bangalore, he bluntly told me that all incidents of his service career had vanished from his memory due to old age but when we would start discussing these affairs, there was every likelihood that it would become normal. He was 85 years old at that time. I told him that I would stay at Bangalore till this task was duly accomplished and all the details were adequately recorded. I suggested to him that I would come to his residence daily in the morning after my morning walk and we would start Yoga at his residence which would also help him to revive his memory fast. Thereafter, I started visiting Nair daily in the morning and after finishing our Yoga and Pranayam, we took morning tea and started discussing all intelligence matters since his joining IB and subsequently R&AW. I was astonished to find that Nair recalled all his past in IB and R&AW after three/four days and he asked me to prepare a detailed questionnaire on all the subjects for which I wanted to interview him. I had already done a long exercise on this matter and discussed in pieces with him. After six days of my stay in Bangalore, Nair was absolutely normal with regard to what he had done in IB and R&AW and what were the achievements of Kao. He gave me copy of his memoirs to get these published from some publisher in Delhi. Later, when I was negotiating publishing his memoirs with some publishers, the then Secretary R&AW, Tharakan took the lead and got it published.

Finally, Sankaran Nair agreed for recording his first ever interview about his achievements in IB and R&AW. I suggested to him first to give audio recording to which he agreed. On May 28, 2005 evening, I recorded his audio interview for more than one-and-half hours in which he answered most of the questions pertaining to some events of IB and R&AW. After this interview was over, he looked quite cheerful and it was decided to record video interview next evening. Next morning, when I went to his residence for the usual Yoga and Pranayam session, his wife told him that he was unwell. I enquired from him about his health. He replied that doctor had advised him to refrain from indulging in any abnormal activity since he had two bypass surgeries which caused him some problem yesterday night. He suggested me to wait for some time till he became absolutely normal in a few weeks of time. I was worried about his health and agreed to come again Bangalore when his health became absolutely normal.

I left his house in a state of utter disappointment since I lost the opportunity of video recording about his outstanding intelligence achievements in R&AW. However, I could grab this chance again when in September, 2005 I enquired about his state of health. I found him perfectly in good health when I sought his permission to visit Bangalore to record a video interview. When I met and discussed about it, he agreed with a rider that he would focus only on the achievements of Kao. I had no option but to agree to his wishes. I recorded a forty five minutes interview of Nair wherein he narrated numerous facts and events relating to the achievements of R N Kao during his service career. He wore his Imperial Police tie along with the light blue suit and proudly displayed it to me of this 1940 piece of memory. I enquired from him as to how many these ties were still left in India to which he replied that another one was Ashwani Kumar from Punjab Police.

Thus ended my anxiety to record the memoirs of this legendary intelligence icon for the future intelligence fraternity of this country. Unfortunately, I could not find any TV channel be it foreign or Indian which had the courage to do some programme on the intelligence achievements since independence. Reluctantly, therefore I converted my research from TV programme to writing this book.

3. N F Suntook – From June 1977 To April 10, 1983 – Second Largest Stint After Kao

When R N Kao and K.Sankaran Nair left R&AW by June 1977 due to the stubborn attitude of Morarji Desai, the Indian Prime Minister, there was search for a new incumbent for this coveted post. Rank of Secretary R&AW was downgraded despite objections by Sankaran Nair who preferred to seek retirement rather than serving in a lower post of Director R&AW. In these circumstances, there was no senior R&AW officer except N F Suntook who was then serving as Chairman of the Joint Intelligence Committee. So, Suntook was appointed R&AW head by Morarji Desai but to the lower rank of Director. His appointment was welcomed by the R&AW hierarchy because there was strong apprehension that an outsider would toe the dictated line of Morarji Desai which could jeopardize the smooth functioning of this organization in that hostile political atmosphere. Even Kao told me that after Suntook took over, he was some what relieved that at least a R&AW man had taken the charge of this organization and would not stoop to harass the cadre of R&AW in general.

Morarji Desai had a strong malice against R&AW and its previous heads Kao and Nair for their alleged interference during Emergency at the behest of Indira Gandhi. After, Suntook took over its regime, Morarji asked him to curtail its budget to its two third with the result its staff was also pruned. Two important divisions, the Political and Information created by Kao on specific requirements were abolished and its staff was either sacked from service or shifted to other branches of R&AW. New recruitment was totally banned. There was a total chaos in the organization. This resulted in complete demoralization of the working conditions and agency's operational functions came to a grinding halt. Morarji also asked Suntook to stop all operational activities inside Pakistan with the result R&AW's important sources were abandoned causing huge financial losses. Although, Suntook was a Gujrati speaking Parsi but he too could not stop the witch-hunting unleashed by the beleaguered Morarji Desai merely on suspicion of R&AW being a tool in the hand of Indira Gandhi during Emergency.

Suntook belonged to the "Nehru Service" i.e. Jawahar Lal Nehru, soon after the independence faced paucity of administrative and police officers to manage the tribal area in North East and Andaman Nicobar island. He picked up some of his own officers from various departments and appointed to a new cadre Indian

Frontier and Administrative service. Suntook, a Metriculate in qualification, was a former Navy officer. He too was appointed to this cadre. He served in many tribal areas of North East prior to the formation of R&AW. Kao was aware of his ability and sincerity. He got Suntook into R&AW soon after its creation. Suntook had great regards for Kao with the result he escaped witch-hunting during Morarji Desai any more. Kao repaid this gesture to Suntook when he continued to remain R&AW Chief during the return of Indira Gandhi in 1980.

I first met Suntook when R&AW staff was on strike in November, 1980. In his South Block office, he was surrounded by his close stooges when a meeting was arranged with him to break the deadlock which prevailed after police action on thousands of hapless employees at R&AW Headquarterss on November 27, 1980. This meeting with Suntook was arranged by some senior officers of R&AW who were averse to ongoing confrontation between the hierarchy and junior/ middle level cadre after the strike. When I went to meet Suntook, the coterie sitting around him portrayed Suntook as a triumphant king interacting with a defeated soldier. When Suntook insisted to impose certain unwarranted conditions to break the stalemate, I refused to agree with those unreasonable conditions and suggested him to resolve the crisis on "forget and forgive" principle. This suggestion was turned down by him after consulting those paper tigers who were instrumental to allow that chaos to continue for their personal gains. Some of those stooges were eyeing for lucrative foreign assignments in UK, USA and other European countries. To their misfortune, Suntook later decided to send the mediocre officers abroad and asked other competent officers to work for rapprochement with the affected staff and restore normalcy inside R&AW at its Headquarterss and other outstation offices all over India.

Second time, I met Suntook in 1981 when Kao discussed the matter with him on my suggestion, to find a via media for a reasonable solution to the ongoing stalemate and media onslaught about the working conditions inside R&AW. Suntook seemed a little reasonable when I met him again at South Block but his coterie again tried to scuttle this move and they succeeded in thwarting to get the matter resolved. After that meeting, I decided not to meet Suntook again till he was heading R&AW. On the day of his retirement, he went to Mauritius on direction of Indira Gandhi to indulge in an ethnic crisis to help Anerood Jugnauth. Some leading newspapers compared this disappearance of Suntook with the CIA defector Aldrich Ames. Other published stories that Suntook perished to USA for a post-retirement assignment. B.Raman, the former officer of R&AW blamed in his book that a union activist spread this rumour through a Kolkata based daily. This was totally humbug. At that time there was a general perception among senior officers of R&AW that whatever news about R&AW appeared anywhere in India was got published by the union leaders of R&AW. If that was the fact then these union activists were more intelligent than these officers, who could manage the press of this country. How foolish observations were floated by these officers to bring disrepute to their junior cadres.

Suntook was a true nationalist and this rumour was cleared when he returned to India after accomplishing his task in Mauritius on April 10 1983. He retired that day and was never heard again. Although I had some differences with him on certain principles but I would exonerate him due to the reasons of his honesty and dignity to his job. Later, it was learnt that he died after a prolonged illness.

4. G.C.Saxena - From April 11, 1983 to 1986

Girish Chander Saxena was the first officer of Indian Police Service to become head of R&AW. Prior to this appointment, he served in the Indian High Commission in London.

Saxena's tenure as Chief of R&AW was the most disastrous in so far as political scenario of this country was concerned. Terrorism in Punjab mushroomed to its maximum where Saxena could not keep tab on its origin from Pakistan. Most of the outposts of R&AW on the border areas were shut down by him fearing safety of R&AW officials there. He posted a low caliber officer Rakesh Mittal at Amritsar which further demoralized the already sagged morale of the junior cadre. Rest is history wherein thousands of innocents were massacred in terrorism in Punjab. Saxena either advised Indira Gandhi to go for operation "Blue Star" or did not warn her of its repercussions. He proved an utter failure to prevent the assassination of Indira Gandhi by her own body guards. These two unprecedented events took place during the period when Saxena was Chief of R&AW.

I met Saxena twice during his term as head of R&AW. First, prior to the killing of Indira Gandhi, when we discussed to resolve the fate of suspended and dismissed employees of R&AW. He recorded our conversation clandestinely and kept in the "archives" of R&AW for future record. I failed to understand how such mediocre level officer was made to enter into the shoes of Kao who was deceitful in his dealings even to junior officer like me.

Just prior to operation Blue Star, Indira Gandhi gave a statement that intelligence agencies like R&AW failed in Punjab due to the recruitment of casteist elements during the regime of Janta Party in 1977 to 1979. Her remarks were directed towards the Sikh community. This statement was issued at the behest of Saxena. I clarified her statement through the editor of Indian Express wherein I stated that there was no recruitment in R&AW during Janta Party regime. Rather its staff was pruned to two third of its original strength. I further stated that either she was grossly misguided by her advisors or words were put in her mouth to misguide the general public. Saxena started a departmental enquiry against me on this account to get me dismissed from service as to why I wrote the article in the newspaper. I got reprieve from Delhi High Court much to his dismay. Later, a senior Sikh officer of R&AW informed me that Saxena, in order to distract his utter failure to quell terrorism, misguided Indira Gandhi that Sikh officers in R&AW at every level were having soft corner to those who were fomenting terrorism in Punjab. This prompted Indira Gandhi to give such unwarranted statements about intelligence agencies in general and R&AW in particular.

General Sunderji, who was incharge of operation Blue Star in the Golden Temple, was holding a press conference soon after army action, when Rakesh Mittal, the local head of R&AW at Amritsar, entered his room. Sunderji shunted him out of his room in full view of media persons accusing him of utter failure to give any intelligence about the fortification of terrorists inside the temple. Sunderji shouted that due to the incompetence of R&AW, his unit lost large number of brave commandos in that operation. Such was the observation of Gen. Sunderji about R&AW during operation Blue Star when G.C.Saxena was Chief of R&AW. I fail to understand as to how a brave lady like Indira Gandhi allowed this incompetent officer to continue after such monumental failure wherein thousands of innocent people lost their lives during Punjab terrorism.

Soon after operation Blue Star, Saxena on his own removed all Sikh officers from sensitive desks of R&AW and an atmosphere of distrust was created by him among this community who were loyal to the core of their heart while working in R&AW. Saxena tried to create a wedge on religious grounds inside R&AW after Blue Star which took years to redeem honour of Sikh in R&AW.

Second time I met Saxena, when Rajiv Gandhi announced general elections in 1984 and campaigning was in full swing all over India. Saxena enquired from me as to which way these elections would go. I was wary that he must be recording my conversation again. I deliberately misinformed him that Congress was going to lose elections under Rajiv Gandhi. Saxena promptly reacted that if opposition would come to power, they would pulverize him beyond recognition. I wanted to gauge his assessment on the prospects of Congress in that election and I found him totally off guard and his assessment was almost negligible on the outcome of election results.

However, Saxena survived when Rajiv Gandhi got massive majority in Lok Sabha in 1984 elections which even his grand father Nehru and his mother Indira Gandhi did not get during their massive popularity in India. Saxena misguided Rajiv Gandhi about the ongoing internal squabblings within R&AW and IB and got passed a draconian Act, Intelligence Organizations Restrictions of Right Act in 1985. This Act made the employees of both the organizations pariah to the press and made it a cognizable offence and criminal conviction if any one from these agencies was found in contact with media. Such nasty embargo is not found any where in the world in any intelligence agencies. This incapable officer tried to seek cover under this Act to hide his incompetence of Punjab catastrophe. Rajiv Gandhi too forgot that Indira Gandhi was misguided by him for operation Blue Star in the Golden Temple at Amritsar and subsequently she was assassinated due to utter failure of Saxena to forewarn her in this regard.

Saxena was made Governor of Jammu and Kashmir on May 26, 1990 for a period of three years by the NDA government of Atal Bihari Vajpayee wherein Shrimani Akali Dal of Punjab was the ruling partner. I fail to understand as to how this political clan of India is working in deaf and dumb manner. Were the NDA in general and Akalis in particular were not aware that Saxena was the R&AW Chief during operation Blue Star when sacrilege was committed in the Golden Temple in June, 1984 and without his recommendation Indira Gandhi would not have taken that drastic step against the Sikh community. These politicians occupy coveted positions without remembering even the sins committed by a particular person against the whole community and decorated him with the governorship of Jammu and Kashmir. Such acts are pardonable or not, should be asked by them from their own conscious, when the whole community of Sikh was traumatized due to operation Blue Star.

5. S E Joshi – From 1986 to July 31, 1987

Joshi belonged to the royal family of Amravati in Maharashtra. He was an expert on Pakistan affairs since IB days. He was a workohlic and fully devoted to his job. He was an upright and straightforward officer who never allowed sycophants to mushroom in R&AW. He was spontaneous to take even the serious decision and never believed to give long rope or to put cart before the horse. He was meticulous in his approach towards operational handlings without wasting time on ifs and buts. According to one senior, Joshi was a no-nonsense fellow whom no one could take for granted since he had his own vision in operational fields.

I first met Joshi at his R.K.Puram office sometime in the middle of 1980 when he was Joint Secretary, Pakistan operations, a highly sensitive branch of R&AW. We had a long discussion on the prevalent turbulence among employees inside R&AW as a result of stagnation caused due to the pruning of staff by Janta Party in 1977. Since, he was not involved in those affairs in R&AW, he was disturbed when full facts were briefed to him. He assured me that he would discuss this issue in the weekly meeting with all his senior colleagues. I understand, he tried his best to take a serious note of the situation but some of his detractors threw his suggestions to the winds.

After G.C.Saxena demitted office, Joshi became the chief in 1986. Criminal cases and departmental enquiries against the suspended and dismissed officials of R&AW were progressing at snail's pace in the court and at various places inside R&AW. Press was reporting all these events at regular intervals. Some of our colleagues were instrumental in the publication of these news items. When Joshi became Chief, one of his rare photo was procured from the photo division of R&AW and a story about his appointment was published in a daily along with his photo. Joshi was irked to see that news report since his photograph was rare to go outside R&AW precincts. He took strong exception to this event and took the Counter Intelligence and Security of R&AW to task for this serious lapse. Instead, he also asked one of his senior colleagues as to why these court cases and departmental enquiries were dragging for long wasting time and energy of the agency. His colleague suggested him to discuss this matter with me to find a way out to wriggle out of the ongoing stalemate.

Joshi sent one emissary to me at my residence. He told me that Joshi was serious to resolve all pending cases be it criminal or departmental enquires against the suspended and dismissed employees. I enquired from him as to what was the hitch for him to resolve these cases. The emissary replied that without my help he would be unable to reach any conclusion since I was leading this confrontation since 1980. When I further asked him as to what I had to do in this regard, he said that Joshi suggested that I should initiate this process and take the lead by seeking an appointment with him to discuss the entire matter. I told him that I would take two days to take a decision in this matter since I had to discuss this new development with some of my confidants in the union.

After two days, I sought appointment to meet Joshi. Promptly, I was called at R&AW Headquarterss a day after and one to one meeting with Joshi lasted for more than two hours in the evening. I found him quite cooperative and sincere in his approach to resolve the ticklish problem which was giving R&AW a torrid time since 1980. I too gave my words that I would honestly help him in this regard. Joshi told me that since he would require the consent of Prime Minister Rajiv Gandhi, he would revert to him in two days after consulting him. Exactly after two days, Joshi called me in his office. After usual discussion, he gave me a third person unsigned note wherein he outlined a four paragraph suggestion to break ice in this imbroglio. He was pragmatic enough to tell me that we might not agree on some of the points which should be left for future consideration and rather strive to resolve those issues on which we both could agree on reasonable grounds. I agreed to his proposal and sought a week time to give my answer to his suggestion to which he smiled mysteriously. I told him that I was leading more than 80 tough R&AW employees who were entangled in that serious situation and it would be a tiring exercise to corner them. He laughed and said I could manage that.

It took me enormous pulls and pressures to bring those affected officials of R&AW to round to accede to the terms and conditions suggested by Joshi for a settlement to resolve the crisis. I had to adopt tough posture to handle some obstinate elements but after a hard work of seven days, I brought all of them to my tunes to agree Joshi's proposal. Thereafter, I had protracted meetings with

Joshi and Balakrishnan, in-charge of administration, who was asked to complete the residuary work of this agreement.

On March 1, 1987, all the suspended and dismissed employees of R&AW were taken back on duties by Joshi. All the criminal cases against the employees were withdrawn. When I took them inside R&AW Headquarterss complex, I gathered them in a corner and gave instructions that since all of them had been reinstated in service, I had disbanded the union and they were individual employees of R&AW and as such they should work sincerely and diligently. Henceforth, there would be no union activity in R&AW because the government had promulgated the Intelligence Organizations, Restriction of Rights, Act, 1985, which forbid such activities being a cognizable offence. Many of them left the service after rejoining R&AW.

Thus, In my opinion Joshi was a daring officer who got resolved the seven years old crisis of union employees which was hanging fire. So, a history was created because MI6 faced this identical situation but Margret Thatcher, UK Prime Minister, did not allow the sacked employees to rejoin MI6 and instead absorbed job to them in other departments. CIA never reinstated some of its sacked officials. Hence, I should salute Joshi who took a calculated risk in this regard because some senior officers of R&AW were then bent upon to brand these employees as rogues and their reinstatement was considered to create unwanted chaos inside R&AW for the future authorities. But nothing of that sort happened in R&AW and most of those employees, despite targeted by some officers, completed their service career and retired merrily after superannuation.

On the day of his retirement i.e. July 31, 1987, Joshi got arrested K V Unnikrishan, IPS, Joint Secretary of Madras office, to Delhi Police when he was found working for CIA at his Chennai office. It would be pertinent to mention here that after his retirement, Joshi returned to his Amravati residence and never came to R&AW Headquarterss. It was learnt that Rajiv Gandhi wanted to extend his tenure as R&AW chief for one year but Joshi refused on the plea that he did not want to create a wrong precedent in R&AW to deny the service right of his next incumbent. Such officers are rarely found in R&AW now where a competition is prevalent to slash the head of each other to get this coveted post. Joshi died this year and no one in R&AW ever knew what was cause of his death and his fate after retirement because he never kept any connection with R&AW thereafter.

6. A K Verma – From August 1, 1987 to May 31, 1990

A.K. Verma was the first Chief who ushered in political indulgence and corruption in the affairs of R&AW. R.Govindrajan, once the Staff Officer of Kao, was set to take over from S E Joshi and all arrangements were made in R&AW for his taking over ceremony. Verma too received him as the future Chief when

Govindrajan returned after his foreign assignment a few months prior to the retirement of S E Joshi. Verma proved a true chameleon. In a bureaucratic coup, Verma through his friend V C Shukla and another Congress heavy weight, launched a smear campaign against Govindrajan about his competence, which misguided Rajiv Gandhi who superseded Govindrajan and Verma was appointed R&AW Chief. This was disgraceful for R&AW because already a panel was in place to select the future heads in order of seniority. This diabolical decision shattered the discipline among the higher officers of South India in particular. A shameful precedent was created by Verma in this coup which boomeranged on him when his arch rival G S Bajpai was got appointed by me as his successor despite the recommendation of Verma to appoint his nominee R.Balakrishnan. Thenceforth, seeds of one-upmanship was sown among the senior hierarchy and indiscipline among them became rampant which was the sole gift Verma gave to the future generation of R&AW.

Verma had a dubious past in his service career. During Emergency in 1975 - 77, V C Shukla was made Information and Broadcasting Minister at the behest of Sanjay Gandhi to curb freedom of press. V C Shukla got A K Verma on deputation from R&AW under his ministry for this job. Verma created a coterie of officers under him who imposed censorship on press during Emergency. Many journalists who were writing against the imposition of Emergency were harassed by Verma and his coterie. Many leading dailies published blank pages on their front pages to protest against this censorship indicating that their news was barred by these officers for publication. When Janta Party came to power in 1977, L K Advani, the then Information and Broadcasting minister ordered Verma's reversion to his parent cadre of Madhya Pradesh but Verma managed his posting in R&AW through his bureaucratic connections. His notoriety during Emergency was overlooked by Rajiv Gandhi and opposition leaders because no one raised any hue and cry against his appointment as R&AW Chief.

Rajiv Gandhi signed the India-Sri Lanka accord with his counterpart Jayewardene wherein there was devolution of powers to the provinces and to make it effective it was decided to deploy the Indian army for its implementation in right spirit. Indian army was sent to Sri Lanka as Indian Peace Keeping Force to contain the LTTE which was trained by R&AW. This terrorist outfit of R&AW had played havoc with the Sri Lankan forces and almost captured the North provinces in their virtual control. Novice Rajiv Gandhi was never advised by A K Verma against this pact since it was impossible for R&AW to stop its cadre of LTTE to cooperate with the IPKF. Due to inept handling and lack of internal assessment by A K Verma to rein in LTTE cadres, 70,000 strong IPKF lost 1,155 army personnel including 5 Colonels, wounded and crippled 3,000 others due to the unimaginative and none-too-productive operation launched hurriedly without any significant motive or purpose. Rupees three crores per day was the burden on Indian exchequer for this futile exercise. In the last three wars with Pakistan, Indian army did not suffer such heavy casualties due to failure of R&AW under A K Verma. This distrust created by Verma with LTTE was evident when their operatives killed Rajiv Gandhi in sheer retaliation since they branded him culprit for their cause of independent Eelam. So, Verma was solely responsible for this big fiasco in Sri Lanka which consumed one of the brilliant leaders of Indian politics, Rajiv Gandhi.

In April, 1988, former Pakistan President Gen. Zia-ul-Haq had planned to "liberate" Jammu and Kashmir through a secret operation codenamed "Op Topac" which was to be carried out by ISI. He detailed out modus operandi of this operation at a secret meeting at his residence. Zia-ul-Haq wanted to liberate Kashmir valley through political subversion, chaos and terror. He schemed out to sanp communication lines inside Jammu and Kashmir, destroying base depots at Srinagar and other places and also putting out of action air fields and radio stations located at vantage points by Indian authorities. Although, this operation was planned in April, 1988, it was highlighted by media in early 1990 when Altaf Gauhar, former advisor to Z.A.Bhutto revealed it in an interview while releasing his book. R&AW under A K Verma could not detect this sensitive operation of Pakistan with the result thousands of army, para military personnel and civilians lost their lives in Jammu and Kashmir.

Militancy in Jammu and Kashmir started after this operation Topac with the result JKLF militants kidnapped Rubaiya Sayeed daughter of the first Muslim Home Minister of India, Mufti Mohammed Sayeed in the newly sworn-in government of National Front under V P Singh. Five hard core militants were forced to bargain to secure safe release of Rubaiya. This was an utter failure of R&AW under A K Verma. Despite such monumental failures during his tenure as R&AW head, Verma manipulated his one year extension in National Front government which was got thwarted by me when his second-in-command sent an emissary to me who gave details as to how Verma was sending exaggerated reports about Pakistan to smell poison in the ears of V P Singh. Through Rajmohan Gandhi, who unsuccessfully contested against Rajiv Gandhi in 1989 elections, I got presented true picture of R&AW which sent Verma to retirement and G.S.Bajpai succeeded him as next chief.

Verma was never an idler. After his retirement, he joined the notorious NRI businessman Manu Chhabaria who was blacklisted for economic offences like FERA and HAWALA cases by various law enforcing agencies of India. Chhabaria was under the scanner of these agencies and raids were conducted on his businesses premises at various cities. Verma became his advisor and constituted a team of former R&AW and CBI officers to work for Chhabaria to scuttle his cases in these agencies through his connections and these officers. This racket was busted when I filed a SLP in the Supreme Court.

Presently, a CBI court has ordered CBI enquiry against A K Verma for possession of disproportionate assets to his known sources of income. He divested the secret service fund via a novel invention when he floated a private limited company in R&AW wherein two serving Joint Secretaries were made directors. This company made investment in the real estate through the secret fund of R&AW. Verma too acquired several properties in his name and in the name of his family members. Most of these properties are located in the capital, NCR region and Bangalore. He was the first chief in R&AW against whom a court has passed order to investigate the assets disproportionate to his known sources of income.

7. G.S.Bajpai - From June 1, 1990 to 1991

How Bajpai was got appointed as R&AW chief by me has been detailed in a separate chapter in this book. Bajpai served under three Prime Ministers, namely, V P Singh, Chandershekhar and P V Narasimha Rao. In these swift transitions, neither did he formulate any policy nor got any direction in this stop-gap Prime Minister appointments towards Pakistan because militancy in Jammu and Kashmir was in the embryonic stage. Moreover, Bajpai was out of R&AW for a considerable period of time when he was on deputation to the Ministry of External Affairs.

Rajiv Gandhi, former Prime Minister of India, was assassinated during the tenure of Bajpai. Congress party had declared to prosecute Bajpai and four other senior bureaucrats for this lapse in the security of Rajiv Gandhi. Such a prosecution of senior officers is hardly done by a weak political system of this country and nothing was done in the assassination case of Rajiv Gandhi against these bureaucrats. I last met Bajpai when Narasimha Rao was Prime Minister. I had good relations with the then Home Minister S.B.Chavan. This fact was known to Bajpai and he shamelessly requested me to get him extension through Chavan to which I laughed away.

However, I salute Bajpai to get his son-in-law, S K Tripathi appointed as nineteenth R&AW Chief in mysterious and intriguing circumstances. Tripathi was ignored for this appointment on February 1, 2009, when K.C.Verma, an outsider, was appointed as chief after 26/11 terrorist attack. According to one senior R&AW officer, Bajpai had confided in one of his confidants that he would get K.C.Verma resigned in December, 2010, prior to his retirement date of January 31, 2011 and get his son-in-law appointed as the next R&AW chief. Subsequent events proved that K C Verma resigned a few days before the retirement of S K Tripathi, to make way for his appointment as Chief and Bajpai got appointed his son-in-law as R&AW head which he had declared two years back. Hats off to him for this manipulation which he has hatched under the nose of Prime Minister Manmohan Singh and his PMO hawks.

8. N.Narasimhan - From 1991 to 1993

Narasimhan was the Principal Director of Aviation Research Centre prior to his elevation as head of R&AW. In the normal course, an officer shunted out in ARC is exceptionally allowed to return to R&AW and he was that exception due to domination of South Indian bureaucrats in Narasimha Rao government. He was stated to be an expert on China affairs. Prior to this appointment, Narasimhan was on a cover appointment in Washington. During his stay there, he managed to settle three of his kins in U.S.A. He also bungled there when in one of the marriages of his dughter in US, he got printed two types of invitation cards. One card was printed in the name of his cover assignment and the second in his original name. When this lapse was known to the R&AW authorities, Narasimhan was severely reprimanded.

Militancy in Jammu and Kashmir mushroomed to its optimum during the tenure of Narasimhan since he had no definite planning to counter the operation Topac unleashed by General Zia-ul-Haq in the valley. Militants were merrily executing their activities since most of the officers of R&AW were withdrawn from the outposts and stationed in Srinagar office. This was a grave mistake on the part of Narasimhan and his advisors.

As usual, Narasimhan also completed his tenure in R&AW leaving a big vacuum in its operational planning towards Pakistan sponsored militancy. After retirement, Narasimhan was roped in by A K Verma to work for Manu Chhabaria, the notorious NRI businessman. He was given assignment to take care of business interest of Chhabaria in Bangalore and other states in South India. Narasimhan was paid ten thousand per month for this job. This is very shameful that these greedy officers would stoop so low to work for a meager amount of ten thousand and that too for nefarious activities. I have documentary proof of his assignment. Such denigration indicates as to how they played havoc with the secret service fund of R&AW while they were in top position of this outfit.

9. J.S.Bedi - In 1993 for five months

J.S. Bedi was an outstanding officer in R&AW. He was known for his honesty, dignity and uprightness. He was in-charge of R&AW office at Amritsar office during the 1971 war with Pakistan. R&AW operatives provided crucial intelligence to the army in this area which enabled them to reach at Ichogil canal on the outskirts of Lahore much to the embarrassment of Pakistan government. Had Indian government allowed the army to cross this canal, there were clear options for Indian army to encircle Lahore but India was playing safe on this front knowing fully well that their position was bound to be retrieved. Bedi played a significant role for R&AW in this war in Punjab sector.

Bedi was also groomed by Kao as his staff officer to take the reins of R&AW in future. He was left with 5 months of service when he was appointed by Narasimha Rao as chief. An understanding was given to him that he would be granted an extension for one year which was later on not given to him. It was against the spirit of this appointment because there was no logic to appoint a head of R&AW for five months. During these five months, Bedi had planned some good operations to counter militancy in the valley which could not materialize after his retirement.

10. A.S.Syali – From 1993 to 1996

Syali was the first Sikh to become head of R&AW. Syali played a very significant role in the merger of Sikkim with India. He was one of the members of Kao's team which accomplishmed this monumental assignment given to R&AW by the then Prime Minister, Indira Gandhi. He was stationed at Gangtok to implement the plans of Kao for this merger. He was later sent for another assignment during the middle of Sikkim operation due to some exigencies and his place was assigned to another Sikh stalwart, G.B.S.Sidhu.

Syali was an expert on China and Nepal affairs. He was a low profile officer with no intention to harm even his arch enemy. But after his appointment as R&AW head, there were some serious failures in Jammu and Kashmir during his tenure, for which Syali was least to blame. Four foreign nationals were kidnapped by the militant outfit "Al Faran". R&AW mounted air surveillance through ARC planes at the behest of Syali and these militants were detected in the valley for which permission was not given in time to attack their hideouts. They perished inside the tough terrain of the valley and were never found thereafter.

There were some immoral rumours inside R&AW by his detractors when Syali was given one year extension of service by Narasimha Rao government. But these rumours were bound to spread when such happenings took place in R&AW but Syali was an honest and peace loving person who served R&AW earnestly.

11. Ranjan Roy – From 1996 to 1997

Ranjan Roy was an intellectual who was least concerned about some dangerous acts of intelligence maneuvering. There was a general impression in R&AW after his appointment that to the good fortune of Ranjan Roy, he got a naïve Prime Minister Deve Gawda. Neither Deve Gawda nor Ranjan Roy had least concern for the ongoing militancy in the valley. They both passed their time without inviting any controversy.

12. Arvind K. Dave - From 1997 to 1999

Arvind Dave did not possess any expertise on any desk of R&AW. He was an expert manipulator and file pusher. Dave was my Under Secretary after Arun Bhagat who subsequently became Commissioner of Delhi Police and Director, IB. I found Dave totally unpredictable and untrustworthy. His uncanny approach to lobby for his own foreign assignments and promotions was remarkable. He was a perfectionist in pursuing his own cause. However, I should give him credit for getting things executed by hook or crook even from the most obstinate official in R&AW.

He worked under two Prime Ministers i.e. I.K.Gujral and Atal Bihari Vajpayee. He got extraordinary benefits from both of them. Gujaral granted him one year extension of service while there was no worthwhile contribution made by him to contain militancy in Jammu and Kashmir.

Dave was chief of R&AW when Pakistani intruders invaded Indian check posts in Kargil which resulted in a two-month conflict between the armed forces of both sides. Indian army lost more than 500 young soldiers in this regional war. There were allegations that R&AW failed to give any intelligence with regard to this intrusion. A committee under K.Subrahmanyam was constituted which severely indicted R&AW for not providing adequate information about the incursion in Kargil area by the Pakistanis. In the normal course, Dave who was head of R&AW during this armed conflict, should have been prosecuted for this grave lapse but the NDA government decorated him with his appointment as Governor of Arunachal Pradesh. A former Special Secretary of R&AW wrote an article in this regard wherein he mentioned that it was a back door deal to cover up R&AW for any judicial enquiry since Governor is immune to depose in it. Brijesh Mishra, then NSA, went personally to get this appointment cleared from the President. A former Secretary of R&AW revealed that he was witness as to how Dave took proper "care" of Brijesh Mishra without the knowledge of Prime Minister Vajpayee. Dave was skill master in that art.

13. A.S.Dulat - From 1999 to 2000

Dulat was the first IPS officer imported in R&AW as its chief by NDA government. This was a severe blow to the RAS cadre of R&AW where its officers were empanelled to succeed in routine manner for this post. There was strong resentment among its top hierarchy with the result Dulat's appointment was a sort of damp squib till his demitting this post. I was told by a senior R&AW officer that it was the game plan of Brijesh Mishra, the Principal Secretary of the Prime Minister which he orchestrated through Farooq Abdullah with whom Dulat had close relations. Even a retired Special Secretary of R&AW wrote a nasty letter to the Prime Minister not to erode the basic fabrics of R&AW by appointing this person.

Dulat had a torrid tenure in R&AW. His compatriot did not allow him to understand even the composition of R&AW in India and abroad. He was a mute spectator in R&AW where the state of affairs was in absolute limbo. All senior officers were firing their shots independently resulting in the intensity of militancy in the valley.

IC-814, the Air India plane Air bus A300 was hijacked by Harkat-ul-Mujahideen terrorists when it was on its way to New Delhi from Kathmandu. There were 176 passengers on board including a senior officer of R&AW, S.B.S.Tomar. This plane landed at Amritsar for refueling but the security forces did not intercept it due to inept handling of this crisis by the then Cabinet Secretary, Prabhat Kumar and his advisors. After seven days of high-pitched drama, three dreaded terrorists, Maulana Masood Azhar, Mushtaq Ahmad Zargar and Ahmad Omar Sheikh were released in lieu of the hijacked passengers. Later, Maulana Masood Azhar founded a terrorist outfit Jaish-e-Mohammed which masterminded attack on Indian Parliament and Mushtaq Ahmad Zargar was charged for his complicity in 9/11 attack in USA. It would be pertinent to reveal here that one junior R&AW officer in Kathmandu had informed his seniors about a possible hijacking by Pakistani terrorists but his information was not given any credence. Dulat was severely criticized for this hijacking since security of Indian civil planes on foreign soils, were the mandate of R&AW where it failed miserably.

On the eve of his retirement, Dulat met the then Home Minister L.K.Advani and suggested to him not to impose any outsider in R&AW where he had the worst experience of his life. Such unimaginative attempts on the part of these so called experts in PMO have further denigrated this coveted post meant only for the professionals who are trained in R&AW for years and not for any Tom and Jerry.

14. Vikram Sood – From December 12, 2000 to March 31, 2003

Vikram Sood was the first non IPS officer appointed to this post. He belonged to the Indian Postal Service. When Sood became chief, Ashok Chaturvedi, got published a series of news article in a Hindi daily exposing some very sensitive inside happenings of R&AW. He branded him as a Dakia, the Postman who became head of this organization. I should give credit to Sood's sheer brilliance as to how he countered the onslaught of powerful IPS lobby since his appointment in a lower rank long back in R&AW. This lobby did not allow any other non IPS, including the direct recruits of R&AW, to reach this post. Confidential reports of these non IPS officers were either spoiled or downgraded resulting in their incompetence to become head of R&AW. So, Sood was an exception to get this coveted post.

Sood found himself in a very piquant situation just after taking over the charge. He had three Bihari IPS Special Secretaries who were out for the blood of each other and were fighting to outclass one another to get number two position. News were got floated in media by one of these officers that Sood was unable to rein them. However, Sood took advantage of their foolish infighting and put them against each other and they wasted their time in the ensuing squabbling which was enjoyed by the junior cadres as the game of these jokers.

This infighting proved very costly to the operational functioning of R&AW. On December 13, 2001, five terrorists of Lashkar-e-Taiba and Jaish-e-Mohammed entered the premises of Indian Parliament in a white ambassador car with labels of Home Ministry and Parliament. Parliament session was in progress on that day and Home Minister, L.K.Advani was inside the building. They got near the entry gate of Vice-President of India and started firing indiscriminately killing a dozen persons, including security personnel and injuring 18 others. They were ultimately gunned down by the security forces inside the complex.

I viewed this ghastly attack on many Television channels whose crews were inside the premises of Parliament House to cover the proceedings. I should give credit to these valient media persons who did not run away while these terrorists were in an attacking spree killing those who came in their way. These brave media persons covered the entire incident at the cost of their life. I salute them for this extraordinary courage.

In my opinion, this media coverage revealed that the terrorists were trained just to enter Parliament premises and fire at insiders indiscriminately and ultimately got killed by the Indian security forces. They were running hither and thither shouting some slogans and killing those who came on their way. I noticed that had they were trained to stop outside the main entrance gate of the Parliament as they could have conveniently entered inside the Parliament because there were limited security guards at that entry point during those days. Had it happened, God knows what havoc would have taken place inside Indian Parliament.

This dastardly act of Pakistan was the result of total intelligence failure of Indian intelligence agencies and R&AW could not absolve its responsibility for this fiasco. How Sood survived this terrible blot, is certainly questionable. These three buffoons working under Sood should be the main culprit since they were irresponsible enough to make R&AW a burden for Indian government. Indian Prime Minister, Vajpayee ordered the movement of Indian army to borders and a state of war with Pakistan was likely to be declared in the coming future which ultimately did not take place due to the presence of US forces on various air fields of Pakistan. But this attack on Indian Parliament was a brazen attempt to undermine Indian sovereignty. There was an unimaginable anguish amongst the people of this country to teach Musharraf, the President of Pakistan who was the mastermind behind this attack, a lesson of his life.

Sood retired leaving this stigma on his tenure. Later on, I was given information by a senior officer of R&AW that Sood, after retirement, was spotted on a secret video recording which was covering the surveillance of Rabinder Singh, the Joint Secretary, who was working for CIA. Sood was seen exchanging some documents with Rabinder Singh which were considered useful for CIA. If this is the fact, then Sood never gave any explanation on this count. However, I noticed that Sood was always writing news articles in a newspaper showering praise on USA for various acts of omission and commission in Asia in general and in Iran and Iraq in particular. These writings of Sood give credence to the fact that his presence in the video with Rabinder Singh had a questionable explanation, which he is bound to give in the near future.

15. C D Sahay – From April 1, 2003 to January 31, 2005

C D Sahay became Secretary of R&AW when the two other Biharis were fighting to outclass each other in bureaucratic jugglery. Sahay was comparatively modest of them with the result the other two made his life hell untill his retirement. This rivalry at the top adversely affected the operational functioning of R&AW at that time since every junior was aware of it. Moreover, to make things worst for him, Sahay found another stumbling block in the form of National Security Advisor and that too the arch enemy of R&AW, M.K.Narayanan. Narayanan's malice towards R&AW is explained in other chapter.

Although, Sahay was an honest and diligent person but these qualities did not qualify him to rule R&AW where a man of different DNA was required to manipulate things. However, Sahay smoothly managed the prevalent hostile atmosphere but his subdued nature could not contain corruption in R&AW. There were press reports that two brothers, namely, J.K.Sinha, Special Secretary and C.K.Sinha, Joint Secretary were stated to have embezzled Rupees 100 crore while handling elections in Bangladesh. A departmental enquiry was duly conducted on this allegation but the matter was put under the carpet to save R&AW from stigmatic situation.

The worst blot that took place in R&AW during the tenure of Sahay was when Rabinder Singh, Joint Secretary, managed to flee to USA with the connivance of CIA when R&AW was keeping a close surveillance on him. Full details of this case are given separately in this book. But why the other accused, who connived with Rabinder Singh, were not brought to criminal justice is still hounding Sahay and others who were responsible for his disappearance.

16. P K H Tharakan – From February 1 , 2005, to January 31, 2007

Tharakan was serving in police in his state. Prior to this, he had a stint in R&AW wherein he was posted in Nepal. He was a capable officer and some of my Nepali friends still remember him for his valiant efforts to help the pro-Indian politicians against the menace of Maoist in Nepal. Tharakan too was an honest and upright officer. I remember him when he was working as Under Secretary in CI&S unit in

1980 and during the strike in R&AW, I had to go inside the Headquarterss for some official work. Tharkan was escorting me inside when he tried to show his police attitude towards me. In the ensuing altercations, he cut a sorry figure which showed that he was a gentleman to the core.

M.K.Narayanan, NSA, deliberately brought Tharakan to R&AW ignoring claims of other suitable incumbents. Although this appointment too was resented to by the seniors but Tharakan was not much traumatized being the old R&AW man. I was given to understand that he tried his best to bring pro-Indian government in Nepal but some officers posted in Kathmandu bungled his scheme to contain the Masoist. He was instrumental in getting an ISI officer posted at Kathmandu in Pakistan Embassy declared as Persona Non Grata i.e. PNG for his active role in the IC-814 hijacking. During his tenure in Nepal, he made concerted attempts to check the inflow of fake currency to India in which he succeeded to a large extent.

Tharakan did a praiseworthy job when he organized an annual lecture in the memory of R&AW founder, R N Kao on his death anniversary which is a regular feature now. But subsequently a chief manipulated this occasion for his personal gains by inviting an industrialist, K.M.Birla to give a lecture on Indian intelligence and on Kao. How such ridiculous adventures are allowed by the government to happen in R&AW. Sankaran Nair gave me his memoirs to get published through some publishers in Delhi but Tharakan outwitted me to get it published.

17. Ashok Chaturvedi – From February 1, 2007 to January 31, 2009

Ashok Chaturvedi was the most controversial and dubious person appointed to this post. He was never in the reckoning for this appointment because his blemished service records but he was selected on the recommendation of B.K.Chaturvedi, the then Cabinet Secretary, who happened to be his close relative. Chaturvedi was vindictive, corrupt and a debauch person whose elevation sent wrong signal in R&AW. He had his own coterie which was hand in glove with him to bring discredit to the organization. I remember during the tenure of G.S.Bajpai, this coterie was eyeing a lady officer who was previously involved with A K Verma and made her life hell. This fact was known to the higher officers of R&AW but they were all scared of the clouts of this coterie.

First time in the 45 years history of R&AW, a senior lady officer of R&AW, Nisha Bhatia tried to commit suicide in the office of the Prime Minister where she was called to narrate her woes as to how Chaturvedi wanted to sexually exploit her. When she was not allowed to meet the Prime Minister, this lady tried to kill her by consuming poison since her dignity was at stake in R&AW. Media played havoc on R&AW after this drastic incident. Chaturvedi and his coterie created an impression in the PMO and at other bureaucratic levels that this lady had some psychological problem due to which she took such a drastic step in the PMO. This was all a concocted theory to save themselves. Supreme court of India had clear directions in this regard wherein there is no scope of relief for such delinquent like Ashok Chaturvedi on such serious charges but he got everything scuttled and on the other hand got criminal cases registered against that lady. I got inside information that Chaturvedi had planned to dismiss her from service. I wrote a nasty letter to the Prime Minister highlighting Chaturvedi's other misdemeanors and asked for a CBI enquiry in this suicide case and demanded stringent action against Chaturvedi and his coterie responsible for forcing her to commit suicide. Chaturvedi got frightened after this letter and relented to take any action against the lady.

Nisha Bhatia fought back valiantly after that incident. She was a brilliant officer and due to this reason she was posted in Indian Mission at Paris in France. After this incident, she took Chaturvedi and his cronies head on and was hell bent to retaliate like a wounded tigress. She filed numerous cases against them in many courts, including the Supreme Court. She contested all these cases in person and made life of these cowardices miserable. Chaturvedi was likely to be criminally prosecuted due to her persistent crusade but he could not sustain the onslaught and died of a cardiac arrest just three years after his retirement. Subsequent R&AW chiefs adopted the dictated approach against her and instead of redeeming her honour, retired her compulsorily from service against which she is fighting a case in Delhi High Court. I fail to understand as to how these demeaning officers are making a prestige point to harass a lady who was traumatized by a former R&AW chief and instead of helping her out, continue to persecute her. Biological DNA of these cowards should be conducted to determine their real origin. Bhatia has completed her law degree with first class from Delhi University and she would prove her mettle against R&AW officers after wearing black coat in the courts.

During his tenure of two years as head of R&AW, Chaturvedi resorted to witch-hunting against his rivals which subdued the morale of the agency to its lowest ebb. He pursued an aggressive, hostile and punishing campaign in going after these rivals. Many complaints were sent to the Prime Minister in this regard but by then his relative B.K.Chaturvedi became the Principal Secretary of Prime Minister but no action was taken to rein him.

Chaturvedi was least concerned about the operational requirements of R&AW. There were reports that many important sources in Afghanistan and Pakistan refused to work for him when their monthly allowances were not paid to them. In this chaos, the worst terrorist attack of 26/11 took place in Mumbai when 10 Pakistan trained terrorists of Lashkar-e-Taiba killed 166 innocent citizens and wounded more than 300 in three days of terrorist attack. R&AW was severely reprimanded for this catastrophe. Some details of this disaster are given in a separate chapter. There were strong indications that the then National Security Advisor, M.K.Narayanan and Ashok Chaturvedi would be sacked for this fiasco but as usual Narayanan was elevated to the post of a Governor and Chaturvedi was allowed to retire merrily in January, 2009. There was a definite information given to me by a senior officer of R&AW that he pocketed Rupees 5 crores of money from the secret fund of R&AW which was meant for the elections of Bangladesh. This fact was revealed to that officer by the Hawala dealer who transacted the money from Kolkata to Dacca in that election.

There was so much resentment in R&AW against Chaturvedi that its cadre boycotted his farewell party on January 31, 2009. In his farewell, Chaturvedi arrived with escorts fearing manhandling from some R&AW officers who were agitated even to blacken his face in the open. His number two, Rana Banerji lambasted Chaturvedi in his departing speech for his unruly behaviour with juniors during his tenure. Rana also criticized Chaturvedi for demoralizing the organization due to his incompetence and stubbornness. Such an undignified farewell was ever given to a retiring chief of R&AW which depraved Chaturvedi shamelessly deserved. This was the darkest period of R&AW.

18. K C Verma – From February 1, 2009 to December 30, 2010

M.K.Narayanan again played havoc with R&AW while a search for the next incumbent was on in the PMO. Rana Banerji, an expert on Pakistan and the first IAS officer was a front runner for this post. He also worked as head in the North-East sector of R&AW. He had an excellent rapport with the Prime Minister of Bangladesh. He managed some of the ticklish problems of the two countries which were haunting their relations for many years. Banerji had a good stint for R&AW in London High Commission where he handled some sensitive operations of Pakistan when Benazir Bhutto was in exile.

Prime Minister, Manmohan Singh was to be operated for his heart ailment in the last week of December, 2009, when selection of R&AW chief was to be finalized. M.K.Narayanan with the connivance of the then Home Minister,

P.Chidamaram, misled the Prime Minister and got K.C.Verma appointed who was working with the Home Minister, as R&AW Secretary. There was strong resentment inside R&AW for the imposition of another outsider after A.S.Dulat.

K.C.Verma was a non-starter in R&AW. He was working on the dictated maneuvering of S.K.Tripathi who was ignored for this appointment. Verma never knew the specialized functioning of R&AW and he was least interested to acclimatize with it and most of the time was confined to his cozy office. He used to depute the desk officer of a particular desk to brief the PMO and Home Ministry and always shied away for his personal appearance on one pretext or the other.

In a dramatic twist to the succession drama in R&AW, Verma submitted his resignation more than a month prior to his retirement scheduled for January 31,

2011, paving way for S.K.Tripathi who was retiring on December 31, 2010. Rumour mongers inside R&AW openly discussed that huge money was paid by Tripathi to Verma for this deal. Even a close associate of Sonia Gandhi was stated to be involved in this manipulation. This money was paid to a close associate of Verma in Bangkok. More details about this transition have been written in a separate chapter. So, R&AW have now become an institution like a PSU where chiefs are appointed by paying hefty amount. Hell to digest this denigration engineered by Tripathi and his father in law, G.S.Bajpai, former R&AW Chief number 7 to get number 19 for him.

19. S K Tripathi - From December 30, 2010 to December 29, 2012

Much has been written about the dubious appointment of S.K.Tripathi in other chapters and not more is required to undress him further. However, it should be noted that he would not lead a comfortable retired life because he is still under cloud for $350 million deal in the purchase of airborne electronic surveillance system while he was head of ARC. Finance department of Cabinet Secretariat has raised objections that these equipment had been purchased from the Israeli manufacturer ELTA without trials and competitive bidding for add-on equipment. Besides this, there were additional allegations of siphoning off secret fund money by Tripathi for which a complaint has been filed in CBI by a R&AW activist.

Tripathi was Additional Secretary in charge of Rabinder Singh when he was working for CIA. There are many circumstantial evidences that it was Tripathi who alarmed Rabinder Singh about the ongoing surveillance on him. Tripathi accorded permission to Rabinder Singh to visit Nepal when he fled to USA with the help of CIA. This issue is still pending in a court in Delhi and Tripathi is bound to get a strong heat of it.

But it is now an admitted fact that parasites like Tripathi have eroded the working culture of R&AW and made it an agency of municipality level where corruption is order of the day. I tried to put forward some logical facts to prove how this august organization which was recognized during the regime of Kao as an epitome of brilliance and dignity has been brought down to that of a crumbling empire when it was ruled by unscruplous successors like number 17 to 19 in particular and some others in general. Government of India should take some stringent measures to bring its bygone glory otherwise future is very gloomy.

20. Alok Joshi – From December 30, 2012 to December 30, 2014

Alok Joshi is 1976 IPS officer of Haryana. He was not a RAS officer i.e. he was not empanelled in R&AW. He was in R&AW in the early nineties but was reverted to his parent cadre when he was embroiled in a controversy of misappropriation of secret fund during his posting in Indian Mission at Brussels. It is learnt that Punjab and Haryana High Court have issued directions to CBI in October 2004, against him on corruption allegations. Status of that case is still under scrutiny. However, Joshi was re-inducted in R&AW by the controversial Ashok Chaturvedi in September, 2007. Immediately thereafter, he was posted in Indian Embassy at Kathmandu. He returned to R&AW Headquarterss in July, 2010. When S.K.Tripathi became chief, Joshi too was groomed by the former to succeed him so that he could put a lid on the corruption charges leveled against him by the press. There are rumours inside R&AW that he was appointed to this post on the intervention of a close confident of Sonia Gandhi and on the recommendation of Tripathi.

Insiders have revealed that while in Kathmandu, Alok Joshi along with his junior Ashwani Saxena misappropriated secret funds by making fictitious entries in the secret fund register and transferred that amount towards the purchase of two flats at Mohali and Gurgaon. On investigation by R&AW, Saxena was recalled to Headquarterss prematurely when his connivance in this bungling was proved but no action was taken against Joshi. There were other serious allegations against him that during the 2007 elections in Nepal, Joshi along with his deputy Alok Tiwari siphoned off the funds meant for certain pro-Indian political parties with the result Maoist were able to manage considerable seats in that election. An enquiry in this allegation was conducted by the senior lobby of R&AW but as usual, it was put in cold storage in the name of secrecy.

If credence is given even to one of the above allegations, there was a serious lapse on the part of the PMO to appoint Joshi as R&AW Chief.

To conclude, in the last 45 years of its inception, denigration of this coveted position of R&AW Chief which was like a place of worship for a person like Kao has receded to that of undignified municipality clerks who only breed corruption in their official duties. Government should take note of these details and help reestablish the much desired sanctity of this organisation.

Events after Publication of First Edition of This Book Up to February, 2014

Alok Joshi was thereafter appointed as Chairman of National Technical Research Organization (NTRO) on 30 April, 2015 wherefrom he retired on 31 August, 2018. Now, I should not hesitate to admit that Alok Joshi could have performed better as R&AW Chief in comparison what I wrote earlier about him. His elevation as NTRO Chairman was particularly based on past performance and not an ordinary appointment because this agency had become a pivotal force to coordinate with other intelligence departments.

21. Rajinder Khanna – 31 December, 2014 to 31 December, 2016

Rajinder Khanna succeded Alok Joshi in view of his impeccable honesty and vast operational experience in the organisation. My inquiry with horses mouth revealed that his records were far more excellent than the other incumbent who was also vying for this coveted post.

During his tenure as R&AW Chief, Khanna proved his mettle not only in operational capability but made financial accountability more transparent at all level. Khanna was a damn honest person. Many R&AW heads are having a number of unaccountable assets in New Delhi but Khanna is said to have no house to live in Delhi. This is a great example of honesty which was rare in this agency.

Khanna was an expert of North-East insurgency. During his first stint in the North-East in R&AW, he made deep inroads into the insurgency groups and won great admiration for his capabilities. His juniors in North-East found him totally committed to their cause in view of hostile terrain and worst working conditions. He commanded deep respect during his stay from his juniors. Since his induction in R&AW, he has been in and around this region be in India or adjoining foreign territory. He had two stints in Thailand and Myanmar to keep tab on the North-East insurgency during his prime days in R&AW. His juniors found him a die-hard workaholic with or without cozy official environment.

With the passage of time, intelligence gathering and working of R&AW has found a sea-change in the last two decades. Social media and inter-netting have drastically affected the blue-book pattern of intelligence all over world and R&AW is no exception. Old ethos of intelligence maneuverings are extinct now and new concept found the intelligence fraternity in a state of limbo and new beginnings are being devised for different types of terrorism, intelligence-gathering and types of infiltrations to gather worthwhile results.

Fortunately, Khanna was an expert in counter-terrorism and had been working tirelessly since the last decade on this desk in R&AW. I should admit without any further hesitation that after his taking over as R&AW head no major terrorist activity took place in India. Many operatives of Islamic jihads were neutralized across the country and some apprehended in various countries and more were feeling the heat and found wanting. Although, there were allegation of failure of intelligence when Gurdaspur and Pathankot attack of Pakistani terrorist took place but I was given to understand that complete information about these infiltrators were passed to the concerned agencies who could not co-ordinate effectively on border to neutralize them.

Uri surgical strike was hallmark of the acumen of Khanna in which Indian Army took revenge of terrorist attack on Brigade Headquarterss in Uri on 18 September, 2016. Around 100 commandos of Indian Army entered more than 5 kilometers in POK territory and destroyed many terrorist launchpads in a daring operation lasting more than 48 hours. R&AW operatives under Khanna very effectively coordinated with Army in this strike providing vital clues about the locations and targets of terrorists. Big success for Indian Army with R&AW help after 1971 war to attack the enemy inside their territory.

But I am usually seen as R&AW basher have no option but call spade a spade that this RAW Chief was totally different in attitude, working and honesty in comparison to many of his predecessors. Ajit Doval rightly choose him as Deputy NSA where he is continuously working as an asset to NSA since January, 2018.

22. Anil Dhasmana - 1 January, 2017 to 26 June, 2019

Anil Dhasmana was obvious selection as next head of R&AW after Khanna completed his tenure. He was an expert on Pakistan and Afghanistan.

Balakot airstrike was his major achievements as operational head after the Pulwana attack on security forces. This airstrike was a bold decision to attack inside Pakistan after the 1971 war. Dhasmana provided all operational help in this brilliant operation of Indian Air Force.

He was due to retire on 31 December, 2018 but in view of the forthcoming Parliament elections in May, 2019, he was given extension of service for six months so that next Government can select the next head of R&AW. Next incumbent Illango retired during this period which was another questionable omission of succession.

However, Dhasmana took some drastic administrative measures during his tenure wherein he removed around 90 odd employees of R&AW invoking even article 311(2)© of the Constitution which is used in rarest of rare cases as penalty when a Government servant is found involved in anti-national activities. Rampant use of this article in the garb of security or secrecy is really dangerous when employee is not given chance to prove his innocence. His successor Samant Goel immediately stopped all this pruning. Many of these employees are embroiled in various court cases which affected the inside functioning of R&AW at all level.

Dhasmana is now appointed as Chairman of National Technical Research Organisation (NTRO) where he would serve till he attains the age of 65 years. This post in Government is exceptional where retirement age is 65 years in comparison to normal retirement age of 60 years. This age consideration is no where clarified in public domain.

23. Samant K. Goel (From 27 June 2019)

There was lot of hullabaloo in media and even in bureaucratic circle about the appointment of Samant Goel as R&AW Chief. Obviously so, because his name cropped up in a telephone interception by CBI during worst ever bureaucratic tussle between the then CBI Director Alok Verma and his deputy Rakesh Asthana. According to evidences which surfaced later revealed that the CBI found link between Goel and money-laundering accuse Moin Querishi's henchmen Prasad brothers. Goel was stated to have managed this issue in PMO.

This was background of the whole controversy. Surprisingly, no evidence was available in CBI interception about any bribery issue with Goel. He became victim of rivalry between Alok Verma and Asthana.

According to my sources, Prasad family is certainly linked with Samant Goel. This link was professional and if Goel helped his previous sources then it is obligatory because usually R&AW always stand with such people. His Gurdaspur encounter case is still under investigation and would reach judicial conclusion perhaps when he would retire from R&AW too.

Samant Goel was perhaps destined to become R&AW Chief. Had Dhasmana not got extension till June,2019, Illango as R&AW Chief would have continued till 2021 and Goel would have retired by then. However, he superseded R.Kumar perhaps on the basis of his exceptional operational capability. On his appointment, most of the media highlighted that Balakot strategist appointed as R&AW Chief which was perhaps best feather in his cap.

I too was given some misconception about him when he was Additional Secretary. But unlike his predecessor Dhasmana who created panic in R&AW

by retiring/ dismissing ninety odd employees, Goel stopped that misadventure. According to insiders, he is quite considerate and having human approach while handling day-to-day affairs of the employees. Every R&AW Chief is somehow other mired in some controversy and Goel was no exception. But if NSA Doval had faith in his capabilities then there was no better choice than him. However, insiders found him as a good police officer rather a perfect intelligence operative because he lacks initiative and innovative qualities.

❑

Sex Escapades

Sex related incidents are a common feature at work places not only in India but world over. This phenomena should not however be an exception in R&AW in this fantasy. In India, this epidemic has been gathering storm in every walk of life, be it politics, defence forces, civilian bureaucracy and other working places. Film industry is the most easy hunting ground for such adventures. Among politicians, we as youngsters often heared stories of L N Mishra, a powerful Minister in the Indira Gandhi cabinet and Narayan Dutt Tiwari using their offices in the Ministry as the safest place wherein they used to call their preys to perform this bravado act. In Nehru's era, we heard that being a widower he himself was blue-eyed figure of some very beautiful ladies and Indira Gandhi then his hostess in Teen Murti Bhavan had to devote her precious energy to keep him at bay from these charming ladies. His Defence Minister Krishna Menon was forthright in this regard mingling with beautiful white ladies in swimming pools in London. We also heard many jokes about Nehru and Rajkumari Amrit Kaur who was Health Minister in his Cabinet. M O Mathai, a close aide of Nehru wrote many such interesting details of Nehru era in his book. But these were only stories floated in good humour unlike the daring acts of Mishra and Tiwari.

Driver of a former Prime Minister who was known to me being a R&AW man informed me that one very leading actress used to come in the morning flight from Mumbai and after spending three-four hours in the company of a former Prime Minister used to take return flight in the afternoon. Nowadays, these allegations are distorted as an attack on the personal life of an individual. Kerry Packer, the leading media baron of Australia wanted to extend his business in India. He sought services of two wheeler-dealer Indian politicians who had good links in all the parties. Kerry Packer sent his own executive plane to carry these politicians to Australia for initial discussion. These politicians had a good company of blonde Australian beauties in this air trip of which they boasted later that they had a very soothing flagrante delicto with these beauties 11 kms above the sea level. One of these politicians was a troubleshooter of Manmohan Singh in his cabinet and the other is a discredited one discarded by every Indian political party. They are at loggerheads now.

Janardan Thakur, a leading Journalist wrote a book after the Emergency of 1975-77 in which he gave a good account of sex related stories of some politicians during that period. V C Shukla, who attained notoriety for imposing censorship during Emergency was the Information and Broadcasting Minister. Films Division of India was also his portfolio. According to Janardan Thakur, while attending an International Film Festival at Moscow in the company of A K Verma (later R&AW Chief), his chum and Joint Secretary in his Ministry asked an Indian actress, who was his halfway namesake, to come to his room in the night which was declined by her. He has narrated a number of similar incidents in his book.

I could recall innumerable incidents which are in my mental achieve heard from R&AW operatives and other sources about sex orgies of leading politicians but it would be wastage of some pages of my book. Kathmandu, Bangkok and Goa have now become meaningless for intelligent politicians for sex encounters or body-to-body message since there are several good places in almost every city for such sojourn.

With all humility and respect I beg to the reverent women folk of this great country, I have no hesitation to say that even some lady politicians too used this ladder to climb highest position in politics and I should be excused in advance for the type of criticism I would face after the release of this book. Few years back, one of my acquaintances went to the house of a leading lady politician of New Delhi and found her in the company of a former Prime Minister with pant down in her bed room. Of late, defence forces social gatherings was touted as another grey area where allegations of these incidents are reported in the media. Nowadays, civilian bureaucracy has outclassed other competitors in this marathon race.

So, R&AW honchos should not be squarely blamed in this game of day to day life because in comparison to other bureaucrats they are immune to be caught by law enforcing agencies. In the name of secrecy in their mission, they have got safe houses in almost all important cities of India where no other agency could dare to enter to catch them. For the top echelons, planes of Aviation Research Centre(ARC), a wing of R&AW are at their disposal which are freely used for this act in the name of operational duties to avoid public glare. Even some powerful politicians have been provided these planes to take their girl friends in the morning from New Delhi to hill stations and return in the evening saving their precious time to serve the poor people of this country. I should not name these hard working politicians since they would rebut it by claiming that their names are deliberately disclosed to malign their respective parties when the next parliament election is round the corner. But these are facts wherein records of these sorties of ARC planes are shown as top secret for important operational duties. Even actual destinations are not disclosed to keep the mission of these politicians as closely guarded secret.

Former R&AW Chiefs, Brief Details

Among the former R&AW Chiefs, its founding father R N Kao and a thorough gentleman, was a one-woman man. He was vegetarian, non-smoker, non-drinker and was faithful to his wife. Such people are extremely dangerous in real life in their professional duties which he proved as R&AW Chief in the liberation of Bangladesh and merger of Sikkim with India. He was quoted as an example of utmost dignity in character by his juniors. K Sankarn Nair although was a little naughty but no such allegations were heard against him in spite of him marrying in his forties. N F Suntook, G C Saxena and S E Joshi subsequent R&AW heads were too men of perfect character and morality.

A charming lady officer of R&AW who was in her early thirties when I had close association with her daringly told me that when she enters R&AW Headquarterss, she is raped by not less than one thousand eyes. When I discussed this matter with another senior lady officer, she told me that even most of the ladies of R&AW used to rape her with their eyes since she was almost naked from the back in specially designed backless blouses. Even her perfume could be enjoyed even from a distance of 50 meters. This lady took full advantage of her charm and became regular companion of next R&AW Chief A K Verma. Tour details by Air of Verma and this lady could reveal that he used to take her everywhere be it in India or abroad for "Operational Duties". Their Madras sojourn was most frequented because Verma was handling LTTE during his tenure. Once at R&AW Headquarters, Verma and this lady were in the bed room which was adjacent to his office room when alarm bell of bed room rang. Counter Intelligence and Security(CIS) staff of R&AW headed by one K P Ramkumar ran to the bed room smacking some trouble and found Verma with pant down and lipsticks on his face and the lady hidden in the bathroom. After Verma retired, this lady found company of a handsome Joint Secretary of R&AW. A former Joint Secretary of CIS unit, S.Soundra Rajan informed me that this Joint Secretary and the lady went to Hong Kong on unauthorized visit and without seeking proper permission from R&AW. On this charge, the Lady was reverted to her parent cadre and the Joint Secretary who was destined to head R&AW later, was asked to take voluntary retirement. Families of both of these have reconciled with their illicit relations and they are now partners in some business activities operating from Indonesia.

G S Bajpai who replaced A K Verma had a very beautiful wife who acted in a side role in film Kabhi-Kabhi. He too was known for his distinction to respect ladies of R&AW. N.Narasimhan, after Bajpai, had some instinct to have sexual link with two ladies who usually made fool of him. According to his Personal Assistant, he was usually busy in watching the printed pornographic material which was sent to him through diplomatic bags by some of his cronies. He was a non-starter but desirous hunter.

Subsequent R&AW heads from 9 to 13 J.S.Bedi, A.S.Syali, Ranjan Roy, Arvind K.Dave, A.S.Dulat, Vikram Sood, C D Sahay and P.K.H.Tharakan maintained proper dignity too certain extent and nothing adverse was heard about them in the sex related affairs. Although there were some incidents when some of them used safe houses of R&AW while entertaining their lady friends.

Nisha Bhatia, Director, Tormented By, Ashok Chaturvedi

In August, 2008, one senior officer of RAW, Nisha Bhatia, working as Director in the Training Branch of RAW at Gurgaon attempted suicide outside Prime Minister office in South Block by consuming poison. She took this drastic step out of frustration and disgust because no criminal action was taken on her complaint of sexual harassment by another R&AW officer. When she went to make a formal complaint to the Secretary of RAW, Ashok Chaturvedi, he used lewd words to get sexual favour from her. She decided to complain to the Indian Prime Minister about her torture by the advances of Ashok Chaturvedi. Instead of looking into her grievances, she was depicted as psychiatric patient by RAW authorities at the behest of Chaturvedi to save their skin. Had she been so or under depression, she would have committed suicide in her house rather than take such an extreme step inside Prime Minister office with sheer anguish and disgust. Ashok Chaturvedi and his coterie tried to take sexual advantage from her due to her being a divorcee which could be the cause of this whole tragic event. She gave in writing in her complaint against another Joint Secretary, M.K.Piyasi's name a close associate of Ashok Chaturvedi, who also tried to take advantage of her plight. Piyasi was known for his links with a Dowood Ibrahim agent, Rakesh Wadhwa in Kathmandu. Details of his mobile records would reveal that he was in regular touch with Wadhwa and his wife. Additional details about sexual harassment and retaliation of Nisha Bhatia have also been elaborated in a separate chapter.

About three months back of this incident, she personally met the National Security Advisor,Shri M.K.Narayanan and the Cabinet Secretary, K.M.Chandrasekhar. She gave this complaint to them also but no action was taken against the delinquent officers. She was so dejected due to the traumatic behaviour of the RAW authorities that she took extreme step of suicide inside PM office when she was not allowed to meet the Prime Minister despite having a formal permission This matter was reported in media but no corrective measure was taken at any level to take cognizance of Nisha Bhatia's complaint.

This was simplest of the simple criminal offence for which Supreme Court of India had laid down clear guidelines to prosecute a person who sexually tries to harass a woman employee in the office. Since, R&AW is a Government within the Government of India, no such guidelines are followed or implemented here. Had the National Security Advisor or the Cabinet Secretary taken this matter out of the purview of R&AW authorities, she could not have taken this extreme step of commiting suicide inside Prime Minister's office.

Next Chief K.C.Verma was new to R&AW and killed his time by drawing official salary only. S.K.Tripathi, the last R&AW head, had a coterie of Gurinder Singh and Ashok Chaturvedi with him who tried to exploit many ladies in R&AW. Although, while serving as R&AW Chief Tripathi maintained a good track record but when I was serving at Amritsar in the late eighties, I was informed by my colleagues that he was having relations with some ladies whom he used to call at his official residence in the absence of his wife.

Other Incidents

Mindset of certain R&AW officers in indulging sex related incidents is reflective of a sex oriented psyche in which they are usually working operationally. Most of the agents they developed during the course of their operational duties, are entertained with all these unethical facilities like providing prostitutes for sex. This sadistic working culture has provoked many of them to exploit their own lady colleagues or they themselves were exploited by foreign agents. There are numerous such incidents in R&AW which have hounded this agency and many officers were even subjected to departmental action and removed from service.

When I joined my first posting at Jodhpur in 1973, one retired army Colonel was my boss supervising Rajasthan sector of R&AW. This Colonel used to call prostitutes in the safe houses which were plush buildings in R&AW. He was an old man and in order to enjoy satisfactory sex, either he was taking sex injections or tablets. I was told by insiders who were guarding the safe houses that while performing sex, this old man was usually tired and in order to complete the sex exercise two strong constables of R&AW were ready at his disposal to physically lift him and push him up and down to give finishing touches in this orgy. When an enquiry was conducted against him for financial irregularities, these Constables were asked to depose and they admitted to this duty which they had performed.

In early Eighties, A.P.Mishra, an IPS officer, working as Director in RAW was posted in Indian mission at Kathmandu. He exploited a lady of junior rank posted in the embassy. Subsequently, when he was reverted to India as Additional Commissioner in R&AW office at Lucknow, he was caught with this lady in

R&AW safe house by some activists of R&AW Employees Association. He was reverted to his parent UP cadre but no disciplinary action was taken against him.

In 1987, K.V.Unnikrishnan, IPS officer, Joint Secretary was working in R&AW office in earstwhile Madras in 1987 where one lady CIA agent exploited and obtained all secret information from him. When detected by the Intelligence Bureau (IB), he was arrested on espionage charges and sent to jail. He was later dismissed from service.

In Early Nineties, P.K.Venugopal, who was serving as Director of R&AW, was divorced by the niece of M.G. Ramachandran, fromer Chief Minister of Tamil Nadu for infidelity. In the normal course, a single working man in R&AW is never sent on any foreign assignment. Knowing this fact, he was sent on foreign assignment by R&AW to Indian Embassy in Tehran. He was caught by the Iranian intelligence officials while womanizing in a hotel and repatriated to India on this charge. Back in India, he was asked to resign R&AW. Subsequently, he kept a Shia lady of Iran with whom she developed illicit relations while serving at Tehran. This lady reportedly entered India illegally with the connivance of Venugopal.

In August, 1997, three ladies of R&AW were arrested from Vasant Intercontinental Hotel by Delhi Police on charges of prostitution. These ladies were heavily drunk when they were taken to the police station. One of them was a Chinese language expert and other two were Personal Assistant. Delhi Police recovered identity cards of R&AW from their possession and the authorities were informed about these arrest soon thereafter. R&AW authorities got this matter hushed up and police was not allowed to register any case in this matter. These ladies claimed that they had gone to hand over some translated documents to one of their acquaintances. The internal enquiry conducted by CIS unit of R&AW, as usual, remained a closely guarded secret. Six months earlier, three ladies of IB were also caught on charges of prostitution and a case was registered under the Immoral Traffic Prevention Act. These ladies disclosed that an Assistant Director of IB forced them in this trade. Next day, that man committed suicide.

R.V.Guge, Director, was dismissed from service when he was found exploiting a lady servant in his North East office. Prior to that there were allegations against him that he tried to develop illicit relations with a lady colleague at R&AW Headquarterss.

In 1998, Suchit Dass, 1971 IPS officer of Orissa Cadre, was caught on videotape for his rendezvous with a lady of Bangladesh Mission in New Delhi on several occasions by the surveillance team of R&AW. This lady was used by Bangladesh Intelligence officials to recruit Suchit Dass as their agent while he was serving in the Indian Mission at Dhaka. When Suchit Dass reverted to India on completion of his tenure, this lady was also sent by Bangladesh Intelligence to continue her liaison with Dass. She exploited Dass and got many secret information from him. No criminal action was taken against Suchit Dass and he was simply reverted to his parent cadre after the exposure of his illicit relations. Surprisingly no criminal action was taken against him despite conclusive evidences of his involvement with a foreign agent.

In 2006, Kishore Jha, IPS, a Joint Secretary in R&AW in the mid-nineties tried to sexually exploit wife of his IAS batch mate. On the intervention of the then Prime Minister, he was reverted to his parent cadre in Manipur when that lady made a complaint. However, he politically managed his re-entry in R&AW and while serving in Jodhpur office, he tried to molest a lady employee of R&AW in inebriated condition. Subsequently, he was transferred to R&AW Headquarterss where he used double meaning words to a lady officer to exploit her for sexual favour. This matter was reported to the then Secretary of R&AW, P.K.H, Tharakan but instead of taking any action against him, he was posted to Germany in Bonn as RAW operative.

In June, 2006, Brig. Ujjawal Dasgupta, Director in Computor Division was arrested for his alleged link with a lady CIA operative Rosanna Minchew working in US Embassy in Delhi. He was arrested on charges of espionage and lodged in Tihar Jail for long time before getting bail.

In October, 2007, Ravi Nair, a Joint Secretary of 1975 batch direct recruit of R&AW was abruptly recalled from Indian Embassy in Colombo for his involvement with a suspected lady Chinese agent. Senior sources in R&AW revealed that this lady got involved with Nair during his Bhutan stint. She wass a North Eastern lady working for Chinese Intelligence. This liaison continued in Hong Kong and detected in Colombo. Nair has a dubious past in R&AW. He was accused by a source of pocketing $40000 of his remuneration. More so, he worked for more than 4 years in Pakistan which no other officer of R&AW could ever complete due to ISI interference. There were allegations of his being hobnobbing with ISI. In the matter of his involvement with a lady spy, no harsh action was taken against him by Ashok Chaturvedi and curiously he was given charge of a sensitive desk of North East.

In May, 2008, M.M.Sharma, Director of sensitive Science And Technology Division of R&AW was videotaped by Chinese intelligence officials while having sex with a prostitute in Beijing where he was posted in the Indian Mission. He was declared Persona Non Grata(PNG) and sent to India. He was subsequently dismissed from service. Sharma disclosed to me that he was framed by the Chinese authorities since he was getting information from that lady who was a teacher in Beijing. He admitted to his sexual relation with her. In sheer foolishness he posted some of their sex performing photographs in his computer which later on were taken into custody by R&AW authorities. This was another bungling by

R&AW because Sharma was a widower and in normal course he should not have been selected for foreign posting.

Gurinder Singh, who was Special Secretary of R&AW was found having sex with a lady on a videotape in the spy camera which was secretly installed at the residence of Rabinder Singh by R&AW authorities to detect his activities. Mysteriously, R&AW authorities did not take any disciplinary action against him and rather sent him on post-retirement assignment with the Mauritius government. I am informed by one of the staff members that while Gurinder Singh was serving as Minister in Indian High Commission at London, a dubious lady of Indian origin got visa from him by developing illicit relations which continued till he stayed there.

In July, 2013. Rachna Srivastava a Linguist in the Language Division of R&AW and Rajesh Kumar a DANICS officer were caught in R&AW Headquarterss while having sex in her room. CIS unit was aware of their affairs and in order to catch them red-handed, secret cameras were installed in the room of this lady. Rajesh Kumar was reverted to his parent cadre immediately after this incident and Rachna was asked to seek voluntary retirement. Surprisingly, when this lady submitted her retirement papers, she was disallowed. Strange are some decisions which R&AW authorities have taken when the delinquent officer were allowed to work merrily even after their offences are proved. There are numerous such examples.

These are some of the instances of senior officers of RAW who were either exploited by lady foreign agents or they tried to exploit the ladies who were working with them. There are other such numerous cases in RAW which would need pages and hours to disclose before the public.

❑

Two Parliament Seats for POK and Gilgit/Baltistan

Author had been continuously raising the issue of creation of two Parliament seats for Pakistan Occupied Kashmir i.e. Azad Kashmir and Gilgit/Baltistan. Text of following letter dated 16 November, 2016, sent to the Prime Minister would unfold the historical facts for which the author wanted Indian Government to amend the Constitution and create these seats in the Lok Sabha. Author filed a PIL in this regard in the Hon'ble Supreme Court on 1st July, 2019 wherein he demanded legal intervention to create these seats in Constitution. But to his utter dismay, the Chief Justice of India Ranjan Gogoi threw the file away in few seconds without allowing the Counsel of the author to bring relevant facts before the Hon'ble bench. He also imposed a cost of Rupees Fifty Thousand on author for wasting time of the Court. Two other Judges of this bench were silent spectators to this autocratic behavior of Chief Justice Gogoi. However, Government of India abrogated Article 370 on 5th August, 2019. But the most pertinent question is still hanging fire as the Delimitation of the State of Kashmir would bring POK and Gilgit/Baltistan in the ambit of Parliament of India particularly in view of the fact that Pakistan has declared Gilgit/Baltistan as its fifth provisional province.

Text of Letter Dated 16 November, 2016 to Prime Minister

"According to article 47 of the Constitution of Jammu & Kashmir, the Legislative Assembly consists of 111 members out of which 24 seats are earmarked for the Pakistan Occupied Kashmir (POK). These seats are kept vacant and not taken into account for reckoning the total membership of the Assembly because this area is under illegal possession of Pakistan and elections in J&K are held on the remaining 87 seats. These 24 seats are earmarked for POK including the Gilgit-Baltistan area which are under the forcible control of Pakistan. Drafters of the Constitution of Jammu & Kashmir at that time must have taken cognizance of illegal occupation of this 78,114Sq. Kms. of area by Pakistan including 5,180 Sq. Kms. which was ceded by Pakistan toChina in 1963. So, for a complete Constitutional framework of the total area of pre-1947 Kashmir, a total of 111 assembly seats were created by the makers of the J&K Assembly Constitution. Many circumstantial provisions not written in this Constitution must have been taken into oral consideration by the then leadership because political situation in this area was under the ambit of UNO resolution on plebiscite. However, they could not create Parliament seats for these 24 assembly seats of POK at that time since it was not a state subject of Jammu and Kashmir Assembly but a constitutional obligation of the Central Government. In view of volatile political situation in J&K, Central Government was wary of the aftermath if such imitative was taken at that time. Pro-Pakistani elements were creating many other unwarranted problems for the J&K administration. Any such move was counter-productive then. Moreover, Sheikh Abdullah was in prison when this Constitution was promulgated in 1957 and Prime Minister Nehru did not want to give him any chance to raise a hue and cry in favour of Pakistan against such provision.

In view of this Constitutional framework of India on Jammu & Kashmir and Assembly composition thereto, I sought information from the Election Commission of India on 6 April, 2016 (copy attached) about the name of 24 assembly seats in J&K assembly which are under the illegal occupation of Pakistan. I also inquired why no Parliament seats were created for these 24 assembly seats with reasons thereof. Also, is there any provision in offing to create Parliament seats for these 24 seats of J&K assembly. Election Commission forwarded this letter to the Chief Electoral Officer, Jammu & Kashmir to provide this information to me. Public Information Officer of Chief Electoral Officer vide his letter dated 24.05.2016 and J&K Chief Minister's Secretariat vide their letter dated 06.06.2016 informed me that such information can be sought by the residents of J&K State only. They added that I am not permanent resident of the J&K State and as such no information can be given to me under the RTI Act. Copies of these two letters are enclosed for ready reference. From the above communications, it is evidently clear that no Indian can seek any information about Jammu & Kashmir under the RTI act. This is stigmatic situation when Indian Government since independence has been claiming that Jammu & Kashmir is integral part of India. How this situation could be acceptable to any Indian citizen when J&K Government is informing me that I can not be provided any information since I am not the permanent citizen of Jammu and Kashmir. This dual relationship with J&K visà-vis other Indian States has to be eliminated if

Government is keen to bring a sense of belonging among the residents of Jammu and Kashmir.

When I persisted with the Election Commission of India to provide me the information sought for vide my letter dated 6 April, 2016, the CPIO vide his letter dated 1 September, 2016 (Copy enclosed) informed me that according to Article 81 of the Constitution of India and the Constitution (Application) Order, 1954 Part V as applicable to the State of Jammu & Kashmir, the constitutional position is as under:

PART V.577 (a) For the purposes of article 55, the population of the State of Jammu and Kashmir shall be deemed to be sixty-three lakhs.

(b) In article 81, for clauses (2) and (3), the following clauses shall be substituted, namely:-

(2) For the purposes of sub-clause (a) of clause (1) -

(a) there shall be allotted to the State six seats in the House of the People;

(b) the State shall be divided into single member territorial constituencies by the Delimitation Commission constituted under the Delimitation Act, 1972, in accordance with such procedure as the Commission may deem fit;

(c) the Constituencies shall, as far a practicable, in geographically compact areas, and in delimiting them regard shall be had to physical features, existing boundaries of administrative units, facilities of communication and public convenience; and

(d) the constituencies into which State is divided shall not comprise the area under the occupation of Pakistan.

This provisioning of Parliament Constituencies has lost all its relevance now in view of many alarming incidents took place in whole of Jammu & Kashmir, be under control of India or with Pakistan and China. Indian Government has to amend this outdated provision if it in real sense claim Jammu & Kashmir as integral part of India. In addition to many other incidents, these two incidents took place in Jammu & Kashmir recently has left India with no option but to redefine its constitutional framework earlier the better:

I. China Pakistan Economic Corridor (CPEC)

In an hidden agenda, Pakistan with the connivance of China has made Kashmir a trilateral dispute before the world community. Pakistan and China, while enacting to enhance the Pakistani infrastructure, signed a $51 Billion agreement known as China Pakistan Economic Corridor (CPEC) which include the up-gradation of Karakoram Highway from Peshawar to the Chinese border through Gilgit and Baltistan, a territory of Kashmir under the illegal occupation of Pakistan. This project proposed to link Indian Ocean at Gwadar port of Pakistan in South-

West region to Chinese province of Xinjiang via a vast network of highways and railways. This pact would reduce the travel length of sea route of 15,000 kms to 1,500 kms by road to the Indian ocean. A railway line linking China's Southern Xinjiang Railway in Kashgar to Pakistan through this region is also part of this project. This pact is part of expansionist strategy of China vis-à-vis India to legitimize the forcibly occupied territory of Aksai Chin which was historically part of India as per the documents of McMahon line, the dividing line between Tibet and India. Most pertinent aspect of this project is its complete violation of the UN resolutions which clearly mandated Gilgit and Baltistan as territorial dispute between Indian and Pakistan. This is mockery of the existence of UNO to have any say when such violations are taking place in a dispute which is affecting peace and security since the last seventy years. Indian Government had mildly protested to the Chinese on this interference on its sovereignty despite many resolution passed in the Indian Parliament that Jammu & Kashmir is integral part of India. I have no hesitation to reiterate that Indian Government has no plan to legitimize this part of Jammu and Kashmir except to the form of debating on international forums. Our future generations would never pardon us for this tame surrender if this CPEC is allowed to be made a reality though construction work in Gilgit and Baltistan whic has already been started by the Chinese and India is none more than a mute spectator watching haplessly.

2. Post 8 July, 2016 (Killing of Burhan Wani) Scenario in Kashmir

Perhaps India had never witnessed such anarchy, sabotage and protest as took place after the killing of the terrorist, Burhan Wani on 8 July, 2016 by the security forces. I fail to understand why this non-existent element was allowed to attain such popularity and fame through social media by the Indian Government and our media that his encounter boomeranged on even the presence of security and armed forces in the valley. Indian army was never found so wanting as we found after this encounter. Even after 4 months of this incident, law and order situation in the valley is a question of uncertainty for our law enforcing agencies. Most parts of the valley are under curfew since this killing. It is estimated that 94 civilians have been killed and around 13,000 injured after this encounter while attacking the security and armed forces. Around 4,000 Indian soldiers have so far also been injured by stone pelting and attack by militants in this catastrophe. Massacring of soldiers at Uri and subsequent surgical strikes on terrorists launching pads in POK by Indian army though engulfed the public euphuism elsewhere to its boiling point but the lull in valley is unpredictable.

Most disturbing aspect in the aftermath of this incident is the burning of schools in Kashmir. So far, 29 schools have been put on flames by the militants in the valley since the start of this unrest. This is alarming situation because such incidents were never witnessed during the worst militancy in Kashmir in the last two decades.

Separatists are still calling the shots. They are making all possible efforts to give new impetus to the ongoing grim situation in the valley. Although, the present PDP- BJP alliance is working in complete allegiance with the Central Government but normalcy in the valley is still a far cry.

Historical Background

4. Pandit Jawaharlal Nehru during his tenure as Prime Minister could not look into this issue owing to volatile political situation in J&K. Sheikh Abdullah, the towering political personality of Kashmir of that era, was kept under detention for treason. Nehru released him only on 8 April, 1964 and sent him to Pakistan to study the state of affairs of POK. Nehru wanted Sheikh to get him back to a proper frame of mind so that he could take a decision whether merger of J&K within India was more realistic in comparison with Pakistan. Sheikh Abdullah went to Pakistan on 25 May, 1964. Nehru died two days later on 27 May, 1964 and his dream of everlasting solution of Kashmir could not materialised. Sheikh Abdullah resorted to his old rhetoric of an Independent Kashmir when he sensed vacuum in Indian politics after the death of Pandit Nehru. He considered all other Indian leaders inferior to his own status and the political situation in Kashmir remained in limbo till Smt. Indira Gandhi became Prime Minister in January, 1966. She too was engrossed in political upheaval since most of other senior Congress leaders wanted her to be a puppet in their hand. However, she could attain full authority in 1969 when she divided Congress and got full majority to outwit other Congress leaders. She took many radical steps of Bank Nationalization, Privy-Purse Abolition and ultimately liberation of Bangladesh. Sheikh Abdullah watched this dramatic political change-over with precision and came in terms Smt. Indira Gandhi. Rest is history but till the death of Sheikh Abdullah in 1982 neither Indira Gandhi nor Morarji Desai ever got them entangled with this sensitive issue of creating two Parliament Seats for POK since they were embroiled in one controversy or the other and did not dare to amend the Constitution to do so.

Pakistan has divided this occupied territory into two different political regions. Azad Kashmir, with an area of 13,297 Sq. Kms. along the Line of Control, is made an autonomous administrative territory where a Parliamentary form of government was constituted. President is the constitutional head and Prime Minister is the Chief Executive of this region. It has its own Supreme Court and a High Court. Pakistan's Ministry of Kashmir Affairs is administrative head of this region. No member is elected to the Pakistan National Assembly from Azad Kashmir. This was a ploy and camouflage by Pakistan to inject a wrong perception in the minds of people of Jammu & Kashmir that Azad Kashmir is a separate entity so that the inherent desire of some separatist elements in J&K continue to abet the slogan of independence for the Kashmiris. Pakistan succeeded in this nefarious design and a section of separatist leaders who are on the pay roll of Pakistan, are still voicing for the independence of Jammu & Kashmir due to this background.

Like Azad Kashmir, Pakistan also maintained Gilgit-Baltistan an autonomous self-governing region under the name "Northern Areas". This region of 72,971 Sq. Kms area was also not integrated as separate entity and is not part of Pakistan's constitution. It has its own Legislative Assembly and Council. Pakistan has maintained its autonomous status like Azad Kashmir to project before the World community particularly the UNO that this region is part of an independent Jammu & Kashmir territory.

Since, both Azad Kashmir and Gilgit-Baltistan were part of the erstwhile Jammu & Kashmir territory, India should bring these regions under its Constitutional obligation like the Jammu & Kashmir Constitution, administrating it incognito with

24 MLAs. Prior to the rule of Dogra Rajputs, this whole region was ruled by Raja Ranjit Singh. This is a historical truth available in various books.

I would like to emphasize that political situation both in Pakistan and China is unpredictable unlike India and these countries would certainly disintegrate sooner or later. Pakistan is facing political dissension in all provinces due to Punjabi domination in all walks of life. Once, its army disintegrate on regional issues, Pakistan would certainly be reduced to two or three independent countries. Likewise, Communism is fading in every respect all over World. China would not remain the same what it is today. Although in 1979, the Tinanmen Square demonstration for democracy by students was crushed by the army but it is not a denying fact that voice for democracy is taking roots in China and communism has bleak future there and its disintegration in future is on the cards. In view of these two adversaries on our two borders, there is every likelihood that the area of Jammu & Kashmir under occupation of Pakistan and China would return to Indian fold. We should create a constitutional disposition for this area to be part of Indian Constitution so that even if we are not alive, we can leave a Constitutional Legacy for our future generation who could portray it as integral part of India. Total area occupied by Pakistan and China is as under:

a. Area occupied by Pakistan:	78,114 Sq. Kms
b. Area ceded to China by Pakistan in 1963	5,180 Sq. Kms.
c. Forceful occupation by China	37,555 Sq. Kms.

At the time of integration of Jammu and Kashmir with India, Raja Hari Singh was ruling over an area of 2.22 Lakh sq. kms. out of which one-fifth is in possession of China. India is in occupation of only 46% territory of Jammu & Kashmir whereas Pakistan and China have captured 54% area by sheer force.

In view of this future proposition, I would request you to create two Parliament seats for the Azad Kashmir and Gilgit-Baltistan region in the following manner:

a. Muzaffarabad Seat: Areas and population

Division	District	Area Kms.	Population	Headquarterss
Mirpur	Bhimber	1,516	3,01,633	Bhimber
	Kotli	1,862	5,63,094	Kotili
	Mirpur	1,010	3,33,482	Mirpur
Muzaffarabad	—d-	2,496	6,38,973	Muzaffarabad
	Hattian			Hattian Bala
	Neelam	3,621	1,06,778	Athmuqam
Poonch	Poonch	855	4,11,035	Rawalkot
	Haveli	600	1,50,000	Forward Kahuta
	Bagh	768	2,43,415	Bagh
	Sudhnoti	569	4,56,7982	Palandri
Grand Total	**10 Districts**	**13,297**	**4,56,7982**	

b. Gilgit-Baltistan Seat:

Baltistan	Ghanche	9,400	90000	Skardu
	Skardu	8,000	219000	-do-
	Shigar	8,500		-do-
	Kharmang	5,500		-do-
Gilgit	Gilgit	16,300	1,48,000	Gilgit
	Diamer	10,936	1,35,000	-do-
	Ghizer	9,635	1,21,000	-do-
	Astore	8,657	72,000	-do-
	Hunza Nagar		20,057	99,000
Grand Total			**72,496**	**8,84,000**

I would not hesitate to point out that every Indian is looking towards you as the only administrator after decades who could deliver what is the need of hour. People have bestowed great faith in you not only in the last Parliament Elections but also in the subsequent assembly elections. You would certainly give proper attention to the aspirations of the people of this country.

12. I am not only hopeful but fully convinced that all political parties in India would support you on this issue. If anyone would dare to oppose it, they would

face unbearable public ire. In the present state of affairs with Pakistan, Indian public is in a showdown once for all. Coffins of Indian soldiers coming from Jammu and Kashmir to various parts of India are causing a sort of feeling in general public that we should resolve this confrontation once for all. Your recent decision of demonetization has also brought a sense of feeling in Indian public that you are capable to act for better cause despite some uncalled for resistance by a section of politicians.

In view of the situation explained above, I would request you to look into my suggestion of creating two Parliament seats in the Pak-China Occupied Kashmir so that future generation of this country could remember you after Sardar Patel as saviour of the sovereign integration of the territorial boundaries of India.

With highest regards,

Yours Sincerely,

(R.K. Yadav)

Copy to: Shri Rajnath Singh, Hon'ble Home Minister of India.

2. Shri Ajit Doval, National Security Advisor.

Following Leaders of various parties. All are requested to please support this issue in national interest.

1. Smt. Sonia Gandhi, President, Indian National Congress.
2. Shri Rahul Gandhi, Vice-President, Indian National Congress.
3. Ms. Jayalalithaa, President AIDMK.
4. Shri Mulayam Singh Yadav, President, Samajwadi Party.
5. Ms. Mamta Banerjee, President, TMC.
6. Shri Prakash Singh Badal, President, SAD.
7. Ms. Mehbooba Mufti, PDP.
8. Shri Omar Abdullah, NC.
9. Shri Nitish Kumar, President, JD(U).
10. Shri Lalu Prasad Yadav, President, RJD.
11. Shri Udhav Thakre, President Shiv Sena.
12. Shri Karunanidhi, President, DMK.
13. Shri Naveen Patnaik, President, BJD.
14. Shri N,Chandrababu Naidu, President, TDP.
15. Shri K.Chandrashekhar Rao, TRS.
16. Shri Abhay Chautala, INLD.
17. Shri Prafulla Mahant, AGP.
18. Shri Prakash Karat, CPI(M).
19. Shri S.Sudhakar Reddy, CPI."

❑

Ajit Doval as National Security Advisor

In the first edition, I have written few pages as to how National Security Advisors degraded R&AW from 1998 to 2014 by retired bureaucrats of MEA and Intelligence Bureau. When Narendra Modi became Prime Minister in May, 2014 I was again apprehending installation of a non-intelligence person on this post. In an interview on 11 April, 2014, before Modi became Prime Minister, I had opined that his agenda had already been outlined by the media on various issues and Pakistan would be on his radar first. It was my conviction because he was a beginner on national scene and as such intelligence and security of India were new subject for him. These delicate matters should be handled by him without much bureaucratic barrier. I professed that he should appoint some former intelligence officer his National Security Advisor because henceforth these appointees proved a liability on the nation which could be assessed by many tragic incidents.

Fortunately, Modi appointed Ajit Doval for this post probably on the basis of his relentless crusade after retirement from Intelligence Bureau to enlighten the policy makers on multiple security and foreign affairs through various write-ups, lectures and briefings to various Government agencies and NGOs. His achievements, past track record and fearsome background were a testament to his intelligence rectitude in the public domains. I hardly need to repeat these well known facts here again. Pakistan media, however, raised a lot of hue and cry after his appointment fearing worst reprisals to their terrorist activities and even every Indian was eyeing for it with Modi as PM and Doval his National Security Advisor.

Since his appointment as NSA in May, 2014, I found many remarkable achievements of Doval in and around India. I would certainly like to elaborate on what I read and heard from some horse's mouth. Before analyzing these facts, I can not digest one happening which I would reveal without fearing any consequences be it political or otherwise.

Around few months after the Modi rule of first term, I was discussing appointment and other aspects of inside issues and Pakistan related policy of R&AW with one of my friends, a senior R&AW officer, who happens to be keeping a close tab on these matters. I told him that my sources revealed that the Government has presently dropped a proposal to eliminate all leading terrorists of Pakistan including Hafiz Saeed & Masood Azhar for which full scale preparation was made after Modi became PM. A full blueprint of this operation was devised under the supervision of then R&AW Chief. That officer corroborated this fact and informed me that R&AW Chief had sent a detailed operational proposal in this regard but after some deliberations, the concerned file was not given consent by the Government. Meaning thereby either this operation was postponed for political or international compulsions or Modi Government decided to afford a chance to make Pakistan senses. Whatever might be the compulsions or considerations for this non-action but it is beyond any doubt that within few months of Modi Government, R&AW was made ready by Doval to eliminate all prominent terrorists inside Pakistan. That was the beginning of an end. However there was another theory that these terrorists should be undeterred to continue terrorist activities which would ruin Pakistan in future. I am assured that this agenda is still in pipeline and could be implemented at appropriate time. This is what I got to know about Doval on Pakistan in the first year of Modi rule.

While assessing the World overview, it is beyond any doubt that Doval in his first term as NSA enhanced Indian prestige and power of India by arranging various tours of Modi in every corner of the World. He attained overall control on internal security as well as on foreign policy. S Jaishankar and subsequent foreign secretaries were working under Doval during his first terms as NSA. Such power centre was created by Modi under Doval that India was considered as a major power in this region. Most of the prominent leaders of the World visited India during this period and signed various trade and other agreements with India.

I would focus on regional aspects of security matters of Modi Government implying how Doval as National Security Advisor resurrected the deadwood of M.K.Narayanan in particular and Shiv Shankar Menon in general, two so-called stalwarts of Manmohan Singh Government. Some details related to neighoubring countries would reflect achievements of Doval as NSA.

Bhutan

Prime Minister of Bhutan Tobgay attended the swearing-in ceremony of Modi in May, 2014. Bhutan was the first country visited by Modi after becoming Prime Minister in June, 2014. Prior to that a move was afoot to open Chinese Embassy in Bhutan when Shiv Shankar Menon was NSA. Soon thereafter, the Prime Minister of Bhutan emphatically denied in June, 2014 that there was no question of allowing China to open its Embassy in Bhutan. This was a major achievement in view of the prevailing bonhomie between these two countries during Manmohan Singh regime. China was thus outmaneuvered by Doval to open a diplomatic channel with Bhutan despite a treaty with India against such provision. All previous trade agreements were given due sanctity by the Modi Government. Bhutan Prime Minister visited India several time thereafter on Indian Government and some State Government's invitation to attend summits and regional inaugurations of various projects.

Sri Lanka

In so far as Sri Lanka is concerned, M.K.Narayanan, as NSA during UPA regime, proved utter disastrous and self-destructive for the cause of Tamil population. Pro-Chinese Rajapaksa Government let loose a reign of terror on civilian population of Hindu Tamils in Jaffna and other northern part of Sri Lanka in the garb of LTTE militancy. Rajakapsa ordered its military to crush LTTE before the results of 2009.

Parliament elections in India were to be declared. He was wary if a non-Congress Government would get elected in India, its foreign policy with Hindu population of Sri Lanka could take a reverse stand to what Manmohan Singh's NSA were pursuing earlier. Sri Lankan army crushed LTTE the day Parliament results in India were announced in May, 2009. Such was a cause of concern of Rajapaksa. He committed worst genocide of Hindu population under the nose of Manmohan Singh Government. In the next five years of Rajapaksa rule, Hindu population was persecuted to the worst of its kind in Sri Lankan history. In order to humiliate India further, Rajapaksa involved China in many economic and strategic projects in Sri Lanka to jeopardize Indian security in this region and development of Sri Lankan Hambantota port and a rail project were prominent among these ventures. Doval was observing these developments when Narayanan was NSA. However, the worst to follow was when Chinese submarines were allowed to be docked twice in Colombo during September, 2014 after Modi became Prime Minister of India.

Rajapaksa was ousted in the general elections of January, 2015. He alleged role of R&AW Station Chief in Colombo to align all opposition parties against him in his defeat. Illango, the R&AW officer was accused of helping and gathering support for joint opposition candidate Maithripala Srisena and managing his defection from Rajapaksa camp. There were media reports that USA and UK diplomats in Colombo too broad-based the election strategy to oust the pro-Chinese Rajapaksa in the elections. India too was on board of this scheme. Ajit Doval visited Colombo in November, 2014, to attend a "defence seminar". He met Former President Chandrika Kumaratunga, Srisena and opposition leader Ranil Wickremeseinghe, head of the pro-US United National Party (UNP) during this visit. Although Illango was recalled after Doval's visit but the die was already cast. He was stated to have encouraged several lawmakers including Srisena to defect from Rajapaksa group. Wickermssinghe was convinced not to contest against Rajapaksa so that "someone else" can take on him to ensure his defeat. Kumaratunga was the linchpin of this plot. Illango played a pivotal role to manage support of the main Tamil party of Sri Lanka the Tamil National Alliance for Srisena.

The author smilingly asked Doval (where is secret) what was happening in Sri Lanka. Doval retorted and said in Hindi "KAR TO DIYA SIDHA" (Taught the lesson). Anti-Indian Rajapaksa was ousted in a bloodless coup in his own turf by Doval. Sri Lanka took a reverse tilt after Rajapaksa's defeat and Srisena restored the erstwhile friendly relations with India de-alienating China which has made its presence felt adversely to India and USA. This was another feather in the cap of Doval during the first year of Modi Government. In this political bonhomie, India and USA were in unison to oust Rajpaksa which is indicative that if such geo-political tensions intensified with China, this trend would continue.

Thereafter, Modi visited Sri Lanka in March, 2015, which was after a gap of 28 years as Prime Minister of India due to internal strife there. Modi gave possession of 27,000 homes to Tamil families which were affected due to conflict of LTTE and Sri Lankan forces. Doval not only had Rajpaksa in political oblivion for his anti-Indian stance but also brought the historical India-Sri Lanka friendship to blossom again.

However, the Rajpaksa brothers won the last elections recently with landslide victory and Modi was the first to congratulate on it. I should reveal here that one of the former Prime Ministers of Sri Lanka contacted the author through his friend in Sri Lanka and sought Indian help in these elections. Since, Rajpaksa were pro-Chinese, the author tried to provide that help to the opponent of Rajpaksa but Indian Government did not respond and author said sorry to his Sri Lankan friend.

Now, Rajpaksa brothers are not keeping balance with India in so far as their relations with China are concerned. Recently, a top Chinese delegation visited Sri Lanka and signed a free trade agreement including revival of Hambantota loan project. This is alarming development for India in particular and USA and its allies in general. India has to resort to counter it and US along with NATO allies should exert political pressure on Rajpaksa in this regard to keep China away from this region. However, Rajpaksa should be on the watch-list of India provided the Doval and Jaishankar policies on this country are evenly matched.

Indian Ocean

Maritime security of Indian Ocean has been a cause of concern for Modi Government due to inevitable China factor, the perennial elephant in the room in any South Asian discourse. China is not an Indian Ocean power and yet it has been continuously enlarging its strategic footprints in the region. In order to thwart this menace, a mechanism by way of Trilateral Maritime Security Cooperation among India, Sri Lanka and Maldives with Seychelles and Mauritius as observers, was put in active existence by Doval. This was a paramount achievement in view of the fact that more than 1,00,000 ships pass through the Indian Ocean every year. Around 66% of the World oil cargo, over 50% of the World container traffic and almost 33% of the World bulk cargo crosses Indian Ocean every year. In order to keep tab on what happens in Indian Ocean this cooperation endorsed training search and seizure operations, training on board of Indian ships, exchanges between think-tanks and participation in adventure activities. It was a master stroke to counter Chinese convoluted designs.

In another major strategic foothold in Indian Ocean, Modi signed a Memorandum of Understanding to develop infrastructure on Agalega Islands in Mauritius and Assumption Islands in Seychelles. Agalega is around 1,000 kms north of Mauritius capital and Assumption is 600 nautical miles south-west of Mahe, Seychelles's capital. India will develop airfields and port facilities on these Islands which would monitor movements of naval activities of other countries. This would be added advantage to an Indian listening post on Madagascar, off the coast of Africa which was commissioned in 2007 to monitor activities of foreign vessels in the Indian Ocean Region. The strategic US military base Diego Garcia is about 600 nautical miles east of Assumption Islands. Increasing Chinese activities in the garb to counter Somali piracy in Indian Ocean Region would be counter-balanced through this strategy. In order to counter-piracy efforts, India gifted two patrol vessels and a Dornier aircraft to Seychelles. The Mauritian and Seychelles armed forces would be the primary users of the facilities which India is creating on the Islands. Indian warships which are routinely deployed to patrol the 1.3 million square km Exclusive Economic Zone of Seychelles and Indian naval hydrographic survey vessels visiting Mauritius would be provided all docking facilities in this region of Indian Ocean.

In November, 2015, India inducted first squadron of 8 Boeing P-8 I Poseidon aircraft at Rajali Naval Air Station about 70 Kms of Chennai. These planes are equipped for long range anti-submarine warfare, anti-surface warfare, intelligence, surveillance and reconnaissance operations. The new unit designated as Indian Naval Air Squadron 312A would be permanently stationed at Rajali to counter any intrusion of Chinese navy. Two of Poseidon 8 aircrafts have been based at the strategically located Andaman and Nicobar archipelago are also a part of this strategy. Unmanned aerial vehicles Searcher-II of Israel and drones have also been deployed in this region to check enemy forays. The Andaman and Nicobar Command has expanded the military infrastructure to accommodate a division-sized military force on the 572 island chains thus covering an area of more than 700 Sq. kms. The P-81 planes would also operate from Indian Naval Air Station, INS Utkrosh, Port Blair to keep tab on maritime security of this region.

US Strategists termed this development as emergence of an Indian "String of Flowers" to counter China's "String of Pearls" for a network of posts, infrastructure facilities and basing rights being built by China in countries in the Indian Ocean. Possibly yes. This is certainly devised by Doval to make Indian Ocean a safe hunting ground for Indian Navy which is being enhanced manifold. Indian navy presently possess two aircraft carriers, INS Vishal and INS Vikramaditya. It is building a 40,000 ton indigenous Aircraft Carrier. It also has 10 Russian and 4 German HDW-1500 submarines. Six French Scorpene Class submarines are under construction at Mazagaon Dock as part of Project 75 and another 6 are being added to it. Indian Navy took on lease from Russia an 8,000 ton Akula Class nuclear powered attack submarine and commissioned it as INS Chakra. Another indigenously structured nuclear submarine INS Arihant is currently undergoing sea trials. By 2022, India plans to have 160-plus ship including 3 aircraft carriers, 60 major combatants and close to 400 aircrafts of different version. Further 5 submarines and ships are being inducted every year for the next five years. Present budget with 18% share of Defence for Navy is further enhanced to make it a formidable entity in the Indian Ocean Region. Remarkable maritime strategy is planned by Doval and implemented by Modi.

Bangladesh (Land Boundary Agreement – Landmark Achievement)

India was aware of the impending danger from the Pakistan soil but prior to Sheikh Hasina Wazed becoming Prime Minister of Bangladesh, this country was a hub of terrorists, insurgents and radical groups which was a serious security threat to India. Islamic groups such as Islamic State, Ansarullah Bangladesh, Jama'at-ul Mujahideen Bangladesh, Harkat-ul-Jehad-al-Islami Bangladesh and Hizbut Tohid had consolidated as anti-Indian outfits mushroomed with the funding of foreign agencies. North-East insurgents like the ULFA, NSCN, MULTA etc. were getting training from these Islamic groups to indulge in proxy war against

India. In order to stop cross-border terrorism of these groups, border fencing with floodlights were becoming deterrent in view of the border demarcation and exchange of enclaves.

Existence of a large number of enclaves on either side of both countries was a major cause of concern to demarcate the border lines. There were 111 Indian enclaves (17,258.24 acres) on the Bangladesh side and 61 enclaves of Bangladesh (7083.72 acres) on the Indian side. The inhabitants of the enclaves did not have full legal rights as citizens of either country and basic facilities like electricity, schools and health care. Law and order were a big problem.

Modi Government entered into a historical agreement when the enclaves on both sides of India and Bangladesh were exchanged on 1st August, 2015 under the India-Bangladesh Land Boundary Agreement which was a rare land-swapping peaceful mechanism adopted by both countries in this era of conflict and confusion prevalent all over World. It also sent a message to the World that India is willing to settle its border disputes with neighbours provided there is same will and desire as shown by Bangladesh. A total border of 4,097 kms between the two countries stand demarcated now for ever without any territorial dispute.

This Land Boundary Agreement would minimize the security concerns of India and facilitate the security mechanism on this border. It will curb illegal movement of humans, drugs, funds and small arms along both sides. A constructive unilateralism has been identified in the neighbourhood policy by Modi Government on the planning of Ajit Doval. Residents of these enclaves have got the citizenship of their desire opted on their choice. A long-awaited dispute beside giving new lease of life to thousands of residents of these areas is the hallmark of this major achievement of Modi for which Doval played a pivotal role.

In December, 2018 general elections of Bangladesh, Awami League of Sheikh Hasina gained overwhelming majority of 288 seats out of 300 seats. There were allegations of managing these elections by ruling party with "Indian Help".

Nepal

Modi's Nepal priority started with a high note when he was accorded an unprecedented rousing welcome just after becoming PM. However, proclamation of a charter for new constitution by the Constituent Assembly in September, 2015, brought spontaneous protests by the Madheshi population which brought the India-Nepal border to a standstill. These protestors felt discriminated by this constitution and imposed a blockade on the movement of vehicles. This blockade continued upto February, 2016 resulting in widespread scarcity of gas, food, medicine and other essential commodities in Nepal. Pro-Chinese Nepali elements triggered this opportunity to defame India for the blockade although it was a self-inflicted hammering. Many unwarranted accusations were heralded against India by a section of Nepalese media forgetting how India went out of the way to provide help in previous year's earthquake within spur of a moment. Communist Prime Minister of Nepal Oli capitalized this opportunity and signed a trade transit treaty between China and Nepal which meant to import goods from third countries via Chinese territories. How it would be counter-productive to historical India-Nepal relations was a matter of concern in India. Nepal raised this blockade issue at the UN Human Rights Council in Geneva further aggravating the volatile diplomatic relations. Communist ruler of Nepal have raised another bogey that China's last-minute intervention has saved the Nepali Government headed by "pro-China" Prime minister K P Sharma Oli else it was collapsing.

During the initial years of Modi rule, the pro-Chinese elements in Nepal along with a section of media have temporarily succeeded in creating a wedge in the historical relations of Beti-Roti among two countries. But Indian Government would never afford to tolerate the increasing Chinese influence in Nepal and Doval was working tirelessly on this sensitive affair. Pushpa Kumar Dahal "Prachand" is old friend of India. his Jabalpur sojourn was a mystery.

Oli was never honest and sincere in continuing smooth relations with India. On Chinese pattern, a controversial map of Nepal was got printed wherein Kalapani, Lipulekh and Limpiyadhura in Uttarakhand were shown as Nepal territory. Oli issued a number of anti-Indian statements against India and even foolishly claimed that Bhagwan Ram was born in Nepal. Indian Government. chided Nepal for such unwarranted and immature actions which brought relations at its lowest ebb. Thereafter, India terminated all sort of bureaucratic and political relations with Nepal. Fearing further deterioration, Oli sought assistance from former diplomats of both countries and some civil society leaders, academics and even scientists were approached to soothe the ongoing bitterness between two countries. Ultimately, despite Nepal Ambassador's request for months, Doval met him and sternly told to stop all anti-Indian narratives at the behest of China. Doval also told him that Nepal politicians should stop adopting jingoistic stance against India for the sake of domestic political compulsions and would never afford to tolerate any political adventurism which Oli tried to portray in the past.

Oli was a stooge of China but in the overall interest of Nepalese population let the good sense among these Nepali leaders should prevail and not been carried away on the influence of certain Indian Communists also who had several unscheduled visits to Kathmandu to add fuel to the fire. My sources in Nepal were joking with me how Oli was totally silent after the visit of R&AW Chief Samant Goel to Nepal and his meeting with Oli. I retorted that it was hidden diplomacy not to be made open.

Pakistan

I have least hesitation to say that though Modi started his Pakistan diplomacy with a positive note when he invited Nawaz Shariff, the Pakistan PM, on his oath ceremony but soon thereafter the game of one-upmanship between the two countries took new dimensions. What I said in the beginning, death warrants of leading terrorist elements were signed at RAW Headquarterss but why these were not executed in the first year of Modi rule is a questionable mystery. Could be presence of Nawaz Shariff in the oath ceremony halted it? Probably also, Big Brother got cue of this execution and amateurish Modi Government was pursued on identical line like the "Aar Paar Ki Ladai" diatribe of Atal Bhihar Vajpayee to a damp squib. This is not sarcasm but a hard truth which I am narrating because I am in the know of it to some extent.

Initially, Modi diplomacy was a soothing balm on the relations of both countries particularly after Modi went to Lahore on an undiplomatic venture to focus World attention for his sincerity to resolve good relations with Pakistan. Although, the tone and tenor of Pakistan establishments including media took a u-turn and altogether new "Spring of Hopes" was attuned at every quarter. But Pakistan army has some more ideas to emulate in its cupboard. Postures of Pakistan diplomacy towards India at that time changed altogether assuming that Modi has engaged himself more in Make in India, Digital India, Start-up etc. to make India economically formidable and Kashmir-related issues have been put on back-burner. With this perception, ISI and Pakistan army enhanced covert operations in Kashmir with the result that those rural ladies of this region who were offering flowers to Indian soldiers during flood were provoked to pelt stones on them when some terrorist were killed in encounters.

Another most disturbing development was major infrastructure work taking place in Gilgit and Baltistan under the 46 Billion China-Pakistan Economic Corridor (CPEC) which was conceptualize in November, 2014 to humiliate India. This corridor would pass through Pakistan occupied Gilgit-Baltistan linking Gwadar Port in Balochistan with Kashgar in China's Xinjiang province. Through this project Pakistan tried to kill two birds with one stone. It would create a triangular conflict involving China in disputed Kashmir area and equally curb the more volatile independence voice of Balochistan which is forcibly kept as illegally captured territory due to Durand Line controversy. Modi Government was initially not pursuing any aggressive policy to thwart this illegal concept of Pak-diplomacy to aggravate the existing disputes in Kashmir and Balochistan. This was a very sensitive matter involving the sovereignty of India. I think Ajit Doval was keeping his cards close to his chest at that time in view of on-off diplomacy of Modi with Pakistan.

Rest is history now. Deterioration of worst ever relations started with terrorist attack in January, 2016 and ultimately reached to a flashpoint to Balakot airstrike. Even High Commissioners were withdrawn.

However, there were some extremely bold actions taken against Pakistan at the initiative of Doval. I learnt from horse's mouth of R&AW that prior information was sent by Doval about possible terrorist attack on Pathankot Air Force station but this was not properly conveyed to the concerned security forces. Thereafter, Doval pursued the "Double Squeeze Strategy" against Pakistan. Uri surgical strike was a bold action against Pakistan and ultimately first time after 1971 war, Indian Air force crossed the international border in February, 2019, and dropped bombs at Balakot in Khyber Pakhtunkhwa province in Pakistan. This was retaliation of Pulwana terrorist attack on Indian security forces. I wish to clarify some political rumour that there was not an iota of truth that R&AW was involved at all in the Pulwana terrorist attack. These rumours were floated for political mileage of 2019 elections by certain elements which were far from any truth.

China

Modi was totally naïve to analyze the Chinese diplomacy when he assumed power in May, 2014. So, Doval was responsible for all the bonhomie that continued thereafter in first term of Modi which was apparently seeming fruitful far from the past decades after 1962. But in my opinion it was deceptive which was not boldly handled much to the adverse actions of Chinese. President Xi Jinping visited India in September, 2014 and Modi ignoring all diplomatic protocol accorded him a warm welcome at Ahmedabad rather to at Raisina Hill. Swinging on bank of Sabarmati river and pouring tea to Xi was background of that bonhomie that Chinese first sent 1000 troops across the LAC in Chumar of South Ladakh and withdrew when Modi raised this issue with Xi. Probably, Indian policy makers were trapped by this action. Even when Modi visited China in May, 2015, he raised border question which was ignored by Xi and later Chinese termed it as historical complex issue needed to be resolved with time. Doval was apprehensive of Chinese intention and turned towards US for major developments.

Soon thereafter, Indo-US relations took a resolute turn when US backed India in getting entry into four global non-proliferation agreements i.e. Missile Technology Control Regime, the Australia Group, the Wessenaar Arrangement and the Nuclear Suppliers Group (NSG). This was great achievement of Doval because Foreign Secretary was working under him then. Irritated China blocked India's candidature for NSG membership and Masood Azhar was not allowed to be a global terrorist in UN. India followed it by refusing to become part of the flagship infrastructure building project of China, the Belt and Road Initiative (BRI).

Doklam crisis of 73 days was though resolved by Doval but Chinese hidden agenda was apparent when they again entered there which India did not resist. This gave a psychological dominance to China vis-à-vis India. Modi's speech at

Shangri-la Dialogue in June 2018 to caution that USA has no role to play in the Indo-Pacific region was to placate Xi but it proved counter-productive. Though Xi was again invited to India at Mamallapuram in October, 2019 probably at the initiative of new foreign minister of India S.Jaishankar who is stated to be having very cordial relations with China. Rest is history now. In June, 2020, Chinese confronted with Indian troops in Galwan valley where 20 Indian soldiers were martyred.

In the second term of Modi, S.Jaishankar, the pro-Chinese Foreign Minister was responsible to the Chinese diplomacy but he has still not succeeded to resolve the stand off with China. . Doval has no role to play in this diplomacy. Now LAC is still hot and next year May would be very vital to watch if there could be a possible war with China.

Abrogation of Article 370 in Jammu and Kashmir

First and foremost big decision which Modi Government took in its second term was abrogation of controversial Article 370 of Jammu and Kashmir on 5 August,2019. Doval played crucial in its pre-and-post implementation. He secretly visited Srinagar in the third week of July, 2019 and coordinated Army, Air Force, Security and Intelligence agencies including selected state bureaucracy high-ups. All surveillance and reconnaissance plans were put on alert in case of any Pakistani adventurism. Drones were deployed to trace the separatists and terrorists. Air Force was prepared to airlift the paramilitary troops from outside J&K. Satellite phones were provided to the prominent security and civil official. More than 45,000 troops were deployed in the valley. Israeli Heron drones of NTRO were put over for mob control. In order to divert public attention and to scare Pakistan, Sukhoi and Mirage 2,000 aircrafts made numerous sorties from Srinagar airport. Security forces mounted attacked in POK on terrorist camps. Doval remained there for many days. He visited Amarnath and later Yatra was discontinued on security reasons.

After implementing the abrogation in Parliament, Doval flew to Srinagar and camped there till 15 August making arrangements to fly National Flag in every corner of the valley so that a right message is given to Pakistan. It was another feather in his cap in the second term of Modi Government.

Earlier Doval got eliminated around 40 separatists of National Socialist Council of Nagaland (NSCN-K) inside Myanmar borders which brought peace to certain extent this age old disturbed area.

In the back-drop of above analysis of Ajit Doval as National Security Advisor, it is heartening to note that he proved much more effective than his predecessors. North-East insurgency is almost under control now. Doval has sanitized the Indian Ocean. Both Sri Lanka and Bangladesh are far more friendly with India in comparison to the UPA Government. Nepal is victim of its own misdeeds but there is no choice but to toe India-dictated line. Pakistan too is wary of the intention of Doval and Balakot airstrikes were a warning of intention of Modi Government. I feel the writing on wall is quite apparent and if Rawalpindi is living in fool's paradise about Modi agenda of economic development, their doomsday are not quite far. But POK-Gilgit Baltistan merger by force is still not the agenda of this Government which I should not hesitate to disclose now. We are destined not to hear decades old sermons that Kashmir was ours, is ours and would be ours. India should capture this region by force and this Government is capable to achieve that.

Two Power Centres

In his second term, Modi abruptly appointed S.Jaishankar as Cabinet Minister of Ministry of External Affairs which was managed by Doval in his first term. Jaishankar virtually worked under Doval then as Foreign Secretary. Murmuring in media was resolved by Government when post of National Security Advisor was elevated to Cabinet rank because Doval was holding State Minister rank then and brought him equivalent to Jaishankar. But Doval-Jaishankar duo is working in tandem and Jaishankar is always respectful to Doval due to his big stature. However, I should not hesitate to mention that unlike Doval's success in first term on foreign policy, Jaishankar is yet to prove his credential. Doval tackled the much more serious issue with China on LAC at Doklam but pro-Chinese Jaishankar is yet to resolve Galwan stand-off with China where 20 of our soldiers were martyred. Whole of country is very curious about the ultimate outcome of this volatile situation on border with China.

❑